W9-CKP-937

Praise for Gordon Kent's

HOSTILE CONTACT

"Kent's clever and complex thriller has one foot in the techno-thriller genre and the other in traditional espionage... top-notch."—*Publishers Weekly*

"[*Hostile Contact*] is high-tech warfare at its best."
—*Abilene (Tex.) Reporter-News*

"Swashbuckling U.S. Navy Lieutenant-Commander Alan Craik returns to earn the thanks of a grateful nation, not to mention his growing fan base.... [*Hostile Contact* has] brilliant scenes and a thoroughly agreeable cast."—*Kirkus Reviews*

TOP HOOK

"The father-and-son former naval aviators behind the Kent nom de plume again mix aviation and espionage as effectively as in *Rules of Engagement* ... characterization and pacing remain superior."—*Booklist*

"The high testosterone doses satisfy."—*Publishers Weekly*

"Another tour de force in the military fiction field."
—*Abilene (Tex.) Reporter-News*

"Snares the reader with a story that is purposefully not over-complicated, unlike the CIA itself."—*Tampa Tribune*

"In this far-ranging, fast-paced novel the dialogue is authentic, fresh from carrier wardrooms and S-3 cockpits."
—Lieutenant Colonel Richard Seamon of the U.S. Naval Institute's *Proceedings*

RULES OF ENGAGEMENT

"Flying, spying and dying—*Rules of Engagement* is the real straight Navy stuff. Better strap yourself to the chair for this one. I loved it."
—*New York Times* bestselling author Stephen Coonts

"Plenty of flying, espionage and a sizable body count . . . this is a can't-put-down book."—*USA Today*

"*Rules of Engagement* has it all—gripping heat-of-battle action and a terrific new hero, a young naval intelligence officer hell-bent on finding the spy who killed his father. A tale of friends and enemies, sacrifice and betrayal, honor and revenge, *Rules of Engagement* is an exhilarating debut."
—*New York Times* bestselling author W.E.B. Griffin

"Fast-moving, heavy with air and land action, and authentic enough to satisfy the most demanding techno-buffs. A nice combination of military thriller and spy novel."—*Booklist*

"The writers' knowledge of naval technology and wartime tactics is flawless, and they work it effortlessly into the plot."
—*Publishers Weekly*

PEACEMAKER

"A fireball of a military thriller . . . few authors integrate multiple plots with such dazzling 3-D realism and technical accuracy. . . . A tour de force with near hypnotic pull, Kent's second outing scores a bull's-eye and saves rocket fuel for a sequel."—*Publishers Weekly*

"Heroes of both sexes to root for, deliciously corrupt villains to create anxiety . . . this rollicking, rousing naval thriller bears comparison to the genre's best."—*Kirkus Reviews*

By Gordon Kent

HOSTILE CONTACT

Gordon Kent

A DELL BOOK

HOSTILE CONTACT
A Dell Book

PUBLISHING HISTORY
Delacorte hardcover edition published July 2003
Dell mass market edition / August 2004

Published by
Bantam Dell
A Division of Random House, Inc.
New York, New York

This is a work of fiction. Names, characters, places, and incidents either are the product of the author's imagination or are used fictitiously. Any resemblance to actual persons, living or dead, events, or locales is entirely coincidental.

Library of Congress Catalog Card Number: 2003043559

ISBN 0-440-23748-3

Manufactured in the United States of America
Published simultaneously in Canada

OPM 10 9 8 7 6 5 4 3 2 1

To those
who tell the truth

HOSTILE CONTACT

Prologue

"THIS ADVENTURE APPEARS TO HAVE GOT US *NOTH-ing,* Mister Craik!" Admiral Pilchard's face was grim. "You get shot up, Special Agent Dukas takes a bullet, we engage two Chinese aircraft and shoot them down for you—and you bring back nothing! Do you know what the Director of Naval Intelligence has to say about that?"

His voice faded in Alan Craik's head as it all came back: Pakistan, night, blood . . .

When a shot from the darkness severed the sniper's spine, they were sprayed with blood. Mike Dukas crouched next to Alan and then moved a step, and the Chinese officer spun and fired his pistol into Dukas's chest from five meters away, knocking him back. Alan raised his good arm and brought the sight down one-handed, leaning forward as Dukas recoiled. He shot once and the officer stumbled back and caught himself against the ruined Islamic prayer screen; he raised his own gun again and then flew forward as a rifle shot from the darkness hit him.

Dukas staggered up and forward. He fell to his knees beside George Shreed, the traitor they had chased all this way. . . .

The admiral's voice stabbed through the memory: "Mister

Craik, I'm sorry for your injury, but what in the name of God did you think you were doing?"

Alan grunted, more an acknowledgment that the admiral had been speaking than a reply. He sat there like a whipped dog, his uniform rumpled, his head down, his injured left hand a white mitten of bandage—two fingers gone. And, as the admiral said, for what?

"We caught a spy, sir. A damned important spy. A traitor." Alan's tone was flat.

"Yes, and I understand he's been comatose since you brought him back and he's going to die within twenty-four hours, and he hasn't said a word! Craik, you can break the rules when you bring back the gold ring, but when you come back empty—!" When Alan didn't respond, Pilchard looked at a stone-faced officer who had come over from ONI to sit in on this chewing-out, then back at Alan, and he said almost kindly, "Didn't this guy Shreed say *anything* while you had him, Commander? Nothing?"

Had Shreed said anything? Alan had desperately wanted Shreed to say things. He had felt his head reeling as his hand had bled, but he had leaned over Shreed and tried to get him to explain. . . .

"Why?" Alan had gasped. "I want to know why. Why did you do it?"

"Do what?" A smile in Shreed's voice, as if he were saying, What, this little thing, these deaths, this meeting a thousand miles from nowhere? *"This op? Because I could. None of those other dickheads had—intestinal—" Shreed rolled a little as if to rise on his elbow, and gasped, falling back so hard his head hit the paving. He wasn't smiling now. He had at least three bullets in him, and Alan was trying to get answers from him before he died.*

"You weren't running an op. You betrayed people."

"China—won't trouble—us—"

"China—!"

"Dickheads. Idiots . . ." The voice trailed off.

Alan was aware that Pilchard had been talking again, had stopped. Alan said, "No, he didn't say anything, sir. Not anything that made any sense."

Pilchard looked at him hard, and Alan realized that he'd lost track and that now he was responding to something already past. Pilchard had the furious look of a senior officer who wasn't being listened to. "Maybe you need to take six months off," Pilchard growled. "You're not what I'd call rational."

"Sir, once I'm back on the boat—"

"You're not going back to the boat! Goddamit, Craik, look at yourself! Your uniform's a mess, you look like an old man, you can't concentrate—! Get a grip on yourself!"

Alan touched his bandages. They were really there so he couldn't see the hand. As if not seeing it denied its reality. "I need work, sir, not six months off." Pilchard looked aside at the man from ONI, and Alan got the message: ONI wanted to see a flogging. "We went to get Shreed, and we got him," he said stubbornly.

The ONI man said, "And he hasn't said zip. You got nothing."

"What did you bring the Chinese?" Alan had said then to the dying Shreed. There were a dozen dead Chinese soldiers around the old mosque, and the Chinese officer who had shot Dukas was lying with his head a foot from Shreed's. Alan thought that Shreed had brought Navy secret codes to give to the Chinese. "What did you bring them?"

Shreed gurgled, turned his head, and spat blood against the wall. "Poison. Brought Chen—poison—" Shreed's head turned, seemed to merge with the Chinese officer's in the darkness, their faces as close as two lovers'.

"He's your control? He's running you?" Alan leaned within inches of Shreed's ear, trying to force the answers from him.

"Chen?" Shreed snarled. He made the name sound like a dirty word. "Never—never—! The money—!" Shreed closed his eyes. His chest heaved, and Alan thought he was laughing. He wheezed and coughed, then quieted, and there was a silence. "You taking me home?" Shreed whispered.

"If we make it."

"You think you're heroes, but you don't—understand—" Shreed's voice faded. Alan heard the rasping breath in the darkness. Abruptly, the voice came back, loud now. "I'll have a monument—like—Bill Casey. You'll see—who the hero—is—"

The wheezing cough came again as if he were laughing, but he wasn't laughing.

The admiral was looking at a photograph of the President on his wall and talking again. "Your 'traitor' was an important man with important friends at the CIA. They deny that he was a spy, and they're saying that the Navy made a huge mistake. And you broke a lot of rules in doing it."

"Shreed said he'd be a hero."

"And to them he is! He's got a big cheering section over there." Pilchard glanced at the ONI man, who nodded gloomily. "Alan, you and this man Dukas broke a *lot* of rules. When you break the rules, you better come back with a diamond in your hand, or you're in the deepest shit in the world."

But Alan went on, like a drunk who doesn't hear what's said to him. "Shreed said he'd be a hero! What the hell, he *was* a traitor. Why would he be a hero?"

"You're not listening, Commander—!"

"They'll come back at us," Alan said. He sat up a little straighter.

"What?"

"The Chinese. They have to come back at us."

"Come back how?"

"Revenge. Like street gangs. They'll take a shot at us."

Pilchard wasn't interested in street gangs. He nodded at the ONI officer; clearly, it was his time to talk, and it had all been arranged before the chewing-out had started. The ONI man said, "Our office would be happier if Shreed had lived to talk. Or if you'd got the Chinese officer—Shreed's control. Chou?"

"Chen."

Shreed saying, contempt in his voice, when Alan had asked if the Chinese officer was his control, "Chen?" as if "Chen" were a word for shit.

"Yeah. We think that if we could get this Chen, we could salvage something here. What happened to him?"

"I was pretty much out of it by then." Meaning that his civilian friend Harry and Harry's assassin girlfriend had had another agenda, and they had been the only good guys left standing at the end of the fight, so they had got whatever was left of Chen.

"If we had him, we'd bury Shreed's buddies over at the Agency." The ONI man, a full captain, shook his head. "Is Chou alive, do you think?"

"Chen. It's Chen."

"Okay, whatever! If there's a chance that sonofabitch is still alive, we want to know. That would be something, if we could bring him in. Commander, you hearing me?"

Alan was hearing a sound and couldn't place it, a distant drone. He was trying to say something to Dukas but he couldn't hear, and then it was too late to ask anything, and the blood was draining out of him and he wondered if the sound was the aircraft that was supposed to lift them out.

"Money," Alan said now to Admiral Pilchard. "Shreed said something about money. When he was talking about Chen and poison. I wanted to ask him about it, but then the aircraft came and—"

Alan stared at the wall of the Pentagon office, still hearing the S-3 that had come to take them out of Pakistan, still smelling the blood and feeling the wound in his hand. He'd thought that he had done some of the best work of his life, and now he was being read out for it. He wanted Pilchard, who was a damned good officer and a "sea daddy" to him sometimes, to say that he and Dukas had done a hell of a job and it wasn't their fault that Shreed hadn't talked. He wanted him to say that Alan should go back to sea and take over command of his detachment again. But what the admiral was dealing with was not Alan Craik, but a turf war between ONI and the CIA, with the Navy looking bad because one of its officers had broken a lot of rules to capture a man who could, in death, be made to wear a hero's halo.

"If you know anything about what happened to this Chen, Commander, you better come out with it—*quick*." The ONI captain leaned in on Alan, and Pilchard waved him off with a shake of the head.

"Maybe I can find out," Alan said. *Maybe*. Maybe Harry

and Anna had nursed Chen back to life and were having picnics with him in Bahrain. Maybe Alan's lost fingers would grow back, too.

"Don't maybe me. *Find out.*" The captain leaned away from him out of deference to the admiral, but he sounded threatening.

Admiral Pilchard stood to show the meeting was over. Alan looked him in the eye. "I'm sorry, sir," he said. "I did what I thought was right."

The admiral gave him a bleak little smile. "The Navy goes by results, Commander."

Out in the corridor, the captain grabbed his arm. He was a big man who used his size to awe people. "Come up with a diamond, Mister Craik," he snarled. "Come up with a diamond, or you're going to be one early-out lieutenant-commander."

PART
ONE

Targeting

400 NM east of Socotra, Indian Ocean.

CAPTAIN RAFE RAFEHAUSEN SLAMMED HIS S-3B INTO the break and thought that he'd done it badly, out of practice, the move both too sudden and too harsh, and beside him he heard Lieutenant jg Soleck give a grunt. Rafehausen had an impulse to snarl and overcame it; he was the CAG and he didn't fly enough and the kid was right—he should have done it better. Although, as he knew from the weekly reports, the kid's landing scores were the worst on the boat.

"Gear one, two, three, down—and locked—flaps, slats out—hook is—*down*—read airspeed and fuel, Mister Soleck—"

The jg muttered the fuel poundage and airspeed, which Rafehausen could have read perfectly well for himself, of course. He supposed he was trying to communicate with the much younger man, who seemed mostly terrified of him.

"Not one of the great breaks of all time, Mister Soleck."

"Uh—no, sir—but good, sir—considering—"

Rafehausen lined up dead-on, said "Ball" when he caught

the green, and took the LSO's instructions almost unconsciously, now into his groove and operating on long and hard-won experience. He caught the two wire, rolled, lifted the hook, and let a yellow-shirt direct him forward.

"Nice landing, sir."

Rafehausen smiled. "Little rough, Mister Soleck. Practice makes perfect." He slapped the lieutenant jg on the shoulder. "Weeklies tell me you need some practice yourself." He would have walked away then, but he saw the kid blush and look suddenly stricken, so he put the hand more gently on his shoulder and walked with him over the nonskid that way, shouting over the deck noise, "Don't take it wrong, Soleck—we all get into slumps! Hey, how about you and me do some practice landings together sometime?"

He debriefed in the det 424 ready room, which was his for the moment only because he'd borrowed one of their aircraft, and then made his way to the CAG's office. He wished, often, that he was a squadron officer again—no stacks of paper, no wrangles with personalities and egos. Now that it was too late, he knew that when you were a squadron pilot, you were having the best that naval air offered; Soleck didn't know how lucky he was. What came later—rank, status, command—were compensation for not being a young warrior with a multimillion-dollar horse and a whole sky to ride it in.

"Another urgent p-comm from Al Craik, Rafe," a lieutenant-commander said as he sat down. "Same old shit—'Request immediate orders,' et cetera, et cetera."

"What's the medical officer say?"

"No way."

"Even in nonflight-crew status?"

"Negative. MO says the man 'needs to heal and overcome trauma, period, and don't ask again.' Another month, maybe."

Alan Craik was a personal friend, and Rafehausen wished he could help him. Craik had been flown back to the carrier with part of one hand shot off and so much blood gone that the medics thought they'd lose him; now back in the States, he was recovered enough to be itching to return to duty. But not enough to serve.

"Send Craik a message over my name: The answer is no, and don't ask again for at least two weeks."

Unimak Canyon, Aleutian Archipelago.

"Depth is 200 meters and steady."

"Steady at 200." The Chinese captain, standing by his command chair, turned and looked toward sonar station three, the towed array whose passive equipment had most reliably tracked the American. His crew had scored more contact hours on an American ballistic missile submarine in the last four days than any submarine in the history of the Chinese Navy. No moment of that time had been easy.

Even when he knew where the submarine would be, it was almost invisible.

Even trailing it by a mere four thousand meters, it was almost inaudible.

He dared not close any more. His own boat, the *Admiral Po*, was a killer, slow but sure—the best his service had to offer, but too loud and too old, and no amount of pious mouthing to the Party would change the fact that she leaked radiation from her reactor compartment. Her condition affected the crew, destroyed morale, made retention of the dedicated specialists vital to the service nearly impossible.

He was going to change that. He was going to follow an American ballistic missile sub, a "boomer," from her base near Seattle to her patrol area, wherever that was. And he was going to take that information home and shove it down the throat of the Party until they paid the money to make his service the equal of her rivals in Russia, Great Britain, and, most of all, America. Because when he had the patrol area where the most precious eggs in the American nuclear basket rested, he would bury the army and the air force.

"She's turning to port."

"All engines stop!" Drift. Every time the American maneuvered, *Admiral Po* had to drift. He couldn't take the risk that the Americans were executing a clearing turn to get their passive sonar on their wake. Twice the boomer had done just that, and he had waited, knuckles white, drenched in sweat as the two submarines passed in silence. He couldn't risk detection. Detection would imperil not only the operation but also its source, a faceless spy whose radio transmissions told him where to pick up the boomer near the American west coast and when.

Admiral Po's secret friend. Jewel.

"Passing 340 relative and increasing engine noise."

"Increasing speed?"

Two men in a darkened ballroom. Each can track the other only when he moves and makes a noise. Where is he? Where is he going? How fast is he moving?

Omnipresent—Is he behind me?

The sonarman, his best, watched his three screens, touching buttons and waiting for the computer to analyze tracking data. Passive sonar was an imperfect sensor that had to detect emanations from the target; only active sonar sent out its own signal and listened for the reflection. Sonarmen on passive looked for certain telltale "lines": auxiliaries, reactors, propeller wash. They hoped for a specific signature that could be reliably assigned to the target, and not, say, a passing whale or a fishing boat on the surface. When they had a library of such noises, they became better trackers, but this endless game of follow-the-leader required constant analysis and perfect guesswork. The cream of the sonar team had been at their stations since they entered the difficult undersea terrain of the Aleutian chain—three watches. The captain hadn't left the bridge for more than an hour in four days. Despite air-conditioning and high discipline, the bridge stank of sweat and shorted electrical power, a faint ozone smell that never left the *Admiral Po*. The captain thought it was the smell of leaking radiation.

"Nine knots and still increasing, turning hard to port. I think he's diving, as well. I'm losing the track in his own wake." The man sounded exhausted. That was not good; the excitement had kept them going through the first bad moment off Kodiak Island. Now that, too, was gone.

"Come to 270 and make revolutions for three knots."

"270 and three knots. Aye."

"Status?"

"He's gone."

The captain rolled his head slowly to the right and left, banished all thought of angry response from his mind, and settled slowly into his command chair.

"He's drifting. He will complete the turn as a clearing turn before running the Unimak channel." The captain didn't feel anything like the certainty he projected, but it was a skill that came with command.

"270 and three knots, Captain."

"All engines stop."

Two of the sonarmen played with the bow sonar, a much weaker engine than the powerful towed array behind them. The tail could be deployed only at low speeds, and certain maneuvers like rapid turns were not possible while it was deployed, but it was their only tool for following the American. The bow sonar had intermittent contact at best. He could hear the two murmuring to each other about the noise that the ocean was making, pounding on the island due north of them. Background noise, a white noise that would cross most of the spectrum, all of the "lines." They were murmuring because sonarmen had a superstitious respect for their opposite numbers, afraid that loud conversation would be heard by the opposing specialists. No one knew how good the American sonars really were, but four days had taught the captain that they were not as good as his worst fears, and their tactics showed that they were cocky.

That still left a lot of room for them to be very, very good.

"350 relative! Range 3500 meters and closing!"

It was eerie, having his prediction fulfilled like that. He had tossed it off, based, yes, on some experience. But mostly to steady the bridge crew. The bastard was coming around toward them, and quite fast now that his engines were driving him again.

"Take us down to 255 meters, bow up."

"255 meters, bow up, aye." The *Admiral Po* began a very slow dive, aiming to get her metal bulk through the deep isothermic layer that would reflect most sonar and greatly hamper passive detection. The captain looked down at his knuckles on the collision bar in front of his command seat and gradually willed his hands to relax.

In the darkened ballroom, there are long, velvet curtains that hide sound if you can get behind them.

"000 relative, 3000 meters and closing. Speed five knots. Vector 190."

The boomer suddenly appeared as a digital symbol on the command screen, with her course and speed displayed next to her. The distance between the *Admiral Po* and her quarry seemed very short, and the captain wondered if they were about to change roles.

"255 meters."

"Try to put the bow sonar up in the layer."

"Bow up, aye."

This was a tricky maneuver and one that couldn't really be accurately gauged for success. It required that the planesman adjust the pitch of the submarine so that her bow sonar was actually above the acoustic layer, allowing that sonar to listen to the enemy while the rest of the submarine's metal hide was hidden below the temperature gradient of the layer. The problem was that you never knew for sure that you had it exactly right; the acoustic layer was simply a metaphor for the invisible line where two different layers of water with different temperatures met. It couldn't be seen, only sensed, and only sensed as a relative gradient. The bow might be in the layer or meters above it, depending on luck and skill and local variations.

He's bow on to us right now. The American, with his infinitely superior equipment, was in the best position he could ask to detect *Admiral Po*.

"Nothing on the tail."

"Bow sonar has contact, 010 relative, 2500 meters and closing. Speed five knots. Vector 180."

He has us. Or he will turn away.

The captain turned to the planesman.

"Well done. Very well done." The bow sonar report indicated that the bow was, indeed, above the layer. But how far? And how reflective was the layer?

He watched the symbol on the bridge screen, the only

visual input that mattered, willing it to continue its turn to port.

"020 relative, 2700 meters. Speed six knots. Vector 160."

Deep breath, long exhalation.

"Make revolutions for three knots. Hold us at 255 meters and pitch for normal."

"Aye, aye." That pulled the bow back under the layer, making them blind, but he had to move or the American would get too far away. Simply avoiding detection was only half the game.

"Three knots."

"Helmsman, three knots for the center of the channel."

"Aye, aye."

He cast an eye at the chart and decided he had a safe amount of water under his keel, even in these treacherous seas.

"Depthfinder off."

"Depthfinder off, aye."

Ahead, perhaps well ahead if he stuck to his six knots, the American would be entering the channel already. The captain calculated quickly; the American would be well over six thousand meters ahead when they were back in the deep water on the other side of the channel, but the captain thought that the risk was worthwhile, and he was a little distracted by the obvious adulation of the bridge crew and his own internal buzz of triumph. He had outguessed an American boomer captain. His crew had reacted well. He *was* worthy.

"Center of the channel."

He waited patiently, following the channel on his chart while thinking over the last set of moves, trying to guess the next. His eyes actually closed twice. Minutes trickled by. He hated letting the American have so much time undetected, but he couldn't risk anything in the narrow channel.

"Bow sonar has possible contact, range 7000 meters, bearing 000 relative."

He snapped fully awake.

"Speed?"

The man looked anguished. The data were too sketchy.

He needed a longer hit, or a second and third hit in quick succession to get a vector and speed.

Seven thousand meters was too far ahead, and too far for the bow sonar to make contact. Unless he was going very fast. It had to be a false contact—a seamount, or a boat. Or another submarine. He struggled with the possibilities as his own boat continued to creep down the channel.

"All engines stop. Planesman, bow above the layer."

The *Admiral Po* seemed to hold its breath.

"Possible contact, range 7000 meters, bearing 000 relative."

The image returned on the command screen.

"Vector 000. Speed twelve knots."

The American was racing away. He would be clear of the channel in moments; indeed, given the vagaries of passive sonar, he might be free now, and increasing speed.

"Make revolutions for four knots. Retrieve the tail." It was useless in the channel, anyway. The American was surely too far away to hear its telltale 44dB line as the bad bearing in the towed array winch screamed.

Were they detected? He didn't think so, couldn't think so. This had the smell of a standard operating procedure, a routine to lose hypothetical pursuit. If so, it was crushingly effective.

"Towed array housed, sir."

"Very well. Make revolutions for six knots."

At six knots, the *Admiral Po* was one of the loudest leviathans in the deep. Her second-generation reactor could not be made really quiet by the addition (and in some cases, the slipshod addition) of the best Russian quieting materials from the third generation—isolation mounts, for instance. The captain *hated* to go above four knots in an operational patrol. He felt naked.

They roared along the channel, a painful compromise, too loud to avoid detection, too slow to catch the American if he was determined to go *fast*.

"How did we miss him going so fast? I make no accusation, understand. I need to know."

"Captain, he is not much noisier at twelve knots than at

six. Even the cavitation noise is, well, muffled. He is very quiet."

No submarine should be so quiet at twelve knots.

In Severomorsk, they had told him about the "steel Sierra," the Russian submarine that would do these things. That had been twelve years ago, before the Soviet Union rolled over and sank. Clearly the American boats could do the same. His antiquated attack boat had just fallen even farther behind, because the ability to run fast without cavitation, the designer's dream since the 1960s, placed the new American boomer in the fourth generation.

He timed out the channel's length on his own watch. The second he was sure he had depth under his keel, his voice rang out.

"Make our depth 300. Turn to port heading 270. Make our speed two knots."

Turning gradually broadside to the expected vector of the target, exposing the length of the towed array to get the maximum signal, diving to avoid an unexpected ambush.

Time gurgled by down the hull.

"All stop."

Nothing.

"Sonar?"

"No contact."

The captain was a thorough professional and he didn't quit. He searched in ever-increasing spirals for twelve hours, sprinting and drifting, risking detection and flirting with disaster if the American sub was lurking in the deep water just north of the channel. But he took such risks only because he already knew the answer: His opponent had raced down the channel and into the deep water and had vanished to the north.

Sleepless, grimy, sweat-stained, he rose from his command chair and addressed the bridge crew.

"This is not a total loss, comrades. We have unprecedented sonograms on the American; we know that he was headed north. We know more about their patrol routes and procedures than any boat in Chinese history. And they have no idea that we're here."

"Do we go north, then, Captain?" asked his first officer.

"No. No, we return to our patrol area, study our sono-grams, and wait."

Until Jewel gives us the next one, he thought. But Jewel was too precious, and he couldn't say that to the crew.

The submarine set a course for the waters off Seattle.

Suburban Virginia.

The gleaming new S-3 sagged a little, turning on final for the carrier; his break had been weak, and he knew that no self-respecting LSO would give him an okay on any part of this trap so far. Now he was in the groove but chasing his lineup like a nugget, all of his motor coordination sluggish and unre-sponsive, like a bad hydraulics system in an old airplane. His brain knew where his hands should go, but his injured hand lagged and the signals seemed to move too slowly, too jerkily, and the plane, like a horse that knows that the hand at the reins is weak, seemed to fight him.

He eyeballed the lineup, called the ball in his head, and tried to recapture the flawless rhythm that he had once had at this game. One mile, six hundred feet, one hundred and forty knots. He knew the numbers, but the response seemed to lag and he wanted to blame the equipment, wanted to suddenly press a button and have all of those reaction times and skills come flooding back, and then he jerked physically to realize that he was there, the deck was THERE....

His angle of attack was too steep, tending to sag at the very end and fighting his near-stall speed for altitude; the plane had nothing to give him; his correction was too late, and the immovable laws of physics and mathematics grabbed his plane and flung it into the back of the ship, just a few feet above the neat, white lettering that said "USS *Thomas Jefferson.*" A brilliant orange-and-white explosion obliterated his con-trol screen—

—and he picked up the joystick in his good, strong right hand and smashed it through the wallboard of the living room, screaming his frustration at the top of his lungs.

"Fuck! FUUUCK! Jesus FUCKING Christ!" He was roaring with anger, sweat and failure dripping from him, and the shards of a piece of expensive computer equipment broken by his own stupid rage prodded him to a sicker, meaner level, as he thought of what he had become with one wound—two fingers shot off his left hand in Pakistan and he was half what he had been. Less than half.

There was a small irregular hole in their rented living-room wall. "Fucking stupid JERK!" he shouted. His face left no doubt whom he meant. He threw the shattered remnants of the joystick across the room, where they left a nick in the paint on the wall under the stairs. He clenched his hands, savoring the awful feeling of the missing fingers. A noise distracted him.

Crying.

His son was standing on the stairs, terrified by a side of his father he had never seen, never should have seen.

"Oh, my God, Mikey!" Alan said, his voice bruised from shouting.

Mikey stood, whimpering, looking afraid. Afraid of his father, the hero. Alan took a step toward the stairs and Mikey bolted for his room, and the front door opened, and there was Rose, beautiful and healthy in her flight suit, the poster child for women in naval aviation. She stopped as soon as the door opened; he could see in a heartbeat that she saw it all, knew it all.

He threw himself into an armchair he didn't like, facing a television he hated. He hated the room and he hated the house. It might have been better if it had been his own house, but this was merely a place they had found in the hectic last days of the Shreed business, when Rose had been temporarily attached to the Chief of Naval Operations, and then he had got hurt. The house was too small and too mean, but it was what she could find in one day. And he hated it.

Now, she came into the room, trying, he knew, to mute her own joy at feeling good about herself and her life, going down to Pax River to fly every day, preparing to get her heart's desire by going to Houston.

She kissed him lightly on the top of the head and went into the kitchen, and seconds later she was back.

"You know"—and she kept her voice light—"you could have done something about dinner."

"Because I don't do anything but sit here on my ass all day? Right!" He shot up and headed for the kitchen. Upstairs, the baby started to cry. "And shut that kid up!" he shouted.

It was as if he hated her, too. As if hurting her, the thing he valued most in the world, was the only way to express his rage. She wouldn't have it, however; she had a ferocious temper of her own, and she could be sweet Rose, forgiving Rose, good-wife Rose for only so long. Grabbing his arm from behind, she spun him halfway around and shouted, just as loudly as he had, "That's *your* kid up there! If you don't like him or me or us, get the hell out!"

"I might do just that!"

"Well, do it! We're all sick of tiptoeing around so you can feel sorry for yourself and stare at your wounded hand and think how bad the Navy's treated you. *Get a grip or get out!*"

And he raised his hand.

Washington.

Mike Dukas came out of his shower, his heavy, hairy body pink except for the livid red scars along his collarbone. Seeing it in the bathroom mirror, he made a face—the first bullet he had ever taken, and it had been a doozy. He still couldn't lift his hands above his shoulders, and drying himself made him wince, and when he went out into the world he still had to wear a plastic harness that held his hands up in front of him so that he looked like the Easter bunny.

"Fucking George Shreed," he muttered.

George Shreed dominated his life now: He had taken the bullet capturing Shreed, and now he was paying for it in the paperwork that waited at his office—reports and explanations and assessments. "The thanks of a grateful nation," he said aloud and thought, *Well, at least I don't feel as bad as Al Craik.* Craik, he knew, was in a deep depression.

He needed a change, Dukas thought. God knows, he needed *something*.

Time was, he would have thought he needed to fall in love. He fell in love easily, hard, usually badly. This time, however, he didn't have the urge, as if scraping death's fender had warned him off the risk. Even now, there was a call on his answering machine that he had started to listen to last night and had switched off because he had recognized the woman's voice. "Hi, Mike," she had said, the voice a little breathy and too bright. "Hi, this is—" and he had turned it off because he knew who it was.

Sally Baranowski. CIA analyst, incipient alcoholic just out of rehab, nice, *nice* woman. They had almost had something going, and then he had got himself shot and she had got herself rehabilitated, and now, what the hell, what good was any of it? Half-dry, his back still covered with water, he wrapped the wet towel around his gut and stalked out of the bathroom as if he meant to punch somebody out, went to the answering machine and stabbed it with a stiff finger and said to himself, *Don't be a schmuck.*

"Hi, Mike—Hi, this is Sally!" A small laugh. "Baranowski. Remember me? Uh—I just thought I'd call—This is awkward as hell; I thought you'd be there. Goddam machines, you can't—"

He switched it off. She must be *just* out of rehab. How long did rehab take, anyway? Thirty days? He didn't want to get involved, was the truth. What he wanted was real work, a case, relief from the mind-numbing reports that filled his days. So far, his boss at the Naval Criminal Investigative Service wouldn't give him a thing; he'd been going into the office for a week, pounding out paperwork, kept out of action. Because he was "awaiting a clean bill of health," his boss said, which had nothing to do with his health and everything to do with the fact that he'd gone into a foreign country (Pakistan) without a country clearance and without adequate authorization, his boss *said*, and got himself shot up and had needed to be flown out by a Navy aircraft that was also there illegally. And, what the hell, the fact that they'd caught a major spy seemed to make no difference. And now Kasser, his boss's boss, wanted to know where the Chinese case officer was. Dukas could see himself spending the rest of his life writing reports related to his trip to Pakistan.

So, Dukas had said, let me go back to the War Crimes Tribunal, from which he was supposedly on six months' leave of absence as a favor to NCIS, but his boss had negatived that as "dodging the issue," whatever the issue was.

"Shit," Dukas said.

And his telephone rang.

"Dukas," he growled into it in his early-morning voice.

"It's Alan."

"Hey, man!" Dukas sounded to himself like a jerk— happy-happy, oh boy, life is great! Trying to cheer up Al Craik because he sounded like shit. "How's it going, Al?"

"Get me something to do, Mike. Anything!"

"That's a job for your detailer, Al."

"My detailer can't do anything; I'm on medical leave and some genius at Walter Reade wants to disability-discharge me. I'm going nuts, Mike."

"Yeah, well—you sleeping?"

"Sleeping—what's that? No, I'm not sleeping. I fought with Rose; I shouted at my kid—" His voice got hoarse. "Mike—I'll do anything to get my mind off myself. Scut work, I don't care."

This was Dukas's best friend. They had almost died together. They had been wounded together. Dukas's own helplessness made him somber. "I'm doing scut work myself, kid. Writing reports on what happened in Pakistan, closing the Shreed file." He sighed. On the other end, Craik made a sound as if he were being wounded all over again, and Dukas, relenting, said, "Come down to the office, what the hell. We can talk, anyway. Okay? Hey, you talk to Harry lately?"

Alan Craik was slow to answer. He muttered, "I don't like begging, Mike. But I'm going nuts. Last night, I—Rose and I had a fight, and I—almost—" He didn't say what he had done. He didn't have to; the tone of his voice said it all.

Then Alan snapped back from wherever he was. Mike heard the change.

"What about Harry?"

"Tell you later."

In the Virginia Horse Country.

A dark Ford Explorer turned into a gap in a wooden fence where a paved drive led away from the two-lane road. There was a line of oaks and more wooden fence along the lane, and up ahead a colonial revival house that needed paint. The wooden fence wanted attention, too, and the pasture beyond it was scraggy with tufts of long grass, and a horseman would have known that no animals were being pastured there.

The Explorer pulled up next to the house and a tall man got out. He waved at somebody by the stable block and trotted up the front steps, nodded at the hefty young man at the front door, and said, "Everything okay?"

"Bor-ing," the young man said. "He's upstairs."

"I'll talk to him in the music room." Balkowitz always talked to Ray Suter in the music room, which had no music but did hold an out-of-tune baby grand that had been pushed against a wall to make room for recording equipment. Balkowitz was a lawyer for the Central Intelligence Agency; the bulky young man was named Hurley and worked for Agency security; the man out at the stable block was a local who took care of the place but wasn't allowed in the house. And Ray Suter, the man upstairs, had been George Shreed's assistant and was wanted by various people for murder, conspiracy to commit a felony, espionage, and perhaps corrupting the morals of a minor. The CIA, however, had him stashed away here, and what they wanted him for was information.

Balkowitz sat on a faded armchair that smelled of its age. He was dressed in jeans and a polo shirt and looked more like a Little League dad than a lawyer. When Suter came in—tall, pale, pinched—Balkowitz got up and waited for Suter to sit. Balkowitz's manner reflected his Agency's own ambivalence—polite and stern, unsure and patriarchal. Suter, to judge from his sour smile, knew all about it and rather enjoyed the situation. "You keep trying," Suter said. "A for effort."

"Mister Suter—"

"Ray." Suter spread his hands. "We know each other well enough. Call me Ray."

"I just want to apprise you of your situation here. Really, you know, if you'd get yourself a lawyer—"

Suter shook his head. "I don't need a lawyer."

"Your situation is serious."

Suter raised his eyebrows. "The food's good. Hurley plays pretty good tennis. Except for the lack of females, it isn't bad."

"Mister Suter, you've been charged in Virginia and Maryland, and we're holding off federal charges until, until—"

"Until I talk?" Suter laughed. "Don't hold your breath."

"I just want to impress on you the legal seriousness of—"

"You say that every time you come. I've told you, I think three times now, I've got nothing to say. You guys are holding me here without a charge; well, okay, I'm suspended from work, anyway. I assume that you want me to get a lawyer because you think a lawyer would tell me to bargain. But for what? With what?"

"If we file charges, you face twenty years to life on the federal issues alone."

"If you do. Right." Suter grinned. "Maybe you should file."

Balkowitz sniffed and reached into his pocket for a tissue. He was allergic to something in the room. "Mister Suter, we're holding off the local jurisdictions with some difficulty." He blew his nose. "Your relations with the young man, Nickie, um, Groski—if you'd be willing to tell us *anything* there—"

Nickie Groski was a computer hacker whom Suter had hired to hack into George Shreed's computers, but Suter hadn't admitted to a word of that. Instead, he said now, "What would you like to hear?"

"You were in the boy's apartment when the police broke in."

"I was, yes." Suter seemed pensive, as if what Balkowitz was saying was a little surprising.

"You paid the rent on that apartment."

"Maybe I felt sorry for him. Or maybe I'm gay. Is he gay?"

Balkowitz stopped with the tissue at his nose. "Mister Suter, we know you chased women all over the place."

Suter nodded almost sadly. "Maybe I'm bisexual. What is it you think I did with this boy?"

"That's what we want to know." Balkowitz got out a document, which he kept tapping as he talked. "If you agree to tell us about Nickie Groski and certain other things, then we're willing to—but you really should have a lawyer to help with this—"

Suter didn't even look at the document. "You'd like me to have a lawyer because then I'd be admitting I was ready to deal. But I'm not. No deal, Balkowitz."

They went around for another ten minutes, Suter seeming to enjoy it all the more as Balkowitz's nose ran and the lawyer's face got red. At the end, the man's patience ran out and he pointed a finger and said, "This is my last visit! You come partway to us or the shit will hit the fan out there!"

Suter gave his thin, acid smile. "I love the majesty of the law." He patted Balkowitz's shoulder. "Have you tried Allegra-D?"

SUTER WENT BACK UPSTAIRS AND CHANGED INTO shorts and took the time to scribble a note on a very small piece of paper, which he signed "Firebird" and stuffed into a chartreuse tennis ball in which he'd already made a slit. When he went downstairs, he told Hurley he was going to practice some serves, and he went out the back door and, passing the stable block, threw the slitted tennis ball for an old golden retriever to catch. The dog lumbered after it, caught up with it, held it down with a paw until he could get his old teeth around it, and then, tail wagging, carried it to his owner, the maintenance man.

Beijing.

Colonel Lao tse-Ku touched the place where the two sides of his collar joined at his throat. The gesture was unconscious, not quite nervous but certainly atypical—a last check of self before opening a door through which you can pass only once.

The door itself was quite mundane—gray, metal, the surface broken only by a small nameplate, INFORMATION DIRECTORATE. The man who held the door's handle, ready to open it, was inconsequential, too, a captain, balding, smelling of cigarettes, but seeming to share the muted panic that Lao felt in Beijing, where heads were rolling and careers were crashing to an end. Now, when the captain opened the door and stood aside, the slice of room that Colonel Lao could see beyond was no more impressive than the outside—yet, again, he checked his collar, wondering if his own head was the next to roll.

And went in.

The General was sitting at a desk of sleek, pale wood, certainly not government issue, the edges of its top slightly rounded, its proportions balanced and delicate. The door closed behind Lao; he braced, his eyes on the bent, bald head of the man behind the desk. Still, Lao's first glance had registered an elegant bookcase, a scroll painting that was either old or well-faked, a silk carpet. All where they were not seen from outside the door.

And, to the right of the desk and slightly behind it, a pale second man in civilian clothes who was smoking.

The General looked up.

"Colonel Lao tse-Ku, sir," Lao managed to say.

The old man smiled. "I know," he said softly. He raised the fingers of one hand off the desk. "Sit." The fingers seemed to indicate a chair to his left. Lao sat. The General looked at him for several seconds and then looked down at an open file on his desk, which he seemed to find more interesting than Lao. After several seconds more, the General glanced over his shoulder at the third man, but he made no move to introduce him.

"You have been called very suddenly from Africa," the General said to Lao.

Lao was confused, uncertain whether he should say something banal about the soldier's life or something enthusiastic about serving the nation, or—by that time, it was too late to say anything, and the General was going on. "You were ordered to Africa only a year ago."

This time, saying "Yes, sir," seemed best.

"You like it?"

What on earth could he mean? The old fox knew perfectly well that at his age and rank, a senior figure in intelligence, Lao wanted to be in a major capital or Beijing, not an African backwater. "The post has interesting aspects," he managed to say.

The General glanced at his file and then at the third man and then said, "You were sent there because you lost a battle with your rival, Colonel Chen. Isn't that so?"

This plain speaking caught him off guard. Although, when he thought about it, the General must know all about the savage struggles for supremacy within the service. He and Chen were on the same course toward the top, two of six or seven who might one day run all of Chinese military intelligence. And, yes, Chen had bested him this time and arranged to have him sent into darkness. Still, Lao said, "I did not question my orders, sir."

He heard the third man flick a cigarette lighter and in his peripheral vision saw a new plume of smoke from that direction. He didn't want to look directly at the man. Clear enough what he was.

The General had a round face made puffy with fat, so that his eyes seemed to have difficulty keeping from being squeezed shut by cheeks and brows. When he chuckled, as he did now, a thousand wrinkles came to life. Smiling, he said to Lao, "Chicks that pecked their way out of the same egg will fight for the dunghill when they have combs and spurs. Rivalry between you and Chen is quite natural. Necessary, in fact. Working together is often required; going where you are ordered is required; rivalry, too, has its uses. You lost the last battle. Now it is your turn." He leaned forward. "Colonel Chen has disappeared."

Lao made his face, he hoped, impassive; in fact, it looked wooden.

"Chen has disappeared," the General said again. "I want you to find him." Lao sensed the third man's movement, perhaps a gesture of a hand. The General frowned bitterly. "Finding him is of the highest priority."

The air of tension, then, the stories of rolling heads and ended careers, might have the loss of a senior intelligence officer as its cause. Even before he had received the orders to come to Beijing, Lao had got ripples of it in Dar es Salaam—somebody's inability to make a decision, the absence of a senior official from his office.

The civilian moved into the space by the General's desk and began to speak in a low, guttural voice.

"Three weeks ago, Colonel Chen went to northern Pakistan to meet with an American agent. He has not been seen since."

The man was tall, rather European in face—from one of the western provinces, Lao thought, feeling the dislike he couldn't avoid for those people, not "real" Chinese. He had rather long and unkempt hair, sallow skin; there was something uncouth about his rapid gestures and his rumpled clothes. His voice was hoarse and heavily accented. An odd type to be a power in military intelligence. Lao thought he must be a party hack.

"The meeting place was a peasant village," he went on. "At night. Chen took twelve special forces soldiers. Nine were killed outright; two have died since; one is not expected to live. We interviewed the people of the village. Typically narrow-minded and fearful, hard to get anything out of." He blew out smoke, made a chopping motion with the hand that held the cigarette. "Still. A few talked. There was shooting, they said. Then an aircraft came in and landed on the road below the village, then took off again." He took two strides toward the door, his big feet making thudding sounds right through the carpet, spun and started back, waving out of his path the smoke that hung there. "One fellow who runs some sort of hostel said he had a 'Western' customer, who rented a bed and then disappeared. Caucasian, he said, didn't speak the language but had a computer that gave him some phrases. We found cartridge cases from Spanish and Pakistani ammunition, plus our own, of course." He blew out smoke and stood by the window, staring out. "Seven local civilians killed—we think by a shaped charge that Chen had brought with him. He blew a hole in an old tower, no idea why. Enemy inside, maybe. Doesn't matter." He turned back to the room and said, seeing some look on Lao's face, "No, hold your questions until I'm done.

"The aircraft. Karachi had had an emergency declared by an American naval aircraft the day before, but the aircraft never appeared. Went into the sea, maybe, they thought. Then, several hours later, an aircraft landed and took off from the village where Chen had been, and then an American naval aircraft exited Pakistani airspace while two American F-18s flew cover. Two of ours tried to engage and were shot down. The American carrier USS *Thomas Jefferson* was within recovery distance in the Indian Ocean.

"Probable scenario: The Americans flew a combat team in under Pakistani radar, using the fake emergency for cover if they were caught, landed the aircraft somewhere up near the village, and later picked up the combat team after they had killed Chen's men—and either killed or captured Chen and the American agent he had gone to meet.

"That is *one* scenario. Knowing American military doctrine, we did not find evidence of American special forces in the village. Ammunition casings were relatively few for so many men, and limited to shotgun, 9 mm, .41 Magnum, and— peculiar—.38 special. The .41 Magnum came from a Desert Eagle that was left behind. Scenario: The American agent brought his own shooters, either as a backup team because the zone was hot or because he feared Chen.

"The agent—now I am telling you facts so tightly held that you will be only the fourteenth person in China to know them—the agent was an American CIA official named George Shreed. He had been giving Chen good material for years. Vetted, checked, proven. He was supposed to have met Chen in Belgrade a day earlier, but he canceled that meeting and set up the one in Pakistan. Which fell apart into a lot of shooting. Only today are we beginning to learn that this Shreed had apparently fled the U.S. two days before, not using the escape plan we had given him, not using our considerable resources, not informing Chen. And he may have offered his services to the Israelis before he finally did contact Chen.

"Scenario: Shreed faked flight from the U.S., with the connivance of his CIA superiors, lured Chen to a meeting, and captured him with the help of a CIA team; they were then picked up by a U.S. Navy aircraft and flown to the *Thomas Jefferson*.

"Or: Shreed, who has shown signs of instability and whose wife recently died, had a mental seizure and set out to destroy his Chinese control."

He took out a wrinkled package of Pear Blossoms and tapped one out. "Or: We have no idea." He flicked the lighter, a cheap plastic one in bright peacock-blue, and lit the cigarette. He stared at Lao. "If the Americans have Chen, we will have been badly hurt. That is not your problem. If the Americans do not have Chen, then your problem is to find him and to bring him back. To fail to bring him back will be to fail the nation and its leaders. Unh?" He smoked, staring at Lao. "All right, ask your questions."

"Can I investigate this village in Pakistan?"

"Yes. I warn you, it is still a hot zone; Pakistan and India are shooting over Kashmir. We will give you everything we found in the village."

"Forensics?"

"Get it done. Our country team didn't have the time or the skill for forensics."

"What about the American, Shreed?"

The man took another turn to the window and stood there with his back to Lao. The General, still smiling, sat looking at Lao. Finally the civilian turned and said, "Shreed is a brilliant man. He has been a productive agent for twelve years. Still, like any agent, he could be a double. Scenario: The shooting in the village was a cover; Shreed and Chen were pulled out, and now both are in America."

"Do you know that?"

"I don't know anything!" A hank of the man's coarse hair fell over his face, and he pushed it back with his free hand, hitting himself in the forehead as he did so, as if punishing himself. "The Americans are saying that Shreed is dead. They are having a funeral, trumpeting the death rites. Is that natural?"

"Do you think Shreed is dead?"

"Don't ask me! What do you think we want *you* for?"

Lao could see that the General was leaning his elbows on a file. The characters on the outside of the file were from an old code word. *American Go.* Lao had heard the name whispered before. High-level material from Washington, sometimes political, sometimes espionage-related. So American Go was George Shreed. Lao wanted to laugh aloud. Chen had been running a penetration of the Operational Directorate in the CIA. No wonder he won every fight in Beijing.

The Westerner and the General talked about details for some minutes—Shreed, Chen, the reason why Chen himself had gone to Pakistan to meet with Shreed. Neither the General nor the civilian was being quite forthright, Lao thought. He wondered if he was simply being set up so that they would have a scapegoat. They talked almost as if he weren't there. He wanted to smoke, felt too junior to light up, although both older men were smoking hard.

"If Chen isn't in America but is dead or wounded—" He pushed himself in like a timid housewife at a fish stall.

"Yes, yes—?"

"I would like to be ready to make a forensic examination, if I have to. If I find him. Fingerprints, DNA—"

The civilian waved his cigarette and growled, "Yes, of course," and muttered something about the files. The General nodded and separated the top three from the stack. Lao could see that he was reluctant, even now, to hand them over. "If you accept, then I suggest you take these with you—you will have an aircraft to fly you back to Dar es Salaam, plenty of time to read in an absolutely secure atmosphere."

"I won't go direct to Dar, General. I'll start in Pakistan."

"Good. Time is short." He hesitated. "These are the communications files that Chen used with Shreed." He put one file down on the desk. "Pass-throughs, cutouts, dead drops." He put down the second file. "Electronic communications, mostly the Internet—Shreed was a master of the computer." He put down the third file. "Communications plans for face-to-face meetings. Three places—Nairobi, Jakarta, and the village in Pakistan where the shootout took place. We consider that the Pakistan site is no longer usable; therefore, Nairobi or Jakarta—" He gave Lao a look.

"These are the original files from American Go? Or substitutes?" Lao was suddenly sharp. He winced at his own tone, imagined that he could be marched from here to a basement and shot, but he knew he was being used and he might as well be used efficiently.

The two exchanged a look. The Westerner wrapped a length of hair around his fist and twisted, gave an odd sort of grunt. "Substitutes," he conceded.

"I want the originals. I want the entire case, not three files." Lao threw caution to the winds. "If you want me to find Chen, I think I need to have everything Chen was working on."

The General smiled, the last gesture Lao expected. "I told you he was sharp," he said, talking to the Westerner as if Lao were not in the room. The General lit himself a Pear Blossom, lit one for the Westerner. Then he reached behind his desk and started to sort folders, old ones with red spines. Lao imagined hundreds of folders in the vast space he couldn't see behind the General's desk, all the secrets of the universe. He shook his head to clear it.

Then they went over some of it again, and the General handed several files to Lao and told him that the entire case would be sent to him in the diplomatic bag at Dar es Salaam. Lao said that he would rather work out of Beijing, and the General's eyes almost disappeared in a smile and he said that, of course, who wouldn't rather be in Beijing, but they wanted him to stay where he was. "For cover." They didn't know if Chen had associates who might smell a rat if Lao worked from the capital. And there were other elements in the People's Army and the Party who might try to interfere, for their own purposes—times were difficult—Lao's mind had caught on the expression "for cover"; you didn't need cover within your own service unless you were doing something fatally risky, he was thinking.

"So," the General said finally, "you will accept this responsibility?" He said it smiling, as if Lao had a choice.

"Of course," Lao said firmly, although he, too, knew they had passed the point of choice when he demanded the folders.

"The people will be grateful."

The third man made another of his chopping gestures. "The people will never know! *We* will be grateful, which is what matters." He began to cough.

"There is another matter, Colonel Lao." The General's aged geniality had vanished. "It actually falls under your responsibilities at Dar es Salaam—a Middle Eastern matter. I speak of the loss of face we suffered when the Americans shot down two of our aircraft and got their agents and Shreed out of Pakistan. We were made to look like *children* in this matter. We were humiliated in front of the Pakistanis. We will pay for this failure for years. Admittedly, we may have been too 'forward leaning.' That is not for me to say. But we have been tasked to register our anger with the power that interfered with us."

Lao had an armful of critically secret folders and was burning to begin his investigation. The idea that there was further business irritated him. "Yes, sir?"

"We are going to target a strike on one of their carriers. The one that was used in Pakistan."

The General opened yet another file and tossed it on the desk.

Lao had to change his grip on his stack of folders and put them on the floor. The Westerner was watching him now, as if judging him. "Yes, sir?" he repeated.

"USS *Thomas Jefferson*. We will hit her through surrogates. The Americans will get the message."

Lao's heart pounded, and he thought, *They'll kill us.* "Has this been approved by the War Council?"

"This operation was planned by the War Council." The Westerner seemed less watchful, as if he had passed some test. "It is called Jade Talon. You will execute it. Use Islamic surrogates. I have appended contacts that we recommend."

Lao opened the new file with trepidation. The first item was a photograph of a Nimitz-class carrier. There followed a detailed analysis of the possibility of crippling a Nimitz-class carrier with a speedboat full of explosives. Lao looked up. "I don't believe this will sink a carrier."

"Sink? Probably not, although we want you to use several

boats. But a nice big hole? Perhaps leaking radioactive mate-rial? Hundreds of dead sailors?"

"And how are these small boats to target a carrier?"

"I'm sorry, Colonel?"

"How are a group of Islamic surrogates in tiny boats sup-posed to find this carrier and strike it?"

"*Jefferson* will be off the coast of Africa for sixty days. We have a method to pass accurate targeting information."

"Is this my operation?"

"Absolutely. Only, do not fail. And make finding Chen your priority. Am I clear?" The General was no longer smiling.

"Perfectly clear, sir."

Lao picked up all the files and saluted and turned. The room wheeled as if he were dizzy, but his mind was utterly clear. He knew that he had been sent to walk a razor's edge.

"DOES HE KNOW WHAT THIS IS REALLY ABOUT?" THE General said when the door had closed. The civilian snorted and shook his ugly hair. He lit another cigarette. The General sat back, hands folded. "He must have heard things."

"He doesn't know about the money. *Nobody* knows about the money."

"Perhaps we should have told him."

"No!" The hoarse voice was rude; the General's eyebrows arched a millimeter. "No. If he finds Chen, he finds the money. If he doesn't find Chen—" He shrugged.

"He is a good man," the General said. "There is no real chance for a speedboat to cripple a carrier, is there?"

"It sends a message. Either way. American public opinion is fickle. It might move the U.S. away from Africa. A lucky hit? It might damage the reactor and kill everyone on board. It might call into question the whole legality of placing a nu-clear reactor on a vessel in international waters."

"But Lao? Whether he finds Chen or not, he loses."

The civilian shrugged again.

Over the Pacific.

"Craik and Dukas," Jerry Piat said to himself, jammed into the middle of the five-across seats in the belly of a 747.

He was traveling economy class to Jakarta. Jerry was just past having been a hotshot CIA case officer. He had always traveled well, first or business class on cover passports or diplomatic ones, and the reality of an economy seventeen-hour flight from Washington with a layover in Manila had settled into his bones. *Being fired from the CIA means you have to travel like this,* he thought. Even walking around the cramped aisles didn't help the swelling in his feet.

Booze cost cash and was harder to get in the back of the plane. It was claustrophobic, with kids screaming and their mothers trying to ignore them, couples chatting or fighting. Too much. Not Jerry's scene.

The flight kept him awake and gave him too much time to think. He kept thinking of the messages and the plan he was on his way to implement. Too Byzantine, he felt. Too complex. The plan of an analyst, not an operator. He didn't like Ray Suter, the desk-driver who had thought it up, didn't trust him, thought him a boob when it came to the street. He didn't like Marvin Helmer, Suter's henchman, who was some big hotshot in Seattle now, but whom Jerry remembered as just one more Ops Directorate cowboy. Jerry wanted revenge against the traitors who had brought George Shreed down as much as anybody, but he didn't like the Suter-Helmer plan—or the planner. Photographs, blackmail, and a smear campaign. *Desk-driver shit. Like giving Castro an exploding cigar. Jesus.* He shook his head, raised the plastic cup of wine to his lips, and hated the taste.

Fuck that. In Jakarta, he would make up his own plan. Anything could happen in Jakarta. He began to shut out the plane as he worked it through. He had twelve hours left in his flight. By the time he landed, he'd be ready to act.

"Dukas and Craik," he murmured to himself, and tasted the wine again and concentrated on a simpler plan.

Kill them.

NCIS HQ.

ALAN CRAIK SHOWED UP AT DUKAS'S OFFICE A FEW
minutes after Dukas got there himself. Alan wasn't a stranger
to the Naval Criminal Investigative Service, even had a somewhat tenuous designation as "agent" because of past work for
Dukas. Still, he had had to go through some rigmarole with
security that had cost him time.

"Hey, Mike."

"Jesus, put out the cigarette! The tobacco police'll be here
with a warrant!"

Alan crushed the cigarette against the sole of his shoe. "I
quit, before—you know—then I—" He shrugged.

"Surprised some turkey didn't collar you out in the corridor." Dukas took the cigarette butt and doused it in a half-full
coffee cup and hid it under some trash, all the while studying
Alan's face. "I've seen you look worse." In fact, he was surprised at how relatively normal Alan looked—drawn, sleepless, but okay except for a new tic that drew one corner of his
mouth down in a kind of spasm and then was gone.

Alan gave a lopsided grin. "Death warmed over?"

"Practically lifelike. Anyway, enough about you; let's talk about me for a while. My injury feels pretty lousy, thanks for asking. And you noticed I'm wearing my Bugs Bunny rig—how perceptive of you."

"Oh, shit, Mike, I'm sorry—Christ, all I think about is myself—"

Dukas raised his hand, palm open, to shut Craik down, and said, "How's Rose?" and Alan said she was fine, fine, doing her fixed-wing prep so she could fly out to Edwards and fly F-18s before she went into astronaut training. "While I sit on my ass and watch reruns," he said, and Dukas knew that he had asked the wrong thing.

He put Alan at his absent assistant's desk and pulled up the drafts of his report on the Shreed affair and told him to read them and make comments. It was make-work, but it was work, and Alan seemed grateful. They worked that way for an hour, Dukas at his own computer, Alan at the other, a wall of white plastic crates between them, no sound but the building around them—footsteps, unclear voices—and the click of the computer keys.

And then the telephone rang.

"Dukas?"

Not a woman's voice. Not Sally Baranowski. A man's voice he recognized. "Hey, Carl."

"Long time no talk."

Dukas cast his mind back. Only a month—just before he'd taken off for Pakistan. Carl Menzes had been in a rage at him then, had called him every bad name he knew, because he had believed that Dukas had blown the investigation of the very spy, George Shreed, that Dukas had then caught up with in Pakistan. "Still mad, Carl?" He wrote "Menzes" on a Post-it and slipped it through the crates to Alan.

"Nah." Menzes laughed, a laugh that sounded honest to Dukas. In fact, he liked Menzes, who was a straight-arrow guy, a real fighter in the CIA's Internal Affairs Division. "How's the injury?"

"I can't scratch my dandruff yet, but I'm healing."

"Lot of people think you can do no wrong, Mike."

"Yeah, fucking hero. In fact, what I hear is, the Crystal Palace thinks we made a huge mistake. What's up?"

"We're sending you some of the paperwork you asked for."

Dukas was instantly on guard. "My experience is, you guys wouldn't toss a used rubber this way. And I didn't 'ask' for it; I got a court order for it. What happened, Legal Affairs decided that ten percent compliance would string it out for another six months?"

"Hey, Mike—! We're doing our best to satisfy you, okay?"

"Oh, yeah," Dukas said. "Oh, *yeah.*"

"I was trying to be helpful." Menzes's voice was cold, and a few seconds later he hung up.

Dukas looked across at Alan. "They're throwing me a bone. Big deal."

"Shreed stuff?"

"Worse—Suter." Ray Suter had been Shreed's assistant at the Agency, a one-hundred-percent bastard who got arrested when Shreed had fled the country. "Suter hacked into Shreed's computers; he's supposed to have killed some guy who helped him; he's *deep* into Shreed's business, and the Agency's got him someplace and won't let me near him. I've gone to court to get anything and everything that Suter had his hands on when Shreed went down." He made a face as if he smelled something bad. "So now they're sending something over. Oh, yeah."

AT ELEVEN, A NAVY RATING SHOWED UP AT DUKAS'S door with a dolly and a wooden crate the size of a refrigerator.

"Messenger service," the rating said. "He could only come as far as the loading dock. Where you want it, sir?"

Dukas looked at the signature sheet and the labels and signed for it. Classified, secure, CIA origin. When the rating was gone, Dukas closed his door and growled, "Ten to one it's a bag of shit." Dukas was at his telephone then, trying to get somebody with a wrecking bar to come open the crate.

"Must hold a lot of stuff."

Dukas made a face. "Probably a collection of Suter's old

jockstraps. You ask for everything, they generously extrude one item after a month's delay. You can bet this is whatever the Agency people thought was least useful."

What the crate proved to contain was a case file. "Case file" implied a folder, something small, but this was folder after folder, pounds and pounds of paper. There was a cover letter to say that it was one case, sent in response to the Naval Criminal Investigative Service request of—et cetera, et cetera. Dukas and Alan peered in.

"Jesus," Alan said. "This is all one case?"

"Wait until you see what the Shreed case looks like when it's done." Dukas shrugged himself out of the Bugs Bunny rig and reached into the crate. "If it's ever done. Old cases never die, and they don't just fade away." He pulled out a folder. "Well, let's see what we got."

Alan started to look in one of the folders, and Dukas said that they should go about it in an organized way, which was to find the inventory folder and the summary folder and get some idea of what the hell the thing was. The summary was at the bottom, of course, and it was only when they had covered the desk belonging to his absent assistant, Dick Triffler, as well as his coffee table and all the chairs, that they found it, and then Dukas sat at his desk and Alan leaned over him from behind, his hand with the missing fingers supporting him on the desktop—the first time since the shooting that he'd forgotten the hand enough to let somebody else see it up close.

"Radio transmissions," Dukas said, reading. " 'Burst transmissions of unknown origin—northwestern North America—' What the hell has this got to do with that shit Suter?" He looked up at Alan. "Can I turn the page?"

"I've been waiting." Alan grinned.

"Speed-reader, great. Okay—'detected by National Security Administration—' I thought this was an Agency case, what the hell? Where's the inventory? Where's the document history?" Dukas began to burrow as Alan read on. When Dukas came back, he had a red folder and a green one, both stamped "Top Secret," and he fell into his chair and opened the red folder. "Okay, yeah—NSA started it and got zip and booted it to the FBI, who made it a case and apparently sat on it for five years.

Then they booted it to the Agency—some great case, it's been through three other agencies and nobody's found out diddly-squat. Oh, swell—here's why they broke down and sent it to me—signed out to Ray Suter two days before Shreed took off for Pakistan. Jee-sus H. Christ, he didn't have it long enough to read the fucking summary. What'd you learn while I was slaving in the folder piles?"

"That it's a case that nobody's solved in nine years. Your big chance, Mike."

Dukas sighed. "I was hoping I'd get something I could, you know, at least use to tie Suter to the Shreed investigation." He threw down the red folder and opened the green one. "Oh, ow," he said. "Ow, ouch, oh, shit—radio interference reports up the wazoo! Ouch. 'Frequency Analysis Tables 1.1 through 1.17.' Oh, shit." He sighed. His right index finger ran down the page and he muttered, "Radio, radio ... interview, interview, interview—" He looked through the wall of crates at the stacks of folders and growled, "They've dicked me."

And Alan said, "What's that?"

He had reached over Dukas's shoulder and turned up the page so he could read ahead.

"What's what?"

Alan turned the page all the way over. " 'Communications Plan, Jakarta, Indonesia.' "

Dukas looked at the entry. "Jakarta, Jesus. That's a long way from northwestern North America."

"Kind of jumps out at you, doesn't it."

Dukas wrote the ID number down on another Post-it and went around the wall of plastic crates and started going through the folders once again. He came back with a slender folder in a white cover with "Top Secret" and "Eyes Only" and "Eurydice" on the front. "You're not supposed to see this," he said.

"What's Eurydice?"

"It's a classification group, which you're not supposed to know about, so don't ask." He sat down again and opened the folder.

"Holy shit," Alan said. "It *is* a comm plan for Jakarta." He looked over his shoulder. "What's Jakarta got to do with the Northwest?"

"More to the point, what's it got to do with Ray Suter?" Dukas wrinkled his nose. "I smell an analyst at work." He opened the folder on his desk, pressing the fold with the flat of his right hand and wincing because the effort hurt his chest. He pointed at the folder, which, opened, had papers attached to both inner sides by long, pointed prongs through holes in the paper. "Right side," he said, "meat and potatoes. Left side, the analyst's brilliant synthesis of materials." The comm plan was on the right side. On the left, on top, was a sheet that said simply, "No action recommended." Below it were several sheets with long numbers at the top. On the top sheet, however, a different hand had written in pencil, "Follow this up—S?"

"Suter's writing?" Alan said.

"Beats me; I don't even have a sample of *that*. 'Follow this up—S, question mark.' S for Suter? S for Shreed? S for shit?" He made a farting noise with his lips and tongue.

"Yeah, but, Mike, at least Suter had it. So why did Suter have it? You say he was into Shreed's business—what was he looking for? Maybe this is something you can run with, after all." Alan began to turn the pages of the analyst's report. "Doesn't seem to be all there," he said.

"It wouldn't be. The number's a high one, meaning that this is part of something else. 'Observation of courier contact site.' See, this is what caught the analyst's eye—actually, probably an abstract someplace. Yeah—here on the second page, see— 'The courier is believed to have visited the U.S., with special relevance for naval facilities in California and the Pacific Northwest.' Aha, says the analyst, that might have a connection— notice the 'might'; the woman—it's usually a woman—is reaching; she's desperate. She gets a copy of the relevant stuff and smacks it into a folder and here it is."

"Who wrote the report?"

"Who knows? Some agent doing his job; he's busted a comm plan, written it up, turned it over to his case officer, and here it is." He tapped the comm plan's several pages of narrative.

Alan reached over and turned the pages on the left side,

reading quickly, then did the same on the right. The paper was slightly brittle, the comm plan itself old enough to have been done on an electric typewriter rather than a computer printer. He lifted the top page on the left again and said, "1993."

"A little long in the tooth," Dukas said.

"But they never checked it out."

Dukas stretched. "So?"

Alan cocked his head. "Well—Somebody, maybe Suter, thought it was worth following up." His old grin, not seen for a month, partly returned. "Doing something is better than doing nothing—right?"

Dukas shook his head. "You're having an idea. I don't like that."

"I just thought somebody could go to Jakarta, check it out—follow it up, like it says here—" He looked like a kid asking for the day off from school.

Jakarta.

Jerry Piat moved his practiced hand from the bargirl's neck, over her breasts, down her flat and naked stomach, his hand always light and playful, never heavy or commanding. He hooked a leg under both of hers and rolled them both over so that she was above him, her breasts heavy against him, her long hair a black cloud that smothered him in incense. At least, it smelled like incense.

He watched her with the detached part of his brain, the part that wouldn't ever turn off, not when he was fucking, not when he was getting shot at, and that part registered that she was fourteen years old and had a Hello Kitty bag for her makeup. She liked him.

The phone rang. His hand found it, lifted it from the receiver, and dropped it back to the cradle. She laughed, happy that she was more important than a *Bule* (Westerner's) business call, but Jerry was just following the signal procedure— his agent, Bobby Li, would give him one ring, and then he would go out to a pay phone to talk. It wasn't exactly Moscow rules, but it was tradecraft, and Jerry was alive and sane where a lot of his peers were either dead or content to run Chinese double agents and lie about their access. Jerry rolled them both over again, still agile at fifty, and kissed her, hard, on the lips, which clearly surprised her.

Her body was still very much on his mind when he cursed the lift and started down the seven flights of cockroach-infested stairs to the hotel's lobby. The lobby was clean and neat, but the stairwell's strong suggestion of urine stayed in his nostrils until the heavy petroleum scent of unleaded car exhaust drove it out as he stepped into the street, still pulling a light jacket over his old silk shirt. The jacket had only one purpose, to hide the bulk of the gun that sat in his shoulder rig. In Jakarta, the only men in jackets were wearing guns, or so Jerry had come to believe during Suharto's regime. The place looked better now, cleaner, richer, even after the collapse in the nineties.

He stopped on the street, lit a cigarette from a nifty gas lighter with a serious torchlight that he had picked up at the airport. You could solder with the damn thing, and that could have its uses. Or you could burn someone's eyes out.

Two cab rides and three bars later, he was getting ready to make his phone call, on his way to start the process by which he would kill the men who had killed George Shreed.

One more stop, he told himself. *For old times' sake.*

And, of course, for caution's sake, because there always just might be that watcher who needed to be convinced that he was bar-crawling and not running an op.

Suburban Virginia.

Alan greeted his wife at the door with a kiss and a suddenly urgent embrace. She leaned back in his arms and looked at his eyes and saw something that made her grab him and squeeze him hard. They stood there, holding each other, rocking, and she said, "Something good happened, right?"

He laughed, a sound she hadn't heard in a while, and he

said, "I went to Mike's office to do some work. He got a new case—it's interesting, there's something in it for me, maybe—"

She was still in her flight suit. She had been out at Pax River, putting in her hours in the T-84 as she transited from choppers to fixed-wing. Holding her, seeing the sudden brightness in her eyes, he understood her misery of the past two weeks, never knowing what she would come home to. "I'm so sorry," he said.

"No, no—"

"Yes, yes." The dog pushed between them then and they both laughed and he pulled her into the house. "I had to leave Dukas early to get Mikey at school; no problem, but Dukas has this case, this crate of stuff! A case, something they dumped on him from the Agency because they can't hack it but I think we can; there's this comm plan in it; it doesn't make sense, but—I'm babbling, right?"

She laughed. "Right." She kissed him. "Keep babbling; it's nice."

"I'm getting dinner."

"I smell it. Risotto with white beans, garlic bread, frozen peas, and a salad, right?"

"I invited Mike for dinner."

That took a beat for her to absorb, sobering her, and she smiled too brightly and said, "Great!"

"To talk about the case," he said.

"Great!" She headed for the stairs. "I'll just change into something glamorous."

Half an hour later, Dukas was there with an attaché and a cell phone, which he dumped on the battered coffee table. He kissed Rose. "Hey, gorgeous, you're breathtaking."

"Did you bring the comm plan?" Alan shouted from the kitchen.

"Like you asked, yes, yes, yes! I always do what I'm told." He glanced toward the kitchen and lowered his voice still further. "This okay with you, babe?"

"If it makes him this cheerful, God, yes!"

"He's a little manic," Dukas murmured.

"I'll take manic," she said. "He's so down when he's not *in* things."

Dukas looked toward the kitchen again. "I used to think it was just, you know, type A behavior. But now I realize he always has to be proving something. To himself." He lowered himself into an upholstered chair. "You know the difference between you two? You've got a plan, an ambition—you're going to be an astronaut. You've built a career around it. He doesn't have a plan. He just has to *go*." Dukas looked up at her. "What's the matter with him?"

Alan shouted from the kitchen, "You talking about me out there?" He appeared in the doorway, grinning. "Speak up, or I'll think you're analyzing me." They stared at him a little guiltily, and the dog got up and sat there looking at him, too, and they all began to laugh.

Jakarta.

"Hey, Meester?" the voice said. Jerry whirled; that hand was awfully close to his pistol.

"Back off, bud." Jerry glared at the boy, but the boy, half Jerry's size and weight, held his ground.

"You memba?" He pointed up at a large sign in Dutch and English, Dutch still first, because this place went way back. ANHANGER ENKEL, MEMBERS ONLY.

"I was a member here when your mom still worked here, bud." Jerry leaned forward. "*Asrama pekerja?*"

Malay was clearly not his mother tongue, but the boy smiled and nodded.

"Go get the missus, then, bud." Jerry waved his hand, palm down, the fingers snapping open, like the locals—dismissed, the gesture meant. Then he turned and walked to the huge teak bar, forty-five feet long and carved from a single tree. He waved to the bartender, a slight youth in a clean white shirt. There weren't many customers, at least in the bar; the rooms upstairs could be full to bursting and you'd never know. George Shreed had waited for him in the spy's seat, there next to the alcove, a private booth invisible from the door.

"Meester?" It was the boy from the alcove.

"Hey, bud, we're done, you and me."

"You memba?" The boy was insistent, and it reminded Jerry of all the time and money he had spent here. He deserved better.

"Go get the missus. You hear me, sport? The missus? Before I bop you one, okay?" He wondered if they had gone to membership cards. Had it really been so long since he was here? Maybe they had fucking plastic IDs with your photo. He felt someone enter silently behind him, back by the alcove, and he turned to see Hilda, the handsomest of the Western blondes of his own day, coming through the door in sensible business attire—not what she'd worn back then, but still attractive.

"Jerry, darling."

"Hilda. Aren't you still too young to be trusted with the keys?"

She laughed; she had natural lines at her eyes and mouth that meant she'd disdained surgery, but she looked good. Really good. "This man is a member. An *old* member who gets anything he wants, *mengerti?*"

"*Yaas, majikan.*"

"Drink with me?"

"I can't—I'm working."

He looked at her and winked. "You were too good for that sort of thing when we were twenty years younger. The missus never made you *oblige* the customers."

"But I'm the missus now, and I have books to do. Come back—come back tomorrow and I'll drink with you."

"I might have to do that, Hilda." He smiled, gulped the rest of his gin and tonic, disappointed at one level, happy to be on with the job at another.

Jerry gave her something like a salute. She had poise, like a runway model; maybe she had been a runway model before she crashed in Jakarta. He didn't really know her, but he liked that she remembered him. Whores and spies; the oldest profession and the next oldest, or so the joke ran. He stopped in the alcove, still smiling because she had remembered him.

Aboard USS Thomas Jefferson.

Rafe Rafehausen pulled a stack of papers toward him, read again the paper on top, and then said, "Get me Admiral Pilchard at LantFleet. What the hell time is it there—? Yeah, you might catch him—try, try." He took the next paper off the stack and started to read, rubbing his eyes and wondering if they'd last through the reams of reading on this cruise, thinking, *Jesus, next I'll need glasses,* acutely aware again that his squadron years were over. He tried to concentrate on VF-105's morale self-study and was relieved when a phone was shoved toward him and the lieutenant-commander said, "Admiral Pilchard."

Rafehausen threw himself back in the chair. "Sir! Captain Rafehausen, CAG on the—Yes, sir." He grinned. "Nice of you to remember. Uh, kind of a personal matter, sir. If I say the name 'Al Craik,' will you—? Yes, sir, that's the one." He nodded his head as he listened. Pilchard was Craik's self-appointed "sea daddy," a kind of naval mentor and enabler. He swung, Rafe knew, between thinking that Craik was God's little cracker-jack prize and that he was a dangerously loose cannon, but he'd concern himself with Craik's welfare if it was threatened. Right now, he was in the loose-cannon phase, and Rafehausen winced at the admiral's sour tone. When the admiral had finished reviewing Craik's recent performance, Rafehausen said, "He's going nuts onshore and he needs something. I can't take him back here yet—med officers won't allow it. If there's something he could do—"

He looked up at the lieutenant-commander, winked as the admiral did some more talking about times in the past he'd gone out on a limb for Craik, and how sick he was of having Craik blue-sky things and act as if rules didn't exist. When the admiral stopped talking, Rafehausen said, "Absolutely, sir!" He grinned again. "What I was thinking, I just received some correspondence about this experimental MARI det that was set up—that's the det that Craik was commanding, sir, when—good, yes, sir, you remember all that. Well, it's gone so well that there's a request about setting up a second MARI det on the west coast; I was wondering if maybe that could be moved up some, then Craik could go out there now instead of at the end of this cruise—Yes, sir, to advise and—No, sir, not as det CO, and not to fly because—Yes, sir. No, sir. Purely advisory, yes, sir, of course they'd pull personnel from the west coast squadrons, and Craik would—Yeah, Miramar, I'm sure that Miramar—Uh—"

Rafehausen signaled to the lieutenant-commander to close the door. Swiveling around, he bent forward as if he had to talk to the floor. "It's a matter of helping a good man, sir. I know Craik—I think we could lose him if he doesn't get something to do. Between you and me, Admiral, I think he got hit harder than we thought on that recent mission. I don't normally put much stock in 'trauma' and all that psychobabble, but he's been sending me p-comms that, well, I think maybe he's lost some faith in himself." Again, he listened, slowly leaning back, and when there was silence on the other end, he said, "Yes, sir. That'd be great. That'd really be great. And absolutely, yes, I'll put the fear of God in him to do it by the book. And if they can see their way to setting up a west coast det with him on board, it would—Of course, of course, these things take time—Yes, sir. Yes, sir. Yes, sir."

A minute later, he had hung up and turned back to the pile of paper, Al Craik now only one of many worries nibbling at the edges of his consciousness.

Jakarta.

He gave terse orders to the third cab of the night, cutting across the city, going twice down *gangs* rinsed clean by the heavy rain, until he was tired of the game. Clean as clean could be. Then he led them back south away from the sea by the toll road, off the Semaggi Interchange and into the gleaming modernity at the heart of Westernized Jakarta. It wasn't his favorite part of the city; he liked the Japanese in Japan but hated them when they were abroad. It never occurred to him that they acted just like him.

"*Wat ingang?*" asked the driver in Dutch. Jerry was white

and coming from Emmy-Lu's, hence Dutch, as far as the driver could tell.

"Hotel Mulia Senayan, *danke*. Simpruk." The Mulia was the newest, flashiest hotel in Jakarta, with over a thousand rooms and the largest ballroom in Asia. It was the multiple entrances and table phones that drew Jerry—a postman's paradise. Simpruk was a broad and well-traveled avenue full of business traffic; he'd leave by the main entrance and go to the cabstand, and while he sat and talked he'd be another business traveler. A little seedy, but hardly the only Westerner in the lobby, and that's what mattered to Jerry. And nice public lines—murder to monitor, and businessmen don't like monitored lines.

Jerry paid the cab before they stopped, was out and up the steps before the cab had pulled away. No time to linger; this was the operational act itself, the very heart of the game. It didn't matter if no one was watching; Jerry played for an invisible audience of fellow professionals he hoped weren't ever there, breezing into the enormous lobby, walking past the desks to the central bar where leather couches held the open space against a jungle of local potted plants. At each end of every couch sat a house phone, and Jerry knew how to use one to get an outside line in Jakarta. He ordered a gin and tonic from a waiter, sat, and looked at his watch.

Two hours and ten minutes since the phone had rung in his room and he had hung it up. The last time he had worked in Jakarta, he'd been following orders from George Shreed. Now he would set up an operation to avenge him. It had an Asian air to it, like an episode in the tale of the Forty-Seven Ronin.

He lifted the phone.

Suburban Virginia.

"Sleeping Dog was an NSA case, and then it was a Bureau case, and then it was a CIA case. And now it's *our* case," Dukas explained to Rose. They were eating in what was called the dining room, which barely had enough room for the table and three people. "Believe it or not, it's nine years old."

"And it's got this comm plan," Alan said. "The first action item."

"Who says it's an action item?" Dukas said.

"Well, isn't it? They should have moved on it when they got it, and they didn't."

Dukas raised his eyebrows. "We've barely looked at the stuff. There could be tons of action items."

"Not according to the inventory." Alan put his elbows on the table and turned to Rose. "The comm plan just leaps out at you; it's the way a courier could meet with somebody else, and it was connected somehow with this Sleeping Dog—"

"We don't know that," Dukas growled. He finished the risotto on his plate. "Who taught you to make risotto?" he said.

"You did."

"Good for me." He held up his plate. "I'll have some more." He watched the plate being heaped with the yellow grains and the dust-colored beans. "Next time, just a tad more saffron, okay?"

Alan grinned at Rose and poured more red wine and said to Dukas, "I want to go to Jakarta."

"To do what, for Christ's sake?"

"To test the comm plan."

"Alan, read my lips: You're not a spy! You're an intel officer!"

"Yeah, but I'm available. And you know you can trust me, which is a big deal for you right now because you think everybody's on your back over George Shreed." He leaned forward. "Mike, it's three days—fly there, nice hotel, take a walk, leave a mark, have a nice dinner, go to the meeting place. Bang, that's it."

"And what happens at the meeting place?" Rose said, scenting trouble.

"Nothing. Ask Mike. He insists it's a dead issue because nobody's done anything with it for years and there's nobody at the other end. Right?"

"Did I say that?"

"You did. Just before I left this afternoon."

"Well—"

Rose was looking at her husband with her head tipped to the side. "If it's dead and nothing's going to happen, why go?"

He seemed to falter, then made an apologetic face. "Because it's something to do," he said softly.

She changed the subject then by asking Dukas about Sally Baranowski, a question that embarrassed him and made him almost stammer. Dukas told them about the call on his answering machine that he hadn't returned and then admitted his doubts about getting involved, and at last he was telling them both that he was still shaken by the shooting and he didn't know what he wanted. "So what is this," he growled, "post-traumatic stress syndrome?"

Rose put a hand over one of his, then over Alan's good one. "You guys," she said. "You guys."

After dessert, when Alan had brought coffee into the living room, he raised the subject of Jakarta again. It was clear to them then that Alan had brought Dukas there that night because he was asking Rose's permission as well as Dukas's: He was trying to get a go-ahead from both of them. "Give Rose and the kids a rest from my bad temper, drink some good beer, do Mike and Uncle a favor." He looked at Rose. "And in case you're worried, this is a no-risk operation—a walk in the park." The appeal in his voice was touching. "It's a walk in the park!"

Dukas snorted. "It's a free trip to Jakarta, that's what it is." He stirred sugar and then cream into his coffee, even though all day long he drank it black. "Well—if you come back and tell me nothing happened, I can close out what you call 'the action item,' that's true. Then I can bore myself stiff with the radio crap for six months and close out the whole file, and then I can go back to writing reports about why I should be reimbursed for ten grand I took on my personal responsibility when we were running after that shit George Shreed. That's your view of it?"

Alan looked at him, then at his injured hand, and then he reached out with his good hand to his wife. "You're flying all day. I just sit here."

She squeezed his hand. To Dukas, she said, "Can he do it?"

Dukas shrugged. "You don't just 'do' a thing like this. You got to have a country clearance. Once we apply, the Agency gets notified, then they want to know what's going on and why they're not the ones to do it. Then we wrangle, on and on."

"They had their chance," Alan said.

"Not the way they'd see it."

"It's *your* case now. You've got a number, what can they say?" He leaned forward. "Mike, let me go. I go, *then* you apply for the country clearance; it's happening too fast for them to do anything."

"No—I don't think so—"

"Mike, Goddamit," Alan snapped, "you lost your nerve? Jesus, you can't apply for a country clearance; you can't even call an old girlfriend on the fucking phone!"

Rose's hand gripped Dukas's. He looked into Alan's suddenly angry face and looked away to keep things from escalating. He sighed. "And if something goes wrong?"

"What can go wrong? You said yourself, it's dead! It's just crossing the *t*'s and dotting the *i*'s! What can go wrong with that?"

Dukas sipped coffee. "Jakarta, that's what." He looked at Alan, and Alan winked. Another first since Pakistan. Dukas put down his cup. "Tell you what. Triffler's back tomorrow. I'll have him check Al out on the comm plan—walk him through it, lay it out on paper. Then it'll be easy. Right?"

He was talking to Rose. She made a face. "It's still Jakarta," she said.

Jakarta.

Just an old-fashioned spy, he thought. The idea delighted him. He was drunk, happy-drunk. *I want a spy/Just like the spy that buggered dear old dad.* He lifted the telephone and rang through, picturing the little man who would be waiting at the public telephone.

"Yes?" The voice was tentative. Bobby Li, the agent at the other end, never seemed quite sure of himself. Well, people who were absolutely sure of themselves didn't make good agents, right?

"Wondering if you've read *Green Eggs and Ham.*"

"Oh, yes, right. 'Mister Brown is out of town/He came back with Mister Black.' Hi!" Bobby sounded distant, but he had the recognition codes right. Good start.

"Hey, Sundance—how're they hanging?"

Bobby Li giggled. George Shreed had given him that code name. "Hey, Butch Cassidy."

"Long time, bud." Three years, in fact. But they'd had some great times before that. "Want to play some ping-pong, bud?" *Ping-pong* was telephone code for an operation.

"Good. Great!" Real pleasure in the high voice. Bobby loved him still.

"I'm going to need a few items, bud."

"Sure thing, boss."

Jerry struggled for a moment with the simple telephone code, trying to remember the word for cameras. Ah. Camera. Hidden in plain sight. He was supposedly in Jakarta to find locations for a Hollywood feature film, as good a cover as he'd ever had, as it excused a great deal of roaming. He was using his old cover name, Andrew Bose, who had always been an antique dealer in the past, but what the hell. Cameras were now a legitimate extension of his cover, so no code word needed. Too much booze, he thought, but wryly, and not really meaning it. Can't really have too much booze. "Need a camera, bud. And a guy to use it, okay? To photograph the ping-pong."

"Sure."

"And an ice bucket, okay?" *Ice bucket* was code for a weapon.

"Oh—okay—" Now Bobby seemed nervous, but, because Jerry was ordering him to find a weapon, that made sense.

"A *big* ice bucket, okay?"

"Sure, sure."

"And some ice." Then Jerry switched to a serious voice. Bobby would be happier if he thought things were serious. "This is a big game of ping-pong, pal." Jerry leaned forward as if Bobby was right there. "You want to play in the big game. This is it, Bobby. The start of a big game." He looked around the hotel lobby for the door to the bar, saw people going up three steps and out of sight and figured it was that way. "Meet me at Papa John's and we'll practice some ping-pong." *Papa John* was code for a place and a time. Would Bobby remember after three years? Of course he'd remember! Bobby Li fucking loved him!

He hung up and headed for the bar. He was still sober enough to have kept from his old agent the fact that the ping-pong was going to end in the death of an American.

BOBBY LI HUNG UP AND FELT EXCITED AND HAPPY. He had thought maybe his friend Andy had forgotten him.

Bobby had lived his whole life in Jakarta. He was Chinese only by ethnicity, but ethnicity made for sharp divides here. Sometimes it was the ultimate arbiter of loyalty.

And loyalty was crucial for Bobby Li, because he was a double agent—for his American friend who had just talked to him on the telephone, and for Loyalty Man, who was Chinese and a right shit and not his friend at all. Bobby was loyal to Loyalty Man because of ethnicity, the powerful force, but he was more loyal to the American because he was his friend and because he also loved George Shreed, who had been Bobby Li's surrogate father. It had been George Shreed who had pulled him out of the gutter of Jakarta and made him a pet, a pal, and an agent. Love trumped ethnicity.

Bobby had worked for George Shreed for two years, and then for both George Shreed and Mister Chen, a double agent already at thirteen, but different then because both men had known he was a double—Chen had made him one and then Shreed had accepted it and become a double himself. And then one day George Shreed had taken him aside and had said that he had to go back to the United States, and somebody else would be there instead. That was the worst day of Bobby's life, when George Shreed had told him he was leaving.

"And a new guy will be taking over," George had said. "Taking you over, too, Bobby. But—" George's eyes signaled the secret look that Bobby loved, the look that said that it was only the two of them against the world. "But we won't tell the new guy about Mister Chen, okay? Mister Chen is our secret, Bobby."

That had been twenty years ago, and he had never told. The new guy had been called Andy Bose, which was surely not his real name, but Bobby knew enough about espionage to understand that, and anyway, he had liked Andy from the start. And then Mister Chen had turned him over to another Chinese, and then he to another, and so on—six Chinese controls he had had, the last one this shit, Loyalty Man—and he had been the whole time with Andy. And now Andy had called him and they were going to do a big operation together, just like old times, and it would be great.

Being a double agent wouldn't matter. He could be loyal to Andy for the operation, and nobody the wiser. It would be great.

Suburban Virginia.

Lying in the dark, Alan could feel Rose beside him, feel her wakefulness and her worry. There had been no sex since he had got out of the hospital. He had been afraid, he realized, confused by why the injury to his hand should make him so.

"Alan?"

He grunted.

"You really want to go on this Jakarta thing, don't you?"

He grinned into the darkness. "Yeah—I confess: I really do."

He heard her chuckle. "Hey, sailor," she whispered, "want to have a good time?"

"I—" He swallowed. "I'm afraid I'll touch you with my ha-hand. . . ." He felt her move on the mattress and heard the rustling of cloth.

He heard the smile in her husky voice. "Just you leave everything to me," she murmured, settling on top of him.

Then he began to slide down that glassy slope that is sex, losing his fear, losing consciousness, losing self-consciousness, merging with her and coming to himself again in warmth and sweetness and safety; and, later, he knew that it was at that moment that his real healing began.

Northern Pakistan.

Colonel Lao stood in the remnants of a street, peering out from under the hood of an American rain parka at generations of rubble. The village had been fought over recently. The mosque had been destroyed years ago. In between, the village had been a focus of violence over and over.

His people had a generator running and spotlights on the ruins of the mosque. Forensics people from State Security were all over the site. He hoped they were working for him. Their team leader had an encrypted international cell phone of a type his department had never heard of, much less issued. Lao watched them with a detachment worthy of the ancients. He didn't even have a cell phone.

"Sir?" His new man, Tsung. Young and competent. A little lazy, but well-trained. He was hovering at arm's length, careful of Lao's silence. Lao appreciated his courtesy.

"Are you waiting for me, Tsung?" He turned, shook rain off his parka.

"I have an eyewitness the Ministry seems to have missed. He says that after the plane left, another car left too, going north."

Lao shook his head again, though not at the rain.

"Well done, Tsung. We needed another complication."

North meant trouble. Afghanistan, Tajikistan, Russia. Lao didn't want to consider what would happen if the Russians had Chen. He followed Tsung toward the ruined tower, stopped by a low wall where a technician in an olive-drab poncho was using forceps to clear something out of the muck.

"Cartridge?"

"That shotgun. The shooter moved all the time."

Lao ducked under the awning and accepted a cup of tea from one of the State Security goons. He had a picture in his head of the fight in the village. Shreed had never moved, firing repeatedly from one position in the open. That made Lao think he had been the first man hit. It also suggested that Shreed had been either ambushed or set up, and that didn't fit any of the theories he had been offered in the office in Beijing.

Chen's opposition had come from only a few men, perhaps as few as three or four. They'd killed Chen's paratroopers with relative ease. Because it was a trap? Or because the Chinese paratroopers weren't all that good? Lao wasn't that kind of soldier. He looked at the trails of tape that marked the movements of individual shooters, traced by the cartridge casings they had let fall, and thought that the opposition had done all the moving.

One of the Chinese, a sniper, had apparently killed two of his own men before he was killed himself. That made no sense to Lao. Lao thought that someone else must have killed the sniper and used his weapon. Perhaps the forensics men would find something to prove his theory—or perhaps they wouldn't.

He used his teacup to warm his hands as Tsung brought him an older man, his thin trousers flapping in the wind. Lao bowed a little and the old man gave him a nervous smile.

"Tell him that I'm a policeman."

Tsung spoke to the old man in careful Arabic. It wasn't his best language, and it was one the old man probably only knew from the Qur'an, but they communicated.

Lao stood patiently, sipping tea and offering it to his witness, while the old man told the story of the evening in halting driblets. Lao taped it. He didn't speak much Arabic and he wasn't sure he'd trust anyone in Dar to translate, but he had to keep a record.

The old man pointed out the commanding view that the little hill village had of the highway below them in the valley. He described the plane's landing on the road, and he described the other car's driving away after the plane had left. Yes, he was sure. No, he had no idea who had been in the car.

Lao swallowed the rest of his tea and spat out the leaves.

Maybe Chen was alive, after all. Lao smiled without humor: If Chen was alive, then he could clean up his own messes. Like the unfinished operation to target the *Jefferson*. Lao disliked executing operations in whose planning he'd had no part—

let Chen be alive and take it over! The operation, he thought, had been put together too hastily, too emotionally—it seemed part of that nervous hysteria he'd felt in Beijing. He never thought he'd be sorry that Chen was dead (if he was dead), but he'd be delighted to have him rise now from the rubble of this Pakistani village and take over.

"Tsung," he said. The younger man came almost at a trot. Eager. Lao was wondering if Tsung could be trusted to take over some of the details of the *Jefferson* operation and free him, Lao, to concentrate on Chen. "You've run agents among the Pakistani military?" he said.

Tsung grinned. "They don't like to call themselves agents. 'Friends of China,' meaning they have an agenda that matches ours somewhere." He made a joined-hands gesture, fingers of one hand inserted between the fingers of the other like meshing gears.

"I have a task for you."

Tsung said something about being honored. Lao ignored it. He skipped details—the name of the *Jefferson*, the use of the submarines to pass data, the agent on the west coast of the United States—and explained about the plan to tap into Islamic hatred of America and to launch a small-boat attack on an American warship.

NCIS HQ.

Alan was in Dukas's office at NCIS headquarters at nine-thirty, eager to hit the road for Jakarta.

Dukas was supposed to be making the travel arrangements; his assistant, the until-then absent Dick Triffler, was going to brief Alan and then go along to ride shotgun.

"Shotgun, hell," Triffler said. "My son's pitching tonight for his Little League team, and being Dad is more important than playing cops and robbers. Sorry, Commander."

Alan grinned. "You wouldn't say that if Mike was here."

"I'd say it in spades if Mike was here! You think I'm afraid of Mike?"

Triffler was a tall, slender African-American with what

Alan had to think of as "class." His skin was the color of caramel; his face was handsome and lean; his voice was a tenor, his enunciation pure northeastern U.S. He was not afraid of Mike Dukas, that was true; in fact, he emphasized their differences whenever he got the chance. Their shared office, for example, was divided by a wall of white plastic crates, into which the obsessively neat Triffler had put potted plants, sculptures, books—anything, in fact, that would block his view of the squalid mess where Dukas ruled.

Alan laughed. "I think you're about as afraid of Mike as I am, Dick. But, uh, this *is* an operation, and I really *am* going to Jakarta, and I really do need some—"

Triffler waved a long hand. "Okay! I know! Uncle Sam says I have to go. *Tomorrow!* Okay? So I get there twenty-four hours after you, so what? You take a nap, have some local beer, watch TV. I'll catch up." Triffler shot his cuffs, maybe to show off his cuff links. "I don't want to spend any more time in a germ pit like Jakarta than I have to, anyway."

Alan didn't comment on "germ pit." He had heard enough about Triffler to know he was obsessive about cleanliness, too—the only man in NCIS who slid a coaster under your coffee cup when you picked it up. "Well—if it'll work—"

"Sure, it'll work. I got here at twenty of eight this morning; Dukas *already* had the file and a memo on top of the pile of other jobs he's tasked me with while I was away, so I've read it and looked at the map and I'm up to speed."

"If you wouldn't take time off"—a voice came from the other side of the room divider—"you wouldn't get tasked."

"Hey, Mike—when did you sneak in?"

"I didn't sneak, Al, I walked; you and Mister Clean were too busy dissing me to notice. And how are you this morning, Mister Triffler?"

"I was telling Lieutenant-Commander Craik that I'm not afraid of you, is how I am."

"Good. Nobody should live in fear. You rested after your vacation?"

"It was not a vacation! It was quality time with my family." Triffler smiled at Alan. "Some people don't *have* families. Unsociable, outsider people."

"Somebody has to do the scut work while you daddies are having quality time," Dukas's voice growled. "Will you guys get to it, please?"

They spent three hours. Triffler explained—redundantly, but there was no stopping him—what a comm plan was and what the Jakarta plan was. He went through the structure that Alan would have to build around the comm plan—walking a route before he left the mark that was supposed to set up the meeting, memorizing codes to communicate with his team (that is, Triffler), planning for a busted meeting and an escape.

"Which won't happen," Triffler said, "because there isn't going to be any meeting to bust, right? This is a dead plan, right? Uncle's paying to send us to Jakarta so Mister Dukas can cross an item off a list, right?" He raised his voice. "IS THAT RIGHT, MIKE?"

"Just do your job."

DICK TRIFFLER WAS DOWN TO SHIRTSLEEVES AFTER an hour more of briefing Alan, revealing wide yellow suspenders to go with his yellow-on-beige striped shirt. His tie looked like heavy embroidery, also brown and yellow with flecks of green. He made Alan feel dowdy, even in uniform.

"Uh, what will you be wearing in Jakarta?" Alan said.

Triffler looked startled. He spread his arms as if to say, *These.* "Work clothes," he said. He looked more than a little like a model in *GQ.*

"I thought I'd wear jeans."

Triffler coasted over that by saying they weren't going undercover, so there was no need to think of disguise. "We're just two guys who happen to work for the Navy, having a look around Jakarta. In and out in two days. One suit, one wrinkle-free blazer, two neckties, four shirts."

"And blue jeans."

Triffler looked at Alan's uniform, then his shirt, then his polyester tie, and apparently decided to say nothing. He got them both coffee—great coffee, because he was also obsessive about that—and sat again at his uncluttered desk. "You go in," he said. "Normally, you'd have watchers. This time, only me. No problem; there's nothing to watch. You do a route to a cannon, or whatever it is where you leave the mark. If we thought the plan was active, we'd have a team to watch the mark to see who picks up on it, but not ap, right? You get a good night's sleep, we rendezvous—telephone codes to come, so you know where and when—and you go to make the meeting, which is in something called the—I had it a moment ago—"

"The Orchid House."

"Right! You're way ahead of me. In some sort of park— theme park? Something. So, you go there, and you walk the route in the comm plan—this is so the other side can look at you if need be; their guy is walking a route, too, in theory, and we'd have a team to watch, but we don't and won't—and you go into this Orchid House and walk to, quote, 'bench by curved path, west side,' where, at ten minutes after the hour, at three stated times of day *precisely,* there would be some guy waiting for you if this was an active plan. Which it ain't."

"What if it is?"

"It isn't; we have Reichsführer Dukas's word on it."

"Yeah, but just suppose—what if?"

"You say your recognition words and he says his, some b.s. about a Christmas party, and then you look at each other and wonder what the hell comes next."

" 'Hi, my name is Al, and I'll be your waiter this evening'?"

"Try 'What have you got for me?' At least that sounds as if you know what you're doing." Triffler closed the folder and slapped his hand on it. "Won't happen. In and out in two days, home again to the rapturous applause of Mike Dukas."

"Ha, ha," said the voice from the other side.

"Okay." Alan grinned. "Now what do we do?"

"Now we go over it again, and then you memorize the codes and the greetings and the route, and then we go over it again, and then we go over it."

"Not really."

Triffler sighed. "Really. You thought signing EM orders was tedious? Try spying."

Jakarta.

Jerry Piat had half a dozen places in Jakarta where he stayed when he made a trip there, places he'd come to like over the years and felt comfortable in. Only one had any class; only one was really a dump. The others were modest little hotels where low-end tourist agents put groups that were doing Asia on the cheap. He had kicked around the East long enough that he spoke the languages and didn't require a block-square chunk of America to sleep in, and he liked the strange mix of comfort and oddness that the places gave him.

The Barong Palas had been built by a Dutch exporter as his city house in the nineteenth century; when the Dutch left after World War II, it had become a whorehouse, then a clutter of ground-floor shops with a squat in the upper floors, and finally a hotel when an energetic Indonesian woman had bought it and kicked everybody out. It still looked Dutch—a stair-step roof, a certain overweight look to the cornices and lintels—but inside it was immaculate, slightly threadbare, secure. They locked the doors at twelve, required that guests pick up and drop off a key each time they went in or out, and paid their own knife-toting guards to patrol the gardens that surrounded it.

Now Jerry woke in one of its bedrooms. The room wasn't much because the hotel—only twenty rooms in all—was full of a Korean gourmet club. He didn't remember that, at first. His hangover was intense—familiar but awful: a headache like an ax in the skull, a swelling of the eyes, a nausea that became vertigo if he moved. Then he remembered where he was and what he had done last night—the bars, Hilda, the call to Bobby Li—and he sat up and let the full awfulness of the hangover grip him like a fist.

"Nobody ever died of a hangover," he said aloud, a man who had suffered thousands. In fact, he thought that people probably had died of hangovers, but not this one, which he would classify as a Force Four, severe but not fatal. Nothing would help, he knew; showers and coffee and deep breathing were for amateurs. He dressed and headed out.

The code he had given Bobby Li, *Papa John's,* meant a

corner by a taxi rank opposite the Import-Export Bank, at ten minutes after seven in the morning, ten after nine, and ten after four in the afternoon. He had already missed the seven-ten. Bobby would have been there, he knew, waited for three minutes, pretending to read a newspaper, and walked away. Jerry felt guilty.

Not professional, missing a meeting time.

He walked slowly, balancing the hangover on his head. He stopped in a sushi bar and had two sea-urchin-egg sushis, supposed to be good for his condition. The green tea seemed to help. Four aspirin from a corner vendor helped still more, and each stop let him check his back trail and see that nobody was following. He then stepped abruptly to the street and pushed himself into a cab that two Indonesians were just leaving, then wove through central Jakarta and got out three blocks from the Import-Export Bank. At nine-ten, he was fifty feet from the taxi rank.

Bobby Li was there.

Jerry got into a cab and told the driver to go slowly. After a block, he looked back; another cab was following.

"Fantasy Island Park," he told his driver. When they got there, the other cab was still behind. He'd noted nobody else. He had the driver go three blocks beyond the park, and he got out; the other taxi pulled up and Bobby Li got out and followed Jerry to the park entrance without acknowledgment.

"Hey, bud," Jerry said when he was standing in the shade of the ornate gate. Bobby Li smiled. Bobby was a smiler, one reason he still seemed like a teenager to Piat, that and his small size. "Hey, Andy," Bobby said. He was pathetically happy to see him.

"Come on, bud, I'll show you where the ping-pong's going to be." They went into the park, which was an old-fashioned fun park crossed with a somewhat corny cultural display, none of it terribly well-maintained. The centerpiece, however, was a world-class collection of orchids.

"Been here before?" Jerry said.

"I bring the kids."

"How're the kids?"

"Good." A big smile. "The boy is bigger than me. Fifteen now."

"The wife?"

"She okay. Working hard." The Lis didn't make a lot of money, Jerry knew. Bobby had a small business, buying and selling exotic bird skins. Jerry, in fact, had set him up in it, persuading the CIA that it was worth the investment to have an agent with decent cover and an income. It amused him that Bobby was a feather merchant, the old term for a bull-shitter. Amused him because that was the last thing Bobby could be.

"How's the business?"

"Pretty good. Lot of problems, CITES, that stuff." He waved a hand. "Big companies cutting all the forest every-place, no birds."

Jerry led them to a kiosk where ethnic dancers performed several times a day. The kiosk was white, glaring in the sun-light, empty plastic chairs around it for the audience. He nod-ded his head toward it. "Our man is going to walk in the gate and sit here—that's in his comm plan." Bobby took it in but didn't ask any questions. Agents got told what they needed to know, nothing more. "I'll give you a photo of him. You get a guy who'll sit here and check him out. I want him checked for guns, wire, walkie-talkie—anything. Has to be visual—can't touch him. Maybe bump him once when the crowd's moving, but they got to be careful, because if it's the guy I expect, he's a pro and he'll know what's up." The guy he expected was Dukas. Dukas was the one who would get the file; Dukas was the special agent. It wouldn't be Craik, who was Navy and would be off saving the world someplace. If Jerry's luck was bad, it would be merely some NCIS nobody that Dukas had got to come over from Manila, and then the whole plan would have to be shit-canned. That was one reason it was a bad plan, as Jerry had pointed out to both Suter and Helmer.

He dug out a photograph of Dukas that he'd lifted from an old Agency file. "That's him." The picture was ten years old, and Dukas looked tough and overweight. Jerry had looked for a photo of Craik but had dug up only a useless old group

photo from a squadron book in which he looked about fifteen.

Jerry led Bobby over to a food concession and bought a
Philippine pancake and two green teas, and he ate the pancake with his torso pitched forward so he wouldn't spill anything on his shirt and pants. "You get the ice bucket?" he said.
They both sipped the tea.

"Not yet, Andy." He didn't say, *It was only last night you
asked for it, for Christ's sake.* Bobby never said things like that.

"I'll show you where I want it." Piat licked his fingers and
walked toward the Orchid House, a greenhouse perched atop
a concrete model of a Javanese fortress, circa 1500. They went
inside, where a broad path covered in bark mold wound
through two full acres of flowers, which rose so high they
screened the turns of the path, preventing long sight lines and
making a perfumed maze with walls forty feet high. Four entrances, each arriving from a separate path through the minipark.

It was one of the most perfect sites for a clandestine
meeting that Jerry had ever seen. It was a site where a man
could meet his agent while the whole world watched him,
never really *knowing* whether they had met. It had George
Shreed written all over it.

Jesus, George knew his craft.

"This is where the meeting's going down," he said. He led
the way along the path, his left hand gently stroking the narrow leaves of a mountain orchid. "I'm going to tell you a secret," he said. Bobby was behind him; when Piat turned, he
saw that the little man looked worried. Agents didn't usually
get secrets. "Who d'you think chose this site? Go on, guess.
Take a guess." Bobby frowned still more. "George," Piat said.

"George!"

"George Shreed picked it." Jerry grinned. The hangover
had receded and was a dull ache with a peculiar peacefulness
spread over it. "I shouldn't be telling you this. No need to
know. But I thought you'd care. Because of George." Bobby
looked flustered and excited. Jerry had paid him a great compliment, made a great gesture of trust. The little man was absurdly flattered. Finally, he was able to say, "How is George?"

Jerry realized that, of course, Bobby didn't know. "George is dead, Bobby. That's what all this is about—the people who killed him are going to make this meeting. Then we're going to get them."

Tears stood in Bobby's eyes. All the pleasure of being told a secret was wiped away. "George *dead*?" he murmured.

"We're doing this for George, pal." He touched Bobby's shoulder. "Okay?"

Piat located the actual meeting place, where the path curved and a bench stood among the orchid plants. He pointed out the main entrance through which their man would come, and then walked to the one at the opposite point of the compass. "And this is where our guy will come in. Then he'll walk around that way, taking his time, back the way we just came, to the meeting place. Got it?"

Bobby nodded.

"Our guy will carry a copy of *The Economist* to identify himself, and he'll also have an envelope stuffed with what will feel like money, which he'll hand to the guy who killed George, and your team with the camera will get a *good* picture. Got that?"

"Got it, Andy."

Jerry smiled. "You haven't asked who's going to be our guy."

Bobby shook his head.

"Go on, ask. You can ask, it's okay."

Bobby knew then that he was supposed to ask. "Who?" he said, like a good stooge.

"You." Piat laughed and slapped him on the shoulder and headed for the far wall of the greenhouse, walked boldly past a young man raking bark mold off the path and another misting leaves with water, both of whom looked at him but were cowed by his eyes. He pushed past them down a maintenance trail and on to a battered sign with TREETOPS painted on it; directly below it was a less old but hardly new sign that said CLOSED. Jerry remembered when Treetops (the name borrowed from the famous African lodge once visited by Queen Elizabeth) was new, a viewing platform out over the entire Orchid House, back when its trees had been young and its vines small. Built cleverly of steel pipe disguised to look like branches, it was meant to recall those game-viewing, tiger-shooting platforms once put up in real jungles. Now, the trees reached to the roof and the vines were as thick as your wrist, and Treetops was old and sagging and probably unsafe.

"Come on."

He climbed the imitation-treetrunk stair, ignoring the thought that every worker in the Orchid House was watching them. The old viewing platform was filled with rolls of hose and cuttings, and the protective railing was broken, and the pigeons that flew in and out of the broken panes of the greenhouse had used it as their personal privy. The platform, however, looked as if nobody had been up there for years, except, he now saw, for the odd, courageous tourist who climbed up to stand in the one spot where you could see through some of the greenery.

Jerry lay full length, looking over the edge of the platform. "They need a few elephants," he muttered. From up here, he could see most of the meeting site—the back of the bench, but not its legs, because of the foliage; about three feet of path to the left of the bench, the side from which Bobby would come; and a little more on the side where he hoped Dukas would come.

"I want the big ice bucket placed up here, okay? Roll it in a floor mat; I can lie on that."

"You going to—?" Bobby stopped himself. He had been about to ask a question. Piat ignored it, concentrated on the bark path beyond the bench. *Have to wait until they've got the photo. Then shoot? Or wait until he starts out*—He tracked an imaginary figure back toward the exit to his own right, seeing the path here and there as a red-brown stain among the green leaves and the flowers. There was one place that might do. *Have to be ready, shoot as he moves into the open. Bang.* Not such a long shot, but iffy because of the visibility.

Then noise and a lot of running around; I leave the gun, just like Oswald in Dallas; I head for the stairs—He raised his head to look at the steep, winding staircase, then craned to look down. There was better cover from the leaves where he was, one now-huge tree masking most of the front of Tree-tops. A sober man without a hangover could shinny down the old scaffolding unseen. *Climb down, no sweat, there's a lot of uproar, our team is making noise and providing a diversion—what?* He looked up at the glass roof, saw the lines of water pipes up there. He studied the vast space. "Can you get a stun grenade, Bobby?"

"Not so easy. Maybe."

"Try." He didn't like the idea of the stun grenade; it was distasteful to him—unprofessional. However, he would have to be out and away before the Jakarta cops arrived. Not good to get caught up in all that now that he wasn't Agency anymore.

Jerry got up and tried to brush the pigeon shit off his front, but the headache knifed back when he bent too far. "I think we'll need four guys," he said. He took ten American hundreds out of his wallet and handed them over.

TEN MINUTES LATER, THEY WERE STANDING OUTSIDE the Orchid House.

"You know Si Jagur?" Jerry said.

Bobby Li grinned. "Everybody in Jakarta know Si Jagur." Si Jagur was a seventeenth-century cannon that sat in a public place and was both a totem and a sort of pet, also a good place to meet for a date—*See you at Si Jagur.*

"Fatahillah Square," Jerry said. "You're going to go check it out every day. Here's the deal: When our man's ready to make the meeting, he'll leave a chalk mark on Si Jagur. A circle with a little tail, sort of a letter Q. Got that? On the left-hand wheel as you stand behind the gun. Okay? He leaves the mark, that means the clock is running and the first meeting time is next morning at nine-ten. Mmm?"

"I got you, Andy."

"I want you to check Si Jagur every day, starting today. You'll have to set up a route that takes you there, going some-place you usually go. Mmm?" Jerry wanted something sweet, which he hoped would absorb or minimize or anodize or do whatever the hell sugar did to alcohol. If the alcohol he'd taken in was still alcohol, and not some poisonous shit that it turned into after it hit the gut. "You know the drill—you make walking by the cannon look normal. Okay, you know all about that." He also wanted a drink. "One of these days, you'll see the mark. Then you let me know *at once*. I'll give you a comm plan."

"Okay I ask a question?"

"Ask."

"How soon this guy going to leave the mark, Andy?"

Piat, hands on hips, inhaled and exhaled noisily. It was another flaw in Suter's goddam plan. "Soon, I hope." *When Dukas gets around to it*, he meant, but Suter had believed that Dukas was smart enough to find the comm plan quickly and to see that it was an anomaly. *Well, maybe. We hope.* "Soon." He liked Jakarta, but he didn't want to grow old there.

Jerry wanted to go back into the Orchid House and sit down. He liked the bizarre mixture of smells—earth, flowers, rot, bark. But he had other things to do. "I'm leaving," he said. "You hang around for fifteen, twenty minutes, check out the way you go into the Orchid House to make the meeting. Then check out Si Jagur, then start to get your shit together. Okay?" He smiled into the small man's eyes. "Good to be working together again, Bobby." He put out his hand.

"Yeah." Bobby's face was sad. "I can't believe George dead."

"For his memory, Bobby. Hmm? Loyalty—that's what this is about. Loyalty to George."

Dulles Airport.

The summer evening looked golden through the great windows. Incoming aircraft winked like stars in a sky still too light to show the real ones. Alan walked with his bad arm around Rose, in the other the carry-on that was his only luggage. "Seems weird, going halfway around the world with less stuff than I'd take to the beach."

She had her right arm around his waist; she squeezed. "I'll miss you."

"Not the way I've been the past few weeks, you won't."

"Even that way. Mikey cried when I told him you were going. It's bad for him, you getting hurt, then you were so—so—"

"Crazy."

"Whatever, and now you're going away. . . ."

There are few good conversations for a parting. Kids, the dog, her airplane, good-bye, good-bye. I love you, I love you.

She stared at the security gate and the metal detector. "Jakarta," she said, as if she could see it there. "I've just never heard anything good about Jakarta."

He kissed her. "You will."

Jakarta.

The next day, Jerry Piat slept until noon. At four, he went to Hilda's and a whorehouse and several bars.

Bobby Li ran around Jakarta, stopping four times at his business, which was only an office and a storage space; a woman old enough to be his mother answered the telephone for him and kept the place clean. He visited Si Jagur; he bought a much-used SKS with a scope and wrapped it in a grass mat and took it out to a suburb where a petty gangster named Ho had a fiefdom of about three square blocks.

"Got a job," Bobby said.

Ho grunted and looked at the rolled mat. "I don't shoot guys," he said.

"Surveillance job. I need you and three others. You use a camera?"

Ho grunted.

"Use it good?"

Ho grunted.

"You use a telephoto?"

Ho grunted, but without conviction.

"Okay, I get you a point-and-shoot."

They talked money. Bobby made a deposit from the bundle Andy had given him. He handed over the roll with the SKS in it. "Pay some glue-head to put this up on the old platform in the Orchid House. You know, the Treetops? Some doper who'll do it but then forget it, okay?" He peeled off another hundred, tore it in half, and put half in Ho's hand. "I'll check five o'clock this afternoon. You get the other half if it's been done right." They talked terms some more, then communications, and Bobby told him he and the team would have to be ready to move on short notice. That required another deposit.

He went to the street market and bought an Olympus point-and-shoot cheap, probably ripped off from some tourist, loaded it with 400-speed film and took it back to Ho, who held it in his fat hand and looked puzzled. Bobby explained how it worked.

He tried to buy a stun grenade.

He told his wife nothing was wrong when she asked what was wrong.

He went to a different street market and bought six Walkabout radios.

He met with Andy and the team. He told Andy he needed more money.

THAT EVENING, ALAN CRAIK LANDED IN JAKARTA.

About the same time, Dick Triffler took off from Washington.

Jakarta.

"HELLO, MISTER!"

Alan tried to ignore the swarm of aggressive children, each with his palm stretched up toward him in supplication. It was the morning after his arrival, stunningly hot, the streets steaming from a ten-minute downpour.

"Hello, Mister! Hello!"

The route on the map looked very clean and neat; here on the streets of Jakarta it was virtually impossible for a foreigner to decipher the name of any road, much less the maze of alleys *(gangs)* that had been marked for him to travel. He did his best, which was usually quite good, and found himself the only foreigner in what appeared to be the courtyard of a colorful and desperate tenement.

"Hello! Hello! Mister!"

Alan looked down at the sea of little faces that moved with him through the *gang* and took a folded bill from his shirt pocket and held it up.

"Anyone speak English?"

"Oh, Mister! Hello, Mister!" Like a children's choir.

"Mister!" Hand raised in the affirmative. A chorus of *Yes*.

"I need a guide." Alan didn't think that James Bond required a nine-year-old to guide him through his surveillance detection route, but he wasn't James Bond.

"Why don't we practice?" he had asked Triffler, back in Washington. Triffler had explained to him that if the Indonesians or the Chinese or any other service were watching them, they couldn't practice in Jakarta, because anyone observing the practice might be set up to watch the real thing. The explanation had confused him, because the military believed that people should *practice* complex evolutions, but he followed his orders, and here he was, lost in Jakarta Barat. At least, he hoped he was still in Barat. And Triffler, who was supposed to be with him, was—Alan hoped—still over the Pacific somewhere.

"We won't even meet." Triffler had been quiet, assured. "You'll see me at the end of the route, because I'll be the signal that you're clean. But we won't hang out; we won't be in the same hotel or travel together; nothing to link us." Nonetheless, Alan was tempted to look for Triffler on every corner.

"I can speak Inglis, Mister!" one kid said. "Real Inglis, like you can understan'."

Alan handed him the folded bill without hesitation, then withdrew a second bill before the boy's eyes wandered or he contemplated flight. This one he held up ostentatiously and then put back in his pocket.

The boy launched into a torrent of abuse at his mates, most of whom vanished in an instant, although a few merely fell back as if waiting their turn.

Alan read the next street on his route to the boy, who nodded and set off at a fast walk. Alan followed, sweating. He liked the sweat. He had been right: It felt good to be doing something, even if he required a nine-year-old to help him.

A minute later, the boy stopped in a *gang* identical to the last, carpeted in the same bright trash that reeked of rotten fish.

"Here, Mister. What we do here? You buy batik? This not a good place for batik."

Alan looked at the wretched row of shops, each offering

its own batik and some of the "cap" cloth that every tourist seemed to want. Alan couldn't see Rose in "cap."

In Washington, Triffler had told him that every stop would "make sense." "These things have to have a logic of their own, Alan," he had said. "We depend on that logic to look natural." Alan saluted him, mentally. *I look like a natural lost tourist.* To keep his cover, he pointed at a piece of cloth slightly less repulsive than the others and nodded at the price.

"He ripping you off," his guide said, turning on the merchant. The exchange went on and on, getting louder and shriller; and then, suddenly, everyone smiled and Alan got a pile of cash back—too much, he thought, but the transaction seemed to have satisfied all parties.

"Now I want this one." Alan pointed at the next destination on the list, marked "Fish Market."

"Okay." And they were off, Alan almost running to keep up, his batik (or cap, he couldn't tell) clutched under one arm.

It certainly smelled like a fish market. This one he had checked out on the Internet—supposedly the oldest part of the city, with some parts dating to the fourteenth century. What was he supposed to do, buy some squid? He walked about for a few minutes, followed by the boy. The fishmongers shouted at him and one another, and he was reminded of his first visit to Africa and how alien it had all seemed. Jakarta was alien, too—almost more alien, with a sturdy structure of the ultra-modern, hung with a great deal of African-style poverty.

Beyond the fish market were boats, old sailing boats with brightly colored hulls and sharply raked bows and masts, and he moved toward them without really thinking. The boy followed, incurious, and Alan walked along the pier, threading through the piles of nets and watching them being mended in much the same way that nets were mended in Mombasa and in Gloucester, Massachusetts. The ocean didn't seem alien. He felt as if he had his feet under him, and he smiled at the boy.

"You plan a hash run? That why you walk everywhere, Mister?"

Hash runs—long cross-city races over a course marked by hash marks—were a feature of expat life from Bahrain to Mombasa. Alan had run a few and had helped mark one, and he smiled at the boy, thankful for a better cover story than any he had been able to concoct.

"Fatahillah Square."

Now for the real thing. Or the thing that probably meant nothing but might lead to something real. What Triffler called the "operational act." As if this were some espionage performance art.

Alan crossed the square under the full weight of the sun and went to the gun, which had been here since the seventeenth century, had been loaded and used to keep surrendering Japanese from resisting in 1945, and now seemed to be the city's leading fertility shrine. Si Jagur was the site he was to mark, the target set for him from the first meeting with Triffler and Dukas in Maryland.

He needed to get rid of the boy.

"Coke?" he said, miming unnecessarily to his guide. The boy stuck out a hand and Alan gave him some small colored bills. The boy vanished, and Alan walked up through a crowd of women, many of breathtaking beauty, to run his hands over the rims of the wheels on the old cannon. He touched it as if he were measuring it, as tourists often do, and many of the women giggled to see a man in such intimate contact with the old monster; things were said that might have made him blush or worse, and the older women didn't hesitate to suggest that men often had their own failings.

This part he did well. He seemed no more interested than any *Bule* tourist, but when he moved back to the boy and his two lukewarm Cokes, he had left a white mark shaped like a Q high on the rim of the wheel.

Game on.

But as he picked his way back toward his hotel, he thought, *I'll like it better when Triffler gets here.*

BOBBY LI WALKED ALONG THE NORTH SIDE OF Fatahillah Square, looking at nothing, moving purposefully toward his next business appointment—at least as far as a watcher would see. This was the third day he had walked through Fatahillah Square. When he came parallel to the ancient cannon, he stopped, covered his look at the cannon by glaring at a little girl who tried to beg, and moved off again, his head down, his stride again purposeful.

In fact, his glance had caught the mark, high on the wheel of the gun, and his heart was pounding because it was too soon—he hadn't been able to get a stun grenade; Andy was drinking a lot and Bobby wasn't sure of him, and he was nervous about actually getting the ragtag team together so fast. Still, he walked on, planning the moves that would take him to another place to leave his own mark to tell Andy about the mark on the cannon. And then Andy would call him. And then tomorrow morning, they'd go to the Orchid House and—

For George.

No reason to bring his Chinese loyalty into it.

FILOMENO HAMANASATRA WAS AN AGED CHINESE agent who had no duties anymore except to monitor three out-of-date, probably dead, communications sites. He walked his dog past them, proudly, even defiantly, because most of his neighbors were Muslims and had little regard for dogs. Mister Hamanasatra was a Christian—well, nominally a Christian, certainly culturally a Christian, inwardly somewhat contemptuous of belief itself—but he loved the presence of the animal and never stopped wondering at the mystery of communication, even affection, between the two different species, his and the animal's. The dog was a cairn terrier, the only one in Jakarta, and, although it suffered from the heat, he walked it every afternoon and then returned it to the air-conditioned coolness of his flat.

Once a week, Mister Hamanasatra walked the cairn to Fatahillah Square. Faithful in his duty, he glanced each time at the wheels of Si Jagur, admiring when he could the women congregated there, and then, seeing nothing on the wheels, moving on.

Today, however, as he glanced at a lovely woman who was probably barely in her teens, and, because he never stopped walking but kept moving so that nobody would think his visit unusual, he was almost past the great gun before he looked down again at it and saw that a mark had been made on a wheel with white chalk. And, yes, the mark looked like a letter Q with an extra bar through the pig's tail that curled down to the right.

Remarkable!

Mister Hamanasatra's aging heart beat a good deal faster. He had seen a mark on the wheel only three times in all the years he had been paid to watch it. He was a romantic: He made up scenarios, stories, of what messages, what events, that mark symbolized. Now, he was so excited that he walked faster, almost dragging the dog, and it balked, sat, scratched, looked at him accusingly.

"Well, well," Mister Hamanasatra said. He scratched the terrier's ears. He walked more slowly to the far side of the square and then, because he wanted to "make assurance double sure" (*Macbeth,* a particular favorite), he walked the dog back past Si Jagur and the women and checked again to make sure, double sure, that the mark was there and that it was really the correct mark and not something a child had done at play.

Then he walked home through the deafening traffic noise and, safe inside his flat, he called a number on his cell phone and said that Vidia had a message from Lakme. Had they got that? Yes, they had.

That was all he did. A widower, retired, he had little else to do, but at least, that evening, he could stare out a window with the dog in his lap and dream of where his message was going and what it meant.

"SHIT!" JERRY PIAT SAID.

He had just heard from Bobby Li that the mark was on the cannon in Fatahillah Square.

That raging prick Ray Suter had been right—Dukas had glommed on to the comm plan first crack out of the box, and here the bastard was, making the mark and no doubt all bright-eyed and bushy-tailed, ready to hit the Orchid House tomorrow morning so he could enjoy a day at Uncle's expense in Jakarta.

Jerry knew that Dukas would believe that the comm plan was dead. In that situation, you left the mark, you made the meeting site faithfully for a couple of days, and, when nobody showed, you went home and checked the box marked "Deceased."

Well, surprise, surprise, Dukas!

Jerry was still sober because it was only late afternoon. Now he wouldn't take a drink until it was all over. He began to strip and change into running clothes—a good run, sweat, exertion to work the alcohol poisons out of the muscles, and he'd be ready to go.

Nonetheless, he wished he'd done a dry run with Bobby's team.

The road to hell is paved with good intentions.

NCIS HQ, Washington Navy Yard.

Mike Dukas had talked to Triffler, who was in Manila waiting for an aircraft to get a hydraulic leak fixed to get him to Jakarta. It was plain that he wouldn't get there in time for the first window for the meeting in Jakarta, and Dukas didn't like it. He wanted Triffler with Alan to calm him down, even though nothing was going to happen, nothing could happen, and the comm plan was strictly what scientists called a chemical stomach.

Dukas sat in his office, one hand on the telephone, wondering if he should call Alan at his hotel. Bad move—insecure phone. Around him, on every flat surface—chairs, desk, file cabinets, computer—were folders from the Sleeping Dog case file. Two days into them, Dukas was bewildered by technical radio jargon and bored by old reports about the futility of an investigation that had gone nowhere. He had read nothing that caused him to worry about Al Craik in Jakarta, and yet—

He took his hand off the telephone and glanced at his watch. Ten-thirty-seven A.M. Meaning that it was ten-thirty-seven P.M. in Jakarta. If Alan had any sense, he had waited for Triffler to arrive before he left the mark on the cannon. Alan had good sense, Dukas knew, lots of good sense—but not always when it came to action. So maybe he had already left the mark, and the clock would start ticking, and tomorrow morning—tonight in Washington—he'd make his first trip to the Orchid House.

And nothing would happen.

Would it?

Dukas told himself that he was suffering case-officer jitters. You sent somebody out, he fell off the face of the earth as far as you were concerned, *of course* you questioned what you were doing. Imagined worst-case scenarios. So what was the worst case here? Dukas frowned. What could possibly be the worst case with an old comm plan that had been unused for seven years? Your man walked into the Orchid House and—

Dukas picked up a folder and got ready to read. He even took out the reading glasses they'd given him at his last physical and that he never used, except that now he was reading all day, day after day, and his eyes felt like hot bullets that had been superglued into their sockets. He started to read about alternative explanations for radio bursts that NSA thought they had detected in western Canada. The prose made him groan. Solar flares! Shifting magnetic fields!

Dukas stared at the telephone. Something was bugging him, and he knew that the something was partly Alan's mission in Jakarta, but only partly; some of it was this goddamned case itself.

"It smells," he said out loud. The smell wasn't strong, and it wasn't bad, but it was there. Dukas actually put his nose down and sniffed the pages in front of him. The odor was slightly musty, slightly dry and woody. Papery. Dukas thought of some storage site in Maryland or Virginia, somewhere secure but unknown to most people at Langley, a dead end for old Agency folders.

He got up and walked along the corridor and swung into another office, one hand low on the doorway to support himself without stressing his injury. "Hey, Brackman," he said.

"Yoh." An overweight black man was tapping a computer keyboard. He didn't look away from the screen.

"How long has the CIA been using computers?"

"Long time, some of them; no time, a lot of them. Computer illiterates, lot of them."

"They still doing files on paper in, say, ninety-seven?"

Brackman turned away from the screen and focused on a half-eaten Devil Dog. "Some of the holdouts, sure." He ate the Devil Dog. "Very conservative place."

Dukas walked back to his office, poured himself coffee from Triffler's machine, and sat on his desk, one hand on the telephone and a look on his face as if some source of deep dissatisfaction had been tapped. He fiddled his fingers on the telephone. He chewed his upper lip with his lower teeth. He made a sound with his tongue and the roof of his mouth, *Tt-Tt-Tt*. He picked up the phone and hit a button and said, "Find out how I get a Nav pilot who's flying out of Pax River. Call me back."

Ten minutes later, the phone rang. He'd done nothing more with the folders in that time but had sat at his desk, staring at the wall. "Okay." He scribbled a number. "Thanks." He called and was put on to a duty officer who told him that Commander Rose Siciliano was in the air but expected back before lunch. Dukas left a message that she should call him, and then he went back to the folders and slogged; when she called at eleven-fifty, he was sighing and groaning, and the first thing he had to do was reassure Rose that he wasn't calling about Alan—nothing had happened, everything was fine, there was no news. "What I want you to do is invite Sally Baranowski to dinner," he said.

"You *still* haven't called her?" Rose snapped.

"I've been busy, babe, plus—you know—"

"You want me to be there so you won't be on the spot, right?"

Dukas sighed again. "This isn't what you think."

"Oh, right."

"It's sort of business."

"Funny business."

"No—damn it, babe—it has to do with the case."

"Alan's case?"

"Yeah."

That was different, she said. She'd invite Baranowski, although she wasn't really running a restaurant. Tonight would be fine, although she'd planned to have a night alone with her kids and then wash her hair. Anything for you, Mike, you coward.

"Six?" he said.

"Six-thirty, and bring some wine and a dessert."

Dukas had a pizza sent in for his lunch, and at one, unable to control his jitters, he decided to call Alan in Jakarta, and then he decided he couldn't.

Dar es Salaam, Tanzania.

Colonel Lao was a day back from Pakistan when the message about the mark in Jakarta came. He was supposed to be an advisor on urban-rural relations, a subject, in fact, in which he had a good deal of knowledge (his training to be an intelligence chief at a foreign station had been excellent), but one that bored him. He had spent part of the day at a village forty miles from Dar, watching a performance of the Chinese-sponsored theater-for-development troupe's *Hope Is the Village*, a play that seemed to him small return for six weeks of work and a good deal of Chinese money. By the time he got back to the office, the message had been on his desk for two hours. It had been rerouted from Beijing, re-encrypted, received and logged at the embassy in Dar, then marked "Most Urgent" and hand-carried to his desk, where it had sat.

Lao looked down at the sealed envelope. *What is the use of all the secrecy and all the hurry if I am out wasting my time in a muddy village?* he wondered. He ripped open the envelope, found himself angered by an inner envelope and its stamps— "Most Urgent!" "Most Secret!" "Unauthorized Persons DO NOT OPEN!"—and ripped it so savagely that he tore part of the flimsy sheet inside. However, nothing was seriously damaged, and he saw that the message within had the class mark Wealthy Songbird, meaning that it had to do with the frightening but glorious task he had been given—finding his rival, the missing Colonel Chen, and the intelligence funds that had disappeared with him.

He had to do his own decoding, Wealthy Songbird being too secret even for the embassy cryptographers, but the message was short, and his interest in it carried him through the drudgery of it. All that it told him was that a mark had been left on an antique cannon in Jakarta, and that the Jakarta watcher had reported it exactly as if to Chen himself, because of course the watcher knew nothing of Chen or his disappearance or, in fact, anything at all. Lao had a moment's envy for the watcher in Jakarta, somebody lucky enough not to be caught up in a tangle of ambition, deceit, strategy. Lao sighed.

He opened the Chen files and searched for Jakarta, found it in eleven of them, found the mark that the watcher had seen in the communications plan called American Go. The plan was not Chinese, Lao recognized at once; Chen's agent in the CIA, George Shreed, must have drafted it, as Lao now knew the agent was named. Who, like Chen, had also disappeared. And who was supposed to have been buried nine days ago in Washington, although that was being checked.

Lao sighed again, wondered if he had caught something in the cold rain in Pakistan. He thought that this was not a real illness but a reaction to the beginning of an operation that would be difficult and long and, quite possibly, disastrous for him.

The immediate question to be answered was, Who had left the mark in Jakarta, and why? Was it Shreed—supposedly dead, but not necessarily so—trying to contact the missing Chen? Chen himself, trying to throw off pursuers like Lao? Some third party, working for both of them? The CIA, using a dead Shreed's files?

What the mark was meant to signal was a desire for a meeting, the meeting place a playland called Fantasy Island Park, something left over from the boom of the nineties and now gasping, he supposed, since the bubble had burst. Such matters had no reality for Lao; economics was somebody else's concern. What mattered to him here was that a meeting had been signaled, and he, as the new master of the plan called American Go, must find out what the meeting was for and who had asked for it.

He sent a message to the intelligence chief at the Chinese embassy in Jakarta, requiring that a surveillance team monitor the meeting site for the next three days; the times, according to the comm plan, were to be ten minutes after nine, two, and six. Parties meeting according to the plan would identify themselves by carrying a magazine under the left arm. The surveillance team was to watch the site without being seen, note all persons who appeared at any of the appointed times, photograph them if possible, and follow them if they were sure no countersurveillance was present (an unlikely possibility). No, he would have to give them more instructions than that, and they'd have to have a senior officer in charge— if Chen actually appeared, there were major decisions to be made very quickly.

Then he sat late, trying to see how it would go and what he could do if the meeting really happened as early as tomorrow. Jakarta was an hour behind Beijing, where an officer would have to be found to fly to Jakarta to oversee the surveillance. Early evening here in Dar es Salaam was the middle of the night in Beijing. They'd be lucky to find anybody at all, much less the veteran officer Lao wanted; then the officer would have to find air transport to Jakarta—he'd be on the run every moment and still be fortunate to get there for the first meeting time. Lao couldn't send anyone from his own office; Dar was an impossible distance by air, and Tsung, in Pakistan, already had an operational meeting for tomorrow. Bad, bad—the last thing he wanted, a tired man arriving late with no time to prepare the surveillance team. Lao smoked and made notes and sent messages. At nine his own time, he got confirmation that an officer was on the way to Jakarta. Lao started to prepare further instructions for him, to be handed to him when he got off the plane. An hour later, he shook his head and threw down the ballpoint pen with which he had been trying to write. The papers were a mess of crossed-out sentences and scribblings over scribblings.

The gist of it all was that he needed somebody on the spot

who could tell him if either Shreed or Chen made the meeting. Somebody who would know at once and somebody who was loyal—not one who would hurry the information to Beijing, and not one who would babble to the officer running the operation.

He dug into Chen's personal file. He knew it fairly well by then, knew that there was something in there—And found it.

"Jiang!"

A captain hurried in.

Lao held out a piece of paper. "This is still active. I want him. Most urgent!"

"Sir!" Jiang vanished, in his fingers the piece of paper on which Lao had written, "Code name Running Boy, name Li, Bobby, agent for Chen 1983."

Jiang was back in ten minutes. "Still in Jakarta, still active, but not used in three years. Control code-named Loyalty Man."

"Get him."

Jakarta.

ALAN LAY IN HIS DARK HOTEL ROOM AND WATCHED Jakarta through the window. It was cool in the room, almost cold. Outside, Jakarta was hot and busy, and Alan watched it for a while, the constant bustle of taxicabs, rickshaws, and vast limousines pulling up to the front of his great hotel, twenty stories below. NCIS seemed to have paid for a really good room in a really good hotel, and it was all wasted; Alan felt as if the huge windows were force fields walling him off from the reality of Jakarta. He wanted to go out and explore, but his instructions were explicit. So he repeated today's operation until he had it to his satisfaction and then reviewed tomorrow's until it bored him.

Buy a copy of The Economist. *Go to the theme park and go to Anjungan Bali. Sit in the dance kiosk and watch the dancers. When they finish, walk across the Anjungan Sumatra to the Orchid House, carrying* The Economist. *When you are inside, walk along the path. If a man approaches you with a copy of* The Economist *and asks if he met you at the AGIP Christmas party, respond that you were there with a Dutch girl. It won't happen, cowboy. It's a fake. There won't be anybody there. Just go and fill the bill, okay?*

He got up and headed toward the door. He needed to walk.

Just stay in your room, Al. Just sit tight and don't get robbed, don't leave your briefcase, don't have any adventures, okay?

Alan walked back and forth in front of the window for the thirtieth time, bored, angry, all keyed up and wanting to discuss the problems of the morning, talk about the tactics for tomorrow, anything. He had been a spy for about thirty hours; so far, it was really dull.

It beat the crap out of flying a Microsoft product in his living room and having rages at his wife, though.

He paced back again. He wanted to go down to the giant lobby; there had to be a kiosk there to buy a paper. Triffler wouldn't mind if he just went and bought a copy of *The Economist.*

He got as far as the door, with his electronic key in his hand, before his conscience stopped him.

Just stay in your room, Al. Just sit tight and don't get robbed, don't leave your briefcase, don't have any adventures, okay?

Triffler wasn't Mike Dukas; he was a thorough, professional man who seemed unimpressed with Alan's reputation and impatience. He hadn't grinned when he spoke about *any adventures,* either. He meant what he said. Alan walked back to his enormous bed and threw himself on it, the expensive pillow-top mattress swallowing him whole.

Too damn soft.

Lying sideways on the bed, Alan stretched out an arm to rifle through his belongings in the carry-on on the floor. Underwear; a linen jacket that Rose had given him a year ago and thought would be perfect in Jakarta; probably would, at that. She'd ordered him to hang it up as soon as he got to a room, and he smiled at the pang of guilt and unfolded it from the bottom of the case.

Something heavy slipped out from its folds and fell on the bed. Alan leaped back for a moment, and laughed aloud.

A book. The cover said *Blue at the Mizzen*. Inside, a feminine hand had written:

All I want you to take to bed while you're away. Love, R.

His grin threatened to crack his face, and he kissed her writing. Deep inside him, more ice cracked.

And he started reading.

In the air, Beijing–Jakarta.

Qiu was very young, as his code name—"young dragon with new horns"—announced. The name irritated him, as it indicated a lack of respect from his superiors. He had, after all, graduated from all the schools; he knew exactly how to perform his tasks. Why such a disrespectful code name?

He knew what he was about to do, to perfection: He would meet with the Jakarta embassy black team in a warehouse near the Jakarta waterfront only two hours before the meeting was to take place, and he would outline to them his surveillance plan as based on a map of the Fantasy Island Park that he had downloaded from the Internet. If, as he anticipated, the local chief watcher was rude, Qiu would step on him hard to make sure that the fellow knew his place. In fact, he planned to step on everybody hard.

This was his first independent assignment.

The local station had reported a certain signal placed on a certain old cannon. They had no idea what the signal meant. Qiu, however, knew, because he had been told in Beijing: It was an old signal from an old comm plan between his service and an American double agent. Qiu was to follow the comm plan and meet whoever had left the mark. No reason had been given for doing so: there was no context, no background, no time for analysis or research. His head swam with questions, but no answers came. He knew enough to do only one thing: follow orders. And, by implication, a second thing: be ruthless, meaning that he wanted an armed team, as if for a hostile meeting, and he wanted absolute discipline.

He went over and over it, and any idea he had had of sleeping on the flight proved foolish. He was awake all the way—awake when the sun rose and still awake when the plane banked and began its final approach into Jakarta.

The local man seemed relieved to be able to push the responsibility for the hasty operation off on him. He was even apologetic, in fact. "But there's been a change," he said.

Qiu bristled. "I will decide that!" he said. They weren't even in the embassy car yet.

"It was decided at a higher level." He handed Qiu a message. Qiu read it, his fatigue suddenly heavy and depressing. He gave an exasperated groan. "Where is this Loyalty Man now?" he said.

The embassy man jerked his head at the car. They walked toward it; the driver, standing by the passenger door, braced and swung it open. A middle-aged man was sitting inside, a burning cigarette in his fingers. He looked at Qiu without expression, making it clear that he was a veteran who would go along with this stripling because he had been ordered to. Qiu settled himself next to him. "Well?" he said. He made it sound like a challenge.

"You are to add one of my agents to your team. He is to be with you at the meeting."

"That is ridiculous!"

"That is the order." Loyalty Man didn't even bother to look at him.

The embassy man got in and sat on a jump seat. The driver got in behind the wheel. Everybody sat there until at last Qiu realized that they were waiting for him to give an order.

"Well, get him!" he shouted.

Suburban Virginia.

Sally Baranowski was healthier-looking than Dukas remembered, but vulnerable, obviously glad that Rose was there with them. She was a fairly big woman, better eyes and color now that she had dried out, good black dress that maybe showed too much of pretty hefty legs. But who was he to notice?

"Did you ever run into a case code-named Sleeping Dog?" he said to her.

"If I did, I wouldn't talk about it, would I?"

"Well, you were Shreed's assistant for a while there, I thought you knew what was going on."

"I knew some things." She was picking at her food, not looking at him. She'd been kicked sideways from her job at the Agency, because when the dying Shreed was brought back as a traitor, there had been a lot of vengeance within the Agency. Some people had been punished for being too loyal to Shreed. She had been punished for being too disloyal. Now, fresh out of rehab, she was working in a nothing job in Inter-Agency Liaison after having been a rising star in Operations Planning.

Dukas wanted to pick her brains—*and* take her to bed— so he tried to explain the case as he understood it. The burst transmissions, the case's being kicked around among NSA, the Bureau, and the CIA.

"*Now* does it sound familiar?"

"Not even remotely. Sorry." She smiled at him. "Why?"

"Because I've got the case, and it seems to me to have a kind of tang. What the Brits call a pong. A hint of fish."

"Like what?"

He was thinking of how to propose that they start over, go to his place, get in the sack—"Like I need your help," he said.

Jakarta.

Bobby Li was awake. He was a nervous man, easily kept awake by the tensions of the family or his business. Now he was awake because of the operation. Nothing would go wrong, but—

The telephone rang twice and stopped. He felt his wife tense beside him; he realized that he had tensed too. The telephone rang again—twice. And stopped.

Bobby sighed.

"You have to go?" she said.

"Only a few streets."

He dressed quickly, not even bothering with socks, and went out into the warm, wet dawn. Three streets away was a public telephone. He leaned into its plastic shelter to escape a sudden patter of rain and dialed. He knew the voice at the other end at once: Loyalty Man, his Chinese control. He flinched.

"The southeast corner of Suharto and Nyam Pareng. *Now.*"

He knew better than to object or ask a question. He hung up, found he was trembling, lit a cigarette in the shelter of the phone, and then splashed off into the night. His sockless shoes rasped on his feet and he shivered as if the warm rain had given him a chill. He was at the proper corner in six minutes, but there was already a dark car there waiting. He saw from thirty feet away that there were three men as well as the driver, and he knew what sort of car it was and what sort of people were inside.

"Get in." A man he didn't know, sitting with his knees drawn up on a jump seat, had opened the door from inside and was holding it open. Loyalty Man was against the far window, a young, foolish-looking stranger closer to Bobby.

"Get in!" the young one screamed.

The air inside was bitter with cigarette smoke. The car pulled away but went slowly, so that he knew they were not really going anywhere yet. Whatever it was, they were going to talk first. Did they know about Andy? Did they know he was helping on an operation he hadn't told them about? He began to think up excuses—

"I am Qiu," the foolish one said. "I am your superior, and you will do precisely what I tell you."

Bobby tried to look at Loyalty Man, through whom this insane youth should have been speaking, but Loyalty Man was looking out the window, as much as to say to Bobby, *I have nothing to do with this.*

"Yes, sir."

"I have orders directly from Beijing. *I* am from Beijing. Flown in expressly for this." Bobby knew he was from Beijing from his accent.

"Yes, sir."

"You have been added to my team. I have a strict plan. You will conform to it. Well?"

"Yes, sir." This didn't seem so bad as he had feared. Nothing about Andy, at any rate. Merely some stupid, extra work. Bobby kept himself from sighing.

"In"—Qiu looked at his watch, which he had to hold up in the light of a street lamp to read—"precisely one hour and forty-three minutes, my team will report to a site for an operation. You will be there." The young man paused, perhaps debating how much to tell Bobby, then, if he was at all wise, seeing that time was so short that he had no choice. "I am making a hostile contact in a place called the Orchid House, in a park called Fantasy Island. My arrangements are none of your affair; however, I have been ordered to allow you to observe the meeting. Therefore, you will make yourself available at the Fantasy Island Park at—" He looked at his watch again. "From precisely ten minutes before nine, local time, until completion of the operation. You will do precisely as I say. At six minutes after nine, I will enter a certain entrance of the Orchid House and will proceed to a certain place. You will go in another entrance and find a place from which to observe. If you get in the way or cause any trouble, you will be dealt with. That is all you need to know. Understood?"

Bobby felt nauseated. Surely it couldn't be happening. Surely—were they testing him? Did they know all about Andy, after all?

"Well?"

Bobby forced himself to mumble, "Yes, sir," and Qiu spoke to the driver and the car rolled to a stop. Again, the man in the jump seat opened the curbside door.

"Get out," Qiu said. "You will be at the Fantasy Island Park in precisely"—pausing to study his watch—"one hour and forty-two minutes. Meet me at the main gate. Now get out."

Bobby Li stepped into a puddle. The car pulled away, sending slow waves over the tops of his shoes. He watched it go, unable even to step up on the curb. At ten minutes after nine, he was supposed to meet an unknown American in the Orchid House for Andy, but at the same moment he was also supposed to watch Qiu meet the same unknown American in the same place. His life had turned into a contradiction. And a mystery: Nobody had told him why Qiu was doing this to him!

He walked home. Passing the telephone, he thought of calling Andy and telling him—what? That he was too sick to go? No, you were never too sick for an operation, not when it was Andy, and not when it was for George. Tell him that his Chinese masters also had a job for him? But Andy didn't know about the Chinese masters, and, because Bobby loved Andy, he couldn't let him know. It would make Andy hate him, and he couldn't bear that.

Loyalty, Andy said. It's about loyalty.

He let himself into his house and sat in the little front room. His wife came in and stared into the dark where he sat, then went away.

Bobby thought it through. He had to do what Qiu said. He knew what the punishment would be if he did not— Loyalty Man's attitude had told him that the thing was serious and out of his hands. To disobey was to end his life here, his family's life. Maybe to see his children shipped to China, to disappear there. Therefore, he would have to do as Qiu ordered. How, then, would he keep Andy from knowing what he was doing? If he stayed far enough back, maybe Andy wouldn't see him through the greenery—was that possible? But even then, there were the photos—Ho was supposed to get photos. Andy would see the photos.

And, of course, Andy would see Qiu meet with the American.

I never saw him before, Andy; he stole The Economist *from me and his guys held me and he went into the meeting—*

Andy wouldn't believe it. Andy didn't believe in unmotivated acts.

Well, the photos. Maybe he could just not hand over the film. No, Andy wouldn't believe it if he said he lost it or Ho kept it. Or he could expose the film—pull it out of the canister. No, Andy didn't believe in accidents, either.

But if the photos were simply bad photos—out of focus, for example—

Bobby went to the bedroom and turned on a light without warning his wife and without apologizing. He took his own camera from his drawer, hesitated, and then burrowed deep under his four shirts and took the gun that was concealed there. In the bathroom, he opened the camera—his pride, a good Nikon, 3X zoom, internal motor drive—and smeared Vaseline on the inside of the lens. He put in a roll of film.

Back in the living room, he sat with the gun and the camera in his lap. The gun had lost most of the bluing at the end of the barrel and a lot along the edges of the slide. It was a thirty-year-old Walther PP .32, an old police pistol from somewhere in Europe in the days when policemen could enforce the law with little guns that were now thought too weak for even ladies to carry. He put on a light. He took out the clip. Seven cartridges, their ends open—hollowpoints, segmented for expansion. Like looking into the heart of a flower. Well, you could kill with those.

It had been so good for the first day with Andy. Now it was all awful. He went back to the bedroom and began to change his clothes.

"Is it bad?" his wife said.

"Don't take the kids to school today. Take them to the place in Tangerang." He had a shack out there under a different name. Sometimes he went there to be alone. He had a garden out there, like his father. "Park the car in the trees, where it can't be seen from the road."

"How bad is it?" she said.

He finished dressing. Out of deference to her, he hadn't brought the gun back into the bedroom. "It will be all right," he said. He kissed her and went into the living room and put the gun inside his waistband just by his right kidney, and he picked up his camera and went out. It was daylight.

USS **Thomas Jefferson.**

Cyclic air ops went on, creating thunder that went pretty much unnoticed in the corridors of the O3 level. In the ready rooms, crews preparing to fly were gathered around the TAMPS; others stood or sprawled to watch ongoing landings on the Plat camera. For the air group commander, a walk past the ready rooms was a mixture of envy, nostalgia, and irritation, the last because every squadron had its own problems, its own flaws, which he was supposed to solve and correct. To Rafehausen, who wasn't flying that day and who could hardly find time to fly enough to stay qualified, the ready rooms were also a nagging reminder of what he had given up.

"Approval came through for Craik's orders to Miramar," a voice said at Rafehausen's shoulder.

"Say again?" Both men flattened themselves against the bulkhead as a cluster of aviators hurried past. "Sorry, Deak, I was woolgathering."

"Not important. I just saw a message that Al Craik's orders to Miramar to advise a second MARI det will be cut in a couple days."

It took an instant for Rafehausen to switch focus. Then: "Oh, sure. Right, I wanted to find something for Craik. That's great!" He detached himself from the bulkhead and started toward his office. "What's being done about the parking problem behind cat three? They were supposed to have the mess there cleaned up by 0600 and now I learn that—"

Overhead, the engines screamed and the colored jerseys moved and spun, and aircraft blasted into the sky, and Alan Craik was forgotten.

Jakarta.

AT FIVE-THIRTY ALAN WAS UP, ADRENALINE AND DE-
layed jetlag combining to get him out of bed and into the
shower. He had been awake for a long time, waiting for the
alarm, and he was charged with energy, like a kid waiting for
his parents to get up on Christmas morning. He shaved and
had a long shower, humming something he had heard the day
before, and then dressed carefully in slacks, a fancy T-shirt,
and the linen jacket Rose had packed for him. He felt that he
looked like Don Johnson in *Miami Vice,* but so did everyone
else in Jakarta. The air outside was already hot and heavy with
moisture by the time he emerged to catch a taxi, almost an
hour early. He told himself that he would spend the extra
time making his route really complex. The truth was, he had
to get out of the room.

Make some stops before you get to the park, Triffler had
ordered without really explaining why. Alan knew it had something to do with helping his minders make sure that he was
clear of surveillance, but Alan couldn't for the life of him see

how he could have acquired surveillance in Jakarta when traveling on his own passport. Nonetheless, he obeyed. Coffee and a decent roll were high on his morning agenda, so he asked the cabdriver where he could get the best cup of coffee in Java. The man smiled wickedly, as if he had just been asked where to find something far more sinister, and he left the curb with a jolt reminiscent of a cat shot.

Twenty minutes later, his insides comforted by a chocolate croissant and a cup of excellent coffee, Alan left the café and walked through the steamy morning. He window-shopped along a closed arcade and made left turns until he found an open news store, the magazines and newspapers international and mostly concerned with the upcoming presidential election in the United States. The subject didn't interest him much, but he had a tiny cup of espresso and bought a copy of *The Economist*, skimmed it to eat the rest of his surplus time, and departed with a much better understanding of the economy of oil in Indonesia.

His second cab of the morning was duller; the driver was quite young and didn't seem to want to talk. He made good time, though, and Alan arrived at the gates of the park that contained the Orchid House with fifteen minutes in hand and a charge from all his energy and caffeine on top. He was beginning to feel nervous, the nerves of inexperience, concern about making mistakes through ignorance—feelings he hadn't had in a long time. Then he told himself, for the twentieth time, that nothing was going to happen, and he sagged and felt the fatigue under his energy.

It was damp and hot. He started to walk.

Washington.

Dukas had got as far as suggesting to Sally, while Rose was out of the room, that they maybe check out his apartment, and then the shit had hit the fan. He had hardly tried his dessert when she had seen something in his open attaché and gone through the roof. "What the hell is this?" she cried.

"Hey, what—?"

"What the hell are you trying to pull?" she said. She didn't seem vulnerable any longer.

Dukas misunderstood. He thought it was something about his clumsy approach to sex. "Hey, I was only—"

She tried to speak, moved her lips to form words that didn't come, and then slapped the attaché and shouted, "This is Chinese Checkers!" She began to scrabble in the old papers, knocking them out of their neat alignment, dropping some on the floor and not caring.

"What the hell?" he said.

"You bullshitter, what have you done to—" She shook the folder. "This is the Jakarta part of *Chinese Checkers*!"

Dukas tried to focus. He had an idea what the code name Chinese Checkers meant. Chinese Checkers had been a CIA operational project—a comm plan that George Shreed had covertly used to meet with his Chinese control. When Dukas and Alan Craik had gone into Pakistan after Shreed, they had known he was following one of the Chinese Checkers comm plans to a village near the Kashmir border. That's how they caught him—because Sally Baranowski had illicitly given Dukas a copy. But he had seen only the Pakistan section, and then only long enough to know where Shreed was going.

But *Jakarta*?

"Chinese Checkers is a defunct Ops comm plan," Sally Baranowski snarled now. "And now here it is! I risked my fucking career to give you this stuff, and you're walking around with it in your attaché!"

Dukas didn't say that everybody walked around with classified material in his attaché. He was too stunned by what she was saying, stunned by the implications. A warning bell was sounding in his head. "This is *Chinese Checkers*?" he said.

"What did I just say?"

"Maybe it's just *like* Chinese Checkers. Sally, it can't possibly be—"

She simply looked at him.

"This comm plan can't—I don't see how it can be part of Chinese Checkers." He grabbed her upper arm, then let it go and leaned back so she wouldn't think he was bullying her. "I just sent Al Craik to Jakarta to road test it. He's there right now."

Sally stared.

"All I'd paid attention to in Chinese Checkers was the Pakistan part. I didn't even read the rest. If this is really—"

Her look told him everything. She said, "I helped Shreed edit Chinese Checkers. I used to pull it up to see why it never got activated. There were three comm plans, Mike—Pakistan, Nairobi, Jakarta." She picked the pages up again. "And why the hell is it typed this way? It's beat-up, like you've had it forever. *I* didn't give it to you like this—I gave you a goddam floppy! Where the hell did you get this?"

"It's part of Sleeping Dog." Even as he said it, Dukas saw the abyss that was opening.

"This was *never* part of Sleeping Dog!" she shouted. "Never, never, never!".

He realized that Rose was standing in the doorway and that she had heard. He ran for the telephone.

6

Fantasy Island Park, Jakarta.

JERRY PIAT WAS UP EARLY AND FEELING GOOD—
rested, strong, wired just enough to stay alert. He got a paper
cup of coffee and walked to the park. He took his time; it was
only a little after seven, the streets already hideous with traffic,
sidewalks still puddled from a rain that now steamed in early
sunshine.

The Glorious Mornings. Title of some book. Nice phrase.

He looked around like a tourist, checked out a couple of
ethnic displays, tossed his coffee cup at an overflowing trash
bin, and went into the Orchid House.

BOBBY LI HITCHED A RIDE ON THE BACK OF A
scooter to within five streets of the park gate. He'd shoved the
gun down into his pants, with a loop of string holding it to his
belt, a trick that George had taught him and that he said his
side had used in World War II. *The Economist* and the envelope full of newspaper that was supposed to be money were
inside his shirt. He kept the camera in view, like a tourist.

His heartbeat was way up. He thought a heart attack might be a good way to get out of this fix. His wife would get the business and a little insurance, and Andy and Qiu would forget him. But his heart wouldn't cooperate.

A woman in a headscarf was sweeping the area in front of the park gate. He went around her and sidled in, looking for Ho, anxious not to miss him. Ho was lazy and would more likely be late than early. Bobby walked around, feeling his bowels get queasy. He couldn't do it, he thought. He couldn't walk in there behind Qiu and risk Andy's seeing him. He was in a vise, being squeezed.

Ho grunted behind him, and Bobby whirled. His breath came too fast, and he had to breathe through his mouth or faint. "Give me the camera," he managed to say. He had just seen, beyond Ho, a Chinese who looked professional and dangerous. But every Chinese he saw today would look as if he belonged to Qiu. "Don't give it to me here; walk down to the toilets and meet me in the men's."

Ho walked away. He was eating an Indian sweet, slender coils of orange jelly. The smell of it made Bobby sick.

In the men's room, he stood next to Ho and tried to piss. Ho was making water like a fire hose. Bobby strained; nothing came out. The vise was squeezing even his piss.

He put his own camera, the one with the grease on the lens, on the metal urinal. Below it was a wall of metal over which water ran, splashing their shoes. "Take this camera. Put yours there so I can take it."

"Why?"

"It's a better camera."

They switched. Bobby said, "Take the pictures, and the moment the meeting is over, get out. Get your people out. You meet me by the east door and hand me the camera, and we're done."

"Not until you hand me the rest of the money." Ho zipped up as if he was tightening a garrote.

"Right. You hand me the camera and I hand you the money."

"Wrong. You hand me the money, and I hand you the camera."

Bobby went out and walked up and down, keeping an eye out for Chinese men, glancing every half-minute at his watch, looking for Qiu. One of Ho's team found him and gave him a Walkabout, which he had altogether forgotten. It seemed like one more terrible thing, one more burden—if the Chinese saw him with the handheld radio, they'd kill him. Or drag him off to the embassy, which would in the long run be much worse. He walked around the back of the toilets and smashed the radio under his foot and threw it into a tangle of weeds, then threw Ho's camera after it. The less baggage, the better.

Washington.

Dukas and Sally Baranowski sat in Rose's living room. It was going to be a long night.

A woman with a young voice and a thick Asian accent at Alan's hotel had assured Dukas that she had tried the room three times, and, yes, she had the right room, and, no, Mist' Cra-ik not answer. Dukas had looked at his watch for the tenth time since Sally had told him; it was by then eight-thirty-five in Jakarta, and Al Craik was already out of his hotel room. *No, no, no,* Dukas was saying. *Don't go this early—!* He had left a message for Craik to call him at once; then he had tried Triffler, but Triffler still hadn't checked in. The duty officer at NCIS told him that the last word they had was that Triffler was still in Manila.

Sally Baranowski now understood exactly what was going on. "How bad is it?" she said.

"Maybe pretty bad. I don't know."

She was an experienced operations officer. "If you don't know," she said, "then it's pretty bad."

"If you're right about Chinese Checkers—"

She was contemptuous. "There is no 'if.' I'm right. So what is part of Chinese Checkers doing in a file about radio intercepts in Seattle?"

Dukas shook his head. Sally had his attaché open on her lap, and she took a sheet of memo paper from the Jakarta folder, smoothing the creases. It looked like the other papers, a little old, a little weary. It had a yellow fold-down FBI tab. "This is an FBI cover sheet," she said.

"Yeah." His voice was empty. "It's supposed to date from the time when the Bureau had the case."

"No way. The Bureau *never* had Chinese Checkers."

She held it up to the light. There were columns for dates and times and signatures—a record of who had seen the pages and when. "Not much," she said. "Only three names. Seven years ago, supposedly." She brought her arm down. "Bullshit."

"Check the document history."

" 'Acquired 24/9/94 via Long Shot from E75P3211. Unverified. Authenticity 3, Reliability 3.' " She looked at Dukas. "What the hell is this shit?"

"What's Long Shot?"

"Long Shot was a big buy from some very questionable sources after the Soviet Union went belly-up. Mostly in the 'Stans,' mostly KGB stuff, but there was some Chinese and Indian material in there, too. We never trusted it, never were able to use most of it. But no way is this comm plan from Long Shot."

Dukas simply looked at the pale wall, waiting. She was sitting there now with her eyes slitted, staring at someplace he wasn't allowed to go. "George Shreed would never have knowingly given Chinese Checkers to anybody," she said. "The only way it could have shown up in the Long Shot buy was if the other side had got it somehow, and then after the end of communism, they sold it back to us." She shook her head. "But it won't wash. George would never have let it get out of his hands."

"Yeah, but if he secretly used Chinese Checkers to meet his Chinese control, then the control had to have a copy, too. It could have got into the Long Shot buy that way." Dukas was eager to authenticate the Jakarta comm plan, to tell himself that, after all, Al Craik was safe.

"You know that's not the way intelligence works! It's not the way *George* worked. If China had a top spy in the Agency— as they did, in him—then, by God, they wouldn't have his comm plan someplace where it could be sold off to the highest bidder."

Dukas stared at a rain-spotted window. "So how did it get into this file?"

She had no answer.

"If you're right," he said, "then the cover sheet and the document history and all that about Long Shot are forgeries." He rubbed his eyes. "Somebody's planted this stuff on me. And I've sent my best friend off to check it out."

Fantasy Island Park, Jakarta.

To Alan, the park seemed empty. The night's rain had left a faint gleam over the stones in the early morning light, but the only people in the park with him were the ground crew and a few Chinese tourists and a school group of local girls in white shirts and ties and plaid skirts. Alan smiled, thin-lipped and tense, and moved on, heading for the first performance of the park's Javanese dancers.

The dancers performed in a kiosk across from the looming concrete and glass of the Orchid House. Alan tried to see inside, but the fog of condensation on the walls of the greenhouse was impenetrable. It was hot already, with the heavy air of full humidity complicated by massive smog, but the lithe girls danced smoothly despite the early hour. The performance didn't last long, and Alan was one of five members of the audience. All the rest were Asian, and Alan wondered if any of them was his target.

BOBBY LI LINGERED WHERE HE COULD WATCH THE front entrance to the Orchid House, knowing the American would go in there. Andy had said so. He was trying to cut down the variables in this horror, even though seeing the man, being able to recognize him, wouldn't help matters much unless Bobby could get inside and get to him before Qiu did. It wouldn't work. Nothing would work. He leaned back in the shadow of a pillar and gave a murmured whimper. A hand closed over his arm.

"Aaah—!" He spun, eyes wide, found himself inches from the face of Loyalty Man.

"Very nervous," Loyalty Man said. "No reason to be."

"Th-this Qiu makes me n-nervous."

Loyalty Man spat and lit a fresh cigarette. "Your job here has nothing to do with Qiu. Qiu knows nothing. Qiu is like the wooden duck you put on the water to bring in the real ducks." He pulled something from his lower lip, spat tobacco flakes. "You are to find if the person who makes the meeting with Qiu is either the American Shreed or Colonel Chen. You know both. That is all." He inhaled smoke and looked at Bobby. "Orders from very high up."

"But—" He started to say *But Shreed is dead,* and remembered in time that he had learned that only from Andy and so wasn't supposed to know it. "But," he said instead, "it has been so long since I saw either."

"I am told you knew both well. Do your job. Call me to report." He walked away.

Bobby's face screwed up as if he was going to weep.

JERRY HAD BROUGHT A PIECE OF NYLON PARACHUTE cord, which he tied across the rickety stairs to Treetops. He didn't want any early tourists stumbling over him. Up on the viewing platform, he drew on a pair of gloves and located the gun and dragged it out, unrolling the mat to lie on. It was nice up there, a feeling of airiness and light, that tantalizing mixture of greenhouse odors in the nostrils. He looked through the scope of the SKS, unloaded it, checked the trigger pull, decided that it would do well enough. He reloaded it and laid the weapon next to him and looked down into the green and flowery target area.

"Report," he said into his handheld. "One here. Report." Bobby was Two. He should have said "Two," but he didn't. "Two?" Jerry said. After a silence, he said, "Three?" Three reported—that was the big ox, Ho—then Four, Five, and Six. "Two?" Jerry said again. Was Bobby out of range somehow?

It was eight-forty-eight. Dukas should be in the park. "Anybody see our target?" He said it again in dialect, or as much dialect as he knew. An answer came, too fast, too local. "Say again?"

"Got a white man at the dancing thing. Not same as the photo."

Shit. Maybe he wasn't going to make the morning time. Maybe he was waiting until later in the day—overslept or got the trots or got laid. Or maybe he wasn't coming. Or maybe he'd sent somebody else.

"Two?" he said. "Two, answer up. Two?"

BOBBY COULD SEE ONLY ONE WHITE IN THE DANCE kiosk, and he was young; his hair was dark and he had his left hand in bandages, none of which matched Andy's description of the man he called Dukas. It suddenly struck him that perhaps the target wasn't going to come, and his heart leaped. It was eight-fifty-three.

QIU WATCHED THE AMERICAN ENTER THE ORCHID House from twenty meters away, leaning over the railing of one of the reconstructed Sumatran houses, the long eaves shading the sun above him so that he could snap his first picture of him. He didn't trust local people to do such things. And the American was carrying *The Economist,* so he was the man. Qiu checked his watch and saw that the man was four minutes ahead of schedule. Most unprofessional.

BOBBY SAW THE AMERICAN CROSS TO THE ORCHID House, and he saw the copy of *The Economist* under his arm. And he was going in early!

ALAN SAW ONE OF THE ASIAN MEN ON THE PLAT-form to his right raise his camera, and his heartbeat rose to a quick march in his chest. *This wasn't a fake, Mike. That guy works for somebody else and he knows who I am. He just took my photo.* Suddenly, Alan's world changed, and the beautiful morning, the lithe dancers, the good coffee, were all erased. He was in a foreign place, and he was *alone*.

JERRY SETTLED HIMSELF ON THE PLATFORM. HE HAD plenty of time to arrange the matting and lie flat so that only a foot of the barrel protruded over the edge, and two small dead shrubs served to camouflage his body. The mat smelled of rice and curry and sweat and dog shit.

Dukas would appear *there*, and he worried about how little time he would have to shoot. Plus, now he would have to identify the guy. Then the main door opened, and he saw a furtive movement. Then the west door opened, and he saw another movement. Jerry brought the rifle around slowly and settled it on a half-hidden figure. The head was turned as if the man was speaking to someone just outside the door, but Jerry knew him before the face turned, clear in the crosshairs, and Jerry's lips moved.

Jesus.

Jerry Piat had worked Jakarta long enough to know most of the Chinese embassy watchers by sight, and he certainly knew the team leader when he saw him.

What the fuck were the Chinese embassy goons doing here?

ALAN ENTERED THE ORCHID HOUSE TOO FAST, MINutes early, and forced himself to slow down. He realized that he had not really expected this meeting to happen at all. Now it was real because of the man with the camera he had seen outside, and he felt exposed. He felt a wave of vertigo. He slowed his pace still further and forced a smile to his face. He began to smell the orchids, and he forced himself to stop and read the cards, admire the rich colors and marvelous shapes. He was so early that he would have to smell every flower on the path to get to his appointed spot at the right time. He dawdled, nervous and bored at the same time.

•   •   •

IT WAS A NIGHTMARE.

Qiu had a hand around his left biceps. Qiu had a copy of *The Economist* in his other hand, also the side on which he wore his watch, which he now raised to read. He held Bobby in place, watching the seconds tick off. Bobby wanted to scream at him—he was wasting time that Bobby could use to find the American inside the Orchid House!

"I will go inside in precisely two minutes and twenty seconds," Qiu said to the watcher by the door. He gave Bobby a shove and let go of his arm. "*You* stay out of my way!"

Bobby ran for the south entrance, all the way around the building.

Now he was in for it.

JERRY SAW THE MAN WITH THE BANDAGED HAND, framed in the bright sunlight of the east door.

Jesus, this thing is fucked.

Jerry's mind was racing through the ramifications of a Chinese surveillance team. Now he had to think who the man with the bandaged hand was. Not your typical NCIS special agent. Military. Fairly recent wound—from the dustup when they'd brought down Shreed? It must be *Craik*. He checked the face against his memory of the old squadron photo. Where was Dukas? Why were the fucking Chinese here?

They could have followed Bobby Li, but his tradecraft made that unlikely. They could be here for another reason entirely. Or one of his own could have brought them. Like Ho. Or—he hated the idea, but he had to consider the possibilities—Bobby Li.

What didn't occur to him, nonetheless, was that it was his own signal, which he had used to draw Craik and Dukas to Jakarta, that might also have drawn the Chinese. It didn't occur to him then, because, if it had, he would have had to consider that George Shreed had actually been a traitor.

QIU ENTERED ON THE SECOND AND HURRIED DOWN the path, wondering where his team was, why none of them was supporting him. He stopped to photograph an orchid, allowing himself twenty seconds of the three minutes' time he had scheduled for the approach to the site. The other man would be doing the same. He was suddenly scared. These tough CIA Americans were legendary—beautifully organized, skilled, always dangerous. Where was *his* team, now that he thought of it?

He looked around. Leaves and flowers were everywhere, like a nightmarish wallpaper; then, glimpsed through them, he saw faces, a hand, an ear. One of his own people? The other side's? He moved more slowly.

JERRY SAW SOMEBODY FLASH IN AND OUT OF HIS chosen killing ground, and he hesitated. His crosshairs registered on the back of Craik's neck and his finger took up the slack of the trigger, but he hadn't decided.

Somebody seemed to step toward Craik—a dark shape, hanging back on the left side of the bench. Jerry saw black hair. *Bobby.*

ALAN GOT TO THE EDGE OF THE CLEARING IN THE center of the maze. A man in a windbreaker was there just ahead of him, panting as if he had been running. He had *The Economist.* Alan shifted his own copy to make sure it would show.

The other man's eyes were wide, almost crazed. *His first meeting,* Alan thought.

"You ever go AGIP party?" the man croaked at him.

That was not quite the code. *AGIP Christmas party* was the code.

Oh, shit.

BOBBY LI HAD REACHED THE EDGE WHERE PANIC becomes madness. Qiu was inside by now, and the American was standing across the space that Bobby knew was Andy's window on the meeting. If Bobby took another step, he would be visible to Andy. *Shoot,* he thought. *Shoot the American!* His life, his family, his future, hung on a gunshot. All because of—not because of Andy. Not because of George. Because of these two outsiders in this Orchid House in this foreign place—these interlopers, these meddlers, these oppressors—

"Did I see you at AGIP *Christmas* party?" he cried, realizing he had said the code words wrong.

The American across the open space looked relieved. He, too, was carrying *The Economist*. He gave the reply signal: "I was with a Dutch girl."

Shoot! Bobby screamed inside his head. Did he say it aloud? No. And then he saw Qiu coming up *behind* the American. Bobby had the envelope full of newspaper in his hand and he stuck it out, shaking so hard the paper inside rustled and crackled. "Take it!" he cried. "Gift—for you—take it!"

The American put out a hand, but didn't take it.

And Qiu, eyes horrified, backed against the wall of plants as if to sidle around the American, but what he was looking at was *The Economist* in Bobby Li's left hand.

Bobby went over the edge.

It was Qiu. It was all Qiu's fault.

Bobby flipped the safety on the Walther and began to shoot.

The Chinese man made a little O of surprise, and the American dove over a table of orchids.

Bobby just went on shooting. Three into Qiu, two down the path, one where the American had disappeared, one into Qiu again, and the slide locked open because the clip was empty.

JERRY HEARD THE FIRST SHOT AND HAD A DIZZY moment when he thought he had pulled his own trigger, and then he recognized the smaller, sharper report of a handgun. Shot after shot. *Jesus!* Then the Orchid House erupted in shooting, at least three guns on the north, west, and northeast. Glass began to break overhead and shower down.

It was a bust.

He rolled the gun in the mat and threw junk over it and swung himself off the platform.

• • •

ALAN LANDED ON HIS MAIMED HAND AND FIRE
raced up his arm, but he rolled clear of a tangle of flowers and
raced down the maze. The bastard had a gun, had fired at
him. *But how could he have missed?*

Alan could hear at least three guns firing then, not all together, but two of them were close. He pressed past a toolshed
and grabbed a pair of wicked-looking scissors from a table.
Any port in a storm. Another shot was fired, so close that he saw
the muzzle flash through the flowers and realized that he was
separated by only a screen of plants from the main trail. He
couldn't tell whether the shot had been fired at him or not,
but he flung himself around the next corner.

BOBBY LI HEARD THE SHOTS AS IF THROUGH DEEP
water, as if they were fired by somebody else. The young
Chinese was down, lying on the trail, and Bobby headed for
the west exit. He thought he was safe, unless Andy had actually seen him fire the gun. If he hadn't, Bobby could blame the
shooting on the American. He could say that the American
had shot Qiu.

But suddenly there was more shooting, all around him.
Qiu's team were now shooting at Andy's team, and he was in
the middle.

ALAN MOVED THROUGH THE MAZE OF TRAILS, UN-
able to consider anything beyond his next cover. His hand
pulsed with pain as he stumbled through a display, knocking
plants in all directions. He threw himself behind a collection
of tools and handcarts right at the edge of the greenhouse
wall, determined to get his bearings before panic and paranoia eliminated his ability to think. He lay panting, trying to
be silent. There was another shot. Were they shooting at him?
He couldn't seem to see the moment of the meeting, as if he
had a spot of amnesia around the first shot.

Something had gone horribly wrong. But the man in the

windbreaker had known the signal. And then the shots—now it was coming back—and a man behind him going down, and the guy in the windbreaker still shooting. At Alan, yes, he thought so, yes. But not really aiming. Looking—crazy. He lay still, his lungs going as hard as if he had run five miles, and tried to imagine where the shooters were, and what they were after. They *had* to be shooting at one another. There was no cover. The plants offered concealment, but in the whole building there wasn't anything that would even deflect a small-caliber pistol bullet. Only the screen of the plants separated the trails. Alan thought there were at least four shooters, spread across the hall. Somewhere, one of them fired and a bullet hit the glass above him and the whole pane crazed, lines of cracks spreading out to the frames.

Part of him wanted to stay and solve the puzzle, but that last bullet made up his mind. *Time to go.* And he realized that he was thinking again, not simply reacting.

He reached across, tore at a wheelbarrow with his good hand and tipped it, with its load of tools, squarely across the path. Then he pushed with his bandaged hand against the shattered pane of glass until pieces began to break out of the frames, and in a moment he had cleared it, although his hand was screaming and there was blood on his arm. There was another shot from twenty meters off, hidden several folds in the trail away. A potted plant burst, spraying him with loam and plant matter.

He rolled through the hole he had made and remembered to hold his maimed hand close with the other as he went. His shirt tore and a pain cut like fire across his back as he scraped through the frame. He fell much farther than he had expected and landed hard on his back, the wind knocked clean out of him. So many things hurt that his hand had to struggle to be heard. He rolled onto his knees and pushed himself to his feet, already plotting his path to the parking lot.

The shooting had stopped, and he had to consider that he *had* been the target, and he had to wonder if there were more of them outside, on the trails and in the parking lot. He balanced waiting in hiding, perhaps in the foundations of the Orchid House, against a run for the parking lot, if he could even run. Despite the pain, the desire for movement won. He'd be damned if he'd wait for them like a cornered rat. He might surprise them. He moved cautiously around the base of the Orchid House wall and then crossed the open ground to the first of the high-peaked roofs of the traditional buildings he had seen. He surprised the schoolgirls there, and his torn shirt and blood and the wildness of his expression shocked them. He took them as a sign he was safe for a moment and he ran along the gravel path, heedless of the looks that other visitors gave him until he made it to the parking lot without another shot being fired.

The cabdriver didn't want him, but Alan shoved cash into his hands and made noises until the cab was moving. He had good instincts, but, because he lacked training and was preoccupied with his injuries, he didn't see a car follow him out of the lot.

BOBBY LI HELD OUT ALL THE REST OF HIS AMERICAN bills as he and Ho collided. Ho grabbed the money and tossed the camera. He was fast for a big man, gone while Bobby was retrieving the camera. Men were pouring out of the Orchid House like ants; a woman was screaming somewhere near the food concession. Small, hollow-cheeked Indonesian men were turned, eyes wide, toward the Orchid House.

He had to get rid of the gun. He had to get out of Jakarta. He had to change his life.

But he hadn't betrayed Andy or George Shreed with the truth.

JERRY HELD HIS GROUND UNTIL THE BUILDING WAS clear. He should have left as soon as he saw the Chinese. He should have shown Bobby Li exactly where to stand. He should have had a better escape route. As it was, he was one step ahead of the Jakarta police. His mind reground the facts on and on, and he blamed himself, and he needed a drink. They all went together.

Washington.

DUKAS GOT THE CALL ON HIS CELL PHONE FROM THE
NCIS duty officer when he had been asleep at his desk and
was dreaming of a house and a dog and was happy, perhaps
because he didn't own a house or a dog and these two seemed
particularly congenial.

"You have a secure call."

"Oh, shit."

Oh, shit. He knew only one person who might want to
call him at the office at eleven at night, and there wasn't supposed to be any reason for him to call.

"What's the number?" he said to the duty officer.

"U.S. embassy. Naval attaché."

Oh, double-shit.

"Dukas, NCIS, I have a message to call you." There was
the usual confusion, nobody at the other end ever having
heard of him, and then they found the person who had asked
him to call, a lieutenant-commander who asked him to wait,
and then Alan came on the line.

"Hey, Mike. You secure?"

"Can't you tell by the sound? You sound as if you got your head in a fifty-five-gallon drum. What's up?"

"Somebody started shooting."

Dukas felt his heart squeeze. "Oh, Christ, Al—"

"I left the mark, no sweat, and then I went to the meeting we said was going to be a piece of cake, and all hell broke loose." He told it quickly to Dukas, what he knew of it from his point of view. "I'm sorry if I screwed it up, Mike."

"But you're okay?"

"Yeah, I'm fine, except for my self-esteem."

"Where's Triffler?"

"Good question."

Dukas felt his blood pounding in his ears. He squeezed his eyeballs with his fingers and felt horrendous guilt. That Craik was okay made him no less guilty: He'd sent a good man into a bad place. "God, I'm sorry," he said.

"I volunteered."

"Yeah, but—you tell the local cops?" Dukas said.

"I came to the embassy; I didn't know what the hell was going on. They've dealt with the locals."

"Come home."

"I hear the ambassador's really ripped—"

"Come home!" Dukas was thinking fast, thinking about his mistake, about something that had seemed small and easy and was actually big and dangerous. "Come home *now*." He saw that his hands were trembling. "Put the lieutenant-commander back on."

Dukas asked the Jakarta attaché to put Alan on the first flight out to anywhere and to provide protection until they were in the air. "This a matter of national security?" the man said. He wasn't unwilling, only a little jaded. Dukas gave him his full name and number and the case number he'd given the Sleeping Dog file, and he told him that, yes, it was a matter of national security.

After he'd hung up, he sat staring at the wall of the duty office for fifteen minutes, and then he went along dimly lit corridors to his own office and spent the rest of the night there. First, he tried to figure out how a meeting taken from a long-dead comm plan could go bad, *really bad,* because he had been sure that nobody would show, sure that the mark itself would go unnoticed. The answer was now easy: because the comm plan had been planted on him and he'd been suckered by it, and the intention had always been that it would go bad.

But who had planted it on him?

The easy answer was Shreed's control, who must have had a copy—but how did a Chinese intel officer insert a comm plan into a dead CIA file, and then get it sent to Mike Dukas?

It didn't make sense. Especially since Shreed's control was probably dead himself, because the last Dukas had seen of him, he was lying facedown in a village in Pakistan with a hole in his back.

Then Dukas spent the rest of the night going through Sleeping Dog, which was supposed to be moribund but suddenly wasn't.

Dar es Salaam.

Colonel Lao had been in his office before the African dawn had broken, because the first meeting time in Jakarta had been close and he wanted to be there for a report. The report would be negative, he had thought: Surely whoever had left the mark in Jakarta would pass up the first meeting time, perhaps appear for the second or third. Yet his secure phone had sounded only fifteen minutes after the scheduled time, and his face had registered the horror he had felt as he had heard the report of the whole bloody, blown operation.

"Who shot first?" he said, hardly able to keep his rage out of his voice. On the other end was the Chief of Security at the Chinese embassy in Jakarta, a man who, at that moment, was facing the loss of his career and knew it. His answer was evasive; Lao excoriated him.

"How can you be sure there was an actual meeting?" Lao demanded. He was certain that there could be only two people who knew the American Go plan other than Lao himself—Chen and Shreed. When the officer insisted that a Westerner had appeared at the appointed time and place, Lao thought he saw it more clearly: Shreed had sent a substitute, meaning that he was alive and thought that Chen was, as well. Had Chen been there? Chen's surrogate?

"Did you have the wits to identify anybody?" Lao growled. So much confusion, the officer whined, and there was shooting—unknown entities, Indonesians working perhaps for the Westerner or the Chinese, undoubtedly counter-surveillance. The embassy hadn't had enough men, and the man sent out from Beijing, Qiu, was an idiot who had antagonized the in-country team and then got himself shot dead. Time had been too short, and—his voice stronger as he began to shift the blame—why hadn't Lao informed them earlier? And why hadn't he expected violence? And after the whining, the face-saving, and the excuses, a nugget of useful fact: One of the in-country team had followed one of the Americans to a hotel. He didn't have a name yet.

Lao sat up and asserted himself. "Did you get photographs? Did you get at least that much?" They had, he learned. "Send them to me at once—have them scanned at the embassy and encrypted. I want them on my desk in twenty minutes. And the ID on the man your one competent agent followed."

The officer protested that the films hadn't been developed; these things took time—and hung up.

It was another hour before Loyalty Man reported that his agent had been unable to identify the man at the meeting. He had been only some American.

Jakarta.

The balls-up at the Orchid House made Jerry Piat angry—enraged drunk was only a couple of swallows away: Well, there you were, in the pleasant fog of booze one second, full-bore rage the next. He was jolting through a bad part of Jakarta in a taxi, a pint of Scotch in his hand and his head full of murderous doubts. Something apparently easy had gone bad—*Jesus, shooting!* It wasn't supposed to be a hostile meet, and somebody had started *shooting!* Of course, he had planned to do some shooting of his own, but that was different. He was a renegade, what the hell. And Bobby Li had gone missing; he hadn't shown at their rendezvous spot and he didn't respond to phone signals.

And, Piat was thinking, he was himself in deep shit with the people who had sent him to Jakarta in the first place. What would he tell Suter and Helmer?

Well, he could tell them that Craik had done it. Some kind of personal thing. Maybe something snapped, he just—

Bull*shit*.

He couldn't help thinking that what it reminded him of was the Watergate break-in. The Gang Who Couldn't Shoot Straight. *Jesus*.

He went through it step-by-step. He had put somebody to check at the cannon, and a guy had come and had left the mark, only it hadn't been Dukas, it had been Craik, which Piat hadn't known until too late. (*First mistake.*) Then, this morning, they'd been at the meeting place, just as they had planned, and the same guy, Craik, had showed up there. Okay. Ho had been ready with the camera inside the Orchid House, too, or so Piat had thought, except that Bobby hadn't got the film to him afterward (*second mistake*), meaning that to date there were no good photos of Craik inside, actually meeting with Bobby Li, which was the object of the whole operation. That had been the object, anyway, back before he had got enraged-drunk and had decided to shoot the sonofabitch—to get a photo of Dukas or Craik with what would look like a Chinese agent, which was what Bobby Li was meant to look like. But somebody had started shooting, and now he had no photos at all. Zip.

How was he to know that a bunch of people—*Chinese*—would fucking start *shooting*?

The thought of it made Piat scowl into the humid heat: He had screwed up—forget the others, he was talking to himself about good tradecraft—he had *screwed up*, and he was ashamed. He had let the booze do his thinking for him, the booze and his loyalty to George Shreed, and he hadn't been on top of things and they'd gone to hell.

But why?

It was really a double screwup: First, he hadn't made sure himself that somebody competent would be taking the photos inside the Orchid House. In fact, he should have been on the camera himself and not dicked around with the fucking gun. And, second, he'd somehow overlooked the possibility that a third party would read the mark on the cannon and know that it signaled a meeting in the Orchid House—somebody Chinese, as it turned out. An idea zinged around his brain: *We set up somebody to fake a meeting with a fake Chinese, and real Chinese show up. How the fuck did the Chinese know?*

Something ugly sucked at his brain. Suspicion.

George Shreed had been accused of selling out to the Chinese. If he'd given the Chinese the comm plan—

He couldn't let himself be sucked toward that. Any direction but that. *Think of something else.*

He'd lifted this old, dead comm plan out of the Canceled file and had laid it on Dukas *because* it was dead, *because* nobody else could know about it, *because* it had been Shreed's creation and therefore beautifully ironic—Shreed striking back from the grave—and therefore it was a safe hunk of bait to lure Dukas into a trap. But somehow the Chinese had known about it and had shown up and had started shooting.

Part of his brain kept picking at the problem of how they could have known, and it was saying, *People know about comm plans because they've either stolen them or been given them, and, because this was a George Shreed comm plan*—But another part of his brain, the part that loved the late George Shreed, was saying, *Don't go there.*

Piat sipped and admitted to himself that he wasn't going to tell Suter and Helmer the truth. Nothing had happened in the Orchid House, he'd say; he hadn't tried to kill Craik and failed. There hadn't been any Chinese.

Think about Bobby Li, he told himself. *Where the hell is he?*

He changed taxis and directed the driver out to an old temple that stood on the edge of a colossal industrial park that was once going to make somebody fantastically rich and that had gone belly-up like the rest of Indonesia in the nineties.

Nature was vengeful in Indonesia: give it a chance to take something back, and nature moved fast. The industrial park now looked like a Mayan ruin, with small trees growing out of windows, and wild pigs running around the decaying roads.

Across the road from the old temple was a cookshed. One old woman had a fire and a pot and a "cooler" full of water with cans of soda in it. You could get a really cheap lunch there, with a case of the shits thrown in for nothing. It was his and Bobby's last-stand, desperation, no-fallback dead drop.

"Package for Mister Brown?" he said. He held up an American five.

"Ten dolla." Prices had gone up.

He handed over a ten and, wonder of wonders, she fished out a brown envelope with a bulge in it. Inside was a plastic canister with a roll of film. *That little sonofabitch!* He took back his doubts about Bobby.

A piece of paper was in the canister with the film. One word had been scrawled on it:

Scared.

It made Piat smile.

He wrapped three American hundreds into a tight roll and stuffed them into the canister and put the canister back into the envelope with the piece of paper, on which he had written,

"I'll be back."

"Give to Mister Black when he comes, okay, Mama?"

"Ten dolla."

Piat headed for the airport.

Dar es Salaam.

Two hours later than he had demanded, as Lao was smoking and staring at the wall, his stomach seething, the photos came through from Jakarta. They were not particularly clear, but one was clear enough for him to see that Bobby Li had been close to both Qiu, the dead man, and the Caucasian. Too close. Had he spoiled the meet?

Lao tried to see the logic of such a thing. He had sent a case officer to Jakarta to run things, and he had got killed; and he had sent Chen's old agent, Li, to identify Chen or Shreed if either showed at the meeting, and—and Li had then intruded on the meeting that was detailed in American Go. Doing so was far beyond the responsibility of an agent. It was a kind of hubris. Had Li thought that Lao wouldn't know?

Or had he had some other, more important agenda? Had he wanted to eavesdrop? But why?

Li's action suggested another set of orders, because Li, in Lao's experience, was an insecure man who always needed orders: The only things he did on his own were acts of desperation. So, who else might be giving him orders? The question chilled Lao because it came from the ice of a case officer's worst fear—that his agent was a double. This led to a second, colder question: double agent for whom? He couldn't forget that Li had been Chen's agent.

He shook his head. He didn't believe in the game of mirrors. He ground out his cigarette and called in Jiang, an aging captain with a good bureaucrat's sense of how to get things done. Lao brought up on the computer screen a photograph of the Westerner leaving the Orchid House. "I want to know who that Westerner is. He was in Jakarta two hours ago: check the manifests of flights in and out for five days back and the outgoing from now on; I have a suspicion he will leave Jakarta soon. Check with embassy security in Jakarta; one of their people followed an American, maybe this man, to a hotel. Get a name if you can. Then check the hotels for Americans who were there yesterday and today. Ask if they have been asking for directions to Fatahillah Square and the Orchid House in the minipark." He squinted at the screen. "This man was probably with somebody else—up to four others, maybe. A countersurveillance team. Maybe traveling together, but not necessarily." He lit another cigarette. "Then get on to the Jakarta police and find out if they have any reports on an incident at the Orchid House this morning."

The captain gave a forward jerk that suggested a bow. Both were in civilian clothes; military etiquette did not seem quite right.

"I am going home for lunch," Lao said. It was, in fact, only nine in the morning. The captain's face was impassive.

Lao drove to his rented house in a suburb where most of the diplomatic community lived (not so with most of his Chinese colleagues, who huddled around the embassy), kissed his wife, American-style, and responded to her questions about his day, then put his finger to his lips as he led her to the bedroom. The house was bugged; the phone was bugged; she had years ago given up trying to know how his days really were. Yet they had great affection for each other, despite their arranged marriage and his profession and its conditions. Sometimes, she knew, he came to her like this to make love when he wanted to make his mind a blank.

Lao wished he could talk about his problems to her. Or perhaps not. She might say, as she had once when they were test-driving a new car in Beijing and nobody could possibly have been listening, "Don't you ever dream of living like other people?"

8

Washington.

ROSE MET HER HUSBAND AT DULLES AIRPORT. HIS EM-
brace was hard, quick, eager. He looked worn out. "Jakarta
was a bust," he said as he settled in the car.

"I thought it was supposed to be a walk in the park."

He folded his arms and sank lower in the passenger seat.
"The case isn't what we thought."

"Mike should have his ass hauled for sending you." Rose
accelerated to get into the traffic heading toward Washington.

He looked out the window. A deer was standing by the
side of the six-lane highway. He frowned. "I wasn't very good
out there." He flexed his bad hand. "I'll tell you the worst of it
up front: there was shooting; a guy was killed; I got out by the
skin of my teeth."

She gasped, bit back some comment. "I'm just glad you're
home." She put her hand on his.

"Everything went wrong," he said. "Triffler never got
there, one goddam thing after another."

"What *happened*?"

"Everything." He turned his hand over—the bad one—

and squeezed her fingers. " 'This time, Amelican Fryboy, you make big mistake!' "

It had started to rain. He stared out the side window again, dimly seeing his own reflection, hers. He put his hand, the bad one, on her thigh, and she covered it with her own. "It was great to be doing something, though," he said.

To his astonishment, she laughed. "You're going to be doing a lot." She reached across him and opened the door of the glove compartment and pulled an envelope into his lap. He saw the naval return address and his own name, and he opened the envelope and began to read, his heart swelling as he did so. "You are ordered to proceed to Naval Air Station, Miramar, California, for a period of—"

"Sonofabitch," he said. He was frowning.

"I thought you'd be beside yourself!"

"I am, I am—but—There's the case, you know—Sleeping Dog—I've got some ideas I want to share with Mike—" He looked again at the orders. "My God, another MARI det—a week ago I'd have killed for this—"

He had called Mike Dukas from the west coast and invited him for dinner, something he broke to Rose only as they were nearing their rented house. "I've got to talk to him about the case," Alan said.

"You've got orders to Miramar."

"I let him down in Jakarta. I want to make it up to him."

"Alan, the Navy's given you a new job—you're not an NCIS agent!"

"Mike's my friend."

"Mike should have his ass kicked."

He kissed her cheek. She steered into their weedy driveway and turned the car off. "I wish you'd told me that you'd invited him," she said.

"You're right; I should have. I didn't think. I was stupid." They were in the house by then. He kissed her again, and she smiled and stood back from him. "Well—if working for Mike is this good for you—"

He embraced her. "I'll get a shower." He grinned. "And I know I'm still in the Navy." As he headed up the stairs, he hugged the orders against his chest with his good hand.

Twenty minutes later, Dukas's battered car pulled up behind theirs in the too-short driveway, and there he was, worried and guilty.

"Hey, babe." He kissed her as he came through the door. Rose held herself stiffly, and he felt it and got the message. "Where's the great man?" He dumped his attaché in one of the ugly chairs. "Rose, what's wrong?"

"If you don't know, there's no point in telling you!"

Dukas blew out his breath and headed upstairs to see Mikey, his godson. Coming down again, he tested the atmosphere—Rose slamming things down in the kitchen, a smell of onions and garlic frying. Dukas positioned himself in front of Alan, who was sitting on the sofa and wincing with each slam of a pan lid in the kitchen. "Al, it was all my fault. I feel like shit about it."

"No." Alan looked up at him. Something thumped in the kitchen, maybe a piece of meat being thrown down on the cutting board. "Let's get on with the case."

Dukas flinched as a cupboard door slammed. "Rosie, can I help?" he shouted.

Rose appeared, no smile, a chef's knife in her hands. "You're unbelievable, Mike. You almost got my husband killed!"

"What can I say?" he muttered.

"Try 'I'm sorry!' "

"Okay—Rosie, I'm sorry."

Rose folded her arms. The chef's knife stood straight up by her right shoulder like some kind of emblem in a statue of one of the more severe saints. "Saying you're sorry isn't enough!"

Dukas tried to grin, and Rose, uncharmed, walked out. "I should have never let you go," Dukas sighed to Alan. "I've already had my ass chewed by two experts at ONI. CIA, Embassy Jakarta, and State all want a piece of me. Rose has to stand in line."

"And I should have told her I'd asked you to dinner. We'll get over it; Rose'll get over it. What's going on with Sleeping Dog?" Alan stood up, restless, wanting to move, but the room was too small. "The way I see it, that comm plan wasn't dead;

it was active as hell, so what about everything else in the file? Let's go through it piece by piece and figure out—"

Dukas tried to raise a hand to Alan's shoulder, winced, and settled for putting a hand on his arm. "I've been through the file—several times. I can tell you this: We thought the Jakarta comm plan was the only action item there. We were wrong. Maybe we were supposed to *think* the comm plan was the action item, but there's also action in Seattle." They sat down, their knees almost touching, their voices low because the small woman in the kitchen was still slamming things around. Dukas leaned forward, his face only inches from Alan's. "After I talked to you in Jakarta, I began to check Sleeping Dog out. I got a retired FBI guy who'd been the case officer in ninety-two. He wouldn't say much, but he'd at least admit that he remembered it—it *was* a real case, meaning that the whole thing isn't a crock of shit. *Some* of it, at least, is real. Sally Baranowski insists that the Jakarta comm plan *wasn't* in Sleeping Dog, but— news from town, kid, here comes a big one—" He bent even closer to Alan's ear. "The Jakarta comm plan was part of Chinese Checkers—George Shreed's personal map for meeting with his control."

Alan stared at him. He was processing it—Jakarta, Shreed, Chinese Checkers. "The Chinese?" he said.

"I think, yeah. Who else has Chinese Checkers?"

"Well—the Agency—"

"Yeah, but the Agency isn't going to lay a Shreed comm plan on us and then use it to try to kill you!"

"Well," Alan said grudgingly, "I'm not sure anybody tried to *kill* me." He was frowning, looking away from Dukas.

Dukas leaned in close again. "It's the Chinese, stupid. Get it?"

Dar es Salaam.

By midnight, Colonel Lao knew enough about what had happened in Jakarta to make him start using obscenities in his conversation—always a sign of frustration in him. Inwardly, he cursed: he cursed the distance between Dar and Jakarta; he cursed the surveillance people there and the fact that he couldn't debrief them himself. Had they been so incompetent that they had got themselves shot at? Had they frightened off Chen and Shreed? Had there been some other failure?

"Unlikely," he said aloud. He believed in likelihoods, probabilities: when you must choose, choose the probable.

Start with the certain, he thought.

Nothing was certain.

Start with the probable, then.

What was *probable* was that the American in the Orchid House had been sent by the CIA. If Shreed was dead, then it was *probable* that the CIA had his files, including the comm plan; it was *probable* that they had tested the plan by planting the mark. Therefore, the man who had appeared at the meeting place with a magazine under his arm had been a CIA agent—unless Shreed was not, in fact, dead. If Shreed was not dead, then what was probable was that the American in the Orchid House had been sent by him.

What was utterly uncertain was why and how the meeting in the Orchid House had degenerated into a shootout. Such things were remarkably rare—so rare that most operations officers hardly ever even carried guns, much less used them.

James Bond, Lao thought with a sneer.

What went wrong?

A fuller report had landed on his computer. The American (if he was) had had no gun and had not fired. Others in the Orchid House, apparently locals, had been armed and had fired. And his people had returned the fire. All this suggested not two sides, but three, with the American seemingly at a different level of involvement—almost, in a sense, a bystander.

A third force. Maddening.

And the Americans as bystanders. Odd.

And then the odd behavior of Chen's old agent, Li.

Analysis of airline manifests showed that an American named Alan Craik had flown into and out of Jakarta on the right days, and a report from the agent who had checked the hotels said that Craik had asked about the location of the cannon and the Orchid House and had then been gone for part of an afternoon. The officer in Jakarta had had to winnow down a list of possibles to get to this one, a list that included a Dutch businessman, an American tourist, two Japanese tarts, and an airline steward, but Craik seemed the likeliest because of the question about the park. Lao himself became convinced when a simple check of a military registry turned up Craik as a serving officer in naval intelligence—not quite real intelligence, to Lao, but close enough. Although why he was traveling under his own name to a hostile agent contact, Lao could not begin to guess. Madness! Amateur!

Currently on medical leave, he had read in the sketchy report on Craik. The Jakarta agent had reported that the hotel staff remembered quite clearly that Craik had had new, livid scars on his left hand and was missing two fingers. Was this relevant? Why would an officer on medical leave be sent on a dangerous mission?

He distracted himself by leafing through the new operational file on Jade Talon. Tsung had done the scut work, locating a local team to do the dirty work and finding an existing agent, a Pakistani intelligence officer with ties to the Islamic conservatives who could be used as the cutout. It wasn't pretty, and the quality of the operational personnel (Somali) wasn't high, but it had the virtue of being totally secure. The Pakistani thought Tsung was North Korean. The Somalis thought they were fighting for Allah. Lao put his chop in the upper right of the document, approving the next step, the passing of targeting data. The quality of the targeting would determine whether the Somalis had a prayer of hitting their very mobile target. It was also one thing that the Americans could use as an indicator of who was behind the attack.

But the real question was what could be done about Chen. Lao thought about that for hours, took it home with him and to bed with his wife, and then he decided that the answer must lie with this Craik.

Suburban Virginia.

Alan and Dukas had been over it all again—Jakarta, Chinese Checkers, the shooting—and had given it up for now, shaking their heads. Dukas was trying to change the subject.

"I understand you got duty orders."

"Yeah, but I got an idea about that." Alan raised his voice. "Rose, what're you cooking out there?"

"Spaghetti, what do I ever cook for your friend in there?" The slamming had pretty much stopped, and she sounded pleasanter.

"Want some help from your thoughtless husband?"

"No." She appeared with two glasses, which she set down on the coffee table. She held a wine bottle as if she'd fill the glasses only if they passed some test first. "What are you guys whispering about?"

"Uh . . . a little debrief—" Dukas mumbled.

"Oh, yeah, I bet."

"Actually," Dukas said, "we were talking about a case called Crystal Insight."

Rose held the wine suspended over the glasses. "That's *my* case!"

Dukas grinned. "Right. That's the NCIS investigation of Shreed's phony-baloney framing of you as a security risk—which hasn't been closed, thank God, although I've been writing reports on it since I was able to sit up in a hospital bed! Because"—he tapped the coffee table—"because, guys, this Chinese Checkers connection drags in George Shreed, and George Shreed was the focus of Crystal Insight, so all of Sleeping Dog and all of Chinese Checkers is now part of Crystal Insight." He looked triumphant.

"What's so great about that?" Rose said.

"It lets him deal from strength," Alan said, turning to look at her. "With an ongoing case, you've already got established tracks, leverage with the other agencies." He looked at Dukas. "Cool. I like it."

Rose poured the wine. "I thought my case was going to be closed."

"Rosie, sweetheart, CNO as much as exonerated you by

pulling you over to his staff for a month and restoring you to duty. But a case is different—a case has a life of its own. Now, it'll go on for as long as there's anything about Shreed out there."

Alan grinned. "Mike's kids will be working on Crystal Insight."

Rose rolled her eyes. "If Mike is going to have kids, he'd better hurry up." She skewered Dukas with a look. "How *is* Sally?"

Dukas pretended not to hear. "And now there's this Seattle thing—"

"I have to go to Seattle," Alan muttered to her.

"*What?*" Her voice was a shriek.

"*I'm* supposed to go to Seattle to investigate Sleeping Dog," Dukas said. "But I don't want to go to Seattle, because I've got to contact every officer who signed off in every agency on this pile of paper, and then I've got to go through the original index of every closeout file—when it left each agency—to make sure that every piece of paper matches. Then, when I'm satisfied that Chinese Checkers is the only clinker in the pile, I'll do something." He held up a hand to keep Rose from tearing into him. "Listen, babe, it makes sense—you don't know the case—

"NSA picked up these burst transmissions on satellite years ago. No idea where they came from, except the satellite was limited by line of sight to the Arctic and North America down to, like, Wisconsin. And not very helpful, because they got the tickle only now and then, sometimes months apart. In fact, for a couple of years, it was so sparse one expert put a note in the file that the transmissions could be a natural phenomenon, although he didn't say what. Prairie dogs rubbing their back feet together, maybe. Anyway, this had no priority, and NSA shunted it over to the Bureau when the Bureau went international and got interested in communications. But nothing much happened. Then came wireless, namely the cell phone, and this case got hotted up along with a lot of other stuff. The Bureau leaned on NSA and got a new fix from them—new technology. Probably what we'd call triangulation, although in fact it was done by figuring the bounce off the ionosphere—you got that? it means zip to me, but I read practically a book about it in the case file—and they got to where they could say it was northwestern U.S. or southwestern Canada, so now they were down to about a million square miles. For a while, the Bureau actually worked on it—there's reams of interviews in my office: RCMP, midwestern ham operators, ships' radiomen, meteorologists, you name it—trying to get the location more precisely. I'll give you the short form: They found *nada*, except for four reports of radio interference along the Canadian coast."

Rose made a show of pretending to yawn. "Really fascinating stuff, Mike. Wow, how do you do it?"

"This is important! Anyway, they didn't get enough for anybody to get the hots about it, so in 1994 the Bureau kicked it to the CIA, because the Agency put out a call for anything on burst transmissions in this frequency range. They were into terrorist groups operating in the Philippines, and there was some shit going around about Chinese intel supplying them with comm equipment that put out a signal more or less like this one." Rose rolled her eyes.

"Wait. Three years ago, the Agency was running some of its ops wannabees from the Ranch through an exercise and they sent eleven students to Seattle to do interviews. Grunge work, real-world slogging stuff. And they used Sleeping Dog as the exercise subject because it was inactive. Now, what the students were supposed to do was make up a plan for interviewing 'appropriate' subjects—that is, ham operators, ships' radiomen, et cetera, et cetera—just what the Bureau had already done. But here's the fascinating part—this is really interesting, really—this one guy, a maverick, he demanded that they be given all the data on every intercept NSA had made, and then he makes out this chart. It's huge; it's got a folder to itself—and *lists* and *time lines*. And then, instead of interviewing like everybody else, he finds where there's a radio telescope at the University of Washington and he goes and he says, 'Give me your records for the last nine years, with every instance of radio interference you've experienced.' " Dukas looked at Rose to make sure she was following. "Eighty-seven percent correlation," Dukas said.

"Wow," she said. She smiled at him.

"Wow, my ass. It means he proved the transmissions originated in Seattle. But the Agency doesn't like guys who don't do things their way, so they bounced him from the program and sent Sleeping Dog right back to the cellar. *Now* it comes to me. Why?"

Rose crossed her eyes and let her mouth hang open. "Why, Professor?"

"Because somebody wants me—or me and Al—to go to Seattle." He waited. "Well? Get it?"

"Well, I get it," Alan said. "*I'll* go to Seattle." His jaw was set in what both Rose and Dukas called "the look"—impenetrable stubbornness.

"You're going to Miramar to set up a new west coast MARI detachment," Rose told him.

"Which I can do just as well at Whidbey Island. Look, Mike, you get DNI to sign off on it, and I go to Admiral Pilchard; Rose pulls her strings in CNO's office—"

Dukas glanced at Rose, who was frowning and shaking her head. Dukas started frowning and shaking his head, too.

But Alan went right on. "You could send Triffler to Seattle undercover to be my case officer. He and I get along. This time I'll do it right—eyes wide open, people at my back all the time—Come on, Mike! It'll be great!"

"Over my dead body," Rose said.

"No, *with* your gorgeous, sexy body. You come with me."

"I've got T-84 hours to fly at Pax River!"

"They've got T-84s at Whidbey and, anyway, you're due to move on to F-18s."

"Alan! The Navy doesn't run to accommodate you and me!"

He grinned. "What d'you want to bet?"

9

Over the Indian Ocean.

PAUL STEVENS KNEW HE WAS THE BEST PILOT ON THE
Jefferson, and he thought that he deserved to be Top Hook if
there was any justice in the Navy. The trouble was, he wasn't
in a squadron, and so he didn't have a squadron CO kissing
the CAG's ass to get one of his own pilots named as Top
Hook; no, Paul Stevens was *acting* CO of a rinky-dink, two-
plane detachment with no clout and no access to the people
who made the decisions, and so he, Paul Stevens, would go on
making great landings, landing after landing, and everybody
on the boat would watch him on the Plat camera and say,
"That guy sure can land an airplane," and then somebody else
would get the glory. The story of his life.

Stevens made a minuscule adjustment in his heading and
brought the S-3 up a hundred feet or so because it wasn't *exactly* on eighteen thousand feet where he wanted it, and he
looked over at LTjg Soleck in the other front seat and wondered why he couldn't make contact. That shit Craik was
fucking *worshiped* by the kid, and he barely gave Stevens the

time of day. And Stevens had been nice to him, he swore he had.

"Want to land her on the boat?" he said now.

"Yes, sir!" Eager kid. Stevens liked that, or at least liked an eagerness to learn to fly as well as he did.

"We're going to have to go in the stack, so don't get too anxious."

"Yes, sir."

"And watch her when you go dirty; the flaps are cranky. Hydraulics, maybe. Just feel them, see what you think. I don't want to ground the goddam aircraft for nothing."

He turned it over to Soleck and stared out at the endless blue smudge that was ocean and sky. It was a hazy day, the horizon invisible, so that they seemed to be flying through an undifferentiated brightness. Stevens was not much for scenery, anyway. In fact, and he admitted this to himself, wondering why it was true, he wasn't much for *anything*—a beer on the beach, TV on the boat, the odd letter from one of his kids. Divorced, so his wife never wrote unless something was wrong.

Get a hobby, the chaplain had said to him. *Get a life.* Actually, he could have said, I got a hobby—hating fucking Alan Craik. He thought about Craik so much they should have been married. Craik was the det CO, when Stevens knew he should have been CO himself. Craik kissed the CAG's ass and said they were "old squadron buddies." Oh, yeah. Craik got the medals, the commendations, the top fitreps, while Stevens, he thought, did the real work and got nothing. Craik couldn't have landed a plane on a carrier if he'd had a fucking angel holding up each wingtip. Craik was a *ground-pounder!*

And here Stevens was, *acting* CO until Craik got over his injury and came back and took over again.

Stevens winced as Soleck dropped too fast out of the stack and then overcorrected; he almost grabbed the stick but caught himself. "Try not to kill us," he growled.

They came around into the break a little fast, therefore, with that much more speed to bleed; Stevens heard the flaps complain and felt them respond just a fraction late. "Hear that?" he said. Soleck shot him a scared look, looked back at the panel, dropped the right wing; Stevens shouted, "No—!"

"One, two, three gear down—" the kid was saying, and Stevens knew he hadn't really looked to see that the gear was down and locked; the kid was doing it by rote, chanting off the landing checklist. That was how you wound up on the deck with no gear. Stevens checked it himself to make sure: down and locked. "Down and *locked*!" he snarled. "You're supposed to *look*."

The lineup wasn't good, and then the kid was chasing the ball. Stevens tightened his sphincter and squeezed his thighs around his penis unconsciously. *Bad, really bad.* "Too far to the left!" Stevens shouted. The kid overcorrected, the LSO saying, "Right—right—" in that bland voice that meant you were about to crash. The kid chased the ball. Lost the ball. Got it again—*oh, shit, he's afraid of the ramp; he's too high*—then dropping like a rock, BANG!, Stevens shouting, "Jesus H.—!"

And abrupt deceleration as they caught the first wire, and Stevens knew they wouldn't give the kid an okay. He glanced at Soleck, who was sweating and flexing his fingers around the stick. The yellow-shirts were signaling. "Lift the hook, lift the goddam hook," Stevens was muttering, wanting to scream it, and at last the kid got it and lifted the hook and taxied them forward until they were parked aft of the number two elevator and the engines could whine down to nothing.

Soleck looked at him. "What'd I do wrong?" he said.

Stevens sighed. He was bathed in sweat himself. "Jesus, I'd need a book," he said. He stared out the windscreen, trying to think of something good to say, the way they taught you to do it. Behind them, the backseaters were cleaning up knee-pads and paper cups and grease pencils. *The hell with saying something nice!* he thought, and he turned to Soleck and said, "You're afraid of the ramp. You can't land an aircraft on a deck if you're afraid. Don't you get it? Why the fuck can't you get it? *Don't be afraid of the fucking ramp!*"

It seemed so obvious to him. Why didn't people understand what was so clear to him?

He went down to the ready room, where there was a message to see the CAG. Stevens groaned aloud so that everybody could hear and took off up the p'way. The CAG was an asshole buddy of Craik's—they'd won the Gulf War together, or something—so anytime that Stevens had to talk to the CAG, he figured the guy was just waiting to hear something stupid come out of his mouth so he could laugh about it later with Craik. What he really feared this time, however, was that Captain Rafehausen would call him in to announce that Craik was returning to active duty, so he, Stevens, should be ready to hand the det back to him in two or three days.

Stevens *liked* being acting CO. In fact, he'd been CO before Craik had ever appeared, and even though Craik and some others said he'd done a lousy job and that was why Craik had replaced him, it was Stevens's view that he'd done the best he could with a lousy lot of castoffs from squadrons that had got rid of their dead wood when they'd been told to staff the det. Anyway, here he was, running the det again and doing a good job, and he didn't want the CAG calling him in to say it was over. Although he hoped that the man would at least have the consideration to call him in when he knew Craik was coming back—not just all of a sudden have Craik the Fucking Hero step out of a COD and take over the det just like that, no warning.

So he rehearsed all this in his head as he walked the p'way, sniffling unconsciously and once running the back of his right hand under his nose because it was running. He still had on his flight suit, his helmet under his left arm—a somewhat deliberate move; his way of saying to Rafehausen, *I'm a pilot, Goddamit!*

"Sir," he said, and sort of braced when he was in the door.

"Hey, Paul." Rafehausen sounded perfectly friendly, an attitude that Stevens didn't trust. "Give me a minute," Rafehausen said. He was going down a long scroll of computer paper, now and then checking something with a pen. Then he tossed the pen down and leaned back and said, "What's up?"

"I got a message to see you."

"Oh, right, right, right—" Rafehausen burrowed under the computer paper. "Got a set of orders—Al Craik—"

Oh, shit, Stevens thought, *here it comes.*

Rafehausen had to call in a yeoman to find what he was looking for; it was on a side table in another pile.

"Craik's been ordered TAD to Whidbey Island—something to do with another MARI det."

Stevens's heart bumped: Maybe Craik wasn't coming back!

"He'll come back to the boat as soon as he's medically sound. Until then, he's doing this job at Whidbey." Rafehausen looked up, eyebrows raised. "You got a problem with that?"

When in doubt, object, was Stevens's approach to life. "I'm doing a lot of work for him!" He shifted his helmet.

"Craik saved your butt, career-wise. Now it's your turn to help him."

"I hear you."

"Good." Rafehausen scribbled on the paper. "I'll tell Al we're all doing fine." He called in the yeoman and gave quick instructions, then turned back to Stevens. "How things going otherwise?"

Stevens said they were going fine, fine, except for the parts he'd been chasing for two weeks. Rafehausen made a note. He looked at Stevens with a sour smile. "How's our Mister Soleck doing?"

Stevens said in effect that Soleck was doing okay, muttering something about his landings. Rafehausen exploded with laughter. "He's got the worst landing scores on the boat!" His face became serious again. "He needs to shape up, Paul. What's his problem?"

Stevens temporized, shrugged, muttered, "I guess he's rattled, is all. He's ramp-shy."

"Who's he flying with?"

"Me, mostly."

Rafehausen cocked his head. The yeoman appeared in the doorway and started to say something about a meeting, and Rafehausen waved him away; Stevens realized suddenly that Rafehausen was actually concerned about the ensign. "You hauling his ass about the landings?" Rafehausen said.

"No. 'Course not."

"You letting them slide?"

"No! I try to teach him as we go—hands-on stuff—let him know when he's wrong."

Rafehausen slit his eyes. "For example—?"

"Just now, we're out of the break, going dirty, he goes,

'One, two, three, gear down.' He hadn't even checked. I told him about it."

"Once he's on his approach, what d'you say?"

" 'Too far right, too low, find the ball—' Like that."

"Isn't that the LSO's job?"

"You saying I should sit there and keep my mouth shut?"

Rafehausen swiveled sideways. He looked tired, Stevens thought without compassion, even old, his hair thinning a little, his eyes pouchy. He was young for a captain, but the CAG's job was wearing him down. And he was worried about a jg! "Maybe he's more afraid of you than he is of the ramp." Rafehausen smiled. "That possible, Paul?"

"What're you saying, I'm a goddam bully?"

"If I wanted to say that, I'd say it. No, I just mean—you're his CO; he's a jg; you're a veteran; he's green as grass. Maybe you make him nervous."

"Somebody better make him nervous; someday he'll be coming in on eight hundred pounds and his hydraulics shot, he'll really have something to be nervous about! What d'you want me to do, tell him he did just swell and forget about almost having to take the net?" Stevens made a face. "Today he put the plane down so goddam hard I thought we were going to lose the hook. He's not going to learn better if somebody doesn't put the fear of God into him!"

Rafehausen nodded, smiling a funny smile, and Stevens realized too late that he'd said something he shouldn't have, and it was only when he was in the p'way again that he knew it was that word "fear." He shouldn't have said that. It had confirmed something that Rafehausen had already had in his mind.

Rafehausen's last words had been "Let's try flying him with somebody else. Just for a few landings, see how he does."

Stevens went to his compartment and threw his helmet against the bulkhead and then stood there, feeling the beginnings of a postnasal drip and wiping his nose on his hand and thinking that he couldn't be getting a cold, not a goddam cold, not now.

Washington.

Jerry Piat checked his apartment to see if his old friends at the Agency had bugged it while he was away, but it was clean. So was the telephone. He'd given up using the remote phone because it was really a radio and could be bugged by remote, no entry, no hardware required. He didn't know why he expected them to be after him, and he had to admit to himself that he was disappointed that they weren't. Old habits die hard, but the fact was, he wasn't important enough for them to care about anymore. He was just one of those old Ops people who had gone quietly into that good night—thanks, Jerry, sorry you got caught in the crossfire; don't call us, we'll call you.

He sat at his computer and scanned in the lousy photos that Bobby Li's people had taken in Jakarta. Really shitty work. As if they were doing it on purpose, the shits. He called up an image-resolution program that George Shreed had told him about—George, who knew everything about computers, always knew the latest and hottest programs. *Good old George,* he thought. He tried to manipulate the right-hand side of the first photo. *Good old George, good old substitute dad.* George had been his first boss on his first assignment—Jakarta. George was a born teacher, tough but brilliant, as demanding of Piat as he had been of himself. Hobbling around on two metal canes because he'd crashed a jet in Vietnam. *You were the best of us, George, and now they're saying you were a traitor.* He turned to another photo. He couldn't recover the clarity that the camera lens had bitched, because it was out of focus, but he could coax the computer program to make sense of the blur and try to pull related pixels into something more like what the camera had been aimed at.

He pointed the mouse and clicked and boxed part of an image and clicked and pulled down a menu and clicked, and a kind of sense began to run through the images—a kind of story, in fact.

The Jakarta police report had said that at least thirteen shots were fired within the Orchid House, six exiting through the glass walls. Four had killed a Chinese national named

Qiu—a Chinese intelligence officer. That was the spine of the story—a Chinese intel officer being shot.

Piat shrank the digitized and doctored photos and lined them up on the computer screen. He tried to read the story.

The first photograph showed what Piat knew was the inside of the Orchid House, lots of dark green and two of the flowers now recognizable by their color and size after his manipulation of them. In the right side of the frame, a human shape seemed to be walking in from offstage; on the left, another seemed to be walking off. Between them, a third. It was these three figures upon which Piat had spent the most time. The faces were unclear, the outlines fuzzy, but Piat remembered Bobby Li's maroon jacket, so he knew that the shape on the right was Bobby. The shape on the left was unrecognizable, but Piat suspected that this was the now-dead Mister Qiu because he was all in gray, and, even out of focus, the gray looked bureaucratic. In the middle, a blur. Short-sleeved shirt, something blue at the top, white rectangle in the middle, white shape where a hand should have been.

Craik in his baseball cap. The rectangle would be the magazine he was supposed to carry.

The photographer must have been using a motor—stupid, too noisy, he thought—and a telephoto to stay at a distance. In the second shot, Li was well into the frame, and the other figure, instead of having walked all the way out, was just at the left edge, no sign of walking—a gray column with a flesh-colored top and a black crest—hair. The doctored photo was clear enough so that one of Li's arms could be recognized, swinging out in front of him, at the end of it a single white star of reflection. *What the hell?* Piat had thought when he played with it, but he was pretty sure what it was. Something bright in Bobby Li's hand. Not a diamond pinkie ring, oh, no. A fucking gun, in fact.

The man on the left was not quite a vertical column in the third picture. His lines had wavered as if he was making some sort of whole-body movement—something in a dance? There was almost an S-curve from shoulder to foot. And no wonder. The star at the end of Bobby Li's arm had become an orange pencil line that reached for the man on the far side of the frame.

Bobby shot the fucker himself!

Then Bobby Li, or a smudge of him, was standing, still at the right side of the frame. The dancing column on the left had metamorphosed into a fuzzy worm that was almost horizontal now, down at the bottom of the frame. A black smudge toward the center might be a shock of Asian hair. Hovering over it was a white moth, or maybe a white bird, something as big as a head but winged, with bits of color over one wing like light through a stained-glass window. Qiu's Confucian soul, caught on the way out? His aura? Craik was reacting away from Bobby and the shooting. Who could blame him?

In the next photo, the bird or moth had flown, nowhere to be seen; Bobby Li's maroon jacket was still identifiable on the figure on the right; the worm had expired into a large pile of gray dogshit. Craik was a mass moving out of the frame, fast. Then Piat understood the white moth-bird with the splashes of color—*The Economist.* The dying man must have let go of it. Meaning that he, too, was there to make the meeting, following the directions in the comm plan. It was like a goddam Marx Brothers movie. *Why?* Bobby Li was supposed to make the meeting with Dukas—now Craik—and hand him a package inside his folded *Economist,* and those assholes were supposed to have got a photo that would make it look as if Craik had been passed something by an Asian. Instead, Groucho and Harpo and Chico had bought out the entire Jakarta stock of *The Economist* and then started shooting at each other!

Piat's focus was on Bobby Li. Bobby was supposed to have been there because he, Piat, had put him there. What the hell game was he playing? Jerry drank a lot more and thought, insofar as his boozy brain could think, about Bobby Li and what the photos really showed. Even drunk, he saw that the fuzziness of the photos was probably deliberate, to forestall the very thinking he was now doing.

Piat poured himself more bourbon. He went to sleep with his clothes on.

In the morning, there was mail in his box, including a

postcard from Seattle signed Bob. It meant that he was supposed to go to Seattle and report.

Fuck, Piat thought. He felt like hell.

NCIS, Washington Navy Yard.

Mike Dukas was eating a glazed doughnut that he'd found in his desk drawer and thinking that it was, in fact, older than yesterday's, and maybe from a batch he'd brought in the day he got the Sleeping Dog file. It was as chewy as a bagel, but at the same time flabby and musty-tasting. Not what a man who loved glazed doughnuts wanted when he was having his mid-morning sugar crash.

"Those things'll kill you," Dick Triffler said from the other side of the plastic egg-crate divider. Triffler had made his way back from Manila. For the moment, he was still Dukas's assistant, but doing everything he could to get assigned somewhere else.

"When we gonna knock down the Berlin Wall here?" Dukas said, nodding toward the divider.

"Your mama ever tell you not to talk with your mouth full?"

"If I didn't talk with my mouth full, I'd never talk."

"Oh, happy day."

"Aw, come on, Dick—! Christ, I'm a wounded veteran!"

Triffler came to the wall and peered through the white plastic crates. "I felt deeply for you when I heard you were hurt," he said. He was quite sincere. He was, in fact, probably the most sincere man Dukas had ever known—distressingly honest, incapable of breaking any rule once he knew of its existence. He had a somewhat flutelike voice that sometimes seemed effeminate but that perfectly conveyed his seriousness and provided a resonant tenor to the Northeast Washington AME choir. "I don't think you should trade on your injury, however. You could have got Craik killed in Jakarta."

"Trade on it! I'm wearing a fucking harness that makes me look like Roger Rabbit, and you say I'm trading on it!"

Dukas was, in fact, wearing the plastic rig that kept his hands high. Dukas sighed. "That was the worst doughnut I ever ate."

"You're getting fat."

At that point, Alan Craik walked in, and after the amenities, he got himself coffee and said to Dukas, "Admiral Pilchard's in my corner. I think we're a go for Whidbey."

Dukas tried to get his elbows on the desktop and gave up. "Triffler's got a mad on about Jakarta, and he didn't even get there."

Triffler looked through the crates at Alan. " 'Mad' wouldn't quite cut it. I told the boss I'd go anywhere, do anything to get out of this office."

"Great! I got just the job for you, then." Dukas grinned through the plastic crate. Triffler, stooping down to look back at him, scowled. Dukas said, "Ever been to Seattle?"

"I didn't like it."

"Couple weeks there, it'll grow on you."

Triffler came around the partition and said that he was a married man and he had social responsibilities; he mentioned his church, the choir, Little League. His father was coming for a visit on Monday.

Dukas was trying to get out of the rabbit rig, which he couldn't stand for more than an hour at a time. "We need you in Seattle."

"No!"

"Yes." Dukas pulled the plastic contraption off his shoulders like a feather boa. "Al Craik needs a minder."

"Oh, spare me—not again." Triffler looked at Alan. "No offense—"

"This time," Dukas said, "it'll work. This time, we know what we're doing; we're focused." He smiled. "Trust me."

Triffler groaned. A few minutes later, he was up the hall, trying again to get a transfer. When he came back, Dukas said, "I got there before you this morning. I told him you're indispensable."

"Yeah, that's what he said." Triffler exhaled, stood with his hands on his slim hips, staring at Dukas. "Mike, you do great work sometimes and you get results, but, boy, do I hate working for you!"

Dukas winked at Alan. "Tell you what I'll do. Because you're good, Dick—there isn't a better special agent in this building, and I think you know it—I need you in Seattle. If you go and if it goes down the way I think it will, when we're done I'll get you out of here. Deal? This one job for me, and then up, up, and away. Deal?"

Triffler came a step closer. "*Promise?*"

"On my mother's grave."

"You had a *mother*?"

"Watch it!" Dukas picked up his coffee mug, which had what appeared to be permanent drip stains down the side he always drank from, moved past Triffler and around the plastic barrier, and poured coffee from Triffler's personal coffee machine.

"You have no shame," Triffler said, coming behind him.

"None." Dukas sipped, made positive signals with his eyebrows at Alan Craik. "Let's put our brains together." Dukas and Alan pulled chairs around from their side of the office and sat, and Dukas told Triffler everything that they had gone over the night before: that the Jakarta comm plan was part of Chinese Checkers, that the likelihood was that the Sleeping Dog file had been doctored, that Dukas was convinced that the Chinese had done it.

"Son of George Shreed?" Triffler said.

"Maybe Ghost of George Shreed," Dukas said. "Anyway, Sleeping Dog gets folded into the ongoing Crystal Insight file, and that way we don't have to make foreign-contact reports for Jakarta and hand it back to the Agency. We get to keep it."

"Why *don't* we just hand it back to the Agency?"

"Because it looks like somebody worked through the Agency to lay it on me. You think I'm going to give it back without knowing who or why?"

"Yeah, but, Mike, what you're saying is that somebody *Chinese* doctored an Agency case file, inserted *another* file that supposedly nobody knew about, and sent it to you as a supposedly all-but-dead horse. That looks to me like a perfect thing to kick back to Carl Menzes. Investigating crap inside the Agency is his life!"

Alan stirred. "Menzes wouldn't know what to do with it. He wouldn't have caught the Jakarta plan, for example."

Triffler sighed. "And now it's sending us to Seattle. Shh-boom, shh-boom." He gave Dukas a fishy look. "Why?"

Alan answered. "Because that's what Sleeping Dog is about—Seattle—and we think that whoever doctored the file chose it on purpose. There must have been lots of files they could have sent over, but this is the one that came, and it's the one that's been doctored."

"You don't know that."

"Okay, that's where the probabilities point, how's that?"

Triffler shook his head. "I don't like it. Jakarta, you had a comm plan—very specific. Seattle, you got nothing."

"I'm trying to get something," Dukas said. "I've got one half-time clerk checking to see if there's another inventory someplace so we can cross-check, because the one we got has obviously been tampered with. Then I'm going to chase down everybody who ever had the file and see what they remember; so far, I've got Sally Baranowski and an FBI guy."

Triffler looked skeptical. "What's in Seattle?"

Alan tilted his chair back. "You mean, for us? If we knew, we wouldn't have to go." He got up and headed for the coffee machine. "Nothing good, I'm sure."

"So I go, and I set up countersurveillance for Al, and I'm—what?"

"Case officer. Op manager."

"With whom? Help from local NCIS?" Triffler actually said "whom." Dukas had learned to ignore it.

"At least two guys, more if I can get them."

"And you think it's the Chinese. Huh." Triffler went down the hall to wash the coffeepot and the filter, and Dukas sat there, massaging his scar and scowling, and Alan took out a cigarette and then put it back and looked sheepish. Triffler came back whistling, and, as he started to make a new pot of coffee, he said, "Has it occurred to you guys that there could be a third party who's been in this all along?"

"Say again?"

"You assume everything's the Chinese because we know they used to be at the other end of the comm plan. But think a minute—Craik leaves the signal, their watcher picks it up, they do everything the same, even *if* they're not behind giving you the Sleeping Dog file. They could be as surprised as anybody by his mark, but they're still going to send people to the Orchid House and then try to get in touch, because they have a copy of the comm plan and that's what they're supposed to do." He measured his custom-blended coffee with the precision of a pharmacist measuring a controlled substance.

Dukas groaned. "Dick, you're making things worse. I don't need a third party!"

Triffler used the spoon like a lecturer's wand. "The Chinese wouldn't shoot their own intel guy. Somebody else did— and it wasn't Al. That says to me a third party. Mike, the Chinese would have been in the Orchid House whether they doctored the Sleeping Dog file or not. They have to have a lot of questions—wouldn't you? Like how come a dead comm plan came alive?"

Alan sat with his legs apart, one hand with the coffee cup between them. "Yeah, like, was it Shreed who left the mark? Or did Shreed tell the Agency about it before he died, and the CIA left the mark?"

Dukas chewed on a finger. "Well, it wasn't Shreed, because we went to his funeral." He handed his filthy cup over; Triffler backed away from it. "Come on, it won't bite you!" He sat back. "Anyway, your point is the Chinese have a lot of questions. So?"

"So all I'm saying is, the Chinese have been alerted by what happened in Jakarta, and they want some answers—but that doesn't mean they're the ones who put the Jakarta comm plan into Sleeping Dog."

Dukas groaned. Triffler leaned his buttocks against his desk, and Alan stared into his cup. After a long silence, Alan said, "Anyway, you and I are going to Seattle."

"So what's waiting in Seattle?"

Alan looked up and grinned. "That's what you and I are going to find out."

Seattle.

His code name was Jewel. He was sixtyish, a naturalized American who had emigrated from Hong Kong before the British left. He had brought money and an entrepreneurial spirit, and now he had his own company and a handsome house right on the water. He also had access to several buildings where it was necessary to have an ID that required prior vetting.

Jewel showed his ID to the watch officer of a downtown building leased by the U.S. Coast Guard and was waved through the turnstile. His crew waited on the quarterdeck as the petty officer of the watch emerged from behind a security desk and checked their equipment. The young sailor was careful, and he had the three chevrons of a petty officer first class on his sleeve. His scrutiny made Jewel nervous.

"You guys are early."

"We got a lot to do," said Jewel, deliberately sounding like a new immigrant. He smiled a lot around the military people. He gave this one a big smile, although one of his hands was trembling. "We got secret plans, heh!"

The petty officer frowned. "I hope not. Petty Officer Nguyen will be with you while you work. You know what you're here for?"

"Sure, sure. Air-conditioning ducts. Clean and purify to prevent against Legionnaires' disease. No problem." Jewel had a lifetime of being scared of authority to fall back on. He smiled like an idiot to hide his fear.

Jewel's people came past the quarterdeck and headed down the hall, following PO Nguyen. She led them past the watch floor, where Jewel was careful to display no interest, past a small room that housed Jewel's target, and through a short corridor to a concrete-floored maintenance area. There were shelves of cleaning supplies and racks of brooms.

He barked orders at his team and they began to unpack equipment. In fifteen minutes they were in the air-conditioning ducts throughout the building, scrubbing away with remote-controlled vehicles. Jewel had considered using the cleaning 'bots to plant bugs or leave remote cameras, but the risk of discovery outweighed the possible gain. PO Nguyen sat down against the wall and read a magazine. Jewel did the job that the Coast Guard was paying for. It would take three nights to complete, and he needed only a few minutes for his real work. He could be patient. His nerves screamed that he should do it now, get it over with, but his training was good, and he kept to his plan, his nerves visible only in a sort of bouncy energy that caused him to overturn his can of Coke early in the evening.

The watch changed at midnight. Forty-five minutes before midnight, PO Nguyen went down the hall to check that her relief was on his way and to use the head. She didn't come back for ten minutes. When she returned, she was replaced by an older petty officer with a deeply lined face. He made a few jokes in bad Mandarin, but Jewel laughed along with him and listened to his stories of Taiwan with interest. He, too, left his post fifteen minutes before the arrival of the oncoming watch.

Jewel had his times. He was able to walk the corridors all the first night, usually under the scrutiny of military personnel, but not always. Now he knew the layout. He knew the exact location of the JOTS terminal that the Coast Guard used to help monitor the traffic in the sound. It was a much more elaborate form of espionage than watching the sound with binoculars or cruising it in his boat with the depthfinder, but he had trained for it twenty years before. He was ready. He reviewed the commands he would give to the JOTS terminal when he got his hands on it. He needed less than one minute.

THE WATCH WAS THE SAME THE NEXT NIGHT. HE HAD hoped it would be. Nguyen was again assigned to them, and she watched them less, going out the back of the maintenance room to smoke at least twice, and leaving them early to find her relief.

The moment she left, Jewel put his tools down and followed her into the short corridor. He didn't try and explain himself to his men. They didn't ask him questions. His hands were shaking again, but his breathing was good. He had had long minutes to prepare for Nguyen to leave.

He emerged from the corridor into a bleak gray room

with a JOTS repeater terminal. JOTS was the Joint Operational Tactical System, a networked military computer system that displayed every unit in the U.S. Navy with its location, course, speed, and the units it had identified in its area of operations. There were repeater terminals on every ship in the Navy and at many shore installations. China had nothing like it.

Jewel didn't hesitate or spend time looking at the terminal. It was on, and focused on Puget Sound. He took a photo of the initial screen in case there was information there that could be deciphered later by Jewel's case officer. Then he reached for the trackball. He had been trained for this, but the training couldn't keep his hands free of the tremor from his neck. There were loud noises from the next room, where the watch did traffic control for merchant ships in Puget Sound. He flinched. The noises calmed. He reached for the ball again and used the mouse pad key to enlarge the view.

All of the West Coast.

All of North America.

He moved the trackball until the cursor was on Africa. He clicked to refine the screen.

Just the east coast of Africa.

Just Kenya and Tanzania and the water off their coasts.

And a little cluster of circles. He ran the cursor over them. As the cursor touched each one, its name lit up next to the circle.

USS *Esek Hopkins*. USS *Yellowjacket*.

USS *Thomas Jefferson*.

Click. Location. *Click*. Course and speed.

Done.

EIGHT HOURS LATER, JEWEL HAD HIS TRANSMITTER out and warm in the trunk of his car, high up in the Olympic Mountains. His message was very short.

WELL OUT TO SEA, *ADMIRAL PO* CAME TO PERISCOPE depth in broad daylight, a maneuver her captain hated like death itself. If Jewel was passing them information on the

American boomers, their ballistic missile submarines, then the risk was worthwhile. His operational clock was running down, as well. He had perhaps twenty days left on station before he'd have to turn for home.

His communications officer nodded almost as soon as the mast was up.

"Message incoming."

He nodded.

"I have it," said the comms officer.

"Dive. Take us down to 250 meters. XO, you have the con. Give me the message."

Ten minutes of laborious decoding later, the short message was clear; the location and course of a nuclear carrier across the world. It made no sense. It was a waste of his effort and the risk to his crew. Jewel did occasionally put them on a U.S. carrier leaving Puget Sound, but carriers, despite their huge crews and vast conventional power, were not *Admiral Po*'s legitimate prey. *Admiral Po* was here to catch their boomers and to keep China safe from the huge intercontinental nuclear missiles that American boomers carried.

He growled, "Waste! We have twenty more days on station. Waste!"

He said this to his cabin bulkhead, of course.

Then he went back to the bridge and put his ship through the laborious process of surfacing to retransmit.

PEOPLE'S NAVY INTELLIGENCE HEADQUARTERS, BEIjing, noted the code on the incoming transmission and sent it through proper channels. In seconds it was decrypted, read at a junior level, noted as being important to a program called Jade Talon and needed for retransmission to a deployed submarine in the Indian Ocean, *Chairman Mao*. A mid-level officer placed it in the daily transmission file for the *Mao*. Then he gave a hard copy to a courier to take across town to the bastards in the old Imperial Palace. It occurred to him that no good could come of State Security's knowing the location of a U.S. carrier, but, as always, he kept his thoughts to himself.

•   •   •

SIX HOURS LATER, WHEN *CHAIRMAN MAO* SURFACED to receive transmissions, Jewel's data was in the first burst. The watch officer read it with the surrounding message and woke his captain, who came immediately to the bridge. There, he gave orders for a significant course change that would take them well down the east coast of Africa. Then he addressed his bridge crew.

"We are going in harm's way. We will be tracking an American carrier battle group. There is no harder target. It will be our duty to get in close to them and provide detailed reporting. I expect every man to do his duty and more."

He said things about home, and wives, and how the republic depended on them. Their faces hardened with determination. They were good men. The captain suspected they were all about to be sacrificed, but he was happy that his ship had been chosen. He began to plot tactics to approach the carrier.

A DAY LATER, CAPTAIN TSUNG WAS STANDING ON A pier in Karachi, holding a briefcase full of money for a greedy aristocrat. He hated Pakistan and cursed his fate that he had learned Arabic and Farsi. Most Pakistanis had little Arabic. Few Chinese had any Urdu. It put him in Pakistan far too often. And his Farsi and Persian features made him perfect to play the part of an Iranian.

Colonel Namjee was the highest-level officer Tsung had ever recruited. He was smart and venal, both virtues in an agent. He was well-placed with the "Islamic hardliners" that U.S. news so often mentioned. Namjee was tall and elegant, fastidious in his dress. He looked like a Mogul prince, and his taste in horses and Patek Philippe watches had led him to this moment.

"You have the men?" Tsung liked things to be clear.

"Yes. Somalis. The best. Well, the best of a bad lot, anyway."

"I'd like to see them."

"I thought you wanted to stay clear of this?"

"I don't intend to wander up and exchange names. I want to see them."

"They will complete their training in the next few days. Then they will collect their boats from another source. Not your business, although I have to pay for the boats and the GPS systems, eh?"

"Yes. I'm prepared to pay."

"Good. Then they have to transit the boats to the African coast. It is the worst part of the operation, if I may intrude my experience here. If we had boats in Somalia already, we'd be safer."

"We don't."

"Exactly. We could send them by ship."

"Too easy to catch, not enough time. Just have your crews wait for clear weather and go. Surely a cigarette boat is safer than a dhow."

"Not necessarily. You are not a nautical man, I take it?"

Tsung shook his head impatiently.

"They cannot just drive as if they were cars. They need fuel. In fact, they will go with the smuggler traffic to Oman, and then hug the coast. I will have to pay for a local smuggler to guide them and open the way. Yes?"

Tsung nodded. Namjee had a way of getting the most possible cash out of every operation. Tsung wondered if the "local smuggler" even existed.

"I want to see them."

"In Mogadishu." Namjee made it clear from his intonation that he did not relish being in Mogadishu.

Tsung was direct. "Arrange it. Contact me the usual way. We will do an accounting there."

"I need fifty thousand now."

"I just gave you fifty thousand last time." Namjee's venality made him easy to manage, but the money portion of every meeting was a drain on Tsung's conviviality.

"I need it. There are expenses, as I said. The smuggler, the boats, the fuel, the extra training...."

Tsung smiled bitterly and handed Namjee the briefcase he had been holding. Namjee smiled broadly.

"Nice briefcase." Then he frowned. "I still don't see how we're going to place our Islamics, no matter how dedicated, in proximity to a U.S. carrier at sea. We need the targeting."

"We'll have it. In fact, I know where they are right now."

Namjee looked impressed.

PART
TWO

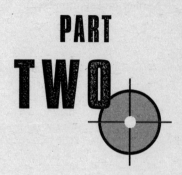

Seattle

Seattle.

ALAN WAS READING *THE RIDDLE OF THE SANDS,* A book about spying on the German Navy in World War I. It wasn't his normal reading, but Abe Peretz, one of his earliest friends from the Navy, had suggested that depression could be answered by changing life patterns. Alan suspected that his depression would be answered only by getting on a ship and going somewhere, but he was willing to try anything. Abe had asked him if he had ever read Jane Austen or the *Iliad,* with a look that suggested that these represented basic life skills. Alan chose *The Riddle of the Sands* because he thought it might be a murder mystery. Now he was lost in it while consuming his fourth packet of airline mixed nuts. He had Rose's hand wedged under his arm.

She was watching him from the cover of her own reading, the most recent copy of *Aviation Week.* He was not recovered, but the ferocity of his attack on Abe's book brought hope, and his absentminded annihilation of packets of nuts was a sign that his full concentration was at work. It hadn't been evident much during his recovery from the wound.

Rose watched the long, slow turn into the military field at Whidbey Island with a critical eye. They were on a Hawaiian Air charter, but the pilot was probably former military. Rose thought that he had made this landing often enough to have his own set of muscle memories for it, because there was no hesitation in his maneuvers. The part of Rose's mind that was a pilot was never off, not even when she was asleep on a plane.

The intensity of her glance drew Alan out of his fugue.

"We there?" he said.

"Almost." She smiled. He smiled back and touched her cheek, her neck. . . . She growled and rolled her eyes.

"Something on your mind, lady?" he said. They both laughed. She pinned his hand, this time, and they both looked out the window while she stroked the top of his good hand.

He worried about whether she would ever do the same for the other one.

Then his attention was grabbed by something on the field. He waited a moment to be sure and smiled and squeezed her hand. The plane began its final descent, and in a moment the wheels touched the runway in a gentle three-point landing.

"See that, honey?"

A lone F-18 Hornet sat on the tarmac near the terminal. Whidbey was not an F-18 base, so there was only one reason for that plane to be there, and that was for Rose. It gleamed in the damp Pacific light, and it had been carefully painted in the gleaming white and red of NASA, although such a paint job was unprecedented and unnecessary. As they rolled past the terminal, the little jetliner slowing rapidly, Alan and Rose could just see the lettering under the pilot's canopy: CDR ROSE SICILIANO.

There was a crowd of people standing around the plane. Alan looked at Rose, his throat full of something heavy. He smiled at her, and she beamed.

"That's my plane," she said.

He waited for the sag of rejection that had accompanied every triumph he had seen her accomplish since his wound, and there it was. He rode it, fought it like a sickness, and hugged her with his good arm, wondering, *When will this end?*

Sea-Tac Airport.

Jerry Piat watched the Seattle sprawl materialize out of the cloud cover and searched for Lake Washington, which should have been a great spread of water behind the city but which he couldn't find. It was, unsurprisingly, raining in Seattle, and visibility wasn't much. Piat was really looking for the places where runners ran, because, along with drinking and smoking, he ran for his health. Or so he said, although he ran for nostalgia as much as anything—the 1964 high school cross-country champion of eastern Montana. He drank too much, he smoked sometimes, but he loved to run. Anyway, Seattle was a running city, and the drizzle would be cool, and the running would be great. He was here for serious business, sure, but he'd see Marvin Helmer and get that crap out of the way, and then he'd hit his hotel and take a little run. And then he'd have a drink. And figure out what to do about Bobby Li.

He got a rental car and drove south on 5, smiling again to remember that there was a place named Des Moines here, a long way from Iowa, then frowning as he returned to the problem of Bobby Li. He was certain now that Bobby was a double. Piat couldn't let that stand. He was out of the Agency, but he couldn't let his own prize agent go on as a double, as a mockery of what he, Piat, had done for his whole career.

He tooled around Tacoma and was in Olympia before the offices broke for lunch. Olympia had the feel of small—small town, small capital. He'd checked out the state police on the Web and noted that most of the senior staff were natives who'd gone to high school here and got such education as they had close by, and most of them had had military experience and come right back home. *Small* town.

And it was in this small town that he had to justify the screwup in Jakarta to an asshole who wasn't half the ops officer that Piat was, but who had the clout to boss him around.

Seattle.

Dick Triffler looked around his hotel room and admitted that traveling at the government's expense had its advantages. He'd miss his wife; he'd miss his kids; but there was always a lift to getting away and being on his own. *Admit it,* he told himself, *nobody can be one hundred percent with somebody else all the time.*

He tried the television.

He tried the phone.

He inspected the minibar.

He admired his French coffee press and the pound of Triffler's Mix he'd brought from M Street Coffees in D.C.— sixty percent dark-roast Colombia, thirty percent Kenyan, ten percent Arabian Mocha Sanani.

"Not bad, not bad," he said aloud. Outside, it was drizzly but bright, and on an impulse he took out running shoes and shorts. He had already unpacked as if he were filing state papers—jackets and suits on hangers; shirts in one drawer, socks in another, underwear in a third—and pulled them on, with a Redskins T-shirt and an L.L. Bean baseball cap. He did some quick stretches, felt wicked and free because he skipped the sit-ups and the push-ups, and almost danced out to the elevator. *Oh, Massa Dukas,* he sang to himself, *if you-all could see me now!*

An hour later, he was in the local NCIS office, getting desk space and a phone and doing some schmoozing with the people who were going to be on his team. Not always easy for a black guy. He scheduled a briefing for after lunch and began to make a list of sites around Seattle that might be the subject of the burst transmissions. His team would have to visit every one.

NCIS, Washington.

With Triffler gone to Seattle, Dukas needed a new assistant. He had begged for a special agent. He got instead a twenty-year-old file clerk named Leslie Kultzke—half-time. After the first day, he decided that she was probably a ditz-brain but maybe, just possibly, God help us, not quite as dumb as she seemed. She was cursed with a trailer-park worldview and an American high school education; her idea of office dress apparently derived from Dolly Parton's idea of swank; her voice was permanently hoarse from trying to shout down all the other girls when she was sixteen; and her idea of culture ended at Britney Spears. She also believed in big hair—dyed the color of borscht at the moment—and very big perfume. As she was a few pounds over the baggage allowance and not what you'd call gorgeous, her short skirts and tight tops seemed a little excessive. Yet she had surprised him by needing to be told things only once.

"Leslie, what d'you do with your other half time?" he said the second morning, deciding that she was actually better than nothing.

"I file." She laughed, also part of her curse—no matter what she said, she laughed. "Sometimes, I do my nails."

"How about I get you full-time, you give up on your nails."

"They're sculptured. See?" Laugh. Dukas looked. Her nails looked as if they had termites.

Leslie wasn't getting along with her regular supervisor, so the only thing between her and full-time for Dukas was turf rivalry, which Dukas figured wouldn't be too deadly because the supervisor, also a woman, despised Leslie. Dukas cleared a place at Triffler's desk, currently loaded with the files from the Sleeping Dog crate, and told her that the desk was hers until his real assistant came back, and she should consider herself full-time there, and they'd wait until her supervisor screamed before they told anybody.

"Terrific," Leslie said. More laughter. By then, she was also chewing bubble gum.

"Here's what I want you should do," Dukas said. He was debating whether he could stand Leslie's perfume full-time, but he needed her maybe even more than he needed a happy nose. "You know the inventory that came with this crate of stuff, right?"

"Oh, yeah?" Nervous laugh.

"Yeah." Dukas in fact had the inventory, which he retrieved from his desk and put in front of her. He tried not to inhale. "This inventory. Remember? You had it yesterday."

"Really."

"Yeah, really. We also have an inventory I got from the FBI."

"Oh, yeah." Laughter. Waves of perfume spread from her, hit the walls, and bounced back on Dukas.

"I want you to compare the two inventories and find any anomalies."

"We already done that, Mister Dukas," she said. He had had to explain the world "anomaly" to her yesterday; today, obviously, he didn't. Not bad.

"No, we compared the two to see if the Jakarta file was on both of them. It wasn't on the old FBI one but it was on the CIA one that came with the crate, which was how I knew the one in the crate had been doctored. Right?"

"Oh, ri-eeght!" Laugh. She rolled her eyes. "It's all rock and roll to me!"

"No, it isn't, Leslie. It's what we're here for. This is serious—okay?"

"Oka-a-a-ay!" Giggle, giggle.

He thought of bawling her out, and instead he found himself laughing with her.

"You're doing a great job," he said, sending her into almost hysterical laughter.

Whidbey Island.

The sounds of a hangar are always the same, with the high roof and endless space both amplifying and dwarfing them. The hangar held two large P-3 Orion aircraft in various stages of reconstruction, and Alan walked past them with undisguised interest. Both birds were clearly in the latter stages of a major refit, and from the new antenna array, it looked as if at least one was to be equipped with an update of the MARI system, the whiz-bang experimental electronics that Alan's detachment was testing on the *Jefferson*. In essence, it was a

high-definition, 3-D, side-looking radar system—the prover-
bial gnat's-ass detector. Tucked into the far corner was a single
S-3 with all her bottom panels off and her nose cone laid on a
skid. She, too, was having a major antenna-array overhaul.
Junior enlisted were carrying cruise boxes like ants at a picnic,
material coming off pallets in the belly of the hangar. Flatbeds
full of more pallets were coming in the wide hangar doors,
and forklifts were buzzing around them like tugboats with an
ocean liner. Alan worried a little about his reception here,
since they would all know that he had been the cause of their
rapid redeployment almost a week ahead of schedule. Dates
would have been broken and lives replanned to make their
schedule match his.

Alan walked briskly across the hangar, his whole attention fixed on the S-3, ignoring the consternation that his rank
caused as he moved through the maintenance space of the VP
squadron.

He approached a young petty officer third class, a woman
who was standing with one hand on her hip and checking
items off a clipboard. "Where the fuck are the maintenance
cruise boxes?" she was shouting. "I have this bird down and
my people need to get to work!"

"Look again." The maintenance chief was invisible around
the other side of the plane but sounded to Alan absurdly young
for his rank, for all that his voice carried authority.

"Chief, this ain't our fault. What if all our wrenches are
sitting on the tarmac out there? Fuck, I hate this rapid-move
stuff. What if we can't get 103 up tomorrow?" she said, obliv-
ious to the lieutenant-commander now parked at her elbow.

"Petty Officer, can I ask—?"

"Wait one, will ya?" She turned to say something more
and froze at his neat khakis and his gold oak leaf. "Sorry, sir."

The chief was coming forward from his position under
the extended MAD boom at the rear of the aircraft, warned by
her last words that there was an officer present.

"I'd just like to locate the ready room or the skipper's office."

The female petty officer waved toward a ladder well.

"Second deck, sir. Go up the ladder and look to your right. They just flew in, but the skipper will be in his office."

The chief was staring at Alan's chest. "You LCDR Craik?" He gave Alan an odd look, as if he couldn't decide whether to frown or smile.

"Yes, Chief."

"Chief Soames. I was at the RAG with Master Chief Craw."

"I'll send your regards, Chief."

"Kinda hoped he might be with ya, sir."

"I couldn't pry him away."

"Sure could use his help. We've got a steep learning curve on this thing." Alan nodded and started up the stairs to the second deck. The drab walls and ancient linoleum floors, polished to a fine sheen by generations of junior sailors, could have decorated any set of hangar offices Alan had ever seen. He passed the det admin office and an empty ready room and found himself eye-to-eye with a compact man with the blond hair and pug nose of a California beach bum, wearing a rumpled flight suit.

"Surfer!" he yelled.

"Spy!" Surfer responded by grabbing him in a bear hug and immediately going for a hold on Alan's leg, starting a wrestling match. Suddenly, the two of them were down on the floor of the passageway, wrestling, pawing for holds, gasping, flailing about the corridor and scattering junior officers and enlisted. The violence shocked them until they understood that the squeals were laughter, may even have guessed that the two had been junior officers together. Surfer's flight suit survived the clash, but Alan's khaki shirt was pulled out of his trousers, and a button popped off in the struggle. He didn't even have the consolation of coming out on top.

"Bastard!" Alan said, smiling like a maniac. "I almost beat you with one hand!"

"Your fucking little wings gouged my eye!" Surfer threw back.

"Get off me! Man, have some people put on weight!"

"Takes one to know one." Surfer made Alan feel young again, as if he were a newly minted jg on his first flight. "I'm supposed to look neat to meet your boss."

Surfer was trying to pull him back into shape. "My boss?"

Alan got it immediately. "Don't tell me they trust *you* with this operation."

Surfer whacked him on the back, hard enough to make Alan cough. "Come on into my office. Hey, Petty Officer Flint, see if somebody has a sewing kit, okay?" Surfer pointed Alan into a big armchair that might have started life in a frat house, as he closed the door and winked. "I got sent here to stand this thing up. I don't know the equipment or the mission, but it's a command, and I want it. But getting sent up here a week early is *not* helping morale."

"Well, I'm here on orders for a few weeks. Fuck, you hurt my hand." Alan looked at the scarring and moved the light bandage to hide the stumps of his fingers.

"If you're here to help, I could use it, man." Surfer was grinning ear to ear. "I'm reading my way through all this stuff," and he whacked a pile of publications. When they had served together in the Gulf War, Surfer had been the most intellectual of the pilots, but he had always hidden it behind his surfer-boy image.

"I have a few irons in the fire, Surfer," Alan said. "But I'm here to help."

"That's great, man. Great. I mean it. Fuck, none of these guys has ever done MARI except on a simulator that runs on a laptop. Most of our maintenance guys never saw the equipment before yesterday. We don't even have an exercise sched yet."

"Got a recognition library?"

"A who?"

"We made a library of recorded images, land and sea targets. A really sharp guy in my det started it on cruise. It's all digital. You want?"

"ASAP, man. ASAP."

"Your admin office open for business? I can send a message."

"You still smoke?"

"No. Yeah. Give me one." He leaned forward.

"We have to go down the hall to feed my habit. We can catch admin on the way." Petty Officer Flint returned with the shirt, button replaced, and Alan tucked it in as they walked down the hall.

"I want to get back in a plane and get an up-check so I can go back to my real job." Alan tried to keep his tone light. He knew he wasn't supposed to fly.

Surfer nodded. "Can do, buddy."

Just like that. Alan was worried that his hands were shaking from relief as he drafted the message in admin. He kept it short, provided a secure link for sending the data, with help from the office data processing expert, and saw the message sent. Surfer held up a pack of Marlboros.

Alan followed him down the passageway to a tiny balcony full of men and women, smoking. The place reeked.

Alan began to enjoy the smell, at least the first sweet smoke of the cigarette as it was lit.

"How bad's your hand?"

"It hurts when people twist it in wrestling matches. Otherwise, except that there's some parts missing, it's okay."

"Want to fly?"

"Sure!" *A little too eager.* "But I doubt the flight surgeon will—"

"Screw that. Short hop, just testing the hydraulics in 702. Maybe forty minutes in the air."

"That'd be great."

"You got flight gear?"

"On the *Jefferson.*"

"Go down to the rigger, get some stuff. Okay?"

Alan was out the door and headed for the rigging shack before Surfer had the pack out for his third cigarette. *Now this,* he was thinking, *is what I REALLY came for.*

Olympia, Washington.

Marv Helmer was an anomaly—not a Seattle-area native, no close connection with the state. Somebody had known somebody, Piat thought as he drove through the city and missed a turn. He was trying to use a GPS with city-map software, and he had to admit he preferred paper. Finally, he pulled over in a park and jabbed the buttons on the device, found the address he'd marked back in D.C., and wrote it down on a torn piece of paper.

The Enright Center was two blocks from the capitol and appeared to be a commercial building that the state had leased when the bureaucracy got too big. Most of the state cops were located somewhere else, as any fool could see from the absence of cruisers with bubble lights or bars. Piat noted a number of plain, dark vehicles that he guessed were under Helmer's thumb, because Helmer was honcho of a division called International Relations and Information, which to Piat meant terrorism and intelligence, with perhaps as much domestic surveillance and invasion of privacy as he could get away with. The Seattle area was big and dynamic, and it had a huge international trade and a big foreign, mostly Asian, population, so the state probably had good reason for wanting its own finger in the Pacific wind. Piat simply thought they'd hired the wrong finger. He thought of what he could do in such a job and was swept by envy.

Helmer had a corner office on the third floor. The suite was surprising after the blankness of the corridors—tile floors, metal doors, plain-Jane signs that said ANALYSIS and FOREIGN ESTIMATE and FILE ROOM RECEIVING with an attached penciled note, "moved to seventh floor," now curled with age. Helmer's part of the building also had a sign, also plain, DIRECTOR, and Piat wondered if Helmer had got to create his own title, which sounded enough like J. Edgar Hoover's to make a skeptic grin. The truth was, he disliked the *idea* of Helmer, which was really the idea of his own loss of clout, so that he was now answerable to this ambitious jerk who was facing him across a desk that Piat had the smarts to know was a good antique.

Helmer was a small man, neat, slender, clearly in great shape. His hair had been cut to the FBI standard, his suit expensive, his tie sober. Everything about him, in fact, was sober. It made Piat feel drunk just to look at him.

"I don't like you coming to my office," Helmer said.

Piat decided to treat it as a joke. "Thanks for the warm

welcome," he said with a smile. He waited. "You messaged me to come here."

"Not my idea. Firebird's idea—safe place, no surveillance." Firebird was Ray Suter. Helmer was LeMans. Piat was supposed to be Mustang, but he didn't deign to use it. Who wanted to be a car, for Christ's sake?

"Firebird's an asshole," Piat said. "He knows about as much about operational intel as a duck. Anyway, as long as this is such a safe spot, let's cut the code-name crap. *Ray Suter* is an asshole." Piat didn't like Suter any more than he liked Helmer, and he supposed it might be for the same reason: George Shreed had recruited Suter, not Piat, to be his assistant.

Helmer sat up even straighter. "Watch your mouth," he said. "Firebird is a fine American."

"Marv—!" Piat didn't like Helmer, but he knew him; they had in common a history in Ops. They had run into each other a lot in the now-defunct West Asia Project, where they had been involved with different groups of mujahedin with different goals. "Suter couldn't find his way through a counter-surveillance route with a map and a guide. He's a desk jockey and a shit, and the only thing going for him is he's loyal to George and he's willing to take on the bastards who hurt him."

"This operation is his to run," Helmer said. "For starters, he's paying the bills."

"Okay, okay, okay." Piat decided that he had made a wrong move, so he tried to make himself sound cordial. "Remember when we had the food fight about the mujahedin?"

Helmer made a gesture, like shooing something away.

Piat smiled even more. He'd said back then that it was a mistake to cut the mujahedin loose, because they'd come back to haunt the U.S.—as in fact they had, so far in Bosnia and Chechnya and Afghanistan itself. "All water over the dam," he said now, not really meaning it. Nothing was ever water over the dam to Piat. But he knew that he had to make nice to Helmer, because he didn't want Helmer or Suter finding out about his screwup in Jakarta and bad-mouthing him all over the intelligence community. He'd *never* get another job if they did. "Old times, right? The good old days."

"Sit down, please." Helmer, his hands clasped in front of his groin, waited until Piat was seated and then lowered himself into his own chair, also a first-rate antique. Windsor, real eighteenth century, Piat thought, although he'd have to see the stretcher to make sure. He'd used antique dealing as cover for quite a few years and learned a lot in the process, enough to think of taking up the trade someday. "Beautiful chair," he said.

Helmer was nonplussed, then said, "Oh, right," and opened a folder on his desk. Piat looked around and figured that Helmer didn't give two cents, either, for the Rowlandson prints of London criminals or the Piranesi prison scenes.

"This is outside the province of my work as director of the state external-intelligence fabric," Helmer said. "I'm really pushing the envelope, meeting on state property for this mission."

Pushing the envelope was nice, Piat thought. *Breaking several laws* was more like it. "I'm comfortable with it," Piat said.

"The people pay me to use my office judiciously."

"Would you like to adjourn to the parking lot?"

"I'm just making clear why I'm going to move things along." Helmer turned a page. "Brief me on the operation to date."

Piat ignored Helmer's implication of superior/inferior and tried to be pleasant. "We're exactly where we were two weeks ago: I doctored the Sleeping Dog file as specified, and then I left the Agency. The word is that Dukas subpoenaed everything in Suter's office; at some point, the lawyers apparently gave him Sleeping Dog, because his pal Craik showed up in Jakarta."

Helmer's little eyes glared. "And?"

"And what? He showed up, my guys there got some pictures, but—" Piat shrugged.

"What the hell does that mean?"

"Pictures are NBG, as the Brits say, old sport. My guys apparently missed the lesson where they taught about focusing. Terribly sorry." Said with a fake-Brit accent. Why had Helmer brought out this Monty Python imitation in him?

"*No* pictures?"

"Absolutely none, old chap. But I'm sure that you'll get brilliant ones here in Seattle. That was the idea, wasn't it, to get two sets?" Piat smiled. He had a hangover headache. He wanted a drink.

"Firebird will be really pissed."

"Oh, hey, I'm heartbroken."

Helmer looked up. "I don't like smartass remarks."

"I don't like dumbass ops. The Jakarta idea sucked, as I've been saying from the beginning." Indeed, he had been so sure that it sucked, that he had hoped to kill Dukas in Jakarta, not take his picture but—but, but, but.

Helmer's cheeks were pink. "It's a good plan."

"It's a plan put together by a desk-driver who's dropped out of sight and is under investigation for everything but buggering altar boys."

"All fabrications by George's enemies. You sound disloyal, Jerry." Helmer folded his hands on the desk and leaned a little, only a little, forward. Piat had heard some gossip that Helmer wanted to move up to the federal level, the Bureau or ATF or even the Agency—somewhere near or at the top, of course—and he was trying to look the part right then, very directorlike, but Piat thought he was probably too small. His eyes were also set a little close together. He had balls, however. "All we need is a photograph of Dukas meeting with a foreigner. If you'd got it in Jakarta, we could have gone forward! Then we drop the money in Dukas's bank account, and he's dead in the intelligence community."

"Yeah, and Craik?"

"Craik goes when Dukas goes. They played into our hands when Dukas sent Craik to Jakarta."

Piat snorted. "Marv, have you and Suter ever heard of 'with severe prejudice'? We should be fucking *killing* these guys!"

Helmer gave him The Directorial Look: two-hundred-yard gaze, dead eyes, furrows of dislike in the small space between them. "Piat, I'm an important public figure. You have nothing to lose and so you make irresponsible comments." They held the look. Piat thought of trying his dangerous smile, but he was already tired of Helmer and of the whole thing. What he cared about right now was Bobby Li. Without breaking the contact, Helmer said, "It's my understanding you want to be reinstated at the Agency. If you want my help, and Firebird's help, you do things our way." He let that lie between them. Piat got it, as he was supposed to; he sighed and broke the eye contact. Helmer, however, decided that kicking a man while he was down was just the thing that an important public figure should do. "You're a has-been and a wanna-be," he said. "You got one thing going for you in this operation— you got canned because you were close to George Shreed. Firebird makes a lot of that. Frankly, I never thought you were that good. However, what's done is done, and you can be useful within certain parameters. To a degree, I have to hold this thing at arm's length, so I can use somebody like you as— as—"

"As the arm?"

"I want to know what Dukas and Craik are doing. I leave it to you to find out."

Piat started to say, *You mean wiretaps and surveillance?* but never got the words out because Helmer held up a hand. "Your play; keep me out of it." Helmer looked at his watch. "I have a meeting with the lieutenant-governor about some very important security concerns." He stood. "We'll leave it for now that you understand that you work for me. The meeting between Dukas and the 'foreign agent' will have to happen here, under my direction. You're to return to Washington and arrange to keep me informed about Dukas and Craik." Helmer held out his hand. And he waited while Piat made a clumsy exit, more a retreat than a withdrawal, until Piat found himself in the corridor, shaking with anger and frustration.

Whidbey Island.

Alan mixed cocoa into his coffee, a trick he hadn't done since his squadron days. The mixed flavors took him back, as did the borrowed flight gear and the foreign taste of his oxygen mask. *Somebody else's spit.* Alan knew he was going along on the flight as self-loading baggage, but he prepped his seat and walked around the aircraft as if it were a mission. He walked across the tarmac to the base Metro office and got a weather report, a process which seemed to call for some humor from the woman running the office. When he got back to the plane, Surfer laughed at him, too. "This is Whidbey, man. It's going to rain. Later, it will be sunny. Whatever. You probably made Darlene's day."

Alan strapped in and they taxied. He was never as comfortable in the front seat of an S-3 as the back, with the unfamiliar small screen and backward computer controls, but he'd been flying front seat more often in the last few months before his injury and he managed the shortened checklist well enough.

"What do you guys plan to use as MARI targets?"

"Lot of freight traffic in and out of Bremerton and Vancouver. We hope we can pick on the big microwave sites along the coast as practice targets, too, because they're pretty real-world. You can get some microwave cuts on ESM way out at two, three hundred miles and then fix the site, put it on MARI, and send it as a target to a strike package."

"Sounds great. You need two planes to get the full effect, especially if conditions are rough. Otherwise all you have is ISAR with a better image quality." The MARI system had been Alan's baby for six months. It was a system that used multiple radars at very high frequency to create a digital image of the target, hence MARI, Multiple Axis Radar Imaging. ISAR was an older system that used one axis, one radar, to create a fuzzy image from the radar returns.

"It ought to be great, except nobody on this coast has done it yet. This bird keeps kicking her antenna, though, and no one knows why. Anyway, MARI is probably on for the budget this year or next, and the P-3 in the hangar is due for the next system. We have to get on top of this ASAP or somebody will take the whole program away."

They had rolled to the runway. They exchanged the last litany of checks, and Surfer put the throttle to full power and the engines raged.

"She looks good to me," Surfer said. He seemed to be waiting for something, and Alan nodded, which seemed to satisfy Surfer, who moved the plane to the runway as Alan called the tower and got permission to take off.

"You ever finish your pilot's license?"

"Yeah. I even started on twin engines. I'm pretty hot in a Cessna."

Surfer laughed. "You're a man of many talents, Al."

"Fuck off." The traditional Navy reply to a compliment. He went back to talking with the tower. He'd filed their flight plan and he had a comm card. He thought about the distant days when this had all seemed so hard. Now he did it while thinking of other things.

"Let's go fly," Surfer said happily.

Alan envied him at that moment, the simple happiness of the craftsman, but he smiled. "Okay, bro," he answered, as if they were both still twenty-three.

Tacoma.

Jerry Piat found himself standing outside the police building, shaking with anger, not least at himself for having screwed up Jakarta so that he was still working with a yo-yo like Marv Helmer. He almost backed into another car in the parking lot and then pulled out too fast into traffic and heard a shriek of brakes and a horn. He blew his own horn in answer and held up a finger. He got lost twice trying to get back to 5 and cursed, feeling his armpits wet with the stinking sweat of nerves and even fear, and he hated Helmer and wondered why he feared him. It was his power—the power to make or break him. He did admit that about Helmer: He had real power, and he could use his connections to get Piat reinstated, or he could get him blackballed from decent security jobs all over the country, much less at the Agency.

He drove at eighty up Route 5 and then forced himself to slow. He thought of Helmer's local power, specifically his ability to command cops. It wouldn't do to get into trouble with the state cops.

He drove north, bringing himself down, forcing himself to think about what he was going to do about Bobby Li, and even before he got to Tacoma he knew that he was being followed. Helmer had laid on a three-car surveillance, for exactly what reason Piat couldn't yet see. Probably to demonstrate his power, because he had to know that Piat would catch on to being followed.

The surveillance actually helped him, giving him something else to focus on. He drove toward Seattle, making sure they could see him and stay with him, turning it into a surveillance exercise where you wanted them to see every move you made. Until you were ready to do something else.

Whidbey Island.

Surfer had taken them off the runway and up to twenty thousand feet without much conversation. Alan was not familiar with the comm card, the local air-traffic control, or the airspace around Bremerton and Seattle, so the plane and the radios had occupied them both. Well out to sea and above any possible interference with civilian aviation, Surfer unclipped his harness and excused himself. "I ought to know better. I need a piss."

"I thought this was a forty-minute flight," said Alan, glad that it was not. Bad hand and all, he was enjoying the return to simple routines. *Punch in the frequency. Get a check. Call the tower. Call ATC Seattle.* It hadn't challenged him since he was a nugget, but it was reassuring to do it. To remind himself that he had been away from his own detachment for only a month and that he might yet return.

"You got it?" Surfer looked meaningfully at Alan, his hands on the controls. "Just like flying your Cessna, huh?"

Alan laid his hands on his set, the left one odd and throbbing. He thought about all his failures on the simulator.

"I've got it," he said tentatively.

If Surfer noticed his hesitation, he didn't pause as he wriggled out of the cockpit into the rear of the aircraft. Alan steadied the plane. He had unconsciously started a shallow turn to starboard. He thought about being away from his detachment and he faced the reality. *He was afraid.* He was afraid every day that a set of orders would arrive, removing him from command of the detachment and sending him elsewhere. He had too little time left. It would make perfect sense. Rose was stateside, attached to NASA, and the detailer might even think he was doing Craik a favor—both Craiks, really. He was afraid of the plane he was in, too. He had a fear of failure that he'd never felt, and his hands were twitchy on the yoke.

He needed to be back in the saddle.

His hand throbbed. Nonexistent fingers hurt.

"Want to look at Seattle?" Surfer said, slipping back into his seat and plugging his comm cord back in.

"You got it?" said Alan.

"I have her. Hey! You didn't lose any altitude!"

"Hey! I have a pilot's license." Alan tried not to sound relieved. "I know what I'm doing." He grinned. "Sort of."

"I know that. Do you know that? Okay, enough adolescent psychiatry, man. Want to see Seattle?"

"Roger."

"Get us an altitude for crossing the bay."

"Roger that."

Alan talked to a controller and got them an altitude. Surfer started to imitate a tour guide.

"Beautiful Bremerton, Washington, home of USS *Carl Vinson* and her battle group. On our left, the submarine base."

"Wow." Bremerton was beautiful from the air, if your taste in beauty ran to giant warships.

"Should have seen it a couple of weeks ago, when *Carl Vinson* and her battle group steamed out for an exercise."

Alan was looking down at the long rows of boomers and attack boats. His first thought was about power, a complex thought about how dangerous warships looked, and how well they suited their role in diplomacy by showing a capability without direct effort. Sending a warship off someone's coast was like showing a gun hidden under your jacket.

"Hey, buddy, if I wanted to fly solo, I'd have left you at home."

Alan ran his hands lovingly over the computer screen.

"This is great," he said, and meant every word.

"What're you thinking?" Surfer said. "You sure ain't talking."

"Oh—what they'd look like on radar—stuff like that."

Surfer turned and smiled at him.

"Ever think you'd be better off as an NFO than a spy?"

"Yeah. And then I wonder about spending the rest of my adult life with people like you."

Surfer laughed. "Don't let anybody tell you you've changed, Spy."

Seattle.

Piat checked out of his hotel, drove to Sea-Tac, turned in the car, and headed for the desk of the airline on which he'd flown in. There, because he'd spotted a pair of Helmer's people— dark suits, sidewall haircuts, sunglasses—he pretended to check in and in fact got the woman there to take back his ticket ("Maybe we can get you a refund—maybe—") and make him a reservation on the next plane out to Las Vegas.

Then he headed toward the security gate, making sure that his tailers saw him go. Very diligent young men, and very bad at surveillance. However, they served his purpose: They'd see him go through the gate of the Washington flight, and so Helmer would now believe that Piat had been so dismayed by the meeting that he'd cut short his time in Seattle and gone home with his tail between his legs to spy on Dukas and Craik.

Which was true, to a point.

The point came when Piat walked back up the ramp and headed for the Las Vegas flight. His tails were gone.

Whidbey Island Bachelor Officers' Quarters.

Rose had spent the day admiring her F-18 and being admired by a lot of male aviators who said they wanted to see the plane. She'd walked around it, felt it, kicked the tires, done a preflight, and spent three hours with a pilot who checked her out on it. She was very full of her day at dinner.

"Enough about me," she said finally. "Let's talk about you. What d'you think about me?" She laughed. "Joke—it's a joke."

"I was going to ask when it was my turn."

"Well, I had a great day!" She made a face. "But I miss the kids. And the dog. Is it wrong to miss your dog?"

"Not if you miss your kids more. My day was great. Just like yours." He told her about Surfer and about being allowed to fly again. He told her about flying over Bremerton, the long line of ships there. Sea power. "I'm reading this book about a guy who spied on the German fleet at Bremerhaven in World War I. It made me wonder when I saw all those ships at Bremerton: How does an enemy keep track of sailings and returns these days?"

"They look at the wives' site on the Internet?"

Alan laughed. "Seriously. There are lots of classified sailings. Think of subs! My God, they dive as soon as they clear the shipping lane."

"Satellites?" she said. She wasn't really interested. She put her hand over his and said, "Want to hear about this really good-looking captain who flirted outrageously with me?"

Mogadishu, Somalia.

Ahmed Fazrahi hated Americans. In fact, what he hated were white Westerners, but he thought of them all as Americans. He was, himself, dark-skinned and handsome in the slender, bony, Somali way, with a long, narrow head and thin lips. His grandfather had hated the British and the Italians, by which he also meant white Westerners, because in his generation it had been the British and Italians who had said they "owned" Somalia, as if it had been something they had bought at a shop, and who had brought their noise and their religion and their power. Now, Ahmed hated Americans, because now they were the ones who filled the air with their godlessness, with images of sex and luxury, with impious songs with the beat of sex and words suitable for a whorehouse, with their material-ism, their advertising, their world of *things,* in which there was no place for God, the only God, the one true God. So he hated Americans.

"I need five hundred kilos of C-4," he said to the man who was supposed to be Palestinian.

The Palestinian grinned, showing a gap in his front teeth. "I need a hundred kilos of refined opium."

"I can move a hundred kilos from Hazara across the bor-der to the tribal area of Pakistan. There is a lab there where you would have to pick it up."

He didn't mean that he would personally move the opium. He meant that he could set in motion a chain of orders, arrange-ments, transactions, that would end with the movement of the opium. It was like the *halal* money system, which also op-erated entirely on trust and which allowed you to move, let us say, a thousand dollars from a conversation in Ibadan to Houston, Texas, without records or checks or bank balances.

"I can get C-4," the Palestinian said. He, too, meant that somebody else would actually get and move the explosive, which, in fact, the Palestinian knew only in theory, having no real idea where it was or how it would be got. In fact, the C-4 that would finally be moved was presently in a former Crusader citadel in the Bekaa Valley, but that was of no conse-quence to either the Palestinian or Ahmed.

"Here in Mogadishu," the Palestinian said, "or—?"

"Here will be fine."

11

Whidbey Island.

SUNRISE REVEALED MOUNTAINS AWAY TO THE EAST, and an endless forest stretching away inland. Rose bounced from their bed with the sun, eager to meet her borrowed maintenance crew and get in the air. She moved so fast that she was in her flight suit and kissing him good-bye before he was shaved, so that he suddenly found himself alone, razor in hand, searching their suitcases for shaving cream that he began to suspect hadn't made the trip.

"*Jesus fucking Christ,*" he muttered, and caught himself. He made himself smile at the face in the mirror. *Smile and forget the anger,* he thought.

He wanted to smoke.

An hour later, he saw a lone F-18 rolling out on the runway, and he watched with love and envy as the plane taxied out, tested its engines to high power and full military, and then rolled out. Rose didn't do anything fancy like pulling the nose straight up into afterburner as soon as she launched, but her takeoff was pure and beautiful, and he smiled to watch her go, the hot wind of her engine check washing over him in waves as he jogged in place. It struck him that, just now, this was an allegory of their lives. He ran back to a second shower. He wanted to get into the air, too.

Las Vegas.

Everything about Vegas made Piat's skin crawl, perhaps because it was so much the opposite of Jakarta and the places where he'd spent his recent life. This was foolish, he knew; the tarts of Vegas were fundamentally no different from the tarts of Jakarta, nor were the hustlers nor the tourists nor the shop owners trying to make a buck. But Vegas still made his skin crawl. Before he ever left the airport, he made himself a reservation for an evening flight to L.A. and Jakarta by way of Manila.

He got in a rental car and drove to a far suburb of Tahoe, where retired middle managers and executives who'd never made the top tier had bought gimcrack houses that were all size and landscaping and that would start to fall down in ten years. But then, so would their owners.

Jill Petrack lived in one of them with her new husband. He was affable, Southern, and discreet, or at least he seemed so, but he was in a hurry to get to the golf course. A handshake and a joke and he was out the door.

"Well, Jerry," she said, "what a surprise!"

"Long time." He'd called ahead and she'd been *really* surprised then. He'd seen her a few times here and there, but it had been twenty-five years since they'd worked together in Jakarta.

"To what do I owe the honor?" Smiling but uncertain. He remembered that about her—an uncertain woman, never quite right with the men she attracted, of whom Jerry had never been one because she was older and he liked a certain sluttishness. She was still thin and a little too tall and much too ladylike for him. But they'd got along. Now, she went through the offers—coffee, tea, booze—and the politeness— weather, old times, did he ever see so-and-so—and then he got down to it, sitting in her somewhat colonial living room with the cactus outside the window and a big TV that he guessed she'd just turned off.

"I'm following something up, and I need your brain," he said.

"Oh, I haven't used my brain in years; it's the nicest thing about retirement." She smiled, but he didn't believe it. Her usual uncertainty was tinged with something more acid, maybe regret. She was a fundamentally negative personality, he remembered, one of those cursed people who never manage to say yes often enough to be happy.

"Jakarta," he said. They'd overlapped there by almost a year; Shreed had been chief of station and she'd been his administrator. Maybe in love with him.

"Poor George," she said. "I hear terrible things, even here."

"Don't believe everything you hear. George was the best. That's sort of what I'm here about." He told her that he was working with some people to clear Shreed's reputation, not quite true but not too far off the mark. "I have to ask you to keep this to yourself, Jill. There are people around who, you know—it's in their interest to smear George. I don't want them knowing what I'm doing." He didn't have to tell her that he'd been retired early because of George. Something she said suggested that she already knew that, so he guessed that she had sources and contacts still. "I'd like to keep my visit quiet," he said.

"Nobody bothers with me anymore," she said. "You weren't followed, were you?" Making it a joke, except it wasn't a joke.

He shook his head. "Jakarta," he said again. "When I got there, you'd been working for George for a good while; you knew what he did and how he did it. You know what they're saying now, don't you? That he was a Chinese agent?"

She shook her head. "That's so ridiculous. We ran ops against the Chinese as hard as we could go. My goodness, the Chinese were running a network right in Jakarta; George was the one who busted it. And Malaysia—Singapore—he had some big successes."

"Do you remember a kid George used, named Bobby Li? Chinese, about five-two, very willing—he was only a kid then."

She thought about that, smiling a little. She was weighing old secrets against the present, he thought, perhaps telling herself that she had been out of it so long that nothing she knew could matter now. But she'd never gossiped, never published a memoir, never broken that oath they'd both signed when they took the Agency's nickel. "I don't think we called him that," she said.

"I inherited him when George left. You were gone by then."

"Yes," she said a little sadly, as if getting out of Jakarta had been a penance. "I think we called him Go-Boy," she said. "I think it started as Gofer Boy and got cut down, because George used him as a gofer. He was only twelve."

"A little older."

"Well. I was never very good at guessing the age of Asians. I didn't deal with Go-Boy that much, either; he was sort of George's dog, you know? He'd send him out for the newspaper if he wanted one. Had him cutting his grass one time, I think. He wasn't really an *agent.*"

"But George used him as one."

"Oh, sometimes, little jobs. Messenger boy, and so on."

"By the time I got him, he was an agent, Jill. Sundance. Because of the movie, *Butch Cassidy.* They said he loved that movie and the name stuck to him."

"I was gone by then. He was Go-Boy when I knew him, if we're talking about the same one." She shook her gray curls. "He was only a kid." She offered him iced tea and lemonade and water, and he took water because of the heat outside, giving her the chance she wanted to leave the room for a while, he thought. She wasn't comfortable with the past, or not with this past. He looked at the room, which seemed to him empty and toneless and bland, and maybe that was what she wanted now, including the man she'd married when she was sixty-seven. Maybe she hated the past, or maybe she simply felt guilt about its secrets. Piat thought he'd kill himself before he'd settle for bland as the only reward at the end of his life, but perhaps for her the blandness was soothing after saying no for so long.

"Did you ever think the kid was a double?" he said before

she even set the water down in front of him. She had a tray with lemonade for herself and a bottle of water for him, and rather good glasses with heavy bottoms.

"He would have been vetted," she said. She put one of the glasses down and poured the chilled water into it. When she was done, she smiled, as if she'd been practicing pouring water and thought she'd done it very well.

"Who by?"

"Oh—me, most probably."

"Did you?"

"Probably. I don't remember. Yes, I suppose, because I remember about his code name, so I must have been close at some point. But he was a kid, so there wouldn't have been much to check, would there?" She sipped the lemonade. "Why?"

"How did he come to us? To you?"

"Oh, gosh—" He thought she was faking how hard she had to think about that. "He may have been a walk-in."

"George never took walk-ins, Jill, you know that. None of us did."

"Well, maybe George felt sorry for him."

"*George* did."

She shook her head. "He was George's little guy. He was, you know, outside the envelope. A kind of pet."

"But he had a code name and you vetted him."

She frowned. "Not a code name, actually. A nickname. I don't think it ever went into a report or anything, because he never got involved in any real ops. Maybe he'd bring George street gossip, stuff like that. He wasn't a real agent, and if he got an agent name, it was after I left."

Piat had been going over it in his head since he had seen the photos of Li shooting the Chinese intel guy. "It was just before George went back to the States, Jill. *I* remember that part. He handed the kid over to me and said he wanted me to take care of him. He gave me a file with 'Sundance' on it, and there was nothing in there but his basics and his contract and an account sheet that had just been opened. I was his first case officer, according to the file, and I said that to George and he said something about—this is a long time ago, Jill, and this wasn't a big thing to me at all. I was taking over a lot more important stuff than this kid—George said something about the kid was growing up and he wanted to see he was taken care of. As if he hadn't been an agent before that."

"Well, that's what I said."

"But you said that George used him sometimes. George was punctilious about things like that. Well, that isn't the point. The question is, was the kid a double?"

"I can't imagine that he was."

"But if you vetted him when he was twelve or fifteen or whatever, when, as you say, there was so little to check, you must have given him a clear bill. Right?"

"I must have."

"But there was no new vetting done when George gave him to me. So we accepted him as 'Sundance' on the basis of whatever you did earlier."

She looked at him without expression. "Do you mean I gave a clear to a double agent? Why would I do that?"

"I don't mean anything, Jill. I'm just trying to find out."

"You think I did a sloppy job."

"No, no. It's possible you thought, 'It's a kid, he's harmless,' and sort of, you know, did it once over lightly. Isn't that possible?"

"I never let a double get by me in my life!"

"I didn't say you had."

"If he turned out to be a double, then somebody turned him later. What you're suggesting is that somebody planted him on us to start with? Never. I'd never have let that get by me. Nor George. George was the devil on that sort of thing. Every agent, I had to cross every *t* and dot every *i*; then George would go over the vetting and give me grief for the smallest little thing."

"A kid? One that George liked?"

She started to flare up, and then he saw her pull back and look at something. She sipped her lemonade, her eyes turned toward the past. She put the glass down and wiped her fingers on a paper napkin and touched her lips, leaving a lipstick stain, and Piat had time to think that she must be seventy and she still used makeup, and maybe she did because it was something to do to fill the time. "It was George who vetted him," she said. Had she remembered that earlier, and had she chosen not to tell him then? Maybe not, he thought. Maybe, in her hero-worshiping memory of George Shreed, she had edited this one out until now. "He gave me some notes and a file. Funny, how things slip away. The file was labeled 'Kim.' You know, like Kipling?"

"And Kim Philby."

"Well, he called himself that after Kipling, too. My goodness, I'd forgotten all about that. Kim. I suppose—George was a romantic in his way, you know. I suppose he had some notion of teaching the boy tradecraft, that sort of thing."

Piat found himself shying away from this memory, too. He didn't want to deal with the questions that spun off from a George Shreed who had vetted an agent himself, however young, and not gone by the book. Variations from routine were things Piat had been trained to look for, but he didn't like this one and it wasn't what he wanted to think about just now. "So what happened to the Kim file?" he said.

"Oh, I don't know. It turned into Go-Boy, I suppose. We must have started paying the boy something—I've some dim memory of authorizing a payment, I think—and you need an account sheet and a proper file for that. All pre-computer, of course." She laughed. "I was using an IBM Selectric. George was the only one who understood computers." She was relaxed now; he guessed that the one bad spot she'd feared had been got over. "Have I been any help?"

He thought about that. "So you don't have any recollection of anything that would have made you suspicious of Li—Go-Boy-slash-Kim-slash-Sundance."

"None whatsoever. He was so close to George, you know."

They talked a few minutes longer. She told him some of it all over again, emphasizing how unimportant the young Bobby Li had been to her. Bobby Li's history as a spy really had begun when Piat had taken him over, and she'd been long gone by then.

She seemed relieved when he left. He saw her looking toward the big television. Outside, the heat met him like a blow. He headed back for Las Vegas, planning how he'd set up a hostile interrogation of Bobby Li, which was the only way to go about it now. He drove along at eighty, looking for a bar, and pretty soon he saw a sign for a whorehouse called the Bar-XXX Ranch, and he went there thinking, *What the hell, I've got an hour.*

Then he was off to Jakarta.

Dar es Salaam.

"Have you got anything new?"

"An interesting detail on Lieutenant-Commander Craik."

Lao raised his eyebrows in question.

"He was serving on the aircraft carrier USS *Thomas Jefferson* when it was sailing off India, about the time that Colonel Chen went into Pakistan. There was a report of an American aircraft that—"

"I remember, I remember!" Lao waved the hand with the cigarette.

"Well, the aircraft flew out of Pakistan and to the *Jefferson.* It was the antisubmarine type known as the S-3B. Craik has served in such aircraft."

"So it could be Craik who flew in and out, maybe picking up Shreed and Chen and taking them to the carrier. And that would explain his wound." He inhaled, spat a bit of tobacco from his lower lip. "Meaning that Shreed could have lured Chen to Pakistan, where Craik captured him." He threw his head back. "Anything new on our third force in Jakarta?"

"The police say they are working on it."

"Keep on them." Lao turned to his computer. He hunched over the keyboard, scowling at the screen. The captain, after several seconds of indecision, went quietly away, and, too late, Lao called after him, "Good work, Jiang—good work—"

Lao scolded himself for not taking more notice of Jiang, who was, at the very least, a potential threat because he was undoubtedly reporting on Lao to another level of military intelligence. Lao had once held a position like Jiang's; he knew how it went. Nothing personal. But there was no point in antagonizing Jiang and making things even worse. He made a mental note, *Flatter Jiang.* Trouble was, he would probably forget it.

Too much to think about. Tsung was in Pakistan again, waiting to meet with his agent and move Jade Talon along to the next step. The agent in Jakarta he had let slip while he worried about these other things. Well, not let slip; he had wanted the man to stew for a few days. That time was over, however.

Bobby Li had behaved oddly, wrongly, badly, in Jakarta. Time now, however, to find out what he had been up to and what he knew. Lao clicked on Li's file. "Prepare a pickup and interrogation in Jakarta," he wrote in a note for Jiang. "I want this man brought in and held. While we're holding him, I want him squeezed dry." He paused and then added, "Excellent work so far on this project, Jiang. I will put a note of commendation in your folder."

NCIS HQ.

"Mister Dukas?" Leslie said from the other side of the plastic barrier. She sounded as if she feared she'd wake him.

He had in fact forgotten that she was there, and he was half-asleep—lunch plus the boredom of the report he was trying to write. "Yeah, Leslie," he said, coming to but not looking up.

"I've compared the inventories." Laugh, as if the idea of her doing anything was hilarious.

Low self-esteem, Dukas thought, even though he didn't believe in self-esteem. He still didn't look up. "Okay, good, very good." He wanted to give in to his sleepiness, but he remembered that she was new and young and looked as if her brain were made of tofu, and he owed it to her not to ignore her. "What'd you find, Leslie?"

"I found an anomaly." Leslie, despite her permanent hoarseness, had a little-girl intonation, and she made "anomaly" sound like the missing rabbit in a child's picture-puzzle. "Want to see?"

Dukas sighed. "You bet." He went around the barrier and waited. When nothing happened, he said, "Well?"

"I thought you'd want to check my work."

"Leslie, I haven't got time to check your work. You check your own work."

"And you trust me?" Wild laughter.

"Leslie, what have you got?"

Leslie was left-handed. With a pencil, she was left-handedly checking pages of a yellow legal pad that she'd covered with entries about the Sleeping Dog inventories. "There's actually tons of anomalies, right? Because you'd expect that two inventories made four years apart would be different, okay? So there's all these items that aren't in the FBI inventory because of course they didn't exist yet, but they're in the CIA inventory because they did. But! There's one item that's in the recent inventory and wasn't in the old one, but it isn't because it didn't *exist* way back then. Even though the item has a date before the FBI one. You get me? What I'm trying to say is, it should of been in the FBI inventory but it wasn't, but it is in the new inventory *as if* it was in the old one, which it should of been because it already existed. Okay?"

"What's the item?"

She put her pencil on a notation. "EF392-94, 'Newspaper Clipping.' " She looked up. "Want me to find it?"

Dukas looked at the stacks of files that had been brought back from the office across the building where she had been working. "Can you?" he groaned.

"Oh, definitely! I rearranged them while you was at a meeting." She caught herself. "*Were* at a meeting." Leslie began walking her fingers down the spines of a stack of files, holding them from toppling with her left hand and revealing more plump thigh than the office dress code would have recommended. Dukas looked quickly away and glanced around her side of the office, the words "sexual harassment" ringing in his brain, and saw files stacked in almost military order. "Here we a-a-a-re!" she giggled. She handed him a file, laughing her ass off, as the saying went.

The left side of the folder held the analyst's additions. The fifth paper down was the news clipping, in a Xerox copy with an NSA flag pasted on it:

Police Arrest Ham Fan

Mercer Island, WA. Mercer Island Police went into a local ham radio operator's home today in answer to neighborhood complaints of interference. "That guy was on my radio every night," complained Henry (Popeye) Ludlam of the Belle Isle subdivision. Other neighbors say that the interference came in short bursts, often of static, lasting only seconds.

Arrested was John Tashimaya, who is a licensed ham operator. "He was just doing his thing, but he was coming through on his neighbors' radios," said Sergeant Jim Kusluski of the Mercer Island Police. "He isn't supposed to even be anywhere near the broadcast bands, but we got these complaints."

Mister Tashimaya was charged with disturbing the peace before Magistrate Helen Malcoway. According to Sergeant Kusluski, the matter will be turned over to the Federal Communications Commission.

Tashimaya had no comment, but his lawyer, Fred Dickers, said the matter is "a tempest in a teapot" and his client is a victim of "ionospheric reflectivity." Arraignment is tomorrow in Seattle.

"Poor guy," Leslie sighed. She was reading over Dukas's arm. "Is it important?"

"I'm allergic to your perfume," Dukas said. He made a great show of blowing his nose. "Oh, wow."

"It's Dope!" she said.

Dukas took several seconds to realize that Dope must be a brand name. "I don't care if it's Chanel Number 5." He shook his head. "It's too much for me."

"I bought it from a really knowledgeable guy on the street. He said it's what Cameron Diaz wears, Mister Dukas!"

"Maybe you could save it for best."

"My boyfriend *loves* it."

"Maybe it's a question of context." Dukas blew his nose again. He waved the paper. "You done good, Leslie. Yeah, this is important."

"Really? Wow, this is exciting!" She leaned in and lowered her crow's voice. "Did he do it?"

"Who?"

"John Tashimaya. Is he the source of the burst transmissions?"

Dukas was sure he wasn't, but he mumbled something about security and high classification and went around to his own side of the office, wondering how a ditz-brain in cheap perfume who had been on the job for a week knew about burst transmissions. Leslie came to the plastic crates and looked through. Her voice was childish again. "I'm awful sorry about the perfume, Mister Dukas. I just won't wear it again while you're here, okay?" She shook her head. "My boyfriend just loves it."

"Well, there's a time and place for everything," Dukas said. His hand was on the telephone. "What's good in the, um, in a relationship isn't necessarily good in the office, right?"

"No kidding!" This was news to Leslie. "Oh, wow." She went back to her desk. "Oh." She sat down. She blew a big pink bubble and drew the bubble back between her made-up lips. "Oh, I see."

Dukas picked up the STU and dialed Triffler's number in Seattle.

Whidbey Island.

Alan half-expected to be told that yesterday's flight was Surfer's gift, a one-shot that wouldn't be repeated, but when he put himself on the flight schedule, nobody so much as blinked. Surfer introduced him around and made more of Alan's expertise with the experimental MARI gear than even Alan's detailer would have thought justified.

Alan found that some of his reputation had arrived ahead of him. A lieutenant named Cunnard said, "Did you really land a light plane on a gator freighter?"

Alan felt his face go red. "I'm afraid I did, yeah—that was me."

To his surprise, Cunnard said, "That was great! Great!" Not a word about his ground-pounder wings or his intel designator. It wasn't quite like coming home, but it certainly was better than landing among a bunch of aviators who resented his very existence. As it was, he found himself viewed as a kind of useful and nonthreatening eccentric—not there to stay, no command responsibility, an old buddy of the skipper's, so okay until proven otherwise.

Somebody out in the Indian Ocean had been right on the ball, because the first data packets from the Det 424 signal library began to arrive while Alan and Surfer were making a second flight. Alan's old friend Master Chief Craw had sent a whole classified addendum on maintenance and tweaking of the MARI gear, too, based on their experience in the Mediterranean. Alan smiled to read it, remembering the hard early days that seemed to be years ago and had, in fact, only happened a few months back.

He showed the new material to Surfer and they went down to the hangar, got Chief Soames going on Craw's information, and got the DP from admin to load the new MARI image material on one of the training computers. In an hour, the backseaters were chattering away and making notes, while Surfer and Alan sat in his office and started to work out the approvals they'd need to use real-life sites onshore for training. It was basic organizational work. It didn't fuel the adrenaline junkie in Alan Craik, but it was a hell of a lot better than flying a simulator and putting his fist through drywall.

"I want you to brief the guys," Surfer said. "Negative is not an acceptable answer."

"Great."

Surfer looked at him. "I thought you might say that hotshots with oak leaves don't do briefings."

Alan laughed. "In the Pentagon, hotshots with oak leaves clean toilets."

NCIS HQ, Washington.

Dukas caught Triffler on his third try at the Seattle office.

"I'm running around like a chicken with his head cut off, Mike. Actually, I've never seen a chicken with his head cut off, but that's what they say. What's up?"

"We got a breakthrough." He didn't mention Leslie, because she was just on the other side of the divider, but he outlined the finding of the newspaper clipping and its contents. "I suspect it's a fake, and I think we're supposed to notice that it has some connection with the burst transmissions."

"How old is it?"

"It's supposed to be from 1996, but the NSA analyst code was missing, and I've checked the wire services. I don't think this story ever existed."

"So somebody wants us to go to Mercer Island."

"Somebody wants us to do something, and maybe Mercer Island is it. Send Craik—that's what he's there for. You'll have to make up a route for him, provide surveillance and security—the whole nine yards. We don't know what's waiting out there."

"This isn't going to result in more shooting, is it?"

"Joke, yeah, ha-ha. He's going to make an inquiry at a police department, for Christ's sake."

"That's what you said about Jakarta."

"Okay, okay, I made a mistake about Jakarta!"

"Your first ever, right? Okay, Mike, I'll run with this, but I tell you, we're busy little beavers out here. You know how many potential targets there are in the Seattle area?"

"Think military."

"I've *thought* military. I sent a guy out this morning to Bremerton, they go, 'Please submit this through channels and we'll clear it with Washington.' Is this the same Navy out here, or are they working for Lithuania?"

He was simply blowing off steam, Dukas knew. He could

tell when Triffler was having a good time. They talked some more about who was out there—Triffler was already impressed with a local NCIS man named Nagel—and what sort of surveillance had to be laid on Craik when he was off the base, and how strict the need was that Triffler and Craik never be seen together. "Use your skills, Dick. You're the control; Al's the agent. Make him follow the rules."

"Will do."

"And don't let him fly. I know him; once he's around those airplanes, he'll want to go up; next thing you know, he'll be gone for good. *No flying*, got it?"

Triffler started laughing, and Dukas hung up too quickly to ask why.

"Mister Dukas?" Leslie said.

Dukas was still sitting with his hand on the phone. "I've been thinking," Leslie said.

Dukas smiled at her, remembered that he didn't want to seem to be valuing her too lightly. "Thinking about what, Leslie?"

She came around the plastic barrier and leaned against the white crates, endangering one of the plants—which she had started to water without being asked—one plump hip cocked and her red-dyed hair like a sunburst around her face. She was holding one hand as far away as possible so she could study the nails. "What d'you think of green?" she said. Before Dukas could answer, she snapped the hand back to her hip and said, "What I've been thinking is that this burst-transmission stuff is *spying*. You know? I think it's some guy hunkered down with some radio, reporting on *stuff*, you know? I ask myself, What is there in Seattle to spy on, and so I go on the Web and, really, Mister Dukas, there's so much out there you wonder the government allows it all in one place. But what I figure is—"

Dukas's face was clouded. "Leslie, how do you know about the burst transmissions?"

"I read the files, don't I? You've had me reading the files for days! I'm cleared." She looked only slightly scared, like a kid who's been caught out but is going to plow ahead, anyway.

"Well, yeah, but—"

"So I figure—Can I go on and tell you my idea? Okay. I think we ought to interview the mave-rick who got canned by the CIA for finding the truth about the transmissions." That was the way she pronounced it—*mave-rick,* to rhyme with pave and brick. "It seems a little fishy to me, by the way, that he got canned. Doesn't it to you? Like he was getting too close?"

Dukas started to laugh a paternal laugh, and he actually said something about the Agency's canning people all the time, and then a voice in his head was saying, *Yeah, but what if she's right? What if—?* "It's mav-er-ick, Leslie, three syllables. Okay? Maverick?"

She said it silently to herself. "How do you know these things?" she said. "I'm so dumb."

"No, no—no you're not." Dukas was on his feet, wincing at the stab in his chest, trying to get to her because he was sure she was going to burst into tears or something worse. Her already low self-esteem would bottom out; she'd quit; and he'd be left with no help. "That was very smart, Leslie, a very smart idea—"

"My ass it is," she said. She laughed. Merrily. "You think I'm a ditz-brain. My boyfriend says I'm a ditz-brain about nine times a day. My social studies teacher said I should sell my brain to science, because I wouldn't miss it." She laughed.

Dukas shook his finger at her. "Don't let people say things like that to you!" he shouted. "You're a very bright girl; you're just—!" He wondered why he was shouting. Why did he care? "It's a *good* idea, but it took me by surprise because I didn't think you knew the case. Um, most file clerks don't, you know, read for content."

She looked at him and stopped laughing. Their eyes locked, and he realized they never had before; one or the other had always looked away, some sort of avoidance syndrome. And he knew it was because he was a very old man to her. Leslie clearly had her own ideas about it, because she went pink and turned away and went to Triffler's desk. "Well, that was my idea," she said and went back to work.

Dukas sat behind his own desk. *What the hell was all that?*

Dar es Salaam.

COLONEL LAO HAD COME TO THE HUMILIATING conclusion that he didn't know quite what he was doing. This realization had come in the midst of a flurry of what he had been thinking was productive work—messages, orders to pursue lines of investigation, study of Chen's files—and he had stopped for a cup of tea and suddenly seen, as if the message had been written on his wall by a moving hand, that he was simply filling time.

The realization was not helped by two messages from Beijing, one from the General and one from the Party man, both stiffer than their last message and both demanding the same thing: progress.

"We're not making progress," Lao said to Jiang. Jiang had become a sometime confidant, a full-time wall against which he could bounce the ball of his ideas. "Progress is not satisfactory."

"Early days yet, Colonel."

"Early days are all we have. Beijing is pressing."

He kept looking for lines along which to make real

progress, and he kept coming back to the same questions: Was Chen dead? Was Shreed really dead? Who was in the car that left the Pakistani village after the plane? Was it really George Shreed who was buried in St. Anselm's Cemetery? Until he knew the answers to those questions, it was difficult to proceed with any confidence. If Chen had been lifted out of Pakistan alive, flown to an American aircraft carrier and then to the United States— He actually shuddered. If such things had happened, Lao's career was over.

Maybe his life, as well.

"Who can tell us if Chen is dead?" he said.

The captain smiled—one of those smiles that can mean anything because he didn't know whether the question was real or ironic.

"Craik," Lao said. "We now believe that Craik was in Pakistan when Chen disappeared and flew out with the S-3B aircraft. So, he is the likeliest one to know what happened. *He* can tell us if Chen is dead."

The captain tried the same smile, because he still didn't understand what the line of attack was here. "Why would he tell us?"

"Because we would give him something that *he* wants."

The captain was now truly puzzled. "What?"

Lao fiddled with his computer mouse. It skated over the rubberized desktop, sending the cursor into wild dances on the screen. "Good question." Lao shot a glance at the captain and made a rare joke. "How about you?" He laughed, but Jiang didn't. Lao made the cursor dance some more. He sucked air between his teeth in little rhythmic pulses. "I think," he said, "it is time to send Lieutenant-Commander Craik a message."

Seattle.

It was a Saturday and it should have been a day off—a no-fly day for Rose and the det, both—but Triffler, energized by the discovery of the fake newspaper report, was hot to trot to Mercer Island. He had laid out a surveillance route for Alan to drive, and he had promised—promised, honest to God, cross my heart—that Alan would be done by four P.M. and he and Rose could have a romantic evening in Seattle. "Just remember, you got to drive the route exactly the way I wrote it down so we can keep an eye on you and scope out anybody who seems to be a tail. Okay? Okay?" When Alan had said that it was okay, Triffler had said, "And no deviations, right? No deviations!"

Alan and Rose were just on the mark of noon when they drove into the parking lot of the Blue Rodeo, which Triffler had thoughtfully put on Alan's surveillance route to check out the fake newspaper story, and the lunch wasn't bad, just yuppier than anything Alan or Rose would have eaten if left to choose for themselves. Alan sensed the finicky Triffler behind every bite of watercress salad, and he wondered if Triffler always led his agents on a trail of gourmet food and expensive coffee. He grinned at the thought.

"What you thinking, baby?" Rose said.

"That we might get a really good dinner tonight, too, if Triffler picked the restaurant." Alan had explained the game to Rose. She seemed to be reserving judgment. But the country was beautiful and occupied both of them as soon as they were clear of the place. The Olympic Mountains dominated the horizon, and the road had enough elevation to offer them tantalizing glimpses of the sea and the mountains and great splashes of trees stretching away as if they would run in a single forest to the edge of the world. It made Alan want to get out in the woods and really gulp the air.

"Smells better without the JP-5," he said, and she clasped his gearshift hand. His other hand, the one he thought of as *the other hand,* rested on top of the steering wheel. Even in an Ace bandage, he could steer the car with it.

SOMEWHERE BEHIND THEM, DICK TRIFFLER WAS happy to be working, too. He had three cars out, one with him and two waiting ahead on Alan's route, where parallel roads would make their actions less obvious. Professionally, it was all going pretty well.

• • •

ALAN FOLLOWED TRIFFLER'S ROUTE EXACTLY, DRIV-
ing carefully and using Rose as a navigator. Unlike Washington, Seattle does not believe that street signs need to be
hidden from foreign invaders. Better yet, prosperity had hit
Seattle recently enough that a ring of well-marked highways
with well-warned exits penetrated most of the city. Saturday
had no real rush hours, and he crossed the long bridge to
Mercer Island well ahead of his time and stopped at the park
at the end of the bridge to sightsee, an unplanned stop that
had Triffler cursing Alan's name as he redirected one of his
two supporting agents into the park behind Alan.

There was no sign of surveillance. Triffler thought about
his wife, and decided that unless he saw something worth investigating in the next two hours, he was calling Dukas and
going home.

ALAN PULLED INTO THE CAMPUS OF THE TOWN OF
Mercer Island and followed the signs to the Police Admin-
istrative Services.

"I'll go for a walk," Rose said, waving her hand at the distant skyline. He nodded and went inside, feeling incongruous
in shorts and west coast shirt. He checked his pocket for his
credentials and went in.

Fifteen minutes of moving from counter to counter finally led him to the office of the administrator, a competent-
looking, middle-aged woman who had a sign on her desk that
announced *The buck stops here.*

"Can I help you?" she asked, as he leaned into her office.
Her nameplate read MS. TENCETI.

"I'm Lieutenant-Commander Alan Craik, and I'm looking for a file that may or may not exist on an arrest made here
on Mercer Island sometime back in the nineteen nineties."

"Can you tell me the name of the man arrested? And may
I ask your interest in our case?"

Alan showed her his credentials. He had a plain set, no
badge, given to him by Dukas with the admonition that he

was to use them only for identification to other law enforcement agencies—not to get out of speeding tickets. She looked at them with something like boredom. "If this is a Maritime Patrol case, you're in the wrong office. We do handle some of their paperwork, but—"

"No, ma'am. This is a matter of national security. I'm interested in a case that involved the arrest of a local man with an Asian name for some illegal ham radio operation that seems to have jammed the local radio station."

"Really?" She perked up. "Can I see your credentials again? Thank you." She put glasses on and read them. "I am sorry to say that I've never *heard* of the Naval Criminal Investigative Service."

"We have jurisdiction over crimes committed by or against members of the U.S. Navy." Alan suspected that he was simplifying.

She nodded. "So you're with the shore patrol."

"No, ma'am. Shore patrol would be the equivalent of your local police. We're sort of the FBI of the Navy."

She frowned. "We're not really big on the FBI, here."

Alan laughed. *Neither are we,* he thought. She handed him his credentials back. He handed her his newspaper clipping, and she pushed her glasses up and read it attentively.

"This doesn't look like any local paper," she said.

"I imagine it was taken from a wire service."

"But what gets me is the content. I've been here fifteen years, as a clerk and as an administrator. I don't remember any such case."

Alan sagged a little, but her fingers were already flying.

"Oh, my goodness. There it is, too. Well, I'll be a monkey's uncle." She turned her screen on a swivel mount so that he could see it.

"Could I have a transcript of the file?"

"According to this, we don't actually have the file. That's marked as being in Olympia, with the state police. That's odd too, unless they made the arrest. Is that why I don't remember it?" She was clearly muttering to herself, and Alan took out a notebook and started writing the file number and any other information he could get off the screen. "Except that it lists an arresting officer by name. Sergeant Kusluski is retired now."

"I may need to interview him. Do you know Mister Tashimaya?"

"Never heard of him. It's all odd, if you ask me."

"Can you get the file from Olympia for me?"

She smiled. "We're paperless," she said proudly. "They aren't. That's a paper file and they won't let go of it unless you go down there. Even then, I suspect that you'll have a hard time getting access to it. Mister Tashimaya was arraigned, according to your article, but he was never tried. That means that Privacy Act laws will protect his paperwork."

Alan shook his head. "Even in a case of national security?"

"We prize our rights here," she said primly.

THEY MADE IT TO OLYMPIA WITH TRIFFLER AND gang in tow, and Alan followed the directions provided by Ms. Tenceti to the state police administration and records section in an office park that would have benefited a minor university.

"There's a *lot* of money out here," said Rose.

Alan surfaced from his thoughts to contemplate the limited time and the ruin of their plans for the day—shopping in Seattle, a romantic dinner—and Rose's apparent acceptance.

"I, uh, don't think you should come in," he said, lamely.

She eyed him steadily. "You owe me, mister. This is my no-fly day. You just remember that."

He kissed her.

BORED, HOPEFUL, AND PROFESSIONAL, TRIFFLER DI-rected his people to form a loose bubble around the office park, and set himself to watch and call them when Alan came out.

•   •   •

THE CLERK AT THE FRONT DESK WAS HELPFUL ONCE she saw Alan's credentials, and she passed him to a file clerk who led him into the basement of the building. No one had bitched that it was Saturday, and Alan wasn't going to be the one to bring the subject up. His guide seemed excited that the case involved national security. "Are you trying to catch a spy?" he said. "Like, a real spy? That is so cool."

"I can't comment on an ongoing investigation." Alan had heard this line a thousand times, on TV and from Mike, and it pleased him to get to use it himself. The truth was, he had only the vaguest idea how this file was going to fit into Sleeping Dog, but the answer seemed to please his guide.

"Right. Of course you can't. Sorry I asked, really. It's just exciting."

He led Alan past enough doors to hide all the secrets of several jurisdictions and finally into a neat cave lined with metal shelves. The dates of the files could almost be taken from the age of the shelves. At one end were metal barrister-style bookcases from the 1950s, and they led to heavy metal units with wood shelves from the 60s, to lighter-framed modular shelves of the 80s and finally to black freestanding shelves that looked as if they had come from IKEA. His guide probed along the last for several minutes until he found a plastic carton and dug inside. He surfaced with a pale green file.

"That's funny," he said.

"What's funny?" Alan said as he reached for it.

"It's color-coded. We didn't start color-coding files until last year."

Alan started to riffle the file, still afraid that it was going to be snatched away, trying to remember everything. "Maybe it was active recently." But the file was virtually empty. It had a report filed by a state police sergeant supporting the arresting officer's report, but there was no investigating officer's report.

"Is that what you needed, Commander?"

"Can I make a copy?"

"I'll copy it for you. Want to wait in the hall?"

Alan walked out, smiling at the ways of bureaucracy and thanking his stars that Ms. Tenceti wasn't the administrator here and they didn't seem to have heard of the Privacy Act. He was also thinking that the file should have had more data, like an arrest report or some surveillance data. Anything. He didn't really know much about cops, but he knew about bureaucracy. The file was a fake. He could feel it by the weight.

BY THE TIME ALAN AND ROSE CAME UP THE ENtrance ramp and got back on the interstate headed for Seattle, Dick Triffler no longer cared that Alan was a hundred miles off his countersurveillance route, because the other watchers had identified two cars following him.

Alan was under surveillance.

And it had started at the state police office park.

"Chinese, my ass," Triffler said to his rearview mirror, but he was smiling. In fact, he was grinning. He thought it was absolutely great that Al Craik had surveillance all over him, because it meant that, by God, things were moving!

Triffler sang. *"Happy days are here again. . . ."*

He got on his cell phone to the rest of the surveillance team. "Just a reminder, ladies and gents—I want license numbers of every car that's after the subject, plus numbers of people in the cars, all relevant data. If you can follow them home when Craik peels off, so much the better."

"Craik may stay out until midnight."

"That's the breaks, folks. Play the game."

ALAN AND ROSE WERE BACK AT THE BOQ BY NINEthirty, unaware of Triffler's followers or Triffler himself. He stood above the computer, expecting there to be nothing, ready to shut it down, but the E-mail inbox came up with "1 New Message" in the window, and suddenly he was staring at a message line that said "From: Rathunter. Subject: Missed You in Jakarta."

> Lieutenant-Commander Craik: Didn't I see you at the AGIP Christmas party? You were there with a Dutch girl. Sorry I missed you in the Orchid House.

Maybe you left town early because some people
did some foolish things there.

We need to talk. Maybe you have something I
am looking for. Send a reply with "Egg Roll" in the
subject line and I will tell you more. Your faraway
pal, Rathunter

When Rose came from her room, wearing only a towel,
he was still staring at it. She wrapped her hands around his
arm and said, "What's the matter?" He pointed at the screen.
    "What does it mean?"
    "It means I have to call Mike."

IT TOOK JEWEL AN HOUR TO DECIPHER THE MES-
sage he had from his case officer. He spent that hour sitting in
his car, drinking coffee and scribbling. He had privacy in the
car. At home, his wife would want to know what he was doing.
    The message was full of praise for his coup at the JOTS
terminal, and he beamed. The message also promised him the
payment of ten thousand dollars immediately, to show the
"satisfaction of the people of China," a phrase he read several
times. It made him very happy.
    In the last paragraph, his case officer ordered him to go
back to watching submarines. That suited him; the nuclear
missile boats were the most important part of the American
arsenal. He didn't understand why the carrier had been inserted into his targeting. They had watched carriers for years
without much result. The submarines, while harder, were a
better target, and ever since he had switched to subs last year,
these messages of praise had been more frequent.
    He finished his coffee, read the phrase about "satisfac-
tion" and the money one more time, and got out of the car
with all the scraps of paper he'd used, headed for the camp-
site's firepit. Jewel was thorough. When he'd burned the scraps,
he broke the ashes up with a stone and then urinated on the
results.

Washington and Seattle.

Dukas was at home. Because Alan insisted on a STU, however, he had to get into his car and drive back to NCIS head-quarters. Already late for a date with Sally, he called her first, then got on the STU.

"This better be good," he said.

To his surprise, Triffler's voice said, "It is."

"I thought I was talking to Al!"

Craik's voice came on. "Conference call, Mike. This is important."

"What the hell?"

"I got an E-mail that uses the Jakarta codes. Right after Dick discovered surveillance on us."

"Uses them how?"

"The recognition codes—the AGIP Christmas party, 'I was with a Dutch girl.' Right out of Chinese Checkers."

"Holy shit."

"Signed 'Rathunter.' He wants a meeting," Triffler said. "As if he missed the Jakarta meeting and now he wants another."

"Chinese," Dukas said.

Triffler gave a disgusted groan. "When Al comes out of that state police parking lot, he's got a tail. I asked you how they would know when Al hit town, well, now I know. And two hours later, he gets an E-mail using the Jakarta codes. It's got to be the same guys, Mike—and they've made Al, for sure."

"Holy God," Dukas said. "Al, read me the E-mail again. Dick, fax me a report ASAP."

Alan read the E-mail in a flat voice, as if it were important to keep any interpretation out of it.

"Rathunter," Dukas muttered. "Chinese."

He heard Alan suck air between his front teeth. " 'Missed you in Jakarta.' As in, 'I aimed at you but I missed you in Jakarta'?"

"Rathunter." Dukas continued to stare at the STU as if Alan's face were there. "The Chinese have a Year of the Rat. That mean anything? What year is it now? Anyway, the 'hunter'

part is interesting. Hunting for a rat? You? Nah. Then 'egg roll.' "
He grinned. "This is a Chinese with a sense of humor."

Triffler groaned. "You're hipped on the Chinese. Mike, what we have to focus on is the tail that was put on him. He follows up the newspaper article about the ham-radio guy, he picks up the tail, *then* he gets the E-mail."

"Mike, Dick's right. We agreed there were three parties in the Orchid House."

Dukas sighed. "I hate ambiguity."

"He says, 'Maybe you have something I am looking for,' " Triffler said. "That could be important."

Dukas folded his arms over his chest with a wince that said that that hurt his wound, too. "Okay, okay. Al, don't answer this E-mail; I'll take care of it. You just forget this part and concentrate on Seattle. Dick, you, too—Al's to have counter-surveillance every step he takes off the base and maybe on it, too. I'll put a request in to the FBI to try to trace the E-mail, but you know how long that'll take." He sighed. "Meanwhile, we try to ID Rathunter." He paused. "What was it, 'your faraway pal'? What does that mean—what's far away—Brooklyn? Beijing? San Diego? 'Faraway pal,' sounds like his English is pretty good."

"How about, he's in Seattle and uses 'faraway' to disguise it?" Triffler said.

Alan spoke up. "How about if Rathunter is Shreed's control, or somebody in his office? I mean, walk the cat back: I leave the mark for the meeting, which we think won't produce squat, but in fact it's a live plan, and a watcher picks up the mark and flashes Beijing or someplace—sorry, Dick, I agree it may not be the Chinese, but I'm just thinking it through—and holy hell breaks loose—wouldn't it? It's like Dick said last week: If we had a dead agent's comm plan light up, wouldn't we come to life? So they cover the meeting, and then, if you're sitting in Beijing, you still want to know what the hell's going on, so you try to set up another meet—right?"

"How'd they know it was you?"

"Oh, come on!" Triffler snorted. "They probably ID'd him before he was back in the U.S."

"Maybe it was Chen himself," Alan said, his voice wry. "George Shreed's control," he added for Triffler's benefit.

"What happened to him?"

Dukas squinted. "He's dead. I saw the body. Harry's girlfriend shot him. My boss asked me just the other day why I didn't bring him home." He sighed.

"But the Chinese or whoever *could* think they're talking to Shreed," Triffler said. "If Chen was Shreed's control, and the Jakarta comm plan was the way they met, then maybe they think Shreed is still alive and they're trying to make contact."

"They're missing both their A-number-one agent *and* his control. They get the signal for a meet in Jakarta. Bingo! It's Shreed making contact! They make the meet, bang-bang-bang, it goes bad, their guy gets killed, *but they didn't do it!* But they know it wasn't Shreed; it was some American Navy guy. So they go, 'Shit, we'll settle for him—maybe he knows what's going on.' So they E-mail him."

"Mike," Triffler said, "would you do that? E-mail another intel agency after what, at best, you have to think of as a hostile meet, just to find out what he wants? No, they have to have a damned good reason to make contact this way."

"Like they're taking a big risk," Dukas said. "I agree. So, something makes the risk worthwhile."

The three voices were silent for some seconds until Alan said, "Shreed was talking about poisoning the Chinese. When he was dying. He acted like he'd done something wonderful. He said that he'd have a monument at the Agency like Casey."

Dukas frowned. "I don't remember."

"Shreed was giving Chen hell about something. And he said to me that he was a hero—as if he really believed it! Jesus, do you suppose he really had done something to screw his control, and now the Chinese are shitting bricks over it?"

"How could he have screwed them?" Triffler said. "He was their best spy!"

"He was saying something to Chen about money," Alan said. "Mike doesn't remember any of this. Do you, Mike?"

"I don't remember anything about money. Maybe I read it in your debrief, but I don't remember."

"Well, you know what they say," Alan said. "Follow the money."

"Yeah, but *what* money?" Dukas rubbed his eyes with his right hand. When he stopped to think about it, he was really worn out. "What money?" he said again.

Alan muttered that he had no idea. Triffler was silent. Dukas sniffed, got a lingering hint of Leslie's perfume, and unaccountably smiled. He had Alan read him the E-mail again, and then again while he copied it down.

Dukas was circling things on his version of the E-mail. *Rathunter. Missed you. Something I want.* "Are we done?" he said.

WHEN DUKAS HUNG UP, HE WAS THINKING THAT the E-mail from Rathunter was either a big break or a scam, and the surveillance on Alan was a satisfying development and certainly significant; and somewhere in the back of his mind he was registering the fact that Triffler hadn't complained and even sounded happy now that he was doing something.

"Win a few, lose a few," he groaned as he got to his feet. Then he sat down again and called Sally. "We still got a date?" he said. Her voice was suspicious, a little shocked, but forgiving. She said she was awake, anyway.

"Half an hour," he said. "Don't decide to take a nap."

He booted up his computer and wrote a brief E-mail and went out the door.

To: Rathunter
From: greekgod
Subject: egg roll
let's meet

Seattle.

When Alan at last got off the telephone, Rose was asleep. She had moved into her own room, he supposed as a way of telling him that it had not been her idea of a romantic day for just the two of them.

Alan got into her bed. "Hey," he said softly.

"You bastard."

"I like you even better without the towel," he said.

Washington.

In the dark, his cheek against Sally's bare ribs, Dukas said, "Can you get Chinese Checkers for me again?"

"You're such a romantic, Mike." He felt her chest go up and down with a wry laugh. "I gave you my only disk."

"I lost it in Pakistan." Sensing the beginnings of her annoyance, he said, "Craik had a contact. I want to see how they react if I suggest a meeting at another Chinese Checkers site."

"Don't you wish you smoked?"

"What the hell's that mean?"

"It was always so cool in old movies when people smoked after they'd, you know."

"They didn't 'you know' in old movies; the production code didn't allow it. They kissed and faded to black."

"Well, after they faded to black, they smoked. I *feel* as if I've faded to black."

"I feel good."

"That's what I mean."

"And you want to *smoke*?"

"No, I—You're a literalist, you know that? You have no imagination." The room was not quite dark, light from a neighbor's backyard spilling in the window. "Is this going to work?" she said.

"It's worked so far."

"I'm trying to get my daughter back. They don't take it too seriously anymore if Mommy has got herself a new guy, but still—I don't want to risk her for something that doesn't work."

Dukas patted her bare thigh. "It's working." He sat up. The bedroom was small and mean; he wondered how three people had ever lived in the house. "Give me the name of somebody who can get the rest of Chinese Checkers for me."

She was silent so long that he said, "I asked if you—"

"I heard you." She swung herself off the bed and grabbed something from the back of the closet door and went into the kitchen. When he followed her, he found her heating frozen eggnog. "That stuff'll kill you," he said.

"It's all I could find that's sweet. I want something sweet." She put out two cups and leaned against the sink, a tall, slightly overweight woman with hair untidy from sex, pale, freckled arms sticking out below the sleeves of a faded shorty robe. "If you could get somebody to process a retrieval request, you could get Chinese Checkers out of storage. Anybody could do it. Anybody with the clearance. But for somebody to have the clout and the knowledge to do it himself, I just don't know anybody. Anybody who'd help, I mean. I'm a bad girl over there." She stirred the mixture, which now smelled like cotton candy.

"If I send a normal request, they'll be a month."

"It's part of Crystal Insight, isn't it? That's ongoing; you can plead urgency."

"Okay, three weeks."

She poured the thick, yellow liquid into two cups. "Ask Carl Menzes."

"He isn't Ops."

"He doesn't have to be Ops—he's Internal Investigations, and he's still running the Shreed case, so he has a reason to ask for it." She sipped and reacted away from the cup because it was too hot. "Anyway, Menzes is the straightest guy at the Agency."

"Yeah, but—" Dukas stuck out his lower lip.

Her face got gleeful. "There's Ray Suter."

"That bastard! He's one of the guys I'm after, not somebody I'm going to ask to get a classified file for me! The word is that Suter knew that Shreed was a Chinese mole, and the Agency has him on ice and is squeezing him dry someplace. I hope he rots!"

"I was joking, okay? My God, talk about overreacting!" She spooned up some of the sticky, sweet mess. "Try Carl Menzes."

Dukas didn't have to tell her about the risk of having your investigation taken over by somebody else, or about the conflict of personalities and agencies, or about stubbornness. "I'll think about it," he said. He put down his cup. "This stuff is terrible." He took her hand and led her back toward the bedroom.

Seattle.

SUNDAY IS A DAY OF REST.

Nonetheless, Dick Triffler called Alan at the BOQ at seven.

"Alan? Going secure." As Alan listened to the *snap-crackle-pop* of encryption static on the STU, he wondered if Triffler ever slept.

"I have you secure," Triffler announced.

"I have you the same." Alan yawned.

"This is about your getting followed yesterday."

"Sure."

"I know why you departed from the route. Totally understandable, but this would be easier if you could signal me, if you—"

"Knew what I was doing?"

"You were very good yesterday."

"Yeah. Yeah, I think I was, but it could be better. How are we going to fix that? And how long is this going to continue?"

"I'd like to get together with you every day, run some exercises. Opportunity to give you some training before we get much further. You sound like you're laughing!"

"I am. Yesterday, I thought I had nothing to do."

"How about tomorrow first thing?"

"Deal."

"I have a map of Whidbey. Can you find the corner of Perry and Lawrence, in officer housing?"

"I'll find it."

"I'd like you to be there from 0702 until 0705. If I'm not there to meet you, try again from 0802 to 0805. I'll have a Seattle Mariners ball cap in the passenger-side visor of my car. Got it?"

"0702 until 0705. If you don't show, try again from 0802 to 0805. Seattle Mariners ball cap. That's early, Dick."

"Want to make it later?" The tone carried a great deal of what Surfer would call "negative energy."

Alan smiled to himself. "I'll be there."

Seattle.

Dick Triffler had called from the empty NCIS office; he was there before any but the duty officer, and he was waiting at a desk when the man he wanted came in to take over, a tall, almost emaciated-looking man of fifty named Nagel, one of the two local agents Triffler had been able to borrow.

"You're kind of a gunner," Nagel muttered. "Not even eight o'clock on fucking Sunday."

"Eager beaver," Triffler said. "I couldn't wait to get back to your coffee." He waved at the office coffee machine, which he had washed and filled and turned on. "What do you guys buy for coffee, old horseballs?"

"Go to Starbucks," Nagel rasped. He had a chronic cough. "Weather here strangles me," he said. He poured himself coffee, paused when it met his lips. "What'd you do?" he accused Triffler.

"I scrubbed the filter."

Nagel sipped. "Tastes weird." He sat at his desk and put his feet up. "I can't surveil your guy today; I got the duty."

"Reason I'm here, man, is I want to know who the cars we

picked up trailing Craik belong to. Any movement on the search?"

Nagel made a face. "This is a joke, right?"

Triffler looked baffled.

"Some search! I picked them up before I knocked off yesterday. Those license numbers are state cop cars, for Christ's sake!"

"You should have called me."

"All day, you got us trailing three cars that belong to the state police! What the hell, Triffler!"

"You sure?"

Nagel gave him a disgusted look.

"What kind of state cops? Off-duty? Plainclothes?"

"They're in a block of licenses issued to the state police. The cars are probably unmarked leftovers from drug seizures or some shit like that. Probably came out of a car pool in Tacoma. We need to trail them back and ID the guys in them— get a few pics, maybe a fingerprint if we can get into the cars."

"Don't let them know. Got it? Until we know better, the state cops are not on our side."

"Jesus, Triffler, I *know* a lot of state cops!" Nagel drank coffee and looked unhappy. "What're they tailing a naval officer for, anyway?"

Triffler rested his buttocks on the desk. "Good question," he muttered. He chewed his upper lip. "Ve-ry good question."

In the Virginia Horse Country.

Ray Suter was lying in the grass that lay at the end of a long slope down from the house toward a meadow where two horses, the only ones on the farm, were standing nose-to-tail. They were way out in the big meadow, as if they were part of a herd of dozens. Always together, the only ones of their kind that either knew, they were called "the boys" by the maintenance man and now by Hurley. Suter, who disliked animals, never referred to them.

He was lying with his hand on his cheek and his back to

the house. A book was open on the ground. To anybody behind him, he seemed to be reading. Nobody was in front of him except the horses.

A palmtop lay on the pages of the open book. Suter was reading a message in the small display window:

> **Subject checked in here today. All OK. Where's Mustang? LeMans.**

"Fuckhead," Suter whispered. He meant Jerry Piat, the missing "Mustang." He stabbed the device with his left index finger, keeping the movement out of sight of anybody in the house. He pretended to stretch and yawn and glanced back to make sure nobody was there. Then he pulled a cell phone from a nylon pouch that was hidden in the grass under the book and pecked a number and put the phone against his right ear as if he were still leaning his head on that hand.

"Say what?" a voice on the other end said. It was male, maybe black.

"Five flies."

"Who's this?"

"Friend of Spanish Fly." *Spanish Fly* had been Shreed's code name when he was dealing with the same people and wanted black jobs done. Suter had learned it from the mass of data that Nickie Groski had hacked out of Shreed's computer. "You hear me?"

"Yeah, ah heard you. Talk."

"I want you to find somebody for me. Name, Piat. First name, Jerry—I think it's Gerald. Address on Millington Avenue, Silver Spring; get it from the phone book. I want to know where he is and what he's doing, and I may want you to deal with him. Okay?"

"Thousand bucks, man; 'dealing' with people costs more."

Suter hesitated, then said, "Same arrangement as before."

"Half up front."

Again Suter hesitated. Anybody seeing his face would know he was angry, but he kept control of his voice as he said, "Okay. Money coming the same route."

He switched the cell phone off. Piat had been one of his

interrogators in the first days after Shreed had fled, even though it had been Agency dogma that Piat had idolized Shreed. We love the enemies of our enemies.

Suter had believed—and still believed—that he could stonewall forever, because he knew too much about Shreed and because too many people still loved Shreed. Once he'd learned that Shreed had died, it had been a short step to the beginnings of the plan to protect himself further, by framing the people who had brought Shreed down. Marv Helmer had been a natural ally because he had thought that Shreed walked on water. So had Piat, especially when he disappeared from the interrogation team and, Suter had learned from Helmer, quit the Agency under duress. Now, however, Piat was proving unstable—not where he should have been, not doing what he was told. We love the enemies of our enemies only so long as they prove useful.

Suter pretended to read for another twenty minutes, then made his way on a long curve to the horse barns, the way a man who had nothing to do might wander on a big place like this. He stayed outside the barns so they could see him from the house, and whistled, walking up and down. He bent and took a stone from his shoe; when he stood, the pouch with the palmtop and the cell phone was on the ground.

The maintenance man came out of the tack room. Unlike Suter, he was nervous and he squinted up toward the house.

"Don't look there!" Suter growled. "How many times do I have to tell you?" He pointed at the two horses far out in the field. "I'm asking you about the horses. You're telling me about them. You're telling me why they're always together." The two men stood side by side, not, in fact, unlike the horses they were looking at. Suter shaded his eyes to look at them and said, "I'll need the checkbook at noon. Bring it to me at the tennis court. Then you'll have to go to the bank and get cash and take it to the same place."

"Jesus God," the maintenance man said, "you think I got nothing else to do?"

"Nothing else you're so well-paid for," Suter said. "Come back and pick up the pouch in twenty minutes. I may need it tomorrow." He shook the maintenance man's hand and gave him a big smile and ambled up toward the house.

Dar es Salaam.

Colonel Lao had got the E-mail from Greekgod and had printed it out and taped it to the wall next to his computer. Above it was a printout of the photo of the American naval officer, Craik, in Jakarta. Lao stared at the two as if expecting them to speak to him, and when they did not, he said, "Jiang!"

The captain put his head in from the outer office.

"What do you have on the E-mail trace?"

"Nothing yet. Too soon. The domain's American, but otherwise, it's too soon."

Lao expected nothing more. He had sent his own E-mail to Craik through a cutout server in Denmark; he was not surprised that Craik had done the same in reply. But he didn't understand the use of the code name. "I don't get 'Greekgod,' " he said.

"The Greeks had many gods, in their classical era," the captain said. "Jupiter, Hercules—"

"Herakles."

"Sorry, sir?"

"The Greek name is Herakles. The Romans called him Hercules." Lao rubbed his hand through his hair and looked up at the clock. "Is Craik a bodybuilder? Does he think he's a Greek god? Maybe it's a joke. The Americans make jokes." He lit a cigarette and tossed the pack where the captain could reach it. "I have to send an answer. We can't waste time here."

The captain, who now knew a great deal about the Chen case because Lao could not do everything himself, said, still standing because Lao hadn't asked him to sit, "Make a meeting."

"Too soon. I don't know what I'm dealing with. Craik must have turned the message over to the CIA; they could have agents all over it. Anyway, a meeting will be hard to arrange." And, he thought, where will it leave me, meeting with a foreign intelligence officer?

"Use American Go. There are three meeting places—
Jakarta, Nairobi, Pakistan."

"Pakistan is where Chen disappeared; I could hardly go
there. Nairobi? Huh." Nairobi was close by; he could oversee
the entire thing himself. The office had agents in Nairobi. It
was a good thought, but premature. "I think we will send him
a cautious answer," he said. "Then we must write a report on
this contact." He said "we" because he couldn't entirely trust
Jiang, and it was best to make him share the burden of contact
with a foreign national.

Cyberspace.

From: Rathunter
To: greekgod
Cc:
Subject: your egg roll
it is a fine time of year for travel/ maybe you want
to broaden your acquaintance? you always learn
something, often things of great value/ we cannot
see forward if we look only over our shoulder/
maybe meet location 2 of the plan you have

Washington.

Dukas slammed ahead despite its being Sunday, sleeping at
his office and getting bad-tempered and frowsy and piling up
work for Leslie to start Monday morning. He pushed the back-
checking of the items in Sleeping Dog, looking for more forgeries; when he had this in train for Leslie to finish, he dug into
Crystal Insight to see what he had missed in there.

And that was how he found out about Nickie the Hacker.
First, however, he had had to read Triffler's report on what
had happened here in D.C. while Dukas was off in Pakistan,
which was so circumspect that Dukas realized that Triffler
was tiptoeing around something, especially in his work with

somebody named Detective Moisher. Dukas wanted to know what.

He called Seattle. "What the hell did you leave out of this report? It's all pussyfooting."

Silence. Then, "I thought it was masterful."

"Oh, smell me."

Triffler sighed. "Because of something my boss, Michael Dukas, had done, an entire evidence trail was tainted. Therefore, Detective Moisher had to be helped along without my hand ever showing. And I did it very, very well."

Dukas could see that. Yes, he believed that the thoroughly honest Triffler would have done that. "So what was the upshot about Suter?"

"Detective Moisher is dumb as a stump, but he's tenacious," Triffler said. "He finally made a connection between a crime in Bladensburg and Ray Suter, which led him to Menzes, with a little help, and Menzes invited him along on the bust. He—"

"This cop was *with* Menzes at the bust?"

"Yes, I think he actually served the local warrant on Suter. Anyway, they got to Suter and the kid and arrested them both."

"What kid?"

"A computer hacker named Nickie—mm, what was it?— Groski, Nickie Groski, who was working for Suter. Remember? You had illegally put a tap on Shreed's phone lines so you'd know when his computers were on? And they showed that somebody else was hacking in? Well, there was this kid who had hacked into Shreed's computers, I think to get things on Shreed for Suter. Anyway, Menzes got Suter and the kid and he wouldn't tell me a thing about any of it. It's locked up tight. You there?"

"I'm thinking," Dukas said, and he hung up. What stayed in his head was "Shreed's computers" and a kid who had hacked into them. Shreed had been a computer nut; he had communicated with his Chinese control by embedding data in photographs and sending them over the Internet. *A hacker who was into Shreed's computers might know a lot. A hell of a lot.*

After a couple of minutes, he called Abe Peretz, a pal at

the FBI, at home and asked if he could get anything on a bust on the date in Triffler's report. Peretz, who was unfazed by the call, came back to him in two hours with the information that two FBI agents had been on the team that had gone in with Menzes, and they had, among other things, charged a juvenile named Nicholas Groski with violation of parole.

"The FBI bothered with a kid who'd violated parole?"

"Computer crime. Federal offense."

"What happened to the kid?"

"I'll find out."

Dukas knew that the Agency could hold on to Suter for as long as they wanted because he was an Agency employee, but they couldn't do that for a juvenile who wasn't an Agency employee and whose only crime was violation of parole. In fact, the Agency wasn't supposed to mess with people inside U.S. borders at all. Oh, yeah.

Dukas went on the trail of Detective Moisher. On a Sunday, that trail was cold and dead. The local police didn't give out home telephone numbers; Moisher was unlisted; and why didn't he call back on a weekday?

PERETZ CALLED A LITTLE AFTER FOUR. "NICHOLAS Groski was picked up when Suter was busted. We—the Bureau, I mean—made the arrest and charged him with parole violation; local jurisdictions in Virginia and Maryland also charged him with local stuff—breaking and entering to get into Shreed's computers, stuff like that. Federal judge slapped a ten-thousand-dollar bail on him; bail was posted by the CIA, and they met him at the door and nobody's seen him since. I think it's what we call 'unlimited detention.' "

"Sonofabitch. How come?"

"I smell a fix with the judge. Also, there's a federal gag order on him—that's a place to start."

"What court?"

"Fourth Circuit, Virginia."

"Oh, shit." That was a tough, conservative court that liked what it heard from prosecutors and the government. "Who asked for it?"

"You need to find the kid's lawyer, if he's got one. Start with the local charges—where did he get arrested?"

Dukas looked at Triffler's report. "Prince George's County, Maryland."

"Okay, check the charge sheets in the county court, that's Upper Marlboro. Don't try to do it yourself; get somebody from your legal affairs that knows how it's done."

"How the hell do they get to keep a kid for a month?"

"They would have said the magic words, Mike—'national security.' "

"Well, I know those words, too."

He called NCIS Legal Affairs and was told to call back in the morning.

So he started calling people at home.

Sunday was a day of rest.

THERE IS NO REST ON A CARRIER AT SEA, AND ON the *Jefferson,* aircraft were being worked on the hangar deck and stashed on the deck and launched off the cats. There could be church; there could be rotation-scheduled leisure; but the Air Ops that were the carrier's reason for being went on. LTjg Soleck didn't fly that day and was glad enough for the rest from the tension of trying to get a landing right. Captain Rafehausen allowed himself time to go to church, but he was in his office and among the ready rooms as if it were any other day.

On Whidbey Island, the det took another no-fly day, but, at Alan's insistence, the flight crews put in a couple of hours on the MARI files from the *Jefferson.* CDR Rose Siciliano flew her F-18 down to Edwards and got herself a room in the BOQ so she could get up bright and early and get checked out on a different airplane.

Sunday was a day of rest.

NCIS HQ.

ON MONDAY MORNING, DUKAS FOUND AN E-MAIL on his computer from another special agent that said:

> Hey, Dukas, how do I get me a teenage sex bomb like yours for my office?

It took him a moment to realize that the message referred to Leslie. *Teenage sex bomb?* Dukas sighed and told himself that he had better things to do than trade insults with assholes.

He got himself an appointment in Legal to talk about Nickie Groski. When he hung up from that, there was a call waiting: Detective Moisher. As Triffler had said, Moisher was a few kilowatts short of a sound-and-light show, but at least he got to work early, and besides, he was thrilled to be called by a special agent. He remembered Triffler with enthusiasm because "for a black guy, he was really, really great." Dukas was tempted to say that *he* was a black guy, but he guessed that Moisher was one of those people who live without irony.

"I want to talk to you," Dukas said.

"You bet. Anything!"

"Nicholas Groski."

"Oh. I can't talk about him."

"Sure you can."

"I'm under a court order. National security."

"Ray Suter."

"I don't dare. They'd crucify me."

"Oh, they would? Well, let me put it this way—I'm going to put a court order under your nose telling you to talk to me in the cause of national security, so get your pipes in order, or *I'll* crucify you."

"Jeez, can you do that?"

"Watch me."

Dukas stabbed the lever on the telephone cradle that disconnected them, and, phone to ear to make a call to Carl Menzes at the CIA, he looked up to see Leslie. She was standing by the end of the wall of crates and she had a silly look on her too-wide face. When she saw him looking, she giggled. "Notice anything?" she said.

It was the question with which old-fashioned women drove old-fashioned men to drink. Dukas was old-fashioned enough to feel panic. "Uhhhh—" he said. *Teenage sex bomb* danced in his brain. He didn't want to look at her.

"It's my hair, stupid!"

It certainly was. It wasn't red anymore. It was an unreal, impossible, sword-and-sorcery, computer-game witch's black. It looked like a pile of wet black asphalt, spiraled up on top of her head.

"He-e-e-y!" Dukas said. He had learned a few things from the many women he'd failed with.

"I wanted cornrows, but there wasn't time," she croaked.

He smiled with false enthusiasm and thought that it was about time he had a talk with Leslie about her public image, and then he got very busy with the telephone, because anything he said was going to sound like sexual harassment. A lose-lose situation, his specialty.

He had decided that Sally was right—he had to ask Carl Menzes to get him a copy of the Chinese Checkers file so he could try to set up a meet with Rathunter. When he got Menzes, Menzes was unenthusiastic about meeting; he temporized, hesitated, finally agreed only if they could meet at "the Annex," actually the Old Commonwealth Tavern, a restaurant and booze salon down the road from the Agency—miles and miles of Beltway driving for Dukas. It wasn't clear whether he didn't want to talk to Dukas or he simply didn't want to be seen talking to Dukas.

"Late?" Menzes said. "I can't make it until about six-thirty." It was clear that he hoped that Dukas couldn't make it at all.

"This is kind of urgent."

"Six-fifteen."

When Dukas hung up, Leslie was on his side of the wall of crates, straightening and sorting the piles of paper that he had on every surface. Dukas dared to glance at her, taking in the whole of her, which was much more than the lacquered, unreal hair. She was wearing shack-up shoes, white panty hose, a black vinyl skirt that stopped about where a purist would think that decency began, and a shiny red T-shirt. *Teenage sex bomb,* oh, yeah!

"Uhhh—Leslie—uh—anything going on I need to know?"

"I've got an interview set up with the maverick. You know, the guy who—"

"You can't have an interview set up. I just submitted the request."

"Yeah, we have. I talked to the agent in Florida, where the maverick is—he's a Marine captain? I called the Marine Corps and found where he was; I, uh, had to sort of fudge a little, like I was his sister? But I found him, so I called the NCIS office down there and—Mister Dukas, you're mad at me, aren't you!"

Dukas was, in fact, very angry, but containing it. "What did he say?" he growled.

"We had a nice talk. He said I sounded, well, I won't say what he said I sounded like, but it was a compliment. He said he'd do it right away *for me*." She laughed.

Dukas frowned, thinking of all the interview requests that piled up on NCIS desks all over the world. *Well, whatever works is good.* But aloud, he said, "Leslie, we have forms and protocols and ways of doing things and whole books about how they have to be done. Don't-you-ever-again-do-something-without-my-permission!" He tried to smile. "See?"

She burst into tears.

Maybe, Dukas thought, he should get Triffler back to Washington and *he* would go to Seattle.

He supplied Kleenex, told her to go to the ladies' room, got himself more coffee, and felt terrible. When she came back, however, Leslie had bounced back with the resiliency of a late adolescent, and she smiled and said she'd *never* do that again. Dukas saw that it was a good time to make a point. "Leslie," he said in what he hoped was an avuncular tone, "um, uh, doing all the filing and, um, carrying and lifting and, um, so on—I'd want to be wearing sort of old clothes, um—"

"My boyfriend and I are going to this new bar after work, sort of like in *Friends*?" This was meant to explain the clothes and the hair.

"You're dressed for your date."

"Ri-e-e-e-ght!"

It irritated him. It irritated him that he'd got that stupid E-mail and it irritated him that she didn't know any better than to dress like a goddam hooker to work in his office. "Leslie, how much time will you spend at this bar?"

"Oh—couple hours, max—I don't drink too much, really!"

"And how much time will you spend here?"

"Nine hours, honest to God—I won't leave early, Mister Dukas—"

"And who pays your salary, us or the bar?"

Leslie looked at him, looked away. She looked down at herself. "Oh," she said. Dukas grabbed a folder from his desk and said, "Take this up to the third office on the right and give it to Mrs. Sandow. While you're in there, have a good look at Mrs. Sandow, okay? A good look." Claire Sandow was the best-dressed woman in the building, at least by the dress-for-success standards of Washington offices.

Whidbey Island.

Alan stood under a large pine tree on a corner in the officers' housing area and yawned. He felt silly, when everyone was either getting up or moving off to work, and he was standing on someone's lawn in the early sun, holding two cups of coffee. He worried that the base police would hassle him. He didn't look like a runner, because he wasn't running. He looked like a guy waiting for someone.

He saw the car turn on his street from a block down and approach him. The passenger-side visor was down and had a Seattle Mariners ball cap hung from it, the agreed safe signal. He walked out to the street just as the car stopped, and he hopped inside. The car was rolling again before he reached for his seat belt. Alan reached into the back and tossed a folder containing all the info he had obtained in Olympia.

"That's all there is to it," said Dick Triffler. "It's all about being on time and in the right place and knowing the signals."

Alan held out a cup of coffee.

"I thought you might want this."

Dick sniffed the coffee through the plastic lid with visible apprehension and a smile lit him up.

"That's all right," he said. "Starbucks?"

"On this base?" Alan chuckled. "This is the Navy, Mister Triffler. No, I bought it in Seattle and made it in our room coffeemaker at the BOQ."

Triffler eased them into a parking lot for a ball field, empty except for two men and a woman running the circuit in the distance.

"That's what we call a drive-by," he said. "It allows me to pick you up and talk face-to-face without drawing unnecessary attention." He drank some coffee and made an appreciative grunt. "Thanks for the coffee."

"Okay, I get the drive-by, except that I was standing on somebody's lawn at 0704 local time, that is."

"If this were real, I'd be picking you up on your normal route. While you were out running, for instance."

Alan nodded.

"Wouldn't somebody think it odd if a runner got into a car? Shouldn't it be done at a supermarket or something?"

"Bingo. That's good, Alan. That's just the way to think. Think about the logic of your actions as perceived by the bad guys. Are you doing something odd? Do you feel exposed? Agents hate to feel exposed, Alan. It makes them uptight and nervous and uncooperative. After a while, they stop bringing you coffee."

"Couldn't we do it someplace more, well, hidden?" Alan was watching the runners and thinking that he'd like to smoke.

"Nothing wrong with some concealment, if it's still natural. Let's drive. I want to show you a few things I've already seen this morning."

He pulled out of the parking lot and drove them back to the base exchange, which was just opening. He continued around to the back and drove slowly by the outside garden department.

"Okay, we're behind the building in this alley, right? So no one in front of the building can see us. If you just stood there and got into my car, it might look odd, even to some busybody employee who might remember it for later. See what I mean?" he said, as a young sailor peered curiously at their car.

"Yeah. When did you scope this out?"

"I got here around five-thirty. So what would make it better?" Triffler took a deep swig of the coffee.

"What, the coffee? I don't know, a better filter?"

"The site. As a place for me to pick you up. How would it look natural?"

"If I walked over from the BOQ, bought something in the garden shop, and then got in your car."

"Exactly. And then it's all timing. If I pull up just as you emerge, then it just looks like one guy's helping another guy get his plant home. No big deal. Natural, and somewhat concealed. And what makes it even better is that when I come out of the alley, here, I'm not in the base exchange parking lot, but on Nimitz Road, headed for the gate. Easy access. Anyone behind me is now way behind, unless they followed me right into the alley."

"Mike's talked about all of this before."

"Good. You understand why we have to meet like this?"

"Tell me anyway."

"In this case, you have a clandestine role. In other words, we're hiding your part from anybody who might be watching you. So you can't just come to my office, and I'm not going to come to the BOQ, although it's unlikely that the bad guys can access this base. Okay?"

"Got it."

"What's in the folder?" Triffler gestured at the copies of the Olympia information that Alan had tossed in the back.

"As best I can see, Dick, there's three action items. There's a case sheet with the ham radio operator's name, John Tashimaya, as well as address and telephone number. That was right on top. There's some sort of action report not related to the arrest but signed by the cop in the wire story, Jim Kusluski, that lists his vital stats. So we could contact the cop. And there's an FCC report that we could use to chase down the putative FCC connection."

"Putative is a very good word, Alan." Triffler began to look at the three sheets. "It's incomplete."

"That's what I thought."

"Exactly. So if there are three action items, one is the trap, whatever that is, and the other two may be traps, may be real, or may just be dead ends."

"My money is on dead ends. The reason the folder is so slim is that they can't afford to have too much data for us to check on or we'll get suspicious."

"Bingo. Exactly. I'd expect it to be John Tashimaya himself, because they've gone to the trouble of providing a name and address."

"So I'll do the other two first?"

"Slowly. Make the calls with me here, on my government-issue phone. As every move might be trapped, I'd want you covered for each."

"Roger that."

"Okay. We'll do the FCC on Wednesday. That suit you?"

"I'm on the flight sched tomorrow, but Wednesday the pilots will have all the planes on carrier quals out in the Op Area."

"Can we concentrate on some clandestine training now, or would you like to explore Area 51 or something?"

"Too far to drive. Let's do some drills."

Off Puget Sound.

Five hours later, a pilot named Cunnard had them straight and level at twelve thousand feet, forty-five miles off the coast. Surfer had another plane twenty miles to the south and higher. Alan switched his intercom so that he was talking on the radio and talking to the other people in his plane.

"Okay, folks. Check your GPS and put your cursors on the following coordinates." He read off a series of numbers that caused the Taccos to aim their radar dishes well inland.

"Roger."

"Roger."

"Radars on," he called, and watched the small screen on his right armrest show a hazy swirl of meaningless static. The S-3's surface-search radar lacked the resolution to do much with land targets. On the other hand, there was a definite spike in the middle of the screen.

"Lock up the central spike and go to your MARI menu."

"Roger," from Surfer's plane.

"Roger," from six feet behind him.

"Key image. A free beer to the first ID." He smiled at what he had given them as their first real-life MARI target. The image came up, so clear that the corporate logo was visible on the front of the building.

"Hey! Microsoft!" Bubba Paleologus, in Surfer's plane.

"Give that man a beer," said Alan. "Now let's look at some shipping."

Twenty miles apart, the two planes turned away from the coast.

"Bubba, you locate a contact and then pass it on the link.

Then both of you lock it up and see what you get. No comms. Go ahead."

"Roger. I'm looking."

Alan switched his screen to datalink and shaded it with his left hand. At their new attitude, the sun shone right on it and made reading characters impossible. After a few moments, a white square appeared on the screen. Alan switched his intercom to airplane only.

"Got that, back there?"

"Yes, sir."

He watched on screen as his Tacco switched to surface search, matched the contact, and imaged it on ISAR. A fuzzy image appeared, but it was recognizable as a big merchant ship with superstructures both fore and aft. Then the screen twitched and it was replaced by a sharp-edged image of the same ship, but correct down to details of antennas and the shape of the bow. Alan switched back to general communication. "Right. Good work. Now show me his ESM signature."

That was not part of the MARI system but used the S-3's powerful antennas to search passively for emitters from other ships—and submarines. He switched to his emitter's screen and watched as his Tacco began to correlate signals, first a surface-search radar and then something in a higher frequency, possibly even a ship-to-shore radio.

"Now you know who he is. You can track him passively with the ESM gear as long as he radiates that surface-search radar, right? And you can pass his location via datalink. You probably won't have to image him again. This is how you can build a surface picture and maintain it without constantly reimaging. Everybody see that?"

A chorus of "rogers." Alan thought for a moment of the problems any navy had in maintaining a picture of the location of ships, their own, their adversaries', and the neutral shipping in between. And then he thought of the difficulties of submarine detection. Something was ticking over in his mind, but he let it go.

"Let's get a few more, folks," he said.

NCIS HQ.

At ten, Dukas was in a tacky office in NCIS Legal, facing a fifty-year-old woman who looked as if she'd heard every hard-luck story ever told and didn't believe a one. "What can I do for you, Mister Dukas?" she said. She looked at her watch.

"I want you to file to have a gag order placed by the Fourth Circuit lifted. Today." He smiled. "National security."

She gave him an unbelieving look. It took fifteen minutes of explaining about Nickie Groski's importance to his case, to convince her that he was so serious he was willing to go to the mat on it. When she said, "O-ka-a-ay," and put her hand on her telephone, he figured she was persuaded. "Be it on your head," she said, and he knew she wasn't persuaded at all—but she'd do it.

When he got back to his office, Leslie was at her desk. She worked for some minutes without acknowledging him and then looked through the plastic barrier. "You want me to dress like her, don't you?" she said, meaning that she'd had a good look at Claire Sandow. Her tone meant that she was very, very disappointed in him. "It's what you said about one thing for the office and another thing for relationships, isn't it?"

"Am I the first one who's ever said it?" Dukas said.

"My other supervisor's always on me about it, yatta-yatta-yatta! But I don't take her *seriously.*" Leslie looked away. Dukas was afraid she was going to cry, but her voice was quite firm, if a little hollow, as she said, "She's like all of them. My mother, my teachers, my aunts. Just *on* you all the time, you know?" She came around the barrier to him, pathetic in her finery, and she said, "You want me to grow up, don't you?" It was an accusation.

Dukas couldn't smile. "I'm afraid so, Leslie." They looked at each other.

She sighed. She headed for her desk. He had the sense that he had toppled from some pedestal.

15

Whidbey Island.

LIEUTENANT-COMMANDER CRAIK HAD LAID ON A heavy training schedule, with at least a flight a day for all the aircrews and a list of MARI targets to image. Surfer's aviators were glad to get the flight time, although LT Cunnard's crew had just been completed with a newbie Senso and, because of his inexperience, they had to fly twice a day. On Monday afternoon, they were the last plane airborne.

The new guy picked his nose, and that was so disgusting that Cunnard was annoyed from the moment they got in the air. The pilot had majored in coeds at Berkeley before finding solace in Naval Aviation, and he couldn't imagine an adult picking his nose. His copilot wasn't happy with the way his wife was behaving at home and her newfound independence since starting university. He ran the checklists on automatic while trying to decide whether a better-informed, better-read Wendy was really an improvement over the original Wendy, a gorgeous high-school dropout who lived for the beach.

"Lieutenant-Commander Craik's something, I guess," said Dice, the copilot, trying to get the subject out of his head.

"Yeah," the pilot said, still pressing buttons on the main radio.

"He seemed okay."

"He seemed like a guy who knows a lot about MARI," said the pilot, who hated gossip in all its forms. "Am I using yesterday's comm card here, Dice?"

Dice flipped through his kneeboard and shrugged. "Sorry."

They were silent for a while, and then Dice said, "He has a kind of ... reputation."

"Uh-huh," Cunnard said, discouragingly, and the yoke twisted in his hands. A little kick from an unwilling plane.

The S-3 was the oldest in their detachment and it lived a charmed life, with more pink slips in maintenance than any other bird in the air wing. Sheila, as Alpha India Seven Zero Three was known to her crew, had a tendency to shed tires on landings and an eternal leakage of fuel somewhere in her belly that had never proved fatal but had tempted many a burger from the stomach of a newbie. The Tacco, Lieutenant Spiro "Bubba" Paleologus, was pretty certain that their newbie Senso would lose his cookies from the smell of JP-5 in the backseat, but he thought that if the newbie Senso picked his nose one more time and ate it, he might decorate the cockpit himself. He dropped another sonobuoy. He was an old-time S-3 guy and wanted to keep their antisubmarine skills honed. He could drop sonobuoys and look at MARI at the same time.

"Don't pick your nose, Airman Lennox."

Lennox looked around, dazed. He looked faintly green at the corners of his nose and mouth.

"Huh?"

"Don't pick your fucking nose." Bubba had done the nice thing, and cut off comms to the front seat so that his pilot and copilot, both officers, wouldn't hear him correcting the newbie.

Lennox looked at him, nervous and edgy. His pinched face was haze gray, and Bubba wondered who the hell had decided that this kid was aeronautically adaptable. He'd probably never left cyberspace in his whole childhood.

"I've—" the kid stuttered. "I've g-g-got a hit."

"Lennox, we are in the western op area and there ain't

nothing but whales out here. We're imaging MARI targets, for Chrissakes. Okay!" He held up his hands, afraid the kid would cry. "Okay! You might have a whale. Let's look. It will make a good learning point."

Cunnard flung the plane into a tight right turn, still following Bubba's sonobuoy pattern, inscribed in glowing green on his tiny display. Lennox got whiter, and Bubba assumed that the Technicolor vomit was next on the program, but the kid took a squeeze on his water bottle and punched out another buoy.

"He's still th-there—sir." The "sir" was an afterthought, so late that you'd think the kid hadn't ever been to boot camp. But Bubba had his own sonar display up now, switching rapidly through analog and digital commands laid out for him in the late 1970s. *High tech,* he thought bitterly. Bubba whistled softly.

"Cunner?"

"Roger, Bubba, how's the nursery?"

"Hey, Cunner, we got two possible contacts on an unknown boat, probably a nuke."

"Shit hot! Log it. We can use the contact time."

"Lennox found it. Is there a boat in the op area?"

The three officers all tried to remember anything that the intel officer had said before they launched. Surely they'd have noticed if he had mentioned an actual sub.

Lennox coughed into his mike.

"He's g-going to t-turn."

Bubba cut the comms to backseat only.

"What do you mean he's going to turn?"

"I heard—his auxiliaries—look at this line."

"Speak up, son, I can't understand you."

"I think he's going to turn."

Bubba hit the comms switch again.

"Cunner, give me a new line. I'm marking it now."

"Roger."

The deep hum of the two turbofans increased, the Hoover noise that gave the plane its nickname. The plane dropped down near sea level and turned sharply.

"We're losing him," said Bubba, now fully engaged. He

was trying to push the new sonobuoys into position by body English while tracking the sub and simultaneously running the grams, comparing them on the screen to known U.S. and foreign types.

"Number sixteen," said Lennox, without a trace of a stutter, and there was the sub, clear as day, with a heavy line in the 40dB and another line way down by 5dB.

Nothing like a U.S. sub.

"He's going fast," Bubba said.

"He's going to turn and drift." Lennox sounded confident.

"If he turns west, he goes right back into our practice pattern."

Bubba mashed the comms button with his thumb. "Turn east," he said. He watched the screen as the contact on buoy 16 began to fade. The plane was racing east to get ahead and lay another line of sonobuoys.

"F-fading . . ." said Lennox.

Bubba counted his buoys, as excited as he had been in a year. He had forgotten the joy of hunting a real sub. The new S-3 community was all about war-at-sea exercises and doing Elint and giving gas. Mostly giving gas. The MARI detachments seldom even used their sonar. As the plane passed his waypoint on the screen, he pressed the drop toggle on his panel and was not rewarded with the heavy *k-klunk* of a launching sonobuoy. Instead, there was a small high-pitched squeak, punctuated by a sharp metal sound.

"Jammed," he said bitterly.

They all listened to the submarine fading, vanishing from their buoys.

"Contact lost," said Lennox, sounding as if he might weep.

And then he threw up on his screen.

Airborne off the Oregon Coast.

Rose stood the C-12 on one wingtip and looked down before putting the plane into a steep dive. The C-12 was NASA's weather-plane version of a popular private jet. As an astronaut, she had to be familiar with it. What she found in her first flight was that she loved it.

"Am I making you nervous, Jack?" she asked her copilot, the field pilot from Edwards. He only shook his head and took a pull from his water bottle. "It's your plane, Rose. I'm just along for the ride. I just want you to think of the age of those wings."

Rose grunted. She could feel that the plane was solid, and the descent was exhilarating. The C-12 had its moments. It was small and reliable and it was going to get her *home*.

"Want to get permission from ATC for us to go whale-watching?"

Jack picked up his mike and rattled through a long exchange with Seattle air-traffic control. She took them down to the operations area's ceiling and cruised, looking for signs on the water. It was an overcast day with rain coming, but for now the sea was flat and calm, at least from the top of nine thousand feet.

"Area's clear. We can go right down to the deck if you want, but tower says turn to one-five-zero first. Two EA-6Bs coming through at twelve thousand in a few minutes. There's an S-3 down on the deck about six miles east."

She turned, barely looking at the compass. Alan lived by the gadgets when he flew, and she supposed that there had been a time when she flew the same way, but she could feel the turn and the course change. Of course, she glanced down at the compass at the end of her turn, just to check.

Right on.

"Spouts!" said Jack. "Right over to starboard. See 'em?"

Rose turned and dove, looking for the EA-6B flight at the same time. She saw them up high, their contrails clear against the cloud cover. Only then did she look down for the whales. Then she put the nose on them and gave the plane some throttle.

Jack winced a little.

"Relax, Jack. You'll never get to do this in the airlines." His ambition was to be an airline pilot.

"Yeah," said Jack, suggesting that might be one of the attractions.

At two thousand feet they could see the great shapes perfectly in the water, four of them swimming along in a shallow crescent.

"Hey, that's a calf. They must be heading north! Cool! I saw something last night on TV."

Rose throttled way down and trimmed up to keep her plane slow. Then suddenly and together, the whales dove. They watched the whales go down, straining their eyes to follow them into the deep blue. Rose had to keep glancing up and away to her horizon to make sure that her hands weren't following her line of sight. Newbies crashed planes that way, and her reflexes were still adjusting to the response of the fixed-wing aircraft.

"Something spooked them. They were basking."

"One TV show makes you an expert?"

"Hey, I know a basking whale when I see one."

Rose was putting power in and climbing, her eyes looking all around for anything in their area, scanning the instruments from habit. Jack was still leaning forward, looking down at the water where the whales had vanished.

"I think one is coming back."

Rose started to turn.

"If we spooked them, we shouldn't stay."

"I've never bothered them before," said Jack. "Whoa!"

Rose tracked his glance, and watched the cigar shape right at the limit of vision, just a mile aft of where the whales had dived. It was deep, and even as she gave the plane more throttle and raced toward it, it seemed to glide deeper and vanished into the same blue that had swallowed the whales.

"Cool," said Jack. "I've only seen a sub one other time."

Rose turned again over the area and clucked in frustration.

200 NM ENE of Mombasa, Kenya.

Twelve thousand miles away, Soleck took his airplane through another hard turn to the right. They were close to the water, not close enough to cause him the perpetual fear that low-level flight gave him, but low enough that every detail of the waves and the seabirds was visible.

He turned again. In the back, AWCM Craw kept his eyes locked on the magnetic anomaly detector, a piece of high-tech gear that seldom functioned and required constant adjustment to keep in tune. The long, retractable boom was an antenna to detect the most sensitive fluctuations in the earth's background magnetic field. It was a piece of technology invented in the early seventies and heralded as a great leap forward in submarine detection, but Craw didn't put much faith in it.

Despite which, every month, their crew got to fly a complex compass rose, with tight turns every few seconds, as the computers recalibrated the magnetic anomaly detector. It was a kind of flying that made some people sick, challenged pilots, and bored the rest of the crew.

Craw was fixed to the screen, as much to have something to think about as because he was the man who could declare the fickle boom to be calibrated. Or not.

Soleck turned again. He didn't lose any altitude and he added speed out of the turn to compensate for the loss of speed in it. He was becoming a more proficient pilot all the time, if you ignored his landing grades. Craw would have liked to say something gentle to young Soleck or ream Stevens for the way he had treated him since he had come aboard. Except that today, Stevens was down sick. And Soleck was visibly more relaxed.

"That'll do her," said Craw, as the nose of the plane passed through north again after thirty cuts across the water. "MAD looks sweet and sweet." He spoke with a heavy New England accent. Soleck leveled the plane.

"Everybody take a stretch. That was a killer," Soleck said. In fact, they'd run a complete calibration set only to find that, despite airsickness and boredom, the boom was still not calibrated. Two MAD comps back to back were something of an achievement. The second should have done the trick.

LT Campbell, the Tacco, had already thrown up, so he felt better. And he needed to show that he was unaffected by his own airsickness. "If we go for three, we might score something like a record," he said with evident sarcasm. The other aircrew groaned.

Master Chief Craw groaned with them.

"I have a spike." Everyone who had a screen up looked at it—the sudden manifestation of another failure. A spike was a magnetic anomaly—a spike of green intensity on the computer screen. Any spike meant that something had caught the boom's attention. Here, in the quiet Indian Ocean off Africa, it meant that their boom was *still* not calibrated correctly.

"Maybe it's a whale," said Campbell.

LT Cohen, the copilot, superstitious like all sailors, muttered something about Campbell and his ill-fated comment about a third MAD comp.

"Master Chief, I think we need a breather before we go around again." Soleck wanted a victory, however small. He wanted to go back to the boat and face the landing with a successful MAD comp, if nothing else, because if he couldn't get the plane down well, he thought it was about time to hand in his wings. The thought made tears come to his eyes, but there wasn't a position in the Navy labeled "copilot." He had to get his landing scores up or he would become a permanent embarrassment to himself and his unit. Or get them all killed. He had to face how bad his landings were.

Don't dwell on it, Commander Rafehausen had said. *Let the landing come to you.*

Yeah. He swore, *swore* that if he ever got through this, he wouldn't give a nugget such trivial, meaningless advice: *Don't dwell on it. Jesus,* Soleck thought to himself. *What the hell else should I think about, sir?*

"That spike is still there, sir. No, she's weakening. Gone." Craw was very contained, but there was something under the New England calm. Excitement?

"Huh?" said Soleck, torn from his thoughts.

"The last time we blew the comp, she only spiked for a second. Now, she's spiking like she means it. We had a MAD trace for about sixty seconds, if I read her right."

"What do you want to do, Master Chief?"

"Pop a few buoys, sir."

"Roger that," he said, and began to turn back over the area. Anything that put the deck off for another few minutes was okay with him.

Craw dropped a temperature buoy immediately. It didn't have to be near the target to give him the temperature and salinity of the water, important issues in searching for a submarine with sonar. And Craw was already sure it was a submarine.

Then he laid out a pattern of sonobuoys on his screen in a rough vee with the open end to the north. He had nothing to guide him except the instinctive belief that if it was a submarine, it must be headed for his battle group, and that was well to the north.

Soleck saw the pattern come up on his screen in the pilot's seat. He bent low and cupped his hand over the screen to take a better look.

"West to east or east to west, Master Chief?"

"Humor an old man and start west, Mister Soleck."

"Roger that." They turned again. Craw split his computer screen, watching the MAD on one screen and preparing his sonobuoy drop on another.

Campbell was calling the ASW module on the ship. "Alpha Xray, this is Gopher, over."

"Roger, Gopher, go ahead."

"Alpha Xray, Gopher advises"—he fumbled with his kneeboards—"Golden Apple." *Golden Apple* meant that they had a pos contact I, the lowest level of submarine contact report, the level that most people ignored, except when you were in the middle of the Indian Ocean and trying to keep your presence a secret.

"Copy Golden Apple," said the ASW watch officer, a Tacco from the S-3 squadron. He didn't sound very interested.

Craw watched the spike grow and he hit the record button on his tape and prayed that it actually recorded. Their tapes were sealed boxes with an early form of eight-track inside, the best of 1965 technology.

He reached over his head for the buoy-drop toggle and began to count to himself, and then he started to drop his buoys. He dropped twelve, scrambling with Campbell to get them all up on the radio link and to read their signals. He looked over the sonograms himself and transmitted them back to the boat while Soleck turned and turned and they dropped more buoys. The MAD didn't spike again.

Less than ten minutes later, Craw got a hit on the 40Db line and passed it to the boat, raising the contact from Golden Apple to Black Knight, or pos contact II. But the contact lasted for only seconds. They dropped more buoys until their light peacetime load was expended. Back on the boat, the ASW module tried to convince the tactical action officer to launch an additional S-3 Viking from the squadron, rather than the MARI det. The VS squadron ought to have more guys who didn't have the flu—and more guys with hands-on ASW experience. Then the ASW module tried to get the TAO to put a helicopter in the air. The TAO was less than enthusiastic. He didn't believe in a submarine out here. He didn't believe that the battle group could be detected this far from the normal routes. He wanted an uneventful watch and no trouble from the aviators.

Craw kept them at it until Soleck revolted at their fuel state. "Master Chief, I've got to take us in."

Craw cocked his head, invisible behind the pilot. Sometimes you didn't need to be an officer to get a point across. Craw intended to focus young Soleck on his fuel. Really focus him. "One more pass, sir."

"We're at three thousand pounds right now, Master Chief!"

"One more pass." Like a devoted fisherman begging for one more cast.

Soleck turned the plane, grudgingly, the whole crew feeling the pilot's displeasure.

They didn't get a sniff of a sub.

Soleck tried to keep his eyes from the fuel gauge, but he couldn't. He turned them back toward the boat and flew straight for the stack, although the late-afternoon calls meant that they would be the last plane on deck, and it would be dark for their approach. Soleck tried not to worry about a day trap becoming a night trap. He boresighted on the fuel and flew every inch of the distance back to the boat on max conserve, trying to get every last mile out of his fuel. It would be no use telling Stevens that Master Chief had wanted to stay aloft. Not if he dropped one of their two aircraft in the water for lack of fuel. He sweated inside his already clammy flight suit and looked at his fuel gauge every scan he made of the instruments.

Craw, deprived of his prey, fiddled with knobs until the last sonobuoy ran out its battery and sank. He couldn't get a thing, so he switched to ESM gear and searched the ocean for anything that might get him back on his contact. But they were low on fuel and out of buoys, and the TAO wouldn't launch another plane.

He got an ESM hit along a promising vector. He played with it, massaged it, but it was well within parameters for a cell phone. Someone on a fishing boat talking to the beach. It struck him as incongruous, but nothing more.

THE LAST LIGHT OF THE SUNSET OVER AFRICA showed Soleck the boat. He had the fuel to make the landing. It occurred to him that what he didn't have was the fuel to fuck up the landing, but he decided that he couldn't do that to himself and he turned out of the stack and headed for his break, which was not shit hot but was accurate, right over the bridge and into his clearing turn.

Of course, he always did this part well.

He began his turn for the deck, his eyes glued to the fuel gauge. He heard Campbell call the ball and heard a little gasp in the mike as the boat got the full implications of their fuel status, and he knew right then that he'd be standing tall before the CAG whether this worked or not. It was all fine. He looked for his lineup and found that it was right there.

THE LSO WATCHED THE LAST PLANE AND CURSED under his breath, because he wanted the day to be over and he had to deal with one of the worst pilots in the air wing as his last call of the day. And now the stupid bastard had no fuel.

"Fuck him," he muttered. If the idiot went in the water, it was his ass.

On the other hand, Soleck was a stand-up guy and had really been working his buns off, and all the LSOs wanted him to make it. Every one of them felt a little to blame every time he blew a landing.

"Come on, you dickhead," he said gently.

The S-3 floated into its lineup as if a real pilot were at the controls. The LSO crossed his fingers and took a swig of water from his bottle.

"Just stay like that," he whispered.

Half a mile and steady as a rock. At a quarter-mile just seconds later, the wings waggled and the plane seemed to sag, but before the LSO could even think the word "power," the nose was up. The engines sounded *just* right and the whole attitude of the plane screamed *right on the money* as it crossed the stern.

Steady as a rock, Soleck sailed into the three wire at one hundred twenty knots and went to full power as his hook caught.

"Three wire and *okay*!" shouted the LSO over the blast of Soleck's engines. Inside the plane, there was something like a cheer.

Safe on deck, Craw smiled to himself and shook his head.

"Good landing, sir," he said, and pushed past Soleck to get to the ASW shack.

FIFTEEN MINUTES LATER, WHEN SOLECK'S OKAY WAS posted in the ready room, there was another muffled cheer from the Det 424 spaces. Soleck was high on it, ready to high-five the CAG himself, ready to get reamed for being low on gas.

Sixty frames aft, the staff was wrestling with the notion that there was a live submarine with them in this empty ocean.

Whidbey Island.

Alan was in his room at the BOQ, showered, hungry, and missing his wife. He'd have been at dinner, but he was waiting for her phone call. When it came, he started to say something loving, and she rode over him with the words, "I saw a submarine today!"

It made him smile. "You and everybody else. We have a busy undersea Navy."

"It spooked a pod of whales. I was whale-watching, and then, there was this sub." She hesitated. "I guess it was one of ours."

Alan didn't want to talk about it on an open phone. He was waiting for confirmation from SubPac that the hit that Cunnard's plane had made that day was a U.S. sub; he couldn't talk about that. "Whereabouts?" he said.

"We were almost up to the Washington border. That C-12 can fly! I want one."

"Couple million bucks, what the hell. Listen, send me the position of the sighting, will you?"

"Why? I'm sure it—Oh. Okay." She would be thinking of what he had said after his first flight over Bremerton. "I miss you," she said to change the subject.

They started to talk about their kids.

Later, in the officer's mess, he sat alone and thought it through. Submarines don't give people pause, because they can't be seen. In fact, they were a lousy deterrent for just that reason. Then his mind ran down several strands of thought at the same time. He thought about how hard it would be to guard a coast from modern subs, especially if you had no real idea of where to start. He thought of the days of gunboat diplomacy. The Opium Wars in China. The use of gunboats and aircraft carriers as a show of force. And on another tack, he wondered why he had thought *Bremerhaven* every time Rose mentioned *Bremerton*. The brain was an odd animal, he thought. *Two weeks.* Bremerhaven had been the great German base, even as far back as World War I. The base that the hero is watching in *The Riddle of the Sands.* His breath caught in his throat for a moment. Bremerhaven and Opium Wars and submarines. And power projection.

How do you watch a coast to track a modern navy? he asked himself. He had asked Rose that question before, but they hadn't had hits on a submarine that time.

Next morning in the hangar, he sought out a radioman. "Petty Officer Kralik, can you lend me your brain for a second?"

Petty Officer Kralik had a reputation as a radio fanatic, but his lack of a sense of humor hadn't been mentioned. He stared at Alan as if he thought he was really going to hand his brain over. "Uuuh—sure—sir—"

Alan put a slip of paper with the Sleeping Dog bursttransmission specs on it. "What's the range of a set in this frequency? Let's say it's something kind of small, maybe ten, fifteen years out of date."

Kralik stared at the paper without touching it. "Why'd anybody want to use something like that?"

"Well, that isn't the question. Range?"

"From where? I mean, if there's interference—a mountain or something, bad weather—"

Alan wished he'd asked somebody else. "Petty Officer Kralik, with an outfit like this, could I reach a vessel at sea from the coast?"

Kralik stared at the paper. "Yes, sir, if the weather was okay and—how far is the vessel at sea?"

Alan folded the paper and put it back in his pocket. "Thanks very much."

As he was going, Kralik said, "An uplink to a satellite would be lots better, sir. You could reach anywhere in the world with that."

Alan smiled and got out of there.

Near Mogadishu.

The lighter-skinned one shrugged. "That's why we have five boats. One will get through."

"We'll never get close enough to the *Jefferson* to do damage," the dark one muttered. "They have smaller ships with guns, aircraft overhead all the time, satellites!"

"We pick the day. We pick the place. Their smaller ships are far out, defending against missiles and atom bombs—you think they fear five little boats like these? Their airplanes are useless in foul weather. Their satellites are your own superstitious obsession—you told me you believed they could track you wherever you went."

"They can."

The lighter one sighed. "You are a great fool, but beloved of God nonetheless, and I need you. There will be credit in Paradise for the act, and your superstitious idiocy will be forgotten there." He patted the dark man as if he were a beloved dog. "We do this for a great cause. God will not let us fail."

Jakarta.

JERRY PIAT HAD BEEN A DAY AND A NIGHT IN JAKARTA, setting up the interrogation of Bobby Li. He had rented a soggy house in Menteng because Jalan Surabaya was close, and he was using his old cover of antiques dealing. The antiques in the market were mostly fakes, but they gave him a reason for being there and for going in and out. The house itself was almost unlivable, the owner absent in Malaysia, he was told; the absence had been a long one, Piat thought, because the furniture had visible mold and the ceiling of one room was sagging down as if the room above it had filled with water and was going to burst. The house had had pretensions, though, probably at about the time Raffles had been in Indonesia; it had a library, the books—mostly French, some Dutch—blue with mold and the pages stuck together; it had a conservatory, from which most of the glass had fallen, so that it was now part of the outdoors, birds flying in and out of the metal frame and monkeys in residence in the trees that had grown up through it. There was also a formal dining room, what may have been a billiard room, but no billiard table, and six bedrooms and sagging baths and dressing rooms. The kitchen, no longer usable, was below the first floor, the servants' cells in a low building in the back. It was, all in all, a ruin, but Jerry rented it because it had a wall and because it was set a little apart and because this was on his nickel and nobody was providing him with a safe house at government expense.

He hired a petty hustler who was recommended to him by Hilda, the new "missus" at Emmy Lu's. She knew well enough what he used to do and guessed what he was doing now. The hustler brought in two other men, and Jerry thought he should have done this the first time in the Orchid House and not used Bobby Li, but that was the brilliance of hindsight.

The hustler, a taut, insincerely smiling Indonesian with a neck that looked as if it were made out of rope and wire, told Piat to call him Fred.

"Fred isn't your real name, right?" he had said.

"Sure, Fred—good name. You don't like?"

"Fred is fine. Who're your two pals?"

Fred had squinted at them. One was young, scrawny as a free-range chicken. "Bill," Fred said. The other one was thicker, older, angrier, with a scowl like a rapper posing for his first CD cover. "Bud," Fred said.

"Good—Fred, Bill, and Bud. Okay. Fred, you're the boss—after me." He handed out five-dollar bills, said in time-rusted Malay, "A gift to start things right." Then he got them to work in the rented house, clearing the old dining room to the walls and wiping down enough furniture for them to sit on. With Fred, he went out along the Jalan Surabaya and bought cots and a mosquito net and used Tupperware and then set up camp in the living and dining rooms. By then, Bud had brought a hibachi from somewhere and set it up in the former garden and was grilling either dog or rabbit, Piat never asked which. Rabbit, he thought, from the hairs that stuck to the meat.

"Every day, bring in food for five people," Jerry said to Fred. "Good food, okay? Don't make anybody sick. Anybody gets sick, I'll tell the missus, okay?"

"Okay, okay, good food." Fred held out his hand for

money. Piat counted out bills, resigned to watching his own money go. Not like the days when it was Uncle's. Maybe he could get Marv Helmer to reimburse him somehow.

Next day, a woman was cooking over the hibachi and three naked kids were running around outside the collapsing servants' quarters. "No problem," Fred said, seeing Piat's frown. Piat was weighing the advantage of a woman and kids as cover against the danger that comes with letting too many people get too close. "Okay," he had said, and added in Malay, "if they ever come into the house, all of you are done, and I will tell the missus. Yes?" Fred had nodded, said "Yes," and gone on hissing "yes yes yes yesssss—" as he walked away.

Hilda also put him on to somebody to partner with him in the interrogation. Piat had had some idea that he would pick up somebody who was also ex-Agency, even somebody he could trust, but a day of looking and asking questions left him defeated. Ex-Agency ODs didn't wind up on the loose in Indonesia, except for Piat, it seemed; these days, they were making good money telling CEOs how to keep from getting their asses shot off. He had gone back to Hilda then, who had sat with him in the spy's corner for old times' sake and had a drink that he thought she didn't really want and in fact didn't drink.

"Lost your taste for it?" Piat had said.

"It's excess calories."

He groaned aloud. "Hilda, what's happened to you?"

"I'm not a whore anymore. I can tell the truth, okay?" She patted his hand. "I can get one of the girls, if you want."

"No, I need advice. The hell with nostalgia." He gulped down his drink and ordered another. He told her what he needed: a Westerner, preferably American, who knew how things were done. Ex-cop would be okay. Maybe ex-mil. Male. (Bobby Li wouldn't take a woman seriously.)

She thought about it and said what he already knew, that she didn't think there were any Americans around like that. Maybe a Brit or an Australian. She didn't like Australians, it turned out, something about the way they treated her girls. She didn't explain. Hilda wasn't much given to explaining things. She lit a cigarette and checked out three Asian men at the bar and nodded some message to the bouncer, and then she said, "There's a fella named Derek, or that's what he calls himself. Pretty good-looking guy, something not quite right about him, though, you know? Always moving house. Always got a couple of girls taking care of him. Different girls at different times; he has a lot of them. Told me a lot of crap about being in Interpol. Then another time he'd been a consultant to the Tokyo police. Actually, I think he's a Russian doper."

"Russian." Jerry hadn't expected a Russian. If the guy was Russian. "A pro?"

Hilda had shrugged. "Ask him yourself." She smiled. "He's looking for work. He's *always* looking for work. He comes in, supposedly to see the girls, and what he really wants is to convince me that I need a security consultant."

Piat ran Derek down in a squat in Sunda Kelapa. Piat didn't see it himself but knew it had to be pretty bad, just from the location. Fred had simply shaken his head when Piat had told him about it. Still, Fred had sent Bill with a message, and a note had come back telling Mister Bose (Piat's operational name) to meet him at the bar of the Aston. The Aston was a five-star hotel—pretty cheeky for a guy who was living in Jakarta's worst slum.

Still, he looked good, sitting at a table away from the bar—a good-looking man, as Hilda had said, not quite a blond, six feet, a bit gaunt. Wearing a double-breasted blazer that looked wonderful at a distance and up close had noodle stains on one lapel and shiny edges to the cuffs, with shirt cuffs under it that were fraying. Something in his cheekbones and the eyes said he might, indeed, be Russian.

"Tell me about yourself," Piat said.

"So much to tell." Derek gave him a big smile. "Which story would you like?"

"The one about being in the SVRR."

That registered but wasn't necessarily a direct hit. "What makes you think I'm Russian?" Derek said.

"Hilda."

"Ah, the missus." Derek stubbed out a Chinese cigarette and touched his glass to suggest that he'd have another. Piat waved at the waiter and studied Derek. There *was* something wrong with him. He was a loser, that was what was wrong, Piat decided. One of those people with a knack for screwing up, probably because he couldn't look beyond the end of his own nose to see what the consequences of his actions would be. Plus he was older than Piat had at first thought, maybe as old as Piat himself, although the mannerisms and the expressions tried to seem younger. Maybe *were* younger, because he'd never grown up.

"I'm looking for somebody to do some work for me," Piat said, "but I need to know who he is. Let's cut the crap. Who are you?"

"What makes you think I'll tell you the truth?"

"Okay. That does it." Piat got up. "Enjoy the free drinks."

He'd gotten almost to the door before Derek caught up with him. Derek didn't do charmingly contrite very well. He was panicking, Piat thought, losing his cool. They stood in the doorway, with Derek's hand on Piat's sleeve. Piat said, "You going to cut the crap?"

"Okay, okay."

Some bullying and some more Scotch revealed that Derek was a small-time SVRR recruit who had spied on his buddies in the Russian army and then had been put undercover, where he had sold out both the SVRR and the Russian mafia, so now they were both after him. Derek had nothing to recommend him except that he was available, and Piat needed a stooge.

So, for three hundred dollars, he was hiring a two-time loser when what he wanted was a pro he could trust. Goodbye trust, good-bye security, good-bye help. Now Piat would have to do the interrogation alone, with this Russian clown stomping in on cue and shouting and getting the hell out again, and that was all he could be used for.

Piat raised his whiskey glass. "If you go one step over the line, I'll get on the cell phone to my old pal Dmitri at the Russian embassy, and you'll be toast. Understood?"

Derek's panicky eyes said that he, too, knew that the local Russian SVRR honcho was named Dmitri.

Piat left Derek to mull that over and went to a pharmacy

to buy an empty syringe, which he thought he'd need if Bobby Li didn't want to talk.

Washington.

Dukas picked his way down wallpapered corridors, between tables, through doorways, getting lost once before he remembered the route to the old pantry behind what, in the eighteenth century, had been the kitchen fireplace. This was Menzes's hangout at the Annex—the Hole.

Dukas collapsed into an armchair. "I'm late."

Menzes nodded. He was a lean, fit man who always wore short-sleeved white shirts and a crisp necktie; in his mid-forties, he looked as if he could run marathons or climb mountains. "How you been?" he said. "Beer?"

"I been shot and put back together, but I was going to be fine until I got this Sleeping Dog mess from you guys. Yeah, Corona."

"Mess?"

"It stinks. Did you know it stinks?"

Menzes tried to look startled. He was a terrible liar.

Dukas started to lunge across the table, felt pain in his wound, and straightened. "I need a favor."

"Do I owe you one?"

"You still got the Shreed file open?"

"I'll be retired when they close it. What's the favor?"

Dukas's beer appeared. He let the waitress pour it for him, because she was pretty and his chest hurt. When she was gone, he said, "I understand you've got Ray Suter, Shreed's assistant."

Menzes held up a hand. "No. N-O. Nothing to say, zero—end of conversation."

"Hey, all I—"

"No!" Menzes could be a hardnose. "Not negotiable. Find another subject."

"How about money? You willing to talk about money?"

"In general? In general, I like it."

"In particular, what's with Shreed and money? When

Craik and I caught up with him, he was babbling about money."

"No comment."

"What the hell! Hey, Menzes, it's me—I *caught* George Shreed! I'm a special agent of the Naval Criminal Investigative Service! I have a clearance!"

"No comment."

Dukas opened his mouth, realized that he looked foolish, closed it. He drank some beer, watched the pretty waitress serve somebody else, and got a smile from her in return. "About the favor," he said. "I need a dead file from Ops."

"Our Ops?"

"Well, whose else, for Christ's sake! Yes, your Ops, the jewels of the Crystal Palace."

"Make a request."

"I'm making a request! Jesus, Carl, what's with you to-day? Give a little, will you?"

Menzes had on a serious face. He picked at the label on his own bottle. "We did you a favor already."

"I must have missed it."

"The case we sent you."

"Sleeping Dog—that was a *favor*? That was the result of a fucking court order!" Menzes was frowning, but his too-honest face showed something—unusual interest? A kind of intellectual greed? Dukas decided to take a chance. "You hear about my guy getting shot at in Jakarta?"

Menzes's frown lessened. "That was you?"

"Craik. What'd you hear?'

"A report, then some bad jokes from some of the Ops guys. State was upset. That was *you*?"

"That was Sleeping Dog, buddy—the favor you guys did me."

Now Menzes was really interested. He pushed the beer bottle aside and leaned toward Dukas. "Tell me. We sent you the case; we have an interest."

"Unh-unh. The case got folded into Crystal Insight, which is open and ongoing and eyes-only."

"That's the Shreed case. That's over."

"The case is not over."

"Why?"

"Figure it out."

They sat there, two stubborn men, glaring at each other. Menzes, Dukas could see, was thinking. Menzes's eyes closed slightly; his hands tightened. He said, "Did you find something in Sleeping Dog that kept Crystal Insight open?"

"Bingo."

"What?"

Menzes was too eager. It was the eagerness that tipped Dukas off, and all at once, he got it. "You guys sent me Sleeping Dog as a ploy, you sonofabitch!" He was laughing, not entirely pleasantly. "What the hell! I wondered why my friend in Internal Investigations called me about an operational case—and now I get it. You're investigating something about Sleeping Dog yourself!"

"Don't go there, Mike."

"I'm already there! You sent it to me because—what?" He was working it out as he talked. "Because of something in the case? No, because it's old and it's ready for the shit can? No, no—you're suspicious *because it was being sent to me.* Right? I can see it in your face; I'm right. Anybody ever tell you you got a face like a light-up sign? Jesus, Carl, you set me up!"

"I didn't set you up; that isn't the way it was."

"Oh, yeah? What way was it?"

Menzes began picking at the label again. Dukas leaned in and tapped the table. "This isn't right, Menzes. You give a little to get a little. You're not playing by the rules!"

"The rules say I don't share information!"

"Yeah, and if we followed that rule, nothing would ever get done. Come on—you tell me what you're investigating in Sleeping Dog, and I'll tell you what's what with the Jakarta thing. Come *on!*"

Menzes shook his head. "Can't. Tell me what the favor you want from me is—I swear I'll do my best for you on that."

Dukas stared at him as if he were his worst enemy. He stood up. "Enjoy my beer," he said, and walked out.

•   •   •

BACK AT THE NCIS OFFICES, LESLIE HAD A LONG TELE-
phone chat with the agent in Florida who had interviewed the
maverick. In fact, the phone call plunged right through telephone flirtation and got on course for telephone sex, which
Leslie saw coming and headed off. Still, the guy down there,
who sounded at least forty and married, mentioned flying up
some time and getting together, which Leslie greeted with
wild laughter and a pretense that she hadn't heard him right.
He did, at any rate, fax her a report on the interview.

The maverick was a Marine officer who apparently
thought that his time at the Ranch had been a hoot, and his
having been bounced even more of one. What came through
the interview for Leslie was a kind of tougher Tom Cruise—
she saw much of the world in terms of movies, the rest in
terms of TV—with no tolerance for Mickey Mouse and a
great love of problem-solving.

A perfect intel officer, she told herself, although she knew
almost nothing of intel officers. She began to script the movie
version as she read the fax, seeing the handsome young Marine
pissing off the ancient gasbags at the Ranch, being disgraced
by being kicked out, then pursuing the source of the burst transmissions in Seattle on his own and, in the final shootout, killing
the master spy who reported on American Navy ships—

Because that was what the Marine officer had found. Navy
ships. He had compared the burst transmissions with Navy
sailings and got a better than fifty-percent correlation with
submarines and carriers, and he had made a separate report
of that and sent it through his instructors at the Ranch. And
then he had got bounced.

Poor guy. The injustice of it burned Leslie. More seriously,
it clashed with her knowledge of the files, because she knew
there was no report there on any correlation between the
transmissions and ship-sailings in Sleeping Dog. Even so, she
checked the index again. And then she thought about what
Mike Dukas would want her to do. Dukas was gone for the
day. Surely this was *important.* Surely the little lecture he'd
given her about going by the book couldn't apply to a situation like this.

She called Dick Triffler in Seattle—on Dukas's STU,

guided only by her memory of watching him use it. Triffler was out, but she left a message that an important classified fax was coming. "Mister Triffler, this is Leslie Kultzke in Mister Dukas's office. He's away just now, but we have something I think you ought to see really quick. So I'm faxing it to you. Please pay attention. Thank you (which came out as *Thannkewwww*)."

Then she had to go up the hall and ask Claire Sandow how to send a secure fax.

TRIFFLER TRIED TO GET ALAN AS SOON AS HE READ the fax. Alan was flying, so they didn't talk until that evening. When Alan heard of the correlation between the transmissions and the sailings, he whooped. "I've got it! I've got it!"

"It's only fifty percent, Alan—"

"If the Navy wouldn't let him in on classified sailings, we're lucky it was that high. Dick, this is great! I see it—I really see it—there's somebody monitoring sailings out of Bremerton, maybe by eye, maybe on a JOTS terminal. Jesus, do we have a spy in the Navy, too?—and he's sending data on sailings in bursts—whoosh, they're outta here."

"You think the Navy wouldn't have caught that years ago?"

"How do we know Shreed wasn't the one who pulled the plug on it? Dick, we need to find out if Shreed was in this somehow."

"But sending the data where? That radio—"

"Would reach deep water. Think *deep* water, Dick."

Triffler thought about Russian trawlers, passing cargo ships. Then he got it. "A sub?"

Alan whooped again. "He got it—I think he really got it—!" Moments later, more soberly, Alan said, "We've got to catch him at it."

"Oh, yeah, great idea."

Alan cackled like a movie fiend. "I have a plan."

Triffler didn't see what it all meant yet—submarines weren't his line—but he knew that if something had been important enough to remove from the Sleeping Dog file, it was important enough for them to take seriously. He didn't try to work out how burst transmissions and submarines correlated; that was Alan's to do. What he was working on was suppressed information in a CIA file.

He sent a fax back to Dukas: *"Find out if George Shreed had control of Sleeping Dog."*

Jakarta.

BOBBY LI HAD GONE TO GROUND, PROBABLY EVER
since the mess at the Orchid House, Jerry thought. He was
certainly hiding from somebody, maybe Jerry himself, maybe
whoever else he worked for. He wasn't in his office; he wasn't
in his apartment. He didn't answer phone calls. Piat got him
in the simplest way possible: He sent him a signal for an es-
sential meeting, not just some casual meeting, but a make-or-
break meeting, the kind an agent would pass up only if he
intended never to make contact again.

And Li showed up. Piat thought he might run, afraid of
exactly what was about to happen, but he didn't really expect
it: Li wanted to be a good dog, not a renegade. Anyway, where
would he run? His life was here, and part of that life was the
stable, long-term relationship with his friend Andy. He'd gone
to ground out of instinct, Jerry thought, but he wasn't ready
to break away from his friend. They went back.

The meeting was in the Dreamland Park at Ancol, the
times at twenty after eleven, one, and four, but Piat had never
known Bobby Li to miss a first meeting time. He put Fred

near the gate to the aquatic show and Bud across the way near a much-frequented toilet, and when Bobby Li appeared, strolling down toward them with a Philippine noodle cake in his hand, Piat nodded at them and made sure they knew who the target was. Just in case. Then he checked for surveillance, making doubly sure, because he really believed now that Bobby had another master, and then he stepped out of the shade of a banyan tree.

Bobby saw him but didn't acknowledge him and went on up the curving concrete walkway, taking big bites from the noodle cake and wiping sauce from his fingers on a paper napkin. When he got to a bright magenta trash container, he finished the noodle cake, licked his fingers, wiped them on the napkin, and dropped the napkin into the trash. Then he turned and grinned.

"Nice day for Dreamland," he said. "You American?"

"Just visiting. Yeah, nice place." He came closer. "Let's walk."

"Okay, okay. Anybody sees us, I'm checking you out on the sights of Ancol. You looking good, Andy. Nice shirt, way cool. What's up?"

They walked along the waterfront, moving from shade-patch to shade-patch because it was already hot and muggy. Over his shoulder, Jerry saw Fred behind them. Bud pushed past like a man trying to find the john, then fell in a dozen paces in front of them. "Anybody following you these days, Bobby?" Piat was still spooked by the Orchid House mess.

"Me? No. Why anybody want to follow me?"

"We need to talk, Bobby. Good, long talk."

"Okay, sure. I can clear couple hours later this P.M."

"I want you to call your wife and tell her you're going to be away for a couple of days."

He felt Bobby's pace falter, as if he'd given a little skip; he actually turned his head and looked back, and Jerry knew that he'd made Fred and Bud, probably had as soon as they'd started walking. "I don't get it," Bobby said.

"We're going to talk. You know how it goes."

"Andy, I tole you everything about everything. If you

pissed off with me about that time at the Orchid House, I tole you, I was as surprise as anybody. Honest to God, Andy."

"Don't make it hard, Bobby. Okay?" Piat moved deeper into the shade of a ginkgo whose big leaves lay on the concrete like open hands. He leaned against the spotted gray bark, willing Bobby to follow him and to take out his cell phone. Ahead, Bud stopped, pretending to stare out to sea, and Fred had pulled into the shade, one tree back. Bobby flipped open his cell phone.

"Keep it short," Piat said. "Slowly, Bobby, so I can follow." Bobby's wife was Straits Chinese and they spoke a lot of Malay between themselves. Bobby called and said in Malay, "Tell lady-boss 'Tiger shrimp are in the market.' Just like that—'Tiger shrimp are in the market.' Say it again. Good." He put the cell phone in his shirt pocket.

They walked on up the dockside avenue and went out by the eastern gate and Bud flagged down a taxi, and all four of them got in.

Whidbey Island.

With a few minutes to spare on Monday evening, Alan leaned forward over the JOTS terminal, one arm on either side of the screen. A few years ago these things had been two-color monitors with confusing graphics, and now this one repeater in the base intel center was a full-color guide to most of the operational units in the Navy and their current locations and activities.

All over the world, ships and planes moved through their respective elements, scouting their surroundings with electronic widgets and human eyes, looking for potential adversaries. When they reported, the report was tagged and placed on this machine and repeated throughout the world to every other machine.

Alan thought that they were like crystal balls, as long as the viewer only sought to see the Navy. He could watch the USS *Carl Vinson* conducting workups out in the local operational area, with pilots doing their qualification traps and launches. Someone out there was running an exercise to detect shipping, because a scattering of merchant ships had been entered as "white" or neutral contacts. He leaned back and took a sip of coffee. One of the planes on the terminal was Surfer's, going out to the boat to run up some quick landings.

He spun the roller ball idly, moving the cursor slowly across the Pacific, noting the movement of Seventh Fleet assets in the Pacific, watching BG12 while they were conducting an exercise in the Philippine Sea. He kept moving west around the world, looking at contacts in the Strait of Malacca that had been entered by a Canadian frigate bound for UN duty off East Timor. He sipped more coffee and flew west toward the Indian Ocean until he found the symbol he wanted, the USS *Thomas Jefferson*. He rested the cursor on her and read her course and speed, right down on the equator and steaming north at a solid twenty knots. He thought of his men and women, their detachment, about Paul Stevens and Soleck and the CAG, Rafe Rafehausen. The circle on the screen and the names were enough to cause a lump in his throat.

He noticed that there was a neutral/hostile submarine symbol in the water a dozen miles aft of the carrier. His interest immediately piqued, he took an unconscious slug of coffee and clicked on the symbol to see it resolve into a three-hour-old possible contact. He started to dismiss it and then saw the contact assignment.

Craw. Not a man to make mistakes.

He sat bathed in the bright glow of the electronic Indian Ocean, and thought.

Then he picked up the phone and called U.S. Submarine Forces Pacific.

Jakarta.

The house in Menteng scared Bobby Li. He told Jerry Piat it was a bad place and he didn't want to go in. His face appealed to Piat to let him off. Bobby was a very clean man, and the house looked like shit even to Piat, who didn't have Bobby's standards, but he simply stood by the rusting gate and waited until Fred and Bud had herded Bobby inside, never touching him, but giving him nowhere else to go. Bobby looked around the jungle that had been the garden and darted a scared look at Jerry.

"You know how this goes," Piat said. He wondered if, in fact, Bobby did know how it went. If George Shreed had never really vetted him, and nobody else had later, maybe Bobby had never been through this particular mill. He almost said, *It won't be too bad,* but he knew he mustn't give comfort yet.

Piat had put two chairs in the dining room with one of the cots. They sat Bobby Li in a chair, a straight wooden one with an elaborately carved, open back, probably one of the old dining set. His hands were trembling.

"You want to pee?" Piat said. "Better do it now."

Fred led him out of the room, and a minute later Piat heard the only working toilet in the house flush. It didn't work very well: You had to dump a bucket of water, brought from a tap in the yard, into the bowl. Bobby Li came back, wiping his hands on his pants. "This place is disgusting," he said. For Bobby Li, that was open rebellion.

"It grows on you." Piat was standing by one of the tall windows that looked out on the jungle. "Sit down, Bobby." He walked around behind him, and Bobby's head followed like an owl's, afraid that Piat was going to do something. Piat said, "Bobby, this is a friendly interrogation. I'm just clearing the air here. There's been some confusion about some things, and we need to talk and clear the air."

"We still frands?" There was pathos in the voice. Bobby had always said that they were "best frands."

"Absolutely. But you have to tell me the truth, or—" Piat came around in front of him. "Tell me what happened in the Orchid House."

"I already tole you. It's just like I tole you."

"Tell me again."

They went around it twice. Bobby had clearly been rehearsing his story. He had new details—the color jacket one of the shooters had worn, the size of the gun the American had used in shooting the dead man—"Big! Goddam big like a Colt, man!"

"You didn't tell me that before."

"I remember it at home. I wake up sweatin', Andy, thinkin' about it."

"The dead guy was shot with a .32, Bobby."

"No, big Colt or something." Bobby's eyes went dim and hopeless.

"Cops took .32 slugs out of him."

Bobby was breathing shallowly. He tried to hold Jerry's eyes but couldn't. The early-afternoon sun was coming through the tall windows, right into Bobby's eyes. He put up a hand and tried to see Piat. "The cops are wrong, Andy. Jakarta cops, they lie alla time. Anyways, Colt comes in .32."

Piat looked at him, let the look extend, grow heavy. "I'm really disappointed in you, man. There's a photo of you shooting the guy, Bobby."

"No way!"

"You've got the gun, and it's firing, and the guy is turned back toward you. He's wearing a gray suit and you're wearing a maroon jacket and you're shooting him."

Bobby licked his lips. "They fake photos alla time." He licked his lips again, then again. "I saw a photo, Marilyn Monroe fucking George Washington, all fake. You saw a fake, Andy." He licked his lips and then got up and ran once halfway around the room and threw up. Piat thought that this was as good a time as any, and he pushed a bell-button under his chair and—late, not right on cue; he'd been dozing off or something—Derek came through the big door and closed it behind him and stood there. That part he did well, Piat thought. Derek was something of an actor. He came through the door, saw Bobby still bent over, folded his arms, and stared at the small man. "What's he said?" he demanded.

"He's getting to it."

"What has he *said*? I want results."

"It's okay. He's coming around to it."

"What's the puke about?"

"He's scared."

"He goddam well better be."

Bobby Li was looking at Derek, then at Piat, then back at Derek. Derek paid no attention to him. It was as if Bobby weren't there. Derek was really pretty good at this. "I told you, he ponies up or else."

"It'll be fine, Jack. Just give us time, will you?"

"I haven't got time!"

"This is very emotional for him, Jack. Back off, okay?"

"Whose ass is it here? Who do you think gets reamed if he doesn't talk? *Get it from him and get it now, or else!*"

Derek, a.k.a. Jack, who had never left the doorway, yanked the door open and walked out, and the door slammed like a gunshot. Piat called Bill in from what had been a pantry, and he got a filthy plastic bucket and some rags and handed them to Bobby Li, who had to get on his knees and clean up his vomit. Piat waited by the window, looking out into the green heat, thinking that he was a manipulating shit and feeling sorry for the little man. But he wasn't going to stop.

When they were back in the chairs, Piat said, "See, I have my problems, too, Bobby."

"Yeah, yeah, I see. I understand, Andy. He your boss?"

"Never mind him."

"What's he mean, no time?"

"Don't worry about it. Just focus on telling me the truth. Okay? Will you do that?"

Bobby Li nodded.

"Tell me what happened in the Orchid House. The truth."

Washington.

Fourth Circuit Associate Justice Bryan Coll lived in Potomac, Maryland, out where the houses were big and the owners either had salaries to match or were putting up FOR SALE signs. Dukas and Pat Feisel, the NCIS lawyer, dragged themselves out there at eleven P.M. because Justice Coll had agreed to hear Dukas's application on an expedited basis. Pat Feisel was not happy.

"Coll's a D.C. operator," she said. "He wants to get on the Supreme Court and he likes to live high, which does *not* include letting riffraff into his house in the middle of the night. He's conscientious; he's hard-nosed; he can be very bad-tempered.

He pals around with a lot of ultras who keep telling him he's brilliant."

"Ultras?"

"Conservatives. He's the Scalia of the Fourth District. Don't even hint at anything about affirmative action or abortion. No Clinton jokes, either—his sense of humor can't keep up with his moral outrage. Stay with national security, which he treats with holy reverence. Don't diss the Agency. Pray."

"Who's going to do the talking, you or me?"

"This is 'in chambers,' so he's going to talk to both of us. There'll be a steno. Don't say anything you'll regret reading in a transcript later."

There was a curving drive from a brick gateway up to a huge front door, but they didn't go in there. "Keep going—he said 'around the side,' " the lawyer said.

"Servants' entrance?"

"Don't make smart remarks, okay?"

There was a porte cochere on a side drive that led off into the darkness and, presumably, a garage or perhaps several garages. Dukas saw the reflected taillights of another car and guessed that Menzes and his legal people were already there. He was right: Inside, an Asian woman led them over carpeted floors, past muted lights on tables whose wood shone with polish, to a paneled door. Behind it, Associate Justice Coll waited with a stenographer, Carl Menzes, a lawyer from the Agency, and somebody else who only later turned out to be a high-ranker from the CIA Ops Directorate. Nobody looked friendly. Off to the side, a wan man in a too-big suit looked as if all were lost already: Ronald Welbert, Nickie Groski's court-appointed attorney. Dukas had had only five minutes on the telephone with him, and all he had really learned was that Welbert hadn't seen his client in twenty-six days.

Associate Justice Coll was late-middle-aged, chunky, with terrific black eyebrows, maybe an Irish jock who'd played halfback at Holy Cross and stayed in shape. In fact, he had; he was still the terror of a weekend touch-football league. He was wearing slacks and slippers and a dark cardigan sweater over a turtleneck. His first words were, "It's half-past eleven, and I want you guys out by midnight."

Coll sat behind a desk that had once been a pine country table and now shone like mahogany. Dukas took in a wall of bookshelves, brass lamps, colored prints of fishing and shooting—a gentleman's study of perhaps a hundred years ago. The justice introduced them, with quick explanations of their presence, except for the senior Ops man, and turned to the NCIS lawyer. "You representing NCIS? Is it Miss or Missus? FEI-sel or Fei-SEL? Okay, shoot." He ignored Welbert.

She gave it to him quickly and a little breathlessly: national security, continuing case named Crystal Insight, suspicion of tampering with files.

"Mister Dukas, you're the special agent in charge of the case?"

"Yes, sir."

"What's the relevance of Nickie Groski? That's a different case."

"He's part of Crystal Insight. He was in at the end, when George Shreed fled the country."

"So?"

"I believe that Nickie Groski can tell us more about Shreed and what he was trying to do at the end."

"But Shreed isn't the focus of your investigation, is he? Shreed is Mister Menzes's focus." Menzes nodded; his lawyer nodded; the well-dressed smoothie who would turn out to be an Ops Directorate heavy hitter glowered.

Dukas, who had been given a chair that was too straight and hard for him, leaned in toward the judge. "Your Honor, I apprehended George Shreed in Pakistan as part of my investigation. Mister Menzes and the Agency weren't there."

Menzes's lawyer started to cluck like a chicken, and Coll waved him silent. He was leaning back, his hands folded over his gut. "You have a problem with the Agency, Mister Dukas?"

Pat Feisel jumped in. "I think Mister Dukas means that pursuing Shreed *was* the focus of his investigation, Your Honor. He took a bullet making the arrest."

The justice nodded, scowled. "Mister Menzes, how come your people weren't in on that arrest?"

"That isn't relevant," the Agency lawyer made the mistake of saying.

Coll looked at him with bright, hard eyes. "I wouldn't advise you to tell many judges that their questions are irrelevant, or you'll have a short career. Mister Menzes?"

That was the way it went. Coll was on the Agency's side, but he didn't like uppity lawyers. They wrangled; Dukas asked that the Agency people leave while he explained Sleeping Dog to the judge; objections bounced around the room like handballs.

"Give me one justification for not letting them sit in," Coll growled.

Dukas hesitated. "I don't object so much to Mister Menzes. Can I ask who the other gentleman is?"

Coll looked at the as-yet-unidentified man and nodded to him. The man never looked at Dukas as he said that he was Deputy Assistant Director for Operational Planning in the Operations Directorate of the Central Intelligence Agency.

"You got a name?" Dukas growled.

"Mister Dukas! I ask the questions." Coll looked toward the Ops powerhouse.

"Clyde Partlow," the presence said. An organizational chart clicked into place in Dukas's brain: George Shreed's boss, or equal—the organizational chart was deliberately vague. Where had he heard the name recently? He looked at Menzes and it came back: Shreed's funeral, Menzes saying, *I thought Partlow might come, but he didn't have the balls.*

Then they wrangled some more, and the judge ruled that the Agency people could stay, but Welbert had to leave. Pro bono lawyers in cheap suits weren't cleared. Pat Feisel wormed an assurance from Menzes that they'd leave Sleeping Dog to NCIS, but Dukas was thinking that Clyde Partlow hadn't given any such assurance. Dukas thought he saw what had happened: CIA Operations had taken Nickie Groski and all or a lot of the Shreed case away from Menzes and Internal Affairs. What he was seeing was the aftershock of an internal CIA battle. No wonder Menzes was behaving as if Dukas were an untouchable. Dukas said, "I didn't hear Mister Partlow signing on to this agreement, Your Honor."

Partlow cleared his throat. "In the interests of national security, Your Honor, I'm really not at liberty to make any such offers. However, Mister Dukas can rest assured that I understand discretion."

Coll shared a look with Partlow and said to Dukas, "You'll have to settle for that, Mister Dukas. Speak now or let us all go to bed."

And so Dukas told them about the Chinese Checkers comm plan and Jakarta, but not about the E-mails from Rathunter, which he didn't want Clyde Partlow to have, because he could see which way the wind was blowing. Ops must have Nickie the Hacker's computer files as well as Nickie himself, he thought, and, primitive as the Agency was in its understanding of computers, it would be trying to winkle out what Shreed had done in his last days—and to use that knowledge to stage its own operation. If Partlow got wind of Rathunter, the Agency would be all over him.

Partlow said, "Mister Dukas is on a fishing expedition."

The Agency lawyer whispered fiercely to Partlow and then stood and said, "We're absolutely opposed to letting Special Agent Dukas talk to Nickie Groski, Your Honor. Our mandate is to protect the interests of the United States."

"By denying a kid his constitutional rights?" Dukas said.

"That's a lie!" The lawyer raised his voice. He was earning his money. "This young man is being held in an entirely appropriate way!"

"So that his lawyer can't even see him?"

"That's a law-enforcement matter. He's been charged in four separate jurisdictions. Your Honor, we are not responsible if there's been slippage in the system."

Pat Feisel was on her feet. "Your Honor, may I ask a legal question?"

Coll gave her a grim smile. "I'd be *grateful* for a legal question."

"Your Honor, I don't understand the Agency's standing here. The Groski boy has been charged with two local violations and with violation of *federal* parole, which was an FBI matter. The Central Intelligence Agency has no standing, as I understand the Enabling Act, to arrest or detain within the borders of the United States."

There was silence. The Agency lawyer glanced at Partlow.

Something like a bitter smile passed over Menzes's face. Dukas gave Pat Feisel a surprised look. Coll fiddled with something on his desk and then looked up and said, "The Agency's interest is legal under the Enabling statute, Missus Feisel."

"And detention?"

"I'm not aware that detention is at issue here. Your application is to lift my ban on communication."

"Your Honor, we can't communicate with a boy we can't locate!"

"But that's a different issue. Don't push me, Missus Feisel."

Another silence fell. Pat Feisel exchanged a look with Dukas, who started to say that detention goddamned well was the issue, and her look shut him up. Instead, she said, "Your Honor, could we have Mister Welbert back? I think what he has to say is relevant here."

Coll looked at his watch and started to say something, and Dukas knew what it was—that there was no point in having Welbert in, because he was ready to rule—but Coll made a face and waved at the door. He leaned back and looked resigned, as if assuring both the reality and the appearance of justice was a strain. Dukas went to the door and waved Welbert in, and he came in with a walk that other people must have made fun of all his life, hitting his feet too hard on the floor, his arms hanging from his drooped shoulders as if he were carrying Willy Loman's sample cases. Pat Feisel murmured to him.

"Can I speak?" Welbert said.

"The very reason you're here," Coll said with something that was not quite a sneer. He gave Welbert's suit a disapproving look up and down.

"Your Honor, I was appointed by the Prince George's County Superior Court to represent Nickie Groski on two charges, conspiracy to commit murder and association with known criminals. Later—"

"Make it short, Counselor; it's late."

"His mother asked me to represent him on all the charges, that's all."

"What's the point?"

"I represent him in four jurisdictions. I haven't seen him

in more than three weeks." Welbert couldn't keep a whine out of his voice.

"Whose fault is that?"

"Your Honor, I can't *find* him! They're keeping him some-place."

"Who's keeping him?"

"The government."

"Mister, mmm, Welbert, you're taking up our time. What's your *point*?"

"Your Honor, I want to be allowed to see my client!"

"Well, I suggest you start with a court that has jurisdiction. The subject tonight is whether I lift my gag order on Nickie Groski, and what you're saying isn't relevant. Now, your last chance—have you got anything to say relevant to Mister Dukas's request?"

"I support an application for habeas corpus, Your Honor."

"Well, find yourself a court to file it in." Coll slapped a hand on his desk. "Mister Dukas, your application is denied." He checked his watch. "We're fifteen minutes over."

WHEN THEY WERE OUTSIDE IN THE WARM NIGHT, Dukas saw Menzes as only a dark shape down by his car. He was being read out by the other two from the Agency. Dukas couldn't make out the words but he got the outraged tone of their whispers. He walked to his own car and said to Pat Feisel, "You want to chew me out?"

"No, you done good."

They both listened to the harangue for a few seconds more, and then the men seemed to run out of rage, and they wandered off into the dark, presumably to other cars. Dukas said to Mrs. Feisel, "Hold on a second."

He walked down to Menzes, who was leaning against his car with his blazer draped over his folded arms. Dukas said, "We need to talk."

Menzes nodded. "What's this shit about faked documents in an Agency file?"

"What's this shit about you guys holding a kid for a month without his lawyer getting to him?"

"Not me."

"Those two?" Dukas jerked his head toward the darkness.

Menzes shifted his weight and arched his back as if it hurt. "The Constitution applies in every case except when we say the country's threatened. God help civil liberties if we ever take a real whack from somebody." He shook his head. "I'm pretty down, Mike."

"Can you be at my office at seven in the morning?"

"Don't you ever sleep?" Menzes tossed his coat into the car. One of the cars started in the darkness and then the other, and the two men watched as the headlights bored toward them, so bright they had to turn their heads away. Menzes watched the red taillights disappear. "Ever have the feeling you're on the wrong side?" he said. "The fix is in, man—the fix is in. I'll tell you in the morning."

Dukas got into his own car and sat next to Pat Feisel without turning the key. "Who overrules Coll?" he said.

"Court of Appeals."

"Welbert's got the right idea—application for habeas corpus on Nickie Groski. First thing in the morning."

"Unh-unh." She wiggled in the seat, pulled her skirt down from behind. "You got to go in with power to do that. I can't do it."

"Who can?"

She saw that he was serious. "You'd have to fight the Agency toe-to-toe. NCIS can't do that. The Navy can. You'd have to go all the way to the CNO."

Dukas started the car. "Watch me." He slitted his eyes, his right hand on the gearshift. "Think the FBI would like to join us in suing the CIA?"

Jakarta.

Piat had Derek wake Bobby a little after midnight by shining a big flashlight in his face and then shouting at him. The house was dead-black inside, no electricity, and when the light went on, bugs headed in every direction. Once he'd shut up and gone out and slammed the door again, the only sound in the big room was skittering bugs and Bobby Li, breathing. They'd left the plastic bucket for him to piss in, this fastidious little man who just wanted to be valued as the best agent in the world.

Piat woke him again at three in the morning, shaking his shoulder and marveling that the little man was sleeping so soundly. Bobby Li came to and looked up into the light, and Piat said, "It's Andy," and saw Bobby's frightened face relax a little. "Get up, man."

"It's the middle of the night."

"Time to go to work."

Piat lit a gasoline lantern and put it on the floor near Bobby's chair. The room still smelled of Bobby's being sick and his urine and his sweat. Piat called in Bill and told him to empty the bucket. He gave Bobby a cigarette. "Kind of hard on you, Bobby."

"I know you doin' it for a good reason."

Piat smoked. Bill came back in and put the bucket down, and Piat told him to make tea. Piat took out another cigarette, offering one to Bobby. Bobby's hands were trembling again and he shivered, although it was a hot night. Piat smoked, looked at him, looked away. Finally, he said, "I want to get you through this, Bobby. I want you to come out of it looking good, so we can go right on like always."

"I still be your agent?"

"You bet. That's the deal. You want to be my agent, don't you?"

"I always try real hard, Andy. I try to be the best. I do good work for you, right?"

"Lots of good work."

"You not going to shit-can me?"

"Not if we get through this okay. Understand me?"

Bobby looked at him and then shook his head. "I don't get it. Why you doing this to me, then?"

Piat leaned forward, hitched his chair closer so that they were bent toward each other over the bright light like two conspirators. "A case officer has to be able to trust his agent. You understand that, don't you?"

"Absolutely. You bet."

"If I can't trust you, Bobby, what have I got?"

"You always can trust me, Andy! Always. I do good work! Don't I deliver?"

"What happens if a case officer can't trust his agent?"

"You *can* trust me. I do very best for you!"

"Bobby, Bobby—you lied to me."

"No—"

Bobby was about to tell him that he hadn't *really* lied, Piat knew; he'd be looking for an excuse to lie, right now, even though before they went to sleep, Bobby had admitted, in tears, that he'd shot the guy in the Orchid House and had lied to Piat about it. Piat waited, and Bobby ran his inventive mind over possible excuses, and he said, "I didn't mean to lie, Andy."

"I know."

"I had to."

"Sure."

"See, I was 'tween the rock and the hard place, no way out. Shooting that guy, that was the way out. Nothing against you, honest, Andy—I doing it for you, too, trying to save some of the op, make it work 'cause I know it's important to you. I want to do good work for you!"

"Why did you have to shoot him, Bobby?"

"Well—He say some bad things to me."

"Bobby, if you don't tell me the truth, we can't go back to the way it was. You see? You know how sad that makes me? This isn't my decision, Bobby. This is out of my hands."

"That other guy. He don't like me."

"It's out of my hands. But if you tell me the truth, we can go back to the way it was before. But there's got to be trust. You follow me?"

"Sure, trust. You can always trust me, Andy."

"Bobby, you lied to me."

"Only 'cause I had to."

"Why?"

Bobby's torso was twisted in the hard chair, mostly leaning to his right, but with the shoulders turned back; his legs went the other way, so that he was a kind of human pretzel. Twisting, turning to find a way out, his arms locked around himself to keep from flying apart. "I had to shoot him. He going to kill you otherwise. I save your life, Andy."

"Bobby, you have to tell me the truth. If you go on lying, we're finished."

"I'm telling the truth! Only one time I don't tell the truth, because I have to do something; I got no choice! I tell you, the guy was going to kill you; I shot him to save my friend Andy! That's the truth!"

"Who was the guy?"

"I don' know, just some guy. Making threats."

Piat leaned back in his chair. He studied Bobby Li. He pushed the chair back six inches so there was more space between them, more darkness. "I know who the guy was, Bobby. So do I. I'd rather that you told me yourself who he was. That way, I can tell my boss that you gave me the information yourself. That'll really help, if I can say that you gave up this information yourself. Okay? Come on, Bobby—who was the guy you shot?"

Bobby looked around the darkness for help. "Very bad guy," he said. "Killer."

"Tell me the truth, Bobby. Who was he?"

"I'm telling you the truth!"

"Who was he?"

Bobby had folded himself into a smaller tangle of arms and legs—one foot up under him now, arms still wrapped around his torso, the left side of his face against the carved chair back. He slowly pulled the other leg up until he was curled entirely within the embrace of the chair, and he lay there a long time, his face turned away from the gasoline lantern so that it was deeply shadowed. At last he said, "Chinese guy."

"Okay."

"Some kind of job at Chinese embassy. You know—like, security, or—"

"Okay."

Piat waited. It was easy to wait, his body heavy from fatigue, the night sounds from the old garden peaceful, Bobby

Li shrunken to something like a child. After a long time, Piat
said, "Why'd you have to shoot him?"

Bobby Li didn't move.

"Are you a double agent, Bobby?"

Bobby began to weep.

NCIS HQ, Washington.

DUKAS WAS IN HIS OFFICE AT SIX-THIRTY ON TUES-
day, puffy-eyed, aching. He had bought a pound of coffee at a
7-Eleven and some pastries that he knew he'd regret, and he
made coffee in Triffler's machine, knowing he would never
clean the filter, although he'd promised. Actually, it tickled
him that coffee from a can was trickling through Triffler's
pristine machine, which had never known anything but cus-
tom blend.

At midnight he had called Rose at Edwards, doubting
that she'd be out of her room with flying to be done the next
day. In fact, her line had been busy for an hour—checking on
her kids in Utica, then yakking with Alan in Seattle, she said.
He had finally reached her a little after one, D.C. time.

"Rosie," he'd said, "where do you stand with the CNO?"

"I worked for him until two weeks ago. He was nice to
me."

"I want to see him, *subito*. He know who I am?"

She laughed. "Your name came up several times during
the Shreed thing. Yeah, of course he knows your name. You're

the guy that arrested Shreed, and that's a very big deal to him. You *and* my heroic husband."

"I need him to back me on a play, babe. Get me in to see him. It's big-time legal stuff, so he might as well have the JAG there, too. Can you give him a call?"

Now he glanced at a set of dailies and ambled down the hall and checked CNN. When Menzes came in at seven-twenty, he was almost alive.

He had dragged Triffler's elegant office chair over and put it so that the two of them could talk face-to-face, no bullshit about the power seat or being separated by the desk. After a few meaningless noises about traffic and weather and how early it was, Dukas said, "Are we on the same sheet of music?"

Menzes was drinking from Triffler's cup. He shrugged.

"Who's up first?" Dukas growled.

"I'm hardly awake."

"Okay, I'll start. What was that last night, a charade?"

"A charade, right."

"Tell me about Partlow."

"It's supposed to be Shreed who called Partlow 'The Velvet Fart,' which still sticks to him. Partlow makes a pained face when you mention Shreed—'poor old George,' that kind of crap. He's a politician and a bureaucrat, knows when to dodge and rope-a-dope, wouldn't cut your throat himself but would probably look out the window while he had it done."

"What's he after?"

"Ops—thanks to Partlow—has swept up everything having to do with Shreed. They've taken over this kid, the kid's computer and his files, and a CD-ROM that Al Craik brought back from Pakistan that was supposed to prove Shreed's guilt. I've been told to mind my own business, which I thought the Shreed thing was, and what's coming across the gossip network is that Ops has found evidence that Shreed wasn't a spy and he was a hero, and they're going to sit on the evidence."

"That's bullshit."

"You know that and I know that, but they've got all the stuff. It's only rumor, but—you know. I don't know what they're doing."

"Where's Nickie Groski?"

"No idea. A safe house someplace. Once, I heard a rumor he was at Quantico."

"They're tromping all over the kid's rights."

"Tell me about it."

They sat there and sipped and chewed and Dukas decided to change the subject. "Tell me why you sent me Sleeping Dog. I was right yesterday, right?—you sent it to me *because* you were suspicious of it? What'd you think, I was going to solve it for you?"

Menzes sighed and reached for another pastry. "Mike—do you believe in will? As in, 'America has to show its will, its resolve,' et cetera, et cetera, blah, blah, blah? I don't. Normally. But I have to say, what's going on at the Agency right now is a loss of will. Lousy morale, indecision, dicking around. The place is shattered by the Shreed thing. People *don't want it to have happened.* I think that's why Ops has gone nuts over Nickie Groski and the computer and that stuff—it's a way out. I think they want to sit on the evidence and make it not have happened."

"What's that got to do with them giving me Sleeping Dog?"

"I've got a boss who's at the head of the line in the loss-of-will department. He keeps saying to go slow on everything and not make waves 'just now.' As if there'll be a better time next year or the year after. If word leaks that I'm suspicious about Sleeping Dog, it's just more grief for me."

"So who's your suspect?"

Menzes frowned and held out an empty cup. "I'm not ready to say—and I'm not freezing you out! I'm not sure, is what I mean. How's 'friends of George Shreed'?"

"Oh, 'Aha!' as they say in the dick novels. 'Friends of George Shreed'—well, well." Dukas poured more coffee. "Friends of George Shreed with a personal mad against Craik and me?"

"Something like that."

Dukas sat down again and the two men stared at each other, both frowning because they were both thinking the same things.

"You might have warned me."

"I might have, but I didn't. Hindsight says I made a mistake. How did it take you guys to Jakarta, anyway?"

Dukas told him again about the comm plan, this time naming Chinese Checkers and explaining what it had been. "It doesn't make sense as somebody's way of getting at Craik and me—unless they wanted to kill us."

Menzes was shaking his head. "Look, Mike, I could name some names, but I'm not going to—not yet, okay? I think it may be some of our good guys—except that they've gone a little bad because you and Craik brought down their hero. But I don't see them as killers. Not the type to lure you or Craik to Jakarta to get murdered. To embarrass you, maybe. Maybe even to implicate you in something. But not shooting." Menzes tapped Dukas's knee.

"You don't want to tell me who they are?"

Menzes shook his head.

"Trade?"

"For what?"

"I told you yesterday I wanted a favor."

Menzes looked skeptical. Dukas started to tell him the truth, and Leslie walked in and went to her side of the office. She was wearing dark blue slacks and a short-sleeved blouse and—yes, actually—a scarf draped around her shoulders. Her hair was down and caught with a rather childish plastic barrette into a ponytail.

Dukas called over to her. "Leslie! Could we, uh—give us fifteen minutes, okay? Have a cup of coffee in the canteen. Okay?" She looked at him, looked at Menzes. She nodded. "You look *appropriate*," Dukas said. Leslie sighed and groaned, "I know," and went out. Dukas turned back to Menzes. "There are two more comm plans in Chinese Checkers. I want them."

Menzes looked weary.

"How hard can it be, Carl, digging two old comm plans out of dead storage?"

Menzes laughed. "Dukas, we're not as smart as you guys over here at NCIS, but we did figure out that a bunch of comm plans that Shreed had squirreled away for his personal use were just a little suspect. They're not in dead storage anymore. They're in Ops, with 'Operational Directorate Eyes

Only' stamped all over them. Everything that Shreed ever touched is now eyes-only." He tried to smile. "File a request, maybe something'll come back in six months."

Dukas hadn't told Menzes about Rathunter and the E-mails. He would have if Menzes had had something to trade, but it looked as if he didn't. Still, Dukas went on probing. "There's a name we need to discuss," he said. "Ray Suter."

"Forget it."

"He was Shreed's assistant and he was the guy who hired Nickie the Hacker. He was there when you guys made the bust; he could—"

"Forget it! Ops has him someplace and is grilling him, but he's one smart shit and he's stonewalling."

"Yeah, but I got Sleeping Dog because I'd asked for everything that Suter was working on when Shreed skipped, meaning that Sleeping Dog came to me just after Suter had it. Okay, you tell me—did it come direct?"

Menzes hesitated. "I had Suter for twenty hours after I grabbed him. I really put the screws to him; I got nothing. Meanwhile, guys from Ops sealed his office, stripped it bare, and the stuff hasn't been seen since, except for Sleeping Dog, which I think they squeezed out because you were making so much noise."

"Ops? Sleeping Dog came to me from *Ops*? Carl, that isn't on the record. Neither is Suter and neither is Shreed, but my guess is that the only reason that Suter had Sleeping Dog was that it had had something to do with Shreed. Am I wrong?" Dukas was thinking of Leslie's idea—that the maverick's discovery in the Sleeping Dog case had been rejected because he had come too close to something. "Carl," he said, "was Shreed the one who terminated Sleeping Dog and sent it to the trash bin?"

Menzes's haggard face said it all. *Bingo.*

"Sleeping Dog was a Shreed case?"

Menzes sighed. "It wasn't Shreed's case, but it was terminated after review by a committee that Shreed chaired. I got the committee's raw notes; Shreed really pressured them to shit-can it. The reasons he gave were good ones—budget, allocation of resources, trivialization of the Agency's mission. But—"

"But when you know Shreed was a Chinese mole, the cancellation takes on new meaning, right? Jesus Christ, Carl, why didn't you tell me?"

Menzes looked at him, sighed again. "It would have given you a reason to fold all that shit into Crystal Insight—and go on with your own investigation of Shreed."

This changed what Triffler and Alan were doing in Seattle. But it didn't change the fact that the Sleeping Dog file, whatever it had been to the dead George Shreed, was a case that had been tampered with after his death. Dukas got them both more coffee and brought it back and sat down and said, "You know that Sleeping Dog was doctored before I got it."

"I do now."

"But you didn't know it when you sent it to me."

"Negative."

"It was in Suter's office. Suter's office gets sealed. The office gets stripped and everything disappears into Ops. Who signed for the stuff?"

"Dukas, you're getting too close to the bone. Lay off."

"Who signed the order to seal Suter's office?"

Menzes compressed his thin lips. "Clyde Partlow."

"Did he sign for the files? Come on, Carl! This is important! I've got two guys in Seattle right now because of what was done to Sleeping Dog. One of them was in a shoot-out in Jakarta because of Sleeping Dog! You say I'm too close to the fucking bone, I say you're endangering my guys! Give me a name!"

Menzes rubbed his forehead. "An Ops officer named Piat. Jerry Piat. He's a hardnose—the kind who still carries a gun everyplace, you know?—but absolutely solid securitywise. A protégé of Shreed's, but straight as an arrow. I'd go to the wall on it." Menzes sipped. "He's a professional case officer, but he was stationed in D.C. on a rotation; he's not one of Partlow's boys, but I suppose that Partlow grabbed him because he was there and because he was loyal to Shreed. Anyway, he signed for the stuff in Suter's office and they carted it away to Ops. Two weeks later, Piat took early retirement—scuttlebutt is, he was forced to because he wouldn't sign on to the idea that Shreed had been disloyal."

"Is Piat one of your suspects?"

Menzes nodded.

"Partlow?"

Menzes shook his head. "Partlow's a shit, but he's too smooth to get involved in anything like doctoring an Agency file or trying to get you guys. I think it's three or four of the old guys who've got a bug up their ass about you and Craik. After the funeral—you remember?—some of the old ones put their intelligence medals on Shreed's grave. *Those* guys. Retired, angry, remembering the good old days in Ops. Action, right?"

"I assume you been surveilling this Piat. Yes?" Menzes, for once, kept his face blank. "He in Jakarta when Craik got into the mess?"

Menzes sighed. "I didn't have anybody to tail him once he left D.C. They're all Ops, and I didn't want to go to Ops, for obvious reasons." Menzes sipped his coffee. "He was back in his D.C. apartment two days after your Jakarta thing. Then he took off. For Seattle." He glanced up, met Dukas's eyes. "I did have somebody there; he tailed Piat to Olympia, to a state police building. Picked him up later and tagged him to the airport, and he flew to Las Vegas. No idea why, although Piat's a throwback, wouldn't be unlike him to go to Vegas to gamble or hit the whorehouses."

Dukas shook his head. "You should have told me all this, Carl. Jeez." Dukas shook his head again. "Who'd he see in Seattle?" It was Menzes's turn to shake his head. "You got some more of your 'old guys' in Seattle, Carl?"

Menzes was silent. Then he said, "There's a former CIA employee working in an important position in the state police up there, and the FBI's already on him for suspicion of abuse of office. They've warned me off and now they're going to warn you off, because when I leave here, I'm going to tell them that you're up there investigating. Okay?"

"You pimping for the FBI now?"

"If you didn't have that injury, I'd fucking deck you for saying a thing like that to me." Menzes's face was cold. "I work with the Bureau and I need them. I don't fight them when they're on a case before me and we have the same goals."

MENZES HAD LEFT, STILL ANGRY. DUKAS WAS ALREADY checking with the liaison office to see what the FBI had going in Seattle. Before the day was out, he had an E-mail asking him to call an Agent Myeroff at the Bureau. When Myeroff heard who it was, they both started shouting. It turned out that Myeroff wanted the NCIS to call off its Seattle investigation entirely, and Dukas wanted the FBI to go blow it out a drainpipe. In the event, they both went to their bosses and did some more shouting and went home with another step down toward ulcers.

IN SEATTLE, TRIFFLER, UP AT SIX, LOOKED AT THE EVIdence they had on state-police surveillance of Alan and the state-police holding of the local police files in the fake newspaper report. He went on the Internet and checked the bios in the state-police PR pages. He found an ex-CIA man there who was now head of the international intelligence unit.

Triffler grinned. "Bingo."

Jakarta.

Late in the day, Piat woke from brief, unpleasant sleep, to face what he thought would be the last round with Bobby Li. Derek had been exiled to one of the upstairs bedrooms with a cot and a cup of whiskey laced with opium, and Bud was sitting on a chair outside to make sure he stayed there. Piat had turned Derek loose on Bobby once more during the day, and he had done his angry-boss act well, but now, Piat thought, no more was needed.

Once Bobby had admitted he was a double, the flood had started. Not a lot of truth, but a lot of apologies and breastbeating, and a lot of tears. That had gone on until Bobby had realized, about the time the sun came up and the day birds began to sing, that Piat wasn't going to reject him.

"It's okay," Piat had said a dozen times. "It's okay to be a double, Bobby, so long as you tell me the truth. So long as I can trust you. See, you're really even more valuable to me as a double, because when you're a double and you tell me the truth, then you and I can play things back to the other side and really turn their heads around. See?" He hadn't said to Bobby that a case officer never could really trust an agent, anyway, and there was only half as much reason to trust a double, and turning him back on the other side probably meant that they were going to turn him back again. And so on.

Nor did he tell Bobby that, in fact, he, Piat, was no longer a case officer.

Bobby had finally told him about having a Chinese control and about the conflicting directions he had had for the meeting in the Orchid House. He'd shot Qiu to get himself out of it. A stupid way of doing it, maybe, certainly a desperate way of doing it. Bobby and Derek had certain things in common, Piat thought, most of all that need to please, to feel love coming back like change from every transaction. *They should have been actors,* he thought as he ate the breakfast of rice and fish that Bud brought in from the hibachi out in back. And Piat thought that actors were the most pathetic people in the world.

Bobby had given him the code name of his control, Loyalty Man, and some of the working details of how they communicated, and, now that they were getting down to it, Piat thought he wanted a record of it. He shopped in one of the flashier malls for electronics and bought himself a small, voice-activated cassette recorder. But Piat also thought that they were brushing up against something much scarier, and for that, he didn't want to have to deal with Bobby's difficulties with the truth. He wanted now to cut through the fears and the lies and reach way back into Bobby Li.

NCIS HQ.

Dukas called Triffler at ten—seven A.M. in Seattle, plenty late for a dynamite NCIS special agent to be awake and alert on a Wednesday morning. Triffler was, in fact, awake and doing push-ups, he said. Certainly, he was breathing hard.

"You could have a great career in telephone sex," Dukas said. "Listen up, we got a breakthrough." Dukas told him what he had got from Menzes. "You were right, Dick. George Shreed killed Sleeping Dog. He's also got to be the one that sat on the guy's report that the Seattle observatory interference coincided with the intercepts. But the people who planted the Jakarta stuff and the fake newspaper story in Sleeping Dog are old Agency guys."

"*Not* Chinese."

"True believers in Shreed's innocence. That's how they made such a balls of Chinese Checkers and then of Sleeping Dog; what we got are two times that these true believers missed what we know is the truth—the Jakarta comm plan, which they didn't get was Shreed's contact with his Chinese control; and now Sleeping Dog, which I think they never suspected Shreed killed, because he was a Chinese agent."

"Then why did they point us toward Seattle?"

"Because: A, they had an old file focused on Seattle; and, B, they have somebody in Seattle who's waiting there to spring something on us. The bad news is, we're not supposed to touch him." He explained to Triffler about the FBI's prior investigation. "I kicked it up all the way to Kasser." Kasser was Dukas's boss's boss. "He says we have to make nice—we continue with the investigation, but we don't do anything."

"Mike, this is *my* case!"

"And I'm your boss. For now, I'm telling you to liaise with the local Bureau office. Inform, but keep your distance. Know what I mean?"

"I know what you mean, and I disapprove."

"I'll make a note of your disapproval."

"Does this mean that we never get to bust these guys?" Dukas sighed. "I'm working on it."

"The Bureau'll take it away from me."

"Over my dead body."

Triffler was silent for some seconds. Dukas had never seen him angry, never seen him throw a tantrum or even raise his voice. The silence from the other end was this quiet man's kind of rage.

Jakarta.

Piat walked through the house as dark was falling—night birds wheeling overhead already, a touch of coolness, just detectable along the edge of the heat, that smelled of the sea. He stopped with his hand on the brass handle of the dining-room door, then took his hand away. He couldn't face it yet. He went into the pantry and got the whiskey bottle and poured himself a tumblerful. Fred was sitting there. Fred said that they had eaten and Bobby Li had been restless.

"And Derek?"

Fred shrugged. "He come down once. I tole him, have another whiskey or Bud knock you out. He sleeping now." He had put more opium in the whiskey, he said.

Piat got a cup and poured some whiskey and pushed it over, then added to his own and went out into the rank garden. A few stars were already visible; the wild trees almost closed above him, one star fading and brightening as he moved around the house and the star flickered behind the black leaves. He planned what he would do now, how he would squeeze the rest of it out of Bobby Li. He didn't like himself much.

Back inside, it was as if nobody had moved.

Piat got his attaché, which held the syringe, now filled with sterile saline solution. He went into the dining room. Bobby was lying on his cot, awake, and when Piat came in, he got up and half-trotted to his chair as if he wanted to show what a good boy he was.

Piat put down the attaché. "How you doing?" he said to Bobby. Bobby looked like hell and smelled worse.

"Wiped, man. Like I been eaten, digested, and shit out."

"You're doing good, Bobby. We're almost there."

Bobby's eyes were larger, darker. They accused Piat, even while appealing to him. "How come we aren't *there* already, Andy? I tole you everything I know."

"Maybe you don't know what you know."

"Yeah, I know what I know. I tole you I'm a double, man—I thought I'd never tell you that. I thought I'd kill me."

"See? I didn't, did I?"

"Now you say gotta be more. I'm wiped, Andy."

"We're getting there, Bobby. We're on a roll. You're doing great. I'm really happy with what you've been telling me."

Bobby folded his arms and pulled his knees up, his heels on the front of the chair seat. "I tole you everything now."

Piat pulled his own chair close. It was almost dark in the room. Outside the high windows, the trees were silhouetted against the last ghost of brightness. "I want you to do something," Piat said.

Bobby raised his head. The eyes were black shadows.

"I want to give you something that will help you remember," Piat said.

"Hey, no, Andy—!"

"It'll wind it up, Bobby. Make it quicker, easier. Get you home by midnight."

"What you want to give me?"

"It's a chemical."

"Aw, no, man—How?"

Piat cleared his throat. "Needle."

"Aw, no, shit! Andy, please! Aw, Andy, no, I tole everything, honest, I tell you the truth."

Piat dragged the attaché case over without getting out of his chair, bending far to his left and reaching with one of his long arms. He put it on his lap and popped the locks, and there, under a folded T-shirt, was the syringe. Piat got up and put the attaché on the chair, bent and picked up the gasoline lantern and shook it, to listen to the slosh of gas inside to make sure there was enough. He pumped it and lit it, and the brightness of the light made them both flinch. When Bobby Li could see again, he stared at the attaché case. He shook his head. "No way."

Piat took the syringe with the saline solution and closed

the attaché and put it on the floor. "I want you to do this, Bobby. For me." Even as he was thinking, *This is cruel; this is shitty; this is sadistic.* "Which arm?"

Bobby held on to his upper arms. "Please don't."

"Bobby, it's better if you help me do it. If I have to call the guys in to hold you, it doesn't look good, you know. Just when you're doing so well."

"No, please, please—Andy, we're frands, *please*—" He began to cry. Piat smelled urine and saw, in the harsh light, a dark stain on Bobby's crotch. Bobby blubbered and stammered *please* and said, "I'll tell you anything, Andy, *anything*, honest, okay, yes, I held back, okay, yes, sure I lie to you before, but now I tell *everything.* Please don' use the needle on me!"

Piat hated himself. What he was doing *was* sadistic—or, because he didn't enjoy it, maybe not sadistic, not quite, but certainly cruel. Bobby was a poor little jerk who had simply wanted, all his life, to trail after somebody bigger and stronger, to be a little accepted and a little loved. Now, Piat was torturing him.

Piat sat in his chair, knowing that, for Bobby, it was like the moment when the dentist stops the drill and you think, *Maybe he's done. Maybe it's over.* He shouldn't give him this chance to recover—but he couldn't stand what he saw of himself. "What have you got to tell me, then?" he said, holding the big syringe so the needle glinted in the light.

His eyes on the needle, Bobby said, "I tole you I was a double. That's true. I tole you I started five years ago. That was a lie. I'm sorry, Andy. I lie."

"Why?"

"I'm afraid of the Chinese guy."

"Your case officer?"

"No, top guy. I go to work for him long time ago now." He was almost whispering. "He kill me, he find out about this."

"Did he recruit you?"

"Yah. Long time ago."

"Where?"

"Here. Jakarta."

"How?"

"Oh—you know—"

"No, I don't know. Bobby, if you're bullshitting me—"

"No, no!" Eyes on the needle. "He jus'—get in touch with me, offer me money—"

"How'd he get in touch with you?"

"Guy I knew, we both young then, playin' basketball. That way."

"What way? I don't get it."

"You mixin' me up! Andy, I tellin' you all about it, the truth! This Chinese guy, he wears a suit, he come by where we play and he buy us Cokes and like that, then we talkin', by and by he offer me money."

Piat knew now when Bobby was spinning a story. When he was making it up as he went along, his voice got a little higher, his eyes a little brighter, as if he liked what he was doing and thought he did it well. And Piat knew it was all invention. "Hold out your arm," he said.

"No!" A scream.

"You're lying. Hold out your arm, or I'll call the guys."

"I won't do it anymore, honest, Andy, no, no—" He was clutching his arms and hugging them to his chest, curling up his knees and rounding his shoulders. He was panting, weeping again, but he said, "The guy took me over! I was already a double!"

That brought Piat up short. "How long ago?"

"Long time." Eyes on the needle again.

"How long, Goddamit? I want answers!"

"Ten years, maybe longer. Twelve. This guy, he really did come where we play basketball; he come around, looked at me, lotta times. Then I get a message to make a meeting, there he is, he says, 'I'm your new officer. You do what I say now.' "

Twelve years! Until then, Piat had thought that maybe Bobby had become a double after Piat had left Jakarta on his second tour. Now he was saying it was before. He sat down again. "This guy is the 'top man' you told me about?"

"Yeah, yeah—the one I tell you, I know he order me to go to the Orchid House, help run that operation with the Chinese guys. I couldn't help it!"

"You've been his agent for twelve years."

"Yeah, about twelve. Last four or fi', he run me through another guy we call Loyalty Man, but top guy still in charge. I think he was in Beijing a lot, from things Loyalty Man say. But this last time, this op where I shot the guy, he's not in Beijing."

"Not Loyalty Man, the top guy."

"Yeah, top guy.

"Was he at the embassy?"

"I don't know. We always meet out someplace."

Piat thought that all this would be great stuff if he had Bobby in a real safe house, with other interrogators and maybe a competent doctor and nurse and maybe a hypnotist to work on Bobby over a long time. It could take weeks to get the details out of him.

"Okay, there was this top guy. He took you over in eighty-seven or so. Who'd he take you over from, Bobby?"

Bobby's body stalled. It was like a hiccup in his physical processes. Piat had seen it before, and he knew it meant that Bobby was scared suddenly and would start to invent. This, then, was a subject that was a bad one for him, one he had planned not to get to. Piat moved the needle forward. "Who'd he take you over from?"

"A Chinese guy."

"Okay. Age?"

"Oh, thirty-five. Forty. You know."

"Bobby, you're tired. When you're tired, your lies show. If you lie, I'll have to use the needle."

"No, you said you wouldn't."

"No, I didn't."

"No, yeah, but I thought you meant we were over with that. I *tole* you the truth. Please, Andy."

"But you're starting to lie again."

Bobby hugged himself, then threw his head back so hard that Piat could hear it hit the wood on the back of the chair. Bobby's black hair, uncombed, sweaty, fell around his face. "Oh, man—" he whimpered. He looked around the room, moving mostly his eyes. "Mister Chen was a guy about forty, forty-five."

"Was that his code name—Chen?"

"No, that his real name—Chen. I find it out one day. I don't remember how."

"Bobby—!"

"Oh, man! Okay, I hear somebody say it one day. He say, 'That's Chen, big shot at Chinese intel.' "

"You could see the guy?"

"Uh—Andy, look—This was a long time ago; I don't remember it good. Maybe I got it wrong."

"Tell me the truth. You do remember it, Bobby; you don't forget things like this. What did he mean, 'That's Chen.' "

"He had a photo. Chen, some other guy."

"You saw the photo?"

Bobby sighed. "I took the photo, okay? Long time ago, Andy. I was just a kid; I did what I was tole!"

"You took a photo of your Chinese case officer?"

"Sort of like that. Not at a meeting. Guy tells me, 'Hang around the Chinese embassy, your guy comes out, snap a pic.' Like that. I pretend to be a windshield kid, you know—rag, bottle a water, wipe down the windshield, ask for money. I do that two, three days, I see Mister Chen go by in a car, I get the pic."

Piat felt dizzy. He was tired, too, and he hadn't eaten anything since morning, and what Bobby was telling him was so new he couldn't make it sit still. He hesitated, letting the rhythm of the interrogation falter. "Who told you to take the picture?" he said. It had been before his time, surely—or had it? His head spun. "Come on, Bobby, who told you to take the picture?"

"Mister Shreed, he tole me."

"George Shreed was running you then?"

"Yeah, he was my frand."

"That'd be twenty, twenty-five years ago."

Then Piat thought he saw it clearly, and his head settled down. Of course, Shreed would want a photo of his Chinese counterpart if he could get one, and using a kid wasn't such a bad idea. "You were Shreed's agent, even then."

"I was his frand. Little kid. He was good to me."

"Was that when they called you Kim?"

Surprisingly, Bobby Li smiled. Through the wetness of his tears, through his swollen eyes and his disordered hair, he smiled. "Yeah. Mister Shreed call me Kim. He read that book to me. I was just a kid. He was my best frand."

Piat let the rhythm go again. He was thinking about what Bobby had said and where it led. Finally, he said, "But even though he was your best friend, you were a double agent, even then."

The small man unfolded himself a little. He even leaned a little forward, moving into the space threatened by the needle. His eyes were somber now, adult, and—another surprise—almost pitying. "Don't go there, Andy."

"I want the truth."

"Maybe not."

"Bobby, come on! We're almost at the end. Don't make me—" He moved the needle. "Don't." Bobby sank slowly back and put his head against the chair back again so that Piat was looking at the underside of his jaw and his eye sockets. Bobby wasn't crying anymore. He wasn't even breathing hard. Looking at the ceiling, he said, "I was a double then, and it didn't bother Mister Shreed, okay?"

"He *knew*?"

Bobby sighed. "Andy—" He sighed again. "He sent me to Mister Chen, okay?"

"Now, wait a minute—Bobby, I want to be clear here. Your story is that George Shreed sent you to this Chen?"

"He did."

"To be a double?"

"Yeah, I guess. It got to be that, sure. He sent me first just to be a gofer, you know? With him and Mister Chen."

"*Gofer*? What the hell does that mean? Spies don't use gofers!"

"I was a little kid, Andy. I—it was—Mister Shreed says to me, 'This is the Great Game, Kim. Now the Great Game begin.' That's what he said. I'm not bullshitting you, Andy. He was *happy* about it, man! And he sends me to Mister Chen with a message. That was the first time."

"Bobby, George Shreed *recruited* you."

"Yeah, when I was a kid."

"And then *Chen* turned you into a double."

Bobby didn't say anything. He sighed. Piat said, "Answer me, Bobby! This was when Chen recruited you—yes?"

"Andy, I tole you not to go there. Don't you get it? Mister Chen never recruited me. Mister Shreed recruited me."

Piat stared at him, the syringe forgotten. "That could be true only if Shreed was a double himself."

Bobby sighed. "I tole you, man. I tried to keep you away."

Piat reached across and smacked him as hard as he could with his left hand. In his right, the needle gleamed.

Washington.

At two, Dukas was in the CNO's office with Pat Feisel, two lawyers from the JAG's office, and the overworked man who was running the Navy. He had fifteen minutes to explain why the Navy ought to go head-to-head with the Central Intelligence Agency in federal court. The lawyers were wary but a little excited, he could see. Suing the CIA was a fairly racy idea.

"And it's the right thing to do," Pat Feisel said. "The boy's rights are being trampled."

That was not as impressive for the other lawyers as she hoped. Nickie Groski was not, after all, a sailor.

"How about we let his lawyer file, and we file an amicus?" one of the JAG's men said.

It was the CNO himself who nixed that. "That's wishy-washy," he said. "The hell with that. Dukas, you really need to talk to this young man?"

"Yes, sir."

"Well, I don't know about you guys, but I'm impressed by the argument that his civil rights are being ignored. This is America. Can you guys handle the Agency?"

One of the lawyers grinned.

"Dukas, give these guys everything they need that can be said in court. Missus Feisel, I'd appreciate it if you'll put full time on this, because you're already ahead. They'll need chapter and verse, the boy's lawyer—"

"His mother," one lawyer said.

"All that. Dukas is in a hurry. How fast can you move?"

The two JAGs looked at each other. "Two weeks?"

Dukas eyed them. "Today?"

The CNO looked from one to the other. "Gentlemen, I trust experts. You're experts in different fields. Dukas, how bad do you need to see this boy?"

"Bad, sir."

The CNO spread his fingers on his desk and stared at them. His head jerked toward the lawyers. "The Shreed case and everything about it is important to the Navy. However, I don't want to send anybody on a suicide mission. If you tell me you can't file ASAP, I'll accept it—but I won't like it."

The two JAG officers looked at each other and the older one said, "Tomorrow?" He smiled, as if he was aware he'd just lost his head over something wild and uninhibited.

Dukas smiled for the first time in two days.

Jakarta.

They had gone around and around it, and it was after midnight. Piat had put away the syringe. He had known the first time through that Bobby Li had at last told him the truth; the blow he had given Bobby was only a reaction to that truth, a blow aimed really at George Shreed and perhaps at himself. He so wanted it not to be true that he raged at the little agent; he walked up and down the empty room, shouting at him; he threatened, cursed, begged. But the story had always come out the same: George Shreed had been a double agent, working with a Chinese officer, Chen. When his tour in Jakarta was over, he had handed Bobby Li over to Piat without telling him of his and the boy's other loyalty, and for more than twenty years, Piat had been using Bobby Li without knowing. Suspecting, maybe—you never really trust an agent—but Christ, not knowing!

At twenty minutes of one, Piat gave it up. He was bathed in sweat; mentally, he was whipped, as if it were he who had been the subject of the interrogation. He woke Bill and told him to get them some food; he gave Bobby a cigarette and lit one himself and fell into the hard chair opposite the little man. They smoked together silently. At last, the cigarette almost gone, Bobby said, "We done?"

"Yeah." Piat's voice was gone. He coughed.

"I'm sorry, man. I know he was your frand, too."

"I'll live." Piat wiped a hand over his face and tried to wake himself up. "You're okay, Bobby. This'll be okay. You've got to go someplace now, that's the only thing. We have to get you out of town." He looked up at the small man's eyes. "Your 'top guy,' Loyalty Man's boss—he's going to try to do the same thing I did. He's got to be asking himself what really happened in the Orchid House, and he's got to be thinking that pulling you in for an interrogation is the right way to go. I don't want him to do that—for your sake and mine, both."

Bobby was crying again. "You going to proteck me, Andy?"

"Who's your American case officer now?"

"Some young guy, not worth shit. He comes to see me every couple months. I don' think he's even here—he flies in and out." Bobby put out his hand for another cigarette. "You gonna take care of me, Andy? My wife and kids, too. I been your man a long time, Andy."

"You got some money?"

"You need some?"

It made Piat smile, despite everything. "No, I thought you might. You got a place to go?"

"A place out beside Tangerang. My wife there now. No way they track me there."

Piat studied his face to see if this was mere optimistic bullshit. The Chinese owned Indonesia; Bobby knew that as well as he did. They'd find him in four or five days, a week at the outside, wherever he went. "Can you go through an interrogation with them?" Piat said.

Bobby curled into himself and moaned. He had an unlit cigarette in his fingers, and it bent, the part between his fingers squeezed flat and the paper soaking from Bobby's sweat. "No, man," Bobby moaned, "no, please—you gotta proteck me—"

Piat stood. He flexed his knees, rubbed one calf. When Piat passed his chair, Bobby grabbed his arm. "We still frands, okay?"

"You bet." The little man's face made Piat hate what he'd done; at the same time, he felt satisfaction—a job well done, knowledge gained—then a pang as he saw again what the new knowledge meant: *George Shreed had been a Chinese agent.*

Piat shouted at Bill to bring in the food.

Whidbey Island.

"Agenda for today. Contact of Mercer Island police officer. Review High Threat meeting plan."

Alan nodded and sipped the coffee that Triffler had handed him. "Hello to you, too."

"I had a little traffic and ran late. I'm very sorry to have missed the first contact." Triffler sounded prim, but Alan already knew him well enough to know that he was angry—with himself. Triffler was not a man to *run late.*

"No problem," said Alan.

"I got coffee for us," said Triffler. He sipped. "News from town: Mistah Dukas, he say that George Shreed was the one who killed Sleeping Dog."

He leaned into the backseat of the car and took out a plastic bag. "This is a clean, one-use cell phone. I bought it at a 7-Eleven, complete with calling card. I was a little overdressed for a drug dealer, but they let it pass."

"So? Oh, I see, this is the phone to call Sergeant Kusluski."

"You ready?"

Alan flourished his notes, written in tiny script on a three-by-five card.

"That's a bad habit, Al. Taking notes to a clandestine meeting—"

Alan held the card up for Triffler, who read it. It was mostly jargon.

"Notes from a sales pitch. I got it off the Internet. Any small-time salesman would carry a card like this. There's no name—"

"Okay, already! I stand corrected. You're the best spy since—"

"Mata Hari?"

"I was going to say James Bond. Ready?"

Alan dialed the number.

"Hello?" It was not a young voice. It was a woman's voice, and she sounded tired. Unconsciously, Alan looked at his watch, afraid he had called too early.

"Hello? May I speak to Sergeant Kusluski?"

Pause.

"Hello? Hello? I cannot hear so good. Hello?"

Alan raised his voice. "Hello! May I speak to Sergeant Kusluski?"

"That's what I thought you said. He was my husband. He was killed in the line of duty two years ago."

Alan hadn't been prepared for this. "I'm sorry."

"I'm sorry, too, but sorry don't make it no better. You sellin' somethin'?"

"No, ma'am. I'm investigating."

"Might be better if you were sellin' somethin'. I was his wife, not his partner."

"Ma'am, might I come out and visit you? I'd like to ask you some questions about an arrest your husband made. Just in case you remember it."

Pause.

"Who do you work for, mister?"

"The U.S. Navy, ma'am."

Triffler was rolling his eyes, but he hadn't said anything.

"I suppose."

"Will you be there today, ma'am? Could I come by this afternoon?"

Pause.

"I'm out this afternoon. My daughter is taking me to Seattle to see a show."

Alan sensed her resistance building, and he pressed on.

"Maybe I could come by tomorrow?"

"I suppose."

Triffler was writing on the notepad. Alan looked at the note, thought about his own schedule, nodded.

"We'll come by at two o'clock."

"I suppose that's all right. I don't really go out much. I really don't want to cancel with my daughter."

"That's fine, ma'am."

"See that you have your badge, though. Our neighborhood association has a paper out on fake cops and pretend investigations as a means of gaining access to people's homes. I'm very up on that sort of thing."

"I'm sure you are, ma'am."

When he was off the phone, Alan was almost wrung out from fatigue. Just from a single phone call.

Triffler grabbed his arm. "You did good. Here, have some coffee."

"Why was that such a wipeout, though?"

"Your brain is on overdrive. Say the wrong thing and *bang* you lose your contact. And she threw you a curve right off. I don't know why we never thought of Kusluski being dead. If I was planting fake officer's reports, I'd make damned sure the reporting officer was dead."

"So we don't go?"

"Of course we go, *amigo*. We just don't expect anything, that's all."

"You don't think this is the trap?"

Triffler shook his head. "Nope. Ready to brief the other part of the agenda?"

"What happened to 'take a sip of coffee and relax'?"

"You have a flight in two and a half hours. I have to lay out a route for this afternoon." He was looking out the window. "By the way, the FBI is trying to horn into the investigation."

"No way!"

"Yeah, they are. Mike's trying to hold them off."

"I didn't come all the way up here to drop something into the FBI's lap!"

Triffler smiled. "Shout louder. Maybe they'll hear you."

Jakarta.

Piat and Fred cleaned the room, trying to eradicate any sign of what had gone on there. Piat smashed the syringe under his heel and carried it over to Jalan Surabaya and dropped it into a sewer. When he got back, Fred, Bill, and Bud were folding up the cots. They'd put Bobby Li into the pantry and given him some of the opium, of which Fred seemed to have a good supply, and he'd fallen into an exhausted sleep.

"Derek?" Piat said.

Fred laughed. He put his head against his palm-to-palm hands. The other men laughed.

"Sell the cots or do what you want with them," Piat said. "Get rid of the woman and the kids. I want this place the way we found it."

Later, they went upstairs and looked at Derek, who was snoring on the last of the cots. Bud and Fred lifted him off and put him on the floor. They folded the cot and carried it out of the house. When they came back, Piat said, "Now him," and the four of them carried the lanky Russian downstairs and out the front door and laid him down just inside the gate. He went on snoring. Piat tucked his money and an extra hundred dollars in his shirt pocket and went inside and paid off the others. He and Bobby Li were the last to leave, Piat locking the doors, listening, aware that the others had already cleared out. Bats were flying in the garden, chasing down mosquitoes and big moths. Piat stepped over the snoring Derek and went out the rusty gate with an arm around Bobby's shoulders, holding him up, protecting him, thinking that everything had changed now—everything had changed.

19

USS **Thomas Jefferson.**

SOLECK DIDN'T QUITE BOUNCE INTO THE READY room, but the knowledge that he'd be flying without Paul Stevens again was enough to make the whole day lighter. Stevens was still sick—sicker, in fact. A lot of people were sick, they said. He sat in the front of the room, facing the television.

Campbell, slated to be his copilot, gave him a nod. "Surface-search exercise," he mumbled, his lap full of cards.

Soleck had already visited the surface module, really just a desk in the Combat Information Center where surface contacts were tracked.

"Yeah. We're picking up the slack for all the guys in VS-34 who're down sick. That's okay; our bird is up for its MARI and we can use the practice. We got a big box north of the carrier, right up the coast of Africa to Somalia. Everybody on board for that?"

The other three nodded.

"This is sort of an exercise and sort of a real-world thing, so we'll track any contact we come up with, even a dhow. I'd like to use the MARI to get right up into the Arabian Sea if the ducts are right. Otherwise, it's business as usual. ASuW at its butt-asleep best. This is a seven-hour flight, so everybody take a piss tube and a candy bar."

They moaned on cue.

"Any more word on that sub?" asked Campbell. He'd missed the flight, but wanted, like every subhunter on the boat, to have a real sub out there. "And how can we use the MARI on a one-plane flight?"

"Intel's still waffling. I've heard some hard things said about us. ASW module says the grams we brought back are 'possible,' and the staff is still sweating it." Soleck shook his head. "One-plane MARI means we'll use it as enhanced ISAR. No problem. Anything else?"

"We ought to be out there dropping buoys," said Craw.

"As Captain Rafehausen just reminded me, we're not an ASW det. We're an ASuW det. And the VS guys have so many down sick—"

Craw merely grunted. Above his head, the closed-circuit television flickered, and they all looked up to get the Metro brief and the intel. A square-faced female ensign rattled through the weather (hot and muggy, with poor visibility at sea level) and the launch cycle. Her voice changed a little at the end, sharper, more resonant, and they all paid closer attention.

"Directive from the CAG. All flights are to scrupulously avoid Kenyan airspace without direct permission from Mombasa Air Traffic Control and the E-2. 'Scrupulously avoid' means don't go there. We're running up a bill of airspace violations and the Kenyans aren't happy. Okay, that's your intel brief. If you have any questions, call me in CVIC. Have a good flight."

Craw was looking wise when Soleck turned around to complete his own brief.

"What's the deal?"

"Hornets have been busting airspace all over the map. First it was a navigation exercise gone wrong, and then somebody doing a beyond-visual-range engagement practice took his section right over the coast where the resorts are."

The aviators shook their heads together.

"Everybody set?" said Soleck, looking over his crew. "Get your cookies and walk. See you in the plane."

Whidbey Island.

"Two-plane flight. Soon we're going to do some drills on what you can get out of MARI with just one plane, but this'll be simple." He smiled at the two crews, both of which had people on their second or third flight with the gear.

"We'll just take a turn through the western end of the op area and see what we see. Then turn back toward land and get some images. Maybe take another look at Microsoft. I'll show you why in the plane. Anybody walk over to the intel center and look at the JOTS terminal?"

Nobody had.

"Okay. MARI is all about surface search, the way sonobuoys are all about submarines. You need to know the surface picture every time you launch. I know this is an exercise area and this is some dumb flight to image helpless merchants, but it's the helpless merchants that you have to know the whereabouts of if you're in a hurry. Question?"

"Yes, sir. LTjg Stern. Nobody will have any stuff in the link about white shipping off Seattle, right?"

"That's more of a statement than a question. Maybe not. We'll fix that. Here's a grid system for our search pattern. For a few hours, we'll locate, tag, and monitor every contact in the western op area. Everybody got it?"

They nodded.

"If you haven't hit the head, then do it. Let's walk."

Off East Africa.

Ducting for radar is related to temperature and humidity and other forces of nature that create a duct that will keep a radar signal bouncing inside it rather than going off over the horizon and disappearing into space. Normally, radar will go only line of sight, so a plane's radar horizon is limited by its altitude. The circle of sea an S-3 can see is enormous at sixteen thousand feet, but still limited, and the tactical problem remains the same as in the days of sail, when the horizon could be extended only by the sailor in the crow's nest at the top of your mast.

With a duct, however, that line of sight can go out beyond the curve of the earth, over the horizon and back. A good duct in the Red Sea can allow a strong signal to find a target three hundred miles away. Sometimes, with good meteorology and good people, you can even predict a duct. Mostly, though, the weather two hours' flight away from the carrier is different enough from the weather back on deck that the predictions are vague. Ducting seems to be mostly luck. Good radarmen hunt that luck, climbing and diving in small increments, looking for the duct that will get them the long look. Good pilots, at least in radar communities, will take the time to fly the difficult patterns to find the duct.

Soleck and his crew found a set of ducts around nine thousand feet early in the flight. Finding them meant that the people in the back end were overworked from the start, able to scan a much broader area of ocean than normal without knowing when they would lose the ducts. Craw worked the MARI while the Tacco, Cohen, ran the surface-search radar. Craw would cycle his screen from time to time to look through his emitters list and see if they had any hits that corresponded to well-known radars of any type. Most of his hit list were old Russian threat radars, with some submarine surface-search radars thrown in for good measure.

Sorting and tagging the contacts took hours for every box in the grid they were forming. Some contacts would prove to be previously identified radar blips, although the MARI's near-photographic resolution made that less common than had been the case with ISAR. Most of the contacts were dhows and deepwater fishing craft from the African coast, although a handful of big freighters bound for Mombasa or Dar es Salaam provided some practice on the bigger merchant types.

Cohen, hot and overworked in the back, went up on the intercom. "What's the point? We could do this all day."

Campbell murmured something about the admiral.

"White shipping, neutral shipping, it's the clutter on the battle group's screens," said Soleck with forced cheer.

"If I wanted a lecture—"

"Hey, you asked. White shipping has to be sorted for both offensive and defensive purposes. You can't fire any over-the-horizon ordnance without a good knowledge of what radar targets the pea brain of a Harpoon might fix on, right? And if you blow a Kenyan dhow or a Pakistani dhow or whatever out of the water instead of your enemy, you get the weight of the world's press, right?"

"And you've wasted your missile," said Campbell, cruelly.

"And the enemy can hide in it." Craw rarely spoke up when the officers were bantering. So they listened.

"Huh? What, hide behind another ship?" said Campbell, but Cohen was right on top of this one.

"No. No, I get what he means. Like when you do a carrier-v-carrier exercise, it can take days to find the enemy carrier because of all the other radar hits."

"Yeah," drawled Campbell from the front seat. "Yeah, okay. I've flown in exercises like that. Hey, Mrs. Luce, I am the Pope, okay? Bears do shit in the woods, I'm convinced of it. But Cohen's point, and my point, is that if you don't get the picture and keep it twenty-four hours a day, then there ain't no point, right? Because as soon as you don't look for an hour, anyone could be anyone. They could all be anywhere."

ON THE OTHER SIDE OF THE GLOBE, ALAN WAS FLYing with an unfamiliar crew, just out into the operations area well off the coast to turn the MARI on and calibrate the system. The other plane flew with Cunnard and a newbie Tacco. Surfer was mixing crews to cross-train.

He sat in back, in the Senso seat, so that he could talk to two MARI operators: Bubba Paleologus in the copilot seat and LTjg Lisa Stern, another newbie, in the Tacco seat. They both exclaimed over the sharpness of the image and how much easier it was to use for real than on the simulator. They imaged a frigate coming into port from duty with Seventh Fleet, and it looked like a photograph in Jane's, the very archetype of the Oliver Hazard Perry class. Then Alan had the pilot turn inland and they imaged some ground facilities, hitting the corporate headquarters of the world's largest software manufacturer again. Alan held up a postcard from the same facility, so that the distinctive architecture was plain to see.

"Not everything comes from a classified pub," he said. "If you had to target that facility overseas, the postcard could make all the difference."

They played with the system, experimented with resolution by imaging fishing boats and pleasure boats. The system lost resolution at about one meter, so that a little wooden dory was just a blob until they flew over it and saw it by eye, where a ten-meter cabin cruiser was easy to identify. Alan found that he could get to all the buttons with his bad hand, using the three remaining digits slowly. He could get there. He could still operate the system faster than the newbies. That, and their attentiveness to his lessons, made him happy.

"See those spikes at the stern?"

"Are those engine mounts, sir?" Paleologus asked.

"Yes, and no, Lieutenant. Remember that MARI is, at its roots, just a radar. You aren't really looking at a photographic image. It's a set of radar returns that a computer enhances to look like an image. So the big metal parts, like the engines, with lots of convoluted metal surfaces to cause a big radar return, those will always appear larger than life."

"I can see that now."

"In the Med we were chasing smugglers in the Adriatic. They were in cigarette boats, and the only real return we'd get, even on MARI, was a pair of big spikes from the engines. The rest was fiberglass and spit and didn't give much of a return. They're in the library you guys have."

"The controls are sure simpler than the old ISAR," said Bubba.

"I wouldn't know," said Lisa, who was in her first operational command, on her first real flight with her det, and didn't want to do anything wrong, especially in front of Craik.

"You never used ISAR? What did they teach you at the RAG?"

"Navigation, sir."

"Nobody says 'sir' in the plane, Lisa," said Alan.

"Bubba called you sir."

"Bubba was temporarily awed by my natural authority. Do you have a nickname, Lisa?"

"No," she said, too quickly.

"Me, either," he said, with a bit of a laugh. He'd had quite a number, and none of them very pretty. "Ready to call it a day? Home, Dice."

The pilot grunted, and they turned toward home.

"HEY, LOOK AT THOSE, MASTER CHIEF," SAID COHEN, now deep in the job. He passed his contacts electronically to Craw's station. There were five of them, all in a neat row, well out in the Indian Ocean toward Karachi far to the north. "Remember that pair of spikes?"

"Cigarette boat, for sure," said Craw. "Moving right along, too. Just like we saw off Italy." Craw said "Italy" in two syllables. *It-ly.*

"Smugglers, I'll bet," said Cohen.

"They're headed for Mogadishu. What the hell would you smuggle into Mogadishu?"

"Or out of it," said Campbell. "Biggest shithole I've ever seen. They have *nothin'*."

They logged the boats, tagged them in the system, and tracked them for the rest of their flight, watching as they moved at sixty knots over the flat, silver sea and close to the port of Mogadishu.

Five hundred and forty miles behind them, the ASuW watch officer received the information over the datalink, and, because the cigarette boats were still listed in his threat log from months before off the Adriatic coast, he placed all five of them into the carrier's tactical picture and then fed their course and speed into his JOTS terminal and linked that picture to the live feed from the S-3.

TWELVE THOUSAND MILES AWAY, ALAN HAD FIN-
ished his flight, landed, showered, and gone to the intel center
to work. He leaned on the JOTS repeater terminal and watched
as the five cigarette boats merged into the coast of Africa. Then
he walked across to the commander's office and asked to use
his message center. In ten minutes, he had requested reports
from all major agencies on the movement of small craft in the
Indian Ocean. He knew that he was trying to maintain some
contact with the ship he loved, with Rafe and his own det.
But another part of him saw the cigarette boats and the three-
day-old pos contact on the unknown submarine, and worried.

SIXTY FEET ABOVE THE DECK AND A FEW HUNDRED
feet from the stern, Soleck doubted himself and attempted a
minute correction. He began to yaw and overcorrected and
his right wheel slammed on the deck alone, taking the whole
weight of the plane. There was a spray of hydraulic fluid as the
left wheel touched, and the hook caught the two wire, and the
whole messy landing became the charge of a chained lion as
the plane surged forward against the last full-power thrust
from her engine and then quieted.

A disgusted LSO shook his head.

"What a dickhead. He was steady as a rock right into the
wake. You have to work to lose a landing that late." Sigh. "No
grade."

Twenty minutes later, Soleck hurt his hand slamming it
into a locker in the ready room.

20

Mogadishu, Somalia.

TSUNG OFTEN WONDERED WHAT IT WOULD BE LIKE to be stationed in Saigon or Paris. Someplace civilized. Instead, he got to visit Mogadishu, a town so poor that most of the metal roofs of the shacks that passed for houses had been sold to Kenya for scrap. Landing, he saw that there were only four dhows and a Yemeni tramp freighter in the main harbor. Mogadishu had very little to offer.

Namjee was waiting amid the broken glass of the airport terminal. He looked dapper in a light wool suit, utterly out of place with his surroundings. He had three thugs attending him. They wore headscarves and were smoking American cigarettes and the oldest of them looked to be fifteen. Namjee spoke to him in Farsi, as Tsung was supposed to be Persian.

"Are you ready to see the products of our labors?"

"Tell me what the cover is?" Tsung wanted to see the operation in its final stage, but he worried about betraying his actions to a third party. Mostly, he worried about the Americans. If their carrier was off the coast, they'd have spies operating here.

"No cover. I tell them nothing. In a few days, they will be dead. They know me as a Saudi businessman. If you like, I'll tell them you're a Saudi. Saudis finance most of this anyway."

"No. Tell them nothing. Just let me see them."

Namjee led the way to an Indian-made jeep, a Mahindi, parked at the end of the runway. "Terrible car, but all I could get here. Not one of India's better products."

Tsung tried not to turn an ankle getting across the rubble.

The boats were gleaming and new, utterly foreign in a small harbor that hadn't had a new building since 1990. There were twenty men with AK-47s guarding the boats, mostly teenagers lying in the warm sun on the stones of the pier. A few older men sat in buggies with heavier weapons. The "technicals." None of them spared Tsung a glance. They were high on khat.

Tsung never got out of the Indian jeep. Namjee waved from the pier and the five boats roared into life and drove around the harbor and then out to sea, their powerful engines churning the brackish water and adding a tang of salt mud to the rotting smell of the port.

"They look fast," Tsung admitted, more impressed than he had expected to be. He raised Namjee's binoculars again to watch them.

"They might actually do the trick," Namjee said with grudging admiration. "Now we just put in the C-4 and go."

"You sound as if you are going yourself."

"Perish the thought, old chap." Namjee smiled. "Leave that for Allah's foot soldiers."

Suburban Virginia.

Sally Baranowski was waked by the ringing of the telephone. She came awake easily, aware of where she was and who she was; she even had time to glance at the orange numbers of the bedside clock and see that it was after four. In the morning. Sometimes, in her drinking days, she would wake and see the clock and not know whether it was day or night—she had time to remember that, too, as she lifted the phone—and put it to her ear and was glad that Dukas wasn't there in her bed, because she had a feeling that Dukas was too much for her; he took up too much space, too much energy. She liked him, but he overpowered her. Putting the phone to her ear, she thought that the call might be from him and hoped not, as it would be exactly the kind of crowding that she was beginning to recoil from, and she said, "Yes?" in a voice made husky by sleep.

A pause followed and she knew it was coming to her from a satellite and so it wasn't Dukas. "Old friend here," a male voice said.

She knew the voice at once. "*Jerry?*"

The pause again, and then his laugh, seeming a little forced so that she knew he'd been drinking—probably was drinking at that moment, the phone in one hand and a glass in the other. "You got me in one, sweetie. I'm kind of flattered. How are you?"

She sat up in the bed, pulling the covers over her bare shoulders and pushing the pillow behind her with a fist. "What're you doing, calling me in the middle of the night— after ten years?" She was laughing, but the sound was half like sobbing.

"Looking for a friend, Sal."

"Who?"

"You. A friend, I need a friend. A 'frand,' as my friend here calls it."

"Jerry, where are you?"

"In a faraway place, love. Very faraway. Exotic. We don't mention it on the phone, okay?"

"You're drinking."

"I'm feeling creative. Trying to get my shit together, and having a little trouble." Now he sounded as if he were half-sobbing. She knew the phases of his drinking, or had known them ten years before; maybe his had got worse, or better, or at least different. When he started to mix laughter with sobs, he was pretty well along but still articulate, often funny, sometimes near craziness. She heard a sound from his end, some sort of horn. Jerry laughed. "Bit of a prang here. *Bang.* Guy in a Toyota took the side off a—what the hell is that, a Hyundai?"

"Are you on the street?"

"You could say that. Yes, you could say that." Using a public telephone because it was safer—she knew that tactic of his, always cautious, sure that private telephones in foreign places were monitored. "I need a friend, love," he said.

"You in trouble?"

"You could say that. But—" He might have been taking a drink then; she heard some indecipherable noise. "Had some bad news," he said. His voice broke. He would be on the edge of self-pity now, she thought. "Some lousy, lousy news." The sound again, and he said, "I couldn't think of anybody who would understand except you. You always understand."

"Jerry, it's been ten years."

"Yeah, yeah. Well."

"I'm sorry if you had bad news."

"Yeah. Oh, yeah." He laughed. "Somebody died." She heard him sniffle. He was actually weeping. Standing there, she thought, on a busy street in some Oriental city, an almost-empty glass in his hand, tears running down his cheeks.

"Can I do anything?"

"You! You already did something. Because you were right, right? You knew what he was, but I didn't believe—I thought he was a fucking god, and now god is dead, right? You knew god was dead. I hated your guts for it; if we'd still been together, I'd have whacked you one for it. But you were right. God was dead all along. You heard I got the ax, right? I got it for believing that god was alive. Well, now I know you and the rest were right—god was dead the whole time. Life's a fucking farce."

"I don't know what you're talking about, Jer."

"Oh, 'course you do!" His voice got loud and it began to swoop, the vowels extending into long, honking sounds. "I'm talking about my i-i-i-dol, about my little tin g-o-o-o-d, about you-know-who-o-o-o—don't you, love? No names, please, we're skittish. No names. No fuck-ing names."

George Shreed. He meant George Shreed. She was slow to get it, but she got it. "What changed your mind?" She still thought then that he had called her for sympathy, nothing more. She was simply talking him along at that point because he was drunk and an old lover.

After the satellite delay, he said more quietly, "A little man. He had privileged information. In a word, he had the goods. He convinced me, see?"

"What little man?"

"My god's first runner, how's that? His gofer. What you'd call a double gofer, because he was a double. You following me, hon? I just learned all this, got a bit-of-a-shock." He exhaled noisily. "I gotta go."

"No, Jerry—!" Because she was getting it by then. "Jerry, you still there?"

Her own echo came back, *still there?* and then his voice, "Still here."

"Don't go away!"

"I need a drink, hon. I'm out."

"Well, hang on just a sec, okay?"

"I'm staying in this really lovely establishment full of young ladies—ready to wait on me hand and foot. For a price. They have lots to drink. Anyway, I've stashed my friend the double gofer with them; I have to check on him. See he's not up to mischief. Sally, I called you because—oh, shit, old times— I need a friend, hon—"

"Jerry, what do you need? Are you in trouble?"

"Not yet. But my little pal won't stay stashed with the young ladies forever, you follow me? His pals from the other side, from my *god's* other side, will catch up with him, and then, oh, shit—How could he do that, Sal? How could he have worked for *them*?" His voice broke.

She thought he meant the "little man," but then she understood he meant Shreed. She revised her picture of the man on the other end of the telephone—Oriental street, glass, telephone, but she added a broken heart.

"Are you trying to find a place to stash your gofer, Jer?"

"Yeah, but it won't work; they're all over this place."

"Jer, where are you?"

"Oh—you know. You know. Where I worked for my god when I was young and handsome."

So, Jakarta. She thought of who was in Jakarta now and thought that nobody there for the Agency now was a friend of his. "Do you want me to go to the home place, Jerry? Ask around among the guys you used to work for?"

"Christ, no. Not a word. They're to be told *nothing*! Why you think I'm calling you? Because *you're* not one of *them*." She heard another traffic sound, more honking. "I need a drink," he said.

"Jerry, don't go. Are you there?"

Silence; then: "I guess I am."

"I know somebody who can help you. Not at the Crystal Palace, okay?"

"He here where I am?"

"Will you promise to call me back?"

"Isn't that how I got in trouble before?"

That one hurt. That was, indeed, how they had got in trouble before: He had promised to call her, and he had whisked off somewhere on an operation, forgetting to call, and she had broken up with him. Then she'd met the man she married, and here she was. "Jerry, I want to help you. I *can* help you. Promise me you'll call me back. Promise."

His silence was so long that she thought she'd lost him, and she said his name a couple of times, and after several more seconds he said, "I'm broke. Cleaned out. I can't protect my guy. What the hell am I gonna do?"

"Jerry, call me back in three hours. Can you promise me to do that? Please?"

"Three hours. Yeah, maybe. Yeah."

"Jerry, promise! I can help you. Okay? Jerry—" She was still saying *Promise?* when he hung up and she was alone with the satellite.

Washington.

Dukas came to from an exhausted sleep, arrested in midsnore with the noise of his own snort in his ears. He grabbed for the telephone and fumbled it, rolling on his side to try to recover the phone and see the clock at the same time. "Dukas," he said in the whisper of a conspirator.

"Mike, it's Sally. I'm sorry for waking you up, but this is important."

"Okay, good—good—" He saw that it was twenty after four.

"Meet me. Now."

"Hey, wha-a-at—?"

"We need to talk. Not on an open phone. Meet me. You know the IHOP on Gallows Road?"

"No—no, can't say as I do—"

"Get on Gallows Road like you're coming to my house; it'll be on the left."

Dukas sighed. There was no point in protesting. She said it was important, and if she wouldn't talk about it on an open phone, then the years-long habits of being in Ops were running things, meaning that she had something good and it had to do with the case.

"I'm on my way," he said.

THE TELEPHONE WOKE THE CHIEF OF NAVAL OPERations at five-twenty-five. He had been dreaming about flying and woke feeling happy.

"Sir, Admiral Rankin here, sorry to wake you. Something's come up."

"Give it to me."

"NCIS has had a contact from Jakarta, Indonesia. An ex-CIA officer has what he says is a Chinese double agent who apparently is connected with George Shreed, the guy the Agency recently—"

"I remember."

"Special Agent Dukas believes that if this is genuine, it's a big break. If the double agent is the real thing, he could walk us right back to the beginning of Shreed's spying. At least that's what the guy in Jakarta is saying, that he goes way back with Shreed."

"How come he didn't go to the Agency?"

"Dukas thinks it's personal. The Agency retired him early. He's looking for help."

"What's he want?"

"This is fuzzy, but apparently the Chinese are after the agent—Dukas thinks they'd want him for the same reason we would. He says the American ex-CIA guy is vouched for by somebody Dukas trusts."

"Dukas in touch with the guy himself?"

"Apparently not. It's coming to him secondhand."

The CNO rubbed his forehead, shielding his eyes from the bedside light. "I don't like it." He gave it more thought. "What can we do?"

"USS *Jackson Baldwin* is twenty hours' steam time away. We could order her to Jakarta, pull the guy out. Pull them both out."

"Indonesians in on this?"

"No, sir. We'd have to declare a port visit, get their permission—the usual. Take them off clandestinely, I assume. Dukas isn't clear on that."

"There's nobody on a frigate can pull off an operation like that. Who've we got out there?"

"I'm having that checked. Nobody in Jakarta itself—maybe the naval attaché—"

The CNO muttered, "Unh-unh," and wrote a note and said, "Man from here can't be out there in time to do it. Got to be somebody already in the area. Get back to me on it." He scribbled again on the pad. "What's the *Baldwin* doing?"

"Far picket for BG 16."

"All right, detach the *Baldwin* and order it flank speed to Jakarta. Get all this sorted out as fast as you can, and have the NCIS guy in my office at 0800. I don't like it one little bit, and if it isn't rock-solid within twelve hours, I'm ordering the *Baldwin* back."

His wife was awake and looking at him. She smiled at him sadly and he said, "Another quiet day in Washington."

Office of the Chief of Naval Operations.

Dukas was supposed to have met with the JAG team about springing Nickie Groski at eight, but the command performance in the CNO's office wiped the board clean. By nine, the

CNO had ordered him to get a team to a U.S. frigate called the *Jackson Baldwin* with deliberate speed, but to be prepared for changes because he might yet call the whole operation off. Dukas had laid out the case, named Jerry Piat and Sally Baranowski, pointed out that anybody connected with Shreed was still in the Navy's universe because he hadn't closed Crystal Insight, and somebody who could really walk the cat back to Shreed's early days in Jakarta was the catch of a lifetime.

"Mister Dukas, this is the second time I've seen you in two days." The CNO wasn't amused.

"Yes, sir."

"I don't want to see you again—clear?"

"Yes, sir."

"If we do this, we have to do the whole thing and pull these guys out clandestinely. I'll be frank with you: I don't like it. It costs a lot of money to send a ship down to Jakarta, not to mention what the BG is having to do to patch the hole in its screen. I don't like doing stuff by the seat of our pants, no planning, and I don't like secondhand data. Has this guy in Jakarta called your contact back yet?"

"Not yet." Piat was, by then, forty-five minutes overdue.

Dukas had tried to assure the CNO that Sally was rock-solid. He had tried to convince him that this guy Piat must mean what he said. He didn't say that the name Piat had rung a bell because he had already heard it from Carl Menzes. By the end of his allowed time with the CNO, Dukas himself was a little dubious—skepticism is catching—but in the meantime, they had an NCIS agent named Ken Huang heading for the *Baldwin* from Manila by way of a COD to the carrier and a chopper the rest of the way.

"If this goes down," the CNO had growled, "*Baldwin* will make Jakarta early tomorrow our time. They'll need twenty-four hours there for appearance's sake, not to mention picking these guys up. That's day after tomorrow, morning, earliest they can weigh anchor. Clear your calendar."

So Dukas had got his boss on a secure line and told him what was happening, and then he'd got his ass back to NCIS,

where he had had ten minutes to leave a message for Triffler
before he got a call from Sally.

"The answer's yes, he called."

Dukas felt his scalp tingle: The operation would go.

"What'd he say?"

"Not much." She was being cautious because of the open
line. "I just told him to hang on and wait because somebody
was coming. I gave him the phone contact your friends gave
me."

Dukas was nodding, looking at his watch. DNI had given
her a telephone cutout where Piat and Huang, the NCIS agent
from Manila, could communicate. "He understand?"

"He's been doing this all his life."

"He sober?"

"Probably not."

She seemed tense and didn't want to make small talk.
Dukas hung up feeling dissatisfied with her and with himself
but excited about the operation. He'd been planning to take
her out to dinner again that night, somewhere decent this
time, and then they were going back to his place for a change.
Now, he'd have to think about it, to think about some guy
named Jerry Piat whom Sally used to sleep with and how
much they still meant to each other if she was the one person
in the world he could call when he was really in deep shit.
Dukas knew that he wasn't in love with Sally, nor she with
him, but he thought they were getting comfortable. He
thought that he was good for her. Was some ex who called her
up only because he was broke and in trouble going to make
waves?

"I look appropriate again, Mister Dukas," Leslie said from
the other side of the office.

"That's fine, Leslie."

"Actually, I look *awful*."

"You don't. You look great." Dukas hardly took in how
she looked—something with a lot of gray. "Keep the phone
available, Leslie—no personal calls, in or out. Something's
happening." Her eyes got big and he turned away. "Tell you
later," he said.

He was worrying about what was happening in Jakarta

when his phone rang, and he flinched when he heard Carl Menzes on the other end. Menzes's voice was like a glass raised in salute. "Hail, the conquering hero!" Dukas didn't get it, and Menzes said, "Navy one, Agency zed. You haven't heard?"

"I'm the last to know."

"The Groski kid has to be produced to his mother and his lawyer. We caved—Legal advised against going against the Navy in court—bad precedent."

Dukas grinned. "You don't sound too shocked."

"You should hear the OD people! They're screaming to take it all the way to the Supreme Court, but I hear that Partlow has already negatived that." He laughed, letting Dukas know that he enjoyed the Ops embarrassment. "Nice move. Applause, applause."

"You bitter?"

"Sadder but wiser. But it's a bad precedent, you know."

Dukas thought about the people whom the *Baldwin* was going to lift out of Jakarta. Dukas was already working to find secure housing for them and a place to run an interrogation. How long could he hold foreign nationals who'd be coming into the U.S. with only notification to Immigration and no paperwork? "Well, for now I'll enjoy winning. It's a nice change."

Menzes laughed. He was, despite everything, a good guy.

"A Mister Welbert?" Leslie said from the other side of the office.

"Welbert, Welbert—Oh, shit!" Welbert, he remembered almost too late, was Nickie Groski's lawyer. "Mister Welbert!" he shouted into the telephone. "Congratulations! When do I talk to the kid?"

Welbert sounded petulant. "They made us wait at the D.C. jail for half an hour. His mother crying her eyes out."

"But they did hand him over."

"Well, he's in the D.C. jail."

"Goddamit—" Dukas banged the telephone down and called JAG and began shouting about habeas corpus. He went through four Navy lawyers before he found the two who'd ramrodded the Groski thing, and then there was shouting at both ends of the telephone when the lawyers realized that the Agency had "released" the kid into the D.C. jail, a zoo where any peace of mind he had left after a month of being kicked around safe houses would be pounded out of him. "I'll have him out of there in a quarter of an hour!" the JAG guy shouted.

"Promise?"

"Try me!"

In the event, it was an hour, but, before noon, Nickie Groski was on the streets with his mother and his lawyer. Dukas didn't see them, but he could picture it, and he had his doubts—a woman who hadn't been able to control her kid up to that point (so why assume she could do so now?), and a hack lawyer with a styrofoam brain, and a seventeen-year-old who was trouble in spades. Still, the kid was out.

"You have him where I can talk to him at five," Dukas said to Welbert in another phone call.

"He's wearing an electronic bracelet."

"I don't care if he's wearing a training bra—where do I meet him at five?"

Welbert cleared his throat with one of those "oh, by-the-way" sounds and said, "What are you offering?"

"Offering? What is he, the recumbent Vishnu? What should I be offering?"

"Nickie will talk in exchange for zero jail time."

"I'll get back to you."

Dukas got on the phone to the JAG office again. "I've got to be able to offer the Groski kid zero jail time."

The JAG officer thought that that was pretty funny. "No way," he said. "The FBI's saying two years for violation of parole."

Dukas got on the phone to Myeroff, his FBI contact on the Seattle case.

FOUR HOURS LATER, DUKAS WAS ON HIS THIRD CALL with Myeroff. His forehead was on his left palm; a pencil and a legal pad were in front of him; and Leslie was looking worried on the other side of the divider because she had heard everything he'd shouted all morning.

"Okay, how bad is it?" Dukas said.

"We'll take your deal."

Dukas sat up. "You will?"

"We drop all charges on Groski. You bring us in on your investigation of the state police in Seattle. When there's a bust, we take part. We do the PR and take the credit in the media. You don't touch Helmer—he's ours and we haven't given him enough rope yet."

Dukas sighed, thinking that it would kill Triffler, and maybe Al Craik, as well. "And I can promise the Groski kid no jail time?"

"You can."

"You got a deal."

Dar es Salaam.

"We have a report from Embassy Washington." Jiang charged into Lao's office with a flimsy marked by a thread of red down the left edge.

Lao was reading a set of agent reports that were all hearsay. None of his officers, spread over a wide theater of operations, seemed to have a single agent who had direct access to anyone who could help him with Chen. "Well?"

Jiang shook his head.

"Craik spends most of his time on the Whidbey Island base, and the one time they managed to lay eyes on him, he had a full countersurveillance team on him."

Lao threw his pen across the room, a very un-Chinese thing to do.

Washington.

At five in the afternoon, Dukas was in Welbert's tatty law office. Convenient to the D.C. courts and five bail bondsmen, the place screamed of exploitation and clapped-out jurisprudence; its walls were drab and chipped, its furniture sagging, its wall calendar a year out of date. The Agency had insisted on sending somebody Dukas didn't know, a young achiever who had decided to dress casual and try to look like his idea of

Welbert's clients, which he succeeded in doing as well as any other white Midwesterner with a college education could have done.

Welbert shook hands with everybody and, apparently cast into deep depression by the effort, leaned against a yellow naugahyde chair.

"Where's his mother?" Dukas said.

"She wanted to see her medical adviser." Welbert looked frightened. "She's bipolar."

They went into Welbert's inner sanctum, which had a desk and some legal-book bindings that may or may not have had books inside them, and a wall map of the D.C. jail so that once Welbert had failed to get you free you'd know how to get around your new home. There was a smell of disinfectant.

Nickie Groski had not so long ago had purple hair, most of which his Agency keepers had cut off; now he had only purple tips, so that he looked as if he were wearing a purple hair net. He also had plenty of acne, and a slouch that suggested that his bones above the waist were bending under the weight of his head and shoulders.

"Yeah" was his response to Dukas's greeting. He was the kind of kid Dukas wanted to slap up into a peak, as his grandmother used to say. Four years in the Navy would do him a lot of good, was Dukas's view, although the Navy probably wouldn't take him.

"Mister Dukas is from the Naval Criminal Investigative Service, Nick," Welbert said. "He's going to ask you some questions. Mister Anderson here is from the CIA."

"I bet," Nickie said. He sneered at young Mister Anderson.

"Let's get comfortable," Welbert said.

Nickie had collapsed into a chair as soon as he had got into the room. Now, the others sat down.

"You understand the offer, Nickie?" Welbert said. "Reduction to one month, of which you've already done the time. And he can get you a job with good money."

"I don't want a *job*," the kid said, making a job sound like an unfashionable pair of sneakers.

"You going to talk to me?" Dukas said.

Nickie glanced at Welbert, who looked at Dukas and then

nodded. This was as precise as the acceptance of the deal got, and Nickie said, "I'm talking, ain't I?"

"You're speaking, but so far you aren't talking." Dukas placed his chair opposite the boy. "Tell me about Shreed's computers."

"C-fucking-IA has them now, I bet. Ask *him*." Nickie sneered at the Agency youth.

"The hard drives were missing by the time the CIA got there. Nickie, don't you want to stay out of jail?"

The kid hugged himself and looked at the lawyer, who smiled. Dukas thought of all the doomed people who must have gotten that smile. Nickie looked away. "CIA fucks wouldn't give me spit when I asked for a deal before."

"I've fixed that."

"How do I know when I've said enough?"

"When I say so." Dukas met the washed-out eyes. "It's my call, Nickie. I'm the cop—you're the one in the shit. I can't change that."

Nickie leaned back in the chair and said, "Oh, man," his spine so profoundly curved that his coccyx was resting on the edge of the seat. Dukas thought he had lost him. But, to his surprise, Nickie rallied himself, dug into one nostril with a finger, and, fortified by what he found, leaned way over toward Dukas and said, "Okay."

Dukas put a pocket tape recorder where Nickie and the lawyer could see it. He turned it on. Behind him, the CIA man was doing the same.

It took an hour, and Dukas had to lead him back from tangents and pull him up when the boy thought he had said enough and Dukas knew he hadn't. Nickie was trying to keep something to bargain with later, for which Dukas couldn't blame him.

Dukas already knew some of what he said, but a lot of it was new. Shreed, Nickie said, would have been tough to crack if he, Nickie, hadn't physically been into his computers and copied their files. What Suter had wanted him for was information about money—not just any money, but big amounts that Suter said were in foreign accounts.

"He never tole me how much or where, man, like that

was *his* business—he was your a-number-one all-time prick, right?—but he expected me to do magic and pull this shit out of the hard drive with my weenie. Suter didn't know zip about computers, so he couldn't help me, but he couldn't tell what I was doing, either, right? So I'm running my own penetration program on his files, right? Man, he had firewalls! Everything was passworded. So, about twenty hours into it—I got his password algorithms, right? So I know what I'm doing—I find this program that takes me to a mainframe someplace. I could tell because I looked around when I was in there; it was fucking *huge*. So Shreed's got this program sitting on the mainframe, but it's firewalled and they don't know it's there. From that, he's sending out a worm whenever the mainframe's on and getting back all this crap. I mean, *code*. A lot of it I can't make shit out of because, I found this out later, it's Chinese code, but my computer won't display the right stuff, so it comes up as fucking chaos."

"What the hell'd you do?" Dukas said.

Nickie's voice had got louder and more confident, and Dukas realized that the kid was a whole creature only when he was playing with or talking about computers. He wasn't talking to hear himself talk, and he wasn't talking to show off: He was making verbal love.

"I said screw it and went for what I could read, which took me where the worm went and then out again. I didn't get it, but it took me to the money. I mean, that's what it was all about: bank accounts. Which I didn't get until the third day. I got a hit on one that came through with a name, and I saw it was a bank. Is there a Maldive Island?"

"Islands, plural," Dukas said. "The Maldives."

"Whatever. That's where this was. So I wrote a little program to watchdog these messages, which were accounts, but I didn't know that then, so the watchdog kept track of the messages going back and forth, including to this Maldive Island, so I figured then these were all banks. These were bank transactions."

"How many?" Dukas said.

"A lot."

"How many is a lot?"

"Like nine hundred?"

Nine hundred bank accounts? Could anybody have nine hundred bank accounts?

"How much money was there?"

"I never seen what was in there, only the transactions."

"For how long?"

"About a day, day and a half."

"And how much money was there in the transactions?"

"If I had it right, about twenty million. That one bank, I mean." Nickie glanced sideways at the lawyer, who looked distressed. The CIA man didn't react, and Dukas guessed that he already knew about the money. Of course—they'd had Nickie for a month.

"Nickie," Dukas said, "you're doing great." His brain was processing what twenty million dollars in a day meant if it was multiplied by all the days that Shreed might have been on a computer. It had to be the money Shreed had talked about to his Chinese control, Chen. *It had to be Chinese money.* "Nickie," Dukas said, "now, this money. Was Shreed just watching this money, or—?" *Or what?* Dukas didn't know.

"He had a worm, I *tole* you. Part of what was sitting there on this mainframe, I couldn't access it, so I figured it was big. You know—important. So then Shreed took off, and he was working from, I think, a laptop someplace, because I didn't get nothing showing on any of the stuff I got from his files, except sometimes he was sending an E-mail. Then, just before the cops came in, this message came in; it was just a password, and all sorts of shit happened. Everything lit up. It was awesome, man."

"What happened?"

"A nuke, man. He nuked it." Nickie snickered. "Suter about shit his pants. I go, 'The money's going, man—the money's going—' And he's going, 'Where, where?' and pissing his pants, because he had an account that he was going to send the money to."

"Suter knew about the money?"

"He knew something he wouldn't tell me. All he said was, Shreed was going to get a lot of money and we were going to take it." Dukas glanced at the CIA man and saw that this wasn't news to him, either.

"So what happened?"

"Suter goes, 'Where's it going, where's it going—? We gotta get it, we gotta get it—' and I was watching what was happening, and he was right, Shreed's worm was sending all the money from the accounts away." Nickie snickered again.

Dukas waited and then said, "Away where?"

"*Away.* See, it wasn't real money, right? It was just numbers—just code. *And he sent the code into cyberspace.* So all the money in all those banks, it just didn't exist no more." Nickie for the first time gave a real grin. "That was some cool hacker, man." Nickie was delighted by the prospect of all that money turned into random charges of electricity.

Dukas looked at the CIA man. He looked oddly embarrassed. The Ops Directorate had had its hands on Nickie's computer and had milked it for data, and they'd had Nickie for a month and undoubtedly got this story, so why was this guy embarrassed? *Because they didn't know what to do next,* Dukas guessed. *They think they should have had an intelligence coup and they blew it!* Five microseconds after the money turned to electrons, it would have been too late to try to get it back; a day later, it would have been too late to jump on the Chinese about it. *They didn't know whether to shit or go blind.*

If twenty million dollars' worth of transactions had gone by in a day, how much could there have been? Dukas's math was not good, but he knew that you could get to a thousand million—a billion—pretty fast at twenty million a day. Billions? *Billions? Was that what Rathunter was after?*

"Okay, Nickie. You done good. We got a deal."

Seattle.

It was the next day. "Four hours' work for that?" Alan asked. He was sitting in the backseat of Triffler's new Buick rental, swallowing an Italian ice that Triffler had provided. He had just finished driving a surveillance route through what seemed like every street in Seattle, with a stop at the Kusluski house to check out the fake newspaper story.

"You ran the route perfectly. On time for every waypoint. The guys had you through the whole thing."

"And?" Alan thought the creamy lemon of the ice was the greatest, *coolest* thing he'd ever had. "This is great."

"I hoped you'd like it. Seattle has some cultural advantages. You were clean the whole way."

"What does that mean?"

"It means that they're waiting for the trap, which is one of the other two action items."

"That's something to look forward to."

"And Mrs. Kusluski?"

"I think she was glad of the company, but she knew nothing about it either way. She didn't remember the case, but she didn't really know that much about the routine of her husband's job beyond that he had a citation for valor. It wasn't exactly an upbeat conversation."

"Welcome to the exciting world of police work, Al."

"Four hours of driving around for a ten-minute conversation?"

"Ah, police work embedded in espionage, I should have said."

"Can I go back to flying now?"

"Tomorrow, we do the call to the newspaper and start part two."

Alan finished the last of his ice.

"I'm meeting with some SubPac guys tomorrow to try to get a schedule on submarine sailings. I hope to get a couple of planes up and see if the uplink shows on our ESM and corresponds to the sailing. That burst transmission is right at the edge of our capability, but we ought to see it."

Triffler leaned over the seat, scooped the finished ice container out of Alan's hand before he could drop it in the back, and popped it neatly in a little plastic trash bag hanging from the driver's-side door. "You really think that will work?"

"I really think so. I'm not so sure that SubPac will buy the sailing schedule part. They hold that stuff very close. And there might not be one for weeks. But all that said, I think it'll work."

"Can you triangulate the position of the signal?"

"From a burst? Maybe, but only to a few miles."

"I sense a deeper plan here." Triffler smiled the way he did when he was leading a witness.

"Yeah. I guess I think that the burst is short-range, so it's meant for a sub off the coast. And if it is, then that sub has to retransmit, so there will be an answering transmission going from the sub back to China. I have no idea what it will look like, but it ought to be VLF, so we'll never see it—but a sub might."

"VLF?"

"Very Low Frequency. A transmission meant to travel through the water. Takes a long time, but it can be done."

"So if you get SubPac to play, and it all works, and you catch the burst transmission? . . ." Triffler left the end hanging, and Alan looked out the window as a new set of clouds rolled in over the sound. They were silent for a moment. "I don't know."

"Catching whoever's sending the transmissions will take years."

"Yeah. I have a better idea, though. Short-term, but effective."

"And?"

"Catch the sub."

They were both silent for a moment, watching the clouds roll in.

"Do you have paperwork on all of this?" said Triffler.

"Not yet. I have to prove the hypothesis."

"Alan, if you're going to work with law enforcement, you have to have a paper trail every time. I'm going to have to get you downtown to see Special Agent Nagel."

"Yeah. Well, if I blow the meeting with SubPac, there won't be a case."

21

SubPac, Bremerton, Washington.

A DAY LATER, ALAN WAS SMILING AT THE TWO SENIOR
captains and an intelligence officer as he accepted a cup of
coffee. He was the most junior officer in the room by two pay
grades, and he felt it. Admiral Smerts greeted him with a firm
handshake and indicated a chair. It had more the air of a
board of inquiry than a meeting.

Submarine officers were a breed apart. Specially chosen,
trained in their own schools, they almost belonged to a different service, and they had their own language and their own
traditions. Alan knew they were far more rank-conscious than
aviators. He felt his lack of knowledge of their ways from the
first but set some interior jaw and determined to win them
over. His wings were of no value here, and neither was his intelligence experience. They cared only about their own vast
element beneath the waves.

"Well, Commander?" The admiral didn't unbend even to
the extent of a smile. Perhaps he already resented the inter-
ruption of his job. Alan had to hope he had the intelligence

officer, Captain Manley, on his side. She had arranged the meeting based on his reports.

"Sir. I'm here today to brief you on NCIS efforts to date on the case we call Sleeping Dog. The case has developed some immediacy because we believe now that it represents the efforts of a foreign power to track the movements of naval units within the Seattle/Puget Sound area, and those units include submarines." *That is,* thought Alan, *I believe the case has developed some immediacy and Mike may have my head.*

The admiral nodded, as if permitting him to continue.

"Sleeping Dog has existed as a case since the early nineties. NSA had occasional hits on a transmitter operating in a footprint so broad that it might have included most of the Northwest of the North American continent. This transmitter was, and is, of an old type that delivers a burst transmission at a high frequency. The signal, while it propagates a long way, would only actually be receivable for information at a fairly short range. So the assumption has always been that the man behind the transmitter was sending his signal to another receiver fairly close. In the last few years, the rate of those transmissions has increased."

Alan opened his laptop and brought up a graphic that displayed the transmissions they had detected since 1993.

"This lists what we've seen." Alan then hit Enter. "This is the correspondence to known sailings of major Pacific Fleet units from Puget Sound."

A set of green and yellow lines enveloped most of the transmission dates. It was an impressive graphic. It had occupied two evenings while Rose was down at Edwards.

"Due to the close-hold nature of the sailings of some units like ballistic missile submarines, this graphic is incomplete, but Captain Manley has been kind enough to confirm that there is further correspondence."

The admiral looked over at Captain Manley, who brushed back her straight gray hair with one hand and frowned. "The correspondence isn't perfect, Admiral, but it's pretty high, especially recently."

"Why recently?" The admiral looked interested.

"Sir, this is more in line of a guess, but I'd say the agent changed his focus from another target to submarines." Alan shrugged.

The admiral nodded. "So you're not suggesting this is a submariner."

Delicate ground. It was a byword in NCIS that the submarine ·community thought it screened its candidates too well to have a spy.

"I don't know that much, sir. It could be a man with a boat, or a man in the harbor patrol. It could be a man with access to a high-level JOTS terminal that includes submarines, although if that were the case, he'd not have to send his reports so close to the sailing dates and we wouldn't see any correspondence. But my guess is that at least recently he's been communicating to a foreign submarine."

"Say that again?"

"Sir, I have some good grams on what appears to be a Chinese or perhaps a Russian attack boat. I have an aerial sighting of a pos sub off Puget Sound. I have a whole body of mythology from the P-3 and S-3 communities going back about four months, suggesting that there is 'something in the op area.' And that signal has to go somewhere."

Captain Manley leaned forward. "Sir, USS *Texas* reported—"

The admiral glared at all of them. "I know. I see the picture." The admiral looked at the graphics. Then he looked at Captain Manley. "Why is this the first we've heard of this? It doesn't look like it took a rocket scientist to make the connection."

Manley looked at Alan.

Alan looked at his shoes for a moment. "Sir, it's really not my place to say, but I'll do my best. We think that a highly placed mole in Washington covered this operation by killing all activity on its investigation."

"Why is this the first I've heard of that element? If you say the words 'need to know,' Commander, I'll ask you to leave. I need to know anything that affects my submarines."

It's not that simple, Admiral. Not a good tack to take. This operation was giving Alan a glimpse into a very dark world, a world of decision-making where things like "need to know" were in conflict, and where no answer was ever easy. It was easy to say that George Shreed was not an issue for an admiral commanding nuclear submarines, but if he didn't have the "need to know," who did?

"Sir, I think you'd need to talk to someone higher than me at NCIS. Can I recommend you speak to Mike Dukas at Counterintelligence?"

"Commander, I may just call the CNO, thank you very much. Maybe he can tell me why I don't know anything about this 'highly placed mole.' "

Mike is going to kill me, Alan thought. "Sir, we're here now, and I'd like to prove this theory right if I can." Manley nodded, encouraging him.

"How's that?" The admiral leaned forward. The two captains, silent watchers, leaned forward as well.

"I'd like to know the date of the next sailing. And I'd like to have some tools in the air and on the ground to be ready to react."

"And that will catch the spy?"

"No, sir. That will prove that there is a spy. I have to shoot straight on this, sir. Catching him may take a long time."

Alan spent half an hour going over why, and where, and who. The admiral wanted to believe that they could catch the spy the moment he transmitted. Privately, Alan thought he watched too many movies. In the end, he agreed to support Alan's project and said that Alan would get twenty-four hours' notice of the next sailing date. And, as Alan left, the admiral leaned out to his secretary.

"Get me the CNO," he said.

NCIS HQ.

"Mike, you're going to kill me."

"Probably. Why now?"

"I just told the admiral at SubPac that a mole in Washington had sat on this investigation."

Silence. Long silence. "Mike? You there?"

"Alan, that wasn't your call to make."

"Jesus, Mike. I know. On the other hand, this is the Navy. They need to know."

"You mean, you didn't want to take the fall or lie, so you told the truth."

"Yeah. The admiral is going to the CNO right now."

Silence. Tinny STU noises.

"Okay, Al. Thanks for giving me a heads up. Don't ever do this to me again, okay?"

Alan couldn't decide whether he was right or wrong, and Mike's anger hurt him. But he fought his own anger. He *was* the subordinate, here. "I'm sorry, Mike."

"Yeah. Don't sweat it, Alan. Things are moving. Just keep them moving."

"Roger that."

IN WASHINGTON, DUKAS LOOKED AT A MESSAGE SLIP: the *Jackson Baldwin* had just left Jakarta—with passengers.

In the Indian Ocean.

Ahmed Fazrahi felt the cigarette boat yaw, and he spun the wheel. He feared the big sea that seemed ready to snatch him, sure that if they turned broadside to the swell, they would broach and go down in seconds. He was trying to find the carrier battle group but had only two-day-old information, and instead of hated American ships, there was only this angry ocean and, on his pathetic little radar screen, some commercial rust bucket five miles ahead.

The stern rose and the twin propellers came free of the water, and the engines screamed like cats. Fazrahi flinched, willing the stern to come down. He hated his fear. It sat inside him, he thought, like a cancer. To kill it, he pushed the throttle its last few millimeters. The stern settled and the engines returned to their working roar, and he swung a few degrees north to avoid the merchant ship, invisible still but only three miles away now.

When he crested the next swell, he looked north and saw

one of the other boats, too far away to wave. There should have been three more.

It was going to be bad out here when the day came, he thought. Bad trying to keep the five boats together, bad trying to locate the carrier, no matter how good the information that was passed to them. Bad when they were discovered—but by then, they would be too close.

Overhead, he heard an aircraft in the cloud, and he thought, *American*.

Seattle.

Alan was early to a meeting with Triffler because he'd passed through the gate of the Whidbey Island base in record time, but he had learned to build some slop into his routes and he went to the magazine arcade next to the supermarket and bought a copy of *Aviation Week* and an *Economist*. Then he was back in the groove. He walked into the mall entrance of the supermarket and picked up the makings of a dinner he wouldn't ever eat because the BOQ didn't give him a place to cook it. Spaghetti. A little sausage. It was a good market. He hummed as he walked with his basket on his arm.

Alan looked at his watch again and noted that the meeting window was one minute old. Good. Perfect. He picked a can of tomatoes off the shelf and walked to the back of the supermarket, turned left, and started up the coffee aisle. Dick Triffler was right on his spot, getting beans from a big brass dispenser.

"Is that stuff really worth the money?" Alan asked, today's signal.

"Depends on how much you like coffee," Triffler replied.

Early on, Alan had questioned all these little verbal signals. "I know you when I see you."

Triffler had shaken his head. "It won't always be me."

This morning, it was still Triffler. Triffler handed him the beans to smell and Alan got another piece of paper with the bag. A message.

"Too rich for me," said Alan, and walked off. In the parking lot, he read the note, which told him to walk over to the Home Depot, where Triffler would pick him up in six minutes. He tossed his groceries in his rental car and walked across the parking lot, zipping his Gore-Tex against the rain.

Triffler picked him up right on the dot.

"Now we call Mister Tashimaya?"

"Yes." Triffler took them out of the parking lot, out of the mall area, and up the ramp to the highway.

"Why exactly couldn't we have done this before?"

"I've been waiting to get all the ducks in a row, Alan. Once we call him, the whole thing starts moving to the end. I needed a bigger team, certain arrest authorities. As it turns out, I needed the cooperation of the FBI. That all took time."

Alan nodded. "I've presented my theory on the submarine to SubPac. If they bite, it could go anytime."

Triffler didn't take his eyes from the road. "One step at a time. I've got the team. We're going to do this today, before people get pulled."

Alan reached for the cell phone clipped to the dash.

"Unh-unh," Triffler said. "We're doing this from the NCIS office so we can run a trace and do it right."

SPECIAL AGENT NAGEL MET THEM IN THE LOBBY OF the Federal Building. Triffler introduced them without comment. Nagel then guided them to a guard desk where Alan drew a big red badge labeled VISITOR and Triffler showed his badge with casual authority. The elevators were huge and covered in some kind of blast-resistant mesh. A computer-generated voice counted off the floors and neither of the two NCIS agents spoke at all.

The squad room of the NCIS office in Seattle reminded Alan of the set of a cop show. There was a map of Seattle and Puget Sound, with inset street maps of Navy facilities. There was a corkboard at the end of the room, with all the local players in the Sleeping Dog case pasted to it, including a photo of Alan himself. There were fuzzy surveillance photos of most of the people who had followed Alan around since he arrived. They had license tags pasted over them and, in some cases, names or ID numbers. Lines had been drawn in red to connect some of the players. Alan went up close and saw a photograph of a man in a dark suit. There was no name, just an FBI case number. Most of the red lines started with him.

"That's Helmer," Triffler said. Nagel grunted. There were other men filing into the room, most dressed in short-sleeved shirts and ties with slacks. There was one woman. One man wore a three-piece suit and flashy shoes. Another wore shorts and a T-shirt and carried an open wallet of electronics tools. Triffler introduced them all quickly, and Alan knew he wouldn't remember their names. They all looked like cops. One was from the FBI, but they all had a certain sameness to them.

The guy with the tools set up a telephone with some electronic equipment attached.

"Okay," Triffler said. "This should be it. Alan will make the call and get us a site, and then we're a go."

"What if they set the meet for next week?" The guy in the flashy shoes. He seemed to want to say more. Triffler cut him off with a wave.

"Let's deal with that when it happens. Everybody ready? Trace on? Let's go." He motioned Alan to the telephone.

Alan had been scribbling a phone script at a desk. He sat, reviewed the script one more time, and was handed a folder.

"Meeting site," said one of the guys. "If he doesn't have his own picked out." Alan riffled through it, saw it was a park in downtown Seattle. He reached for the phone.

"It'll dial itself. Just let it do its thing," said the tech guy.

Alan picked up and listened to the phone dialing. It rang three times and there was a distinct click, as if it were going to an answering machine, and then it rang again.

"Changed lines. Fancy," said the tech guy, doing something on a laptop.

"*Hello,*" said a strong male voice. It echoed a little in the squad room, broadcast on speakers.

"Hello? May I speak to Mister Tashimaya?"

A slight hesitation. "Speaking. May I help you?" The voice was strong, just barely accented. Educated.

"Mister Tashimaya, I'm investigating a series of incidents regarding radio transmissions in the Seattle area. I understand you had a problem with your ham radio license that might have a bearing on my study. Could we get together?"

"To whom am I speaking?"

"My name is Alan Craik. I'm an officer in the Navy."

"Yes, Mister Craik. Am I under investigation?"

"No, sir. I'm just interested in hearing about your ham radio problems." Alan didn't like this part, because if it were all for real, they'd have another level of cover to keep Mister Tashimaya from knowing why they wanted to talk to him. After all, they were supposed to believe he *might* be a foreign agent. But the wheels within wheels meant that it shouldn't matter. Mister Tashimaya should *want* the meeting.

"I'd rather not talk about this here," the voice said. "Perhaps we could meet. I have some things that might interest you."

Alan wondered if Mister Tashimaya was reading from a script. He looked up at Triffler, who made a motion with his hand that meant *go on*.

"That would be fine, sir. Where would be convenient? I could come to your house, if that would be easier."

"No, please. I would prefer my part in this was not known at my house."

"Would you like to meet at ..." Alan had looked at the meeting site under his hand. "Do you know Falkland Park?"

Alan looked at Triffler, who looked at Nagel. Nagel nodded and went to the map. "Yes, I do."

"I'll meet you at the fountain there. How will I know you?"

"I'll be wearing a blue ball cap. Please, you carry a copy of *Time* magazine."

"Sure." Alan felt like he was getting instructions from Triffler. He scribbled it on his script, *blue ball cap* and *Time*. Around him, ten cops were doing the same.

"I will identify myself by saying 'There are rats and alligators in the subway here.' You will please further identify yourself by saying 'There are vultures on the high buildings.' "

Something about the diction of the sentence and the use of the word "further" made Alan sure that the voice at the other end was reading from a script.

"When?" he asked.

Another hesitation. It occurred to Alan that Tashimaya was in a room like this one, looking at others for confirmation just as he was. "Friday," said the voice. "I would like to meet you Friday, at one-fifteen."

"Friday at one-fifteen," Alan said, writing on his pad.

"I'll have something for you," the voice said.

"That's great," Alan said. "I'll be there." He put the phone back in the cradle and waited.

"He's off. Connection cut," said the tech guy.

Triffler clapped his hands together. "Okay, folks," he said. "We have a lot to do."

400 NM NNE of Mombasa, Kenya.

Soleck was afraid to land. He couldn't get around it. The nearer the landing came, the more he thought about it, and the tension in his gut had gone from a little flutter to a cold knot. Every time he touched the subject in his mind, he felt it in his gut.

Don't dwell on it, Rafehausen had said. *Don't think about the landing.* Nice. Really helpful.

His hand still hurt from the last landing.

It didn't help that he had six hours to think about it as he bored holes in the sky over the western Indian Ocean. The S-3s were out constantly, flying ASW missions over the open ocean to clear safe boxes ahead of the carrier. When they weren't searching for the submarine, they were flying surface-search missions, identifying every potential adversary in the sea around them. Lack of aircrew meant a lack of aircraft, and the aviators who weren't sick were flying nearly around the clock. Soleck tried to believe that his bad landings might have something to do with fatigue. He tried to believe a lot of things, but, inside, he had begun to doubt that he could put the plane on the deck.

His stomach gave another lurch.

"I've got two of those cigarette boats coming out of Mogadishu," Craw said.

Soleck was glad for a moment. The cigarette boats were a hot topic in the intelligence spaces. LCDR Craik had sent them reports on cigarette boats all the way from his temporary duty station in Washington State. Soleck was a reader, and he had read the traffic and the background. He'd tried to dump tension by building computer sims of cigarette boats for the MARI computer. He had wasted a day on it.

"They're really goin'," said "Baldy" Baldwin, a borrowed Tacco from the VS squadron. He wasn't sick. That made him aircrew. "Hey, this MARI thing is somethin' else. Hell, you can see the engines clear as day!"

"How fast are they going?" asked Soleck.

"Almost sixty knots, due east into the sunrise."

"Now they're turning south."

They watched the boats. Craw swept other sectors, but the attention of the crew was on the two cigarette boats. Even Soleck began to watch them as it became clearer where they were headed. They weren't headed for the carrier.

But they were headed for where the carrier had been *yesterday*. Craw saw it first, and put a marker on the screen.

"How do they know?" Baldwin asked. "Those boats don't even have a surface-search radar that will reach out fifteen miles. No masts."

Somehow, it made the boats more ominous, and their presence was like the threat of some little, poisonous insect out on the ocean. The flight back was silent.

Soleck brought them in to an adequate landing, and Baldwin left them to debrief in the intel center and pass the word. Someone was giving the CV's location to the boats. Ninety frames farther forward, Soleck got out of his flight harness to find that the LSO thought he had been too slow into the break and too long in the groove and hadn't given him an okay on the landing. Soleck shook his head, wanting to whine that it wasn't fair. He wondered what the hell he was doing wrong.

NAS Whidbey Island.

Alan watched the JOTS terminal repeater with a cold cup of forgotten coffee in his hand, his eyes tracking the movement of the two cigarette boats identified by his S-3s half a world away. They came out from Mogadishu and then ran down the coast for hundreds of miles before making their dash out into the open sea. It took hours.

Alan couldn't figure their role. Either they were trying to locate the carrier for some other attack, or the carrier was already located and they were the attack. The danger of small boats loaded with explosives had been present for the Navy since their first hostile encounters with the Iranian Republican Guard boats in the Persian Gulf way back in the eighties. Most sailors thought of small, fast boats as potential threats. But Alan couldn't work out how a handful of cigarette boats planned to threaten the battle group in the open ocean.

He laid a hand on the terminal as if to encourage it, much as he would when he was in a plane with a reluctant back end. He thought of Soleck and Craw and Stevens and the rest of his det. Then he scrolled the roller ball across the Indian Ocean to India and then past Sri Lanka to the Strait of Malacca and so west of Borneo, where he could see a detached circle marking a friendly surface ship. It was so far from the Seventh Fleet exercise area that he clicked on it, and it identified itself as USS *Jackson Baldwin*.

And the STU next to him rang. It wasn't his, so he let it ring twice, and then, when no one else picked up, he answered.

"Whidbey Island Intel Center, Lieutenant-Commander Craik speaking; this is not a secure line. May I help you?" The spiel reminded him of being a squadron duty officer, back in the day. He hadn't done the phone routine in months.

"Lieutenant-Commander Alan Craik, please."

"Speaking."

"Going secure." By now, Alan knew the voice belonged to Captain Manley at Bremerton, and his stomach gave a little flutter.

"I have you secure."

"I have you the same, ma'am."

"There's an attack boat going to sea in two days. It will weigh from Bremerton at 0400. As soon as she's clear of shipping, she'll trail a VLF/ULF antenna."

"Thanks, ma'am."

"You'll be ready?"

"Ma'am, this is put together with some spit and some baling wire. But yes, ma'am. We'll be ready."

"Then go get 'em, Commander. I doubt there's another gold oak leaf in the Navy who could get our sailing schedule changed."

"Yes, ma'am."

"This is on my dime, Commander. If you fuck up, the head rolling around on the floor is mine."

"Won't happen, ma'am."

"Glad to hear it. Go get 'em."

She hung up. Alan felt a surge of loyalty toward her, although he had met her only twice. She had come through. He didn't need to be told how much she had risked. But he was so sure. His stomach gave a little twinge, and he wondered how sure he was.

Manila.

A Navy COD came in over the city as a cluster of moving lights in the darkness, turned into its final approach, and glided down to kiss the concrete far out on the runway. Instead of taxiing toward the terminal, it turned toward the cargo area. Blue lights showed it the way. Again, however, it turned aside and moved carefully toward a charter jet that was waiting by itself.

Six NCIS and Master-of-Arms Program specialists ringed the aircraft, all armed. When the COD cut its engines and the door opened, two trotted forward to lead the way to the bigger jet. Jerry Piat, the Li family, and Special Agent Ken Huang walked behind them into the darkness.

Twenty minutes later, the jet was airborne for Washington.

22

Patuxent River Naval Air Station.

SPECIAL AGENT KEN HUANG WAS BIG IN ALL DIREC-
tions, maybe part-Polynesian, Dukas thought, like one of
those six-by-six tackles who show up in Big Ten starting line-
ups. They shook hands; Huang punched his shoulder. "Good
to go, man!" Dukas thought that Huang wanted to high-five
him, and he winced away.

"How'd it go in Jakarta?" Dukas asked, to distract the
huge man.

"Piece a cake. Little spicy at the end, no problem." Huang
grinned.

"What's this guy Piat like?" Dukas said. He had started to
sweat; the day was hot, a ferocious sun beating down and the
wind like a slap from a hot towel.

"Better now he's sober. Okay guy. Bitter about the Agency.
Doesn't trust us much, either." Huang grabbed Dukas's elbow
as if he were going to pitch him over his shoulder. "The guy he
brought in is the real thing, Dukas. Piat's very protective, plus
the guy's dependent, so I didn't get much yet."

"Where have we got them?"

"About a mile away. Former officer housing. Kind of run-down, but it's isolated."

"Keep on him."

They went inside. They were keeping Piat in a former EM barracks that had been opened for the purpose. He was the only man in it, with four guards, and visitors like Dukas who came and went. The place smelled musty, and their footsteps echoed in the old wooden building. Huang opened a door, and Dukas stepped inside and saw Jerry Piat.

Dukas felt a pang of jealousy: If looks were what mattered to a woman like Sally Baranowski, Piat swept the board. He had gray-black hair, a chiseled face, knotty arms below a black T-shirt. If he was a regular boozer, he somehow kept in shape. When he looked at Dukas, his face showed a small, fleeting spasm of surprise, like a tic.

"Mike Dukas, NCIS." He showed his badge.

Piat didn't look at the badge.

I would have looked at the badge, Dukas thought.

Piat, a small, confused frown on his face, slowly touched Dukas's hand, then took it in his and gripped it. "Thanks for getting us out." He sounded not so much grateful as resigned.

Well, that was a start.

There were three straight chairs and a metal Navy table with a gray rubber top that had probably felt the imprint of signatures on orders for the Korean War. Dukas sat on one side and Piat sat on the other, and Dukas made some small talk about the accommodations, the food—was it okay?—the weather—too hot for you? How was the flight? Piat was a pro; he knew what they were there for. He sat in a hard chair, legs crossed, answering meaningless questions meaninglessly. Then there was a hesitation, and Dukas said, "Okay."

Piat grinned. "Okay."

"How long did you work for George Shreed?"

Piat frowned. It was not what he had expected. "Year. Fourteen months. Look, Li—"

"In Jakarta. You worked for Shreed in Jakarta."

"You know all this, right?"

"That where you met Bobby Li?"

"Right."

"He worked for Shreed."

"He was a kid, yeah." Piat meant that Bobby Li had been *only* a kid and had been easily influenced. "Bobby lo—" He had started to say "loved" and stopped himself. "George was a father figure to him."

"For you, too?"

Piat shot him a look, the first forthright one he had given. *Stay out!*

"What are your plans?" Dukas said.

"What the hell does that mean? I don't have any plans! Why the hell do you think I called Baranowski?"

"You mentioned money to her. Said you were broke." That was a question, although he didn't make it sound like one.

Surprisingly, Piat smiled. "Flat," he said.

"We can help."

"You're goddam well going to help." Piat laughed again— the real thing this time. "Look, Dukas, let's be clear here: You're any port in a storm, okay? Baranowski said she knew somebody who could help. I needed help! I didn't know—" His voice petered out. He looked away.

"You didn't know it would be me." Dukas leaned forward so that his head was only eighteen inches from Piat's. "So what?"

"We were talking about money."

"No, we're talking about you and me. You said, 'I didn't know it would be you.' "

"I was going to say that I didn't think it would be the Navy."

"So, how much money?" Dukas said. He was thinking that he didn't want to let Piat know yet that he knew all about Jakarta and Sleeping Dog and Seattle. Everything in good time, and this was not a good time. Huang or somebody else could get all that. What Dukas needed was the comm plans in Chinese Checkers so he could make a date with his Chinese E-mail friend.

"I just dropped thirty thousand bucks in Jakarta. My own money. That cleans me out. And no, I didn't get receipts."

"Write me a narrative of where it went; I'll get it back for you."

"Just like that?"

"If Li is what you say, I don't think they'll nickel-and-dime me." He said "me" deliberately, so that Piat would understand that it was his operation. Piat looked skeptical, and, in truth, Dukas was skeptical, too, but he thought that with the CNO's office behind him, he'd get the money. It would take shouting and paperwork and endless bullshit, but he'd get it.

Especially if the comm plans in Chinese Checkers were the tradeoff.

Seattle.

Falkland Park was sunken below the level of the street, more on one end than the other, its trees pushing up so that in their maturity they shaded the sidewalks around the park. It was no bigger than half a football field, hardly more than a stretch of bright green grass surrounded by a walk and the belt of trees, with beds of cannas breaking the expanse of grass. A railing with stone balusters surrounded it at street level, above, broken by an entrance at each of the four corners.

From the sidewalk above the park's lower end, you could look through breaks in the trees and see three of the four flower beds, most of the walk, and the stone fountain at the far end, where a bare trickle of water ran from a grotesque mask down over algae-covered stones to a basin where, for some reason, people had thrown coins. A photographer had stationed himself at this point with his camera.

He seemed to be photographing everything but the park. He turned his back to it and focused on the clouds, then on a 1930s art deco facade, then on the long vista of the street and the sound beyond it. Every now and then, however, he turned, resting the camera on the stone balustrade and glancing down into the park. He could see two men working at the flower beds and a jogger. None seemed worth photographing.

After fifteen minutes of this, Alan Craik entered the far

left corner of the park, as the photographer saw it. The photographer glanced at his watch. So did both of the gardeners. The jogger was gone, but as Alan came down to the park's level, another jogger entered down the three steps to the photographer's right and began to jog, with the slowness of a big man, up toward the fountain.

The photographer got interested in the fountain. He picked up the camera and focused. The grotesque mask, eyes running black tears of pollution, stared back.

A dark man, probably East Indian, leaned on the balustrade next to the photographer. He was wearing cross-training shoes and jeans and a Mariners T-shirt; he had dark-rimmed glasses that made him look like a computer geek. He smiled at the photographer. "Beautiful day, eh?" He sounded Canadian.

"Great day," the photographer said. He was watching a slender Asian man come down the steps opposite to those Craik had used. Craik was now standing by the fountain. The photographer raised the camera.

The man next to him turned his hand over on the balustrade. "Look at my hand, please," he said. The photographer's eyes darted over the way they do when people have lived a long time in big cities and know how many crazies there are. He had his camera just below his chin, in both hands.

"Look at my hand, please, sir," the man said.

The photographer glanced down. In the man's hand was a small leather case, open to show a card and a badge.

"Special Agent Mubarak, Federal Bureau of Investigation. Don't do anything to signal to the others, please. *Please.* Just take your pictures. I have to warn you that anything you say from now on can be used against you; you may remain—"

SPECIAL AGENT NAGEL ENTERED THE PARK FROM the southeast, at the end opposite the fountain, ten seconds after Craik had entered. He was wearing a pale gray summer suit and a button-down blue shirt and a tie, as if perhaps he were a businessman from the East who had time to kill. He carried a computer tote over his shoulder. When he came opposite the flower bed where one of the gardeners was working, he stopped to watch him. The man was on his knees, working with a trowel but with his eyes on the fountain. He was very fit-looking, quite young, his hair cut so short he looked as if he should be a Marine, not a gardener. Nagel said, "Those are canna lilies, aren't they?"

The gardener grunted something. Nagel took a step closer, right to the edge of the flower bed. "What do you feed them?" he said. The gardener didn't seem to know, mumbled something. Nagel was bending over by then. He held the computer tote so that it hid his right hand from anybody at the fountain, where Al Craik had now been joined by a thin Asian. Nagel's right hand held a dark blue leather case that he let fall open in front of the gardener.

"Special Agent Nagel, Naval Criminal Investigative Service. You're a material witness to a crime against the United States. Anything you say may be—"

THE JOGGER HAD THE BEST VIEW OF EVERYTHING, because he kept moving and so saw all the entrances in sequence. It didn't take long to make a circuit, even at his pace. He didn't see the arrest of the photographer, but he saw Nagel, and then he saw that there was a woman standing at the top of the steps of one entrance into the lower end, and a short, squat man at the other. He increased his speed, turning the corner and heading up toward the fountain end, aware that two other joggers were now coming toward him, running the opposite way and not looking as if they were going to give him any room—

ALAN FELT THE COOL WAFTING OFF THE ALGAE-colored wall below the fountain's spout. It looked slick and as green as a piece of plastic jewelry. He licked his lips, telling himself that it was stupid to be nervous but he wanted to be in an airplane, where he felt at home.

He watched Mister Tashimaya come toward him. Mister Tashimaya was tall and a little stooped, wearing thick glasses that made him look clichéd. He was about sixty. He didn't look happy.

Tashimaya came within three feet of him. He stared at Alan. Alan was carrying a copy of *Time*. Tashimaya had on a blue baseball cap with his ratty dark suit and no tie.

"There are rats and alligators in the subway here," Tashimaya said in a surprisingly deep voice.

Alan heard the two FBI agents who were impersonating joggers come down the steps behind him. He hurried through his part of the codes, not wanting Tashimaya to think something was up. "There are vultures on the high buildings," he said.

Tashimaya reached into his jacket. He was about to hand Alan something that would look incriminating in a photograph. Alan reached his left hand into his back pocket for his temporary NCIS badge.

"Please take this as a gift," Tashimaya said. He held out a business-sized envelope that was thick with whatever was inside. But Tashimaya's attention was wandering: the two joggers had collided with another jogger coming this way, and somebody had shouted.

Alan closed his right hand around Tashimaya's thin wrist. "Don't run off." He couldn't think of anything else to say. The code phrases were so foolish that anything else he said sounded the same. He was holding up his badge and actually pulling the other man toward him; Alan was a former wrestler, most of his strength recovered since the shooting in Pakistan. "You're under arrest," he blurted.

Tashimaya tried to pull away. One of the gardeners stood up and reached inside his coverall, and two voices shouted. The joggers were struggling and then one of them was down, arms behind his back, and Triffler was running down the far steps and heading toward them.

Alan yanked Tashimaya's wrist. The man came back toward him, stumbled and almost fell. Twisting the hand that still held the stuffed envelope, Alan said, "You have a right to remain silent. Anything you say can be used—"

But he was thinking, *Well, hell, that's half my job done.*

Patuxent River Naval Air Station.

"Chinese Checkers," Dukas said.

But Piat had had some sleep, too, and had had time to focus, and his face was perfect for somebody who was confused by the words. "That mean?" he said.

"Chinese Checkers. Tell me about it."

"It's a game, right?"

"It sure is, and you're playing it."

"You're talking mysteries, Dukas. I'd rather talk money."

"You want your money, you talk to me about Chinese Checkers."

Piat spread his hands and did the things you supposedly did if you were confused and then irritated and then outraged. He was very good, in fact convincing, but Dukas knew he was lying. He got up. "That was swell, a real class act. Let me remind you that you're on a Navy facility and you're not going anywhere until I say you can. I'll be back, and I want to talk about Chinese Checkers."

"You can't keep me here, Dukas."

"Who says?" As the words left his mouth, Dukas thought of Nickie Groski and the NCIS lawyer who had told the CIA that they couldn't hold an American citizen without legal counsel and without charge, no matter how loud they screamed national security. How was Nickie the Hacker different from Jerry Piat? Or Dukas different from the CIA OD people who had moved Groski around like a pea under the nutshells? He wanted to think that this was different, *he* was different, but he couldn't convince himself.

"I'll give you something to think about," Dukas said, "and then we can shorten the time you're here and we can get you your money. One, you doctored a file called Sleeping Dog and put two booby traps in it for me—the meeting in Jakarta that went wrong, and stuff in Seattle. Two, your head was full of shit, because you thought George Shreed was a hero, so it never occurred to you that the comm plan you stole for Jakarta was in fact Shreed's comm plan for meeting with his Chinese control, and it never occurred to you that Sleeping Dog was a case that Shreed had terminated because it was getting too close to something the Chinese were running in Seattle. That is, those things never occurred to you unless you're also a Chinese spy yourself."

Piat allowed himself an angry glance at Dukas, who allowed himself a smile. "On the other hand, if you're a straight arrow who got suckered and now realizes that Shreed was a traitor to everything you believe in, then you'll tell me what I want to know and we'll all go our merry ways."

Seattle FBI Office.

Three-quarters of an hour after the bust in Falkland Park, Triffler was in the Seattle FBI office, facing an FBI agent who was smiling with relief but still worried about his own case.

"We got four material witnesses," Triffler said. "Three off-duty state cops and the photographer."

"It's a good bust, but you came awful close to Helmer."

"The deal was, we stay away from the top man. We did."

"Yeah, and you scared him so shitless he's left town! I'm not ready to arrest him yet."

"So, don't."

"What if he doesn't come back?"

"Oh, lighten up. It'll be great." Triffler stretched and, for the first time since he'd got to Seattle, relaxed. He was thinking that he'd go for a nice, long run down by the water. He wasn't happy about giving up Helmer, but in fact he didn't care about the PR aspect or who got the public credit. They'd kept the FBI from taking over the case—indeed, there was chitchat now about folding the FBI case into Sleeping Dog, because Sleeping Dog was national security and the FBI case was white-collar crime. But Triffler knew that the FBI would never give up a case they were close to solving.

Who cares? the relieved Triffler thought.

Washington.

After lunch, Dukas drove out to Pax River again, the news that Triffler and Al Craik had made arrests in Seattle buoying him along. It was a fine summer day, the humidity low for a rarity but the temperature climbing, and he put the windows down and enjoyed the illusion of coolness that the dry breeze gave. The rural landscape said that Washington didn't exist, that there was life beyond agencies and offices and bureaus. He pulled over and looked at a bend in the river where there were grasses and cattails and a sweep on the other side across rolling farmland. He hadn't called Sally Baranowski yet, and he realized that he'd forgotten her all last evening, which he'd spent setting up legal protection for Nickie Groski so the Agency couldn't stick him down a hole again. There had been too much going on, but to say that that justified his forgetting Sally meant that she wasn't really part of what was going on. What was she, then? Only something peripheral, accidental? A hell of a way to think of a woman you were sleeping with, if true. Dukas felt guilty and then felt tired of feeling guilty.

He put the car in gear and drove to Pax River.

He didn't have Piat meet him in the interrogation room but instead waited for him in the car and, when he came out, said, "Let's drive around."

Piat sat beside him and waited for him to talk. Dukas was in no hurry. He found a dirt road down to the river, still on Navy property, and he parked by a teetering dock where somebody in shorts and a T-shirt, probably a sailor with some free time, was fishing. Without looking at Piat, Dukas turned the engine off, leaned back, and said, "I know you borrowed Chinese Checkers and put the Jakarta comm plan into the Sleeping Dog file. I know you did it because you loved George Shreed and because other people were helping you. Internal Affairs at the Agency want to hang you for it, but I think I can hold them off. I want your help, Piat. I don't want to interrogate you and I don't want to keep you here. But I want your help."

"What makes you think I'd help you?"

Dukas tapped the bow of his sunglasses on the steering

wheel. "I don't know. I guess basically I think you're a good guy." He smiled. "Strange, right?"

But the words had made Piat frown. He looked out the window on his side. "Can we walk?"

"Sure."

They left the car and strolled along the river, where a fisherman's path took them close to the brown water. "How bad do they want me at the Agency?" Piat said.

"You know Menzes?"

Piat nodded. He, too, had put on sunglasses. He looked up and inhaled deeply. "What d'you want from me?" he said.

"Truth. Like who else is in on the Seattle scam."

Piat leaned against a willow and looked out at the river. A fish made a plopping sound at the surface, sucking in an insect. "You going to give me cover?"

"I have in mind something short-term." He rested his backside on a fallen log.

"Long-term?"

Dukas shook his head.

Jerry Piat looked at the brown water and sighed and began to tell him about the plan to get photographs of Alan Craik meeting with somebody who looked like a Chinese agent. He wouldn't give any names, and Dukas figured that no matter how disenchanted Piat was about George Shreed, he kept the old Agency habit of loyalty. You didn't rat on other people unless you had a personal reason. Piat started to go on and on, spinning out things that Dukas already knew, and Dukas cut him off by saying "Chinese Checkers."

"Yeah, I borrowed it."

"And set up Jakarta. What was the plan?"

"Bobby Li was supposed to meet with you—we didn't know you'd send Craik, but once he was there I gave the okay on him—and we'd get photos and pass them around with some gossip about a meeting with a Chinese agent."

"But the shooting started."

Piat hesitated. Dukas sensed that he was holding something back. "Yeah."

"Why?"

Piat plucked a stem of grass and put the end in his

mouth. "Bobby's a Chinese double. I had him there to impersonate the Chinese agent for the photo. His Chinese control had him there to see what was going on, because they'd seen the signal for the meeting, too." He made a face. "That was the first inkling I had that Shreed had been something I never dreamed he could be—these other guys showed up at the meet, meaning somebody else had the comm plan. I tossed that around in my head, and I saw that Bobby was the likeliest weak link." He chewed on the grass. "Bobby shot the Chinese intel officer who'd been sent, because it was the only way he could think of to get out of the bind of being there for both sides." He chewed. "Bobby isn't very smart that way."

"Two of the three sides," Dukas corrected. Piat shrugged. Dukas waited, because he thought that Piat was still holding back something about the Jakarta meeting; but nothing came. "So you grilled Bobby Li about it," he prompted. Piat nodded. Again, Dukas waited, and again nothing came. He was thinking that Bobby Li's control was probably Rathunter. "Who's his control?" Piat shook his head. "He must have said something."

"All he talked about was two people; I think that's all he's had since he was recruited. The guy who sent him to cover the Jakarta meet he calls Prayer Wheel. His first control was an officer named Chen." Piat seemed in despair. "Shreed sent him to Chen."

Dukas made some notes. "About Chinese Checkers," Dukas said. Piat looked at him. "You used only one part of it in the plan to get Craik and me. Where's the rest?"

Piat looked back at the river. "I only needed one part."

"Where's the rest?"

"I only took what I needed."

Dukas put on his sunglasses but deliberately turned away from Piat, stretching, staring across the water at the fields on the far side. "Afraid this is a precondition, Jerry. I've got to have the rest of Chinese Checkers."

"Get it from the Agency."

"From you."

"No can do."

"It's a precondition. Produce it, or you stay on this base

until Menzes pries you out with a writ of habeas corpus, and then you'll go straight to the L Street federal holding cell." Dukas looked at him—sunglasses staring into sunglasses. "This is hardball. I need Chinese Checkers. Give it to me or I'll make sure you go from here to a federal prison and don't come out."

Piat wasn't a whiner, at least not when he was sober. He didn't say any of the things about *You can't* or *This wasn't what you said* or any of that. He leaned his head back against the rough bark of the willow and stared up through the narrow green leaves, and after some seconds, he said, "If I produce it, I walk?"

"You walk with an NCIS agent on each side of you until they bring you right back here."

"Bullshit."

"You'll be here, and Carl Menzes won't be able to get at you." Dukas looked at the now-unhappy face. "You're in trouble, Piat. I can't make the trouble go away. I can offer you protection—for a price."

"Yeah? And for how long?"

"Long enough for me to put a file together that says you cooperated and you're a good American and NCIS believes that whatever you did with Sleeping Dog is water over the dam. You were a bad boy and now you're a good boy, and the Agency is just trying to cover its own shit if they prosecute you. The alternative is I turn you over to Menzes today and say you refused to cooperate and I hope he hangs your balls on the Langley doorpost for a bellpull."

"I could tell you a lot about Shreed, Dukas. You don't want to give that to Menzes."

"Your man Bobby Li can tell me more. Anyway, Piat, I know more about Shreed already than you ever dreamed." Dukas leaned forward and raised his right index finger. "The only thing I need you for is Chinese Checkers. Produce it or sweat."

Piat pulled away from the tree and straightened his sunglasses and then brushed his shoulders with his hands. "You see any ticks?" he said. "In Texas, the Spanish moss is full of them." He pulled at the top of his blue jeans. "Chinese Checkers is on a disk in my safe-deposit box. Let's go."

In the Virginia Horse Country.

Ray Suter stared down at his palmtop with disgust and something like horror.

> **Project blown. Competitor swept the board. Am out of my office. Don't contact. Where is Mustang? Le Mans**

Suter's sallow face flushed. "Project blown!" For Christ's sake, how? There was only one way that they could have known enough to screw him—if Piat had gone over to the other side. That must be what happened, he told himself: Piat had chickened out. He had gone to Dukas and told him everything. Now Helmer was "out of his office," meaning he was holed up with a lawyer someplace, and they'd come after Suter himself now.

Suter stared past the horses at the faraway trees, willing the people he had hired to find Piat. He worked the palmtop back into the pouch and took out the cell phone and dialed.

"Yah?"

"Five flies."

"So?"

"You're doing a job for me."

"So?"

"Find him and do him!"

There was a second's silence. "All the way?"

"All the fucking way." Suter's anger was in his voice; he was thinking of the message from Helmer. *Project blown.* No, Suter couldn't allow it; nobody could do that to him now.

More silence, and the sense that the man on the other end was consulting somebody else.

"Five down, five after."

After he had put the phone away, Suter realized that he was trembling. He loved control, and he was helpless. It enraged him that a stupid Ops jock like Jerry Piat could screw him, could undermine his control. Suter forced himself to breathe more slowly. *Leave it to the pros.* He had tried killing somebody himself once, and he had really blown it. *Leave it to the pros.* Control at long distance.

But he was still trembling.

Washington, D.C.

Dukas drove Piat into D.C. in his beat-up car, Piat looking around as if he were on a vacation tour, and two NCIS agents grumbling in the back about the heat. They were loaners whom Dukas had gotten because he had caught a Chinese double and his boats were rising, but they weren't happy about it. Babysitting a former CIA Ops puke, as one of them put it, was right up there with working security at the mall.

They went first to Piat's apartment, which was in the inner corner of North East not far from the Supreme Court, in a 1950s building with glass-block inserts in the walls. Dukas left the agents in the car and went in with Piat and waited while he took much time getting out his keys and caught Piat's eye on the upper part of the doorjamb, where, he guessed, Piat had put something—a hair, a sliver of sticky tape, a fake spiderweb—that wasn't there anymore. So somebody had been into the apartment—Menzes?

Three minutes later, they were out on the street again.

"HE'S IN HIS FUCKING FLOP," A HEAVYSET BLACK MAN said to his partner. "He set off the sensor, man."

"Oh, shit, man, four days he doesn't show, now he turns up the only day I got a hangover that'd fucking kill a moose."

They were down the street in a Jimmy with dyed windows. The first man looked in the side mirror to see if he could spot Piat. The other man fiddled with a control on an electronic box that took up too much of the space where he wanted his feet to be. "He's in there, but he ain't doing much." He turned the volume up still further, and the electronic sound of silence filled the car, broken by a kind of pop and a grinding sound. "The fuck's he doing?"

"He don't come right out, we go in and do him now."

More silence, then the jingle of keys. "He's comin' out. The fuck's he doing?"

The first man was watching in the side mirror. After several seconds, he said, "Shit, he's got somebody with him—gettin' into a car, that cream-colored heap—Don't look, for Chrissake—let 'em go past."

They watched the car go past them. They saw Piat clearly, then the silhouettes of the two men in the backseat.

"This gonna be hard, man." He handed over a cell phone. "Get on to Robert, tell him we need another car. Those guys are cops."

PIAT LAUGHED WHEN THEY ALL WENT INTO THE bank with him, but of course he'd understand that Dukas wasn't enough of a fool to let him out of his sight. Dukas sent one of the other agents into the vault with Piat, and, when the man pissed and moaned, Dukas hissed, "Go with him, God-damit!" and then leaned against a counter and watched the stainless-steel grid of the gate until Piat came out again.

"So?" Dukas said.

Piat grinned. He had the disk in a side pocket. "Thought I'd make you sweat a little," he said. He handed over a disk that could have had anything on it from kiddy porn to a list of synonyms for the word "sucker."

"Afraid you stick with me until this checks out," Dukas said. "You didn't have any plans, anyway, right?" Dukas some-what understood Piat now, recognizing the tense look of a man who was being guarded. He drove Piat to the Ethos Security computer office, a littered place in a ratty building not far from the National Gallery. Within a minute, a former Navy EM named Valdez had the disk up on a screen, and two minutes later Dukas knew that it checked out as the complete Chinese Checkers comm plan. He put the disk in his own pocket and nodded to Piat. "Don't get cute, okay?"

They walked out to the street, and Piat squinted at the two agents standing in the too-bright sunlight. "Never liked this city," he said.

"What're you going to do?"

"Run for it." Piat waited for a response, apparently got it, and said "Joke." With a grin, but not much of a grin. Piat put his hands in his pockets and looked up and down the broad, sunny avenue. "I'm going to go someplace and have a drink, is what I'm going to do. Come along?"

Dukas shook his head. "Stick with him," he said to the two agents. "He goes right back to Pax River."

DUKAS HAD HARDLY WALKED THROUGH THE DOOR of his office when Leslie was shouting at him.

"Mister Dukas, Mister Dukas—!"

Dukas was still drying his hands on his pants after a visit to the head.

"Mister Dukas, you got a call, he's very upset and got to talk to you! Special Agent Gandry?"

Gandry was one of the lard-asses he had left to bring Piat back to Pax River. Dukas's hand grabbed for the phone as he fell into his chair.

"I'm, uh, afraid we lost him," Gandry muttered.

Dukas stood up as if he'd been goosed. "How?" he said, his voice cold.

"He ran." The man was defensive, trying to cover himself. "The fucker was wearing fucking running shoes, we were in suits and street shoes, for Chrissake. He just took off. The sonofabitch runs like a rabbit."

Dukas was thinking that he should go through the ceiling and then thought it wasn't worth it. Still, he was enraged. He thought of the two of them—both big men, late forties, big in the ass and gut. And Piat as lean as a greyhound. "Get your asses back to Pax River," he growled. "Write it up for me. And don't expect to have any time off for the next couple of years."

And part of his mind was saying, *Still, it might be for the best. How was I going to keep him?*

JERRY PIAT HAD PUT DOWN FOUR SHOTS AND WAS feeling better. He had found a bar that was dark and a little sleazy and no more like Washington, D.C., than it was like

Syracuse or Duluth. Piat had drunk his whiskeys and sipped some water and then he asked the barman for some change, and he went to the wall phone and called Sally Baranowski.

He went out into the hot sunshine and found a cab to take him to a cheap car rental near the Convention Center.

"SO WHERE'S HE GOING?" THE BLACK MAN SAID. They were following Piat's rental car, staying way back, waiting for the second car to check in and take over. "Where the fuck's he going?"

"Not to his flop, for sure. So who cares? Maybe he's going shopping. Who cares? We found him, we're on him, now what?"

The black man stared through the tinted windshield, watching as the Beltway exits slid past. They were heading for Virginia. "Where the hell's he going?"

Suburban Virginia.

Sally Baranowski awoke after midnight and tasted the alcohol residue in her mouth and felt guilt settle over her like a collapsing balloon. The memory made her almost groan aloud. She had fallen off the wagon with a real *thump*. She ran her tongue over her teeth, around her gums. Bourbon. Why had she been—?

Then she remembered Jerry. She put her hand behind her and felt the warm, hairy leg. Not Dukas. Jerry.

He had called her and she had come home early, thrilled and appalled, and then he had shown up. With a pint of bourbon. Only a pint, as if he were willing to go easy if she was, not knowing she'd been dry but somehow sensing it. He was already a little in the bag, but it didn't matter. It had taken them all of two minutes to get from the front door to the bedroom.

Oh, shit, she thought. It had been clear that Jerry didn't know about her and Dukas. She'd told him later, sometime around ten-thirty, when they'd finished the bourbon and she was making scrambled eggs. Ironic: The only reason she'd had eggs was that Dukas had scolded her for her empty refrigerator.

I want a drink, she confessed to herself. It was the old story. If you drank, you kept on drinking; if you were dry, you tried to stay dry. Then you got wet and you wanted to drink forever.

"What's up?" Jerry whispered. Had he been awake the whole time? Had she moved? She felt his hand on her shoulder, then her breast. "What's wrong?"

"I need a drink," she said. She rolled away, laughed to cover her own feeling of guilt, and began to pull on warm-ups. "You got me started, Jerry—sorry, I'm a girl who can't say no. I *need* a drink."

"I'll go."

"No!" She was pushing her feet into Birkenstocks. She wanted to get away from him for a little, as if he were the source of the guilt that had collapsed around her. "Get a little air," she said.

"Get some cigarettes, will you. Marlboros."

"I remember, I remember—"

Her purse was on the kitchen table. She burrowed in it for her wallet and keys, not wanting to turn on a light, not wanting to see herself even in the reflection of a window. Street light illuminated the living room enough for her to see—and what was there to see, anyway? The room was tawdry to her just then; what she had done that evening was sordid; what she was about to do was pathetic. At the front door, she looked out through the single pane and saw his car, pulled into her weedy driveway behind her own, its tinted windows black, and as reflective as mirrors where the light hit. She pulled on a hooded sweatshirt.

"I need your keys," she said. He was asleep again. She remembered that trait, an ability to sleep like a cat, probably because he was always tired. She said it again, and he opened his eyes and said he'd go, but she said that all she wanted was his keys, because his car was in the way.

"Right pants pocket," he said, his voice hoarse. "Is it worth it?"

"You ever been detoxed and stayed on the wagon for a

month?" She found the keys. "No, it isn't worth it, because I'm going to be really sorry tomorrow or the next day or whenever, but, right now, I need it."

He looked at her in the gloomy little room. "Hurry back."

"Twenty minutes," she said.

"HE'S OUT," THE BLACK MAN SAID. HE MOVED SO suddenly that the panel truck rocked. "Get it started, for Chrissake—!" He looked out again and saw the dark figure get into the rental car they had been following.

"Don't have a fucking cow, Jesus Christ—"

The engine caught. The black man was taking a shotgun from a toolbox fixed to the inside of the truck. "Hold it until he's at the end of the block, see which way he turns."

"Want to wipe my ass for me after you're through telling me how to do my business?"

The shotgun was an old Stevens double twelve-gauge, the barrels cut to eighteen inches. The black man popped it open and shoved in two buckshot shells and snapped it shut as the truck pulled out, did a U-turn, and started up the street. He cranked the side window all the way down. "This has to happen fast," he said. He was nervous now—not scared, only keyed up. He talked too quickly. "Don't pull up on him and sit there; you got to pull up and out and right next to him, all at once, or he'll catch on. Even *then*—"

"Shut up," the other man said. "You give me the jumps."

They picked up the taillights a block away. The panel truck moved up until it was fifty yards behind, and then the black man said "Go!"

The panel truck accelerated. It was out in the other lane in less than a second, then pulling even with the left rear panel, then right up alongside. The black man had waited to point the barrels out the window until they were that close, and then they were beside the car, still accelerating, going right past, and he pulled both triggers.

Dar es Salaam.

Captain Jiang scuttled into Lao's office, his sallow face flushed.

"I have a report from our people in Afghanistan. They have a border-watcher report—it's flagged here—indicating that a car crossed the Afghan border on the date Chen disappeared. A white Toyota Land Cruiser, old model, two passengers, one a woman."

"A woman?" Lao was interested. "I can't see Chen traveling with a woman. He was never the type." He chuckled. "Never mind, Captain. Please go on."

"The vehicle went north across the mountains. I have the same or similar vehicle crossing into Tajikistan the next morning at about five o'clock, at the border post near Quaraval."

"And then?"

"And then nothing."

Lao read through the report, noting the agent's number and checking it against the reliability chart. Pretty good score. Then he composed a quick cable for Beijing, asking for Chen's prior operational involvement in Tajikistan.

23

Over the Pacific.

ALAN'S ESM SCREEN WAS AS EMPTY AS THE DAWN-
lit sea beneath his plane.

They had been in the air since two-thirty in the morning.
They had launched in the cool, moist air of night, and somewhere in the flight the burdens of fatigue and full bladders
had been relieved by the glory of dawn. And there was no sign
of any action.

It made Alan Craik, ordinarily immune to introspection,
ponder the different qualities of waiting. He thought of his
last missions off Bosnia, just a few months back, and the heavy
tension of waiting for cigarette boats smuggling arms to appear on radar. There, the pressure had been self-induced; he
had needed a mission for his detachment, and the possible existence of cigarette boats had opened new vistas for their systems. But the quality of the waiting had been different. It was
full of action. The det's planes had been in the air constantly,
plying up and down the Dalmatian coast like cats searching
for a lost mouse. They had known that smuggling was real. They

had been in constant communication with other planes, ships, even the Italian Guarda Costa.

This was different. Alan had had no contact with SubPac since his telephone call from Captain Manley yesterday, and the events in the park had served to separate it so much that it seemed like another world. They were looking for a potentially hostile submarine that *might* exist; they were using an American submarine as bait but had no contact with her, so that her existence, too, seemed merely *probable*. There was no one to talk to, no potential allies beyond the borrowed P-3 from the local squadron, waiting over to the west with her bigger payload of sonobuoys.

Alan had added to the silent quality of the waiting by suggesting that they practice Emcon (emissions control) during the whole of the search. It seemed possible to him that if the potential submarine were near the surface to receive a transmission from the supposed Seattle spy, it would be listening for radio signals. Especially for any sign that aircraft or surface ships were searching for a submarine. It occurred to him (not that he could do anything to check his hypothesis) that the dates where sailings and transmissions did *not* correlate might relate to exercise activity off Seattle that had scared the submarine away, except that as the dawn came up around them without a sign of transmission, the likelihood of the whole theory seemed to diminish. Now, in the warm light of dawn, Alan saw holes in his theory broad enough for the supposed submarine to drive straight through.

Surfer popped his shoulder harness and rotated his butt on the ejection seat, then scratched vigorously at some areas best left undescribed.

"When was that sub coming out?" he asked, his hand selecting "Front Seat Only."

"Yeah, man, I hear you. She should be leaving port right now, and that means my *supposed* spy should have sent his transmission an hour ago. Longer. Three hours ago would have been nice."

"We're going to need gas soon, buddy."

Alan was used to carrier ops, where gas was available in the air. Whidbey Island didn't offer much in the way of airborne refueling, and what it did have was beyond his capability to pry loose in the three-hour telephone spree he had logged as soon as Triffler had dropped him back at the base. He had had to cut several details because they were not doable. Fuel was one.

"We've got gas for another hour and a half."

"I don't mean to burst your bubble, buddy, and you know I'll go to the mat for you. But this is my Optar we're burning." "Optar" was a Navy unit's monthly allocation of things like fuel and spare parts. In a peacetime training cycle, a small, two-plane detachment had very limited amounts of Optar and had to choose its flights well. So far, Alan's plan had both planes and a borrowed P-3 aloft for five hours without any use of the MARI or any other system. It wouldn't look good on a monthly report, and both Alan and Surfer knew that, while it could be covered, it could also be used by the Fleet Imaging Command as a further argument for their superior management skills to be placed in operational control of the MARI detachment. Alan felt the pressure like a knot of rubber bands in his stomach. Sometimes he'd think about the tactical details for a moment and the knot would squirm a little and loosen, and then he'd think about Surfer's det, or his responsibility to Captain Manley, and the knot would tighten.

"Damn it, Surfer, I can't *make* the spy transmit."

"Whoa, man, I—"

"Yeah. Yeah, I know. But, damn it!" Alan pounded his open hand on the canopy support. "I still think I'm right. Maybe the spy is so far up in SubPac that he's already on to our little operation and he won't transmit. What do I know?"

"I was just venting. I'm here with you on this. And my det is fried unless we get a miracle, anyway, so I'd rather burn my Optar trying this harebrained stunt than logging training hours that won't mean much." Surfer sounded tired. Alan turned and looked at him, really looked past the stylish wraparound shades and the suntan. Command was taking its toll on Surfer, even now as they flew. Just as it was on Alan. The lines around Surfer's mouth weren't all laugh lines anymore.

"Can we send oh-three back to the beach for gas?" Alan

felt a little guilty asking for Surfer's supply of Optar, but he couldn't see any help for it.

Surfer gave him a look. It was lost in the helmet and the sunglasses, but Alan suspected that Surfer was adding up his dwindling resources and his trust in Alan. They both thought about tired crews and no replacements, and lost training, and the odds.

"In for a penny," Surfer said, and called the other plane.

NCIS HQ.

Dukas was in his office at seven, telling himself after a night's sleep that they'd survive Piat's flight—it wasn't the end of the world, although it was going to cost him an ass-raking by Kasser, his boss's boss. He was riding on two intel coups, however, the ID and capture of the fake "agent" in Seattle, and the acquisition of the Chinese double, Bobby Li. Piat must have decided to run when he told Dukas he'd turn over the Chinese Checkers disk. Well, that wasn't such a bad trade.

Leslie came in half an hour early. She seemed to have decided that "appropriate" meant looking like an overweight nun in casuals, but she was so eager that Dukas felt he shouldn't tell her that drab and appropriate didn't have to be the same thing. As it turned out, she was way ahead of him.

"Claire's taking me shopping Thursday after work."

Dukas had to think who Claire was, then got it—Claire Sandow, the best-dressed woman. "Good," he said.

"My boyfriend's pissed." Leslie made a face. "I'd been saving this money for, you know, *special* clothes, and he goes, 'What about us?' and I tried to tell him some things were more important than other things—you know, *appropriate*— and so we had this big fight, and—" She shrugged, but Dukas knew she was hurt. He was thinking about what "special clothes" could mean, and then he had a vision of Leslie and her boyfriend shopping at Victoria's Secret, picking out "special clothes" to satisfy his fantasies—maybe hers, too, but on her nickel—

"You'll make up," Dukas said. He found himself hoping they didn't.

And then the telephone rang.

"Dukas," he said.

"Carl Menzes. You heard?"

Dukas didn't let the possibly threatening question deflate him. "Heard what?"

"Piat? Woman named Baranowski?"

Dukas felt himself go still. "What am I supposed to hear?" He tried to think. What did Menzes know—that Piat had called Baranowski from Jakarta? That they had picked Piat up? But he wouldn't have said "Have you heard?" if he had meant that. Dukas was trying to put Piat and Sally together, trying to get it—

And Menzes said, "Sally Baranowski, Agency employee. She was found dead in a rental car last night. Professional hit."

"Wha—But—Hey, I sort of knew her—" His heart was saying, *No, God, he's lying; these things don't happen*—

"Yeah, I thought so," Menzes was saying. "She'd been Shreed's assistant. Christ, I'm sorry if she was, uh, close—"

"Oh, no, no—" *Why was he denying it? Or was that the truth, that they hadn't ever been close?* "But still, Jeez, she was—I don't get it, Carl—a professional hit?" *Dead* is a hard word. A hard concept. Dukas had seen *dead* a few times, had probably even caused it once or twice, but *dead* didn't apply to a woman he liked, had treated badly, wanted, had wanted, what the hell—

Menzes made it quick and as clean as he could: shotgun through the driver's-side window, massive damage. "Cops ID'd her from her wallet, but confirmation had to be done from fingerprints. But they called us as soon as they saw her Agency connection. We got to her house about an hour later. Nobody there, but signs, you know. Cups and glasses, couple plates—two people in the bed, we thought. Our guys went through it, looking for anything as to why she'd be hit like that. Lifted some fingerprints from a glass and got them back about an hour ago. Jerry Piat." Menzes cleared his throat. "You remember I told you about Piat?"

Dukas was trying to think of what to say. He didn't want

to tell Menzes right then that he had had Piat and had lost him. When had Menzes told him about Piat? When he was talking about who had had contact with the Sleeping Dog file. "Yeah, uh, some Ops guy who, let's see—signed off on the stuff in Ray Suter's office, right?" And what Menzes was saying was that Jerry Piat had been in Sally's bed. And then she had been in his car. So probably they had both been in her bed. Did that make her a slut? A dead slut? Was that what broke his heart, that she had betrayed him?

"Right. We thought he was in Jakarta. Piat and Baranowski were an old number, long time ago before she got married. I guess they got it going again. Anyway, we goosed the local cops to get active on the prints from the rental car she was killed in; they got at least one print that's Piat's. Pretty clear, I think, that it was his car—hers was still in her driveway. The way I reconstruct it, she comes out, it's night, she takes his car because hers is blocked. Then—*boom*."

Dukas flinched. *Boom.* "I—" Dukas cleared his throat. "Why'd you call me, Carl?"

"I know you're hot to trot on the Sleeping Dog thing; I heard your guys made a good arrest up in Seattle; I thought there might be a connection."

"You heard about that." Dukas was seeing Sally walking into her kitchen in the middle of the night, sipping horrible eggnog, kissing him with the sweet taste of it on her mouth—

"Yeah, your people are blowing their horn. I thought, if Piat was in on Sleeping Dog early, maybe somebody from up in Seattle thought he'd blown the op or something, they'd tried to, you know, get back at him."

"*Kill* him?"

"Stranger things have happened. You haven't arrested the top guys up there, have you?"

"Not yet." Dukas didn't say that the FBI wouldn't let him. His head was still swarming with ideas about Sally and Piat. It astonished him that she had gone from him to Piat in a matter of days. She wasn't that kind of woman, he'd have said, and then he wondered what he meant by that. *She was a vulnerable, lonely woman that I didn't do enough for,* he told himself. *Maybe he did.*

Was that why Piat ran away? To be with Sally? And was that why she hadn't called him? Oh, shit—

"So where's Piat now?" Dukas said.

"No idea. Rental car's not in his name. Apartment's empty. He's got to be on the run."

Dukas waited for Menzes to say that they'd found bugs in Piat's apartment, some sign of entry, but there was nothing. Was Menzes holding back? Well, there was no point in letting his own people try for a FISA warrant to go in anymore. The silence got too long, and Dukas said, "I'm afraid I can't tell you anything, Carl. Piat was just a name to me. I heard it from you."

"Yeah. I thought you might have made some kind of connection."

"No, sorry." Dukas scowled at a new idea. "Any chance Piat killed Baranowski?"

"Local cops like that, but I don't. Full of holes." Menzes hesitated. "You'll tell me if you learn anything, won't you?" He sounded doubtful, as if he already suspected something. Dukas told him he would, absolutely, and hung up. He sat there, staring at his desk, then put his face in his hands, and he was silent so long that Leslie came to the plastic barrier and peered through and then came around it and said, "Mister Dukas? Mister Dukas, you okay?"

Dukas sat up. He tried to smile at her. She told him that he was working too hard, and he, thinking of Sally Baranowski in the night, sitting safe and isolated behind the window of a car, and then the gunshots blasting the window and her head, blowing out the far window and the windshield and spattering her over the grass and the trees and the pavement outside, decided to tough it out. He opened his mouth to say something like, *Little setback in a case, nothing,* and he said instead, "My girl was murdered last night."

He said it because he knew that he could say that to Leslie and she'd get it. "Oh, you poor guy," she said in her little-girl voice, and he cracked. She kept her emotions so accessible that they jumped the distance between them like a spark, a permission to feel, and he felt his face crumple.

Seattle.

Marvin Helmer had holed up for a day and a night at a cottage in the Olympics. His bowels were bad; his hands trembled; he had three too many drinks. He thought he was going to be busted. But, then, nothing happened.

Federal agents—his lawyer said "Navy cops," which made no sense, but Helmer thought of Alan Craik and saw where there might be a connection—had arrested two of his undercover officers as material witnesses. And they'd got poor old Tashimaya, who had to be the most harmless illegal in Seattle, plus a department photographer who was so out of it he might as well have been dead. *But they hadn't come after Helmer.*

What did it mean? It meant either, A, they had more on him and were waiting to lower the boom; or, B, they had nothing and were waiting to sweat the material witnesses. Who knew nothing: Tashimaya thought he was working out a debt to the cops; the two material witnesses believed they were on a legitimate stakeout; the photographer didn't know zip and thought he was simply recording a crime for use in court.

"They haven't got anything," Helmer said to his lawyer. "They *can't* have anything."

"I'll check."

So, after twenty-four hours, he told Helmer that it would be better if he came back to Seattle and went to his office and did his work just as if nothing had happened and he was the most innocent man in the world. "Which of course you are, of course you are—!" the lawyer said. He made a lot of money by never really asking his clients if they'd done the things that prosecutors said they had.

"It was all part of a legitimate investigation," Helmer said.

"Of course."

"A naval officer we had reason to believe was conspiring with a foreign power."

"Of course."

"Which is why I can't talk about it. National security."

"Of course."

So Helmer kept saying "legitimate investigation" and

"national security," and finally he really did come to believe that, Goddamit, it had all blown over, and he was home free. He was sheathed in Teflon. The Teflon cop.

Which would have been news to the FBI, who had a tap on his phone at the cabin, at his office, and at his home.

Off Seattle.

The other det plane, oh-three, landed first, got gas, and the crew stretched their legs. The tower at Whidbey gave them a priority channel to stay in touch. As the day got brighter, the possibility of a transmission seemed to wane. Alan checked his signal library for the seventieth time, checking yet again to be sure that he had not dropped a zero on the signal's frequency or made another attention-to-detail error, but the ESM equipment was old hat to the Taccos and most of the Sensos, and he had lots of backup. The library was correct. The equipment was working. The enemy was just not cooperating.

The tower kept them current with oh-three's progress, without breaking their emissions plan. Oh-three was off the ground again by 0600, and Surfer turned them in toward Whidbey as soon as oh-three had her wheels in the well. The sky was fully lit and there wasn't a trace of cloud. Alan played with his radio, tempted to broadcast a request to the tower that they call SubPac, but, even encrypted, the message would be long and identifiable. He told himself repeatedly that he had to stay with his plan, and that if SubPac had not sent a boat to sea, they'd have warned him of the fact. The backseat was quiet. The other planes were quiet. Alan Craik was alone with the responsibilities of his decisions, and worry ate at him.

Ding.

The tone sounded in his helmet. He looked twice at his tiny front-seat screen to make sure that the vector displayed there was within parameters. He heard a whoop from the backseat. The vector pointed over the ocean toward land, Puget Sound and Seattle.

Somewhere over toward Seattle, someone had activated

the uplink transmissions that were the trademark of Sleeping Dog.

"Game on, Surfer," he said, and felt like whooping himself.

Under the Pacific.

The Chinese captain kept his boat just above periscope depth, his antenna peeking above the water. He surfaced three times a day to receive transmissions, and the tension of these moments got worse every time he did it. But it was always this third time, when daylight made any surfacing attempt doubly dangerous because of the risk of visual detection, that really preyed on him. The aggregate of tensions from the previous attempts seemed to float in his bloodstream like a toxin that grew stronger with each success. He had started afraid, and now his fear was a choking thing that filled his mind every time he was forced to execute his orders. Sometimes he hated the spy code-named Jewel. And as the days ticked down to the end of his operational time in the danger zone of the American coast, his fear mounted. The odds were rising. He could feel them.

He had his antennas up less than a minute before the message came. It was a burst transmission that lasted less than two seconds. He would have to wait for some minutes while his technicians turned the burst into a usable code, and then he would have to make sense of it himself, in his cabin, and re-transmit if the message justified such an action.

"Down antennas. Down periscope. Make revolutions for two knots and dive to 250 meters."

He had no intention of spending that time biting his nails on the surface, and his boat fled for the safety of the deep.

THERE WAS NO REPEAT OF THE TRANSMISSION. ALAN looked at the one line on his screen and thought again of the beauty of the system. It was unlikely that they would ever triangulate the transmission, although the three widely separate aircraft had immediately shared their vectors via datalink.

Alan switched his radio to the prearranged frequency and clicked his mike.

"All aircraft, this is Red Jacket. Go. Repeat, go."

All three immediately began to sweep their surface-search radars and MARI systems over the ocean. But their target had already gone deep, and there was nothing to see, not even a periscope.

Alan turned to Surfer. "He's out there, damn it. He must have been up near the surface to get the transmission."

"And he'll have to come up to retransmit."

Alan grunted. "Of course, we're searching four thousand square miles of surface with three planes. He could be well off to the south of here." He was going down his own lines of disbelief. He'd set the surface-search boxes based on prior contacts—none of which was a reliable guide.

"Hey! Relax, Commander. Your guy did his signal. You said the rest was gravy."

"I want him." Alan sounded fierce, predatory.

"*I* want some fresh coffee. I'm going to get gas."

"We haven't finished our box!"

"We need gas. He ain't right here, and he won't go anywhere fast. Look, Alan, I believe. He transmitted. There may be a sub out here. If so, we have several chances at him, as you said yourself. Stay the course, man. Let's get some gas."

Alan nodded, silent, as all his doubts came back to plague him.

NCIS HQ.

Dukas had talked himself down from his reaction to Sally's death; he had left the office, driven around, actually gone into a bar—something he had not done in years—and had one drink. He'd made it last an hour, and then, dry-eyed and gloomy, he had driven back to the office. He had a million things to do, and he put them all aside and called Myeroff, the FBI honcho in Seattle.

"I want Helmer," he said to Myeroff.

Myeroff started to shout. He must have been in a lot of confrontations; he believed in going directly for the kill. The sense of his shouting was that they had an agreement, which was that Helmer belonged to the FBI no matter what the NCIS had on him.

"I want him."

"You goddam well can't have him! We agreed!"

"Things have changed."

"Nothing's changed!"

"I got a new charge."

"Oh, yeah—what?"

"Murder." Dukas had worked it out that Helmer had tried to kill Piat and had gotten Sally instead. It was the least he could do, grabbing Helmer.

"That is new," Myeroff said more calmly. "But you can't have him. Two weeks. We need two weeks. Then you can get in line."

"He contracted out a murder."

"I don't care if he contracted out World War III. We got an agreement. He's ours."

They both shouted for a while. It made Dukas feel tired. Finally, he said, "Go to hell," and hung up. *So this is grief,* he thought. *Can't even manage a little revenge.* Made worse by the fact that he knew that Myeroff was right.

He tried to distract himself by absorbing what was on the Chinese Checkers disk. The three meeting sites were in Jakarta, Pakistan, and Nairobi. Pakistan was out because it was too hard to get in and out of, way over by the Kashmir border. Jakarta was bad because the Chinese were thick on the ground and the other meeting had gone so wrong there. He liked Nairobi, and he guessed that Rathunter might, too. If not Nairobi, then Jakarta, but it was a distant second.

He would need a countersurveillance team in place, plus the extra eyes and muscle to carry off a hostile meeting. He ran quickly over the possibilities, made a list, the first name Triffler's, then Huang's, which he lined through almost as soon as he had made it because Huang was needed with Bobby Li. He put down three special agents he knew could be made available from D.C. and then wrote "three from Naples/ Bahrain," if they met in Nairobi, and "three from Manila" if the meet was Jakarta. He stared at the scanty list and then added Harry O'Neill's name.

Could he make it work?

Under the Pacific.

It took more than an hour to decrypt Jewel's transmission. The captain read the message twice and his gut clenched. An unexpected deployment of an American attack boat was relatively unprecedented and had to be relayed to Beijing immediately, which meant surfacing again in broad daylight. He debated holding the message until dark and decided that such an action would be in breach of his orders about the sensitive nature of Jewel's transmissions.

He didn't want to be ordered to follow the attack boat. It was far quieter than he was and would dive better. It would be quiet at speeds where his boat's cavitation and auxiliaries would give him away like a beacon. Any order to shadow an American hunter-submarine would quickly result in his detection and prosecution. Humiliation. The captain did not think his masters were above such decisions.

His face was pale from being too long undersea. He was losing his hair. He thought of Jewel, alone among the enemy and living at risk of instant capture and humiliation, if not worse. He bit the nail on his left thumb, chewing it so savagely that his thumb began to bleed again. He had virtually no nails on his left hand.

He swept the remnants of his decoding into his safe. He spun the lock and walked slowly from his cabin to the bridge. The officer of the watch leaped from his command chair and stood at attention, even as a sonarman called for "attention on deck, captain on the bridge."

"Helm, bow up. Bring us to periscope depth."

"Aye, aye, sir."

NAS Whidbey Island.

Alan never left the plane while it was on the ground, and he kept the back end live on auxiliaries through the turnaround. The rest of the crew ducked out to refill thermoses. Alan never took his mind off the problem. They were gassed and in the air in less than thirty minutes, one of the acts of efficiency that marked the naval service at its best and never drew rewards or even comment, apart from some mumbled praise from hurrying aviators. Alan swore he'd get the crew chief something if they got the still-uneventuated submarine.

Other planes were launching now, and they had to wait in line as a series of EA-6B Prowlers launched ahead of them into the morning breeze. The EA-6Bs had the most powerful ESM suites in naval aviation, and Alan wished, again, that he had had the prep time to involve them. They turned out over Puget Sound and hurried west into the bright light of full day.

Alan had switched himself into the backseat, trading the place of honor for a full screen and control of his own ESM gear. He checked the library and then set his screen to show every contact, no matter what frequency it represented, within the parameters identifiable by his plane. Instantly the space around Seattle began to fill with hits representing cellular phone users. He thought he saw a millimeter-wave police radar away toward the Olympic Mountains before their altitude cut those signals off, and he began to sort generic surface-search radars out to sea. He wasn't sure what he was looking for, but he wanted to see everything in his search box.

Then he ran his radar and compared. The computer in his back end compared the data and began to match emitters and radar blips, automatically sorting merchant ships. Alan killed the automatic sorting and did it himself. There weren't so many emitters and radar returns that he couldn't do it himself, and he wanted an anomaly. He didn't know what he was looking for, but he knew he wanted something out of the ordinary.

•   •   •

AW3 LENNOX FOUGHT THE URGE TO PICK HIS NOSE and watched LCDR Craik as he raced from screen to screen, picking up data and depositing it on classification pages, locating radar bananas and comparing them, imaging blips with the MARI gear and then adding emitters. He classified twenty-two surface contacts in less than ten minutes. Lennox couldn't even follow his fingers. "Awesome," he muttered, and then looked panic-stricken when he realized he had spoken into a live mike.

"Know what I'm doing, Mister Lennox?" Craik sounded happy. Lennox couldn't remember if anyone had ever called him "mister" before.

"Classifying surface contacts."

"Can you do it?"

"Not that fast, sir."

"Can you use the imaging function on MARI?"

"Oh, *yeah*! Yes, sir." He mumbled the last.

"Then start imaging anything I've marked, okay? Just get an image and give it a number corresponding to the ID I've given it, so I can compare it to my emitters, okay?"

"Roger that, sir."

"Get the IDs right, mind you, Mister Lennox."

"Why—?" Lennox had a question, but the inhuman concentration on the officer next to him reminded him of Mister Data on *Star Trek,* and it was a little scary when it was for real.

"Why what, Mister Lennox?"

"Nothing. Sir."

Alan leaned back and stretched his arms over his head.

"Why what, Mister Lennox? Don't get shy on me."

"Why not let the automated system do it?"

"I don't know what I'm looking for, Mister Lennox. So I want to see it all for myself, just in case the automated system classifies something in a way I might not agree with."

Lennox was already imaging his third blip, working around the screen in the order of LCDR Craik's ID numbers. He had no idea what Craik was after, but he thought he might learn something, so he put his head down and went to work.

Pax River.

Special Agent Huang hid his own frustration at being kept in the States. He wanted to be with his family, but he had to put on a good face with Bobby Li if he was going to get information from him. It pissed Huang off that Li *was* with his family, but he knew you can't fight city hall.

"Hey, Bobby," he said. It was their second session of the day. Bobby Li looked at him with something like relief because it was Huang and not one of the two other NCIS interrogators, who were both Anglo and playing tough. Huang knew that he was being set up to be Bobby Li's "frand." He could be here for months. But he'd damned well get his family there, and good housing, too, if he was going to be the new tin god to this pathetic little jerk.

"How we doing, Bobby?" He asked some polite questions—were his kids okay? Anything they needed from the PX? His wife happy? Anybody want to see a chaplain or a doctor? Then he got down to work.

"Your Chinese control, Bobby."

"Yeah, Mister Chen."

"No, the other one." Dukas had already given Huang what Piat had told him. "The one who told you to be in the Orchid House."

"Loyalty Man."

"No, the one above him. Come on, Bobby, I know about him. I want some details, you know?"

Bobby got the panicky look that Huang knew meant that things were moving too fast. Bobby's face seemed to get longer, and he wet his lips; his eyes flicked around the room as if looking for something he had misplaced. He said, "Where's Andy?"

Andy was Piat—Huang always had to remind himself of this. "Andy's busy."

"I like to see him."

"Hey, Bobby, I asked you a question, man. Let's focus, okay?"

Bobby had some idea of his value to them. Received wisdom in the spy business said that he should spin out what he knew for as long as he could. Now, he was being asked to give up really good stuff on only the second day. "Not sure what you referring to," he said.

Huang laughed. He had to force the laugh at first, then got it more easily as it went on. Finally, Bobby Li was laughing, too. "You can't shit a shitter," Huang said. He whacked Bobby on the shoulder. "You doin' good, man, and I don't blame you for not givin' the store away. But I got a boss wants this stuff today, you know what I'm sayin'?" Huang poured them both tea from a thermos and set out a plate of sweet cakes that he had had sent in from Chinatown. "Give me this stuff today, I'll lay off. How's that? Give you a day off tomorrow, you help me out today. How about it?"

"Andy's my frand," Bobby said.

"Right, Andy's your friend, but Andy's got troubles of his own. You got to think of his side of it, Bobby. Andy's got troubles of his own. Hey, we're friends, aren't we?"

"Oh, yeah, yeah. Kind of." Bobby's smooth face creased with unhappiness. He wanted to be back in Jakarta, clearly. "I never going home, right?"

"I won't shit you, Bobby. *I don't know.* You're a smart guy, lot of experience. Figure it out. If the Chinese get you, your ass is grass, do I make myself clear? Your balls nailed to the gate of the Summer Palace. On the other hand, times change, people change—maybe down the road you go back to Jakarta and be a double again. But I won't shit you. It's likelier you get a new name and a new life in the U S of A."

"I don' want to be an American." Bobby looked at him with despairing eyes. "My wife, she cries at night. My boy say he kill himself if he have to stay here."

"Yeah, well, it's early yet, you hear what I'm saying? Lotsa water to go over the dam before we start making decisions. Your wife, your kid—" Huang made an impatient gesture. "Bobby, my wife and kids are in Manila. You think I don't want to see them? You think I don't want to leave this rundown goddam base? Come on, man, we're alike. Let's do this together."

Bobby ate one of the cakes. He sipped tea. Huang let him take his time. He could sense an important moment, a decision being made. Then Bobby Li said, "You understand me."

He said it as if it were the wisdom of the ages. "We two Asian guys."

"Right."

Bobby ate another cake and then told Huang that the top Chinese's code name was Prayer Wheel.

"This is Mister Chen?"

"No, the new guy. Guy who send the word I gotta go in the Orchid House."

"Prayer Wheel."

"Prayer Wheel, that's his code name. Funny name, huh? He say, when we meet in eighty-seven, it's because he go round and round. But he isn't in Beijing no more, because Loyalty Man gets mad, messages taking so long, and he says to me everything goes long way around getting to him now. That's a good point, isn't it? Isn't that good stuff—this top guy was in Beijing, now he's not in Beijing—isn't that good stuff?"

"Where is he?"

"Loyalty Man don't say."

Prayer Wheel would be pretty well along in his career, Huang thought, if he'd started running Bobby Li a dozen years before. "When he first took you over, Bobby—"

"Yeah, eighty-seven."

"How old was he when he took you over?"

"Maybe thirty-five. Chinese look young, you know. But I think, yeah, maybe thirty-five. He married. He show me picture once of baby, say it's his, new. That helps, don't it? New baby, twelve years ago?"

That would help. Yes, that would certainly help. Huang thought there was more. Bobby was risking a throw on him, but he was holding something back, as people always did. Huang led him and coddled him and all but held his hand, and finally Bobby told him that Prayer Wheel had been in Canada for six months in ninety-three. Huang told him he was a great guy and gave him the rest of the day, and the next day, off.

Under the Pacific.

The captain watched his command screen as his submarine rose beneath the waves and then leveled, her bow just slightly down to ease his descent when the message was sent. He looked over at the comms officer and wondered if he looked as gray and forlorn.

"Do we have a satellite?" he asked testily. They had to linger on the surface during those moments when none of the system's uplink satellites was in view. On a brilliant sunny day like this, the surface was poison.

"Yes, sir."

"Ready to transmit?" he asked formally.

"Sir!"

"Go ahead."

THIRTY MILES TO THE WEST OF THE WESTERN EDGE of his search box, Alan saw a cell-phone-related signal pop up with a set of vectors and some frequency data on his ESM screen. He put his radar cue on the ESM symbol and turned on his surface-search radar.

No return.

Well, not *no* return. Just less return than an outboard motor. As if someone in a rowboat, forty miles at sea, were using a cell phone.

"Blue Jacket, this is Red Jacket, over."

"Go ahead."

"Blue Jacket, please set radar to periscope and target my ESM cue. Do you copy?"

"Copy."

"Go for MARI and image, over." His heart began to thud in his chest, and his hand was shaking as he lined the image cue up with the barely existing contact and switched to MARI mode. He already knew what he wanted to see.

He hit the *image* button.

There were two minuscule returns, standing a little above the black static that represented the shifting surface of the water. One was straight, and the other had a bulb at the top. He keyed a switch to save the image and another to pass it to the other planes.

He was looking at the antenna array of a submarine at periscope depth.

He started to call it in on the radio while he entered the possible submarine datum into the datalink, and Lennox looked on in awe. Blue Jacket, as the other det plane was called, whooped with glee, any thought of Emcon out the window.

"We've got him!" called Dice, over in oh-three.

"We don't have him yet," said Surfer. But he was turning as if he were headed for the break, and his grin filled all the helmet that his sunglasses didn't.

The P-3 was the farthest away, well up to the north, almost in Canadian airspace. Alan had worried from the first that the sub, if it existed, would hide in Canadian water. He could see the P-3 turning toward the datum. It was seventy miles away, twenty minutes at its best speed.

He flipped back to his emitters page and saved several seconds of emission from the datum, all in a common cell phone frequency, and then imaged it again. The same two antennas stood above the sea. Alan had never used MARI for anything related to submarine detection, and he didn't have a library devoted to antenna placement. It would take research and some of Soleck's magic to get one together. He made a note on his kneeboard card.

It said something for Alan's belief in his own theory that the grainy reality of the two antennas on the MARI display had a dreamlike quality for him. It wasn't that he couldn't believe it. It was more that he didn't really have an endgame plan for a reality in which the sub was located and real.

"He's diving," Bubba Paleologus said from the other plane.

Alan watched on his MARI as the two antennas slipped into the grainy black of the water.

"All planes, I want passive contact only," he said. They rogered up.

Alan sat back and watched them work the datum. Oh-three was first on station. They had a course and a last location less than three minutes old, and they laid a V-shaped sonobuoy pattern well ahead of the sub's expected location and fairly deep, on the hunch that any sub so close to a hostile coast would dive as soon as he made his transmission.

Alan and Red Jacket were next on station, and they stayed to the south, laying a barrier that would catch the sub if she turned away to starboard in her dive. Before they were through their pattern, the P-3 was laying hers to the north, one that would cut both the port axis and a sudden clearing turn, effectively surrounding the datum in sonobuoys.

Whoever was down there was cunning. They waited in silence long enough for Alan to bring up his twenty-minute-old image of the original antennas and study it to see if he could have been mistaken.

"Red Jacket, this is Big Orca, over," called the P-3.

"Big Orca, this is Red Jacket, go ahead." Alan perked up again.

"Red Jacket, this is Big Orca. We have pos contact two, repeat pos contact two. We have contact on two buoys, over. Do you copy?"

"Copy pos contact two, contact on two buoys."

Surfer called him on the intercom. "Are we asking for permission to go active? Can we go in on him?"

Could they? He hadn't made a plan to contact SubPac once the event had started, which now looked like a serious oversight. He was left with the hard call to make all by himself. He'd put it off as long as he could. The Navy side of his brain called out for continuing prosecution. He had no idea of the nationality of the submarine below him, although he thought that it was probably Chinese, but the potential in intelligence was vast. He could vector in other planes, perhaps even the attack sub whose morning departure had started the entire process that led to this. They could go active and scare the submarine into leaving the area.

The other side of his brain, the side that Triffler and Dukas had spent so much time taming and training, pondered the results if the submarine realized that it had been detected. Detection would lead the adversary, whoever it was, to change his signal system or replace the agent who made the burst transmissions. As of that moment, Alan and the Navy knew there was a spy and how he communicated. If Alan prosecuted the submarine, as instinct demanded, then the spy would almost certainly remain undetected.

On the other hand, the submarine was there *right now.* Even with triangulation data and the keys to the agent's comm plan, Alan knew he might take months or even years to catch.

But, once warned, he might come up with another system as subtle as this one.

Alan couldn't imagine all the potential scenarios for damage, and he suddenly understood in a way that he never had before that some big decisions had no right answers. He could see possible ramifications from either decision that would make him friends and enemies, would satisfy some communities in the Navy and offend others. For a moment, he almost wished that the decision could be taken from him, but there was no one there to take it. He could share it with Surfer and include him in the blame. He could hide behind his status as an intel officer. He thought of many ways that he could weasel on the hardest professional decision of his life, but he didn't really consider any of them.

The submarine, or the spy.

Alan thought of something he had heard in his first tour. *You're an intelligence officer. Be intelligent.* The submarine was a fleeting victory. He could prove it existed, and twenty hours of sonograms wouldn't tell the Navy much more than twenty minutes. The spy was the long-term problem. He thought of Soleck's ghost sub out in the Indian Ocean. He wondered how many other American ships or subs had a little friend, a silent threat lurking in their wakes like a shark following a passenger ship.

"All planes, this is Red Jacket, break off. I say again, break off. Cease all prosecution and break off. Exit the datum at your best speed. I repeat, break off. Do you copy?"

Alan had a fleeting memory of Rafe's recent decision to break off an action against a Chinese surface-action group in the Indian Ocean. He understood now what that decision must have cost him. He felt that he understood something indefinable about the harshness of the way the world really worked, and he suddenly felt his youth slipping away with the terse confirmations that his order was being obeyed.

TWELVE THOUSAND MILES TO THE EAST, RAFE STOOD over a JOTS repeater and watched the S-3s off the U.S. West Coast.

"That's Alan Craik?" Rafehausen asked Soleck, who was watching the action.

"Yes, sir. He's in oh-two." Soleck clicked on the little symbol, and it displayed as *S-3 (Det 423) 102 Surfer/Craik/Lacey/Lennox.*

"And he's flying?"

"Yes, sir."

Rafe smiled, thinking of his workload and the problems the now-sick Stevens had, and had caused, in his det. He turned to his ops officer, who was standing at his elbow with tomorrow's launch cycles.

"That's Al Craik, in an airplane."

"Yeah?"

"Get his ass back to the boat."

NCIS HQ.

Dukas got the message from Huang at four-thirty: "Bobby Li gave us enough stuff to ID the Chinese who's run him since Chen. Details were: age now about 47, one male child born 1987, not now stationed in Beijing, made a 6-mo trip to Canada in 1993. This checks with known details about a lieutenant-colonel in mil intel named Lao tse-Ku. Analysis rates this a 3.7—solid, Mike."

Dukas smiled for the first time since he had heard of Sally's death. *Gotcha!*

He sent an E-mail to the other agents on his D.C. team:

Check with Canadian cops/RCMP re any connection between Sleeping Dog burst transmissions and six-month visit 1993 Lt Col Lao tse-Ku, Chinese mil intel. Dukas.

Leslie looked around the barrier. "You wanted me to remind you, Mister Dukas. The, uh, funeral is tomorrow."

He managed to smile. "Thanks."

"I sent some flowers. I hope that was okay."

Was she merely dumb, or was she really angelic? How would he ever know?

Whidbey Island.

When the backslapping and the congratulations were over, the triumph rang hollow for Alan. SubPac acknowledged tersely that the submarine contact had been real. Captain Manley had verged on effusive in her praise for Alan's efforts, and he understood from her that SubPac had briefed the mission and its results to the CNO. But the result at Whidbey Island was a ream of paperwork and a flurry of NCIS agents demanding their sonograms and the tapes from their aircraft, and a stack of classified papers that looked like contracts and required that the signee keep silent on all matters related to such and such a mission and such and such a disclosure.

"Till the sun dies," said Surfer, and threw his across the room. Being paper, it didn't go very far.

Alan felt that he had to defend himself. "I never promised you an air medal."

"Fuck, I *hate* this spy shit. We should have gone active on the datum and screamed it out. Then they'd have to make us heroes."

"Surfer, I told you what's at stake—"

"And I know it. I just hate it. It's dirty."

Alan nodded. He felt curiously distant from Surfer, as if he had seen a vision that Surfer didn't share. He wondered if this was something that happened to every officer. *Beyond glory,* was how he described it to himself. Beyond where the medals mattered. "You'll get a lot of recognition in time, and from pretty high up." He sounded lame even to himself. Surfer didn't want recognition. He wanted *glory*.

Surfer just looked at him, and Alan gave up. Surfer knew that Alan was right, and Alan knew that Surfer didn't care. He wanted a different kind of glory, and he seemed to be disappointed in Alan, and that hurt more than anything else.

"No, *you'll* get the recognition from high up. You got a message from the CAG on the *Jefferson*." He tossed it to Alan with barely hidden disgust.

"I do?" Alan tried not to look too eager.

When he had read it, he called Triffler.

Then he started to pack.

Three hours later, he was on the phone to Rose. She had been in Houston overnight and had got back and still had put in her time on the F-18. When she heard he was heading for the boat before she could get up to see him again, she began to cry.

"I thought you'd be mad," he said.

"I'm happy for you! But I'm not very happy for me."

"You'll be left with the kids, everything—"

"Oh, I can cope with that shit! I got driven around the NASA ghetto in Houston; they showed me houses, malls—it's like I'm being sucked into this big, happy family. There'll be so many people to take care of me and the kids, it'll be a piece of cake." Her voice got small. "I love you."

He said that he loved her, too—that necessary response that, spoken into a telephone, is like kissing a mirror. His orders said he was to report "with all deliberate speed" and gave him three days to wind up his affairs in Seattle, plus one to report in to NCIS in D.C. Wasn't Rose part of his "affairs"? If they gave him three days, couldn't he take one of those three days to be a husband? His desire for action said, *No, go!* His desire to be with her overcame the voice.

"I'm going to fly down. Can you get the morning off?"

"Fly here? I thought you were hot to—"

"Get me a room at the airport motel. *Be there!*" Then his own voice got small. "I love you, Rose."

NCIS HQ.

TWO DAYS LATER, MIKE DUKAS HAD A MEETING with his boss and, more importantly, his boss's boss. He and his boss went together the next step up the chain of command. Dukas, known now to have brought in a probable Chinese double and run the team that had cracked Sleeping Dog, was suddenly a star. It didn't hurt that the CNO daily intel report had carried a watered-down version of Alan's Sleeping Dog success, either. His boss's boss, Ted Kasser, rubbed the top of his bald head and actually seemed pleased to see him.

Dukas got right down to it. "I want to make a hostile meet with a Chinese intel officer in Nairobi, Kenya." Dukas didn't look at his immediate boss, who, he knew, would be shaking his head and scowling as if group sex had been suggested. "This officer is the one behind the shooting in Jakarta that involved Lieutenant-Commander Craik, you remember—he was there on our nickel. We're ahead now—we know who the officer is, a lieutenant-colonel named Lao; we know he's currently stationed in Tanzania; and we're trying to get something on him that we think is going to nail the coonskin to the wall. I think it's so important that there's a hell of a good chance he'll defect."

His boss now looked pop-eyed. Ted Kasser looked cautious. Dukas took them through it step by step: Shreed, Chen, Sleeping Dog, and the references to money that had convinced him that Colonel Lao thought he was trying to find Chen, but that, in fact, he was being played for a sucker by his own people and was really supposed to learn the truth about the mysterious money.

"What money?" Kasser said. He had a nasal, upstate-New-York voice. He had pulled a pipe out of his pocket and was sucking on it, unlit.

"We think it's Chinese money that Shreed stole somehow. We're trying to nail it down." He explained about Nickie Groski.

Kasser sucked and looked skeptical. "In five days?" He shook his head.

"We brought in Bobby Li in three." He didn't say that Bobby Li had fallen into his lap.

Kasser leaned his elbows on his desk and hunched his head down between his shoulders. "What do you need?"

Dukas asked for a contract with the Bahrain security company run by Harry O'Neill, the ex-Navy, ex-CIA man who had been with them at Shreed's and Chen's deaths. And the money to back it up. "O'Neill knows East Africa and he's got great people for a hostile meet. And we owe him a contract." He didn't say that O'Neill was the only man who knew what had been done with Chen's body, and that a contract might make him more amenable to sharing what he knew. He looked from one man to the other. He didn't trust his immediate boss, who worked entirely on fear—fear of being reprimanded, fear of not being liked, fear of doing something different. The man next up the ladder was a different story, however, a tough but fair old bird. To him, Dukas said, "I need a team."

"How many?"

"At least eight, better if it was twelve and better yet if it was sixteen. I figure three from here, three from Bahrain, six from O'Neill's outfit because they know Africa—for a start."

"It's a budget-buster," his boss said.

"If it works, I'm going to bring Lao's scalp home."

"All pie in the sky," his boss said.

"Interesting," his boss's boss said. He cocked an eyebrow at Dukas. "But you need to know what happened to this guy Chen before you go into any meet."

"He's dead."

"You got it on the word of this guy O'Neill that Chen is dead! But you tell me that a lot of money may ride with Chen. What if Chen didn't die, but paid O'Neill to say so?"

Dukas groaned and made a face. Kasser wasn't going to let it go. "All right, Mike—*prove* to me he's dead. Find out. What if he's really alive someplace and has the money?" He made a note. "I'm going to send you a memo telling you that if you don't know for damned sure that Chen is out of it, the operation is threatened and you should abort. You follow me? What I'm saying is you need to cover our ass."

"O'Neill wouldn't lie about it," Dukas objected.

"Oh?"

"He's a buddy."

Kasser smiled. He wrote another note. "What else do you need?"

"Country clearances, and a firewall to keep the Agency out."

"They have to be told," his immediate boss said.

The old bird kept his eyes on Dukas and said, "Why?"

"This impacts what they're doing about Shreed, which is nothing. They're kicking dirt over it. If they hear I'm meeting with somebody, they'll put two and two together and take it away from us," Dukas said.

"They have to be told!" his boss cried.

Kasser said, "Yes, Don, but they don't have to be told the *truth*." He smiled at Dukas. "Suppose you got country clearance to look into threats to Navy security over there. We *are* having some trouble, in fact—there's an alert out on a threat to ships. I don't suppose it would be entirely out of the ballpark for an NCIS special agent to check with the Chinese, would it?" Dukas said it wouldn't, and he could live with that.

The old man said he'd take it to ONI that afternoon. They shook hands on it. Holding on to Dukas's hand, Kasser said, "Prepare a briefing on the operation. I want you to be very specific about this Chen and the money—I think that's key to everything." He glanced at Dukas's boss and then smiled at Dukas, who realized that they shared contempt for the third man in the room. "Probably have to brief this to DNI tomorrow. You better be awful, awful good."

"I think I can handle that." Dukas looked at his boss.

"Any way you can angle this to include the submarine and the west coast spy?"

"Sorry?" Dukas was still working through the money angle in his mind.

"The intel community may be hot about your Chinese double, Mike, but over in CNO-land, the news is all about Sleeping Dog paying off with a real spy."

"Yeah?"

"DNI thinks that there may be other Chinese subs out there, tailing other ships. He thinks this may be part of a Chinese intel program, with port-watchers keying ships like we'd have an agent making calls for a surveillance team. *Jefferson* had a pos sub hit a day or so ago which they played down, but now they're not so sure."

Dukas nodded. "Chinese?"

Ted Kasser enjoyed knowing things that other men didn't know.

"The DNI put this in the CNO daily report." The CNO daily report had code words all over it. Only about forty offices received it, which Mike thought was twenty-five offices too many. On the front cover was a picture of two antennas sticking up out of a grainy sea of black. Dukas realized that the image must be Al Craik's. A computer-generated circle glowed around the two antennas. Next to it was a mensurated satellite photo of a submarine at pierside, with distance notes and measurements listed below. "LI PO CLASS SSN," the headline said.

Dukas nodded. "It might relate."

"Okay. I'm a little blindsided by this angle on getting a

Chinese officer, though. And I want *proof* Chen is dead. You got that?"

"Sure." Dukas felt like a whipped dog.

"Good. Separate issue. Seattle. Where is Craik now?"

"He ought to be in the building any minute. We're having lunch—he's on his way to sea."

"I want to see him." Kasser called someone, muttered into the phone about sending LCDR Craik on from Dukas's office here. "What do you see with Sleeping Dog in Seattle?"

"See?" Dukas felt as if he had some kind of intelligence senility; Kasser jumped subjects and left him behind at every jump.

"It's going to be a major case, Mike—CNO loves it. It'll be tough to make, but it's a legwork case. We'll get the guy in time, as long as we stay on top of his transmissions. Are you going to follow it up? Who's going to run it?"

Don cut in. "I thought we'd run it from here. It belongs to this office."

Kasser shook his head. "Too big, Don. CNO and the sub community want to see a 'dedicated effort.' I want to be seen to give it to them. Mike, Crystal Insight is beginning to take this agency over, and I need to see a plan for breaking it up and moving the pieces away. What's up with this Jerry Piat, by the way?"

Again, the question came out of the blue. Dukas had been worrying about how to broach it; now it was in his lap. His boss turned away, as if denying he even knew Dukas.

"We lost him."

The words just sat there in the air. Kasser sucked at his empty pipe, and, when he spoke, his voice had the flatness of restrained emotion. "That's not good. How long have you known about this, Don?"

"We were still—"

"How bad is it, Mike? Will he run to the Agency? Are we going to jail?"

"It won't put us in jail. He came willingly; we haven't hidden any evidence; he's a material witness in an ongoing investigation, and frankly, we didn't have anything legal to hold

him on. Suspicion of framing Al Craik? I wouldn't even want
to make that case, at this point. We'd get screwed in court on
the classified angle alone."

Kasser puffed at Don, as if weighing him for slaughter.

"So your angle isn't that he's escaped, but that we couldn't
hold him."

Dukas nodded.

"But you and I know you fucked up, right?"

Dukas nodded again.

"Who lost him?"

"Not really the issue, sir." Dukas said *sir* about ten times a
year. "It was my fuck-up. I didn't give them enough background on him. He slipped them."

"And we weren't really holding him, right? Just watching
him."

Dukas got the hint—holding Piat would have been illegal. "That's right."

"Any idea where he is?"

Dukas shook his head. "He knows Asia like a backyard.
He probably picked up a passport and money when he got me
the Chinese Checkers disk." He looked Kasser in the eye and
waited for the hit. "I screwed up."

"Okay, Mike." Instead of exploding, Kasser made another
of his zigzags. "How's Dick Triffler?"

"Great!"

"Good enough to run Sleeping Dog to earth?"

"No problem. But he might not want it. He's set in D.C.
and wants to be with his family."

"He can take them. It'll be a three-year job anyway, between catching the spy and writing the damage assessment,
right?"

Don waved his hands. They ignored him.

The speakerphone gave a squawk. "Lieutenant-
Commander Craik to see you, sir."

"Hold him a minute and then send him in." Kasser never
took his eyes off Dukas. "Mike, do you believe in this Chinese
officer enough to walk away from Crystal Insight?"

Dukas realized that this was hardball. Kasser was really

saying, Do you believe the crap you just spouted enough to dump a brilliant case that will make your career to chase the possibility of a Chinese officer in Nairobi?

"Yes, I do."

"Good. Don, give me a list of people eligible to take Crystal Insight minus Sleeping Dog."

"Sure, Ted."

"Right now, Don."

Don all but bowed on his way out, and Alan Craik came through the door, his hat under his arm, crisp and slim in his sparkling whites with short sleeves and shoulder-boards. He made Dukas feel rumpled, but Dukas shot up and grabbed his hand. Kasser came around his desk, the copy of the CNO daily report in his hand. "Well done, Commander."

"Thank you, sir." Alan looked at the cover of the daily report and smiled. Kasser sat back down.

"You going back to your detachment?"

"I'm on the way!"

"Had some downtime, I hope?" Suddenly, Kasser was treating Al Craik like one of his agents—which, in a way, he was. Kasser believed in downtime and families.

Alan looked at Mike, who winked. Alan grinned. "I saw my wife for twenty-four hours on the way. She's a Navy officer, too—on her way to Houston for astronaut training."

Kasser nodded. "You going to your boat via Bahrain?" He was at it again, but this time Dukas was with him.

"Ye-e-e-s—"

"You're still on our dime, you know. Mike's going to want you to run an errand in Bahrain."

"I want to get back to my boat as fast as I can, sir."

"Sure you do. But I'll see that you get a concurrent fitrep on all this, Alan, and I guess it's clear to you that Sleeping Dog isn't really over. We need you to stay on a few things—even when you're back at the boat."

"The Seattle office is all over Sleeping Dog, sir."

Kasser sucked his pipe again. He looked at Dukas. "Bring him up to date. Tell him about Nairobi. And get him to carry the contract out to your Mister O'Neill—who's a personal friend, I think?"

Dukas nodded. Alan looked worried.

"I'm due to catch a plane to Bahrain in Philadelphia tonight."

Kasser stood up again. "Then I'll save my paeans of praise for later. You two have a lot to discuss, and you better get moving." He shook hands with both of them and gave Dukas a look that might have meant a lot of things. What he said was, "I need to *know* that Chen is dead."

Dukas nodded again. Alan looked blank.

They were both talking as they moved out of Kasser's office and down the hall.

They went to lunch at a halfway-decent place near the fish market on the river. Alan's delight at going back to the boat was plain, but he was also clearly guilty at leaving Rose. When he stopped beating himself up to eat some shrimp, Dukas told him about Sally Baranowski.

"My God, Mike. I'm so sorry."

"I'm sorry for her. But her and me—" Dukas shook his head. "I was going to say something stupid like we were just friends. Jesus, I'd like to crucify the guy who did it."

"A *professional* killing?"

"The cops say so. Menzes says it was aimed at Piat. Maybe Helmer hired somebody after you guys busted his operation in Seattle. I don't know; it doesn't make much sense. Anyway, the Agency's throwing dirt over it with its back legs because they don't want to be connected."

"I'm sorry, Mike."

Dukas looked at his plate. "She was a nice woman." He pushed a piece of squid around. "What the hell kind of epitaph is that?" He looked at his friend. Anguished. "I wasn't in love with her, but—shit, you can't go to bed with a woman and have some-b-b-body—!" He heard himself stammering and realized that "in love" didn't cover what she had been to him—his response to her vulnerability, his admiration for her skills, his distaste for her drinking—but whatever it had been, her death had left him emptied.

• • •

HOURS LATER, DUKAS SENT AN E-MAIL:

> To: Rathunter
> From: greekgod
> Meet 5 days from this date at site 2 of plan you have

PART

THREE

Nairobi

25

Bahrain.

ALAN HAD NEVER LANDED AT THE INTERNATIONAL airport in Bahrain. Navy people did, when they joined their ships here, but he'd missed that step. He had always come in on one of the military fields or taken a helicopter from the boat or from Saudi Arabia, just a few miles over the strait. The international airport was modern but spartan, with a different mix of technology than he was used to and more people employed at every level—more porters, more security guards, and more kiosks changing money. He saw a few Palestinians, a handful of Filipinos, and a great many Pakistanis. Their numbers stood out because the airport itself was as empty as a set waiting for actors. There weren't enough passengers to give the terminal any sense of life, and the handful of businessmen passed through the web of service personnel without appearing to need any of them.

Customs was thorough but courteous. He wanted to compliment the young Pakistani man who checked his bags but suspected that it would put him on a profile and let the moment pass with nothing but a very small smile, which the man returned. Then he was through the bleak customs area and walking through engraved glass doors to find a second section of empty airport. Lounging in a chair sat onetime Petty Officer First Class David Djalik, now a very tanned and relaxed-looking man in a suit so good that it made Alan feel cheap.

"Dave," he said somewhat self-consciously, sticking out his hand. The military didn't have a code for dealing with former subordinates who had saved your life and were now prosperous. It seemed better to go with first names, anyway. Djalik hadn't been warm after their experience in Africa. After all, it had cost him part of his hand. And he hadn't volunteered for it.

"Mister Craik." Simple and a little distant. But he smiled, and took one of Alan's two suitcases. Djalik was still all muscle, a former Navy SEAL who looked the part even when expensively dressed.

Djalik turned away and strode out to the next set of sliding glass doors and then out into the open, out of the air-conditioning and into the hammer blow of Bahrain's desert day. Alan followed, angry that Djalik didn't intend to talk. At the curb was a heavy luxury car, big—Mercedes. Alan didn't know the type, but it looked bigger than anything he had seen in the States. Djalik placed the luggage in the trunk and gestured for Alan to climb in the passenger door, tipped a waiting security guard, and got in. The interior was cool and tinted; the car was running.

"Gas is cheap here." He sounded faintly guilty.

Alan thought a few seconds and decided to risk rebuff.

"You still don't like the pollution?"

"I got to run here. The stink is everywhere. Jesus, sir— Mister Craik. Bahrain would make anybody a believer in the environment."

"But you like it here?" Alan tried to keep his tone light. They were rocketing along a highway through packed ranks of new cars, all parked in shipping lots. They seemed to go on for miles.

"My wife loves it. She gets to be a colonial lady with a big house and servants. My kids like it, too."

Djalik didn't say anything about himself.

"And Harry's the best. Cool, professional, but always there for us. If I'd known more like him in the Nav—"

That was a little below the belt, as Alan had also been his boss. The tone didn't indicate that Djalik meant anything in particular, but Alan knew Djalik and knew that he was sharp enough to land a punch, under the guise of a passing remark, without fear of consequence.

"Dave, do we have a problem here?"

"Nope." Smile from Djalik. "Nope. We did, but time gives me a new perspective. Harry told me some things, too. Changed my view a bit. And you got whacked in Pakistan." Djalik nodded toward the remnants of Alan's hand.

Alan shook his head. "Does that make me less of a glory hound in your eyes?" There it was, right on the table. Because Djalik, the SEAL, had thought that Alan was a glory hound, not a real professional. What hurt was that he had a point, although Alan hadn't seen it at the time.

"Yep."

"May I ask why?"

"That's a nice phrase, 'May I ask.' Carries a lot of content. But, yeah." He swung the wheel as they entered a roundabout with six other cars. The roundabout had stoplights, an insane arrangement that Alan thought must have represented the collision of British and American road engineering. All six cars ignored the traffic light as it turned red. Djalik accelerated so hard that Alan was pushed back in his seat as if by a cat shot from a carrier. They had left the rows of cars and were passing shacks on both sides of the road, many selling tea and Cokes. In the distance, housing developments rose above more shacks. Djalik saw Alan's eyes move.

"Shia. All the folks who live here are Shia, except the rulers. They're Sunni."

"I know."

"Recipe for disaster, if you ask me."

Alan just shook his head.

"But to get back to the matter at hand. Yeah, my view changed when you lost your fingers, because you've paid the price, and you're still here, still in the Nav, still in the game.

That's okay. I can deal with that. You aren't a *glory hound,* Mister Craik, you're a different breed of bastard altogether—an *adrenaline junkie.*"

"And you think that's better." Alan was ready to be angry, because Djalik was, knowingly or unknowingly, parroting Harry O'Neill, his best friend and Djalik's boss. And Alan resented it. He didn't like to think of himself that way. It detracted from his image of himself, and it hit him hard enough that he had to suspect that it was probably true. Truer than *glory hound,* and even that had some truth in it.

Glory had a different taste since his moment of decision on the Chinese sub.

Djalik laughed and turned to look full at Alan, the car roaring along a straight stretch at more than one hundred miles an hour.

"Fuck, yes. My wife sleeps with one every night; I see one in the mirror every morning. Much better."

He laughed again, and it was a true laugh; the kind that makes other men laugh, too. Alan finally had to give in. It was all true.

They were still laughing when they passed through Manama and headed out to the country, where Harry had his house.

Harry met them in an elegant Islamic foyer decorated with hanging rugs, a silvered censer that Alan thought he recognized as Byzantine, and a small marble fountain in the center. The foyer was the size of Alan's house.

Harry O'Neill was Alan's best friend. They went back to his early days in the Navy, when Harry had been a junior intelligence officer in the same air wing as Alan. Harry had never flown, but he had a remarkable mind for facts, and they had developed a friendship that started as a working relationship and just kept on. Alan had rescued Harry in Africa, but this served only to strengthen their friendship. That Harry was prosperous was obvious. That he was very popular at the Crystal Palace in Langley was less so, but equally true. He was now a Muslim. He was black. He was a complex, fascinating, brilliant man, and he didn't meet any stereotype of race or education.

Tall, heavily built without fat, handsome, with aristocratic manners and all the grooming money could buy, Harry looked like a poster for success. If he had troubles with his identity, his parents, his adoptive religion, or his friendship with Alan, a lifetime of racial dissimulation and six months at the CIA charm school kept them well hidden.

"Good to see you, bud," said Harry, grasping his hand.

"And you, Harry," said Alan. They beamed at each other.

"Glad you came. Glad Mike Dukas sent you. Whatever— we get some time together."

"I thought the same when Mike suggested it."

"How's Rose?"

"She's great. Sends her love."

"Dave, anything at the airport?"

"The usual. Mister Craik came off alone and came here alone."

"You two talk on the way here, or just hiss like cats?" Harry was smiling, using his size to make disagreement impossible.

Alan looked at Djalik and smiled.

"We're halfway there."

"That's fair," said Djalik.

"Okay," said Harry. "This is my house, and I ordain that to celebrate being 'halfway there,' Dave is going to call you 'Al' and Al is going to call you 'Dave.' *Right.* Let's have a meal and look at this contract. I assume Mike sent you with a contract?"

Alan smiled up at him. "I'm all for the meal, but I've been up for hours and I'm jet-lagged."

Harry turned away, walking through the foyer toward a hallway that seemed to run on forever. "Bud, in this business, you're always coming off a plane, you're always jet-lagged, and the bastards never seem to care."

"But this ain't my business, Harry."

Harry stopped and gave him an odd look. He grimaced a little, a very unusual expression from Harry O'Neill.

"Yes, it is. Don't kid yourself, Alan. Don't hide in jet-jock land. This is your business. You aren't a little pregnant, you don't lose a little of your virginity, and you can't be a little bit of a spy."

Dar es Salaam.

Lao was getting together the team that would back him in the Nairobi meeting with Greekgod. They would be locals; the embassy had only five resident agents, and they weren't his to command. He had two men scouting a countersurveillance route in Nairobi, another seeing about weapons. Suddenly, he didn't like the comm plan and wished they were meeting in a place he really knew—Hong Kong, perhaps. Something like home ground.

Jiang put his head in, grinned. "News!"

"You have found him?"

"Craik has flown to Bahrain."

Not the ordinary route to Nairobi. "Half the American Navy passes through Bahrain."

"Do you think he's going to meet with Chen?"

"Anything is possible, Captain." Lao didn't say that he thought it unlikely that Chen, if alive, would be in a place like Bahrain. "Tell the station in Dubai to put a team out in Bahrain. Tell them to take care, you understand me? The Americans own Bahrain, and the Bahraini Service itself is nothing to sneer at. And they play rough. Take care, but do the legwork. Find out where he went, when he landed, and see if we can track him to anything. If he's going to Nairobi, maybe we can surveil him all the way—gain an advantage."

Bahrain.

"You look better, bud. Sleep well?" Harry was a morning person, and the magnificent smell of really good coffee floated from the cup he had in his big hand.

"Damn it, Harry, if I looked like hell, perhaps it's because I had to work a fourteen-hour day with Mike before I flew here."

"Sucks to be you, bud."

"But, yeah, I'm better. Slept like a log. Great bed. Great house. I should've said that before. The carpets are beautiful, the water is a nice contrast to the outdoors, and the colors are—"

"Vivid?"

"Not what you see at home."

"Ready to travel?" Harry was brisk, bouncing with energy.

"Travel? Uh, I just got here."

"Mike says I have to get you to Chen. Says it is the most important part of this contract right now. I've talked to him twice while you slept like a log. We have to go. I have a whole operation to build in Dar es Salaam and I can't start it until you and I go to Tajikistan."

"Tajikistan?" Alan gulped some coffee and wondered if he was still asleep. "What's in Tajikistan?"

"Chen."

200 NM ENE of Lamu Island.

SOLECK'S CREW HAD RED EYES AND TWITCHY HANDS after seven and a half hours aloft. Soleck had hit a KA-6 tanker midway through the flight, and then they had gone back to watching the cigarette boats as they drove over the heavy swells that had formed in the last hours. Soleck wanted to drive in close and let the boats see that they had been seen, but so far the admiral had forbidden such an action.

Soleck hit the tanker with élan, but, as the moment for the landing approached, his flying got stiffer and he began to find his mind drifting from details. His right-seater kept him reminded of the fuel, but he was so far gone in worry that he had to be reminded of course corrections.

Just after noon, local time, the carrier got a second S-3 off the deck with a snuffling, bleary-eyed crew, and Soleck turned for home. The cigarette boats, after quartering the seas around yesterday's carrier location, had turned for the coast of Africa and were now plowing through heavy seas toward Lamu Island off the northern coast of Kenya.

The carrier deck was pitching through a remarkable distance, given that the sky was still clear. The wind across the deck was rising but wasn't more than fifteen knots. But as Soleck flew into the break, a sudden gust rocked his wings and moved the plane *sideways* in the sky, the gust cutting directly across the path of his flight. He steadied up and flew into the break, his worry about landing now overlaid by concern about the conditions.

His break wasn't shit hot but it was good, and he flew down the side of the carrier just right, calling his numbers softly to himself and his hands moving almost unconsciously through the pre-landing checklist. The wheels went down with a satisfactory *thud,* and the flaps were set, tabs trimmed, engine good to go, and then he was turning into his lineup. Even a mile out, the boat was really moving, her stern rising twenty feet and then falling.

Instead of increasing his tension, the movement of the stern focused him. Soleck didn't watch the stern. He flew the plane. A half-mile out he was good for lineup, his wings solid, as if the plane were riding tracks into the landing.

The first crosswind gust hit him ten seconds from the deck. It challenged him, because it pushed his plane down twenty feet and moved him well off the lineup for his landing. He made two minute course corrections, one to get back toward lineup and another to reclaim the attitude needed to land after the gust pushed his nose down.

Now Soleck was three seconds from the deck. The giant, deep-ocean roller that the carrier was riding was rolling just under the stern, and the carrier was at the apex of her pitch. As Soleck pressed his final descent, the whole deck began to drop out from under him and he chased it, suddenly lost in a landing he had flown with perfect competence, and the attitude of his airplane slipped away. The nose came down too far, the wheels just touched the deck, and the hook slapped the deck *hard* just aft of the three wire and bounced right over, so that as Soleck slammed his throttle to full power, he felt the plane bounce past the point where he should have felt the comfort of the wire dragging her to a stop.

His plane shot down the deck, her tailhook blazing

sparks as he fought for airspeed. The "tower flower," a fellow pilot who often provided advice (needed or not) to pilots, waited until he was clear of the deck before commenting.

"Not your fault, Soleck," said the voice. "The boat just dropped away. LSO saw it."

The man might as well have said, *Don't lose your nerve.* Soleck shook his head, bitter that he had to be coached through a landing. Behind him, the carrier turned to get a better attitude to the wind and waves. Another gust shook the plane.

"Fly for the middle of the deck. Leave the rest to the ship," said a new voice.

Soleck didn't stow his gear and he didn't return to the stack. Gritting his teeth, he went around immediately to try again. There didn't seem to be any other planes, anyway. The sea was now too rough to make landing a safe activity. He flew down the length of the ship off the port side, counting his numbers again, and started his final turn. A gust threw the plane across the sky, and suddenly his numbers were out the window again; he was well up on the starboard wing and looking down at the sea, which was *right there,* and he got the nose up and added power and got back some altitude, but now he was far off lineup, way too high and ten knots too fast, and he had about seventeen seconds to correct. The stern was moving everywhere and he vowed not to chase it, just put his nose at the center of the deck, a few meters beyond the three wire. The middle of the deck moved less, he saw now. But his lineup was still late and he was *chasing the deck.*

Less than a mile away, the LSO began to curse. He knew who was in the plane, and he could feel the gusts that were wrecking every attempt Soleck made to land. Even the LSO felt the unfairness of it.

"Wave him off before he makes a mistake," came a voice in the LSO's ear. That was the CAG.

Late, high, too fast, Soleck struggled to catch a landing that he would have let go by in a simulator. The cut lights and the LSO's voice saved him from the struggle.

"Wave off," said the LSO, who had never called a correction. The landing had been too bad to correct.

"Fuck," said Soleck, quietly, but the cockpit was so still that his one curse caused Craw to twitch in the backseat.

"How bad are those gusts, Mister Soleck?"

Soleck was crossing the stern of the carrier, a hundred feet up and climbing.

"Bad," he said tersely. That was Captain Rafehausen he was speaking to. The CAG. He felt humiliated all over again.

"Need to go to the beach?" Rafehausen's voice said.

Soleck wanted to cry. He was not given to self-pity, but he was *sure* that the first landing would have been an okay on any reasonable day. The second landing had been screwed by the gust of wind.

"I want to keep trying until I get it," he blurted out.

"Good. That's what I wanted to hear, Mister Soleck. Because Kenya isn't being too friendly to us right now, and putting you on the beach would be a little international incident of its own. So I need you to fight the gusts, pick your moment, and get that plane on the deck."

"Aye, aye, sir."

"How's your gas?" Rafe knew that launching another tanker would be trouble. Recovering it would be worse.

"Seven thousand pounds." Two more looks at the deck and he'd start to be in trouble.

"Better bring her aboard this pass, then."

Just like that. Rafe sounded *positive* that Soleck would do it, almost as if he had been messing around up until now and it was time to get serious.

Soleck ground his teeth, felt the bile at the back of his throat and the weight in his gut. Then he was back on his routine, flying down the port side. He wasn't even mouthing the numbers now, because it was automatic, and the gust that caught him three-quarters of the way through his downwind leg was less of a surprise. He beat it to the corner, already back on his game.

He came upwind, right on the money, attitude and altitude, and ready to correct if the crosswind hit him. He was counting down in his mind, mentally trying to keep one of the big storm gusts at bay as he did his cockpit scan, *felt* his angle of attack, *rode* his plane at the pitching three wire. He felt a kind of calm, as if the odds were now stacked so high that he couldn't be blamed for anything and could only do his best, fly his landing, and hope for luck. He didn't actually have any part of his mind thinking these thoughts, because his whole attention was on the plane, wrapped up in it like a trained rider on a mettlesome horse.

Later, he would realize that he wasn't really *thinking* about the landing.

The plane came down. The LSO was silent. The stern of the *Jefferson* started to rise.

Soleck saw the movement of the deck and didn't even twitch. He was committed.

The LSO started to crouch, willing the plane into the wire.

The stern rose. The plane dropped. The tailhook touched the deck inches aft of the three wire.

Soleck felt the harness grab at his chest and rocked forward. He had forgotten to lock it. He didn't care. They were down.

Fifty feet away, on the LSO platform, the LSO took off his helmet and wiped the sweat off his face. "Three wire and okay," he muttered. "If at first you don't succeed—"

Up in the tower, Captain Rafehausen breathed again. He thought that Soleck might make a good pilot, but the boy was losing his nerve. If it got any worse, he was going to have to go.

Dar es Salaam.

"Craik has a new set of airline reservations, sir."

"Oh, well done, Jiang."

The rare note of praise caused Jiang to smile broadly. "Thank you, sir."

"Well? And the airline reservation?"

"Tajikistan, Colonel."

Colonel Lao looked at Jiang for a moment and rubbed his chin. He was thinking that if Craik was really going to meet Chen, and he could capture both Chen and Craik, then there would be no reason at all to go to Nairobi. "Now, I *can* believe that Chen would be in Tajikistan. What do we have there?"

"Nothing. Too close to both the Russians and the Islamics."

"Send a foreign team. Any foreign team. No, send Russians. If this goes bad, I don't want it coming back on us. Use the Russians you picked up on the drug matter. Get permission from Beijing if you have to. We have to beat Craik there and pick him up at the airport. Our people will have to stay close."

"He'll see them."

"Perhaps. If he takes them to Chen, grab Chen. If Craik goes down, so be it. Tajikistan is what Americans call the Wild West."

Jiang looked at his boss with renewed enthusiasm.

"We're going to get him, aren't we?"

"It seems possible, Captain. When that team is in-country, I want them to call. I want to brief their leader in person. I do *not* want another episode like Jakarta."

"Where Craik killed one of ours."

"Possibly. Either way, he's about to pay the price for playing."

In the Virginia Horse Country.

Jerry Piat came to the boundary of the safe-house property where they had stashed Suter and stopped in the woods across the road. He had walked down from Warrenton, where a bus had left him two days before, cutting cross-country and moving along back roads and farm fields by night. He had a small backpack, hardly more than a book bag, and he was rumpled and soiled and looked like somebody who had had the bottom drop out of life.

He waited until there was nobody on the road and then crossed quickly and slipped under the wire fence. Six weeks ago, when he had still been in the Agency and he had come out here to help interrogate Ray Suter, he had asked for a tour of the place out of boredom because nothing else had been happening. Suter wouldn't talk then; it was only when they were alone a couple of days later, and Piat could see the handwriting on the wall and knew that he was going to get the ax, that he and Suter had found a common interest despite disliking each other. The tour of the safe-house property had shown Piat how porous the place was. He had even written a memo on it, but nobody had cared.

The place had been used by the Agency off and on for thirteen years. It may once have been secure enough to hold defectors or important acquisitions, but now it was a place where they mostly held low-level retreats and the odd farewell party. They'd stuck Suter here because Suter wasn't quite a prisoner, more an in-house embarrassment, and they were fighting over what to do with him. The security was good enough, they said.

Piat knew that there was a zone of motion sensors in the woods where he had entered. On the side farthest from him, there were also a stone wall and the gate through which visitors came. The motion sensors were post-Vietnam but not by much; they were monitored from the basement of the house by a security guard who had half a dozen other duties. Most of the sensors had been set to minimum because there were so many deer.

Piat waited inside the fence, screened from the road by leaves and high grass. Cars passed with hissing sounds. When he felt secure, he moved into the woods. He moved slowly, the way deer do—a few steps, look around; a few more steps, look around. He would freeze in place for a minute at a time, like a deer. Or, for a few paces, he brought his feet down harder to mimic the mincing, stamping gait of a suspicious buck.

He gave himself an hour to get through the woods. He had lots of time.

A security man patrolled the grounds every three hours. The original directive had specified two men on foot; now there was one in a golf cart. He stayed out in the meadows, where the cart had worn itself a more or less smooth track. In his memo, Piat had recommended that the guard go back to foot patrol and that he get a dog. Now he waited in the fringe of trees before the woods gave way to fallow ground, to see if that part of his memo had been adopted.

Half an hour later, a golf cart came over the rise to his left and started toward him. No dog.

Wooden fence surrounded the meadows, board X's between upright posts, everything needing paint. The golf cart came along on the other side of the fence, passed him, went on another hundred yards, and then turned up an internal fence to get to the gate that was two hundred yards into the meadowland, toward the house. Piat waited until it was gone, then slipped through one of the peeling X's.

He set himself up in a clump of trees that grew out of an old sinkhole, a geological oddity twenty feet deep, bowl-shaped, some of the trees eighteen inches around. Nobody had ever wanted to plow down there. From the sinkhole, he could watch the house and the horse barns and the tennis courts and the place where he and Suter had sat on the grass and made the plans to screw Dukas and Craik.

Dumb, he told himself. He'd been drinking heavily in those days. He wasn't quite rational, he decided. *My own dumb fault.*

He had MREs from a surplus store, a sheet of plastic to sleep under, a pair of plastic gloves from a roll he'd bought at a Safeway. A roll of duct tape. A pair of binoculars. A knife with a can-opener. His gun. He didn't need much.

Piat watched the buildings through the binoculars. He ate an MRE. Cold. He saw the maintenance man come and go around the horse barns. Later the man got out a riding mower and dicked around some flower beds with it. A couple of horses, alone in the next meadow, came up to their fence and looked over toward Piat's hideaway. He figured they had smelled him. Nobody paid much mind to those horses, he knew.

At about two o'clock, Suter came out the back door of the house and lay down on the lawn with a book. Piat's pulse picked up, then settled down. The maintenance man was mowing along the far side of the house now. Piat watched Suter pull a bag from the grass and get a cellphone from it and talk. *Some security,* he thought. Suter was like somebody who runs a drug operation from prison. *Safest place in the world.*

Much later, when Suter was gone and long shadows were painted along the lawns from the buildings, he saw the maintenance man drive his riding mower near the place where Suter had lain and, parking the mower so it screened him from the house, retrieve the bag with the cellphone from the grass.

Not bad. Suter must have been paying out a lot of money. His savings? His retirement? Maybe he thought he was going to make a big score somehow.

After dark, Piat made himself a bed in the leaves in the bottom of the sinkhole. He pulled the plastic dropcloth over himself and went to sleep.

Tajikistan.

THE BEST EASTERN IN DUSHANBE WAS PROBABLY BE-
low Harry's standard, but the food was acceptable and the bar
well stocked and pleasant. The hotel itself looked like every
major concrete structure of its age anywhere in the world: a
rectangular box with recessed windows that could have been
in Peoria, Illinois. They checked into three adjoining rooms
and ate in the restaurant while Dave made calls to secure the
Toyota Land Cruiser they had been promised.

"Dress warmly and leave the rest of your luggage here,"
Harry advised Alan. He wouldn't be more specific, and his
vague motions to the east annoyed Alan a little. But they were
still moving toward Chen, or his body, and that was enough.
He was enjoying himself. It was the longest he had had with
Harry in years. Rediscovering at least the possibility of friendship with Dave Djalik was icing on the cake.

By early afternoon they were on the road. Djalik drove
them through the city, past reminders of the country's recent
civil war that were visible on every street, and then to one of
the central markets. Dave hopped out, and Alan kept listening

to Harry until it struck him that Dave wasn't just checking a tire.

"Where'd he go?"

"Buying guns. Sit tight, Alan. He does this easy as breathing."

Dave was gone almost an hour. He came back with a satchel that proved to be a Russian rucksack. It held several pistols, a pump shotgun of U.S. manufacture, and a small machine pistol of a type Alan had never seen before.

"Polish," said Dave. "I got it for you, Al. Folds up neat as a pin, but you can shoot one-handed. I love 'em. Commies handed 'em out like candy, so you can get one anywhere in the East. See? Push the safety, flick the handle, and, *voilà*, it's a gun."

"Can't fold it with a full magazine."

"Well, no. But you can shoot one-handed."

Harry took the shotgun. Dave probably had a variety of weapons, although none of them showed. Dave taped the extra Tokarov pistols to various positions in the car.

"Old habit," he said. "Humor me."

Washington, D.C.

The CNO was looking through the thick folders on his desk. They represented the lives of some of his most senior officers, men who had given their whole careers to the service of the sea. He knew them all as men, and, although there were a few he didn't like, there were none he couldn't respect.

He consulted with the Joint Chiefs when he appointed the numbered fleet commanders, the men at the very top of the operational control of the Navy, the commanders whose powers were often greater than that of many nation-states in their areas of operation. Sixth Fleet, in the Mediterranean, controlled more ships than any country in that ocean. Third Fleet, in the Pacific, had a vast array of forces and one of the greatest bases in the world at Pearl Harbor under his authority. Seventh Fleet shared a coast with Russia, China, and North Korea—all potential adversaries. Fifth Fleet, in the

Persian Gulf, faced a constant series of crises with Iran, Iraq, Pakistan, and India.

He didn't need to look at the folders to know the men, but he riffled through them anyway, his eyes catching on words from old fitness reports written in places like Saigon and Manila, Newport News and Naples, by other officers long-retired or long-dead. Keegan, one of the oldest of the names before him, had got a Silver Star in Vietnam as a lieutenant jg on a riverine patrol. The admiral who had signed his fitness report at Cam Ranh Bay had served under Nimitz on a destroyer in the Pacific. It was like looking at history.

He already knew whom he wanted. He'd got most of them. Keegan was one he'd lost. The army hated him, and he was not acceptable as a joint force commander. He'd have to retire, because there wasn't really anywhere else for him to go. The CNO knew he'd gone to the wall for Frederick William Keegan, but it wouldn't matter soon, despite the man's bravery, his record, and his spotless honor.

And he'd lost other battles besides.

Two of his deputies sat in front of him, their attention on the folders. They weren't in this hunt, but they were in this peer group, and they were eager to know.

"Pilchard for Fifth Fleet," he drawled. His DCNO for Naval Aviation nodded happily. One for the good guys.

"He already said he wanted Anne Siddons for his Flag Staff and Al Craik for Intel if he got the nod."

The CNO nodded. He knew more about both than he usually did about commanders and their ilk.

"Yeah, I expect he would. Siddons is on track to have her own fleet one of these days. And Pilchard can keep Craik out of trouble. Where is he now?"

"Headed back to his detachment on the *Jefferson*," his assistant cut in smoothly. He was pointing at a blue folder on the CNO's desk. Craik was already moving back to his det, doing something that only people with the blue folder knew about.

"We could just cut him short and bring him here while Pilchard gets his staff together." This from the DCNO.

The CNO looked out his window and thought about an

intel officer's commanding an aviation detachment. It might
have been hell for the man. Or it might be the command of
his life. Intel officers were odd fish, in the CNO's experience,
and many were totally unsuited to command a lifeboat on a
millpond, but Craik struck him differently. He turned to his
assistant.

"Ask Craik if he really wants to be an intel officer."

"Sir?"

"Something about him—we gave him temporary unre-
stricted line status for this job. Ask him if he wants to keep it,
or take his flight training and be an NFO. And don't cut him
short unless he asks for it. Pilchard won't get Fifth for four
months. Ask him."

"Aye, aye, sir."

Tajikistan.

Once the drive started in earnest, it seemed to go on forever.
The road was flat, although mountains were clear in the distance to the north, and just visible to the south before the sun
went down. Alan couldn't stop rubbernecking.

"Welcome to Central Asia, bud. The new scene of operations for all the big players."

"Harry, sometimes you give me the creeps."

Harry just smiled. "I calls 'em like I sees 'em."

Alan continued to look around him until the light failed,
and he began to notice other features besides the windswept
landscape and the distant mountains.

"That car back there has sure been behind us a long
time."

"Give that student a cigar," said Harry, and Dave smiled.

"He or his buddy the blue Volvo have been with us since
the airport," said Dave.

Alan shook his head.

"I've been talking too much."

"Don't sweat it, Alan. You caught on. This is our business.
Dave's just hoping that they sent somebody into the market to
check up on us, aren't you, Dave?"

"I left a little suggestion with our friends in the arms business that anyone asking after us was from the local police." Dave chuckled. "I don't think we'll see the blue Volvo again this trip."

"How much longer *is* this trip, friends?"

"Another couple of hours." Harry leaned back over the seat. "Need to pee? I do."

"That's a big roger, Harry."

Dave had the Land Cruiser over to the shoulder in a minute. The distant headlights pulled off, too.

"If they want us, this is perfect for them," said Dave, looking into the now-silent dark. "Dark and cold. No witnesses." Alan saw that Djalik had an Ingram M-10 cocked and locked on his lap.

Alan looked back and forth between Dave and Harry. Harry was pissing in the gravel ditch by the road, a big pistol in one hand, while the other helped with the business of the stop. Dave was slumped down in the driver's seat. Behind them, the other car's lights went off.

"Is this serious?" Alan asked, incredulous. "We're about to get hit by a drive-by on a highway in Tajikistan?"

He pushed the long clip into his Polish pistol, where it went home with a very satisfying *click*. He worked the slide. The gun was beautifully made, with a deep black-blue on the receiver that bespoke quality and sparkled even in the dark.

"Probably not," said Dave. "But this here is the Wild West of the world, right now, and it would be foolish not to be ready. Those guys were waiting for us. We don't know if they're following us because of something we did, or you for something you did. Maybe they want the car. Maybe they just want to whack a foreigner. Maybe they have the wrong guys. Doesn't matter, at this point."

Alan got out and pulled down his zipper. His shoulder blades protested as he turned his back to the road. It just didn't seem possible that they were this close to combat and they were relieving themselves.

"I take it we don't want them to know we're on to them?"

"Exactly." Harry was done, was blowing on his hands. Alan was still trying to force back what had been a tidal wave a moment before, when they were stopping to relieve themselves and not to be shot at.

Djalik came out last, when Alan had finally convinced nature to take its course.

"Don't look back," said Harry.

Nothing happened.

In a minute, they were rolling again.

And a minute later, the headlights were there again.

FORTY MINUTES LATER, DJALIK'S LOCAL CELL PHONE rang. He fought with it for several minutes and finally gave up.

"We're leaving the coverage area. It's tough to build infrastructure here."

"Yeah?" Alan was mildly interested in why there were any cell phones here.

"Yeah. We got the security contract for the Pakistani firm building the towers."

"Who was it?" asked Harry.

"Sorry, Harry. I don't really know. I got to figure it was Georgi back in the market. So he's probably had problems with our friends in the blue Volvo. But it could have been a telemarketer."

The phone rang again and Dave slowed the Land Cruiser while he listened. He looked at the faceplate of the phone briefly, saw that he had a signal, and stopped. Alan watched the headlights behind them stop, too.

Dave listened grimly for a moment and then said, "I see. Do what you have to, Georgi." He hung up. "They shot one of Georgi's guys," he said. "Not a great loss to society, but Georgi thinks they're hard guys."

Harry looked at Alan.

"Who knows you were coming here?"

"You and Mike and me."

"Okay. Even I trust that group." Harry smiled, a flash of white in the front. "Get some sleep, Al." His voice took on a throaty growl. "It's going to be a bumpy night."

•   •   •

ALAN DRIFTED IN AND OUT FOR HOURS AS THEY continued to speed down an empty two-lane road. In another hour they made a turn that woke him up, and they left the asphalt for a gravel road that swiftly became dirt, and their pace slowed. The headlights were still there, and Alan was surprised every time he came awake that he had been sleeping in the midst of such an obvious emergency, but it was one of those slow emergencies that he had so frequently experienced in the cockpit of an S-3. It wouldn't resolve itself immediately, and no amount of worry could fix the problem.

Harry snored.

When Alan next woke, Dave and Harry were talking quietly in the front. He woke slowly and didn't get the gist of their quiet conversation, except that Dave was now really worried about the car behind them. Alan sat up, undid his seat belt, and leaned into the front seat. It felt as if he were back in an S-3, going up to talk to the pilot.

"What's the problem?"

Dave spoke quietly. "That car behind us is the problem, Al. They aren't even pretending to be stealthy. They just stay right on us, same distance, on and on. We're getting close to our target and I'd rather not take them right in."

"I say we stop here and go after them."

Harry seemed to be considering the possibility.

"No. We can't afford to be wrong. Just drive up to the old well."

"You're the boss."

Dave made another turn, this time on a tiny track just wide enough for their truck. They were at the base of a high hill, or perhaps a mountain. Its looming bulk couldn't be made out clearly in the night.

"Is this where Chen is?" Alan asked. He was full of adrenaline, ready to go and do—something.

"And will be for some time to come," Harry said with deliberate ambiguity.

The car stopped, and Dave killed the engine.

Dave was out of the car immediately. He did something with a flashlight for a moment and then got down in the scrub next to the driver's-side wheel. Harry pulled on tight gloves and then got out, and Alan did the same.

"Follow me, Al," Harry said, and he was off, moving low. Alan copied him, the machine pistol in his good hand, and his maimed hand out for balance. He could just see the gleam from Harry's leather jacket. Everything else was dark. The lights that had been behind them for hours were gone, as was the engine noise. Alan could smell wood smoke.

"Friends of mine use this place," said Harry.

"Smugglers?"

"Like that. I want the bozos behind us to think we're clueless. Just go inside."

Alan went through the door slowly, his senses hyperalert. He scanned the interior of a small wooden shack. There were coals still warm in the woodstove, but no other signs of life. Harry went immediately to a window and tried to see outside without disturbing the shade.

"Build up the fire, Al. It's cold and it won't get warmer."

"Where's Dave?"

"Scouting. Dave can take care of himself."

Alan took split wood from a stack next to the tiny stove and built a log cabin on the coals. Then he blew on them until the kindling caught. It reminded him of childhood camping trips.

"Anything?" he whispered to Harry.

"Nothing," said Harry."

"Is this where we find Chen?"

"Yeah. At first light, we'll dig him up. He died on the way here and we buried him in the yard."

"That'll be nice."

They were silenced by the sound of a single shot.

Alan was already out the door, because Djalik was alone in the dark, and Alan owed Djalik.

He saw the muzzle flash off to his right. Alan was almost frozen by the knowledge that his own movement might draw fire from Djalik himself, but he had to assume that Djalik knew where they were. He ran toward the last firing, crouched low. He felt that Harry was behind him, but he didn't dare tear his attention from the patch of darkness where the muzzle flash had been.

Crack-crack. That was Djalik, shooting double-tap with a small pistol. Alan had heard him shoot this way in Africa; he knew the exact timing of the sound. It was like a signature. Djalik was well off to his right.

More shooting from the darkness in front of him. Someone firing at Djalik's flash, or even at the sound. Not anyone really dangerous, then. Alan stopped, checked over his unfamiliar gun in the dark until he found the safety, and pushed it off with his good hand. He listened for Harry and didn't jump when Harry's bulk came up behind him.

Harry touched his shoulder and pointed at the area where the nearest shooter was. Alan nodded, and then, afraid his nod might be invisible, touched Harry's hand once, twice. *Yes.* Harry patted his back softly and vanished into the dark. Alan got down and began to crawl as fast as he could.

There was another burst of fire. He couldn't really see it from the ground, although it did still provide a glow. Shooting in this mixture of grass and gorse would be tricky. Every blade of grass would deflect small-caliber stuff. Alan knew he was making noise, but experience had taught him that against most opponents, speed counted more than perfect stealth, and so far he hadn't had the ill luck to meet the other kind. He kept moving, crawling and rolling along the ground, and twice having to pick himself up and roll over obstructions.

Crack-crack from the right. Then the *boom* of Harry's shotgun off to the left. His man whirled, closer than Alan had expected, clearly worried that he was surrounded. He continued to move his head. Alan took a deep breath and tried to find a way to take the man without killing him, but Harry would be moving this way and there wasn't time. The man rose in a stance and aimed off toward Djalik.

Alan rolled to a crouch and fired the little machine pistol. It had no recoil and surprisingly little barrel rise. Alan had got close because the gun was unfamiliar and he didn't want to miss, but the first bullet hit the man just below the throat and the next two rose right across his forehead. He bounced when he hit the ground and flopped a moment, a sickening sound.

Dead.

The steppe around them was silent.

Alan lay still and shook with delayed reaction. The man had been too close and lay less than ten feet away, and Alan could smell him, the blood and the wounds.

Time passed. His shaking stopped.

Then more time.

Alan began to get cold. *Could they both be dead? Harry and Djalik? Was he too late? Were there still men on the hillside?*

Alan raised his head a little to look over the top of the gorse. The dark hadn't changed, and he saw nothing.

He waited.

He raised his head again and saw a flash of red light off to the right. He took a deep breath, his adrenaline charging through his arteries again, and kept his head up.

The light went on and off again. Alan thought it was Djalik's flashlight. Djalik was signaling to someone. Alan waited another moment and then decided that Djalik could be signaling only *him*. He moved up cautiously, trying to breathe through his mouth and listen at the same time. Djalik was giving one quick flash and then moving the light slowly off to the left. Alan stopped behind a rock and considered. The long movement always went to the same place. Djalik either meant there was another bad guy there, or that he wanted Alan there. Alan had to assume that Djalik wanted him to move there, and he crawled around the rock in front of him.

Bang-bang-bang. A short burst from an assault rifle, followed by a yell in a language that sounded like Russian. Alan thought that the man was losing his nerve, but, now that he had given his position away, Alan could see why Djalik wanted Alan well off to the left. Alan scrambled along a shingle of gravel and over a low rock. The man fired again, this time in his direction, uncomfortably close. Gravel pounded away at Alan's shins, where bullets kicked it up. Alan shot back on instinct, and, suddenly, Harry's shotgun roared. Then silence.

"Dave?" Alan called as softly as he could.

"Roger!" Dave called confidently, and rose slowly to his feet. "Didn't really know what happened over here."

Harry was with them in an instant.

"Let's get you a tissue sample and get the flock out of here," said Harry.

Alan looked back to where his first target was dead in the grass. He felt ill, almost morally ill. It had been too easy, now that it was over. The man hadn't needed to die. He just hadn't been able to think of a way to take him.

"They all dead?" he asked. He didn't like the way his voice sounded.

"Yep," Dave said. "There were three of them to start, and then the driver came out of the car, and you and Harry put him down. I was trying to take him alive, but whatever. I'll check the bodies, Harry. You and Al do what you came for. Like you said, let's get gone." He looked at Alan. Whatever he saw, he must have liked, because he punched Alan's shoulder and headed off into the dark.

After the terrors of the fight, the wait, and the reaction, the mere process of opening a grave and taking a piece of the contents had less horror than Alan had expected. The corpse was dry, mostly, and the smell merely sweet and cloying. There were things living in the corpse, but nothing glistened wetly or hissed. He took a button from the jacket. He closed a plastic bag around the fingers of the corpse's right hand and cut one off with his clasp knife. It was quite easy, the sinew separating immediately, already rotted through. Alan dropped the bag into another bag. Then he got some of the short, black hairs from the skull, with a little tissue clinging to them, as well. Then came the worst part. He took a deep breath, reached his gloved hand into the body cavity and found a vertebra high on the back, and pulled. Something moved across his wrist and he flinched. His gorge rose. He steadied himself and pulled. The vertebra came free with a soft, yielding feeling that was far more horrible than the sight of the corpse had been. He got the vertebra into a different bag, put all of his evidence into a third bag, rolled it all up inside his rain slicker, and put the whole thing in his pack. He'd buy another slicker at REI, he promised himself, and threw up on the tall grass beside the grave.

He and Harry and Dave weren't quite as loud going

home. But twelve hours after the graveside, when they finally touched down in Bahrain, they were back to rapid conversation, changing topics as fast as they found them. If Alan was troubled, he had pushed it far down. If Harry still had questions, he didn't ask them. And Dave seemed happy, as if he'd made peace with something.

Harry used the brief stop to talk about the events of the day before, which all of them had avoided on the trip back.

"Those guys weren't locals," Harry said. Alan just kept packing, used to Harry's mercurial changes of subject.

"No?"

"No, bud. They were Russian, I think. Probably hired guns."

"Any idea who hired them?"

"No. Do you, Alan?"

They looked at each other, but the look was not adversarial.

"No idea."

"I just want you to note, on behalf of the U.S. Navy, that I have once again helped Mike Dukas, and once again been shot at," said Harry, with the old smile.

"Roger that," said Alan, fervently. They embraced.

"I expect I'll see you soon. After all, you'll be on the *Jefferson*, and I'll be in Africa."

It was dark humor, given the past. It sat with Alan on the plane, Harry's parting shot and the dead face with the three holes in it. Sometimes the adrenaline wasn't enough even for a junkie.

Nairobi.

A DAY ROOM AT A HOTEL AT BRUSSELS AIRPORT HAD
done little for Dukas's jet lag, and the dozen hours it took to
fly on to Nairobi would all but kill him, he thought. He had
the window seat, but with nothing of course to look at until
morning. Triffler dozed beside him. Triffler had slippers, eye-
shades, and earplugs; he didn't eat airline food and had brought
his own; and he washed his hands every time he touched a non-
American surface. Triffler, Dukas thought with grim satisfaction, was going to *hate* Africa.

Dukas tried to stretch and succeeded only in pushing his
seat back into the knees of the person behind him. He got a
hard thrust back, and he grunted. His wound ached. His head
ached. His mouth tasted like old mummy wrappings. The
memory of Sally Baranowski was like a sore.

When the sun at last rose, he found himself looking down
at endless red desert. It was shockingly beautiful, shocking because stark and unpeopled and alien, undulating away to the
horizon without a hint of green or a suggestion of movement.
Shadows, exaggerated by the early sun, made a moonscape.

Only once, an hour after sunrise, did what might have been a road appear, going from somewhere to somewhere all by itself, unpeopled, undriven, unwalked.

"What d'you see?" Triffler said in a hoarse voice.

"Africa."

Triffler craned across Dukas's lap and looked down. He made a sound like a groan.

"When the Brits made maps of it," Dukas growled, "they wrote 'MMBA' on the empty places." He grinned into Triffler's worried eyes. " 'Miles and Miles of Bloody Africa.' "

Then there were hills and dusty green off to the plane's right, and then a river and intense green, and he thought they were skirting the Sudd, the part of the Nile in southern Sudan where weed grew so thick that it used to close the river. And then there were mountains below and a great dry plain and a vast lake in it, which he thought was Turkana, teeming with fish and crocodiles, its successive levels over the millennia marked by terraces of dark stone that had once been beaches where, when this had been lush savanna, the first humans had lived and died and left their bones for the twentieth century to find.

Dukas had been to Kenya four times and he knew the terrain by car, but from the air he got lost. When they got too low for him to follow the escarpment of the Rift, he had to guess where he was, hoping that the rounded green mountains were either the Aberdares or the Matthews, and the still-greener hills with fields and houses that looked like specks, and the roads that had movement on them now like ant trails were the Kikuyu country, the old white man's country, with lakes to the west and savanna to the south. Then they were lower still, houses and cows below, and roads and fields, and buildings and streets and throngs of people and then grassy prairie again; they banked and turned and turned again and came in on the final approach into Kenyatta, and he saw the other morning flights turning in the sky above them, and two already on the ground below, bright silver and tan dust, the look of drought, acacia trees casting thin shade on dry earth, and then concrete and wire and the hard whack of the first touch and the roar of the engines.

"Welcome to Africa," he said.

"They wouldn't give me a polio shot," Triffler said. "I should have had a polio shot."

"You had polio shots when you were a kid; you're immune."

"I should have been given a booster if I wanted one." Triffler was dodging people who were jerking baggage out of the overheads as if the Mau Mau were about to attack the plane. Triffler got hit in the shoulder and sat back down. "Africans have no manners," he said in a loud voice, but, as most of the people on the plane were Americans, nobody cared. Dukas started to say that in his experience Africans were the politest people in the world, but then he thought that that wasn't quite right, either. Africans could be the politest people in the world, he decided, but they also could be the most shortsighted, the cruelest, the stubbornest, and the least caring, and the best way to bring out their courtesy was to be their guest.

"Remember, we're guests here," he muttered to Triffler as they passed the weary cabin attendants and started up the tunnel.

"I read the State Department booklet," Triffler said. "Do you suppose there's a Starbucks in Nairobi?"

"Dozens of them," Dukas said. Fatigue was pressing on his shoulders like two big, nasty birds perched there. "Starbucks on every corner." They trudged through endless corridors to the dark shed where customs officers glowered. "Better get your passport out of your panty hose," he whispered, "so they'll know you're a rich foreign devil."

Triffler had stopped to stand and sniff. Other people were going around him, banging him with carry-on luggage, muttering. Triffler was taking in his first smells of Africa. Dukas could get them faintly, too—dust, smoke, sourness, altogether a smell that is mostly pleasant and utterly unforgettable. Triffler sniffed again. "It's a blend," he said, as if he were talking about coffee. "Interesting."

A man with a sign that said DUCKAS PARTY was standing in the crowd where immigration disgorged tourists into Africa. Other men held up sticks with signs that read TRANSSIMBA

TOURS and BWANA TOURS and BESTWEST HOTELS, and a man was shouting "Beckstein! Beckstein!" as if he had Beckstein for sale somewhere, and taxi drivers with hot eyes and lean, muscular bodies were darting forward to grab half of the handle of a piece of luggage so they could rip it from the owner's hand and shout, "This way! This way—taxi, best taxi—!" Dukas pushed Triffler ahead of him, dodged a taxi driver, and shouted, "Duckas! Hey! I'm Duckas!"

"Duckas?" Triffler said. "*Duck*as?"

"In Africa, you learn flexibility," Dukas said as their greeter pumped his hand and introduced himself as Mister Ngugi and then began to load himself with baggage. He wore a tan safari suit with short sleeves and *Ngugi* and *Rolls Rentals* embroidered on the pocket. They tumbled out into the morning heat, and the smell was stronger, and Triffler sniffed some more. Minivans were darting in and out; horns were blowing; black men in green uniforms were stepping from Range Rovers with zebra stripes painted on their doors to pick up stunned and grinning whites.

Kenyatta is a more or less modern airport, but it sits near a city of only modest modernity, which is confined to a central area of about six blocks where the Euro-American hotels and the upscale shops huddle; beyond them, poverty and the Middle Ages fight an often-winning battle with the twentieth century. Between Kenyatta and the city is paved highway, scrub savanna, lots of trucks, and some of the worst driving in the world. Once the city itself is reached, armed soldiers start to appear—a truckload at this roundabout, a trio at that intersection.

"Teenagers with assault rifles give me the willies," Dukas said.

"What's going on?" Triffler said.

"Nothing. They're always there. That's why nothing's going on." Dukas could tell that Triffler was thinking of walking these streets with a gun hidden in a holster, and of what it would mean to start shooting here. Their guns would be in a safe at the embassy now, waiting for them. "One shot, you could start a war," Dukas said. "How do you deal with a high-risk meeting in Nairobi?"

"Verr-ee carefull-ee," Triffler murmured.

"Hilton Hotel?" their driver said. Mister Ngugi was polite and brisk and spent his working life driving Americans around Nairobi, on contract with the embassy. He probably knew more about what spooks were in and out of Kenya than the local CIA station did.

"Of course, the Hilton," Dukas said. Mister Ngugi would know as well as Dukas did that all Americans who worked for the government *had* to stay at the Hilton or one of a couple of other central-city, upscale, expensive hotels for reasons of security. Mister Ngugi would know it, the Kenyans would know it, the Chinese would know it. *You staying at the Hilton? What agency you work for?*

They pulled into one of the modern streets that surrounded the modern hotels, and Triffler sat up a little and looked hopeful. "I wonder where you run here," he said.

"Not in town; the muggers wear track shoes. Run in the boonies—the lions give you a hundred-yard head start."

They pulled up in front of the Hilton. Mister Ngugi jumped out, and baggage began to pass from black hands to black hands. Triffler stood on the sidewalk and said, "So this is Africa!"

Dukas took his elbow. "No, this is Kansas City. Africa is about three blocks that way."

They headed into the hotel.

AFRICA AT SUNSET. GLORIOUS COLORS AS ALAN landed at Jomo Kenyatta, the remembered red earth and green foliage, even in local winter. He smiled to himself before the smell had even reached him, because he always loved to return to Africa, and his mood lightened at once. It was more than just a land of adventure. It was a place where anything could happen.

Nairobi after sunset. Darkness covered everything, seemed to flow through the doors of the Hilton, darkening even the electric light. No streetlamps, and cars without headlights. It reminded Alan of a city under siege. Across the square from the Hilton, the *matatus,* tiny buses built of pickup trucks and

minivans, honked for passengers and bowled off into the night.
Most had only one headlamp and marginal brakes. He stopped
just outside the entrance of the Hilton and lit a cigarette,
peered off into the dark for a moment as he inhaled, and then
walked a few steps to a bedraggled flower border armored in
brick that marked the edge of the Hilton's efforts to maintain
North America in Africa. Through the smoke of a trash fire
and the screen of untended acacia trees in the park, he could
see the dark yellow lights of the Ambassadeur Hotel, an Indian-
run institution where he'd have stayed except that it wasn't
approved by the U.S. government. It cost less, offered less, and
pretended to less. It also housed the best restaurant in Africa,
the Safir.

Alan took another drag on his cigarette and mashed it
under his foot, as if destroying the butt could destroy the
habit. Then he turned back for the lobby to find his friends.

DUKAS'S ROOM HAD BECOME HIS OPERATIONS CEN-
ter, and it was packed with people. Dick Triffler was sitting
primly in a chair, holding a STU to his ear and taking notes.
Two overweight white men were poring over a plastic-coated
map of downtown Nairobi, while a young black woman
cleaned an automatic pistol on a chair near the bathroom.
Mike sat at the tiny, inadequate desk, the whole awash in paperwork and what appeared to be stacks of dinner trays.

Alan felt that they had all frozen at his knock, and the
small man who opened the door was hesitant to let him in,
but Dukas shot out of his seat and moved faster than his bulk
would have suggested, only whacking his shin once in his
move to the door. He engulfed Alan in a brief embrace, and
Alan returned it, surprised at Mike's vehemence, then realizing that it was Dukas's apology for jerking him around.

"Boy, am I glad to see you," Dukas said. "We need you."

Alan tossed his big backpack on the bed and opened a
zippered pocket. "Want to sign for this stuff, Mike? I'd like to
get it out of my pack before the rot spreads."

The rest of Mike's team had gathered around. Alan was
holding an opaque plastic bag and a pill bottle.

"Everybody, this is Lieutenant-Commander Alan Craik of the Navy. He is, at least temporarily, a sworn agent of the Naval Criminal Investigative Service. Alan, the dangerous woman with the gun is Margo Simcoe, the fat guys are Frank Rcozy and Bob Lightner. That's Brian O'Leary who let you in."

Dick Triffler leaned past all of them to shake Alan's hand. "Long time, no see," he said with faint sarcasm.

"What's in the plastic?" asked Margo. She had reached the point where she had to put the spring back into the slide and run the slide back into its grooves when the door had opened, and as soon as she had fired off her question, she finished the job so that the slide made a little click of emphasis. She smiled. Alan thought she might have watched too many Dirty Harry movies.

"That's Colonel Chen. That is, those packets contain some small part of the rapidly rotting mortal remains of Colonel Chen."

"Oooh," said Rcozy, stepping away from Alan's out-stretched arm. "Yech."

"Give me that," said Mike. "Got a chain of custody?"

"Yep. There it is. Sign there. It's your problem now."

"Great job, Al. How's Harry?"

"He says to tell you he knew he was working for you when he got shot at. I thought I'd just echo his sentiment."

"Shot at?"

"Yeah, in Tajikistan. Local shooters, probably Russian." Alan didn't dwell on it. "When's my plane out of here?"

Dukas put the two packets on top of his room's refrigerator. "Bob, get part of the skin sample off to the Legal Attaché at the embassy in the morning, okay?"

Bob nodded, already back to his map.

Dukas was searching the piles of paper on his desk. "Dick, do you have any stickers?"

Triffler opened a zipped leather notebook, carefully removed two round stickers, affixed one to each of Alan's packets and wrote something on them. Then he put them into the freezer.

"When's my plane to the boat?" Alan asked again.

"Where's Harry now?"

"Probably Dar es Salaam with his team. He'll send a coded call when he has Lao in sight. When's my plane?"

"Day after tomorrow," Dukas said. His smile was hesitant.

"Come again?" asked Alan. He had suspected something like this.

"I need you, Al. We have a lot to do and we're thin on the ground."

"Giving me a badge doesn't make me an agent! What the hell can I do that these folks can't?"

"Fly." Dukas opened his hands in mock apology. "We've got to have somebody in the air if we do a second meeting."

"HERE'S THE OUTLINE AS I SEE IT." DUKAS WAS SITting in the desk chair, the rest of his team perched on furniture or leaning against the walls. "I could spend all night on the maybes and the possibilities. Lao may not show, or he may wreck the meeting. He may not bite. Forget all that. We need to plan as if he makes the meeting, takes the hook, and shows some willingness to meet again or come straight over. So this is how I want to play." Dukas flipped a big map of East Africa on the bed.

"Chinese Checkers has a meeting site in Nairobi. The site is the Safir Restaurant in the street level of the Ambassadeur Hotel. It's an interesting site choice, as it's very public. That should work in our favor. Nobody should be shooting in a crowded restaurant. It'll limit conversation. It makes a snatch unlikely. That said, we have to be on our toes, especially as it's just across the park. Tomorrow, I'll spend all day moving, going to the game park, seeing the sights, and visiting the public market. Frank and Bob have built me a route. You guys will all play countersurveillance. As we begin the final run, you have to watch me and watch for Lao. And, of course, watch for Lao's watchers, as well. Once he's in the Safir, you have to try and tag as many of his guys as possible. His team could be local or Chinese. We're going to stand out—in case you haven't noticed, most people outside the walls of the Hilton aren't white—which is why we're limiting my route to tourist spots."

Dukas took a sip of water and stared off into space for a moment.

"You'll all have cell phones and headsets. I can't guarantee the headsets will work. Margo and Brian tried them this afternoon in the park and had some problems. So stick to cell phones when you can. Everyone in Africa has one, so they won't stand out. You'll have weapons. *Don't* use them. If you're fired on and have any choice at all, just run. I want to say that again. Anybody shoots, for any reason short of the preservation of national security, and I'll have your badge. The FBI guy at the embassy moved mountains to get the weapons to us, and I don't want to piss on his trust. Okay?"

Everyone nodded. Alan snuck a look to see if Margo was disappointed, but she wasn't; her attention was fixed on Dukas. Triffler nodded at him. What did that mean?

"When Lao walks in, Triffler calls him in on his handset. He'll be sitting right there, at another table. My backup."

"Kind of hard to call him in when he's eight feet away."

"Just one word. Just say 'in.' I want everybody to know when it starts. And when it ends. You call him out, too."

"And then I say 'out'?" Triffler was deadpan.

Dukas blew right by it. "Right. If he comes and stays willing, we'll talk, and I'll tell him some home truths. That is, I'll tell him that Chen is dead, offer him proof, and suggest what happened to the money. If he bites, he'll take a second meeting. If he really takes the bait, he might offer to defect right there. If so, I'll give the word—'Christmas.' *Christmas* means we're taking him out of the Safir and straight to the embassy. We'll take him out through the kitchen and put him in a panel van with hotel markings. Frank has that part arranged."

Dukas swept the room with a glance. He looked at his watch, fidgeted a little, and looked at the map. "The hard part will be *after* the meeting. Any funny business will happen then. If I've called it wrong, and he gets the wrong message or has something bad in mind, we'll see it at the end. Short of him trying to snatch *me*, you take no action. If he runs screaming from the building, let him go. If you've tagged one of their agents—"

"Tagged?" asked Alan. "In the Navy, that means 'destroyed.' "

"Let's not have *that* misunderstood." Dukas laughed grimly. " 'Tagged' means identified and kept under your eye. If you've tagged one, remember that there's an intelligence value to having a photograph for future identification. That's one. Two is that you can try to surveil your man, if you have one, back to his transport. That will depend on the situation, and every one of you will have to make that call for yourselves. If you see a probable, and I stress *probable,* you call him. The word will be *cat.*"

"Cat?" asked Triffler. "I thought we were on a holiday theme."

"Lao calls himself Rathunter. We'll call his people cats. Cat one, cat two, etc. Okay? Everybody still with me? I'd like to stress that most of us stand out like a sore thumb, and that it might not be worth your while to get aggressive. Whenever you break off contact, you run your own clearing route to make sure you're alone and come back here. Odds are they know perfectly well where we're staying. The necessity of playing ball with our own government makes stealth kind of impossible, but play the game, folks. We'll rally here and talk it through. 'Christmas' means we're now doing an extraction. 'April Fool's' means we're aborting. 'Easter' means one of you has spotted Lao. After that, he's the rabbit. Any questions?"

"If we're a go with Christmas?"

"Then watch your cats and keep them away from the action if you have to."

"Without any shooting, of course." Brian hadn't spoken until now. He seemed a quiet man.

"Exactly," said Dukas.

"What if he agrees to a second meeting?" Triffler leaned forward.

"That meeting will be down at the border between Tanzania and Kenya." Dukas pointed to an empty spot on the map. "Lake Magadi. Here's the airstrip where Alan will land the plane. We meet at the border. Both sides will have to be on foot. We talk, and he comes with us, or not. There's some cover, big hills, but mostly a flat, rubble-filled plain with the lake in the distance. Not much high ground, either. We'll cover that later, but I thought you'd all like to see where we're going. If it works, and he comes across at Magadi, we'll fly him to the coast and move him to the *Jefferson*."

"You'd rather have him on the *Jefferson* than at the embassy?" Alan sensed that Mike didn't see any real chance of getting his man at the Safir and was pinning his hopes on the second meeting.

"If we take him to the embassy, chances are really strong we'll lose him immediately to the Agency. I can take that. We all work for the same country. But this time, it's my case, and I want to—" Dukas looked off for a moment, out the curtained window over the dark city.

"Nobody has ever induced the defection of a Chinese intel officer. Not ever. We can do this, folks. And if we get some luck, we will. I suppose it's just team pride that makes me want to do it all Navy, but every time we blink, somebody over at the Crystal Palace seems to still be in love with George Shreed, so I'm keeping this our show till the very end."

"Where's the plane coming from?" Alan asked.

"You have to go rent it tomorrow morning. We have it set up at the airport. Ordinarily it comes with a pilot. We've paid a sizable retainer to get it without."

"I didn't bring my license."

"Can you fly a Cessna 186?"

"Sure. Should I?"

Mike and Alan stared at each other. Alan owed Mike plenty, both good and bad. He nodded.

Dukas went on. "If we're going to Magadi, you and Triffler pick up the plane and check it out day after tomorrow. You fly down, get a sense of the area, come back by car, and spend the night here."

Alan nodded again. The boat was getting farther away. Dukas went on. "I'll need a *Jefferson* bird to land somewhere and take Lao and me out to the boat. That's how I see it now. I've already got the CNO, the admiral, and the air wing on board. Plane'll be an S-3—only aircraft big enough to carry us. Worst case, there's no bird and we take Lao back to the embassy."

"And Harry?" Alan was looking at the map, looking at the hundred kilometers of emptiness that separated Nairobi from Lake Magadi. To the south, at Dar, Harry would be watching Lao's family.

"If we get Lao, we'll have to take his family. He'll insist on that. Any defector would. That's for Harry. It has to be done at the same time as we get Lao, or there'll be hell to pay. Any questions?"

"What happens if they start shooting and it all goes to crap?" Margo sounded bored.

"Don't shoot back, stay low, and go to the embassy."

"That's it? What about you?"

"I'll worry about me. You aren't a rescue team. I just want to hear, early and often, where Lao is and that he's on his way. We *have* to know where his team is to have a prayer at extracting him if it goes that way. Other than that, you guys are wallpaper."

Silence followed. He looked around, recognizing that there were hundreds of possible questions, and that no one wanted to ask them. "This was put together fast. The odds are definitely against us, and as time goes by, the odds will get worse. None of this plan will survive contact with the enemy, and then we'll be thinking on the fly. What can I say? We have a decent chance of doing something great. Get some sleep."

There were some murmurs, and some movement, and suddenly it was just Triffler and Alan and Mike.

"That Margo shouldn't have a gun," Triffler said. "She's liking it too much."

"She's fine," Alan said. "She former military?"

Dukas waved Triffler's worry away. "Treasury. She came from the President's security detail. She's used to guns. She's cool."

"You want me to play tomorrow?" Alan was hesitant.

"Yeah. I've got two places for you to watch, one during the day and later when we're moving to the Safir. They're both stationary and won't stretch your fledgling skills."

Alan nodded to himself and read Triffler's troubled look. "I can do it, Dick."

"I'm sure you can."

"What's bothering you?"

"Anytime I'm working with Mike, I spend my time waiting for the disaster."

"Hey, Dick, that's not fair."

"No, it's not. That's why I'm still waiting."

29

Dar es Salaam.

HARRY O'NEILL WAS STANDING IN A SMALL *BANDA*, A little house built of brush and mud and grass just a field away from the Laos' fortified suburban housing development, one of a hundred such dwellings. Most of Harry's neighbors worked as servants or day laborers in the Chinese-only suburb enclosed in rusting barbed wire and stone only seventy feet away.

The *banda* had cost him less than ten dollars, and although his presence was an unavoidable three-day-wonder to the other *bandas* along the dirt track, Harry expected to be gone before his presence came to the attention of the suburb. He had a poor view of the Laos' ranch house, but an excellent view of the one entrance to the community. At the gate, a dusty African guard sat in the shade under a corrugated iron shack, opening and closing it for the inhabitants in their polished European cars.

Alice, one of Harry's people, was sitting in a Land Rover parked in front of Ngonga's Auto Motive Repair, a thriving business with a lurid sign. She was on a small rise that allowed her a clear view over the stone wall and the wire, past another house, and into the Laos' yard. If the repair shop noted that she was an automotive hypochondriac, they didn't seem to mind; each day, they let her sit in front until late in the day, then repaired whatever complaint she had brought, accepted the payment gravely, and let her go on her way.

"Contact," Alice said, her gravelly English voice clear through Harry's headset. "I have the wife. She's leaving the house for her car."

"Roger," said Harry. He picked up a cell phone and told his team that Lao's wife was out the gate, giving his watchers her license plate and the make and model of her car. The Laos had two, and Harry's watchers already knew them well.

As his lead watcher called Mrs. Lao on the highway toward town, Harry noted the time on his laptop, took a sip of water, and sent Mike an E-mail to indicate that he was established. Then he went back to watching.

USS Thomas Jefferson.

The heat on the O-4 level was overwhelming the air-conditioning of a nuclear aircraft carrier, no mean feat. Almost every man and woman in the admiral's day cabin was in some stage of the flu, and the combined effects rendered them all listless and silent. Everything seemed faintly damp, because when the air-conditioning came, it came in blasts of chilled air that left condensed water on the surfaces and convinced the flu sufferers that they were in for another bout of fever.

"Idem one," said the flag captain through a stopped-up nose. "This black operati—*shud.*" Sneeze.

"I've got it for action," said Rafe, trying not to move his head. "If I have an S-3 crew who can fly, they'll be there. LCDR Craik is supposed to be in Nairobi now. He'll give us six hours' warning to launch."

"The CNO wants this done. He sent the admiral a very definide message—*sage.*" Sneeze.

Rafe nodded. He'd heard the item briefed twice now, and he knew how close to nonoperational the carrier was because of the flu. The medical personnel were scrambling to identify it and prepare a shot to prevent the healthy personnel from joining the sick list. It reminded Rafe of an episode from *Star Trek*.

"Idem two," the captain continued. "These damned ciga-redde boads. Where are they? We need more ASuW coverage up the coast." Sneeze.

"I have two working S-3 crews, mixed from VS-34 and LCDR Craik's detachment. I've got them flying as often as I can, consonant with crew rest. We're trying to fill the gap with F-18s and F-14s. I've got six events today and they're all focused on the ASuW threat."

"Keep theb off the Kenyan coast. If we have anudder dab airspace violation, Kenya's going to go through the roof." *Sneeze.*

The air wing had continued a string of unlucky, or perhaps ill-judged, near-overflights of the Kenyan coast. Rafe bore the brunt of the flag's irritation; he'd already punished the offenders. But his temper was fraying, too.

The flag intel officer dragged himself to the front of the room and put up a computer-generated image showing the last known movements of the five boats that had first been located off Mogadishu. His movements indicated that it was an effort to stand straight and read from his own notes.

"Office of Naval Intelligence didn't have much to add, so we've been punching pubs from the Tanker War in the eighties to get a grip on the threat. These are fast movers, and LTjg Soleck's missions reported the boats to be capable of moving between sixty and eighty knots on calm water."

"Shouldn't we move farther off the coast?" asked a staff officer.

"We have do be here do support the CNO's direcdive," droned the flag captain. "We're as far out as we can ged."

"Our escorts will get them if they get out this far," said another staff officer.

"Led's not led it ged to thad, okay?" The flag captain looked around. "I don' wan those boats gedding near the escort screen. We've had two days of calb weather, but there are storbs coming, and if they have the guds to come oud, we'll have a hard time dracking theb." Sneeze, sneeze.

"How the heck are they tracking us?"

Rafe and the intel officer exchanged glances. The admiral, silent until now and unconsciously holding his head, watched their interchange and waved a hand.

"What's on your mind, Rafe?"

"Al Craik sent us a theory from Seattle. It's kinda hush-hush, but it fits with the evidence we've seen here. We think we might have a Chinese sub on us, passing our location."

"And the Chinese are passing it to the cigarette boats?"

"I didn't say it was a great theory, sir." Rafe focused. "Craik said that out on the dark fringes of every service are people who might do this kind of thing, sir. They might pass the info to the Pakistanis, who would have a natural interest in our movements. And then some Pakistani guy who's a fundamentalist might pass the info to a buddy in the mujahedin."

"Sounds like Cold War paranoia. Why would a bunch of ragheads be looking to take on a carrier group? No facts. Okay, watch the damn boats. I suppose we don't have the crews to mount an ASW effort."

"Not and keep our screen on the cigarette-boat problem."

"Stay on it. Okay, folks. Drink lots of orange juice and get well. Intel, stay and give me what you know. Let's get this Nairobi thing done and get out to sea." The admiral drank off a glass of orange juice as if to emphasize his point and waved his hand. Then he pointed to Rafe.

"What can those boats do to us?"

"Pack 'em full of C-4 and one of them could put a hell of a hole in the *Jefferson*. Take out steering? Maybe get lucky and fry the reactor? I don't know, but it wouldn't be pretty."

"So six of them could kill us. Right. Draft some expanded rules of engagement for those cigarette boats and put rockets on the S-3s, okay?"

"Aye, aye, sir."

NEXT MORNING, THE SUN ROSE BEHIND A DARK BANK of cloud to the east and cast little light, merely paling the gray. Underneath, a fitful pink colored the clouds and made the line moving in even darker. The swell pitched the smaller escorts, and even the mighty carrier moved enough for her more in-experienced crew to turn pale and hurry to the heads.

On the bridge wing, Captain Rafehausen turned to the flag captain, up too early and deep in his coffee, and said, "Red sky in the morning, sailor take warning." He was the first to say it.

But not the last.

THE WINDS WERE HIGH ON THE COAST ROAD AS THE sunrise, gray and dull, swept west ahead of the line of storm. There were breakers on the beaches, and the trees leaned away, seeking shelter on the land. Colonel Lao watched the white-capped ocean, so rare on the east coast of Africa, and thought that the leaden sky was beautiful in all its potent majesty. He stopped his car on the empty road and got out, walked to the edge, and stared at Shimoni Island, just to the east, as the little island bore the first of the storm surge. Then he looked back down the road toward Tanzania, from where he had just come. He was in Kenya, and a six-hour drive from his meeting with Greekgod. His team was well ahead of him. He had time in hand and knew it. He stood in the wind and let it rush over him, thinking how far it had come, and that it came from the east.

Nairobi.

Alan slept late and missed the dawn. He rose to a cool, gray day, typical for the Kenya highlands at the onset of winter, and prepared himself for a long day with a hot shower and a long breakfast in the hotel's café. There was a note under his door in Mike's spiky writing.

*Harry called 0430L Lao prob. enroute have a great day
Mike.*

He was enough into Dukas's scheme now that it made his heart beat faster for a moment. Then he dressed in shorts, heavy shoes, and a sweater, a choice of clothes appropriate in few places outside the African highlands, and went to do his job. *Lao enroute* meant that it wasn't merely an exercise with Dick Triffler.

He had the easiest role, as befitted the least-trained of Mike's people. He had two static surveillance points to watch on Mike's complex and daylong route, and then he had the grandstand seat in the final drama, the high watch-point from the terrace of the Hilton itself. His job would be simple. He had to watch Mike go by the static points and see if anyone else who passed matched his earlier sightings or suspicions called in by the other watchers.

Alan left the hotel and collected his car and a driver from the stand at the back and tried to brush up on his Swahili while they drove through boulevards to the highway, then out on Ngong Road to the racecourse. He established that the driver's name was Jim and that he, Alan, didn't like being called *bwana*. This was greeted with a deep roar of laughter. Perhaps the man had heard it all before. Alan spent the drive looking at pictures of Jim's children.

Alan had been to the racecourse once before and had felt then that it was a bastion for white Kenyans in denial about independence. It had changed in six years, and there were more black Kenyans with money, but the boxes were still white. Alan mixed with the crowd on the benches and watched two races, both enlivened by the occasional cough of a lion in the park, before getting back in his car (the perfect white tourist) and asking his driver to take him to the arboretum. Jim looked puzzled, as if he had never been there, then spoke softly to another driver in Kikuyu. Five minutes later they were flying through a vast sea of *bandas* on a dirt road connecting the major paved thoroughfares. In the distance, he could see sub-urbs like patches of fortified prosperity, each surrounded by its own town of slums. His driver probably lived in one of them. At any rate, the man knew his path, and they bounced along the red dirt road, their horn going to keep the way clear of children and animals, until they emerged on Mandera Road, a two-lane highway that had developed two extra lanes in the hard-packed dirt on each side, at least until the first rains came.

The arboretum appeared on the right, first gardens and then well-watered trees like an English park.

"Where we go now, *bwana*?"

"Just park, Jim."

"Not very fun place, this arboretum. You want the tour?" He laughed the deep laugh again.

"I just want to walk around."

"Sure." Hesitant. And then, "Nairobi can be a dangerous place." Nobody in Africa encouraged whites to walk. It made Alan laugh himself, one of the thousands of details he had forgotten, like the man cooking field mice and the smell of his fire just over by the gate to the arboretum.

"I'll be okay. *Ni nataka Coca-Cola,* okay?"

"Sure, *bwana*."

"Get one for both of us."

"Sure, *bwana*."

Alan walked away from the car and checked his watch. Fifteen minutes early, thanks to the local knowledge of his driver. Alan had learned in Seattle that early was as bad as late and could lead to all kinds of complexity. Right now, it meant that he had to keep his driver entertained while he dawdled in the parking lot of a set of gardens. He lit a cigarette and watched the sky, then crossed the parking lot and watched the old man cooking the field mice. The man pointed at one of the mice and gestured to Alan, who was touched and revolted by the man's hospitality. His offer was obvious and generous. Alan smiled and almost bowed, an awkward, formal movement meant to indicate distress and hide distaste.

Jim came up with their Cokes. "Don't eat that!"

I've eaten worse and lived, Alan thought, the memory of Zaire suddenly in his nose and eyes like the old man's fire.

The old man had a perfect view of the road. Alan went up to him, bolder now, somehow getting back into Africa.

"*Habari, m'zee.*"

The old man nodded and smiled, showing his complete lack of teeth. He might have been sixty or ninety or simply worn down at forty. The boy with him took courage and held out his hand, begging for both of them and protecting his elder from having to beg. Alan gave him some Kenyan shillings and took a mouthful of sweet Coke. The old man's little fire felt good. There was a dampness in the air that made it seem cold. He looked at his watch. Still eight minutes.

The boy jabbered something that Alan couldn't make out. The language sounded familiar.

Jim looked at him patiently. When Alan showed he didn't understand, Jim pointed his chin at the old man. "Boy say if you give them another fifty shillings, they can buy dinner."

"Why don't I understand?"

"He's Luo." The last said in a tone that suggested that anyone should have known where the man was from.

Alan turned away abruptly, walked across the tarmac of the parking lot to the food stand, and bought two more Cokes, a burger, some fries, and a bag of chips. It took five of his remaining minutes, but he was the only customer. Then he walked back and delivered the food to the old man, who gave him a courteous inclination of the head and began to wolf the burger. Alan glanced at his watch and looked up to see Mike Dukas's red pickup truck coming down the road. He let it pass without another look, then knelt by the fire and used an ember to light another cigarette. Jim bantered with the boy while the old man ate. Alan watched the traffic on the road for five minutes, noting each car as it passed, looking for anything out of the ordinary. He didn't see anything worth calling in, but he counted the cars and thought he'd recognize particular makes if he saw them again, although the preponderance of white Toyota pickups full of round-headed Kikuyu men reminded him of the difficulties of surveillance in a foreign country.

When his cigarette was gone, he smiled at the old man and headed back to the car. Jim hurried to open his door. "Not so much fun," he said again.

"It was fine." Alan closed the door, feeling he was back in Africa.

"You want to go to the city park." Not a question, almost an order.

"No, *rafiki*, I want to go to the city market."

"Some bad people there. I can take you better places."

Alan leaned forward and put a U.S. twenty-dollar bill in Jim's visor.

"City market. Find a good place to park, where I can see the place."

"Sure." Jim laughed the big laugh. "Sure."

TWO HOURS LATER, ALAN HAD ALL THE WAXED COTton prints he could handle, some soapstone he knew he would dump as soon as he was clear of the market, and two treasures, a good, old Masai sword with a forged blade, and a King's African Rifles cap badge bought from an old man who claimed that it had been his own. Alan doubted it, but the man knew a little Italian and he charmed Alan with a half-hour's tales of the Kenyan frontier in 1939, the march through Eritrea, and the attacks in Somalia. Alan had fought in Somalia, and he spoke Italian with confidence. His Swahili was coming back, too, and they jabbered away like old comrades, to the point the man began to include Alan in his stories, as if they had served together. He passed the time happily and exited the old colonial building of the market on the dot of two o'clock.

The sky was getting darker and a damp wind was blowing the dust off the surface of the market and along the street, little swirls like tiny tornadoes. Alan looked at the sky and prepared to be wet. He looked at his watch, a new habit formed today. One minute. *Much* better than at the arboretum.

Dukas was late. Alan was beginning to have to fend off offers for everything from safaris to sex by the time Mike strolled by. He was wearing an absurd ball cap and shorts with socks, the sort of clothes that Mike wore quite naturally. No one would have taken him for a dangerous agent of the United States. Alan persuaded a young hustler that no, he didn't want a nice, clean girl with no HIV, by pushing him away.

"*Kwa sababu sitaki!*" he said with unpleasant emphasis. The man sneered, but desisted. Alan affected to watch him depart, since he was walking right down Mike's back trail. There were hundreds of people behind Mike, almost all Africans. None of them was Chinese, but Alan tried to see a pattern of movement that would mean something to him, some determination of walking that would indicate intention. He couldn't find it. Most were chatting with someone near them or walking briskly with their heads down, like inhabitants of major cities all over the world. On a whim, Alan started walking the same way, although more slowly because of his armload of purchases. He walked for several minutes, watching the taxis and *matatus* unloading on Tubman Road. He didn't see anything worth reporting. A carload of white male tourists caught his eye, but by the time he saw them they were so far behind Dukas that they couldn't have anything to do with pursuit.

Alan raised his load to get a look at his watch. Mike was thirty minutes from starting his final run. Alan had to move. He dropped the soapstone on the curb and started back to where Jim was waiting with the car, all the way across the market square on Mbingu Street. He had gone a few steps before a crowd of boys surrounded him, two holding his discarded soapstone collection and the rest demanding reward and portage fees. He bargained as he walked, paying again for worthless soapstone carvings because it amused him and it wasn't his money. The boys followed him to the car. At the hotel, he overtipped Jim on the way and asked him to send the packages up to the room, conscious that Triffler, his instructor on these matters, would have castigated him for his obvious and uncharacteristic hurry after a day of apparent leisure. Jim didn't seem to care.

Alan went straight to the rooftop café, eighteen stories above the street and almost cold in the early evening wind. The rain was coming. He opened his cell phone and dialed a number, and it rang, and all over downtown Nairobi, NCIS agents added him to a multiparty call.

"Hi, everybody," he said. They had decided against any obvious use of radio code, on the very real chance that the Kenyans monitored them. "Nothing to see at the market."

He could hear an odd buzz, the digital combination of all the background noise from six phones.

"Nothing to see anywhere," said Bob.

"Big, lonely city," said Frank.

"Some dickhead thought he was going to mug me on River Road," said Margo.

Alan had binoculars and a camera, as did several other rooftop patrons. He used the binoculars, looking down at the *matatu* stand and across the little square of acacia trees at the entrance to the Ambassadeur Hotel.

"Jambo!" said a young woman at his table. He tried not to snap around. She was the waitress, dressed in a black skirt and white shirt. *Some spy. I almost shot the waitress.*

"Are you watching the vultures, yes?"

He nodded. Then he smiled. She was pretty, and her whole face was active, pleasant rather than beautiful. She looked like a woman who liked people, liked her job.

"I am. And watching the people. Nairobi is great." He sounded like he meant it. "*Mzuri,*" he added, unnecessarily. Really, just then, he did mean it. She nodded back.

"What can I get for you?"

"Tonic water over ice."

She smiled again. "Sure. Will you be eating?"

It was an odd thing, another tiny African thing, but she balanced her tray and stood with her hand on her hip just *so*, in a way that no one in North America would do. "Yeah. When it's dark."

"Sure," she said. East Africa's universal word.

He went back to watching the vultures. And the people.

MARGO WAS THE FIRST OF THEIR TEAM HE FOUND. He knew where she was supposed to be, across the park near the *matatus,* like many other employed women waiting for her ride home. She mixed easily, because fashion in Kenya's black middle class was last year's American fashion, and because she slumped her shoulders a little and stood with her hand on her hip. She already had it. Alan nodded to himself. She was watching the door that Lao ought to approach if he was coming.

Frank and Bob would be invisible, he thought. Frank was outside the service entrance of the Ambassadeur, with a hired panel van and a driver who was heavily bribed. Alan was no part of that and suspected that Mike was in pretty deep there if something came to the attention of the embassy. Bob was across the street from the service entrance in a car, the mobile reserve, the chase car if they took Lao tonight, and communications hub until then. And the eyes on the back door. Brian ought to be visible walking along the edge of the City Square Park. Alan couldn't find him, but Brian hadn't been happy with his post from the start and Alan looked up and down, trying to find him anywhere. Whites weren't thick on the streets because it wasn't tourist season.

And Triffler would be in the restaurant, already seated. Already eating. Dukas's backup.

He looked down again to check Margo, and she was moving across the square, a very convincing portrayal of a woman missing a *matatu*. She had already learned to blow by men trying to talk to her as if they didn't exist, so she made it across the square and back without a problem, returning to her post with a little shrug of the shoulders. Alan took a sip of his tonic water and shifted his gaze up and out, looking across the park and then down Daniel Arap Moi Avenue. He had no idea what he was looking for, but he knew it when he saw it.

One car, one driver, face pale. It was a small European sedan, not a common sight at this hour. The car had a shiny finish but was covered in dust.

It all reminded him of ASW. Looking for patterns that didn't match other patterns. This car was not going at the speed of other cars. That got his attention first. Then the color and the polish, not the dead matte of dust-blown Nairobi. The race of the driver, possible as he turned off Moi, probable as he parked a block away. Alan knew he was craning over the edge of the roof, aware he might be attracting attention, but this was the job.

"Margo. Behind you, parking off Moi. Metallic green sedan."

"I don't see him. I'm moving."

Pause.

Alan lost the man as he parked. He thought it was a man, and his heart was beating because the time was close and this would be it, and because he suddenly remembered that he was supposed to be watching for Lao's backup, but he wanted to know this was right before he switched his gaze.

Don't bore sight, Triffler had said. Hard to obey when he had the target in sight. He tore his eyes away from the screen of the acacia trees and looked north. The laminated map on his table said that the building blocking his view of Moi Avenue was Unlon Tower. He looked at the tower.

"Easter," called Margo. "Rabbit is locking his car."

Alan looked away from an interesting balcony on the Unlon building and swept the street. Then he looked south on Moi.

"I have a cat," said Brian. "Jungle Garden Club, patio."

That was the other side of the square, and to see it Alan would have to cross his side of the roof and lean out. He sat tight and looked back at the balcony on the Unlon building. As it was a commercial building well after business hours, any movement on a balcony was worth watching. The cloth curtain of an open window flapped like a flag in the wind. A man came through the window, noticed the curtain, and tried to hold it still. He was talking to someone else. Alan raised his binoculars, lost the balcony for a moment, and brought it into focus.

"Is cat one Asian?" Alan asked quietly.

"Roger."

Alan took a deep breath and looked again. A short, balding man was watching the square through a camera. He was crouched below the balcony, but Alan was above him. He waited, and watched. *Turn around,* he thought. *Move the curtain again.* And he wondered if he had imagined another man.

"Rabbit is walking east on Kuanda Street." Margo, calm as a relief pitcher.

"Cat one has a camera." Brian sounded a little excited.

Alan wondered where Brian was. He had a moment of disorientation, both physical and mental, and he had to put the binoculars down and look around him. He found that his glass was empty. He turned to look for the waitress and looked around again, suddenly conscious that he might have a watcher right here on the roof of the Hilton with him. If he did, the other watcher was German. Everyone on the roof of the Hilton was German. He listened for a moment, watched the other couples, wanting to raise the binoculars, and suddenly self-conscious. He reached out to the big camera and saw his waitress and smiled at her. It was a forced smile, and he thought his lip must be trembling visibly.

Worse than a night carrier-landing with a bad pilot, he thought. The same sense of having no control. He reached for his earlier reaction to the waitress's natural openness, found it, used it to calm himself.

"Can I have another tonic water?" he asked.

"Sure."

In his earpiece, Margo said, "Rabbit is crossing the *matatu* station. He doesn't want to get his shoes dirty."

Alan looked up at his waitress. *"Jina lako nani?"* What is your name?

"Janet," she said. She gave him the broad smile that Africans always give people trying to use one of their languages and walked off, businesslike. Alan picked up the camera under his hand and pointed it at the Unlon Tower. He found the balcony the first time, focused as he found it. His hands were calm and sure. *Turn around,* he thought again, snapping his first picture, and the man did, calling something to a shadowy form behind the flapping curtain. The wind was rising.

"I have cat two on the balcony of the Unlon building," he said with certainty, and took a picture.

"Rabbit's going in the door," Margo said.

"In," Triffler said.

30

USS **Thomas Jefferson.**

"WINDS RISING TO THIRTY-FIVE KNOTS, SIR."

Captain Rafehausen had been in the combat information center for three hours. He nodded to the tactical action officer.

On the big blue screen, a flight of two F-14s was marked as two half-circles well up by the coast of Africa. Behind them, halfway to the carrier, a single S-3 was another friendly half-circle. Otherwise, the sea was empty.

"One-oh-four says he can't even see the deck. He wants permission to go over the coast and look at the islands." An air operations officer was speaking softly from his station a little in front of the TAO.

"Negative." The TAO sounded angry.

"Seven-oh-three has no contacts."

"Everybody else is scurrying for port or getting some water between them and the coast. This is going to be a nasty blow."

Rafe thought about their fuel state and the likelihood that the F-14s could get gas in the air with a thirty-five-knot wind and gusts to fifty. He picked up a red phone and waited for the admiral to pick up on his end.

"Tell me."

"No contacts, Admiral. Wind rising and thirty-five knots. I want to get them aboard."

"Call 'em home."

Out on deck, the wind rose again.

The Safir Restaurant.

"Colonel Lao, I presume?"

Thrown off guard, Lao stared at the American. The use of his name unbalanced him; it was bad enough that the man in front of him was not Craik, whom he had expected, but it was humiliating that this low-browed, brooding Caucasian knew who he was. To cover his confusion, Lao recited the recognition code: "I have been here six times and it has never failed me."

The American had eyelids that looked too thick and eyebrows that loomed over them like cliffs. The face, by Lao's standards, was not intelligent; the body was too heavy, too broad, the arms almost apelike. Lao detested him on sight.

"Nobody comes here only once," the American said—the other part of the recognition code. He put out a hairy hand. "Bob Michaels."

Lao ignored the hand. "I am Wu. I am, alas, not a colonel." He turned and signaled to a waiter. "Table for Mister Wu," he said.

"Table for Mister Michaels," the American said over his words. "I got a reservation. Michaels—for two."

The African waiter looked at them and hesitated, in the end thought it best to go away. Lao and the American who called himself Michaels and who was undoubtedly named something else stood awkwardly together, isolated in the half-filled dining room, whose other patrons were now staring at them. Lao heard the American give an exasperated sigh.

"Patience is a valuable lesson," Lao said. Saying it helped to restore his self-assurance. Still, he was off balance. Clearly,

Craik had turned his messages over to the CIA: How long had Lao been corresponding with some committee at Langley, he wondered. He glanced aside at the American, again feeling dislike, some of it the inherited dislike of all Chinese for the barbarians, the dislike of a millennia-old civilization for these Caucasian upstarts. Some of it was dislike for American power and American lack of respect for China. Some of it was dislike of losing the lead.

"About time," the American said. A headwaiter was waving them toward a table at the front. Lao, to assert himself, turned aside and headed for a smaller table by the wall. "This one," he said in the voice that Captain Jiang would have known meant business. The headwaiter recognized it, too, and waved the American that way.

One goal for China, Lao thought. He sat, allowed a large menu to be put in front of him, put his hands together above it, and said, "I was told that this is the best Indian restaurant in the world."

"No kidding." The American's face was turned down to the menu. He looked up; under the black brows, the eyes in their thick lids were sharp and hard. "It seems unlikely, here in Africa."

"Many Indians were compelled to emigrate by the British during colonialism," Lao said. "Theirs, like mine, is a very old culture—one that transplants well into new soil." He tried to smile. "I am told that the lamb curry is superb but should be ordered a day ahead to let the flavors blend."

"Wish you'd told me that yesterday, Colonel." The American gave him something like a grin. "Maybe I'll have the chicken."

When the waiter appeared, Lao leaped in first and ordered a tray of pakoras and samosas for both of them; the American interposed his heavy voice and demanded Kingfisher beer; Lao asked for Indian tea. The waiter wanted to take their orders for a full meal. Lao started to order the lamb curry, and the American said, "Later," and the waiter withdrew.

"It takes time to make the dish," Lao said with some asperity.

"We maybe don't have time. Let's cut the crap, Colonel; I don't do small talk very well. What do you want?"

Lao was mortified. He had had a scenario prepared for Craik—a review of the unfortunate incident in Jakarta, leading up to questions about what really had happened in the Orchid House, which would lead in turn to a mention of George Shreed and then the real question: Where was Chen? For an answer to which Lao was willing to trade away his Jakarta asset, Bobby Li—once he found him. The question of Chen was everything. Lao believed now that Chen was in Tajikistan, and that it had been to see Chen that Craik had flown there from Bahrain. Doing so just before the meeting had looked to Lao like preparation, perhaps, for the meeting itself—perhaps Craik had been bringing a message from Chen? Perhaps, having had Chen for a month, they were ready to trade? Perhaps Chen himself had something to propose? He was about to speak when the waiter put the American's beer down between them, then a plate of pakoras, a plate of samosas, and a gleaming tray with pickles and sauces in small dishes. Leaning forward again to speak, Lao was almost struck by a plate of papadums that was making its way to join the other food. "Enough!" he said in the voice that Jiang would have recognized.

"You got tea coming," the waiter said, stubborn as, in Lao's experience, only Africans can be. "Coming right away."

Lao's momentum was lost again. Had the waiter been bribed by the American to distract him? Lao hadn't entirely thought through the problems of meeting in the restaurant— oh, yes, he'd thought of exits and approaches, watchers, security—but he hadn't thought of the waiter. Intrusive. Embarrassing.

"You said that I might have something you want," the American coached him. "In your first message."

"The message was not to you."

"As good as."

"I was communicating with Lieutenant-Commander Craik."

"What you see is what you get. American TV joke. Think of me as Alan Craik, if that makes you feel better." The

American poured beer from the big Kingfisher bottle. "What d'you want, Colonel?" he said again before he drank.

"I want to know what happened in Jakarta. The unfortunate incident at the Orchid House."

"Your man got shot." The American put down his glass, wiped his lips. He looked around at the dim, handsome room, which was much more like a room in Bombay than one in Nairobi. On the far side, a party of African businessmen and two Germans were laughing; in a corner, a lone black man in a safari suit ate his dinner; nearer, three Indians in English suits were spooning tiny puddles of sauces next to each serving on their plates. "Not our doing," the American said.

"My embassy—my government—was very angry."

"Tell them to be angry with themselves. It was one of your guys who did it." The American leaned forward. Despite himself, Lao was impressed by the power of the eyes. "What d'you want, Colonel?"

"I think it is for you to tell me what *you* want, Mister Michaels. You, after all, have led me along this trail of messages." Lao was determined to control the conversation, to work his way slowly and artfully to the question of Chen.

The American gave him a lopsided half-smile. He put a fingernail under the edge of the Kingfisher label. "Isn't that a little like telling the rape victim that she led the rapist along?" He turned his head back to look at Lao again, and again Lao felt the power of the eyes and, for the first time, the intelligence behind them. "What d'you want, Colonel? You want Chen?"

Lao's face remained bland, but again he was stunned. He managed to say, "Who is Chen?" but he sounded unconvincing.

"Aw, come on! Chen, as in the Chinese half of the comm plan we're executing here! How many times do you think Chen and Shreed met in this same room? Maybe they sat at this table—maybe they got to know it well enough that they called a day ahead of time so they could enjoy the lamb curry! Come on, Colonel, we're wasting time. We didn't walk through this lousy city for blocks so we could play Chinese Checkers."

The waiter put Lao's tea beside his right hand. He groped

for the handle without looking away from the American, who, though a barbarian, was taking on more and more the look of an extremely clever and experienced man. *I underestimated them,* Lao told himself. *I made a beginner's mistake.* He felt the ground starting to slide from under him. "Yes," he said, "I want to know about Chen."

"Chen's dead. He's buried in a field in Tajikistan. I assume it was your guys who tried to burn my guy up there." The American shook his head. "Not smart." He reached inside his coat where, Lao thought, he would be carrying a weapon, but of course there was no reason for him to use a weapon in the restaurant. Still, Lao tensed and moved his own hand toward his coat. But the American extracted a sealed, padded envelope from his jacket, not a gun. "The contents are a little gross, but we're not really here to eat." He tossed the envelope on the table. "Chen," he said.

Lao looked at the envelope. He looked up at the intelligent eyes. "I confess, you are ahead of me, Mister Michaels."

"Open it."

Lao reached across and picked up the envelope. It was light, yet bumpy with hard contents. Lao put a forefinger under the flap but found that it was sealed with some sort of super-cement that wouldn't separate. He then tried to tear it and succeeded only in making a hole in the outer skin, through which some gray stuffing fell on his plate.

"Pull the string," the American said. "At the bottom, where it says 'Pull Tab.' "

It was unfair to make him go through this in public, Lao thought. The envelope was unfamiliar; the light was low; it was unfair! He pulled the tab, and a string cut through the length of the envelope and allowed him to look inside.

"What we call in the States 'giving somebody the finger,' " the American said.

Lao tipped the contents into his plate. A button came first; then three inch-square plastic cubes; then a small plastic bag; and last, a larger plastic bag with three inches of brown, lumpy stick inside. Lao looked at it more closely and recognized that it was, indeed, a human finger, partly mummified.

The plastic boxes held pieces of what looked like leather; the other envelope, hair.

"Tissue samples?" he said.

"I thought you'd like to do a DNA check."

Lao studied the button. It was Chinese, current military but of high quality, probably an officer's, possibly from a uniform of the military intelligence service.

"These could be from anyone," Lao said.

"DNA will show they're Chen's. What else do you want?"

Lao knew that the man had to be telling the truth. It would take only three days to a week to have a DNA test of this importance done in Beijing; there was no point in his trying to lie about such a thing. If Chen was dead, Lao wondered, had he therefore failed? Would the samples satisfy the people who had given him this mission? Or would only the live Chen have satisfied them?

"We got Shreed," the American said. "He's dead, too—buried in the U.S. You've lost your top American spy *and* his control. We also, by the way, have Bobby Li—the double who did the killing in the Orchid House. He was your agent, wasn't he, Colonel? Didn't you inherit him from Chen?" The American sipped his beer, then nibbled on a pakora. "Looks to me like you're up shit crick without a paddle. That's an American way of saying you're in trouble."

"I am hardly in trouble!" Lao snapped. He began to put the remains back into the envelope.

"Try this, then." The American pulled out a piece of paper and pushed it across the table. It had been folded into four and, unfolded, it sat on the apex of its folds and spun slowly. Lao looked at it, looked at the barbarian, touched the paper.

"Is this computer code?" he said. He knew very little about computer programming, but he thought he knew enough to recognize it.

"From George Shreed's computer. It shows a quantity of money leaving an account in the Maldives. *The* money."

"I do not understand *the* money, Mister Michaels."

The American had his forearms across his chest now, resting them on the table. It occurred to Lao that the American had something wrong with his arms; certain movements seemed to cause him trouble. Not relevant, but perhaps useful sometime. The American looked almost amused. "*The* money. I make it to be at least twenty billion dollars, of which that piece of code shows only a little bit. Very little bit. Twenty billion dollars is a lot of money, Colonel Lao. Not the kind of money that most of us collect in a thousand or so bank accounts. So much money, in fact, that I'd have to conclude that it was put there by something pretty big—like the Communist Party of China, for example." The dark, intelligent eyes held his own. "Or the Intelligence Service of the People's Army."

The ground cascaded away under Lao's feet. He felt as if he were falling in a dream. At once, he knew that he had been made a pawn by the General and the man from the Party: that it had not been Chen that he was supposed to find, but money. Money had been all the buzz when he had been in Beijing; heads had rolled, careers had been ended. Something about money had been in everybody's mouth.

And now he knew.

"I know nothing about such money," he said.

And the American gave a flicker—a slight movement of a facial muscle, barely a tic—and Lao saw that the American had thought that he, Lao, knew what "*the* money" meant, and now he knew that Lao had known nothing about *the* money. And now Lao was in his fist.

"The money is gone," the American said. "I think Shreed did it for revenge. What the code shows is that the money was pulled out of the bank account and was sent into cyberspace. Made not to exist. Twenty billion dollars." He hunched forward. "Chen is dead. The money is gone. What are you going to tell your government?"

Lao tried to rally himself. "That is, of course, not your business."

"Chen is dead; Shreed is dead; the money is dead. You're empty, Colonel. You're going to go back to them empty. You came for something and you've got nothing. What are you going to do?"

Lao grabbed the envelope and the paper. "I am going to end this meeting!"

"Before you do—" The American hadn't moved; now he

put one hand on the envelope, as if by doing so he could hold Lao. "I think it would be wise to meet me again."

It was impossible for Lao not to meet his eyes. *He knew.* Lao knew and the American knew: He couldn't go back empty from this meeting and survive for long. Still, Lao said, "We have nothing to talk about now."

"I think we'll have something to talk about." The American lifted his hand from the envelope; Lao put it inside his coat. He folded the slip of paper and put it with the envelope. The American put his hands flat on the table. "You know Lake Magadi and Lake Natron, Colonel? Magadi's in Kenya; Natron's in Tanzania. A river runs down a flatland between them, and the border runs right through there. There's a hill called Shompole. I'll meet you on the border by Shompole at eight o'clock. Day after tomorrow morning."

Lao stood. "I have no reason to meet you again."

"I think you will when you've thought about it." The American stood, too. He held out his hand. "Sorry we didn't get to try the lamb curry. Maybe next time."

"There will be no next time!"

But almost unconsciously, his hand reached out and took the American's hand. He could see his own fate reflected in the American's eyes.

Lao fled.

Across the room, Triffler spoke into his microphone. "Out."

Nairobi.

There was a knock at the door, and the wind pounded on the glass of the hotel windows. Alan thought he might have dozed, moved the muscles on his face, and opened the door. Margo slipped through, followed immediately by Brian.

"Good to see you guys."

They were both wired, on edge.

"What happened at the meeting?"

Margo shook her head. "He never called Christmas, that's

all I know. Dick called the rabbit out and I saw him get in his car."

"Cat one got in a taxi. I let him go. Mike said to take them to their transport."

Alan nodded. "I got a photo of cat two and maybe something on another. I didn't try to follow them."

"Yeah. Too right. I hope they didn't make me, though. Gawd, it gave me the willies, knowing that there was a guy right above me with a camera." She smiled at Alan. "Great that you called him, though. Better to know than not to know."

For a moment, they all were talking at once, and then there was another knock at the door. Alan looked through the spy hole. Bob and Frank.

"Hey!"

"Where were you—"

"What happened when—"

"—never called Christmas—"

"—I'm watching this guy sweep the pavement and—"

"—looked around the damn restaurant, I was so freaked—"

"—Everybody does that—"

More knocks, this time not so gentle. Alan looked again. Triffler.

"Hey, Dick."

Triffler was smiling. He cut the babble with a raised hand. "Wait for Mike."

"You see him?" asked Margo. She was pacing the room, sitting for a moment on the bed, then up and moving again. They all were. Alan had never seen this part of the spy game before—the teamwork, the postoperational locker room. Yet it was familiar to him, like a good aircrew after a great flight. They were *on*.

"I passed him in the lobby. He'll be up." Triffler was relaxed, a little detached, but his smile was fixed to his face. He might have just had a really good cup of coffee. "I saw you on the street, Margo. I looked right past you. Good cover."

"Thanks, man." She took the compliment with poise, but it clearly pleased her. They were all doing it in a moment,

praising one another. Alan kept his eye on the corridor and let
Dukas in without a knock. He was smiling.

"Okay, people, settle down. Sit on something. Margo,
stop bouncing."

They sat, or leaned against things, unconsciously finding
their positions from the evening before.

"Well?"

"We met. We talked. He took some of the bait. I think I
got to him. He took the second meeting."

A mutual breath, and they all looked around. It had to
take the place of a cheer.

"I want everybody to get to bed. Tomorrow we do the
prep for Magadi. Alan, you and Triffler prep the plane and go
look at the site. The rest of you get there by car."

"I like a man with a plan," said Margo.

"Anybody get his people?"

A chorus of responses, gradually petering out into individual reports.

"Write it up, just rough notes, before you sleep. We'll
drop a report on the embassy *after* this is over. Go to bed."

It took fifteen minutes, several rehashes of the important
moments of the evening. Dukas didn't discuss what he had
done, simply insisted that they were a go for Shompole. Finally he was authoritative. One by one, he drove them from
his room. He kept Alan back to the end.

"Alan, I need you to contact the boat and give them a
timeline. The meeting is for eight A.M. day after tomorrow
morning—"

Alan looked at the map on the bed.

"If we get him, that's a two-hour flight to the coast.
Maybe three. How long will the meeting take?"

"No idea. It could take forever. It shouldn't take long. He
might have backup that has to be dealt with, or he might
be followed without wanting it." Dukas rubbed his chin. He
looked worn, still running on the energy from his meeting,
but tired. "I expect I'll have to sell him on the spot, even
though by coming he's made a statement. It could take some
time. He'll want to talk about his family." Dukas rubbed his
eyes. "Give me a second."

He walked into the bathroom and Alan heard the sound of running water. Dukas emerged rubbing his face.

Alan was buzzing with questions. "Can we bring an S-3 down on a Kenyan field in broad daylight? Where do you see us bringing the Navy plane in?"

Mike reached over him and pointed to the coast road that joined Kenya and Tanzania. "There's a field built into the road right here. Straight stretch of road, with grassy savanna on both sides. Easy."

"Easy without a crosswind, Mike. You seen the weather out there? Do you see us doing this in daylight?"

"Yeah. It's right on the coast. By the time the Kenyans complain, we're gone."

Alan gnawed his thumb and wished for a smoke. "I need to know if the Kenyans have any radar coverage down there. They used to worry about narcotics coming ashore in that area. Okay, we bring a plane in late afternoon. I land; we call him from a rally point off the coast, maybe here."

"Rally point?"

"S-3s carry a lot of fuel, Mike. We can have him turning and burning a hundred miles off the coast waiting for our call. We bring him in; he's on the ground for a minute."

"I like that."

Alan wrote himself a note.

"What if it's dark?" he asked suddenly.

"Why would it be dark?"

"What if Lao's late? Or he wants to talk? Or we're late, or the plane breaks down. I don't know."

"Can't you land in the dark?"

"On a dark stretch of road? In Africa? Just for starters, what if we hit a civilian? I don't like it. I'll talk to Rafe, but Jesus, Mike, this landing is thin. We have to get there first. That's easy. But if it's getting dark, we'll have to illuminate the strip. That will take time, too, while Lao sits in the plane. Will his friends come after us?"

"If they know where we are."

"Are you sure it isn't better to just fly him back to Hunter Field and give him to the embassy?"

Dukas rubbed the back of his neck, then his chin. He was

wasted. The fatigue was setting in. "Fuck it, Alan. I'm not sure. This is the fucking wilderness of mirrors, isn't it? If Shreed left anybody behind, then Lao would be dead in the embassy. That's as far as I can think it through. I want him for the Navy, Al. So does the CNO."

"I better call the boat."

"You do that. I'll be the one asleep on the bed."

Alan glanced over his notes and realized that they were all written as questions. He shook his head.

THE STU MADE REASSURING ENCRYPTION NOISES. Alan's digital readout said "Carrier Intelligence Center, USS *Thomas Jefferson*." He wondered what Rafe's said at the other end.

"Rafe?"

"Glad to know you're alive."

"I'm *trying* to get to the boat. James Bond has shanghaied me."

"Don't disappoint me, Spy. I thought *you* were James Bond."

"Not this time. Are you up to speed on why we're here?"

"I know that I'm supposed to send a plane to an unspecified location at an unspecified time."

"The location will be a small roadside landing strip on the Kenyan Coast Highway. The time will be 1600 local, day after tomorrow."

"Well, at least the worst of our storm will be past. I hope I have some aircrew left."

"Sorry?"

"We've got a flu bug knocking aircrew down like something from outer space. Right now I have two S-3 crews flying, if I pilot one. You get me?"

"Loud and clear. I'd like to have that plane wait at a rally point from 1530 local to 1930 local."

"Got you. Where's the rally point?"

"You fix it. Somewhere no more than thirty minutes out from the landing field, well out of Kenyan airspace and low."

"Roger that. You know we've been racking up airspace violations with the Kenyans. They aren't too happy with us."

"How bad is it?"

"Bad enough that they might turn down an overflight request. Bad enough that we're going to hear about this for a long time if we get caught."

Alan nodded to himself. "So that's why Mike isn't just doing this at Moi International at Mombasa."

"You got it. We talked about it. I don't even want to ask."

"Who's going to fly the plane?"

"Me."

"Sounds good. What's happening with the cigarette boats?"

"They're still out there, Spy. Somewhere between Mombasa and Mogadishu. I can't put guys in the air in this weather, but the bright side is they can't go to sea, either."

"How's the det?"

"Don't ask."

"Sorry, *sir*. I want to know." *I ought to be there.*

"Most of the aircrew are sick. Soleck is the only pilot fit to fly, and he's—he's having some real landing problems."

"Still?"

"Serious as a heart attack. I may have to pull him. He took three passes to get aboard the other night. Not all his fault, but his confidence is shot."

Alan felt very far away. He wanted to be there on the boat, talking to his det, talking to Soleck. *Pull him* was the kiss of death, the end of Soleck's career. It meant that Rafe couldn't trust him to land, or that Soleck couldn't trust himself.

"Jesus, Rafe."

"Sorry, Al. I've got cigarette boats and flu, a no-fly storm, and an unlocated submarine. I don't have time to fix Soleck."

Alan had forgotten the submarine. "Tell me about the sub."

"It's out there, somewhere. If I had six S-3s and enough A-6s to tank, we'd go find it and maybe ping it until it went away. I don't. Not much we can do till the weather changes, anyway."

"Is it passing targeting to your cigarette boats?"

"Damn it, you're asking me? Aren't you the spy?"

"But it might be. Thirdhand, or firsthand, it might be."

"Who sent the cigarette boats, Alan?"

"No idea. Pakistan, maybe. Damn, Rafe, that's not even my job right now."

"Are they to do with what you're doing?"

"I can't see how." Alan tried to grapple with it all, Lao and Seattle and Shreed and cigarette boats and a possible submarine. Too many layers. The Gordian knot.

"Have you guys tried looking for his uplink?"

"His what?" Rafe sounded uninterested, like he was at the end of his rope and just wanted to be *done*.

"Do you have the files from our prosecution off Seattle?" Even as he said the words, Alan realized that no one had them, because they'd never been sent. They were material to an ongoing espionage investigation. Alan shook his head.

"What prosecution?"

Alan held the phone against his chest and looked at Dukas, who was awake, sitting up on his elbow. "You following this?"

"You think Rafe needs to know about the cell phone signal to find his sub?"

"This is the Navy, Mike. The same one that you need to get your guy. If that sub out there is providing real-time information to those cigarette boats, this is a force-protection issue."

Dukas threw off his covers and swung his feet to the floor with a snort.

"If your friend Rafe uses the uplink to catch that sub and drives it off with an active sonar—that is what we're talking about, right? Okay. I do read messages. If he does that, you're jeopardizing Sleeping Dog. The spy you proved to exist. The Chinese will know we're on to the uplink and change the comm plan."

"Or not. They might not. We're a long way from Seattle, and the carrier might just find the sub anyway."

Alan put the phone back to his ear. "Stay with me, Rafe."

"I could be in my rack."

"One minute, okay?" He put the phone against his chest again. "That carrier should be running at thirty-five knots right now. She should be out to sea, well out from the coast, safe from the storm, beyond reach of the boats, too fast for the sub. Instead, she's tied here by us, Mike. She's waiting to do this thing for us. She's a sitting duck. I insist we pass the uplink information. Is that clear enough?"

"Or what?"

Alan took a deep breath. "Who's flying your plane tomorrow?"

"Fuck you."

They glared at each other. Then Mike shrugged. "Sorry. No, you're right. It's a force-protection issue. That comes first. Don't get your back up. I'll call and get the uplink data sent out right now."

Alan put the phone back to his face.

"Okay, Rafe, let's start solving your problems. There's an uplink code that a Chinese sub used off Seattle—"

Five minutes later, the air-wing commander was banging on the door of the electronics warfare shack.

In the Virginia Horse Country.

Jerry Piat had been watching the routine of Suter's safe house for two days. The stubble on his cheeks was long now, and he smelled pretty bad. He rather enjoyed that part of it. Like Afghanistan in the eighties. It had rained yesterday; he had got chilled and thought maybe he was sick, but today he was okay. He ate an MRE for breakfast and told himself that today was the day if everybody kept to his routine. Anyway, he was running out of food. He finished the MRE and put the empty can into the backpack with all the others. *Pack it in, pack it out.*

At noon, satisfied that things were normal, he went through the high grass in a duckwalk until he reached the fence between his pasture and that of the two horses. He crawled through and started to duckwalk across it, but the horses trotted up and stood close to him, watching.

"Hi, boys." They merely looked at him.

Piat duckwalked some more. The grass got thinner because the horses had eaten it. They followed, swishing their tails. They thought he was the most interesting thing they'd seen in months. Piat duckwalked to the length of fence closest to the horse barns. The horses followed. When he crossed the few feet of lawn to the barns, they put their heads over and watched him go, like people waving good-bye to the pier in an old movie.

Piat had made a note of a door that the maintenance man used. It was unlocked, and he went in, then stood still until his eyes were accustomed to the gloom and he knew that everything was silent. The maintenance man would be in here somewhere, eating his lunch. Piat had seen him carry his lunch in each day and spend an hour or more at noon. Where?

Piat found him in the tack room. There was a desk in there and a chair. The man was using the telephone to complain in a nasal voice that somebody—the person on the other end—never did anything for him. The conversation went around and around, the subject always the not doing by the somebody on the other end. "Talk to you tomorrow," the man said, and hung up. *Talk to you tomorrow about the same subject? Talk every day on this subject?* Piat waited until the man came out of the office and got him in a choke hold and squeezed until he passed out. He could have died; Piat knew that—he'd killed a Russian that way on a bet with the mujahedin—and he didn't really want the man to die, but if it had happened, he wouldn't have changed anything. As it was, he stripped the man and tied him securely, then blindfolded and gagged him with duct tape and dragged him to an unused stall, where he tied his ropes to the saddling rings.

Piat checked the house, first from the window of the tack room and then from a window of a stable fifty feet along. Nothing. He checked his watch. He was ahead of schedule. Suter wouldn't be out for at least twenty minutes.

He checked the maintenance man and changed into his clothes. The man was a little taller and had a gut, but Piat stuck his own clothes down there and thought they'd suffice. He pulled the tractor-driver cap down. He tried the maintenance man's glasses, found he couldn't see anything with them, and smashed the lenses out with his heel. The frames would have to do. Then he checked out the riding mower and saw how it worked. Then he waited.

Suter would come out and lie down, and after fifteen minutes to half an hour, he'd look for the cell phone. Piat didn't know whether it was out there or not: once, he'd seen the maintenance man plant it in the morning, but once he'd actually done it as Suter came down the lawn. No matter; he'd do his business before Suter went looking for it.

Today, of course, Suter was late. Piat couldn't go through this again; the maintenance man couldn't be revved up for a second try. Piat had a fallback, which he'd execute if Suter wasn't out here by seven, but it was crude and he didn't like it. He waited. And waited.

At a little after three, he heard a car. The engine started, and then it faded away. Somebody visiting Suter? Piat had a vision of that shit Partlow. *Here to try to find what the hell went on with Baranowski? Or had they figured that out yet?*

Suter came down the lawn at three-twenty. He looked drawn, perhaps angry. He flopped down on the grass, and Piat couldn't see if he felt for the cell phone because his body was in the way.

Better move a little fast here. Man could do anything if he's upset.

Piat put on the gloves and started the riding mower and steered it out of the barn into the full glare of the afternoon sun. He had to cross two hundred feet of lawn in full view of the house. He tried to sit the way he had seen the maintenance man sit. The mower moved as slowly as an invalid. The yards between the barn and Suter decreased, decreased, but he was still far away. The sound of the motor was loud. He jolted on the hard seat. The machine clanked and coughed.

Twenty feet from Suter, he thought the man was going to turn around, but Suter was simply shifting his weight. He was lying, as he always did, on his side with his back to the house, a book open on the other side of him. *If he turns and recognizes me, I'll have to—*

The front wheels came even with Suter's feet. His knees.

His buttocks. Piat shifted out of drive and the machine stopped, no coasting. A beast.

Piat got down. Suter was six feet in front of him, head to the right, feet to the left. Now was when he would turn around if he was going to. One stride—two strides—squat—

Piat pulled Suter's head back by the hair, whispering, "This is from Sally," and he drew the razor-sharp knife across Suter's throat and threw him forward across his book. Before the jet of blood hit the white pages, Piat saw "You and Your Money" at the top of a page.

He got back on the mower and drove across the lawn and around the flower beds, where he turned the machine off.

A SECURITY GUARD WENT OUT TO RAY SUTER AT five-thirty because he'd been out there longer than usual and it was time to wake him up for supper. He thought Suter was asleep. Then he saw the flies and the drying blood.

USS Thomas Jefferson.

In the Navy, there is always the sea.

By four in the morning, heavy rain had calmed the wind. This wasn't a true typhoon, but only the hint of one, out of season and off its track. Metro blamed global warming. Heavy seas rose under the stern of the ship and raced down her sides, raised the bow through fifteen degrees, and then ran ahead. Visibility was near zero. It wasn't even cold.

Rafe had a float coat on over his flight gear, drenched to the skin from the moment he came on deck. He walked around his plane slowly, trying to see potential problems through the rain and spray. He had a catch in his throat and the sniffles, and he worried that he was finally losing his immunity to the crud, whatever it was. He ran his hand down a landing-gear strut, trying to detect the slick feel of leaking hydraulic fluid by touch. He shone his flashlight into an engine intake. He felt like crap. Lightning flickered off to the east, farther out at sea, briefly illuminating the whole deck and the silent figures moving purposefully to a one-plane launch. His plane.

Satisfied and soaked, he crawled up the ladder into the cockpit and checked his seat. Campbell was already there. Craw was belted in the back, and Ms. Hetzer, a jg from VS-34, was trying to keep up with the master chief.

The inside of the plane was quiet. The wind gusts were gone, and the noise of the rain on the canopy was almost pleasant. Campbell had started the auxiliaries the moment he came into the hatch, and a dim red illumination filled the plane.

"What you got, Master Chief?"

"Captain, the EW guys have two cuts on the uplink. We got a lucky break because the *Fort Stanwix* was on the ball and got a vector, too. This is ten minutes old." He held up a damp sheet of paper with a latitude and longitude.

"Let's get him."

THE HARDEST PART OF THE LAUNCH WAS IN THE seamanship it took the bridge to get the carrier headed into the wind, a maneuver that required unpleasant moments while the ship was broadside to the huge rollers coming in from the open ocean. In his mind, Rafe could see the formation turning. In his new role as air-wing commander, he had to think about the whole picture. The small boys would be hating the turn.

Once they were bow on, they taxied to the cat through a haze of rain and spray and waited. The air-conditioning was working far too efficiently, and Rafe was already freezing cold inside his wet flight suit.

"Ready to go for a ride?" Rafe asked his crew, and waited for the response. Then he snapped a crisp salute.

The launch officer waited until the bow began to rise for a wave, then fired the cat, and they launched just at the top of the rise, giving them a few feet of extra altitude. Rafe made a mental note about the launch officer, a man on the ball. Then he got his altitude and raised his gear and headed for what he hoped was the location of the sub.

•   •   •

"YOU'RE GOING TO HAVE TO BE PRETTY LOW TO drop buoys," Rafe called back to Craw. "If we drop them high, the wind might put them anywhere."

"You let me worry about that," said Craw. Rafe had been flying with Craw for ten years. He checked that off as *not his problem*. If Craw said he could do it, it would be done.

The wind, though weaker than yesterday's, was still enough to move the plane around. Rafe didn't go too high, and he didn't have to travel far. The sub was right with them, six miles to the south. Even now the *Esek Hopkins,* an aging Oliver Hazard Perry-class frigate, was trying to get her tail in the water to join the search. Rafe didn't envy the men on that tiny ship, tossed by the waves, drenched to the skin, pitching and rolling in a way that a carrier never would. They would have to maneuver, too, to get the best out of their sonar tail, and that might mean endangering the ship. Man had his technology, modern equipment like gas-powered turbines and nuclear engines and jets and radar. And then there was the sea.

"He'll be deep," said Craw.

Campbell was trying to stifle a sneeze, and Hetzer stayed silent, a very young woman in the company of giants. This would be her first war story. She was a little afraid, mostly of screwing something up. Captain Rafehausen and Master Chief Craw were legends. But Craw had told her to ask questions, and so she did. "Why?"

"Why deep? Because there's a storm, young lady." Hetzer blushed, glad the darkness and the helmet covered her embarrassment.

"Ever been on a sub, Ms. Hetzer?" asked Rafe.

"No, sir."

"The weather just below the surface is as bad as on the surface. Those rollers will be screwing up the sea for eighty meters down. Think of how much it must have sucked for them just to go to periscope depth and transmit in a storm."

Craw laughed his deep New England fisherman's laugh.

"What's so funny, Master Chief?"

"You people think this is a storm."

THEY DROPPED A FULL FIELD OF BUOYS TO THE WEST in a wide V. None of them got a hit, which didn't seem to faze the master chief at all. Rafe just let him run. He was in his element, doing what he knew best, and this was his battle. Craw muttered to the ASW module on the boat and talked to the *Esek Hopkins,* and all the while he made notes on his kneeboard and dropped more buoys. A second field grew to the north, between the carrier and Craw's expected position for the sub.

Usually, there would have been two or three planes on an operation this important. They didn't have a P-3. S-3 crewmen joke about P-3s, but they carry more fuel and more gear and more sonobuoys. The nearest one was in Bahrain, a little over two thousand miles of mostly unfriendly airspace away. They didn't have a second S-3.

Rafe noticed that Craw dropped an active buoy in each field. He thought Craw must be very sure of himself, or pretty desperate. Usually, if they were going active to warn a sub off, they dropped it last, right on the target, like a torpedo. Craw had only one left.

"Okay, then, sir. I'm ready."

"Where do we go?"

"Right on the datum. He's deep, too quiet for *Esek Hopkins* to hear. He's got to find us in the morning, and he has to be able to hear the carrier. He's not going to be far from where the Elint guys put him."

"You sure?"

"No, but it sounds good, doesn't it?" Craw laughed again. He had no nerves at all.

Rafe turned south, broadside to the wind. He had to yaw the plane to keep his heading. Maintaining an altitude down low was like playing a video game. Everything moved, from the air to the surface of the sea.

"Ready for drop," Craw called from the back. He dropped only two buoys. They had five left, four passive and one active.

They flew on another mile and Craw dropped another while Hetzer brought the two new buoys up on his screen. She felt a little sense of competence when she managed it; then she lost one. Craw cursed.

"Big seas. Buoy just sank. Something must have happened when it hit the water."

"Problem?" asked Rafe.

"Maybe. Anybody have any coffee? The show's about to start."

Campbell passed his thermos back with some cookies.

"Almost as good as having Mr. Craik." Craw was talking with his mouth full.

And don't I wish he was here, thought Rafe.

"I've got something on the 40dB line." Hetzer began to be excited.

"On buoy fifteen?"

"Twelve."

"Can't be right all the time. Sir, please come to 270 true."

Rafe brought the plane up sharply, almost spilling Craw's coffee. A wind gust threw them back into their seats. "Sorry about the ride, folks. Just a little turbulence."

"Ready for drop."

Thunk. Thunk.

"He'll drive through those in about two minutes, and then we'll get him."

Every eye in the plane was glued to the screens, except Rafe's. He couldn't even look at his tiny screen. He had to fly. This flight, he had to fly every meter.

"Now that I can see his grams, I can see he's on fifteen and eleven, too."

"Good on you, Ms. Hetzer. We'll make a subhunter of you yet."

"*Esek Hopkins* say they have contact." Hetzer was busy on the link, more than holding her end up.

The noise of the engines and the rattle of the rain on the canopy.

"Here he comes." Lines on the master chief's screen resolved themselves into a single point of green with a numeric marking. "Put that in the link, Ms. Hetzer."

Hetzer started to process it, her fingers flying. In a moment, every terminal in the world showed a hostile red half-diamond, point down. *UnID Sub. Rafehausen/Campbell/Craw/ Hetzer.* She felt a moment of pride.

"Permission to go active?"

"Go ahead." Rafehausen sounded sure.

"Ready for drop."

Thunk.

"Care to do the honors, Ms. Hetzer?"

"Master Chief, if it's all the same to you, she's your sub."

"That's kind of you, Ms. Hetzer. Going active."

A hundred meters down, a narrow tube of electronics let loose a banshee wail.

Shreeeeeeeeep.

"Now he'll turn for the coast," said Craw.

"Where do you want us, Master Chief?"

"Anywhere you like, sir. We're just ruining his day, from here on. The traps are out, an' he's our lobsta'."

"He's turning west!" Hetzer was pounding her armrest with her fist. "How'd you know?"

"I ain't done yet, neitha'." Craw's accent betrayed his excitement.

"He's coming up on buoys three and four." They were the southernmost buoys from their first field.

"Permission to go active?"

"Damn, you're good, Master Chief."

"I have my good days, Captain."

"Go ahead."

Craw tabbed up the first active buoy he had dropped, more than a half-hour before.

Shreeeeeeeeep.

"Now he'll turn north." Craw's north sounded like "no-ath."

"He's getting louder and moving. Maybe twelve knots."

"*Esek Hopkins* has him off our active and on passive."

"Fourteen knots."

"He'll turn. He thinks he has a sub after him."

The half-diamond jumped on the screen, moving another half-inch in a new direction. North.

"Wow!" said Hetzer.

"Buoys six and seven should have about ten minutes left before they sink."

"No one is ever going to believe this back in Jacksonville." Hetzer was so excited she had forgotten her mike was on.

"Permission to go active on buoy eight?" asked Craw formally.

"Go ahead, Master Chief. Have a ball."

"Going active."

Shreeeeeeeeep.

"An' now he has just one place to run," said Craw, deeply satisfied. "Can't go north, can't go south, can't go west."

"We don't have another active buoy."

"Don't need one. He can run east until he gets home to China, for all I care. We're done, Mr. Rafehausen. Out of buoys."

"Let's go get some coffee."

It was a short flight back, but Craw was asleep when they landed. He woke up to the tug of the harness as Rafe caught the wire, and he had to think back a ways to remember the last time he had slept through a landing. He never did with Mister Soleck, that was for sure.

"Nice landing, Cap'n."

Rafe sneezed.

Coast of East Africa.

COLONEL LAO DROVE SLOWLY AND CAREFULLY PAST the potholes that marked the neutral zone between Tanzania and Kenya. Neither country excelled at road maintenance, but the short half-mile around the border seemed to suffer from utter neglect, as if neither country would admit responsibility for the road. There were other patches in Tanzania that were much worse, but something about the ruined macadam and foot-deep holes on this stretch made Lao fear it more than any other. That, and the constant, nagging fear of border crossings that had been with him since his first mission to Hong Kong as a very junior officer twenty years before.

The bored Tanzanian guard waved him forward, looked at his passport, and collected the U.S. ten-dollar bill folded inside. Lao was traveling under his cover name, Wu, with a diplomatic passport. He had nothing to worry about, but that didn't keep him from worrying through the guard's careless walk around his car.

"Have a good day."

Lao accelerated away into Tanzania, passing the rows

of vendors who waited at the border. His hands were shaking
on the wheel, and eventually, Lao had to admit that it was
more than his habitual fear of border crossings. It was the
meeting—and the barbarian.

Colonel Lao was not a bitter or a cynical man. He was an
idealist, and, if asked to describe himself, would happily have
used the rhetoric of the Cultural Revolution. He was a patriot,
a true believer. He knew that there were aspects to his beloved
Chung Kuo that were unsavory, but China was, to him, "all
under heaven."

It was difficult for him even to frame his thoughts about
what he had just learned, because they did far more than
threaten his views of himself or his country. They as much
as threatened the idea that cherry blossoms would bloom in
their usual color, or that Li Po had been the greatest admiral
of all time. It was as if it were now possible that the universe
was a distinctly different place.

"And yet," he said aloud, the words startling in the quiet
car. He pulled over on the grass at the verge. His hands were
shaking. He rubbed the top of his head for a moment, wished
for a cigarette, though it was years since he had indulged himself.

He had always been suspicious of this task. He had always
been suspicious of Chen and his "friends," those party mag-
nates and corps commanders whom the young openly and
derisively called "the warlords." He had always avoided any
sense of faction in his own work, staying to the simple com-
mandments of the party. Because of that, he was a lieutenant-
colonel with no friends. He had no mentor to call, and no
relatives.

He looked out over the savanna. He and his wife had both
hated Africa when he was first assigned here, as much because
it was the lowest priority in Chinese intelligence as for itself,
but time, opportunity, and education had brought them both
to a love of the place. He could walk here, watching the insects
and the smaller animals, in total contentment. For a moment,
he allowed himself to consider leaving his car and walking
into the bush. Managing his own death. He touched on both
the real and the fake death, but the real death doomed his wife

and his son, and the fake death left him staring at the same impossibilities he had been staring at since meeting the barbarian in Nairobi.

Meet me again.

How often had he used those words himself, when he had had his prey trapped in a web of his own devising. "Meet me again" meant that you had the target in a position where his only choice was to come over.

If Chen was really dead, and the money was the real object, he was dead right now. He could predict the chain of events, from his own report to Beijing to the recall for "consultation." His wife a widow in a reeducation camp, or worse. His child an orphan on a farm.

He had condoned such actions against other men, not because they themselves were in any way guilty, but because it was for the good of the whole. He was disappointed with himself that, having seen his fate, he now flinched from it, but behind the flinching was a pit of anger. This was not for the good of China, or for his party. This was so that a group of men who defied every principle of good living could hide their crimes.

He couldn't fully form that thought. His mind touched it, licked around it like a flame on a new piece of wood, but he wouldn't quite finish it. If he admitted that those men were rotten, the cherry blossoms might change color. He took a deep breath and put his car in gear, resolved to submit his reports and follow the path of the patriot to the end.

He would not go to meet the barbarian again. That would be a small victory, all of its own.

Seattle.

Marvin Helmer had a telephone call. His secretary put it through, but when Helmer heard the voice, he frowned. "I told you not to do this," he said. He meant, *You were told never to call me here.*

"This is urgent." There was a silence. Helmer waited. The caller was male, educated, middle-aged or older, from the voice. Helmer looked at his call recognition and saw that at least the fool wasn't calling from his office at Langley.

"Ray Suter's dead," the voice said.

Helmer stiffened. "How?"

"They won't say. Foul play, it sounds like. Did it themselves?"

But Helmer wasn't really listening. He was thinking, *Suter's dead!*

And then, not being able to suppress a smile, *I'm home free!*

Over Southern Kenya.

Alan cleared the Hunter-Nairobi airspace in the rented Cessna and picked up the A104, the main north-south road that runs from Arusha in Tanzania through Nairobi and all the way to the Uganda border beyond Eldoret. He knew some of the country from the ground but was not so secure from the air; the highway below them provided a clear pointer.

"We'll head south as far as Kajiado and try to pick up the road west to Magadi there," he told Triffler, who was sitting in the right-hand seat. It was a plane Alan knew well; he had flown Rafe's for almost two years when he was at the Newport War College. And it was the aircraft he had landed on a marine helicopter carrier two years before. "You got it on the map?"

Triffler, looking African and elegant in a short-sleeved safari suit that he had bought within an hour of arrival, pursed his lips. "Of course I have." One long, brown finger was resting on the map, an intricate shading of yellow and the palest green, with Mount Kilimanjaro a cinnamon oval rising from a ring of bright green. They would stay well east and north of Kilimanjaro, but they could see it clearly off to their left. "Beautiful," Triffler said. "I wish my wife was here."

"Me, too!" Alan said. "My wife, not yours, I mean." He glanced aside at the map. The road from Kajiado over to Magadi twisted like a snake, a sure sign of fast descents as it went down into the Rift Valley. Alan pointed to their right.

"You can see the far wall of the Rift—the forest off there, see it? Sort of blue-green? We're heading just this side of it." He couldn't see Lake Magadi yet in the ground haze. A car would be waiting for them there. "Tomorrow, we get to drive past Kenyatta's presidential guard's camp. Tough guys—until he died, they were the terror of the country. Still are, to some extent, but they're getting old."

Triffler was silent, looking out, and then he said, "Difficult for me to come here."

Alan digested that and then said, "Too primitive?"

"Too African. I told my wife on the phone, it's not at all like 'coming home.' A black man in a black country, you'd think I'd be walking on air."

"*They* think you fit in." Wherever Triffler had gone in Nairobi, the locals had thought him local. He had the long, thin face of the northern people, the Rendile and the Ethiopians. His slender body was like the Masai and Samburu. If he had spoken good Swahili, he could have passed. "You could have a great career running agents over here, Dick." Triffler made a face.

Harry O'Neill had been a CIA case officer in Tanzania. Alan had heard the same reaction from him. "It's when you find what the limits on being black are, and where being American kicks in," O'Neill had said.

Alan saw what had to be the roofs and trees of Kajiado below him, and he banked and picked up the concrete ribbon of the Magadi road, losing altitude as the land dropped beneath them and the Rift opened. They could see the lake now, a skinny ribbon of white and pink with a rim of startling white in the sunlight. Magadi was a soda lake, home of one of Kenya's major industries, a jarring industrial landscape in the middle of wildness. Alan turned north and then west again so they could look at the lake from the top. The town, little more than the buildings of the soda works and the houses of its executives and workers, sat halfway down where a causeway ran all the way across the three-mile-wide lake.

"That's water?" Triffler said. The surface looked scummy with soda crust. "What's the pink?"

Alan flew the length of the lake, dropping altitude.

Toward the south end, thousands—hundreds of thousands—of flamingos waded in the shallow water. "That's the pink—the birds. Mike says it stinks down there," he said.

"Birds or potash?"

"Dunno, maybe both." He glanced at the map and then swung sharply west toward the forested escarpment on the far side of the Rift. "Pick up a river running north-south," he said. "Runs down toward Lake Natron—"

"Got it—"

"Natron's in Tanzania, but it pushes right up almost to the border, so Lao's got to come up one side or the other of it. We pick him up there, before he reaches Mike." He swung south again, the Ewaso Nyero River winding through green swamp below him. He was flying at a thousand feet above the terrain, the wall of the escarpment rising well off on the right, twenty miles away. Lake Natron was straight ahead, a broad, dead-looking expanse of water in an arid plain. The river seemed to disappear into the swamp; if there was a channel that actually ran into Natron, it was invisible. Immediately ahead, guarding the passage to Natron, were two fifteen-hundred-foot hills, one in Kenya and one nominally in Tanzania. Alan pointed at the hill on the left.

"Shompole," he said. "That's our landmark. The meeting's at the foot."

"Got it, got it—there's a village of Shompole, too—"

Tin roofs flashed beneath the wings. He banked around the flanks of the big hill, which had put out ridges like the roots of a big, old tree. Between the ridges were clustered huts and a corral. Alan could see lanky cattle among the acacia trees. "Masai," he said.

He flew into Tanzania. There was no border post, no fence, no marker, no radar. There might as well have been no border. Lao would be coming from the east, their left. "See any roads down there?"

Triffler was craning over to look down. "I don't even see a rut, man! That is *desert* down there!"

"That's Africa, Dick." There were a few acacias, their shade probably sheltering a cheetah or a zebra they couldn't see. Natron, also a soda lake, had a broad, white rim, and the land around it was gray with soda dust. Alan banked and flew over the lake, circled and came back and dropped down to five hundred feet. "Think I could land down there?"

"Don't!" Triffler almost squealed. He looked at Alan with horror. "You wouldn't, would you?"

"Not this trip. But suppose Lao gets cute? We might want to put down."

He went down to three hundred feet and flew back and forth south of Shompole. There was no road anywhere. "He's going to have to bring a four-wheel drive, and I think he's going to have to walk the last click or two." He banked and pointed. "See those gullies? I don't think you'd get a four-wheeler out of one—too steep." The rains, which came in November, had cut deep, straight-sided erosion gullies in the now-parched soil.

When they had seen enough, he flew back to Magadi and put down on the strip there. Triffler, who'd never landed on an undulating dirt surface before, sat up very straight. They'd been given a radio frequency for the field, but nobody had answered. Alan taxied the plane close to the only building, a prefab the size of a one-car garage, and shut down.

"There's our ride," he said. A Land Rover was parked in the shadow of the building. Leaning on it was the head honcho and general factotum of Magadi International, a well-fed Kikuyu who spoke to Triffler in Swahili and Alan in English; Triffler answered in English, Alan in Swahili. The man seemed delighted that they wanted to leave the plane there overnight. *Hakuna matata* was said several times—"no problem." The parking fee was less than he'd have paid for a car in Washington.

"I want to drive down to Shompole," Alan said to their driver. "*Mzuri?*"

"Okay," the driver said. He was a Masai. He eyed Triffler speculatively and decided something, thereafter spoke to him in beautifully accented English.

They drove the length of the lake on a pretty good road. The smell was, indeed, harsh. Flamingos rose in great clouds, swirled like pink leaves, and settled again on the water. Below Magadi, the road got narrower, became a sandy depression between scrub-grass banks. Nonetheless, the village of Shompole had shade from big trees; they passed a school—mud walls, windows without screens or glass, tin roof—and a store with a Somali name on it.

"Somali?" Alan said.

"Somali," the driver said, as if the word were a curse.

"I thought all the *dukas* were run by Indians."

"Somali, Somali. Somalis taking over everything."

They drove beyond the village. The hill of Shompole, now sensed as a mountain, rose on their left as they curled around it. The clusters of huts and corrals they had seen from the air proved, from the ground, to be small Masai hamlets, each, according to the driver, occupied by one extended family. Nobody waved or came running with tourist trinkets. "This is real Masai country," Alan said, meaning that it was not touristed like the lands to the north and west.

"All Masai here," the driver said. He waved a hand that took in everything from Shompole to the distant escarpment. "Down there, too." He nodded toward Tanzania. A minute later, he pulled up at what was clearly the end of the road.

"*Kwisha barabara?*" Alan said.

"*Kwisha, kwisha.*"

"Let's walk."

Triffler looked pained but got out. They walked along the shoulder of Shompole, on their right the river, which seemed hardly more than a creek now, most of its water sunken into the ground to supply the coarse, lush grass that grew around it. "Where does Tanzania start?" Alan said.

The driver laughed. "Who knows?" he said. He waved his long, graceful hand again. "To Masai, no Tanzania, no Kenya." People lived their lives and died here. When a man wanted a new spear, he walked down into Tanzania because there was no smith nearby on this side. Some of the families slept in Kenya and drove their cattle into Tanzania every day.

"A perfect place for a high-risk meeting," Triffler muttered. "Beautiful, absolutely beautiful. We'll see Lao coming miles away with all this dust. Any surveillance, too." Then he saw a scorpion in the shade of an acacia, and he decided that it wasn't quite so perfect.

Alan walked out of Shompole's embrace to the flat plain by Natron. He was certainly in Tanzania by then; no matter. The landscape was flat; the trees were few; but there were volcanic rocks everywhere, thrown, he thought, by the dead volcano that bulked on the other side of the lake. The lakeshore beyond Shompole was mostly semi-swamp, and it was cut by erosion gullies. Turning back, however, he saw a strip of soda-encrusted lakeshore that was flat and treeless and, he thought, mostly rock-free because the thick soda crust had covered everything. He moved out to it, thinking he might sink through if the soda was only crust over more muck, but it held him. He jumped. The sun beat down. He had a boonie hat and a short-sleeved shirt, but he was baking. He jumped again.

Triffler, who had waited in the mangy shade of an acacia, made a megaphone of his hands and shouted, "The heat's boiled your brain!"

Alan laughed and jumped again. When he got back to the tree he said, "I could land out there," and Triffler rolled his eyes. "You're crazy with the heat," he said. "Let's go."

They walked back to the driver, who was sitting in some real shade, smoking. He handed them a water bottle. He had driven Americans around before.

Dar es Salaam.

Colonel Lao entered his office early. He had not slept. He walked with dignity into his inner sanctum and placed the remains of Colonel Chen in a sealed plastic box, then taped the box into a plastic envelope and affixed a brief contact report about the meeting. The report was factual. He left no nuance of the meeting undescribed, clearly stating that the barbarian had dangled at him and had suggested the existence of vast sums of party money. It gave him some secret satisfaction to know that, somewhere, a clerk would read what were, in effect, his allegations of corruption among the warlords, as stated by the barbarian. He hid *nothing*.

Except that, whether by intent or forgetfulness, he did not include the details of the meeting site at Magadi. No, not forgetfulness, of course. Shame, perhaps. And fear, for his family if not so much for himself. It made him smile—fear was what he felt at border crossings. Well, death was a border crossing.

When Jiang arrived more than an hour later, Lao had already passed his report, the package, and the slip of paper containing what the barbarian alleged to be computer code to a diplomatic courier. It had already disappeared into the embassy. It might already be on its way to China.

Jiang regarded him with something like suspicion, because Lao refused to tell him what had happened. He told Jiang that he had already filed his report. It amused him that Jiang suspected him, because he was taking this action to keep Jiang and Jiang's loyal service well clear of what he now expected to be a blast from Beijing.

And yet—yet he still hoped that he was wrong, that the message back from Beijing would be different. He wondered how long it would take. He could still hope. He went to work on reports of insurgent activity in Somalia and northern Kenya, and Jiang watched him warily.

The morning passed away. For minutes at a time, Lao forgot his predicament. He wrote a report and did a week's work, reviewing backlogged agent reports, making comments, and signing them off. Jiang was unable to keep up. At mid-morning, they shared a cup of tea while Lao read Jiang's surveillance report from Nairobi and suggested some changes.

Lao read on, flipped through Jiang's photos. The barbarian entering the restaurant. He looked dangerous, low-browed, but relaxed, and it crossed Lao's mind that whatever their problems of racism and capitalism, his current predicament was unlikely to happen to the barbarian. He would not be summoned home for "consultations." He banished the thought.

He looked at another photo of a small man in a safari vest holding a camera. In a second photo he was using the camera.

"Are you sure that this man was not just a tourist?"

"Look at the next one."

In the next frame, the small man was pointing his camera directly at the photographer. Lao smiled. "Something of a double kill, I think. But well-done. You needn't put the last in your report. Just the first two."

Jiang beamed at the unexpected praise. "Won't you tell me what happened?"

"I have made my report, Captain."

That ended any possibility of conversation. At lunch, he went home to spend an hour with his wife. She was delighted to see him, and he was attentive, so that partway through the meal they changed their minds and went to the bedroom. It was not epochal, their lovemaking, but it was friendly. He whispered in her ear. She laughed. Then he dressed and went back to work.

He was late, but he couldn't regret it. As he walked into his outer office, however, he noticed a difference—the silence.

There was no one there.

There was no one anywhere. He smiled grimly, understanding at once, understanding everything. Nonetheless, he didn't regret sending the report.

He was going back to talk to his wife.

He was going to Shompole, after all.

Somewhere in the private recesses of his mind, the color of the cherry blossoms changed.

Dar es Salaam.

"Heads up."

The brief equatorial sunset was coloring the western sky, the first sun color to touch the slate clouds in two days. The wind was less, and the palm trees were no longer whipping themselves into a frenzy overhead.

Harry was still at his post in his *banda.* Local Africans were getting curious, and he had had to deal with a queue of vendors attempting to assess his willingness to buy their goods earlier in the day. It was getting to be time to wrap this up.

"Subject is moving."

Lao had come home twice, once at lunch for a long time, and then just after five. Now he was pulling the car out, carefully backing down his short, weed-strewn driveway. Harry had low-light binoculars and other toys denied to Dukas's team in Nairobi. Not least of Harry's toys were voice-activated wireless mikes that were invisible to onlookers and that broadcast an encrypted signal for a relatively short range. They were illegal in Tanzania, but that didn't trouble Harry much. He didn't expect to get caught.

He swept the high ground beyond the housing development and saw lights that he hadn't expected.

"Bravo, this is Alpha. What's that vehicle near your position?"

"Wait one." Bravo was Alice. She would be moving around inside her parked Land Rover, trying to get a sight line.

"Please describe."

"Vehicle looks to be a white Toyota pickup with a red stripe over the hood."

"Wait one."

Harry watched the top of Lao's car picking its way through the housing development and out to the gate. He could just see the tip of the gate as it swung up. He now owned the gatekeeper, or at least was in a position to get reports from him through a cutout. Details mattered. Mike Dukas was getting his money's worth.

Alice's voice came again, describing the hostile pickup truck. "Vehicle has two male passengers, one Asian, one local. Vehicle is flashing its lights."

"Copy."

Harry watched the white Toyota with the red stripe pull out on the road about two hundred meters behind Lao.

"Bravo, pick me up at the road. Delta, take the con." Delta was Dave Djalik.

"Roger, Alpha. Delta taking the con."

Harry picked up a bag from a folding table, glanced around the *banda* for anything he might want, chose a flashlight and a heavy knife, and ran down the little dirt street to the road. Alice arrived a few seconds after he did. She didn't even stop her truck, and Harry was in. They had chosen the pickup point for its screening, a slight bend in the road with palms on one side and acacia on the other. Harry pulled on a ball cap for an Italian soccer team.

"Sorry, Harry. I don't get it. I thought we were here for his missus?" Alice's gravelly voice and English accent floated out of the dark on the other side of the cab.

"Something's going down. Lao's going somewhere with a travel case, and those guys aren't guards. They're following him."

"Following him?"

"They're doing exactly what we're doing. I had a bad moment when I thought they were watching us. Now I'm sure they're watching Lao."

"What's that mean?"

"I think it means that Mike Dukas is about to be a very happy man." He opened his satellite phone and began to call Dukas in Nairobi.

ALICE DROPPED HARRY AT A SECOND VEHICLE, KEPT well out of town, and then sped ahead to maintain contact with Lao, or at least the truck following him. Once the chase had begun, Harry and Alice were both constantly reminded of the hazards of surveillance in Africa. There was no road net, only single tracks across vast, empty spaces. In the mountains, it was possible to hide your vehicle from the person you were watching, but on the flat roads near the coast and up by the great plains of the Serengeti, there was no place to hide. Your target could look in his rearview mirror and see every car on the road for ten kilometers.

Harry took his time catching up to Alice. His own truck was a locally purchased white Mahindi jeep with a cheap plastic top. It was covered in rust and had very little to offer in terms of comfort. It was one of the commonest vehicles in Tanzania, however, far more common than Alice's colorful Land Rover. It was hard to shift, had heavy manual steering and a poor turn of speed. Driving it a long distance would be work. It was a price Harry was willing to pay to blend in.

Once he started to get close, he tried Alice several times on his radio. Static told him that Alice was still well ahead. Short range wasn't always a disadvantage, however. Harry had chosen these little radios because they were difficult to detect beyond a mile or so. He drove on, his low-set headlamps punching through the early darkness to illuminate potholes. Every few miles, a row of *bandas* would appear by the side of the road, sometimes announced by the smell of wood fires. Every little *banda* would have a few candles or paraffin lamps burning. Harry always thought that driving through Africa at night was like driving into the past—his past, in at least one sense: He had been a CIA officer here, driving these roads for months to set up routes. But, now, it was tiring to worry constantly about the possibility of children on the road, or adults, blending with the night. Twice he passed groups that he had to fight the wheel to avoid.

Roadside towns had a different feel. He caught Alice in Korogwe, a crossroads with a gleaming, modern truck stop and a row of shopfronts that would not have disgraced the set of a spaghetti western—tall false fronts all along the road.

"Bravo, this is Alpha, over," he said for the eighth or ninth time.

"... broken, Alpha," he caught. He hit the accelerator, but she was getting gas and he pulled in behind her at the AGIP station a minute later. He got out and nodded to one of the attendants, who started to fill his tank. It was cooler in the hills away from the coast.

"Just the one truck," she greeted him.

"Any chance it's with him?"

"Not bloody likely, Harry. They hang back and hang back."

"What's your read?"

"They want to know where he's going."

"Unless they're going to grab him somewhere ahead."

"Ooh! I hadn't even thought of that."

"I think we have to be ready. Did they stop for gas?"

"No."

Harry looked up the road into the dark. "We'd better fill our jerry cans, too. Stations will be closing in an hour."

"There's gas at Moshi. All night. I've been there."

"That's four hours. I like to be safe."

•   •   •

THE TERRAIN ROSE AROUND THEM IN THE DARK until mountains loomed, heavy shapes in the moonlight. Harry took the lead for a couple of hours, making contact from time to time but otherwise staying back. He knew where Lao was going, and that allowed him some caution. He didn't want the white pickup with the red stripe to make him.

The road wound on and on, climbing away from the coast until even in the moonlight Harry could see the shapes of Kilimanjaro and Meru ahead. An hour to Moshi. He accelerated, caught a glimpse of the now-familiar red taillights, and slowed again. He would have liked to kill his own headlights when he approached them, but the road was too difficult, and he hadn't driven it since he was a young case officer years before. Even in the dark, a few things were familiar, but never familiar enough that he could relax. There was never a stretch where he could simply drive, and he began to get tired. Somewhere in the fourth hour after Korogwe, he drifted off for a moment. He awoke with a sharp jerk of the head to find the little Mahindi jeep was bouncing along the steeply angled verge. He got back on the road without losing the undercarriage, suddenly sweating with adrenaline. He rolled the jeep to a stop.

"Bravo, I've got to stretch my legs."

"Roger."

He got out into the African night, quiet after the rush of the car and yet full of its own motion and noise. He filled his tank from a jerry can and waited for Alice to catch up. He drank some rancid coffee from his thermos and smiled at the rush of memories it brought. It tasted like the Navy.

Alice pulled up behind him and cut her lights.

"Your turn," he said. "I'd like you to stay in contact for a while. If it's going to happen, it will be right after Moshi."

Alice looked exhausted. Her eyes had pouches under them, and her normally sharp features were bloated, thick.

"You okay?"

"Don't worry about me, Harry. I'll be fine."

"That's not some stiff-upper-lip crap?"

She lit a cigarette. "Sod off, Harry. If I wasn't fine, I'd say so."

"Those things'll kill you, Alice."

She laughed, took another drag.

"You awake?"

Harry was down on the surface of the road, doing push-ups. It helped dispel the lethargy. He got up and dusted his hands. "Be careful, Alice."

"Sure." She said it with all the feeling that everyone did in Africa.

COMING DOWN INTO MOSHI, THERE WAS A DOUBLE switchback on a big, long hill. He remembered it, looked forward to it as the sign that they were nearing their goal. Moshi was at least three hours' drive from the meeting at Magadi, and, even at this rate, Lao would be lucky to be on time, but that double switchback would mean that they were entering the last leg, the endgame. Harry was wide awake, now. It was still long before dawn, but there was some hint of light to the sky that promised that dawn was on its way. They hadn't seen a vehicle in hours, but now two big trucks laden with logs passed him, the glare of their headlights giving warning. The second one forced him over to the shoulder, where his little jeep bounced along for a moment, hanging on the edge and spitting gravel before he fought his way back on the road.

Suddenly there were more lights ahead of him. He wondered if the trucks had spilled Lao, or the white pickup, or even Alice into the ditch by the side of the road. He slowed warily and heard a shot, then another. He cut his lights even as he gunned the engine. Something heavy hit the front of his jeep and he ducked. A branch. He skidded the Mahindi to a stop. Two sets of taillights were going away down the switchback. A stream running off to his right covered most of the sound of the night. He cleared his shotgun out of the bag on the seat next to him and cocked it.

Alice's Land Rover was in the ditch. There were a few logs on the road, as if a truck had gone over there or lost a part of its load. Lao's little green car stood in the middle of the road with its lights on. Harry got low, cradling the shotgun. It looked as if whatever had happened here was already over, but he was wary.

Of *course* they had made the grab before Moshi. He cursed his own lack of foresight and scrambled along the ditch until he reached Alice's car. The glass of her windshield was punctuated with stars. Someone had fired through it repeatedly. He walked around, sure now of what he would find, anger growing in him. She had been hit, had rolled into a ball, and been executed. Someone would have leaned in and shot her in the head. He was so angry at himself, he missed her first call.

She was lying under the car, holding a big Colt Python two-handed.

"Jesus, Alice. I thought you were dead."

"Dirty, yes. Dead, no."

"Did they shoot?" He was already holding her left hand, helping her crawl clumsily out from under the back of the Land Rover.

"What do you think, *bwana?*" She leaned against the back of her vehicle and started to shake a little. She reached into her pocket and got out her pack of local cigarettes. After a moment of watching her try to light a smoke, Harry lit it for her.

"You return fire?"

"I was trying to play dead. They weren't really interested. I never saw the grab, just drove right into the end of the whole thing."

"We've got to clear the road. Or rather, I do. You just rest."

He lost track of time for a little while, came back to himself to find he was rolling the logs off to clear the road. He was sweating, and his thoughts were coming sluggishly. He shook his head. His hands hurt from the logs.

He didn't want to be found here by the next truck. He also didn't want the little Suzuki to kill a trucker belting down the hill, and he took it out of gear, gave it a little push, and let it roll away over the edge of the road.

The men who had followed Lao had had friends in front. They had ambushed Lao, and Alice had driven right into it. Perhaps they had made her earlier, or perhaps she had been shot at to prevent some other trouble. Perhaps they had thought her to be an American. It didn't matter now.

Right now, he wanted the men who had done it, and the mission was still there.

He walked back to Alice, who was deep in her second African Dunhill.

"I thought I was dead. Goddam, I thought I was dead. And they just didn't come. The doors slammed and they were off, and I could already hear the little fucking Mahindi coming."

"I was wrong, Alice. I thought it would be after Moshi. Can you keep going?"

"Fuck, yes! I'm immortal right now. My truck is past history, though."

"Leave it. Somebody will strip it and we'll charge the loss to our contract." He smiled at her in the first tinge of light. Then he pointed off to the east, toward Kilimanjaro. She laughed.

"Beautiful," she said simply. "I'd forgotten what it looked like."

"Me, too," he said. She walked off beyond the ditch and he crossed the road to give her privacy, had a piss, then walked back to his jeep. The men who had grabbed Lao were perhaps a half-hour ahead. He thought he knew what they'd do. He got back in the Mahindi, wiped his hands on his spare T-shirt and threw it in the back, worked the throttle until his engine came to life, and Alice jumped in. He didn't think that Lao's kidnappers knew he was behind them.

"Start trying to raise Dukas," he said to Alice, handing her the sat-phone. She couldn't get a satellite, so he kept driving.

The sun was above the mountains by the time they came into the outskirts of Moshi. Harry pulled them into the first truck stop and got water and gas while Alice played with the sat-phone. Harry asked the attendants if they had seen two vehicles full of Asians.

They had. They waved at a back road stretching out east of the town. It was a dirt track that ran down toward Same and the coast, nearly parallel to the road they had been on for sixty miles before it ran along the north side of the Pare Mountains. They had come up the south side. Harry pulled out his Michelin guide to Africa and looked at the road. It improved south of Same, ran on as a broad two-lane to the coast at Tanga. There weren't any branches.

It could be done.

"I've got a connection," Alice shouted. She ran over to him and gave him the phone.

Shompole.

DUKAS STOOD UNDER A GNARLED TREE THAT GAVE its shade as if it had to pay to do so. He was a few yards up the slope of one of Shompole's outriders, high enough to see out over the plain to the north and west of Lake Natron. Lao would come, he thought, from the east, from the way he couldn't see, but Alan and Triffler were up in the aircraft to spot him, and he'd put Margo and O'Leary in the swamp grass down where they could see around the mountain's flank to the east.

"Three, this is One," he said into his Walkabout. Three was Bob.

"Loud and clear."

"Can you see me?"

"Got you." Bob was higher up the slope. He had wanted to have a rifle up there. Dukas had thought the idea was asinine, but had said only that it was too risky. If Lao came with muscle, intending something ugly (kidnapping Dukas would be a nice thought), they'd see everything long before it got here.

"Four?" Four was Frank, who should be in place by now, farther around the hill.

"Yo."

"You there?"

"Yeah, I'm here, but I'm fucked if I know where here is."

"Can you see Margo and O'Leary?"

"I can see Margo's hat if she moves around."

"Well, so can I, so you're not too far away. Okay, radio check, folks—let's go by the numbers—can everybody hear?"

Everybody could hear.

"I got meeting time minus one hour thirty. Settle in, stay cool, and be alert."

Twenty minutes later, he heard the aircraft droning behind him. Dukas had been concerned about gas; Alan had assured him he could stay aloft for six hours if he had to, but Dukas didn't want any emergencies, so he'd told him to leave Magadi later than everybody else. Now the Cessna flew over him at a thousand feet and headed over Natron, then swung east. Dukas did a radio check with them and got a partly garbled reply from Triffler in the right-hand seat. The plane went out of sight behind the hill, and he could hear it for minutes afterward, going away and then coming back as if Alan had wanted to take another look at something.

Then they all settled down to wait.

Alan was flying some sort of Navy-inspired grid, Dukas thought. The plane would appear as a speck, higher and smaller now, fly a leg up the middle of the lake and then swing east and disappear, its sound fading; then it would come up the lake again and swing west and disappear behind the volcano.

It was all very boring. Also tense, and somewhat depressing, as if a kind of fatigue set in from the heat. Dukas was not a worrier about what might be, but it was only human to want something to happen and to want it to be over.

He did another radio check. Everybody was awake, at least, but the voices sounded drowsy.

Dukas watched birds in the marsh grass. He watched an eagle overhead. He watched a pack-train of ants labor past.

And then his cell phone rang. There was no way that a

cell-phone call could be anything but trouble at this point, and the vague depression of the wait was dispelled by the hammering of his heart. He fumbled with the unfamiliar satellite phone, finally pressed the receive switch, and got the call.

"One, this is Alpha, talk to me! One, talk to me!" It was Harry.

"Alpha, this is One—"

"They grabbed him, Mike! No question, it's his own people; they grabbed him. You're busted—he's a no-show. You read me?"

"Jesus, yes, loud and clear! What d'you mean? Where?"

"I'm at Moshi. Maybe two hours from you. Two cars, four guys, not locals; they just grabbed him!"

"Pursue."

Without hesitation, Harry said, "I'm on the way. The vehicles are a white Toyota pickup with a broad red stripe on the hood and some kind of long cab pickup, maybe an Isuzu, white with some pale-blue trim. Maybe the trim's green. Got all that?"

"White Toyota with red stripe, stretched-cab Isuzu with blue or green trim. Copy all. Keep him in visual; we'll do what we can. If we can't catch up, break off. I'll let you know."

"I read you." Harry said something to somebody else. "They shot at one of my people."

"Be careful. Harry, don't try this on your own."

"You aren't paying me enough."

"Exactly. I'll see what I can put together. Keep in touch."

"Out here."

Dukas stepped out of the shadow of the tree and shouted into his Walkabout, "Two, Three, Four, Five, this is One. Abort! Acknowledge: Abort!" His mind was tumbling over itself, sorting and seeking, looking for a way out. He didn't have a contingency for this, except to wish that he'd scheduled the meeting earlier, before anybody in Beijing could know what was going on.

He hurried down the slope. Margo and O'Leary were pushing through the livid swamp grass. Margo was still a hundred feet away, but she was making some signal to him.

Dukas was too busy trying to raise Alan to acknowledge her. Even out in the open, however, he couldn't raise the aircraft, which had made the turn west behind the volcano and was probably well west and south now.

"Hey, Mike," Margo called, "what the hell—!"

"Get in the cars!" Dukas shouted. He was looking around for the others. Bob was coming down the rocky slope with his eyes on his feet. "Where the hell's Frank?" Dukas raised the Walkabout again. "Four, this is One—acknowledge! Four! Four, this is One!"

"One, this is Four. I fell over a goddam boulder—"

"Well, get your ass back here!"

Margo was standing with her hands on her hips. "Okay, we go to the cars, so? Then what?"

"Find a route and head for Dar es Salaam. The only sure border crossing's Namanga; you'll be way the fuck west of Dar, so go to Arusha—"

He heard the plane before he saw it.

"Eight, this is One! Do you read me?"

Garble from Triffler. At least he'd heard.

"Eight, this is One! You're not clear. Do you read me?"

More garble, of which he got "miles" and "minutes."

Frank was limping toward them by then, Bob standing under the nearest tree, Margo and O'Leary close to him.

"Listen up! O'Neill called. It looks like Lao's been grabbed by his own folks. O'Neill's tailing them, but I'm not sure what he can do otherwise. We'll do the best we can. I'll be honest with you—our chances aren't good. Plus we're busted on the pickup from the carrier, because they'll head for Dar, plus we don't have country clearances for Tanzania. Anybody wants to drop out can do so."

They all simply looked at him.

"Frank?"

"I'll live." He had a bloody spot on his khaki pants leg.

"Let's get going!" O'Leary said. "Cut the talk."

Dukas came close to reading him out and then saw that the man was right. "Okay, both cars—Namanga, Arusha, Dar. It's a long trip—six hours if we're lucky."

"You?" Margo said.

"I don't know yet." Dukas pushed his radio switch and called the aircraft again, which he could see clearly now.

"Read you," Triffler said. *Jesus, thank you.* Dukas gave it to him in three sentences.

"What ... to do?" Triffler sputtered.

"Not reading you good, Dick." What was this line-of-sight shit? He could *see* the fucking plane well enough! The plane went into a dive and turned toward them. The reception brightened. Dukas hit the switch again. "Ask Al if he can pick me up, or do I have to go back to Magadi?"

Dukas watched the aircraft. Something was going on up there, he thought. Was Alan unwilling to land? No, it would be Triffler, not because he was frightened but because he liked things right—runway lights, radar, control towers with good radios.

"We'll pick you up. Head for the northeast shore of the lake."

Dukas looked that way. Trees and soda crust waved in the heat ripples. Above them, the plane was already heading downwind to set up for an approach.

Dukas looked at the others. "I'll meet you in Dar." He started running into the rippling oven.

Twenty minutes later he was airborne, headed for Dar on an undeclared flight plan. Alan was on the radio with what passed for air-traffic control, refiling his flight plan as if he were a tourist who had changed his mind and wanted to see Kilimanjaro from the air. Dukas got cooler as they climbed, until the sweat from the soda flats began to run like ice down his back and his shirt was cold. Alan turned back and took his headset off. He had to shout over the noise of the engine.

"*Hakuna matata, bwana.*" He gave Dukas a big thumbs-up; Dukas nodded and unbuckled his seat belt as if he were taking his life in his hands. Triffler was still sitting erect in the front seat, as if he didn't plan to be taken by surprise again. He hadn't liked the landing or the takeoff.

"I want to contact Harry."

"Keep trying his cell phone. If we have to use radios, I'll only be able to get him within a couple of miles."

Mike shook his head emphatically. "I can't get him."

Alan held up a road map. "I can take us right down the road he's on. We ought to find him. He'll be between Moshi and Same for the next two hours. I'll fly right down the road."

Mike shook his head, unconvinced by Alan's eagerness. "I'll keep calling."

Tanzania—on the Same Road.

Every time they reached a little hamlet, Harry asked about the cars ahead of them. Probably the only ethnic group that stuck out in Africa more than whites was Asians, so he always got a report. Something about the two trucks raised the suspicions of every hamlet they passed, so that Harry had to listen to long-winded suppositions about the intent of the passengers. He stuck to it. He couldn't afford a mistake. He couldn't let them slip down some dusty side road to a safe house in the hills. He hoped they were going for Tanga, but he couldn't be sure, and he couldn't raise Dukas to ask for support. He tried to imagine how he could grab Lao on the road without a major international incident developing. He didn't have the numbers or the ability to get ahead and lay an ambush.

It was nine in the morning when they reached Same, where the road divided. The northern road ran to the coast, while the southern ran down to Dar. It was the decision point he had dreaded, because without some luck, he'd never be sure which way they were going. Harry guzzled water and Alice pumped gas, and suddenly he heard his radio crackle. He grabbed for it.

"Alpha, this is . . . over?"

"This is Alpha!" he all but shouted into the headset. He sat on the seat and pulled his headset over his ball cap. "This is Alpha, please say again. You're broken and garbled."

"Alpha, this is Eight." Clear as the great red hump of Kilimanjaro. Alan Craik, a man with a mission. He made Harry smile.

"Where are you?"

"Overhead. Where are you?"

"Gas station just north of Same."

"I'm taking One down to Dar. I can be back in three hours."

"Can you see the roads south of Same?"

"Sure."

"There are two. One runs north of the Pare Mountains, one runs south."

"Got it."

"Try and get a spot on the subject vehicles, copy?"

"Wait one."

ALAN TURNED TO TRIFFLER AND SLID HIS HEADSET back. "Harry needs us to find the guys who have Lao. Road splits at Same."

Dukas leaned up, apparently impressed that Alan had found Harry in the mountainous desert. "Has he lost them?"

"I think he's just too far behind." Alan dove for speed and turned southeast, then steadied up to get a long, clear look at the two roads. He turned north and climbed again, cresting the first ridges of the Pare range and watching the long red road.

Even from three thousand feet, the two cars were obvious. They raised plumes of dust, and the red stripe on the Toyota was like a beacon. Alan turned back immediately, diving to drop back behind the ridge. They flew for a few minutes until they had the range of Harry's radio.

"Maybe fifteen miles ahead, Harry. They're on the north road."

"Then the only place they can go is Tanga. That's a four-hour drive for them."

Alan looked at his instruments, turning slowly over Same. He read his fuel gauge and did some calculations. "Hang on, Harry. We need to have a little talk."

He pulled off his headset and leveled the plane. "What's it going to be, Mike?"

"Where are they going?"

"Tanga, on the coast. Maybe Dar after that, but they took the Tanga road. They'll be there in four or five hours."

Mike Dukas thought with his chin sunk on his chest. The plane circled above Same.

"We have two problems, and they both look huge. We have to get Lao, and we have to get his family."

"I can get us to Dar in another hour, maybe a little more." Alan looked at his fuel gauge again. "Then I'll have to get gas. Then I'll have to get back to the road and find Harry. And then what the hell do we do?"

"Grab Lao." Mike didn't hesitate.

"How, Mike? Damn, do you know what you're asking?"

"Why don't we take him now?" asked Triffler.

"Because we'll need to get him and his family at the same time, Dick. Once we have Lao, the family will be disappeared."

"I don't like this," said Triffler. He set his jaw and looked out the window, then turned back. "I think we're over the edge. We don't even have an operational clearance for Tanzania."

Dukas looked at Alan. Alan played with the controls. "We're out on a limb, Mike. I don't really like it, either."

"We can still do it. You and Dick and Harry get Lao. I get the family."

"And if we screw up, then what?"

Dukas shook his head.

"Mike, what's our job here? Do we know Lao's trying to defect? If we kill some Chinese spook, is that going to spark World War III?"

"Didn't you just give me the patriotic speech the other day, Commander? That we needed to do something 'for the Navy'? This is it, Alan. This is the biggest thing I'll ever do, maybe the most important. I'm not ready to bag it. I still think it can be done."

Alan turned the plane again, looking down at the sunlit plains rolling into Same, and the mountains beyond.

"I'd rather not get killed here, Mike," Triffler said. "And I don't really see any way this will come out happy. I think we should abort." Triffler sounded like the voice of reason, calm and solid. Dukas ignored him and leaned forward until he was looking into Alan's eyes.

"I followed you into Sudan on less than this."

Alan kept glancing away, looking out of the cockpit and

then back at Dukas. It made him look shifty, which he wasn't. He was worried about the plane, and something else was nagging at him. He was surprised at his own lack of response to the crisis. Something profound had changed. He wondered if he was getting old.

"Okay, Mike. I'll try. Harry will try. But if it won't go, you *have* to back off. Think of your career, if that helps."

"I can't believe I'm hearing this from Mr. Gung Ho."

"You are. There's more here than just the mission." He put his headphones on and called Harry again. "Alpha?"

"Go ahead."

"We're a go. Stay with them. I'll be back in three hours, maybe less. We'll keep trying to reach you on the phone."

"Try in an hour, then. I'm worried about the battery."

"Roger that. Stay safe, Alpha."

Harry laughed.

IT WAS A LITTLE MORE THAN AN HOUR BEFORE ALAN was in the pattern for Dar. "You better call the carrier and change the plane."

Dukas nodded. He seemed deep within himself. Alan wondered if five years of shared dangers hadn't finally stretched them to where the ties would begin to fray.

"What's the earliest you might have him on the spot?"

Alan looked at the map and did the numbers again. "Sunset. We'll call the plane in, just the way we planned. I'll get there first and put out some lights. Then Rafe brings the plane in and we're done."

Triffler barked, a short laugh that took them all by surprise. "You guys make it all sound so *possible*."

Mike smiled back at him. "We've done worse, with less."

TEN MINUTES LATER, MIKE WAS STANDING ON THE general aviation tarmac at Dar. The wind from the propeller whipped his clothes tight around him, and he held his baseball cap on with his free hand. He made a move to shut the door, then pulled it back and leaned in close to Triffler and shouted so both men could hear, "Oh, by the way, Ray Suter's dead! I got the word just before I left Nairobi!"

Alan looked at him, blank. Triffler wrinkled his nose. "Well, that solves a big problem for the Agency, doesn't it!"

"Yeah. Funny coincidence, huh?"

He slammed the door and the little aircraft rolled.

USS Thomas Jefferson.

Everyone on the boat knew that something was going down, because there was an alert S-3 on the cat early in the morning, and most of the air wing couldn't remember the last time there had been an alert S-3. They made jokes about it. Some word of the presence of a potentially hostile submarine had leaked out of the ASW module, though, because as the day wore on without a launch, scuttlebutt had it that the plane was carrying a live torpedo.

LTjg Evan Soleck was too deep in his own personal gloom to hear much about the plane. He was in a special hell reserved for aviators who can't land; most of the other pilots couldn't meet his eye in the dirty-shirt wardroom, and no one sat with him. He was beyond being joked with. He was beyond a slap on the back. Most of the pilots knew he was close to losing his wings. He wandered to the library and got a book he didn't read, and then he lay on his rack, waiting for the call. He knew the call was coming. He was almost past the tears and the frustration, although every time he let his mind go, he relived every missed landing he had had in the last two weeks. He flew them all again. He saw where he'd overcorrected. He saw things he could have done better. He cursed some private bad luck, he cursed a call or two by LSOs, but he was an honest young man, and mostly he cursed himself.

He wondered if the CAG was waiting for him to do the right thing and call it himself. He thought it might be better that way.

He'd always taken pride in the ribbing from other aviators. They joked that he was so good at intel he ought to consider it as a designator change. EW guys joked that he had a better grasp of electronic warfare than they did. Even Alan Craik had suggested to him once that he might be happier in a more intellectual part of the Navy.

None of that seemed funny now. Here, at the bitter end, he knew he could hand in his wings and be accepted as an intel guy or something else, and he knew he never could take it. He loved to fly. It was all he'd ever really wanted to do, and if he didn't fly, he'd just sit on a succession of boats, eating his heart out that he was a ground-pounder and not a man with a plane. He wondered how long it would take to get free of the Navy, and what the hell he'd do with his life. Maybe he'd have time to date, or something. He couldn't see it. He couldn't really see anything.

Ring.

Ring.

He picked it up. Not answering wouldn't delay the inevitable. Now that it was on him, he wished he'd done the deed himself.

"Soleck?" The voice on the other end had a very stopped-up nose. Everybody did. Everybody but Evan Soleck.

"Speaking."

"This is Captain Rafehausen. Please come up to my cabin."

"Yes, sir. On my way."

He didn't linger. He even nodded to some guys he knew. Campbell smiled back, already suited up to go flying. Soleck turned his head away, afraid that emotion was going to get the better of him in front of all these guys. He knocked at Rafehausen's door. He felt as if every eye in the passageway were watching.

"Lieutenant Soleck reporting as ordered."

"Have a seat." Rafehausen blew his nose, powerfully and repeatedly, and then drank some tea. He gulped it.

"I'm supposed to be the pilot on the alert 60 S-3," he said. He sniffed experimentally. "God*dam* I hate this cold." He blew his nose again.

Soleck only nodded.

"I need you to do it."

Soleck didn't really even hear the words. He was in a bad

place. He wasn't really listening, simply hoping it would all go by.

"I need you to take the flight."

"Me?" The second time, something in his brain made contact.

"No one else sitting here. You. You are the last healthy S-3 jock on this boat. Your landing grades suck. I have a flight laid on that has the CNO's attention, and the flight plan says 'national security.' So you have to fish or cut bait right now. Can you fly?"

Soleck looked at the floor. It looked really different. He'd never noticed that the O-3 decks had white flecks in the blue. The bad place fled away. "Yes, sir."

"Good. I'm not going to give you any shit. Just go fly. You'll have to land on some pissant road in Africa, get whoever is there, and bring 'em back here. The weather is still breezy. I don't want to hear about it. I don't really give a shit how often you look at the deck as long as you get that plane aboard. Got me, mister?"

"Yes, sir."

"Good. Because I've got to have a nap. I've pretended all day I could take this flight. I can't. Go get your flight suit on and get ready. If we're a go, you'll be off the deck in two hours."

"Yes, sir."

"Don't sit there beaming, Soleck. Go."

Captain Rafehausen hadn't even got into his rack before his phone rang.

"Captain Rafehausen?"

"Shoot."

"The *Esek Hopkins* reports a possible surface contact bearing east-northeast. Might be the cigarette boats."

Rafe blew his nose. "I'm on my way."

Tanzania, Over the Same Road.

ALAN CAME OUT OF THE SUN AT THE ROAD, TRYING
to stay invisible to Harry's targets. He was guessing at Harry's
location and he guessed wrong, because after two passes he
had no radio contact.

He went high and started back up the Same Road, already
worried that Harry had passed his intercept position and that
he was now flying the wrong way. They didn't have any time
to waste. Beside him, Triffler was silent. Alan had been surprised when Triffler had climbed back into the plane in Dar,
but he hadn't made a comment. Alan thought that perhaps
Triffler just couldn't leave a job until it was finished.

Too high, and every vehicle looked the same. The dust
they raised hid them, and Alan tried to get behind them before diving, still trying to hide his presence from Lao's cap-
tors. Intellectually, he knew that most people never look up,
but the big sky over Tanzania felt naked. There were no clouds.
He fought the occasional wind gust, the last remnants of the
storm, and scanned the road again.

They flew up the road for twenty minutes, well over an hour of car travel. Time was leaking away.

"Everything's always slower than you think," he said to himself. Triffler had told him that, about surveillance. If he turned back now and was wrong, by the time he recorrected, it would be too near dark.

"I think that must be them," Triffler said.

On the last shoulder of the Pare range were two trucks. Well behind them was another. Alan turned out to the west and tried to be patient, flying to the west before he turned the nose of the plane back to the east and started to call.

He was still high, almost directly behind Harry and less than two miles away, when he got an answer. It didn't sound like Harry at first, and it took him a moment to realize that he must have someone with him.

"Eight, this is Bravo. Go ahead."

Bravo?

"Bravo, can you see Alpha?"

"He's right beside me." Alan could imagine Harry, driving with both hands on the wheel for the treacherous road. They had twenty kilometers of hill country left, and then they'd be on the coastal plain.

"Go ahead, Eight." That was Harry.

"I can see you, and I can see them."

"Roger."

"Can we take them?"

"What do you think?"

Alan looked at Triffler, who gave him a slight nod.

"I think we can take them. I have a spot in mind."

"Tell me."

"Just before you come down from the hills at Lushoto there's a straight stretch. Then another five kilometers of broken country, and then, bang, you're on the plain. Copy?"

"Roger, Eight."

"Just before the straight stretch is a long climb. I'll land on the straight, walk up the hill, drop a tree just over the top so they never see it coming. You come up behind them."

"That's the best you can do?"

"Pretty much."

"Better than my idea, anyway. Let's do it."

"You start calling as you move uphill, and I'll talk back if I can."

"Roger."

"Fifteen minutes or less, Alpha."

"Roger, copy all."

Alan went west again, using the last ridge of the mountains to hide his plane. He came back low and crossed the road, then turned back from the east. He was going to treat the road as if it were a carrier. Closer up, he could see the potholes and the two elevation changes on the "flat" stretch, but there was no time to make a new plan. He went into a break over the road and turned downwind, racing along the road at six hundred feet. Just before the last hill he turned again, powering through 180 degrees with his throttle at full and then using his flaps and easing the throttle until he was all but gliding. His angle of attack was too slow, but he had the whole of two kilometers of road to cover and it would be easier in the air than walking.

"Extend," he muttered to himself, as if he were his own LSO and this were really the boat. Triffler was holding the instrument panel with both hands. The nose obscured the road, and dust began to rise. There were trees on both sides, though thankfully several meters beyond the wingtips. He pulled out the throttle a little more, and his wheels touched. He skipped, right at the top of one of the invisible gentle rises. He let the plane sink away, and it went down farther than he expected, so that he was almost ready to give it more power when the wheels touched again.

Bam!

He had to compensate for the first pothole, which tried to turn the whole weight of the plane. But he was just touching the top of the road after that, and he slowed the plane gradually over the second kilometer, taking his time. He expected the Chinese to come over the hill at any moment, but he kept his mind on the landing. When the plane was taxiing well below seventy kilometers an hour, the bumps turned into a jolting accordion, and Triffler began to bounce in his seat. Alan finally used the brakes and brought them to a stop, afraid for his landing gear. He powered down the engine, but left it idling.

He was out in a moment, grabbed his bag from the back, and ran once around the plane, looking for cracks or danger signs. The plane seemed to have held together. Alan gave the plane a slap. Then he took an ax and a saw from the emergency bag and pulled on his backpack. He grabbed the spare chocks from the cockpit and put them under the wheels.

"Coming?" he shouted at Triffler. By his calculations, they had eight minutes.

Triffler started to run up the road toward the big hill. He took the saw from Alan and powered along, breathing through his nose and running like a champion. Alan couldn't keep up. Triffler simply ran by him and went straight up the hill as if he were running on flat ground. Alan put his head down and followed.

Viewed from the plane, the hill looked small, the last outrider but one of a mighty range of hills. Closer up, the steepness had been clear, but with his feet on the road, Alan felt as if he were trying to run up a cliff. Any moment he expected to hear the clash of gears coming up the other side. He looked up. Triffler was at the crest, his hands on his knees. Next moment, he was off the road and cutting with the saw. Alan concentrated on his legs. Left, right, left, right. He remembered being at officer candidate school, and how he had hated to run, and a Christian officer had run along beside them saying, "Oh, Lord, thou art my hope of Glory" to the rhythm of the feet. He hadn't let them sing the usual songs, which he proclaimed "profane." The man had been a great instructor, though. Alan had forgotten him, but the running brought him back.

Hope of Glory, he said to himself. Left, right, left. He looked up again. There was something droning in the distance. He plodded on. He had a hundred meters to go, and then fifty.

Hope of Glory. Left, right, left.

He was there. He was shaking all over, bathed in sweat. Triffler had a tree wavering. Alan plodded to the other side of the road and tried to remember everything he knew about cutting wood. He chopped at the base of a big African softwood tree. It was soft and pulpy, and three bites of the ax cleared a third of its diameter. He missed a swing and wiped the sweat from his eyes. The droning was a little louder. Behind him, he heard Triffler's tree fall with a crash. He kept cutting, missed again, and then got the head of the ax just where he wanted it. He moved around behind and cut again. The ax stuck in the soft stuff and he couldn't get it free, couldn't seem to concentrate on pulling the handle. It came free after what seemed like minutes.

The tree moved. He cut again. The road noise was louder. He wanted to peel the headphones off because they were hot as hell, but the static noise promised him an instant's warning when Harry was in range.

If they were even listening to the right cars. He tried not to think of what would happen if they drove a car full of innocent Tanzanians off the road. He cut again and his tree stirred, and he breathed, aimed, and cut again. And again.

Crack.

It was going. He jumped clear and watched it. It fell across Triffler's tree, completely blocking the road just over the crest.

"In the ditch," he panted.

Triffler, apparently unwinded, nodded.

Alan tried again. "We get in the ditch right at the crest. The moment they stop, we're at the doors. Never let them think."

"What about the second car?"

"You take the first car. I'll take the second. Harry'll be here before they have time to react." He leaned over and dripped perspiration on the road, gasping. Then he climbed the last few feet of the hill and got in the ditch.

"Eight—"

"Roger, Alpha. Trees are down. We're a go. Do you copy?"

"Copy go."

"How far are you from the crest?"

"Can't—"

"How long?"

"—come!"

Alan could hear the cars. He didn't feel any surge of adrenaline. He was too tired. He just lay in the ditch as the afternoon became evening all around him. There were ants in the ditch and he watched them, because he didn't want to move his head. He heard a truck shift gears, and then another shift.

"They'll be on you in less than a minute." Harry's partner. It must be Alice, because the voice sounded English.

"Still a go," he said clearly. His heart began to beat hard. So the adrenal gland still worked. He pulled out his pistol, a Smith and Wesson nine-millimeter automatic, and wondered how the FBI would feel about the use he was about to make of it. They'd be heroes if it worked. They'd be fired if they failed and lived. He worked the slide. The first truck seemed to be right on top of him.

And the noise continued to grow. The trucks must have been farther away than he thought. Now he could hear the second gear change, and the sound of the tires on gravel, and then the first vehicle was *there* at the top and saw the tree. He heard the brakes go and the spray of gravel and a crash, and the second vehicle was on him, skidding past, trying to stop, visible even from the ditch, and he was up and after it as it rammed into the first and stopped. Triffler was ahead of him and Alan got up to the door of the second truck, the Isuzu, and pushed his pistol into the cab at the driver.

"Out of the car now!"

Triffler was screaming behind him, the loudest he had ever heard him yell.

"Down! Out and down in the road!" Triffler fired a shot in the air. Alan grabbed the door open and pulled the man at the wheel right into the road, charged with adrenaline. In the backseat, a man cleared a weapon from his holster and started to point it at a third man, an Asian. Alan shot the one with the gun. He didn't think it through, simply fired point-blank. Then he grabbed the man he had just shot and pulled him out by the passenger door. He screamed when Alan twisted his arm.

"Lie down!" Alan bellowed. Then there was a new shower of gravel and another car, a small, rusted, white jeep, skidded sideways across the road. Alan lost the man who had been in the front passenger seat. He was off, out his own door, and trying to scramble across the ditch. Harry fired his shotgun in the air. The man threw himself down. Alan turned back to Triffler.

"I lost one." Triffler pointed into the brush. "Passenger bolted."

Alan grabbed the man in the Isuzu.

"Colonel Lao?" The man, slight and balding, nodded, as if nothing could surprise him.

"Cars off the road. We'll leave in the plane. Get the trees off the road, too."

Alice took the shotgun from Harry and stood over the three men lying in the road.

"Come on," said Alan, and he and Harry started to clear the road. The trees were hard to move, and Alan was sagging, and it took Triffler's help to get them clear enough to prevent an accident in the oncoming dark. Harry pushed both trucks off the road with his little jeep.

"I'm going to miss this car," he said.

"Drive us to the plane?"

"Sure. I'm coming with you. Alice'll take the car. No point in lingering here."

"I hear that."

Triffler tied the three Chinese together. Harry shouted at him in Swahili a few times and Alan looked at him as if Harry had lost his mind. "Dick doesn't know any Swahili."

"Does the phrase 'plausible deniability' mean anything to you?"

"Huh?"

"You look like shit and we're both black. We might be locals."

"They'll never buy that." But Alan got it. They didn't have to buy it. Someone just had to say it and stick to it.

Triffler ran up. "That guy is bleeding pretty fast." He looked at Alan. "You just going to leave him?"

"Yeah."

"Give me your medi-pac, for heaven's sake."

Alan reached into his backpack and took out his medi-pac. He tossed it toward the three bound figures and pulled Triffler into the back of the jeep. "Screw them, Dick. They'd have done the same to us."

"We're not them," Triffler snapped.

The overloaded Mahindi started down the hill toward the plane. Harry reached out from the front, a long arm extending into the back.

"Dick Triffler? I'm Harry O'Neill. You like working for NCIS?"

Triffler shook Harry's outstretched hand. "It has its moments."

Harry laughed and got on his cell phone.

Dar es Salaam.

Dukas was standing inside the mud house that Harry had paid ten dollars for. Outside, a man named Djalik, with whom he'd talked on and off for a half-hour on the cell phone before he ever met him, was giving final, whispered instructions to Harry's people. Djalik struck Dukas as one of those people who love to sneak around in the dark and go *Boo* when you least expect it, but Harry trusted him, and Dukas didn't plan to make a lifetime pal of him. For now, creeping around the dark was a valuable skill.

"Okay," Djalik said in the doorway. It was dusk under the trees, dark inside the lightless house. "I got three people out there. *They* got three people out there—locals, and we don't know if they'll shit or go blind if we make a move. Far as I can tell, they don't know we're here. One of my guys thinks they might be Hutus, some of those hotshot militia bastards who've been on the run since Zaire, but we don't know that. Hardcases if they are. On the other hand, they could be guys with ax handles and a free shirt from some Tanzanian rent-a-cop shop, in which case they'll take one look at a gun and puke."

"I don't intend to show a gun," Dukas said.

"Neither do I. On the other hand, I'm not going to let some Hutu shithead kill me."

Dukas felt a hand on his arm, then a firm grip pulling him toward the doorway. Djalik's voice dropped to a whisper. "We've found a route to the back door of Lao's house that's just out of their lines of sight. It means going on your hands, but it's okay. The wife and the kid are in there alone—he came home from school two hours ago, everything normal. Then a black woman left—maid or a cook; my guess is she got sent away. I think the woman knows what's going down with her husband."

"We don't do anything until they grab Lao," Dukas said. It seemed exotic, alien, the idea of grabbing somebody. Not the way he had wanted it to go.

"The longer we wait, the better the chance that the Chinese embassy is going to send their guys out. And they're heavies."

Dukas guessed that the Chinese embassy was like all bureaucracies—slow and confused. Even if they had a direct order from Beijing to seize Lao's family, the op would take time. And Dukas was counting on a bureaucracy in Beijing, too. Whatever had sent Lao to him to try to make the second meeting, it hadn't so upset Beijing that they had killed Lao outright. Rather, he thought, the team that had taken him must have had orders to get him to a safe house someplace up the coast, or they would have brought him right back to Dar. A safe house meant delay—bureaucratic waffling. "We wait until we get the word," he said.

"You sure you don't want a gun?" Djalik said. Clearly, he couldn't believe it, because this was the third time he'd asked.

"I couldn't raise it to sight it, and I couldn't take the recoil," Dukas said for the third time.

They waited. Against the steely sky, the leaves got blacker, then began to fade as the light slid down the sky. He looked west and saw glorious red and orange.

If they get him, they're going to have to do the carrier-plane pickup in the dark. Not going at all the way he'd wanted.

His cell phone rang.

"One," he said.

"We got him."

Dukas felt a rush of heat down his body, and his scalp crawled. "Say again."

"We got him. We're headed for the rendezvous."

Dukas put the phone in his pocket. And took a big

breath. "We're on." He took Djalik's arm. "You guide me to the house. I'll explain to the woman what's going down. If she resists, we've got a problem. But we have to get her to the American embassy, *capisce?*"

Djalik led him forward, Dukas bent over with his left hand on Djalik's right shoulder. The position hurt, but Dukas ignored it. *High stakes, screw the pain.* They went under the fence, then right along it for a distance that Dukas realized Djalik had already measured and was now doing by duckwalk paces. Then they turned left, were able to walk almost upright for five steps between black banks of undergrowth in a kind of no-man's-land between the good houses and the mud huts, until Dukas could see the lights of the Lao house and open space. He smelled water—somebody watering a garden.

Djalik touched his hand, pushed down. Dukas got down. *More,* the touch said. Dukas was on his knees.

They went along the ragged edge of the no-man's-land, then to a wall that surrounded Lao's house. Along the wall to a gate. Djalik had already cracked the gate's lock.

Inside the wall, Djalik pointed up at a neighboring house—only a corner visible. "Window," he whispered. "He can see us unless we belly-crawl."

There was thirty feet of straggling grass between them and the house. Dukas belly-crawled. He felt water soak into his clothes. It was the Lao lawn that had been watered, the woman coming out here and doing it, maybe trying to seem normal to the watchers she knew must be out there. *Gutsy lady.* Halfway across, he allowed himself a look toward the other house. If there was a window there with a watcher in it, they were just below his line of sight.

Djalik stood. "Golden from here," he said. He pointed. An opening in the building made a sheltered portico; on one side was a huge plastic trash can. A basketball backboard and hoop were silhouetted against the darkening sky.

Dukas moved along the wall to the opening and stepped in, almost falling over a bicycle. Straight ahead was a door, on his left another. Light spilled into the yard farther along, and he heard the chink of a dish on a utensil.

He knocked on the door.

She was small, bosomy, frightened. And she had a gun.

"Missus Lao? Your husband sent me." He was aware of the light spilling out of the house on him, but he thought the portico would hide him from the watcher at the window. "Missus Lao, I'm here to help you."

Her eyes were too big. She had been weeping. Over her shoulder, Dukas saw a boy of twelve or thirteen. "Do you speak English?" Dukas said to her.

"I do," the boy said. The woman said something in Chinese that sounded brutal to Dukas.

"Please tell your mother that there are men outside who want to hurt her, and I want to help her."

The boy said something. The woman only stood there, the gun held out as if she were going to push Dukas away with it. He figured it was a .32 but didn't want to find out the hard way. "Please tell your mother that your father is safe and is flying to an aircraft carrier. Right now." *Not quite true, but getting close.*

The woman listened to the boy. She began to sob. She backed into the house, the gun still on Dukas, but she didn't shoot when he came in or when Djalik came in behind him.

Dukas talked to the boy, who translated. Dukas lied some—he disliked that, but he did it—and told the boy that his father was coming to the States, and he wanted them to come, too. Dukas didn't say "defect." After the boy translated for his mother, she nodded sadly, and Dukas realized with relief that Lao had told her what he was going to do. And had depended on Dukas to get the family out—until Beijing had decided that the defection wasn't going to happen.

"This man is also your friend," he said, indicating Djalik, who was prowling around, muttering to his people over a headset. "Doesn't your mother speak *any* English?"

"Sometimes."

Dukas absorbed that, realized this wasn't one of the times, because she saw him as an enemy. But not, maybe, as big an enemy as some others. "Please ask your mother if we can have a dress that will fit that man." He nodded at Djalik.

The boy got unhappier as they talked. Whatever she had told him, it was only now coming to him that his father was a traitor, Dukas the living symbol of his treason. Yet, as the boy got farther from Dukas's grasp, the wife came closer. He knew she was in his hand when she produced a dress that she had got from the maid's room, and, at his request, her car keys.

"Djalik, you go out in that and drive off in her car. When you clear the driveway, send your vehicle in. We're going out, and they aren't stopping us. Okay?"

"Got it."

"Your people ready?"

Djalik only nodded. He put on the sacklike dress as if it were something he did all the time. "Want me to take the lady's gun?" he said.

"Not yet." Dukas figured it made her feel better. She was holding it at her side. When Djalik went out, she picked up a handbag and put the gun in it.

"Tell your mother we're going. Is there anything else she wants?"

She looked around the living room. If she saw a life, the years put in with a man, the experience of Africa and other places—Dukas noted Indonesian shadow puppets, Chinese watercolors—she gave no sign that she would miss them.

"Let's go, then."

He heard the car start in the driveway and back out. There was a momentary silence, then a screech as it took off, answered by another as another car followed it. Within seconds, a heavier engine got louder in the driveway, then dropped and purred. Dukas opened the door.

They had to cross twelve feet of gravel to get to the Toyota Land Cruiser. A Caucasian was crouched beside it, gun out in combat position, scanning the top of the wall and the house beyond. On the other side of the car, another man was just visible. Where the driveway met the street, an African was just visible against the lights of the house opposite. His hands were out, moving up and down uncertainly; his head was turning from side to side. *Not one of Harry's. And not sure of what to do now the ball's dropped.*

Dukas led Mrs. Lao out as if he were escorting her to lunch. The boy came close behind. Dukas waited for shots.

His shoulders wanted to hunch. Shot once not very long ago, he hated to have it happen again.

"Get in the car, get in the car," the white man was growling.

The African at the end of the driveway turned and ran.

Dukas put the woman into the car and then the boy. "Let's go."

The two men jumped in and the doors slammed, and the car was moving at the same time. It accelerated backward down the driveway and swung hard to the left, just in time to meet a smaller car that was coming with no lights on. The two men with Dukas both screamed "Go!" and leaned out the side windows with their guns. There was a *smack-thud,* and the smaller car was driven backward, and Dukas's driver shifted and accelerated, and they were tearing along the street, and the smaller car was rocking as the driver tried to start the stalled engine.

"American embassy," Dukas said. He patted Mrs. Lao's hand.

Seattle.

Marvin Helmer's secretary buzzed him. Helmer ignored her; he was still smiling about the death of Ray Suter. He had reviewed his options and had decided that, except for Piat, who was by now in Mongolia or someplace, there was no way, *no way,* anybody was going to pin any of the Sleeping Dog crap on him.

The Teflon cop, he told himself.

Of course, there was Suter's cell phone, and his palm-top, on both of which he might have left some numbers and E-mail addresses. But those would slip off him, too. He'd used electronic dead drops and pass-throughs. *Teflon.*

The secretary buzzed again.

"Yes?"

"Agent Myeroff of the Bureau to see you, sir?"

Helmer frowned. "Does he have an appointment?"

"No, sir, he's very apologetic, really, but he says it's important and it just came up."

"He should have telephoned for an appointment." Helmer wondered what Hoover would have done. Been magnanimous? Why not? "Send him in."

FBI Agent Myeroff was short and a little thick at the waist to be convincing. His hair looked a little unkempt, too, Helmer thought. Helmer was standing behind his desk, frowning, back straight, hands joined in front of his privates. An example to slovens like Myeroff.

Agent Myeroff held up a badge. "Dick Myeroff, FBI."

"Normally, I expect visitors to make an appointment, Agent Myeroff."

"Yes, sir. But this wouldn't wait." Myeroff got a paper from his left-hand, inside jacket pocket. His jacket was unbuttoned and his tie wasn't quite straight. Hoover would have dressed him down, right there.

"Well?" Helmer said.

"Mister Helmer, this is a federal warrant for your arrest." Myeroff smiled, not at all pleasantly. "The charge is criminal conspiracy and abuse of office."

Helmer's frown wavered. The hands joined over his privates got a better grip on each other.

"You have a right to remain silent. You have a right to a lawyer. Anything you say—"

34

USS **Thomas Jefferson.**

"HEY, MAN, GET YOUR GEAR ON!" BRIAN CAMPBELL was bouncing in the ready room while Soleck read the ASW board. Soleck waved a hand and ran down the corridor to the ASW module, with Campbell right behind him. "Hey! Soleck!"

"You got an emitters list, Brian?"

"What?"

"Get a tape? A good one?"

"Huh?"

Soleck pounded off down the port-side passageway. Campbell caught him hovering over the chart table in the ASW module.

"Hey! We just got upgraded from Alert 60 to Alert 30! We're supposed to be in the goddam plane!"

Soleck nodded and frowned, ignoring him. He ran his finger down the last location of the sub on the ASW chart and got a nod from the warrant officer who owned it. Then Soleck stepped through the tall knee knocker to the Combat Information Center. The TAO glared at him. "Aren't you supposed to be on deck?"

Campbell muttered something behind him. Soleck waved nervously and moved into the ASuW module, a brightly lit desk manned by two officers and two enlisted, where they tracked surface contacts. In the harsh blue glare of the JOTS terminal, Soleck looked at the whole picture, with possible contacts labeled *hostile fast mover*. Those would be the cigarette boats. To the south of them was a tramp freighter just out of port in Mombasa, headed north with a load of fuel oil for Mogadishu, and there were other contacts appearing.

"You guys the alert? As soon as you launch, you have *got* to clean up this picture. There's a fair amount of surface haze and no one can pick out the cigarette boats for sure. If they're even out there and the *Esek Hopkins* isn't just seeing her own shadow."

Soleck collected a printout from the JOTS. Then he went down a narrow passageway to a locked door, where he knocked. Campbell was just opening his mouth when the door opened. Soleck held up a colored tag he had around his neck and was allowed in. Campbell was stopped at the entrance.

"Damn it. I'm flying on the same mission."

"Do you have a Top Secret Code Word Clearance?"

"I'm cleared Top Secret for the MARI project."

"Where's your tag?"

"Fuck." Campbell appeared to be searching himself. In fact, he never wore it.

The chief petty officer seemed to consider for a moment, but then Soleck was back in the passageway, shouting, "Thanks, Chief," over his shoulder. He ran right past Campbell and kept running until he reached the parachute rigger's space behind the det's ready room.

Two parachute riggers were waiting with his gear. The moment he entered, they began to put it on him over his flight suit. First he got the nylon webbing harness that would be his parachute harness if the ejection seat fired. Helmet. Comm cord. Nine-millimeter Beretta in holster, small clip folding knife in his right sleeve pocket. Campbell was watching from the passageway, his own helmet under his arm.

"We don't even have backseaters. What kind of mission is this? Why are you wasting time with this crap?"

"Someone needs to do it. If we have to launch, they'll call us. Got a gun?"

"A *what*?" S-3 aviators almost never flew anywhere that required them to carry a gun.

"A gun. Petty Officer Lorenz, get the man a gun."

Campbell raised his arms and the PRs strapped the weapon on his harness.

"You got coffee? Cookies?" Soleck realized he was talking to dispel his nerves.

Campbell just looked at him.

"Okay, okay. We've got to go." He picked up his helmet bag, weighted with publications and kneeboard cards, and started up the ladder to the flight deck. One of the PRs blew his nose.

"Good luck, *th*ir," he slurred.

SOLECK DUCKED INTO HIS SEAT, CHECKED THE spreader pin to make sure that he would have a parachute if all went ill, and then ducked back out the ladder and started around the plane. He checked the sonobuoy load and the chaff/flare mix, and he looked at the fans in the engines and he looked at the hydraulics. It was the fastest walk around of his life. He spent some time on the wheels and he paid attention to the state of the tailhook, which was intact and showed no signs of breaking. Then he gave the tail a slap and smiled anxiously at the gray evening, already on the landing. He wriggled up the steps and into the plane. Campbell had the auxiliaries up. Soleck plugged in his comm cord and buckled his harness to the seat.

"Ready to fly?"

"You worry about your part, I'll take mine."

Soleck turned and looked at Campbell. "What's that supposed to mean?"

"It means, I want to get back without ejecting, and I want you to get this fucking plane off the deck and back on it without making ten passes, Soleck."

Soleck glared back. Anger helped. He refused to let Campbell deflate him. "Okay, Brian. In the meantime, you do your job and don't leave it to me to get your emitters from the EW module, your surface picture, and your ASuW info. You don't have Craw to back you up here. Understand me?"

"Yes."

"Good. I'll worry about my landing when I get to it."

A hesitant intake of breath. "Sorry, man." Still resentful. *Maybe still afraid of Soleck's landings.*

"No problem." To Soleck, anger felt better than the fear. They started to go through the checklist.

"NOW LAUNCH THE ALERT THIRTY. NOW LAUNCH THE ALERT THIRTY."

"That would be us."

Someone passed under the nose and Soleck could feel the minute change in weight as the chocks were removed. He powered the engines up to full. "Ready to go for a ride?" he asked, unconsciously echoing Captain Rafehausen.

"Good to go."

Soleck snapped a salute at the launch officer, and the plane slammed forward down the cat. Ten seconds later they were going for altitude.

"How's the back end?"

"Sweet. MARI will be up in one. ISAR up. We're good."

Soleck turned east and headed for the last reported position of the *Esek Hopkins*.

"Get Alpha Xray on comms." Alpha Xray was the coordinator for surface contacts.

"Got 'em." Campbell switched off to talk and Soleck could see his lips moving. Soleck's screen began to show the datalink, and contacts popped up all over the sea between them and the coast. Still climbing, Soleck used his minimal pilot controls over the MARI to image and tag two contacts while Campbell talked. The contact marked as a white merchant ship in the ASuW module was a dhow. He marked it as such, looked for a bigger banana on surface-search radar and found one, miles farther out to sea than the former contact. He imaged it. Merchant. The big superstructure aft was clear as day.

"No contact on the cigarette boats, if they're even out." Campbell began to target and image every contact on the screen. The sea was still running high, although not enough to move the carrier around. Campbell stopped a moment, listening to some communication from the boat.

"We're going to Emcon Charlie. Admiral thinks that cigarette boats might be targeting our comms once they get close."

Soleck passed over the gator freighter, USS *Yellowjacket*. "Lots of seasick jarheads," he noted. *Yellowjacket* carried the battle group's detachment of Marines and their air support, mostly CH-46 helicopters. He continued to turn east and climb slowly.

"*Esek Hopkins* reports a fast-moving surface contact on radar. I've got it in link."

Soleck looked down at his screen, even as Campbell was trying to image the contact.

"Try ISAR, Brian." Without a second plane, MARI would seldom give a good image of a fast-moving target.

"I can't get a lock with the surface-search. I'll try periscope mode. Got it."

The image was a blob with a tall radar spike at the stern, hardly a clear picture like the one MARI provided, but enough to guess that this was a small, fast boat with a huge engine. Both of them had seen similar images in the Adriatic, hunting smugglers. Campbell called in his confirmation.

The contact was given a neutral symbol, a white square with a dot. Campbell began to search the waters around it.

"*Esek Hopkins* is requesting permission to fire if it enters the battle group's formation." Campbell sounded tense. "Damn! Where are the others?"

Soleck looked at his tiny screen and whipped his head back and forth, trying to keep his instrument scan good while looking for surface contacts and trying to think through the problem. The cigarette boats had to be coming down the coast from the north and then heading at them the shortest possible distance. He wondered again how they were targeting. It *had* to be the submarine they had tagged two days back, which would explain why the boats hadn't got to them in the night. Their targeting was old, the carrier had moved, and the boats were trying to find them. If the carrier had been north two days ago—"Look north," Soleck called.

Soleck turned north, listening for instructions from the tower. They were the only aircraft in the air. The *Jefferson*, now alarmed, was launching two F-18s. The F-18 pilots were as sick as the rest of the aircrew, and Soleck hoped no one was about to blow a sinus and end his career. Soleck ran an emitters check, just letting the ESM equipment show him every electronic signal coming off the water. The battle group was relatively quiet, with Emcon Charlie keeping signals to a minimum. He could see a surface-search radar on the merchant ship, and he quickly logged it in the link. That would prevent future mis-ID.

Out to the northwest, ahead of the battle group, was a small, anomalous signal in a radio frequency. Soleck tracked it with radar, using the periscope mode that had worked for Campbell. He got a hit, a small hit, and imaged it with ISAR.

"Bingo. Brian, look at that."

AHMED FAZRAHI WAS TIRED, WET, COLD, AND ANGRY. The fatigue, wet, and cold were all the results of three days spent continuously on the water, looking for the American ships. It seemed like a remarkable coincidence that the Iranian men who had sent him on this mission should lose their ability to track the Americans just a day before they had to launch the mission. Because of the lost targeting, he and his men had spent days tracking the American battle group, strung out in a line forty miles long and using satellite cell phones provided by the smooth Colonel Namjee to communicate. They had a radio direction finder to try and find their prey. It was nerve-racking, dangerous work, and one of their boats had vanished in the storm. Twice they had had to put in to harbors on the Kenyan coast for fuel and food.

No one complained. The younger men prayed to Allah or simply stared into the endless sea. The older men made jokes or talked about normal things. The market. Funny people from their villages. Fazrahi listened, but he was silent. The anger grew. He knew he was being used. As long as Americans died, he didn't care who used him. But the lack of targeting made the mission almost impossible, and he thought he and his boats would be dead if they were discovered. For nothing.

The big powerboat slammed over a wave and he kept his hand light on the wheel, ready to respond to her tendency to yaw at the crest. And then, just for a second at the top of the giant wave, he saw a low gray dagger shape off to the south. A warship, pale gray on the dark gray of the horizon. Not his target, but surely a picket ship for the target. He raised his cell phone to his lips and used his thumb to hit the call button.

"Close in on me. Full power! I have the enemy in sight." He drove the boat forward, powering through the trough of the great waves. "Go for the carrier's stern. If you can't hit that, go for the big ship with the Marines, the one that looks like a smaller carrier. Acknowledge."

Three boats responded.

CAMPBELL PUT THE NEW CONTACT IN THE LINK and tried to pass it to Alpha Xray on the ship. Both of them were trying to do the work of two men and they had never had a chance to run the postlaunch checklist.

"Got another, north of the first," Brian said.

"Tell Alpha Xray they're spread in a search line over thirty miles of sea."

"Contact Two is turning in."

"Contact One is increasing speed." That in a tinny voice from *Esek Hopkins*.

"Okay, Brian. Get us our engagement rules."

"Roger. *Hopkins* is asking the same. F-18s are two minutes to launch."

One minute too late, Soleck thought. He made his decision and turned north, leaving Hostile One to the *Esek Hopkins*. They had a 76mm radar-guided deck gun that ought to be crushingly effective against a fiberglass boat. He put the nose down and pushed the throttle past military and down to max. The twin turbofans roared.

"Contact Three has gone to seventy knots and turned south."

"Contact One has entered the formation. She's passing *Hopkins*."

Going for the carrier? Contact One was emitting constantly now on a radio frequency. Somewhere in the battle group, someone was trying to talk to her. Maybe she would turn.

"Contact One is two minutes from *Yellowjacket*." Someone on the *Hopkins* was on the ball.

Campbell labeled a new contact "Contact Four," just north and west of the formation and already coming south and east. Soleck now had the rooster tails of Contact Two in visual sight, and he began to dump speed, easing the throttle back and using his flaps and his attitude. It was a very pretty piece of flying, if he had to say so himself. He turned hard to the east, almost crossing the cigarette boat's stern, and then ran up her wake. He was trying to frighten her off. She didn't change her course.

"Alpha Xray, this is Alpha Hotel One-Zero-One," Soleck called. "Contact Two is still on course."

"All units, this is Alpha Xray, over. Weapons free. Repeat, weapons free." On the screen, Contacts One through Four blinked from squares to red diamonds. "Contact are designated hostile. Repeat, contacts are designated hostile. *Esek Hopkins* will engage Hostile One. Alpha Hotel One-Zero-One, can you engage Hostile Two, over?"

Soleck finished his turn, having flown through one hundred and eighty degrees on a wingtip, only meters above the wave crests. He was looking at the stern of the little boat, less than a mile away.

"Engaging."

He had to find a balance between too much speed, which would ruin his shot, and too little speed, so that he wouldn't catch his target in time. He could see the big gray shape of the carrier through the haze ahead of the cigarette boats.

"F-18s are launching."

The S-3 doesn't have a bombsite, and shooting unguided rockets requires a steady hand, practice, and a lot of luck. Soleck ran off most of the mile of separation. He was dead astern. He could see a man on the boat. If they turned, he'd lose his shot.

"*Esek Hopkins* is firing."

He pushed the throttle back down and used his flaps to slow until he was barely moving relative to the boat, like a hawk swooping on its prey. Four hundred meters. A man on the stern raised something to his shoulder and fired. Soleck hoped it wasn't a missile.

"Weapons hot," called Campbell.

He fired his whole left pod, every rocket in succession. He'd never have another chance.

The plane moved as they rippled away. The first struck just to the right and the second a little farther to the right. He touched the stick, trying not to overcompensate, and his aim point drifted over the boat just as the rocket's force caused it to deviate from its course. The third hit right in the crew compartment, and the fourth disappeared into a secondary explosion.

"Hostile Two destroyed." He pulled them up and hard to port, turning to look for the other two boats. Campbell dropped chaff and flares in case the boat had shot a MAN-PAD, a man-portable air defense missile. He managed to get his chaff/flare combination going and use his screen while communicating. It was as if he had three hands. "Hostile One destroyed. *Hopkins* shot her."

Soleck and Campbell were leaning forward now, trying to find Hostile Three in the haze. Soleck looked down on the screen. Somebody's radar was still tracking Hostile Three. He pulled farther to port.

An F-18 flashed by under his wing, only a few meters away.

"Fuck!" Campbell shouted, slamming back in his seat. "Where's his wingman?"

Soleck saw the second F-18 firing something under his wing at a point off to the west.

"Hostile Four destroyed."

Where's Hostile Three? Soleck was still turning. The haze was thicker here, as if there were a low-lying cloud right in front of the battle group. He saw the F-18 come out of the haze, very low and climbing. Soleck steadied his turn into a very slight descent and waited. If Hostile Three was still in the game, she'd come out of the haze right—

—there. He gave himself an "A" for situational awareness. Now he was broadside on to a target moving at sixty knots and he had four rockets left. This was going to be the deflection shot from hell.

Hostile Three was turning a little to port. She was planning to bypass the carrier. She was going for the *Yellowjacket* and two thousand Marines.

AHMED FAZRAHI WATCHED HIS MEN DIE. HE HAD never expected more of them than this, that they die bravely, pushing their boats at the foe. He hated the Americans for the casual way their superior technology, their planes and their guns, swatted at his boats until the other three were just plumes of dirty black smoke on the water.

There was nothing he could do to make it better. With targeting, he might have hit the enemy in the dark, which he had thought was their best chance when they were training. Now he had one boat and he elected to go for the nearest target, a small carrier. A "Marine Landing Ship." He remembered it from the recognition cards in training.

"*Allahu Akbar!*" he shouted at the wind and shoved the throttle all the way forward.

THE *YELLOWJACKET* WAS HUGE IN SOLECK'S WIND-screen. On the deck, someone was firing a thirty-millimeter grenade launcher. It made tiny white puffs and the shells made an inferno of explosions in Hostile Three's wake. Soleck changed his lineup so that all his shots would go wide of the gator freighter if he missed his target. The grenade launcher kept firing and something else was coming in, probably deck guns from somewhere else in the formation. It occurred to him that he was in danger from friendly fire.

The cigarette boat staggered a moment and then drove on. *Fort Klock* had turned out of her place in the formation and her bows appeared with a huge wave as she drove toward her target, her deck gun firing. Hostile Three was definitely slowing. Soleck got his wings level and fired.

Whoosh.

Way off, far astern.

Whoosh, whoosh. Overshot ahead and then closer.

Whoosh.

Hostile Three blew up in a spectacular explosion that rocked Soleck in his plane and showered the flight deck of the *Jefferson* and the *Yellowjacket* with debris. Everyone claimed the kill later. There was no way of saying whose shell or rocket hit the cigarette boat as she made her final run at her own target. But Campbell and Soleck were always sure it had been theirs, and so was the rest of the S-3 community.

Campbell reached over and slapped his back.

"Shit hot!"

Soleck grinned at him and turned east for the coast.

"Hey!" Campbell looked over at him, tension still leaving little white lines around his mouth. "Hey! Where do you think you're going?"

Soleck was looking north and south. "Ask Alpha Xray if they think there were only four contacts. We need to be released for our mission. We're late."

"We're what? What mission?"

"Did you read the classified mission briefing I handed you?"

Campbell looked contrite.

"No wonder you asked why you were wearing a gun, Brian. We're going in over the coast to pick somebody up. Spook stuff."

"No shit."

Behind them, the sun started its final descent toward the deck.

South Coast of Kenya.

The Cessna was heavy with passengers, and the fuel had gone from marginal to critical in the last half-hour. Alan kept the plane flying right along the coast road once he was safe in Kenya's airspace, ready to land the moment his engine coughed. By his calculations, Mike's roadside field was only a few miles farther along. He let the plane sink lower.

Lao was silent, withdrawn. Harry was sitting next to Alan in front, equally silent, and Alan wondered if he was thinking about the last time they had landed on a road in Africa. Alan was past exhaustion, into some new place where his mind worked but his body responded very slowly to new stimuli. He was flying almost exclusively with his right hand, because every movement hurt the left. He rested it on the yoke for balance, but he no longer trusted its grip.

The terrain was getting dark under his wings. He wondered if he'd be able to see to land. They had to get down soon. At one level, he was confident in his GPS and his instruments, but he wanted to be there. It would be bad if the S-3 beat them to the road.

He looked down again, saw the bulk of Shimoni Island against the darkening sky, and matched what he saw to his map. The GPS beeped.

He was there.

He flew down the strip, passed it by a mile and turned back to minimize the crosswind that was coming straight off the sea. The plane, though heavy, seemed fine. The fuel gauge said empty, but he probably had gallons of reserve and he couldn't spare time to worry. He used his flaps to slow and fought the breeze off the sea until the plane was settling on the road almost diagonal to the pavement. A gust from the sea hit him and moved him off center and he put both hands on the yoke to steady up, almost flinching from the pain in his maimed left hand as he gripped with it. And then the wheels touched and they were down, suddenly changing from slow flight over a calm landscape to a very fast drive down a narrow road in a vehicle that wanted to blow right off with every gust. Alan rocked them back and forth, dodging potholes and fighting the sea breeze until they stopped, then taxied them right off the road and into a rocky field with some cassava, where the wheels began to sink into the thin soil. He didn't care. The plane's work was done.

"That concludes your chartered safari," he said. Triffler already had his door open and was out on the field. Alan thought he might kiss the ground. Harry was slower, but he was the first into the storage compartment. Alan killed the engine, and suddenly the night was quiet. He looked at his watch for the millionth time that day.

"Maybe thirty minutes. We need lights."

Triffler flourished a bag of metal coffee cans and a jerry can of fuel.

"I'll see if I can tap what's left in the reserve," Alan said. He got another gas can and opened a wing panel.

Harry was already chopping brush, and Lao simply sat in the plane, watching them.

Alan was running on empty, but he kept at it, got the can filled, and followed Triffler around, filling the old coffee cans with aviation fuel. Then they ripped Alan's khaki shirt up for wicks while Harry continued to pile brush for a bonfire at the start of the runway section of the road. Local people began to appear out of the dusk, first two young boys and then an older man. Alan could hear Harry talking to them.

"Got any Kenyan shillings?" Harry called to Alan. Alan trotted over and gave Harry a wad of local bills. He overheard Harry telling the local man that they were with the Kenyan Air Force. The man laughed. It was like Jim's laugh in Nairobi, the pan-African polite laugh of disbelief. Alan ran back to the plane and got the signal pistol. Then he trotted back to Harry.

"If they want to help, get one of them to stand by every coffee can. When I fire the flare, they can light the wicks. Somebody needs to keep the road clear of traffic."

There turned out to be no lack of willing hands. Just a lack of lighters. Finally, when Alan and Harry and Triffler had all passed theirs out, Lao contributed one.

"I thought America was all high-tech," he said quietly.

A boy ran up with four bottles of Coke. Alan laughed, too loudly, fatigue and a little insanity mixed.

"He asked if we wanted them," Harry said.

Alan popped the top off his bottle while he scanned the sky. They stood in a little clump in the falling dark, Africans and Americans and one lone Chinese. Alan drank off half his

Coke and handed the rest to the tall man standing next to him, who nodded his thanks and finished the bottle. Alan pulled a pack of cigarettes from his pocket and came to a decision. He handed them around until they were all gone. Then he crumpled the pack in his hand and stuffed it in his pack.

They all watched the sky. Triffler took Lao back to the Cessna and sat him in it.

Alan heard the engine noise first, a low hum well out to sea that quickly resolved itself into the familiar vacuum-cleaner noise of the S-3. He checked the cartridge in the flare pistol and, as if that itself were a signal, the local people trotted off into the near dark. In the west, the last of the sunset made a brilliant line of pinks and reds.

He could see the plane. A wind gust caught at the dust of the cassava field and it swirled around him so that he had to turn his head, and he thanked God that it was Rafe coming to land in the crosswind. The landing had been one of the hardest he'd done.

He raised the pistol and fired, and the flare arced high and ignited in a brilliant spark that brought a shout of approval from the locals. Alan forced himself to run to the Cessna and turned on its lights to mark the end of the runway, and all along the edge he saw Triffler's makeshift can-lights flame into action. He looked back at Lao, who was silent, immobile. Then he watched the S-3 as it made its approach slipping crab-wise toward the makeshift runway as some of the coffee cans blew out. The S-3 was whispering along, throttles low, and he watched a gust pick it up and move it, but the S-3 was heavier than the Cessna and the pilot got his correction in time to put the plane on the tarmac in a three-point landing, far more elegant than what Alan had managed.

Alan took Lao by the arm and started to run for the plane. In a moment, it was turning around at the end of the road, lit by the dying headlamps on the Cessna, and Harry and Triffler appeared out of the dark. Alan got the safety hatch open and pushed his head up inside the cockpit. He had a moment of shock when he saw that the face under the pilot's helmet wasn't Rafe's. The landing had been *all* Rafe.

"Soleck!"

"Sir. Hope we aren't late." Soleck spoke with a smile, as if he were bursting to say something.

Alan raised his hand. "We've got to get out of here. Ah, Mister Campbell. Please get this gentleman belted in. You brought a spare harness? Too big. Do your best." He backed out of the well and pushed Lao up into the plane. Back on the road, he began to climb into his own familiar harness, so much better-fitting than the one he had worn at Whidbey Island. It felt like home.

He pulled the top over his shoulder and zipped the front.

"We've got to find another way of getting some quiet time," he said to Harry, and hugged him. Harry embraced him strongly.

"Soon, Alan."

Alan didn't know if Triffler would want to be hugged, but Triffler was there ahead of him.

"We did it," was all Triffler said.

"What about the plane?" Harry asked.

"Mike's problem. I'm out of it. Ask the locals to call it in." Alan smiled at the two of them. "You guys going to be all right?"

Harry nodded. Triffler looked at Harry. Alan gave them a tired salute and crawled back into the tunnel and then right up into the Tacco seat. He checked Lao's harness and then pulled the hatch closed, settled into his seat, and clipped his own harness. His helmet rested under the seat.

"Do you get airsick, Colonel?"

"Not that I know of. Where are we going?"

Alan let that go and pulled on his helmet. *His* helmet.

Alan plugged in his comm cord to his helmet. He hit PTT (push to talk) on his cockpit display. "Let's go," he said.

They started to move. Lao, odd-looking in a borrowed flight helmet, tried to get Alan's attention. He pointed at Alan's helmet, with his name emblazoned in reflective tape.

"*You're* Alan Craik," he shouted, and started to laugh. Alan didn't get it.

They bumped down the road, and then the ride was smooth and they were in the air. In the front, Campbell switched his intercom to FRONT SEAT ONLY and looked at Soleck. When they were less than eighty miles from the boat, he asked, "You okay to land?"

Soleck laughed. "After this flight?"

Campbell called their ETA and got a radial for approach. The battle group was on full alert. They had a limited combat air patrol up and an engagement zone set around the carrier. They were ready for a second attack. Soleck wondered where the aircrews were coming from. The air wing would be flying any qualified pilot; men and women on tours as fuels officers with the ship would find themselves in a cockpit if their sinuses were clear.

"I'm serious."

"So am I. What the fuck—" Soleck felt the fear grab at him again, this time injected by Campbell. He'd been *fine* until *someone* had to remind him—

"Open mike." *Al Craik.* Soleck suddenly realized that he had his commander on board and that he had just heard Soleck's fear and Campbell's doubts.

"Sorry, sir."

"You still having landing problems, Mister Soleck?"

"Yes, sir."

Alan laughed in the back. It was a rich, free laugh, the laugh of a man who has been under tension for a long time and is now free of it. "Mister Soleck, I want to get back to the boat ASAP with Mister Lao and get some sleep. I don't want to worry about a landing. Do you get me?"

"Yes, sir."

"See to it, then."

Twenty miles out.

Soleck took a deep breath and turned for his radial. He wasn't going to fuck this up. He was going to be good, and lucky, and get the wire just right. He'd shot the cigarette boats; that had required skill and luck.

He started doing the pre-landing checklist.

THE LSO WAS HAVING A BUSY DAY, AND HE SNEEZED and wheezed his way through landing F-18s flown by guys who hadn't seen a deck in three or four months. It was crazy, because they were flying pilots who weren't in flying billets this tour. He had to make some hard calls. His temper was frayed and his nerves weren't all that good.

He brought an EA-6B down, gave him a late power call, and then gave him a no-grade, the worst thing that a pilot could get from an LSO, short of a crash. It wasn't a fair call, but the LSO's temper got worse with every landing.

"Dickhead," he muttered. He pulled a wad of dirty Kleenex from his flight suit and blew his nose into the sodden mass. Behind him, two junior LSOs tried to hide from the rain in the shelter of the deck edge. They were all wet. No one could get a cigarette to light.

"FAG in the break," one of them called to him. He looked up, watched the F-18 break. Sad. The hottest airplane in the world, and that was the guy's best break? Then the guy was low in his downwind and slow into the groove.

"Call the ball."

The F-18 called it, with fuel and weight. Somewhere else, another officer with an equally runny nose checked her clipboard and yelled at her chief to get the tension set for an F-18 on the arresting gear. The plane itself dropped toward the deck, his angle of attack excellent but his wings wobbling with overcorrecting.

The LSO cursed. The F-18 added power when he should have kept his hand still on the throttle and boltered, missing the wires by five feet and thundering off the deck in a shower of sparks. The deck left twilight behind and entered full dark.

The LSO pounded his fist into the steel side of the ship and hurt it. "For the love of Christ!" he bellowed. "Can't anybody land a fucking plane?" He looked at his watch, which shone red in his deck light. Ten more minutes on duty.

He watched the F-18 climb out of his bolter. "Send him around again," he said into his mike. "Who else is in the stack?"

"S-3 waiting. Last plane this event."

The LSO groaned, knowing full well who was in the S-3. He thought for a moment about "flogging the glass" and handing over the LSO watch to his relief before the S-3 landed. His relief was standing behind him already, staring out into the night and already soaked to the skin. But the LSO had a keen sense of honor, and he knew he was the better LSO. He didn't shirk.

"Okay. Give me the bolter again and then we'll get to the S-3."

He watched the guy come around again, still low in the downwind, still flat in the groove.

"Steady up," he said quietly. He tried to sound encouraging. The guy's wings rocked back and forth like a bird's. It was a dirty night, and the deck was pitching, and this poor bastard probably hadn't looked at a deck this tour.

"Good lineup," he said. He didn't usually say things like *good lineup*, but this was the time for encouragement. Somewhere in the back of his mind, he thought, *I'm practicing for the S-3.*

Not great, but steady into the deck and two wire. Too short, too far left, too wobbly. "Two wire and no grade," he called to his assistant, who wrote it out in grease pencil. His relief muttered.

"What?" he yelled at her. "What?"

"You tell him he's good for lineup and then give him a no-grade?"

"I told him he was good for lineup, to stop him from fucking with his stick. His landing sucked."

Rather than arguing, she nodded. "Yeh. Yeh, it did." She smiled. "Learn something every day."

He turned back to the night. Women as LSOs? The world was coming to an end.

"S-3 is next," his assistant called. "Are we taking it or turning over?"

"We'll take it," the LSO called. His assistant and his petty officer both groaned. A bad pilot could extend them on deck by thirty minutes or more, missing landings, getting fuel. You don't switch LSOs in mid-landing. No one said the name aloud, but everyone knew who was in that plane.

"Jus' get Tholeck on deck," Stevens said from the tower. He had a cold from hell. He also sounded resigned and angry all at once.

• • •

"WE'RE NEXT TO LAND," SOLECK CALLED FROM THE front. "Everybody ready?"

Alan unclipped his harness, leaned over the aisle, and checked Lao. Lao looked glassy-eyed and a little airsick. His skin was gray. Alan smiled at him. He felt on top again. Lao represented a major victory, one that would be felt for a long time. He tugged sharply on Lao's harness and then sat back and belted in to his own. In his ear, he could hear the tower flower coaching Soleck. It wasn't bad advice, just stuff calculated to send a calm pilot over the edge.

". . . and watch the set of your flaps on the downwind. You know the drill. . . ."

Alan listened for a moment, anger rising. Soleck was as ready to land as he ever would be. Soleck was a trained pilot. Alan didn't hear Stevens giving advice, he heard Stevens trying to avoid responsibility for Soleck's failure. Alan hit PTT (push to talk).

"Break. Tower, this is Alpha Hotel One-Zero-One."

"Roger, Wud-Thero-Wud." Sounded like Stevens, even through the cold.

"Paul, shut up." Alan disengaged PTT. He hit INTERCOM. "Just land the plane, Mister Soleck. Wake me up when we get there."

Soleck smiled so wide that his cheeks hurt. "Everybody ready?"

Campbell and Craik both responded.

"Let's rock," said Soleck.

"S-3 IN THE BREAK," CALLED HIS ASSISTANT. THE LSO knew it. He'd watched the plane's lights, listened to the exchange between the tower and the plane, smiled when someone told the tower to shut up. He agreed. Soleck sucked, but he didn't need to be babied. He needed to make a good landing. He needed confidence.

He sure did suck, though. The LSO thought of his last few landings.

"Here we go."

The S-3 rotated from horizontal to vertical in one quick motion and went to full power in a turn right over the bridge of the ship. The timing of the break and the smartness of the rotation and the turn made it an excellent break. Soleck was great at the break.

"Shit hot in the break," the LSO said. Ordinarily, he would have been too busy with other planes to watch the whole downwind leg, but Soleck was the last plane in the event. He watched as Soleck dumped speed and altitude toward his turn into the groove.

"On the numbers at the stern," he called. He was smiling a little.

A mile away, Soleck turned into the groove. All over the boat, sailors watching the Plat camera from boredom or interest saw the first twinkle of Soleck's landing lights. He was thirty seconds from the deck.

"Call the ball."

"Roger, ball."

Their wires were already set.

His angle of attack was good. Not great, and there were two little hiccups right out at the start of the turn, when he was correcting something. A little rough.

Don't fall apart. Just like that. JUST LIKE THAT.

Ten seconds from the deck. Down in the ship, on the TVs that blared in every berthing area, Soleck's lights filled the screen. In the ready rooms, men and women covered their ears.

Good for lineup. He looked good. The LSO's heart was in his throat. He wanted to say something. He didn't.

The roar and flash of light from the landing S-3 went by and he clapped his hands together in glee.

"Three wire and *okay*!" he shouted.

He slapped the female LSO on the back. "All yours, bud!"

HARRY AND TRIFFLER HAD WATCHED THE LIGHTS OF the plane until they disappeared into the dusk. Then they took a few minutes to disperse the locals, paying each of them a few dollars and thanking them. You never knew when you'd pass this way again.

Triffler had felt good, the kind of happy fatigue he got after a long run. He had just extinguished the last of the runway lights. The Africans were gone.

"What do we do now?" he asked Harry. He'd just realized they had no transport.

"We're two black guys in Africa, man. What d'you think we do?" He put his arm around Triffler's shoulders. "We walk."

Coda

Washington.

"I WANT TO BE A SPECIAL AGENT, JUST LIKE YOU."

Leslie had developed a look of almost-religious adoration that she turned on Dukas like a spotlight every time she saw him now. Back for one week, with Lao and his family parked at Pax River, Dukas thought that all his office needed was incense and a few candles for him to feel like a plaster saint.

"You *don't* want to be just like me. For one thing, I don't look good in a dress."

"You're my role model."

That seemed to clinch it for her—if she could use a cliché, it must be true.

Leslie was holding enough textbooks against her front to cover her from thighs to throat. She had just announced that she was starting night classes in criminal justice and wanted to get her degree so that she could, yes, be a special agent just like Dukas.

"What does your boyfriend say?"

"What boyfriend?" she laughed. *Oh. So it's like that.* Dukas growled that they had work to do, and she backed away from his desk, grinning, hugging her books, adoring. She wasn't using Triffler's desk anymore because Triffler was there, but she'd been put in a cubicle two doors down to help with the transfers of Sleeping Dog and Crystal Insight. She looked back at him, balancing the books, and giggled again. When she was gone, he could hear Triffler laughing.

"Not funny," Dukas said.

"It is to me."

"Keep that up, you'll be back in Seattle."

"No, I won't. Kasser said I can have anything I want; I said I want only one thing, and that's not to work for the now-famous and much-decorated Michael Dukas. So I'm being given the intelligence medal and three weeks in beautiful Egypt as a member of the Bright Star team, and you can kiss my pinkie."

"Yours isn't a pinkie; it's a brownie."

"Racist." Triffler came to the end of the wall of crates and lounged against it. He was wearing a glen plaid suit, gray-blue with a minuscule red stripe, a blue shirt with a white collar, a thick silk tie of swirling clarets, and brown wingtips. "Free at last," he said with a smile, "free at last."

"You'll miss me when you're gone."

"I'll learn to live with the heartache." He came a couple of steps closer. "Actually, what you pulled off with Lao and Bobby Li has me kind of dazzled. Kasser, too. I guess you can have anything you want now, right?"

Dukas shrugged. "What I want is to lose twenty pounds and still eat all the Dunkin' Donuts I can hold." He stretched his arms and didn't wince at the small residual pain in his chest. "Actually, getting rid of my rabbit rig is enough." He was afraid that Triffler was going to say something else nice, so he changed the subject. "Al Craik'll be in this morning. He's in town to testify for Sleeping Dog. You know they arrested Helmer?"

"I know it second-hand. Menzes. He thinks Helmer got Piat to waste Ray Suter, but the Bureau won't let him interview Helmer. You think Piat did it?"

Dukas shrugged again. Piat was a painful memory to him,

partly because of Sally, partly because he'd got away when Dukas was responsible for him. "I don't know what they got. Agency's very tight-assed about the whole thing."

"But Piat was for sure in it with Helmer—trying to get something on you and Craik."

"Yeah, but how do you tie them to Suter? The guy gets killed while he's in Agency custody, at a fucking Agency safe house, and the only explanation is that he was involved in a scam *from their safe house*? No matter where they turn, they look like shit. So they're saying nothing."

"Menzes is pissed."

"Not the first time."

Triffler sat in the visitor's chair and dusted one wingtip with a handkerchief. "Thanks for recommending me to head up the Seattle thing, anyway."

"You could have made your career on it. Whoever runs Sleeping Dog to the end will be able to write his own ticket."

Triffler licked the handkerchief and removed a spot visible only to him. "My boy's going to make first team this year. Can't pull him out and throw him into a new school three thousand miles away, Mike. These things are important."

"I hope you won't be sorry."

"I won't."

"I would."

"Yeah, but you'd have Leslie to comfort you."

"Oh, Goddamit—" Dukas was halfway to his feet. He slowed, stood with his knuckles on the desk as Alan Craik walked in. Craik looked from one man to the other, grinned, and said, "You two guys squabbling again?"

Triffler stood. "I do not squabble." He and Craik shook hands, and Triffler excused himself and left the office. Looking after him, Alan said, "He figures we want privacy. Nice guy." He looked at Dukas. "You know Harry O'Neill offered him a job? Twice what he makes here?"

"His kid's going to make the first team. They don't play football at Bahrain High." He waved at the chair.

"I hear you walk on water," Alan said. "It's all over the Navy. 'The biggest intelligence coup in a decade.' "

"Yeah, completely forgetting about us bringing back

George Shreed. Which everybody wants to do—forget, I mean. Win a few, lose a few. How's Rose?"

"Just checking into our motel, I hope."

"I won't ask you to have dinner with me, then. Say hello for me." Dukas left a gap for Alan to say something, and he didn't, and then there it was: Dukas was going to be alone, and what the hell good was it to have pulled off the biggest intelligence coup of the decade if the only way you knew to celebrate was to give a party for yourself and a bottle of Wild Turkey? "I got things to do, anyway," Dukas said lamely.

"I'm back to the boat tomorrow," Alan said. "I dotted the i's on Sleeping Dog, gave somebody a deposition on Helmer." He, too, must have understood about Dukas's being alone, because he said, "Anything on who killed Sally Baranowski?"

Dukas shook his head.

"Maybe you ought to—"

He didn't finish, although Dukas was sure he was going to say either *take some time off* or *get yourself a girl*. Instead, Leslie came in, this time without the books but with a bundle of mail. She was wearing a tailored blouse in a color like the inside of an egg cream, bitter-chocolate slacks, and a scarf whose ends hung down between her substantial breasts. She stood quite close to Alan and smiled down at him and said in her little-girl voice, "Hi." She looked at Dukas. "You want anything?" Her eyes were bright, her lips parted.

Dukas was leafing through the mail. Halfway down was a postcard. A postcard was an oddity, at best. This one was even odder—an old one from the 1950s in bright colors that made it look as if it had been computer-generated, and a texture like fine linen. A big green cactus stood in yellow sand in front of an aluminum-sided diner that looked more blue than silver. Above it was a sign in what was supposed to be red neon: JERRY'S EATS AND GAS.

Dukas turned it over. It had been mailed in Macao a week before. There was no signature, but there was a scrawled message that said, "I didn't know she was your girl."

Dukas tapped it on his lower teeth and then dropped it in the wastebasket.

"Junk mail," he said.

Alan looked at Leslie, apparently saw something in her face, because he smiled. When she had left the office, he said, "Just when I start to worry about you, I see that everything's going to be fine. Everything'll be great."

"She's a kid." He tried to stare down Alan's smile. "I don't do kids."

Alan went right on smiling. "In this case, I don't think you have anything to say about it."

GORDON KENT is the pseudonym of a father-and-son writing team, who both have extensive personal experience in the U.S. Navy and are former intelligence officers. The son earned his Observer Wings in S-3 Vikings and left active duty in 1999. They share interests in history, fishing, and Africa, where they have spent considerable time, in and out of military service. Both live in the United States.

Read on for an excerpt of
Gordon Kent's next global thriller
featuring power couple
Alan Craik and Rose Siciliano ...

FORCE PROTECTION

coming from Delacorte Press
in August 2004!

FORCE PROTECTION

GORDON KENT

Author of *Hostile Contact*

FORCE PROTECTION
On sale August 31, 2004

THE OLD BULL ELEPHANT STAMPED.

The matriarch let the stripped acacia branch drop at her feet and turned her head a little. The bull stamped again, snorted. She took a step toward him and then looked down at her calf, unsure. He stamped again.

All through their band, heads came up.

The old bull's ears shot forward, full display, and he stamped louder, and trumpeted. There was a noise now, a noise they all knew, and the alien metal smell. *Too close,* the old bull was saying. She turned away, her calf at her side, and began to move along the nearly dry watercourse, away from the noise. She was the matriarch, and the others followed her lead. She moved quickly, easily, fitting her bulk between trees, or just knocking older wood down. She wanted to get into deeper cover first, while the bull did his job.

Braaat. A noise like a tree being torn out of the ground right beside her. She whirled and her calf was gone. She started to go back. She could smell her own fear and that of her sisters all around her. Her calf was kneeling at the base of a tree, slumping down slowly, and she knew he was done. She keened a little, and *Braaat* sounded again. Something punched her in the head and stung her ear and she bellowed her pain. One of her sisters stumbled, fell, didn't rise. The ripping noises were all around her, everywhere, and she watched another, younger bull go down heavily, his feet thrashing and tearing at the dry earth even as he gave his death cry. All their shrieks tore the air, audible for miles, the message clear to other elephants. *Panic and death.*

Angry and afraid, she whirled her bulk back and forth, looking for her assailants, looking for the predator killing her family. She hated with a wild hate, and called, standing over her dead calf, until the *braaat* finished her, too.

HE WAS A BIG, CONFIDENT WHITE MAN WITH A sneering smile. His black soldiers feared him. He walked through the carnage, his "boys" already cutting the ivory and in two cases taking the hides. Younger men were cutting the tails for bracelets. He shook his head at the two dead calves.

"That's a waste of ammunition," he said to a young black man, his own South African accent plain. "No reason to shoot 'em. Nothing on 'em worth taking back." He made "back" sound like "beck." The boy nodded, his eyes still wide from shooting the elephants. The South African thought that killing elephants was an excellent way to train his men. He walked back to the big truck that they had come in to lay their ambush hours before, took a long drink of water to wash the red dust from his throat, and reached for the cell phone on the seat.

SIXTY MILES DOWN THE COAST OF KENYA, IN THE small city of Malindi, a man also reached for his cell phone. He was dark with sun but not African—Mediterranean, rather, perhaps Maltese or even Spanish. His English was accented but clear, slightly Americanized. He was a small man, not quite middle-aged, muscular. He was sitting in the well of a thirty-foot power boat in the Malindi marina, sipping Byrrh and looking at a handsome black woman in a thong.

"Uh," he said into the phone.

"This is Cousin Eddie."

He knew the voice and the South African accent. A prick, but a necessary prick, was his view. "Uh," he said again. The topless woman was lying on the deck of the next boat over. Her nipples pointed skyward like little antiaircraft guns, he thought. He'd had experience of antiaircraft guns.

"We got eleven nice pianos." "Pianos" were elephants (because piano keys used to be made from elephant ivory).

"Send them down. Everything okay? The kids, they're okay?" The "kids" were fifty adult mercenaries, mostly Rwandan Hutus.

"Kids are fine. They're playing every day."

"Ready for the celebration?"

"Can't wait! Everything going nicely."

"I sent you three new kids with toy boats."

"Yeah, got here last night. Very eager."

The man in Malindi thought that for what he was paying, they should have been very eager indeed, but he didn't say anything about that. Instead, he said that the kids should be kept busy with their toy boats, and he didn't want anything to go wrong at the celebration, was that perfectly clear? The South African at the other end said that was perfectly clear, in the voice that men use to show that they don't take shit from anybody, to which the man in Malindi responded by grunting and shutting down his cell phone and watching the topless woman grease herself with lotion. Then he turned the phone back on and put in a call that went by way of a pass-through in Indonesia to a number in Sicily.

CARMINE SANTANGELO-FUGOSI WAS THE SON OF A small-time smuggler who had been born in a mountain village and who now lived in an eighteenth-century palace that had been built by the family that had once ruled this part of Sicily. The head of the family had been called "Count;" that had lasted almost until Carmine's father had been a young man. Now Carmine lived there, and people showed him even more reverence than they had shown the counts, and they called him *Don*.

He was tall for a Sicilian, slightly stooped, fifty, a solidly built man with thick features and a head of graying hair that he left long because he was trying to hide pattern baldness. He wore a collarless white shirt and pleated trousers and felt slippers, and from time to time he spat on the floor of his own terrace, big gobs, to show he was a peasant and came from peasants.

"This is very nice," a small Lebanese man said in French from the shade of an umbrella, ignoring the spit. The umbrella was fixed in a cast-iron table with a glass top and rather too much filigree work in the legs—more of Carmine's peasant taste—and matched by the chairs around it. The Lebanese wore sunglasses and a weary-looking cotton suit the color of muddy water. With him at the table was an almost pretty man who translated the French into Italian for Carmine Santangelo-Fugosi.

Carmine looked around at his terrace, his eighteenth-century palazzo, his flowers and his French doors and his tiled floors. Of course it was *nice*. Carmine was a fucking billionaire—what did he expect? "I don't want any shit from Hizbollah," Carmine said.

The Lebanese made a gesture that indicated that shit was something that Hizbollah would never in a million years give him. He said in French that none of this would ever get back to Hizbollah and that if it ever did, he, the Lebanese, swore on his mother's grave—he was a Christian—that he would kill himself.

Carmine looked at him as the translation came and said, "Tell him that if Hizbollah finds out, he'll wish he'd killed himself today."

Then Carmine's cell phone went off and he turned away, the phone at his ear, and walked to the edge of his terrace, where a balustrade separated him from the twenty-meter drop to the town below. Down there was a street, a café, roofs, and then the port and the Mediterranean, sparkling away to Africa.

"And?" he said into the phone when the man in Malindi had finished his report. Carmine kept his voice low and his back turned to the table, which, because the terrace was so big, was too far away for anybody to have heard him, anyway. Plus the Lebanese wasn't supposed to understand Italian, but

Carmine never trusted things like that. People lied about themselves all the time. He leaned on the balustrade and carried on his side of the conversation in grunts and monosyllables, turning slowly to look around the terrace. Two other men were there, one at each doorway, arms folded, impassive, both the children of his father's relatives. Both armed.

"So," he said. He covered the phone with his other hand so he could look at the Lebanese while he talked. The Lebanese was getting a lot of money to do the job, but could he do it? Carmine wondered if he should get rid of the man and start over. No, there wasn't time. "I don't care about that," he said into the phone when the other man started to give him details. "All I want is your assurance that everything will be ready for the celebration. Your *absolute* assurance." When he heard the reply, he grunted and switched off, but the grunt was a positive one. He trusted the man in Malindi.

He spat. He couldn't spit like that without a certain run-up, a certain amount of sound not unlike retching. He went back to the table and waved a hand at one of the other men, who came over and poured him more coffee and then backed away.

Carmine took a biscotto in his right hand and, holding it between his thumb and third finger, used it to lecture the Lebanese. "I want the only face on this to be Muslim, you follow me?" Carmine came from a village where they had still now and then been visited by puppeteers who did plays from the romances about Saracens and Christian knights; his sense of Islam was based in that half-sophisticated, half-ignorant past. "That's what the world is to see. That's what Jean-Marc is for." He gestured with the cookie at the handsome translator, who was actually a freelance television journalist and who smiled at them as if he was on camera. "You deliver Mombasa," Carmine said to the Lebanese. He dipped the biscotto, sucked the now-soaked end. "No mistakes. You don't get a second chance. Eh?"

"Of course, of course—" The Lebanese was afraid of him and showed it—never a bad idea with Carmine, who liked fear in the people around him. The Lebanese tapped the glass top of the table. "I have everything arranged—" He stopped. The translator was shaking his head at him.

Carmine hawked and spat and waved his left hand. "Don't tell me details. Tell Carlo or somebody. Get out." He looked toward a door. "Carlo!"

The Lebanese was hustled out, his right hand halfway up to give a parting handshake, his mouth still open. He would be back in his Christian village in Lebanon by midnight. It might seem he would have nothing to fear there from somebody living in Sicily. But he knew better.

Carmine sat at the table with the translator, wiping his mouth with a cloth napkin. "What do you think?" he said.

"I think I don't understand what is going on, *Don,*" he murmured.

"You don't need to understand!" Carmine's head was down like a bull's. "You do what I pay you to do—you talk nice, look pretty on the camera, you keep saying what I tell you. You don't hear nothing, you don't know nothing, you weren't here today, and you didn't meet this no-balls Lebanese! Yes?"

"Yes, yes—of course—*Don.*"

Carmine sat back. He fingered a cigarette out of a pack on the table without looking. "You want to keep a secret, you chop it into pieces and you give each guy a piece. They look at it, they say 'I don't know what I got here.' That's how it stays a secret."

He lit the cigarette and turned and looked across the terrace at the sea, his legs spread, his forearms on his knees and his hands joined, smoke blowing from the side of his mouth. The sea was empty but he seemed to see something there, because he said, "The U.S. Navy, that's what I worry about. Fucking U.S. Navy."

1

LAURA HAD TARTED HERSELF UP SO THAT SHE WAS
quite a distraction, he thought, watching her approach the
passport-control slot with her hidden contraband. She walked
with a bouncy stride that wasn't really her own, chest up and
out, her rear also very much on view in tight yellow shorts that
barely reached her hips. Her navel rode calmly in all this motion, its ring with the diamond chip winking. Laura had made
herself, in fact, *all* distractions, and every male eye in the shed-
like arrival area was on some part of her. The fact that she didn't
have a really pretty face was irrelevant.

Alan Craik grinned despite himself. She was enjoying it!
He, on the other hand, was nervous, for her as much as for
himself, and he tensed as she sashayed to the passport-control
booth and started to chat with a security officer. More balls
than he had, he thought. He had only to move a 9mm pistol
through; she had something far more dangerous.

He flexed his fingers to relax them, felt the odd sensation
in his left hand where two fingers were missing. Or, rather,

were red stumps. He forced himself to look at them, felt disbelief, slight disgust. *My hand.* The fingers had been blown off by a bullet seven weeks before. There had been talk of his leaving the Navy.

He balled the hand into a fist and forced himself to concentrate. *Back to work.*

Alan laid his U.S. passport, a twenty-dollar bill sticking from its top, in front of the black man at passport control. The man, too, had been looking at Laura, and Alan grinned.

"*Maridadi,*" Alan said. *Pretty.*

The man's eyes flicked over Alan's shoulder again to Laura, fifty feet away, and he growled *Whore* in Swahili, which Alan wasn't supposed to understand. He stamped the passport and waved Alan through. The twenty had disappeared.

Alan took three steps, clearing passport control, and looked for her. For a moment he lost her, then saw the bright yellow of her buns swinging up the stairs to the balcony above. He guessed that she had seen the sign up there for a ladies' room, used that excuse to bypass customs temporarily. Up there, however, farther along the balcony, was a uniformed Kenyan soldier with an automatic weapon, strategically located between the stairs and the exit at the far end that led directly to the terminal. He was there to turn back anybody who tried to get out that way.

The yellow shorts flashed and the door to the ladies' room closed. Alan turned and walked out.

He waited for her in the terminal hall. His pulse had leveled off again, and the sweat that had threatened to leak down his sides had stopped. His part was over: he had moved the weapon and fifty cartridges through the airport's security. Now, if Laura didn't get arrested for moving drugs—

A WOODEN DHOW MOVED SOUTH ALONG THE Kenyan coast, nearing Mombasa. It was going slowly under motor power, its sail useless in the humid breeze that blew from the shore. The men aboard could smell the land beyond, an odor slightly spicy, smoky, earthy, overlaid with the moist decay of the mangrove swamps where Africa met the ocean.

A dark man sat at the foot of the mast, waiting for the first sight of the city. Just now, he could see only blue-green haze where the land lay, and here and there a darker mass where a point thrust out. He had binoculars hung around his neck, but he did not use them. He was in fact seeing far more clearly with an inner eye, which looked beyond the haze, beyond Africa even, into his future.

In four hours, he would be in paradise.

He believed this more completely than he believed that he was sitting on a ship on an ocean on a ball rolling through space. He believed with both passion and simplicity; he believed utterly. He had no fear of the destruction of his physical self that would send him there. They had assured him that he would feel nothing: a flash, a pressure, and he would wake in paradise.

Another man approached him. He had a bag of tools in one hand and, in the other, a black plastic case that held a detonator. "Time," the man said.

The dark man shook his head. "Not yet." He returned to his contemplation of paradise.

"HEY, MAN," HE HEARD HER VOICE SAY BEHIND HIM. "My God, you made it!"

"Piece of cake!" She shrugged. Grinned. Held up a hand so that he could see that the fingers were trembling. "Little reaction after the fact." Laughed. Her distractions bounced, and Alan Craik, loyal husband, father, moral man, pursed his lips and thought that it was going to be a long three days—and three nights—before she went on to other duties.

"How'd you get by the guy with the gun?"

"Walked." She moved a little closer. "Want to see how I walked?" She wasn't wearing a bra, he knew—she had told him earlier—and her silk T-shirt was definitely a little small.

"I think we ought to do our report."

"You're a great partner, Craik. I tell you, man, I sure lucked out with you!" She sighed. Laura Sweigert was a Naval

Criminal Investigative Service special agent, good at her work, tough, but she had a reputation for liking what she called "contact sports" when the workday was over. "I just scored big, man—you think I want to write some fucking report?" He remembered a news report about a female tennis star who, after a big win, said she just wanted to get laid.

A *long* three nights.

He was saved by a voice, calling his name. Behind them and to their right was the exit lane from immigration, lined on both sides by a crowd of greeters—family, hustlers, tourist reps, women in saris, men with hand-lettered signs that said "Adamson" and "Client of Simba, Ltd." The voice calling "Mister Craik! Mister Craik!" came from there, and Alan searched the two crowds, feeling Laura's hand on his bare arm. He thought he recognized the voice and searched for a face, a white face in the mostly black crowd, and then he saw a Navy ball cap and knew he had the right man, and he waved.

"Craw! Hey, Craw!"

Master Chief Martin Craw had been one of the people who had got him through being an ensign. Craw had taught him the back end of the S-3. Craw had shown him how to massage old tapes and older computers and pull up targets from electronic mush. Craw had given him an example of what a Navy man should be.

Now Martin Craw came toward them, a little grin on his face as he took in both Alan and Laura, hand outstretched.

"Laura, I want you to meet the best master chief in the U.S. Navy. Martin, this is Laura Sweigert, who just brought a kilo of white powder through Kenyatta arrivals."

"Ma'am." Craw was in his early forties but seemed an ancient to Alan because of his great, quiet authority. His grin, however, and his quick appraisal of Laura, were not an old man's. "How'd you do that?"

Laura rocked back a little and smiled at him. "I think it was the T-shirt."

Craw reddened only a little. "Kinda dangerous." He didn't make clear whether he meant the T-shirt or the white powder. Craw was from Maine.

She made a sound that pooh-poohed the idea. "Hell's bells, Craik brought through a goddamned gun!"

"Not so loud—"

"And bullets!"

"Laura, hey—"

She held up her hands. "Okay, okay." Her fingernails, like her toenails, were painted a glittery red. Her lipstick was pink, her eyeshadow violet, her hair a mousy brown that you ignored because it was gelled to look as if she'd just got very, very wet. "Entirely legit," she said. "We're testing airport security for NCIS."

"I figured." Craw grinned. He jerked his head at Alan. "He's always legit."

Laura made a face. "So I'm discovering." She put a hand through Craw's arm. "What are your plans for the next couple of days, sailor?" Alan, caused abruptly to see Craw through her eyes, realized that the senior chief was a damned good-looking man.

Craw saw Alan's look, blushed. "I'm goin' to be working for Mister Craik."

Alan bent and picked up his helmet bag, which held the H&K. "You want to bring me up to date, Chief? Like, um, what you're doing here?" He had last seen Craw on board the USS *Thomas Jefferson* a week ago, when he had had to fly back to CONUS to be deposed for a national-security case.

With Laura leaning against him, Craw explained that he had flown into Mombasa the evening before from the CV to set up the U.S. hangar there as their home base while they shore-deployed. "Orders from the CAG." He raised his free hand, which held a black attaché case.

"Yeah, I know, I got 'em, too. But I didn't expect to be met at Nairobi."

"Thought I could brief you flying back to Mombasa. The admiral's goin' to inspect us tomorrow." Again, he gestured with the attaché case. "Got some paperwork—"

"What the hell, we just got here!"

"Well, he's makin' a shore visit, so it's some ship today, us tomorrow."

That changed the price of fish. What he and Laura had

just done—moving illicit items through airport security for the Naval Criminal Investigative Service—was a peripheral responsibility, a test of local conditions that would become part of a report. He had treated it as a game; however, with this return to the realities of his detachment, the pleasures of the game faded and the serious trivia of Navy life took over.

They began moving away from the arrivals area. "What's our space like down there?"

"Kinda filthy. One of the old air-force hangars at Mombasa airport. Not been used for a while—dust, gear missin'—been a lotta thievin', I'd guess. I put everybody to cleanin' up, but the place is big—room for a couple P-3s in there and to spare, if you had to."

They were walking toward the Air Kenya desk now to start the flight to Mombasa. "How many personnel?"

"Aircrew for one plane plus seventeen—other plane comin' in a few days."

"Staying where?"

"Nyali International." American military, like government people, got put up in the big international hotels on the beach because they were supposed to be more secure than hotels in Mombasa itself. "But I told 'em, you boys just plan to be in this hangar nonstop till the admiral's blown through, then I'll get you some rack time. They're all good boys."

They were, Alan thought; they were all good boys now, although when he and Craw had first encountered them some months before, they had been pretty bad boys. Detachment 424 was a one-shot unit put together to test-drive a 3-D radar-imaging system called MARI, and it had been almost run into extinction by its acting officer-in-charge before Alan and Craw and a few others had been able to shape it up. Now deployed with the *Jefferson* in the Indian Ocean, it had been ordered to fly off to Mombasa for two weeks as an advance party for a visit by the entire battle group.

"Give me a rundown."

Don't miss these bestselling superthrillers by

ROBERT LUDLUM